Between the Dark and the Daylight

AND 27 MORE OF THE BEST CRIME AND MYSTERY STORIES OF THE YEAR

EDITED BY
Ed Gorman and Martin H. Greenberg

TYRUS BOOKS

Published by
TYRUS BOOKS
923 Williamson St.
Madison, WI 53703
www.tyrushousebooks.com

Printed in the United States of America
12 11 10 09 1 2 3 4 5 6 7 8 9 10

978-0-9825209-5-6 (hardcover)
978-0-9825209-4-9 (paperback)

ACKNOWLEDGMENTS

Thanks to Janet Hutchings and Linda Landrigan

for their invaluable assistance.

And a special thanks to John Helfers

for his considerable help with this volume.

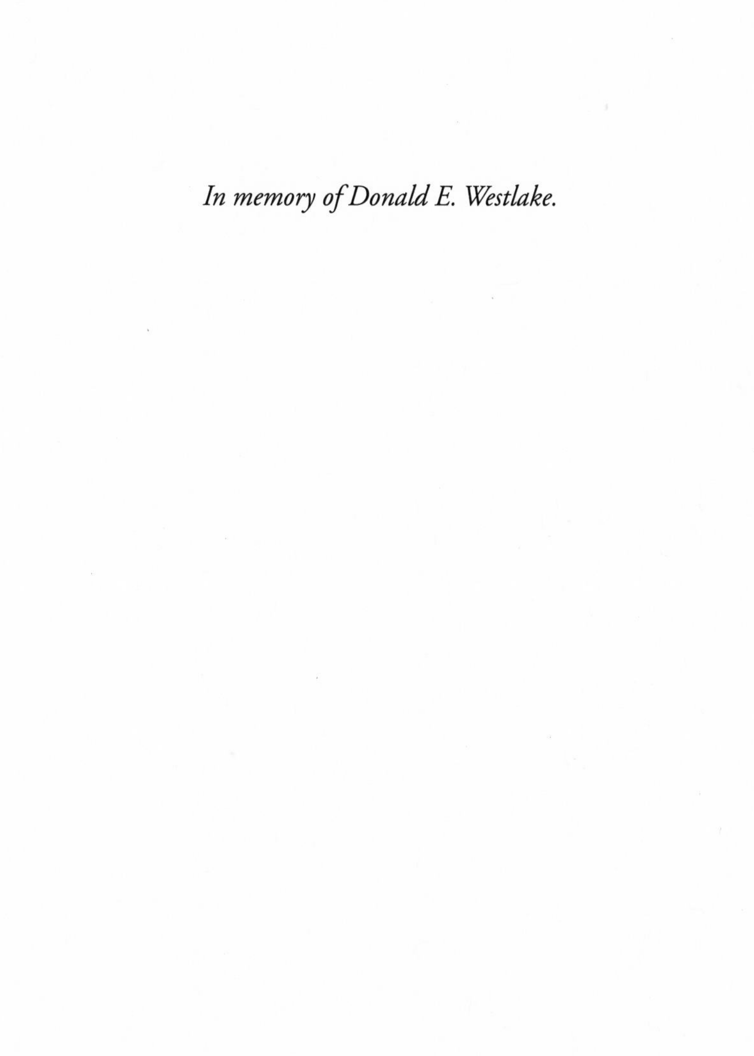

In memory of Donald E. Westlake.

Contents

The Year in Mystery: 2008

BY JON L. BREEN

While no year goes by in any field without the sadness of loss, the mystery world was especially hard hit in 2008, which must be dubbed the Year of Lost Masters. No fewer than five winners of the Mystery Writers of America's Grand Master Award died during the year.

Short story wizard Edward D. Hoch, age 77, died suddenly on January 17. Phyllis A. Whitney, arguably the foremost American writer of romantic suspense, died on February 8 at the remarkable age of 104. Tony Hillerman, whose novels about the Navajo Tribal Police presaged a whole subgenre of detective stories about Native Americans, died at 83 on October 26. Police procedural pioneer Hillary Waugh, 88, died on December 8. Finally, on New Year's Eve, Donald E. Westlake, master of crime fiction both grim and comical, died at 75. Where Whitney and Waugh had published their last books more than a decade ago, and Hillerman was known to have had numerous health problems in recent years, Westlake and Hoch were cut down while at the height of their powers. One of Westlake's novels as by Richard Stark, *Dirty Money*, appeared in 2008, with a new title as Westlake announced for 2009, and Hoch's 35-year record of appearing in every issue of *Ellery Queen's Mystery Magazine* continued through the end of the year and beyond.

Also mourned in 2008 were Julius Fast, winner of the first Edgar Award for his novel *Watchful at Night* (1945); perennial bestseller Michael Crichton, whose Edgar winner *A Case of Need* (1968) pioneered the contemporary medical thriller; Gregory Mcdonald, whose first and most famous comic mystery was *Fletch* (1974); James Crumley, who took the private-eye genre in new directions, beginning with *The Wrong Case* (1975); Stephen Marlowe, who went from private eye Chester Drum of '50s paperbacks to hardcover thrillers and historicals in later decades; George Chesbro, creator of the memorable dwarf private eye Mongo Frederickson; and Janwillem van de Wetering, Dutch-born writer who wrote in English about the Amsterdam police team of Grijpstra and De Gier.

The centenary of Ian Fleming was observed by a trade paper reprinting of the whole James Bond saga, including all the short stories in one volume for the first time in *Quantum of Solace* (Penguin); several secondary sources, including Philip Gardiner's *The Bond Code: The Dark World of Ian Fleming and James Bond* (New Page) and updated editions of James Chapman's excellent *License to Thrill: A Cultural History of the James Bond Films* (Tauris) and Alastair Dougall's *James Bond: The Secret World of 007* (DK Adult); a new faux Bond novel, *Devil May Care* (Penguin), by Sebastian Faulk; and Daniel Craig's second film outing as 007, *Quantum of Solace*. I'm sure there's more—after all these years, the Bond industry remains nearly as hard to keep up with as the Sherlock Holmes industry.

It was something of a landmark year for serious consideration of non-fictional crime writing, with a major historical selection, *True Crime: An American Anthology*, edited by Harold Schechter (Library of America), and a highly praised critical study, Jean Murley's *The Rise of True Crime: 20th-Century Murder and American*

Popular Culture (Greenwood). While Schechter's compilation was denied an Edgar nomination in the true-crime category, Murley's work received an unprecedented nod in the biographical/critical category, usually devoted to studies of fictional subjects. In both these categories, edited collections of whatever excellence have been at a disadvantage.

The year's major non-literary world news event, the financial meltdown, will inevitably have its impact on publishing, as on every other sort of commerce, in ways yet to be fully realized.

Best Novels of the Year 2008

Before unveiling the fifteen best new books I read and reviewed during the year, here's the boilerplate disclaimer: I don't pretend to cover the whole field—no single reviewer does—but if you have a better list of fifteen, I'd love to see it.

Benjamin Black: *The Lemur* (Picador). Booker Prize winner John Banville's pseudonymous novel is notable for its style, characterization, brevity, and respect for mystery conventions.

Andrea Camilleri: *The Paper Moon*, translated from the Italian by Steven Sartarelli (Penguin). Sicily's Inspector Montalbano is one of the great characters in European police procedurals.

Megan Chance: *The Spiritualist* (Three Rivers). This unpredictable and beautifully written historical gothic is set in the claustrophobic world of 19th-century Manhattan society associated with Edith Wharton.

Michael Connelly: *The Brass Verdict* (Little, Brown). The second novel about L.A. defense attorney Mickey Haller is nearly as good as his debut in *The Lincoln Lawyer*.

Patrick Culhane: *Red Sky in Morning* (Morrow). Writing under a pseudonym, Max Allan Collins tells a World-War-II sea story that is one of his finest novels.

Christa Faust: *Money Shot* (Hard Case Crime). Set in the pornographic film and "adult modeling" industries, this woman-on-the-run story combines sex, violence, humor, style, and humanity in an irresistible combination.

Arnaldur Indridason: *The Draining Lake*, translated from the Icelandic by Bernard Scudder (St. Martin's Minotaur/Dunne). A masterful police procedural, with an old skeleton to be identified and Cold War flashbacks, is second only to Oates's novel (see below) as this reader's book of the year.

Asa Larsson: *The Black Path*, translated from the Swedish by Marlaine Delargy (Delta). Cold weather and Nordic gloom often make for great detective fiction. Among Scandinavian practitioners, Larsson strikes me as vastly superior to the more highly publicized Henning Mankell.

Steve Martini: *Shadow of Power* (Morrow). California lawyer Paul Madriani is back in court, courtesy of one of the very best legal thriller writers.

Joyce Carol Oates: *My Sister, My Love* (Ecco). This account of a child ice skater's murder is my book of the year, an extraordinary semi-satirical novel of contemporary America and a genuine mystery, with solution.

Leonardo Padura: *Havana Gold*, translated from the Spanish by Peter Bush (Bitter Lemon). The brilliant Cuban writer never puts a foot wrong in his Mario Conde novels—but his translator needs to work on getting the baseball lingo right.

Justin Peacock: *A Cure for Night* (Doubleday). The best first novel I read in 2008 gives a realistic view of the public defender's work.

Bill Pronzini: *Fever* (Forge). San Francisco's venerable Nameless Detective continues in top form. Pronzini could as easily have been represented on this list by the non-series *The Other Side of Silence* (Walker).

Ruth Rendell: *Not in the Flesh* (Crown). Chief Inspector Reg Wexford, who debuted in 1964, has been around even longer than Nameless. His creator is still one of the best.

Fred Vargas: *This Night's Foul Work*, translated from the French by Siân Reynolds (Penguin). Going gloriously over the top in plot and personnel, Vargas works her magic.

Sub-Genres

Private eyes. Among the sleuths for hire in commendable action were Laura Lippman's Baltimorean Tess Monaghan in *Another Thing to Fall* (Morrow), Betty Webb's Lena Jones in *Desert Cut* (Poisoned Pen), Ken Bruen's Galway-based Jack Taylor in *Cross* (St. Martin's Minotaur), and Domenic Stansberry's San Franciscan Dante Mancuso in *The Ancient Rain* (St. Martin's Minotaur).

Amateur sleuths. Non-professionals in good form included Bill Moody's jazz pianist Evan Horne in *Shades of Blue* (Poisoned Pen), Parnell Hall's faux Puzzle Lady Cora Felton in *The Sudoku Puzzle Murders* (St. Martin's Minotaur/Dunne), Katherine Hall Page's caterer Faith Fairchild in *The Body in the Gallery* (Morrow), Aaron Elkins's bone detective Gideon Oliver in *Uneasy Relations* (Berkley), Kate Charles's Anglican curate Callie Anson in *Deep Waters* (Poisoned Pen), JoAnna Carl's chocolate shop proprietor Lee McKinney in *The Chocolate Snowman Murders* (Obsidian), and Barbara Allan's (i.e., Barbara and Max Allan Collins's) mother and daughter antique dealers in *Antiques Flee Market* (Kensington). Loren Estleman's vintage film hunter Valentino made his novel-length debut in *Frames* (Forge); Carolyn Hart introduced heavenly emissary Bailey Ruth Raeburn in *Ghost at Work* (Morrow); and Toni L.P. Kelner's *Without Mercy* (Five Star) unveilled a promising new character in entertainment journalist Tilda Harper.

Police. John Harvey featured a new male-female police team, Will Grayson and Helen Walker, in *Gone to Ground* (Harcourt).

Reginald Hill's Yorkshire sleuths Dalziel and Pascoe were involved in a completion of Jane Austen's *Sanditon* in *The Price of Butcher's Meat* (Harper), published in Britain as *A Cure for All Diseases.* Tennessee sheriff John Turner returned in James Sallis's contemplative *Salt River* (Walker), while Bill Crider's laid back small-town Texas sheriff Dan Rhodes appeared in *Of All Sad Words* (St. Martin's Minotaur). Also in action were Detective Superintendent Harriet Martens in H.R.F. Keating's *Rules, Regs and Rotten Eggs* (St. Martin's Minotaur), Peter Lovesey's Inspector Hen Mallin in *The Headhunters* (Soho), Baantjer's long-running Amsterdam sleuth in *DeKok and Murder on Blood Mountain*, translated from the Dutch by H.G. Smittenaar (Speck), Christopher Fowler's Bryant and May in *The Victoria Vanishes* (Bantam), Stuart M. Kaminsky's Russian Porfiry Petrovich Rostnikov in *People Walk in Darkness* (Forge), Ben Rehder's Texas game warden John Marlin in *Holy Moly* (St. Martin's Minotaur), and Linda Berry's small town Georgia policewoman Trudy Roundtree in *Death and the Crossed Wires*, (Five Star).

Lawyers. In addition to the characters of Connelly, Martini, and Peacock in our top fifteen, counselors in jurisprudential trim included Martin Edwards's Harry Devlin in *Waterloo Sunset* (Poisoned Pen), Paul Goldstein's Michael Seeley in *A Patent Lie* (Doubleday), Sheldon Siegel's Mike Daley in *Judgment Day* (MacAdam/Cage), Lisa Scottoline's Mary DiNunzio in *Lady Killer* (Harper), and Michael A. Bowen's Rep Pennyworth in *Shoot the Lawyer Twice* (Poisoned Pen).

Historicals. Anne Perry's best recent case for Victorian cop Thomas Pitt was *Buckingham Palace Gardens* (Ballantine). Steven Saylor's Roman Gordianus the Finder made a welcome reappearance in *Caesar's Triumph* (St. Martin's Minotaur). Jeanne M. Dams's former servant Hilda Johansson has moved up in the world in *Indigo Christmas* (Perseverance). Sam Stall's dossier-format *Dracula's Heir* (Quirk) was set partly in the present, partly in the world of Bram Stoker's classic novel. Gyles Brandreth's *Oscar Wilde and a Game Called Murder* (Touchstone) featured many real people apart from the titular sleuth in a mystery of 1892 London. Steve Hockensmith's Old Red and Big Red again practiced Sherlockian detection in the 1890s Old West in *The Black Dove* (St. Martin's Minotaur). C.S. Harris's Sebastian St. Cyr was in action in 1812 London in *Where Serpents Sleep* (Obsidian). Looking at times more recently gone by were David Fulmer's *The Blue Door* (Harcourt), about the Philadelphia popular music scene circa 1962; Max Allan Collins's *Strip for Murder*, illustrated by Terry Beatty (Berkley), set in the Broadway world of the 1950s; David Ossman's *The Ronald Reagan Murder Case* (BearManor), set in 1945 Hollywood; and Carlo Lucarelli's *Via Delle Oche*, translated from the Italian by Michael Reynolds (Europa).

Thrillers. I seem to have read more books that might be categorized as thrillers than in past years, but not everyone will necessarily share my definition (i.e., anything that doesn't fit the other categories). Charles Ardai's stunt novel to commemorate a milestone of his publishing line, *Fifty-to-One* (Hard Case Crime), proved a fine comic crime novel on its own merits. Larry Beinhart's *Salvation Boulevard* (Nation Books) took on political and religious issues. Insider knowledge of how a political campaign is run added to the merits of Ed Gorman's *Sleeping Dogs* (St. Martin's Minotaur/Dunne), while Robert S. Levinson's *In the Key of Death* (Five Star) benefited from the author's music industry background. Joe L. Hensley's final novel was the remarkable account of the challenges faced by senior citizens, *Snowbird's Blood* (St. Martin's Minotaur). Mary Higgins Clark's *Where Are You Now?* (Simon and Schuster) was a gem of deceptive plotting and cross-cutting structure. Karin Alvtegen's Edgar-nominated psychological thriller *Missing*, translated from the Swedish by Anna Paterson (Felony & Mayhem), featured a homeless protagonist. Asa Nonami's *Now You're One of Us*, translated from the Japanese by Michael Volek and Mitsuko Volek (Vertical), was a gothic horror story of considerable power. Max Allan Collins provided a prequel to the rest of his novels about a killer for hire in *The First Quarry* (Hard Case). They don't come much noirer than Ken Bruen's *Once Were Cops* (St. Martin's Minotaur).

Short Stories

Single-author short story collections, rather sparse in 2007, rallied in 2008. Walter Mosley's *The Right Mistake: The Further Philosophical Investigations of Socrates Fortlow* (BasicCivitas) was the third collection about the guilt-ridden ex-con who may be Mosley's greatest character. Others from major imprints included Henning Mankell's *The Pyramid and Four Other Kurt Wallander Mysteries* (New Press) and Laura Lippman's *Hardly Knew Her: Stories* (Morrow). Significant imports were Peter Corris's *The Big Score* (Allen & Unwin), new cases for Australian private eye Cliff Hardy; *The Edogawa Rampo Reader* (Kurodahan), gathering eight short stories new to English along with ten essays by an iconic Japanese writer; and Christopher Fowler's *Old Devil Moon* (Serpent's Tail). Anton Chekhov's *A Night in the Cemetery and Other Stories of Crime and Suspense* (Pegasus) included some early stories by the Russian master not previously translated into English. The extraordinarily prolific Ralph McInerny had a new collection about his famous priest detective in *The Wisdom of Father Dowling* (Five Star). Mixed collections of interest included F. Paul Wilson's *Aftershock & Others* (Forge), Joyce Carol Oates' *Wild Nights!: Stories About the Last Days of Poe, Dickinson, Twain, James, and Hemingway* (Ecco), and MWA Grand Master Stephen King's *Just After Sunset* (Scribner).

As usual, small and specialty presses carried most of the load. New from Crippen & Landru were Mignon G. Eberhart's *Dead Yesterday and Other Stories*; Peter Lovesey's *Murder on the Short List*; Richard A. Lupoff's *Quintet: The Cases of Chase and Delacroix*; Hugh Pentecost's *The Battles of Jericho*; and Walter Satterthwait's *The Mankiller of Poojegai and Other Stories*. Book of the year for C&G was actually a collection of stage plays: *13 to the Gallows* by John Dickson Carr and Val Gielgud.

The extremely active print-on-demand publisher Ramble House offered Bill Pronzini's *Dago Red: Tales of Dark Suspense*, James Reasoner's *Old Times' Sake*, Ed Lynskey's *A Clear Path to Cross*, 1940s Australian writer Max Afford's *Two Locked Room Mysteries and a Ripping Yarn*, and Fender Tucker's *Totah Six-Pack*, adding three stories to the 2005 collection *The Totah Trilogy*.

Others from small presses included Michael Mallory's second Sherlockian collection, *The Exploits of the Second Mrs. Watson* (Top); Dennis Palumbo's *From Crime to Crime* (Tallfellow), inspired by Isaac Asimov's Black Widowers; Hal White's *The Mysteries of Reverend Dean* (Lighthouse Christian), and John M. Floyd's *Midnight* (Dogwood).

There were also notable reprints and regatherings. Two volumes of early stories by Lawrence Block, previously published in limited editions by Crippen & Landru, were brought together in the trade paperback *One Night Stands and Lost Weekends* (Harper). Volume Six of *The Collected Stories of Louis L'Amour* (Bantam) was devoted to the prolific pulpster's crime fiction. Ramble House reprinted Harvey O'Higgins's 1929 collection *Detective Duff Unravels It* and, under the new Surinam Turtle imprint edited by Richard A. Lupoff, Gelett Burgess's 1912 *The Master of Mysteries*, listed by Ellery Queen in *Queen's Quorum*.

It was another good year for anthologies. Joining Akashic's wide-ranging and seemingly endless original city noir series were *Toronto Noir*, edited by Janine Armin and Nathaniel G. Moore; *Las Vegas Noir*, edited by Jarret Keene and Todd James Pierce; *Paris Noir*, edited by Aurélien Masson (not to be confused with an earlier non-Akashic anthology of the same title edited by Maxim Jakubowski); *Brooklyn Noir 3: Nothing But the Truth*, a crossover into true crime edited by Tim McLoughlin and Thomas Adcock; *Queens Noir*, edited by Robert Knightly; *Istanbul Noir*, edited by Mustafa Ziyalan and Amy Spangler; and *Trinidad Noir*, edited by Lisa Allen-Agostini and Jeanne Mason.

The Mystery Writers of America's annual anthology had a theme of the policeman's lot: *The Blue Religion* (Little, Brown), edited by Michael Connelly. A star-studded line-up contributed forensic mysteries to *At the Scene of the Crime* (Running Brook), edited by Dana Stabenow. In *Killer Year* (St. Martin's Minotaur), edited by Lee Child, established thriller writers introduced new stories by some younger colleagues. Another showcase for lesser-known writers was the Chicago Contingent's *Sin: A Deadly Anthology* (Avendia). Notable Italian writers contributed to *Crimini* (Bitter Lemon), edited by Giancarlo DeCataldo. The six British writers known as the Medieval Murderers got together on *The Lost Prophecies* (Simon and Schuster UK/Trafalgar), which is either a group novel or a collection of linked short stories. *Killers: An Anthology* (Swimming Kangaroo), edited by Colin Harvey, was devoted to "speculative mystery," crossing crime fiction with science fiction, fantasy, and horror.

As for the reprint anthologies, comparing selections of the best of 2007 reveals the usual disparity. The precursor to the present volume, *A Prisoner of Memory and 24 of the Year's Finest Crime and Mystery Stories* (Pegasus), edited by Ed Gorman and Martin H. Greenberg, and *The Best American Mystery Stories 2008* (Houghton Mifflin), from guest editor George Pelecanos and series editor Otto Penzler, had only one story in common: Michael Connelly's "Mulholland Drive." Joyce Carol Oates contributed to both books but with different stories. Maxim Jakubowski's *The Mammoth Book of Best British Mysteries* (Running) was comprised of stories from 2006.

The Akashic Noir series has also branched out into reprint collections, including *Manhattan Noir 2: The Classics*, edited by Lawrence Block, and *D.C. Noir 2: The Classics*, edited by George Pelecanos.

Important volumes for serious genre scholars were *Early German and Austrian Detective Fiction: An Anthology* (McFarland), edited by Mary W. Tannert and Henry Kratz; *Gang Pulp* (Off-Trail), edited by John Locke, history and examples of a Depression-era magazine category of short duration; and LeRoy Lad Panek and Mary M. Bendel-Simso's gathering mostly from 19th-century newspapers, *Early American Detective Stories: An Anthology* (McFarland). Recycling a familiar title while combining anthology standards with less familiar stories was *The Rivals of Sherlock Holmes* (No Exit), edited by Nick Rennison. While the older stories in *Murder Short & Sweet* (Chicago Review Press), edited by Paul D. Staudohar, have been reprinted over and over again, they would be a treasure trove for the newer reader who has never encountered them before.

Reference Books and Secondary Sources

Books about mystery and detective fiction had an exceptionally strong year. Mystery critic and veteran stage director Amnon Kabatchnik produced two superb references on theatrical crime: *Blood on the Stage: Milestone Plays of Crime, Mystery, and Detection: An Annotated Repertoire, 1900-1925* and *Sherlock Holmes on the Stage: A Chronological Encyclopedia of Plays Featuring the Great Detective* (both Scarecrow). The creator of Rumpole of the Bailey, who died in early 2009, was the subject of a major biography, Valerie Grove's *A Voyage Round John Mortimer* (Viking). Kathy Lynn Emerson's *How to Write Killer Historical Mysteries* (Perseverance) was one of the best technical manuals for crime writers I've ever read. And yet, in a competitive year, none of these even managed an Edgar nomination.

By far the most prolific publisher of books about mystery and detective fiction, ranging from the lightly fannish to the heavily academic, is McFarland. Their 2008 highlights included two of the five Edgar nominees: Frankie Y. Bailey's *African American Mystery Writers* and David Geherin's *Scene of the Crime: The Importance of Place in Crime and Mystery Fiction.* Also on their extensive list were Jeffrey Marks's *Anthony Boucher: A Biobibliography*; *Dissecting Hannibal Lecter: Essays on the Novels of Thomas Harris*, edited by Benjamin Szumskyj; *Marcia Muller and the Female Private Eye*, edited by Alexander N. Howe and Christine A. Jackson; the same Alexander N. Howe's *It Didn't Mean Anything: A Psychoanalytic Reading of American Detective Fiction*; *Minette Walters and the Meaning of Justice: Essays on the Crime Novels*, edited by Mary Hadley and Sarah D. Fogle; *Nancy Drew and Her Sister Sleuths: Essays on the Fiction of Girl Detectives*, edited by Michael G. Cornelius and Melanie E. Gregg; Mark Connelly's *The Hardy Boys Mysteries, 1927-1979: A Cultural and Literary History*; Stephen Sugden's *A Dick Francis Companion: Characters, Horses, Plots, Settings and Themes*; and James Zemboy's *The Detective Novels of Agatha Christie: A Reader's Guide*.

University press offerings included Leonard Cassuto's Edgar-nominated *Hard-Boiled Sentimentality: The Secret History of American Crime Stories* (Columbia); and Sari Kawana's *Murder Most Modern: Detective Fiction and Japanese Culture* (Minnesota).

For those interested in the intersection of fiction and film, Kevin Johnson's *The Dark Page: Books That Inspired American Film Noir [1940-1949]* (Oak Knoll), a beautiful coffee table book originally published in 2007 as a $450 limited edition, became available for a mere $95.

Among the always plentiful Sherlockian volumes were Leslie S. Klinger's *Baker Street Rambles: A Collection of Writings About Sherlock Holmes, John H. Watson, M.D., Arthur Conan Doyle and Their World* (Gasogene); Gary Lovisi's *Sherlock Holmes: The Great Detective in Paperback & Pastiche: A Survey, Index, & Value Guide* (Gryphon) and Richard L. Kellogg's *Vignettes of Sherlock Holmes* (Gryphon). A landmark volume had a 75th anniversary edition: Vincent Starrett's classic 1933 study *The Private Life of Sherlock Holmes* (Gasogene).

A Sense of History

For all the high-quality new work being published, there is always plenty of past crime and mystery fiction that merits rediscovery. While the major publishers occasionally contribute something important to the process, most of the load is carried by proprietors of small and specialty presses.

Tom and Enid Schantz of Colorado's Rue Morgue Press introduced important new names to their impressive list: John Dickson Carr with two classic locked-room mysteries, *The Crooked Hinge* and (as by Carter Dickson) *The Judas Window*; and Golden Age giant H.C. Bailey with a pair of books about Reggie Fortune, *Shadow on the Wall* and *Black Land, White Land.* They also added three early titles by contemporary traditionalist Catherine Aird, four 1940s spy novels by Manning Coles, two classical puzzles by American Golden-Ager Clyde B. Clason, two by quirky British novelist Gladys Mitchell, and single titles by Glyn Carr, Delano Ames, and Colin Watson.

Greg Shepard's Eureka, California-based Stark House continued its two-to-a-volume reprinting program with titles by Gil Brewer (including the 1950s paperback writer's previously-unpublished *A Devil for O'Shaugnessy*), Mercedes Lambert (*Dogdown* and *Soultown*), Wade Miller (*The Killer* and *Devil on Two Sticks*, with an introduction by surviving partner Bob Wade), Richard Powell, and Peter Rabe.

Then there's Charles Ardai, whose Hard Case Crime alternates new material with important rediscoveries. In 2008, he revived Steve Fisher's *No House Limit*, with an afterword by the author's son; Lawrence Block's *A Diet of Treacle* and *Killing Castro*, two of his many early novels originally published under pseudonyms; and Shepard Rifkin's civil-rights-era novel *The Murderer Vine.*

A very specialized reprinter (limited to one author) is Hollywood's Galaxy Press, devoted to reviving the pulp stories in various genres of Scientology founder L. Ron Hubbard. A sampling of his mystery and thriller fiction, including the novellas *Spy Killer*, *The Chee-Chalker*, and *The Iron Duke*, makes a strong case for his versatility and talent. Another pulpster paid new attention was Norvell Page, author of the short novels in *The Spider: City of Doom* (Baen).

Vampire fiction giant Bram Stoker got new respect in a couple of scholarly volumes: *The New Annotated Dracula* (Norton), edited by Leslie S. Klinger, and *The Jewel of the Seven Stars* (Penguin), introduced by Kate Hebblethwaite. Michael Dirda's introduction to a new edition of Vladimir Nabokov's *The Real Life of Sebastian Knight* (New Directions) highlighted that world-famous author's connection to detective fiction.

At the Movies

In a weaker than average year for motion pictures generally, the crop of crime films was terrific. The Edgar selectors came up with an excellent slate, and there was no shortage of other viable possibilities.

First the five nominees, a group that reflected variety as well as high quality. *The Bank Job*, directed by Roger Donaldson from a script by Dick Clement and Ian La Frenais, was a British big caper in which the targeted bank was on Baker Street. The Coen Brothers' *Burn After Reading* was an espionage spoof with an ex-CIA agent's memoirs as the MacGuffin. Martin McDonagh's *In Bruges* was a darkly comic hitman story. Guillaume Canet's *Tell No One* (original French title *Ne le dis à personne*) was a Gallic adaptation of a Harlan Coben whodunit. *Transsiberian*, directed by Brad Anderson from a script by Anderson and Will Conroy, offered two sure-fire elements for a movie thriller: trains and snow.

But there were plenty of other films that might have been honored in a weaker year. Guy Ritchie's *RocknRolla* was a welcome return to noirish comedy by the former Mr. Madonna. Director Clint Eastwood had two good films during the year: *Changeling*, scripted by J. Michael Straczynski, was a strong fictionalization of a notorious Los Angeles kidnapping case of the late 1920s, while the less obviously criminous *Gran Torino*, written by Nick Schenk from a story by Schenk and Dave Johannson, starred the director himself in a sort of coda to his Dirty Harry persona. Phillipe Claudel's *I've Loved You So Long* (original French title *Il y a longtemps que je t'aime*), about a woman released from prison and the gradually revealed nature of her crime, starred Kristin Scott Thomas, who these days seems to do as many French as English language films. The Tom Cruise vehicle *Valkyrie*, directed by Brian Singer from the script of Christopher McQuarrie and Nathan Alexander about wartime attempts on the life of Hitler, turned out much better than its negative advance buzz suggested. *Body of Lies*, directed by Ridley Scott from William Monahan's screenplay of David Ignatius's novel, and Jeffrey Nachmanoff's *Traitor*, from his story with Steve Martin, were good and very serious contemporary espionage thrillers. On the other hand, André Hunebelle's *OSS 117*, written with Raymond Borel and Pierre Foucaud, was a broad and funny spoof of Jean Bruce's novels about Bondish special agent Hubert Bonisseur de la Bath.

Two of the Oscar nominees for Best Picture arguably fall in the crime genre: the biographical film *Milk*, directed by Gus Van Sant from Dustin Lance Black's script, concerned in part the murder of San Francisco supervisor Harvey Milk, brilliantly played by Sean Penn; while the mystery of a woman's Nazi past is at the center of *The Reader*, directed by Stephen Daldry from David Hare's adaptation of Bernhard Schlink's novel.

John Patrick Shanley's *Doubt*, adapted from his play, was overlooked by both the Edgar and Oscar Best-Picture selectors, but for me it was the best mystery film of the year. One could argue that the mystery isn't really solved and indeed there may not have been a crime at all. But the author and the great performers give the viewer-detective plenty of clues, maybe more than the stage version did, as to whether Father Flynn (Philip Seymour Hoffmann) was actually guilty of the child molestation he is suspected of and exactly what Sister Aloysius (Meryl Streep) means in her final anguished speech.

Award Winners

Awards tied to publishers' contests, those limited to a geographical region smaller than a country, those awarded for works in languages other than English (with the exception of the Crime Writers of Canada's nod to their French compatriots), and those confined to works from a single periodical have been omitted. All were awarded in 2008 for material published in 2007. Gratitude is extended to all the websites that keep track of these things, with a special nod to Jiro Kimura's Gumshoe Site.

Edgar Allan Poe Awards (Mystery Writers of America)

Best novel: John Hart, *Down River* (St. Martin's Minotaur)

Best first novel by an American author: Tana French, *In the Woods* (Viking)

Best original paperback: Megan Abbott, *Queenpin* (Simon and Schuster)

Best fact crime book: Vincent Bugliosi, *Reclaiming History: The Assassination of President John F. Kennedy* (Norton)

Best critical/biographical work: Jon Lellenberg, Daniel Stashower, and Charles Foley, eds., *Arthur Conan Doyle: A Life in Letters* (Penguin)

Best short story: Susan Straight, "The Golden Gopher" (*Los Angeles Noir*, Akashic)

Best young adult mystery: Tedd Arnold, *Rat Life* (Penguin-Dial)

Best juvenile mystery: Katherine Marsh, *The Night Tourist* (Hyperion)

Best play: Joseph Goodrich, *Panic* (International Mystery Writers Festival)

Best television episode teleplay: Matt Nix, "Pilot" (*Burn Notice*, USA/Fox)

Best motion picture screenplay: Tony Gilroy, *Michael Clayton*

Grand Master: Bill Pronzini

Robert L. Fish award (best first story): Mark Ammons, "The Catch" (*Still Waters*, Level Best)

Raven: Center for the Book in the Library of Congress; Kate Mattes, Kate's Mystery Books

Mary Higgins Clark Award: Sandi Ault, *Wild Indigo* (Berkley)

Agatha Awards (Malice Domestic Mystery Convention)

Best novel: Louise Penny, *A Fatal Grace* (St. Martin's Minotaur)

Best first novel: Hank Phillipi Ryan, *Prime Time* (Harlequin)

Best short story: Donna Andrews, "A Rat's Tale" (*Ellery Queen's Mystery Magazine*, September/October)

Best non-fiction: Jon Lellenberg, Daniel Stashower, and Charles Foley, eds., *Arthur Conan Doyle: A Life in Letters* (Penguin)

Best Children's/Young Adult: Sarah Masters Buckey, *A Light in the Cellar* (American Girl)

Lifetime Achievement Award: Peter Lovesey

Poirot Award: Linda Landrigan, editor of *Alfred Hitchcock's Mystery Magazine*, and Janet Hutchings, editor of *Ellery Queen's Mystery Magazine*

Dagger Awards (Crime Writers' Association, Great Britain)

Duncan Lawrie Dagger: Frances Fyfield, *Blood From Stone* (Little, Brown)

International Dagger: Dominique Manotti, *Lorraine Connection* (Arcadia Books)

Ian Fleming Steel Dagger: Tom Rob Smith, *Child 44* (Simon and Schuster)

Best short story: Martin Edwards, "The Bookbinder's Apprentice" (*The Mammoth Book of Best British Mysteries*, Constable, Robinson)

Gold Dagger for Non-fiction: Kester Aspden, *Nationality: Wog; The Hounding of David Oluwale* (Jonathan Cape; Random House)

New Blood Dagger: Matt Rees, *The Bethlehem Murders* (Atlantic)

Diamond Dagger: Sue Grafton

Ellis Peters Award (formerly Historical Dagger): Laura Wilson, *Stratton's War* (Orion)

Dagger in the Library (voted by librarians for a body of work): Craig Russell

Debut Dagger (for unpublished writers): Amer Anwar, *Western Fringes*

Anthony Awards (Bouchercon World Mystery Convention)

Best novel: Laura Lippman, *What the Dead Know* (Morrow)

Best first novel: Tana French, *In the Woods* (Viking)

Best paperback original: P.J. Parrish, *A Thousand Bones* (Pocket)

Best short story: Laura Lippman, "Hardly Knew Her" (*Dead Man's Hand*, Harcourt)

Best critical/biographical: Jon Lellenberg, Daniel Stashower, and Charles Foley, eds., *Arthur Conan Doyle: A Life in Letters* (Penguin)

Special Services Award: Jon and Ruth Jordan for *Crimespree Magazine*

Lifetime Achievement Award: Robert Rosenwald and Barbara Peters

Best website: Stan Ulrich and Lucinda Surber, *Stop You're Killing Me*

Shamus Awards (Private Eye Writers of America)

Best hardcover novel: Reed Farrel Coleman, *Soul Patch* (Bleak House)

Best first novel: Sean Chercover, *Big City, Bad Blood* (Morrow)

Best original paperback novel: Richard Aleas, *Songs of Innocence* (Hard Case)

Best short story: Cornelia Read, "Hungry Enough" (*A Hell of a Woman*, Busted Flush)

The Eye (life achievement): Joe Gores

Hammer Award (for a memorable private eye character or series): The Nameless Detective (created by Bill Pronzini)

Macavity Awards (Mystery Readers International)

Best novel: Laura Lippman, *What the Dead Know* (Morrow)

Best first novel: Tana French, *In the Woods* (Viking)

Best non-fiction: Roger M. Sobin, ed., *The Essential Mystery Lists for Readers, Collectors, and Librarians* (Poisoned Pen)

Best short story: Rhys Bowen, "Please Watch Your Step" (*The Strand Magazine* #21, February-May)

Sue Feder Historical Mystery Award: Ariana Franklin, *Mistress of the Art of Death* (Putnam)

Barry Awards (*Deadly Pleasures* and *Mystery News*)

Best Novel: Laura Lippman, *What the Dead Know* (Morrow)

Best First Novel: Tana French, *In the Woods* (Viking)

Best British Novel: Edward Wright, *Damnation Falls* (Orion)

Best Paperback Original: Megan Abbott, *Queenpin* (Simon and Schuster)

Best Thriller: Robert Crais, *The Watchman* (Simon and Schuster)

Best Short Story: Edward D. Hoch, "The Problem of the Summer Snowman" (*Ellery Queen's Mystery Magazine*, November)

Don Sandstrom Memorial Award for Lifetime Achievement in Mystery Fandom: George Easter; Bill and Toby Gottfried

ITV3 Crime Thriller Awards

Author of the Year: Ian Rankin, *Exit Music* (Orion)

Breakthrough Author of the Year: Stuart MacBride, *Broken Skin* (Harper)

International Author of the Year: Stieg Larsson, *The Girl with the Dragon Tattoo* (Quercus)

Inducted into the International Crime Writing Hall of Fame: P.D. James

Writer's Award for Classic TV Drama: Colin Dexter for Inspector Morse

Film of the Year: *The Bourne Ultimatum*

TV Crime Drama of the Year: *Criminal Justice*

International Crime Drama of the Year: *The Wire*

Best Actress and Actor Awards: Hermione Norris and Rupert Penry-Jones for *Spooks*

Arthur Ellis Awards (Crime Writers of Canada)

Best novel: Jon Redfern, *Trumpets Sound No More* (RendezVous)

Best first novel: Liam Durcan, *Garcia's Heart* (McClelland and Stewart)

Best nonfiction: Julian Sher, *One Child at a Time: The Global Fight to Rescue Children from Online Predators* (Vintage Canada)

Best juvenile novel: Shane Peacock, *Eye of the Crow* (Tundra)

Best short story: Leslie Watts, "Turners" (*Kingston Whig-Standard*, July 7)

The Unhanged Arthur (best unpublished first crime novel): D.J. McIntosh, *The Witch of Babylon*

Best Crime Writing in French: Mario Bolduc, *Tsiganes* (Editions Libre Expression)

Thriller Awards (International Thriller Writers, Inc.)

Best novel: Robert Harris, *The Ghost* (Simon and Schuster)

Best first novel: Joe Hill, *Heart-Shaped Box* (Morrow)

Best paperback original: Tom Piccirilli, *The Midnight Road* (Bantam)

ThrillerMaster Award: Sandra Brown

Silver Bullet Award: David Baldacci

Ned Kelly Awards (Crime Writers' Association of Australia)

Best novel: Michael Robotham, *Shatter* (Little, Brown)

Best first novel: Chris Womersley, *The Low Road* (Scribe)

Best non-fiction: Evan McHugh, *Red Centre, Dark Heart* (Viking)

Lifetime achievement: Marele Day

Dilys Award (Independent Mystery Booksellers Association)

William Kent Krueger, *Thunder Bay* (Atria)

Lefty Award (Left Coast Crime)

(best humorous mystery novel in the English language)

Elaine Viets, *Murder With Reservations* (Signet)

Nero Wolfe Award (Wolfe Pack)
Jonathan Santlofer, *Anatomy of Fear* (Morrow)

Hammett Prize
(International Association of Crime Writers, North America Branch)
Gil Adamson, *The Outlander* (House of Anansi Press)

JON L. BREEN was first published in 1966 with a quiz in *Ellery Queen's Mystery Magazine*, followed the following year by his first short story, a parody of Ed McBain's 87th Precinct. Around a hundred short stories have followed, plus seven novels (with an eighth on the horizon), three story collections, several edited anthologies, three reference books on mystery fiction (two of them Edgar winners), and more book reviews and articles than he can count. In 1977, he became the proprietor of *EQMM*'S "Jury Box" column, which he has contributed ever since, save for a few years in the mid-'80s. He also contributes the "What About Murder?" column to *Mystery Scene* and has been an occasional strictly non-political contributor to *The Weekly Standard.* Retired since the dawn of 2000, he lives happily with his wife, Rita, in Fountain Valley, California.

Father's Day

BY MICHAEL CONNELLY

The victim's tiny body was left alone in the emergency room enclosure. The doctors, after halting their resuscitation efforts, had solemnly retreated and pulled the plastic curtains closed around the bed. The entire construction, management, and purpose of the hospital was to prevent death. When the effort failed, nobody wanted to see it.

The curtains were opaque. Harry Bosch looked like a ghost as he approached and then split them to enter. He stepped into the enclosure and stood somber and alone with the dead. The boy's body took up less than a quarter of the big metal bed. Bosch had worked thousands of cases, but nothing ever touched him like the sight of a young child's lifeless body. Fifteen months old. Cases in which the child's age was still counted in months were the most difficult of all. He knew that if he dwelled too long, he would start to question everything—from the meaning of life to his mission in it.

The boy looked like he was only asleep. Bosch made a quick study, looking for any bruising or sign of mishap. The child was naked and uncovered, his skin as pink as a newborn's. Bosch saw no sign of trauma except for an old scrape on the boy's forehead.

He pulled on gloves and very carefully moved the body to check it from all angles. His heart sank as he did this, but he saw nothing that was suspicious. When he was finished, he covered the body with the sheet—he wasn't sure why—and slipped back through the plastic curtains shrouding the bed.

The boy's father was in a private waiting room down the hall. Bosch would eventually get to him, but the paramedics who had transported the boy had agreed to stick around to be interviewed. Bosch looked for them first and found both men—one old, one young; one to mentor, one to learn—sitting in the crowded ER waiting room. He invited them outside so they could speak privately.

The dry summer heat hit them as soon as the glass doors parted. Like walking out of a casino in Vegas. They walked to the side so they would not be bothered, but stayed in the shade of the portico. He identified himself and told them he would need the written reports on their rescue effort as soon as they were completed.

"For now, tell me about the call."

The senior man did the talking. His name was Ticotin.

"The kid was already in full arrest when we got there," he began. "We did what we could, but the best thing was just to ice him and transport him—try to get him in here and see what the pros could do."

"Did you take a body-temperature reading at the scene?" Bosch asked.

"First thing," Ticotin said. "It was one oh six eight. So you gotta figure the kid was up around one oh eight, one oh nine, before we got there. There was no way he was going to come back from that. Not a little baby like that."

Ticotin shook his head as though he were frustrated by having been sent to rescue someone who could not be rescued. Bosch nodded as he took out his notebook and wrote down the temperature reading.

"You know what time that was?" he asked. "We arrived at twelve seventeen, so I would say we took the BT no more than three minutes later. First thing you do. That's the protocol."

Bosch nodded again and wrote the time—12:20 p.m.—next to the temperature reading. He looked up and tracked a car coming quickly into the ER lot. It parked, and his partner, Ignacio Ferras, got out. He had gone directly to the accident scene while Bosch had gone directly to the hospital. Bosch signaled him over. Ferras walked with anxious speed. Bosch knew he had something to report, but Bosch didn't want him to say it in front of the paramedics. He introduced him and then quickly got back to his questions.

"Where was the father when you got there?"

"They had the kid on the floor by the back door, where he had brought him in. The father was sort of collapsed on the floor next to him, screaming and crying like they do. Kicking the floor."

"Did he ever say anything?"

"Not right then."

"Then when?"

"When we made the decision to transport and work on the kid in the truck, he wanted to go. We told him he couldn't. We told him to get somebody from the office to drive him."

"What were his words?"

"He just said, 'I want to go with him. I want to be with my son,' stuff like that."

Ferras shook his head as if in pain.

"At any time did he talk about what had happened?" Bosch asked.

Ticotin checked his partner, who shook his head.

"No," Ticotin said. "He didn't."

"Then how were you informed of what had happened?"

"Well, initially, we heard it from dispatch. Then one of the office workers, a lady, she told us when we got there. She led us to the back and told us along the way."

Bosch thought he had all he was going to get, but then thought of something else.

"You didn't happen to take an exterior-air-temperature reading for that spot, did you?"

The two paramedics looked at each other and then at Bosch.

"Didn't think to," Ticotin said. "But it's gotta be at least ninety-five, with the Santa Anas kicking up like this. I don't remember a June this hot."

Bosch remembered a June he had spent in a jungle, but wasn't going to get into it. He thanked the paramedics and let them get back to duty. He put his notebook away and looked at his partner.

"Okay, tell me about the scene," he said.

"We've got to charge this guy, Harry," Ferras said urgently.

"Why? What did you find?"

"It's not what I found. It's because it was just a kid, Harry. What kind of father would let this happen? How could he forget?"

Ferras had become a father for the first time six months earlier. Bosch knew this. The experience had made him a professional dad, and every Monday he came in to the squad with a new batch of photos. To Bosch, the kid looked the same week to week, but not to Ferras. He was in love with being a father, with having a son.

"Ignacio, you've got to separate your own feelings about it from the facts and the evidence, okay? You know this. Calm down."

"I know, I know. It's just that, how could he forget, you know?"

"Yeah, I know, and we're going to keep that in mind. So tell me what you found out over there. Who'd you talk to?"

"The office manager."

"And what did he say?"

"It's a lady. She said that he came in through the back door shortly after ten. All the sales agents park in the back and use the back door—that's why nobody saw the kid. The father came in, talking on the cell phone. Then he got off and asked if he'd gotten a fax, but there was no fax. So he made another call, and she heard him ask where the fax was. Then he waited for the fax."

"How long did he wait?"

"She said not long, but the fax was an offer to buy. So he called the client, and that started a whole back-and-forth with calls and faxes, and he completely forgot about the kid. It was at least two hours, Harry. Two hours!"

Bosch could almost share his partner's anger, but he had been on the mission a couple of decades longer than Ferras and knew how to hold it in when he had to and when to let it go.

"Harry, something else too."

"What?"

"The baby had something wrong with him."

"The manager saw the kid?"

"No, I mean, always. Since birth. She said it was a big tragedy. The kid was handicapped. Blind, deaf, a bunch of things wrong. Fifteen months old, and he couldn't walk or talk and never could even crawl. He just cried a lot."

Bosch nodded as he tried to plug this information into everything else he knew and had accumulated. Just then, another car came speeding into the parking lot. It pulled into the ambulance chute in front of the ER doors. A woman leaped out and ran into the ER, leaving the car running and the door open.

"That's probably the mother," Bosch said. "We better get in there."

Bosch started trotting toward the ER doors, and Ferras followed. They went through the ER waiting room and down a hallway, where the father had been placed in a private room to wait.

As Bosch got close, he did not hear any screaming or crying or fists on flesh—things that wouldn't have surprised him. The door was open, and when he turned in, he saw the parents of the dead boy embracing each other, but not a tear lined any of their cheeks. Bosch's initial split-second reaction was that he was seeing relief in their young faces.

They separated when they saw Bosch enter, followed by Ferras.

"Mr. and Mrs. Helton?" he asked.

They nodded in unison. But the man corrected Bosch.

"I'm Stephen Helton, and this is my wife, Arlene Haddon."

"I'm Detective Bosch with the Los Angeles Police Department, and this is my partner, Detective Ferras. We are very sorry for the loss of your son. It is our job now to investigate William's death and to learn exactly what happened to him."

Helton nodded as his wife stepped close to him and put her face into his chest. Something silent was transmitted.

"Does this have to be done now?" Helton asked. "We've just lost our beautiful little—"

"Yes, sir, it has to be done now. This is a homicide investigation."

"It was an accident," Helton weakly protested. "It's all my fault, but it was an accident."

"It's still a homicide investigation. We would like to speak to you each privately, without the intrusions that will occur here. Do you mind coming down to the police station to be interviewed?"

"We'll leave him here?"

"The hospital is making arrangements for your son's body to be moved to the medical examiner's office."

"They're going to cut him open?" the mother asked in a near hysterical voice.

"They will examine his body and then determine if an autopsy is necessary," Bosch said. "It is required by law that any untimely death fall under the jurisdiction of the medical examiner."

He waited to see if there was further protest. When there wasn't, he stepped back and gestured for them to leave the room.

"We'll drive you down to Parker Center, and I promise to make this as painless as possible."

• • •

They placed the grieving parents in separate interview rooms in the third-floor offices of Homicide Special. Because it was Sunday, the cafeteria was closed, and Bosch had to make do with the vending machines in the alcove by the elevators. He got a can of Coke and two packages of cheese crackers. He had not eaten breakfast before being called in on the case and was now famished.

He took his time while eating the crackers and talking things over with Ferras. He wanted both Helton and Haddon to believe that they were waiting while the other spouse was being interviewed. It was a trick of the trade, part of the strategy. Each would have to wonder what the other was saying.

"Okay," Bosch finally said. "I'm going to go in and take the husband. You can watch in the booth or you can take a run at the wife. Your choice."

It was a big moment. Bosch was more than twenty-five years ahead of Ferras on the job. He was the mentor, and Ferras was the student. So far in their fledgling partnership, Bosch had never let Ferras conduct a formal interview. He was allowing that now, and the look on Ferras's face showed that it was not lost on him.

"You're going to let me talk to her?"

"Sure, why not? You can handle it."

"All right if I get in the booth and watch you with him first? That way you can watch me."

"Whatever makes you comfortable."

"Thanks, Harry."

"Don't thank me, Ignacio. Thank yourself. You earned it."

Bosch dumped the empty cracker packages and the can in a trash bin near his desk.

"Do me a favor," he said. "Go on the Internet first and check the *LA Times* to see if they've had any stories lately about a case like this. You know, with a kid. I'd be curious, and if there are, we might be able to make a play with the story. Use it like a prop."

"I'm on it."

"I'll go set up the video in the booth."

Ten minutes later, Bosch entered Interview Room Three, where Stephen Helton was waiting for him. Helton looked like he was not quite thirty years old. He was lean and tan and looked like the perfect real estate salesman. He looked like he had never spent even five minutes in a police station before.

Immediately, he protested.

"What is taking so long? I've just lost my son, and you stick me in this room for an hour? Is that procedure?"

"It hasn't been that long, Stephen. But I am sorry you had to wait. We were talking to your wife, and that went longer than we thought it would."

"Why were you talking to her? Willy was with me the whole time."

"We talked to her for the same reason we're talking to you. I'm sorry for the delay."

Bosch pulled out the chair that was across the small table from Helton and sat down.

"First of all," he said, "thank you for coming in for the interview. You understand that you are not under arrest or anything like that. You are free to go if you wish. But by law we have to conduct an investigation of the death, and we appreciate your cooperation."

"I just want to get it over with so I can begin the process."

"What process is that?"

"I don't know. Whatever process you go through. Believe me, I'm new at this. You know, grief and guilt and mourning. Willy wasn't in our lives very long, but we loved him very much. This is just awful. I made a mistake, and I am going to pay for it for the rest of my life, Detective Bosch."

Bosch almost told him that his son paid for the mistake *with* the rest of his life but chose not to antagonize the man. Instead, he just nodded and noted that Helton had looked down at his lap when he had spoken most of his statement. Averting the eyes was a classic tell that indicated untruthfulness. Another tell was that

Helton had his hands down in his lap and out of sight. The open and truthful person keeps his hands on the table and in sight.

"Why don't we start at the beginning?" Bosch said. "Tell me how the day started."

Helton nodded and began.

"Sunday's our busiest day. We're both in real estate. You may have seen the signs: Haddon and Helton. We're PPG's top-volume team. Today Arlene had an open house at noon and a couple of private showings before that. So Willy was going to be with me. We lost another nanny on Friday, and there was no one else to take him."

"How did you lose the nanny?"

"She quit. They all quit. Willy is a handful . . . because of his condition. I mean, why deal with a handicapped child if someone with a normal, healthy child will pay you the same thing? Subsequently, we go through a lot of nannies."

"So you were left to take care of the boy today while your wife had the property showings."

"It wasn't like I wasn't working, though. I was negotiating a sale that would have brought in a thirty-thousand-dollar commission. It was important."

"Is that why you went into the office?"

"Exactly. We got an offer sheet, and I was going to have to respond. So I got Willy ready and put him in the car and went in to work."

"What time was this?"

"About quarter to ten. I got the call from the other realtor at about nine thirty. The buyer was playing hardball. The response time was going to be set at an hour. So I had to get my seller on standby, pack up Willy, and get in there to pick up the fax."

"Do you have a fax at home?"

"Yes, but if the deal went down, we'd have to get together in the office. We have a signing room, and all the forms are right there. My file on the property was in my office too."

Bosch nodded. It sounded plausible, to a point.

"Okay, so you head off to the office . . ."

"Exactly. And two things happened . . ."

Helton brought his hands up into sight but only to hold them across his face to hide his eyes. A classic tell.

"What two things?"

"I got a call on my cell—from Arlene—and Willy fell asleep in his car seat. Do you understand?"

"Make me understand."

"I was distracted by the call, and I was no longer distracted by Willy. He had fallen asleep."

"Uh-huh."

"So I forgot he was there. Forgive me, God, but I forgot I had him with me!"

"I understand. What happened next?"

Helton dropped his hands out of sight again. He looked at Bosch briefly and then at the tabletop.

"I parked in my assigned space behind PPG, and I went in. I was still talking to Arlene. One of our buyers is trying to get out of a contract because he's found something he likes better. So we were talking about that, about how to finesse things with that, and I was on the phone when I went in."

"Okay, I see that. What happened when you went in?"

Helton didn't answer right away. He sat there looking at the table as if trying to remember so he could get the answer right.

"Stephen?" Bosch prompted. "What happened next?"

"I had told the buyer's agent to fax me the offer. But it wasn't there. So I got off the line from my wife and I called the agent. Then I waited around for the fax. Checked my slips and made a few callbacks while I was waiting."

"What are your slips?"

"Phone messages. People who see our signs on properties and call. I don't put my cell or home number on the signs."

"How many callbacks did you make?"

"I think just two. I got a message on one and spoke briefly to the other person. My fax came in, and that was what I was there for. I got off the line."

"Now, at this point it was what time?"

"I don't know, about ten after ten."

"Would you say that at this point you were still cognizant that your son was still in your car in the parking lot?"

Helton took time to think through an answer again but spoke before Bosch had to prompt him.

"No, because if I knew he was in the car, I would not have left him in the first place. I forgot about him while I was still in the car. You understand?"

Bosch leaned back in his seat. Whether he understood it or not, Helton had just dodged one legal bullet. If he had acknowledged that he had knowingly left the boy in the car—even if he planned to be back in a few minutes—that would have greatly supported a charge of negligent homicide. But Helton had maneuvered the question correctly, almost as if he had expected it.

"Okay," Bosch said. "What happened next?"

Helton shook his head wistfully and looked at the sidewall as if gazing through a window toward the past he couldn't change.

"I, uh, got involved in the deal," he said. "The fax came in, I called my client, and I faxed back a counter. I also did a lot of talking to the other agent. By phone. We were trying to get the deal done, and we had to hand-hold both our clients through this."

"For two hours."

"Yes, it took that long."

"And when was it that you remembered that you had left William in the car out in the parking lot, where it was about ninety-five degrees?"

"I guess as soon—first of all, I didn't know what the temperature was. I object to that. I left that car at about ten, and it was not ninety-five degrees. Not even close. I hadn't even used the air conditioner on the way over."

There was a complete lack of remorse or guilt in Helton's demeanor. He wasn't even attempting to fake it anymore. Bosch had become convinced that this man had no love or affinity for his damaged and now lost child. William was simply a burden that had to be dealt with and therefore could easily be forgotten when things like business and selling houses and making money came up.

But where was the crime in all this? Bosch knew he could charge him with negligence, but the courts tend to view the loss of a child as enough punishment in these situations. Helton would go free with his wife as sympathetic figures, free to continue their lives while baby William moldered in his grave.

The tells always add up. Bosch instinctively believed Helton was a liar. And he began to believe that William's death was no accident. Unlike his partner, who had let the passions of his own fatherhood lead him down the path, Bosch had come to this point after careful observation and analysis. It was now time to press on, to bait Helton and see if he would make a mistake.

"Is there anything else you want to add at this point to the story?" he asked.

Helton let out a deep breath and slowly shook his head. "That's the whole sad story," he said. "I wish to God it never happened. But it did."

He looked directly at Bosch for the first time during the entire interview. Bosch held his gaze and then asked a question.

"Do you have a good marriage, Stephen?"

Helton looked away and stared at the invisible window again.

"What do you mean?"

"I mean, do you have a good marriage? You can say yes or no if you want."

"Yes, I have a good marriage," Helton responded emphatically. "I don't know what my wife told you, but I think it is very solid. What are you trying to say?"

"All I'm saying is that sometimes, when there is a child with challenges, it strains the marriage. My partner just had a baby.

The kid's healthy, but money's tight and his wife isn't back at work yet. You know the deal. It's tough. I can only imagine what the strain of having a child with William's difficulties would be like."

"Yeah, well, we made it by all right."

"The nannies quitting all the time . . ."

"It wasn't that hard. As soon as one quits, we put an ad on craigslist for another."

Bosch nodded and scratched the back of his head. While doing this, he waved a finger in a circular motion toward the camera that was in the air vent up on the wall behind him. Helton could not see him do this.

"When did you two get married?" he asked.

"Two and a half years ago. We met on a contract. She had the buyer, and I had the seller. We worked well together. We started talking about joining forces, and then we realized we were in love."

"Then William came."

"Yes, that's right."

"That must've changed things."

"It did."

"So when Arlene was pregnant, couldn't the doctors tell that he had these problems?"

"They could have if they had seen him. But Arlene's a workaholic. She was busy all the time. She missed some appointments and the ultrasounds. When they discovered there was a problem, it was too late."

"Do you blame your wife for that?"

Helton looked aghast.

"No, of course not. Look, what does this have to do with what happened today? I mean, why are you asking me all this?"

Bosch leaned across the table.

"It may have a lot to do with it, Stephen. I am trying to determine what happened today and why. The 'why' is the tough part."

"It was an accident! I *forgot* he was in the car, okay? I will go to my grave knowing that *my* mistake killed my own son. Isn't that enough for you?"

Bosch leaned back and said nothing. He hoped Helton would say more.

"Do you have a son, Detective? Any children?"

"A daughter."

"Yeah, well then, happy Father's Day. I'm really glad for you. I hope you never have to go through what I'm going through right now. Believe me, it's not fun!"

Bosch had forgotten it was Father's Day. The realization knocked him off his rhythm, and his thoughts went to his daughter living eight thousand miles away. In her ten years, he had been with her on only one Father's Day. What did that say about him? Here he was, trying to get inside another father's actions and motivations, and he knew his own could not stand equal scrutiny.

The moment ended when there was a knock on the door and Ferras came in, carrying a file.

"Excuse me," he said. "I thought you might want to see this."

He handed the file to Bosch and left the room. Bosch turned the file on the table in front of them and opened it, so that Helton would not be able to see its contents. Inside was a computer printout and a handwritten note on a Post-it.

The note said: "No ad on craigslist."

The printout was of a story that ran in the *LA Times* ten months earlier. It was about the heatstroke death of a child who had been left in a car in Lancaster while his mother ran into a store to buy milk. She ran into the middle of a robbery. She was tied up along with the store clerk and placed in a back room. The robbers ransacked the store and escaped. It was an hour before the victims were discovered and freed, but by then the child in the car had already succumbed to heatstroke. Bosch scanned the story quickly, then dropped the file closed. He looked at Helton without speaking.

"What?" Helton asked.

"Just some additional information and lab reports," he lied. "Do you get the *LA Times,* by the way?"

"Yes, why?"

"Just curious, that's all. Now, how many nannies do you think you've employed in the fifteen months that William was alive?"

Helton shook his head.

"I don't know. At least ten. They don't stay long. They can't take it."

"And then you go to craigslist to place an ad?"

"Yes."

"And you just lost a nanny on Friday?"

"Yes, I told you."

"She just walked out on you?"

"No, she got another job and told us she was leaving. She made up a lie about it being closer to home and with gas prices and all that. But we knew why she was leaving. She could not handle Willy."

"She told you this Friday?"

"No, when she gave notice."

"When was that?"

"She gave two weeks' notice, so it was two weeks back from Friday."

"And do you have a new nanny lined up?"

"No, not yet. We were still looking."

"But you put the feelers out and ran the ad again, that sort of thing?"

"Right, but listen, what does this have to—"

"Let me ask the questions, Stephen. Your wife told us that she worried about leaving William with you, that you couldn't handle the strain of it."

Helton looked shocked. The statement came from left field, as Bosch had wanted it.

"What? Why would she say that?"

"I don't know. Is it true?"

"No, it's not true."

"She told us she was worried that this wasn't an accident."

"That's absolutely crazy and I doubt she said it. You are lying."

He turned in his seat, so that the front of his body faced the corner of the room and he would have to turn his face to look directly at Bosch. Another tell. Bosch knew he was zeroing in. He decided it was the right time to gamble.

"She mentioned a story you found in the *LA Times* that was about a kid left in a car up in Lancaster. The kid died of heatstroke. She was worried that it gave you the idea."

Helton swiveled in his seat and leaned forward to put his elbows on the table and run his hands through his hair.

"Oh, my God, I can't believe she . . ."

He didn't finish. Bosch knew his gamble had paid off. Helton's mind was racing along the edge. It was time to push him over.

"You didn't forget that William was in the car, did you, Stephen?"

Helton didn't answer. He buried his face in his hands again. Bosch leaned forward, so that he only had to whisper.

"You left him there and you knew what was going to happen. You planned it. That's why you didn't bother running ads for a new nanny. You knew you weren't going to need one."

Helton remained silent and unmoving. Bosch kept working him, changing tacks and offering sympathy now.

"It's understandable," he said. "I mean, what kind of life would that kid have, anyway? Some might even call this a mercy killing. The kid falls asleep and never wakes up. I've worked these kinds of cases before, Stephen. It's actually not a bad way to go. It sounds bad, but it isn't. You just get tired and you go to sleep."

Helton kept his face in his hands, but he shook his head. Bosch didn't know if he was denying it still or shaking off something else. He waited, and the delay paid off.

"It was her idea," Helton said in a quiet voice. "She's the one who couldn't take it anymore."

In that moment Bosch knew he had him, but he showed nothing. He kept working it.

"Wait a minute," Bosch said. "She said she had nothing to do with it, that this was your idea and your plan and that when she called you, it was to talk you out of it."

Helton dropped his hands with a slap on the table.

"That's a lie! It was her! She was embarrassed that we had a kid like that! She couldn't take him anywhere and we couldn't go anywhere! He was ruining our lives and she told me I had to do something about it! She told me how to do something about it! She said I would be saving two lives while sacrificing only one."

Bosch pulled back across the table. It was done. It was over.

"Okay, Stephen, I think I understand. And I want to hear all about it. But at this point I need to inform you of your rights. After that, if you want to talk, we'll talk, and I'll listen."

• • •

When Bosch came out of the interview room, Ignacio Ferras was there, waiting for him in the hallway. His partner raised his fist, and Bosch tapped his knuckles with his own fist.

"That was beautiful," Ferras said. "You walked him right down the road."

"Thanks," Bosch said. "Let's hope the DA is impressed too."

"I don't think we'll have to worry."

"Well, there will be no worries if you go into the other room and turn the wife now."

Ferras looked surprised.

"You still want me to take the wife?"

"She's yours. Let's walk them into the DA as bookends."

"I'll do my best."

"Good. Go check the equipment and make sure we're still recording in there. I've got to go make a quick call."

"You got it, Harry."

Bosch walked into the squad room and sat down at his desk. He checked his watch and knew it would be getting late in Hong Kong. He pulled out his cell phone anyway and sent a call across the Pacific.

His daughter answered with a cheerful hello. Bosch knew he wouldn't even have to say anything and he would feel fulfilled by just the sound of her voice saying the one word.

"Hey, baby, it's me," he said.

"Daddy!" she exclaimed "Happy Father's Day!"

And Bosch realized in that moment that he was indeed a happy man.

MICHAEL CONNELLY'S 19th novel, *The Brass Verdict,* was released in October 2008, and debuted at #1 on the *New York Times* bestseller list. It introduces Lincoln lawyer Mickey Haller to LAPD Detective Harry Bosch in a fast-paced legal thriller. Michael's 20th novel, *The Scarecrow,* will be released in May 2009, and reunites reporter Jack McEvoy and FBI Agent Rachel Walling for the first time since *The Poet.* His books have been translated in 35 languages and have won the Edgar Award, Anthony Award, Macavity Award, Los Angeles Times Best Mystery/Thriller Award, Shamus Award, Dilys Award, Nero Award, Barry Award, Audie Award, Ridley Award, Maltese Falcon Award (Japan), .38 Caliber Award (France), Grand Prix Award (France), Premio Bancarella Award (Italy), and the Pepe Carvalho award (Spain). Michael was the President of the Mystery Writers of America organization in 2003 and 2004, and edited both the MWA anthology *The Blue Religion* and the Edgar Allan Poe anthology *In the Shadow of the Master.* He lives with his family in Florida.

Walking the Dog

BY PETER ROBINSON

The dog days came to the Beaches in August and the boardwalk was crowded. Even the dog owners began to complain about the heat. Laura Francis felt as if she had been locked in the bathroom after a hot shower as she walked Big Ears down to the fenced-off compound on Kew Beach, where he could run free. She said hello to the few people she had seen there before while Big Ears sniffed the shrubbery and moved on to play with a Labrador retriever.

"They seem to like each other," said a voice beside her.

Laura turned and saw a man she thought she recognized, but not from the Beaches. She couldn't say where. He was handsome in a chiseled, matinee-idol sort of way, and the tight jeans and white T-shirt did justice to his well-toned muscles and tapered waist. Where did she know him from?

"You must excuse Big Ears," she said. "He's such a womanizer."

"It's nothing Rain can't handle."

"Rain? That's an unusual name for a dog."

He shrugged. "Is it? It was raining the day I picked her up from the Humane Society. Raining cats and dogs. Anyway, you're one to talk, naming dogs after English children's book characters."

Laura felt herself flush. "My mother used to read them to me when I was little. I grew up in England."

"I can tell by the accent. I'm Ray, by the way. Ray Lanagan."

"Laura Francis. Pleased to meet you."

"Laura? After the movie?"

"After my grandmother."

"Pity. You do look a bit like Gene Tierney, you know."

Laura tried to remember whether Gene Tierney was the one with an overbite or the large breasts and tight sweaters. As she had both, herself, she supposed it didn't really matter. She blushed again. "Thank you."

They stood in an awkward, edgy silence while the dogs played on around them. Then, all of a sudden, Laura remembered where she had seen Ray before. Jesus, of course, it was him, the one from the TV commercial, the one for some sort of male aftershave or deodorant where he was stripped to the waist, wearing tight jeans like today. She'd seen him in a magazine too. She had even fantasized about him, imagined it was him there in bed with her instead of Lloyd grunting away on top of her as if he were running a marathon.

"What is it?" Ray asked.

She brushed a strand of hair from her hot cheek. "Nothing. I just remembered where I've seen you before. You're an actor, aren't you?"

"For my sins."

"Are you here to make a movie?" It wasn't as stupid a question as it might have sounded. The studios were just down the road and Toronto had almost as big a reputation for being Hollywood North as Vancouver. Laura ought to know; Lloyd was always telling her about it since he ran a post-production company.

"No," Ray said. "I'm resting, as we say in the business."

"Oh."

"I've got a couple of things lined up," he went on. "Commercials, a small part in a new CBC legal drama. That sort of thing. And whatever comes my way by chance."

"It sounds exciting."

"Not really. It's a living. To be honest, its mostly a matter of hanging around while the techies get the sound and light right. But what about you? What do you do?"

"Me?" She pointed her thumb at her chest. "Nothing. I mean, I'm just a housewife." It was true, she supposed: "Housewife" was just about the only way she could describe herself. But she wasn't even that. Alexa did all the housework, and Paul handled the garden. Laura had even hired a company to come in and clear the snow. So what did she do with her time, apart from shop and walk Big Ears? Sometimes she made dinner, but more often than not she made reservations. There were so many good restaurants on her stretch of Queens Street East—anything you wanted, Japanese, Greek, Indian, Chinese, Italian—that it seemed a shame to waste them.

The hazy bright sun beat down mercilessly and the water looked like a ruffled blue bedsheet beyond the wire fence.

"Would you like to go for a drink?" Ray asked. "I'm not coming on to you or anything, but it *is* a real scorcher."

Laura felt her heart give a little flutter and, if she were honest with herself, a pleasurable warmth spread through her lower belly.

"Okay. Yes, I mean, sure," she said. "Look, it's a bit of a hassle going to a café or pub with the dogs, right? Why don't you come up to the house? It's not far. Silver Birch. There's cold beer in the fridge, and I left the air-conditioning on."

Ray looked at her. He certainly had beautiful eyes, she thought, and they seemed especially steely blue in this kind of light. Blue eyes and black hair, a devastating combination. "Sure," he said. "If it's okay. Lead on."

They put Big Ears and Rain on leashes and walked up to Queen Street, which was crowded with tourists and locals pulling kids in bright-colored carts, all OshKosh B'Gosh and Birkenstocks. People browsed in shop windows, sat outdoors at Starbucks in shorts drinking their Frappucinos and reading the *Globe and Mail,* and there was a line outside the ice-cream shop. The traffic was moving at a crawl, but you could smell the coconut sunblock over the gas fumes.

Laura's large detached house stood at the top of a long flight of steps sheltered by overhanging shrubbery, and once they were off the street, nobody could see them. Not that it mattered, Laura told herself. It was all innocent enough.

It was a relief to get inside, and even the dogs seemed to collapse in a panting heap and enjoy the cool air.

"Nice place," said Ray, looking around the modern kitchen, with its central island and pots and pans hanging from hooks overhead.

Laura opened the fridge. "Beer? Coke? Juice?"

"I'll have a beer, if that's okay," said Ray.

"Beck's all right?"

"Perfect."

She opened Ray a Beck's and poured herself a glass of orange juice, the kind with extra pulp. Her heart was beating fast. Perhaps it was the heat, the walk home? She watched Ray drink his beer from the bottle, his Adam's apple bobbing. When she took a sip of juice, a little dribbled out of her mouth and down her chin. Before she could make a move to get a napkin and wipe it off, Ray had moved forward just as far as it took, bent toward her, put his tongue on the curve under her lower lip, and licked it off.

She felt his heat and shivered. "Ray, I'm not sure . . . I mean, I don't think we should . . . I . . ."

The first kiss nearly drew blood. The second one did. Laura fell back against the fridge and felt the Mickey Mouse magnet that held the weekly to-do list digging into her shoulder. She experienced a moment of panic as Ray ripped open her Holt Renfrew blouse. What did she think she was doing, inviting a strange man into her home like this? He could be a serial killer or something. But fear quickly turned to pleasure when his mouth found her nipple. She moaned and pulled him against her and spread her legs apart. His hand moved up under her long, loose skirt, caressing the bare flesh of her thighs and rubbing between her legs.

Laura had never been so wet in her life, had never wanted it so much, and she didn't want to wait. Somehow, she maneuvered them toward the dining room table and tugged at his belt and zipper as they stumbled backwards. She felt the edge of the table bump against the backs of her thighs and eased herself up on it, sweeping a couple of Waterford crystal glasses to the floor as she did so. The dogs barked. Ray was good and hard and he pulled her panties aside as she guided him smoothly inside her.

"Fuck me, Ray," she breathed. "Fuck me."

And he fucked her. He fucked her until she hammered with her fists on the table and a Royal Doulton cup and saucer joined the broken crystal on the floor. The dogs howled. Laura howled. When she sensed that Ray was about to come, she pulled him closer and said, "Bite me."

And he bit her.

• • •

"I really think we should have that dog put down," said Lloyd after dinner that evening. "For God's sake, biting you like that. It could have given you rabies or something."

"Don't be silly. Big Ears isn't in the least bit rabid. It was an accident, that's all. I was just a bit too rough with him."

"It's the thin end of the wedge. Next time it'll be the postman, or some kid in the street. Think what'll happen then."

"We are not having Big Ears put down, and that's final. I'll be more careful in future."

"You just make sure you are." Lloyd paused, then asked, "Have you thought any more about that other matter I mentioned?"

Oh God, Laura thought, not again. Lloyd hated their house, hated the Beaches, hated Toronto. He wanted to sell up and move to Vancouver, live in Kitsilano or out on Point Grey. No matter that it rained there 364 days out of every year and all you could get to eat was sushi and alfalfa sprouts. Laura didn't want to live in Lotus Land. She was happy where she was. Even happier since that afternoon.

As Lloyd droned on and on, she drifted into pleasant reminiscences of Ray's body on hers, the hard, sharp edges of his white teeth as they closed on the soft part of her neck. They had done it again, up in the bed this time, her and Lloyd's bed. It was slower, less urgent, more gentle, but if anything, it was even better. She could still remember the warm ripples and floods of pleasure, like breaking waves running up through her loins and her belly, and she could feel a pleasant soreness between her legs even now, as she sat listening to Lloyd outline the advantages of moving the post-production company to Vancouver. Plenty of work there, he said. Hollywood connections. But if they moved, she would never see Ray again. It seemed more imperative than ever now to put a stop to it. She had to do something.

"I really don't want to talk about it, darling," she said.

"You never do."

"You know what I think of Vancouver."

"It doesn't rain that much."

"It's not just that. It's . . . Oh, can't we leave it be?"

Lloyd put his hand up. "All right," he said. "All right. Subject closed for tonight." He got up and walked over to the drinks cabinet. "I feel like a cognac."

Laura had that sinking feeling. She knew what was coming.

"Where is it?" Lloyd asked.

"Where is what, darling?"

"My snifter, my favorite brandy snifter. The one my father bought me."

"Oh, that," said Laura, remembering the shattered glass she had swept up from the hardwood floor. "I meant to tell you. I'm sorry, but there was an accident. The dishwasher."

Lloyd turned to look at her in disbelief. "You put my favorite crystal snifter in the *dishwasher?*"

"I know. I'm sorry. I was in a hurry."

Lloyd frowned. "A hurry? You? What do you ever have to be in a hurry about? Walking the bloody dog?"

Laura tried to laugh it off. "If only you knew half the things I had to do around the place, darling."

Lloyd continued to look at her. His eyes narrowed. "You've had quite a day, haven't you?" he said.

Laura sighed. "I suppose so. It's just been one of those days."

"This'll have to do then," he said, pouring a generous helping of Remy into a different crystal snifter.

It was just as good as the one she had broken, Laura thought. In fact, it was probably more expensive. But it wasn't his. It wasn't the one his miserable old bastard of a father, God rot his soul, had bought him.

Lloyd sat down and sipped his cognac thoughtfully. The next time he spoke, Laura could see the way he was looking at her over the top of his glass. *That* look. "How about an early night?" he said.

Laura's stomach lurched. She put her hand to her forehead. "Oh, not tonight, darling. I'm sorry, but I have a terrible headache."

• • •

She didn't see Ray for nearly a week and she was going crazy with fear that he'd left town, maybe gone to Hollywood to be a star, that he'd just used her and discarded her the way men did. After all, they had only been together the once, and he hadn't told her he loved her or anything. All they had done was fuck. They didn't really *know* one another at all. They hadn't even exchanged phone numbers. She just had this absurd feeling that they were meant for each other, that it was *destiny.* A foolish fantasy, no doubt, but one that hurt like a knife jabbing into her heart every day she didn't see him.

Then one day, there he was at the beach again, as if he'd never been away. The dogs greeted each other like long lost friends while Laura tried to play it cool as lust burned through her like a forest fire.

"Hello, stranger," she said.

"I'm sorry," Ray said. "A job came up. Shampoo commercial. On-the-spot decision. Yes or no. I had to work on location in Niagara Falls. You're not mad at me, are you? It's not as if I could phone you and let you know or anything."

"Niagara Falls? How romantic."

"The bride's second great disappointment."

"What?"

"Oscar Wilde. What he said."

Laura giggled and put her hand to her mouth. "Oh, I see."

"I'd love to have taken you with me. I know it wouldn't have been a disappointment for us. I missed you."

Laura blushed. "I missed you too. Want a cold beer?"

"Look," said Ray, "why don't we go to my place? It's only a top floor flat, but it's air-conditioned, and . . ."

"And what?"

"Well, you know, the neighbors . . ."

Laura couldn't tell him this, but she had gotten such an incredible rush out of doing it with Ray in *her own bed* that she couldn't stand the thought of going to his flat, no matter how nice and cool it was. Though she had changed and washed the sheets, she imagined she could still smell him when she lay her head down for the night, and now she wanted her bed to absorb even more of him.

"Don't worry about the neighbors," she said. "They're all out during the day anyway, and the nannies have to know how to be discreet if they want to stay in this country."

"Are you sure?"

"Perfectly."

And so it went on. Once, twice, sometimes three times a week, they went back to Laura's big house on Silver Birch. Sometimes they couldn't wait to get upstairs, so they did it on the dining room table like the first time, but mostly they did it in the king-size bed, becoming more and more adventurous and experimental as they got to know one another's bodies and pleasure zones. Laura found a little pain quite stimulating sometimes, and Ray didn't mind obliging. They sampled all the positions and all the orifices, and when they had exhausted them, they started over again. They talked too, a lot, between bouts. Laura told Ray how unhappy she was with her marriage, and Ray told her how his ex-wife had ditched him for his accountant because his career wasn't exactly going in the same direction as Russell Crowe's, as his bank account made abundantly clear.

Then one day, when they had caught their breath after a particularly challenging position that wasn't even in the *Kama Sutra,* Laura said, "Lloyd wants to move to Vancouver. He won't stop going on about it. And he never gives up until he gets his way."

Ray turned over and leaned on his elbow. "You can't leave," he said.

It was as simple as that. *You can't leave.* She looked at him and beamed. "I know," she said. "You're right. I can't."

"Divorce him. Live with me. I want us to have a normal life, go places together like everyone else, go out for dinner, go to the movies, take vacations."

It was everything she wanted too. "Do you mean it, Ray?"

"Of course I mean it." He paused. "I love you, Laura."

Tears came to her eyes. "Oh my God." She kissed him and told him she loved him too, and a few minutes later they resumed the conversation. "I can't divorce him," Laura said.

"Why on earth not?"

"For one thing, he's a Catholic. He's not practicing or anything, but he doesn't believe in divorce." Or more importantly, Laura thought, his poor dead father, who *was* devout in a bugger-the-choirboy sort of way, didn't believe in it.

"And . . . ?"

"Well, there's the money."

"What about the money?"

"It's mine. I mean, I inherited it from my father. He was an inventor and he came up with one of those simple little additives that keep things fresh for years. Anyway, he made a lot of money, and I was his only child, so I got it all. I've been financing Lloyd's post-production career from the beginning, before it started doing as well as it is now. If we divorced, with these no-fault laws we've got now, he'd get half of everything. That's not fair. It should be all mine by rights."

"I don't care about the money. It's you I want."

She touched his cheek. "That's sweet, Ray, and I wouldn't care if we didn't have two cents between us as long as we were together, honest I wouldn't. But it doesn't have to be that way. The money's there. And everything I have is yours."

"So what's the alternative?"

She put her hand on his chest and ran it over the soft hair down to his flat stomach and beyond, kissed the eagle tattoo on his arm. She remembered it from the TV commercial and the magazine, had thought it was sexy even then. The dogs stirred for a moment at the side of the bed, then went back to sleep. They'd had a lot of exercise that morning. "There's the house too," Laura went on, "and Lloyd's life insurance. Double indemnity, or something like that. I don't really understand these things, but it's really quite a lot of money. Enough to live on for a long time, maybe somewhere in the Caribbean? Or Europe. I've always wanted to live in Paris."

"What are you saying?"

Laura paused. "What if Lloyd had an accident? . . . No, hear me out. Just suppose he had an accident. We'd have everything then. The house, the insurance, the business, my inheritance. It would all be ours. And we could be together for always."

"An accident? You're talking about—"

She put her finger to his lips. "No, darling, don't say it. Don't say the word."

But whether he said it or not, she knew, as she knew he did, what the word was, and it sent a delightful shiver up her spine. After a while, Ray said, "I might know someone. I did an unusual job once, impersonated a police officer in Montreal, a favor for someone who knew someone whose son was in trouble. You don't need to know who he is, but he's connected. He was very pleased with the way things worked out and he said if ever I needed anything . . ."

"Well, there you are then," said Laura, sitting up. "Do you know how to find this man? Do you think he could arrange something?"

Ray took her left nipple between his thumb and forefinger and squeezed. "I think so," he said. "But it won't be easy. I'd have to go to Montreal. Make contact. Right at the moment, though, something a bit more urgent has come up."

Laura saw what he meant. She slid down and took him in her mouth.

• • •

Time moved on, as it does. The days cooled, but Ray and Laura's passion didn't. Just after Thanksgiving, the weather forecasters predicted a big drop in temperature and encouraged Torontonians to wrap up warm.

Laura and Ray didn't need any warm wrapping. The rose-patterned duvet lay on the floor at the bottom of the bed, and they were bathed in sweat, panting, as Laura straddled Ray and worked them both to a shuddering climax. Instead of rolling off him when they had finished, this time Laura stayed on top and leaned forward, her hard nipples brushing his chest. They hadn't seen each other for a week because Ray had finally met his contact in Montreal.

"Did you talk to that man you know?" she asked after she had caught her breath.

Ray linked his hands behind his head. "Yes," he said.

"Does he know what . . . I mean, what we want him to do?"

"He knows."

"To take his time and wait for absolutely the right opportunity?"

"He won't do it himself. The man he'll put on it is a professional, honey. He knows."

"And will he do it when the right time comes? It must seem like an accident."

"He'll do it. Don't worry."

"You know," Laura said, "you can stay all night if you want. Lloyd's away in Vancouver. Probably looking for property."

"Are you sure?"

"He won't be back till Thursday. We could just stay in bed the whole week." Laura shivered.

"Cold, honey?"

"A little. Winter's coming. Can't you feel the chill?"

"Now that you mention it . . ."

Laura jumped out of bed and skipped over to the far wall. "No wonder," she said. "The thermostat's set really low. Lloyd must have turned it down before he went away." She turned it up and dashed back, jumped on the bed, and straddled Ray. She gasped as he thrust himself inside her again. So much energy. This time he didn't let her stay in control. He grabbed her shoulders and pushed her over on her back, in the good old missionary position, and pounded away so hard Laura thought the bed was going to break. This time, as Laura reached the edges of her orgasm, she thought that if she died at that moment, in that state of bliss, she would be happy forever. Then the thermostat clicked in, the house exploded, and Laura got her wish.

• • •

TWO DOGS PERISH IN BEACHES GAS EXPLOSION, Lloyd Francis read in the *Toronto Star* the following morning. *HOUSE-OWNERS ALSO DIE IN TRAGIC ACCIDENT.*

Well, they got that wrong on two counts, thought Lloyd. He

was sitting over a cappuccino in his shirtsleeves at an outdoor cafe on Robson Street in Vancouver. While the cold snap had descended on the east with a vengeance, the West Coast was enjoying record temperatures for the time of year. And no rain.

Lloyd happened to know that only one of the house's owners had died in the explosion, and that it hadn't been an accident. Far from it. Lloyd had planned the whole thing very carefully from the moment he had found out that his wife was enjoying a *grand passion* with an out-of-work actor. That hadn't been difficult. For a start, she had begun washing the bedsheets and pillowcases almost every day, though she usually left the laundry to Alexa. Despite her caution, he had once seen blood on the sheets. Laura had also been unusually reluctant to have sex with him, and on the few occasions he had persuaded her to comply, it had been obvious to him that her thoughts were elsewhere and that, in the crude vernacular, he had been getting sloppy seconds.

Not that Laura hadn't been careful. Lord only knew, she had probably stood under the shower for hours. But he could still tell. There was another man's smell about her. And then, of course, he had simply lain in wait one day and seen them returning together from the beach. After that, it hadn't been hard to find out where the man, Ray Lanagan, lived, and what he did, or didn't do. Lloyd was quite pleased with his detective abilities. Maybe he was in the wrong profession. He had shown himself to be pretty good at murder too, and he was certain that no one would be able to prove that the explosion in which his wife and her lover had died had been anything but a tragic accident. Things like that happened every year in Toronto when the heat came on. A slow leak, building over time, a stray spark or naked flame, and BANG!

Lloyd sipped his cappuccino and took a bite of his croissant.

"You seem preoccupied, darling," said Anne-Marie, looking lovely in a low-cut white top and a short denim skirt opposite him, her dark hair framing the delicate oval face, those tantalizing ruby lips. "What is it?"

"Nothing," said Lloyd. "Nothing at all. But I think I might have to fly back to Toronto today. Just for a short while."

Anne-Marie's face dropped. She was so expressive, showing joy or disappointment, pleasure or pain, without guile. This time it was clearly disappointment. "Oh, must you?"

"I'm afraid I must," he said, taking her hand and caressing it. "I have some important business to take care of. But I promise you I'll be back as soon as I can."

"And we'll look into getting that house we saw near Spanish Beach?"

"I'll put in an offer before I leave," Lloyd said. "It'll have to be in your name, though."

She wrinkled her nose. "I know. Tax reasons."

"Exactly. Good girl." It was only a little white lie, Lloyd told himself. But it wouldn't look good if he bought a new house in a faraway city the day after his wife died in a tragic explosion. This called for careful planning and pacing. Anne-Marie would understand. Marital separations were complicated and difficult, as complex as the tax laws, and all that really mattered was that she knew he loved her. After the funeral, he might feel the need to "get away for a while," and then perhaps Toronto would remind him too much of Laura, so it would be understandable if he moved somewhere else, say Vancouver. After a decent period of mourning, it would also be quite acceptable to "meet someone," Anne-Marie, for example, and start anew, which was exactly what Lloyd Francis had in mind.

• • •

Detective Bobby Aiken didn't like the look of the report that had landed on his desk, didn't like the look of it at all. He worked out of police headquarters at 40 College Street, downtown, and under normal circumstances, he would never have heard of Laura Francis and Ray Lanagan. The Beaches was 55 Division's territory. But these weren't normal circumstances, and one of Aiken's jobs was to have a close look at borderline cases, where everything *looked* kosher but someone thought it wasn't. This time it was a young, ambitious beat cop who desperately wanted to work Homicide. There was just something about it, he'd said, something that didn't ring true, and the more Bobby Aiken looked at the files, the more he knew what the kid was talking about.

The forensics were clean, of course. The fire department and the Centre for Forensic Sciences had done sterling work there, as usual. These gas explosions were unfortunately commonplace in some of the older houses, where the owners might not have had their furnaces serviced or replaced for a long time, as had happened at the house on Silver Birch. An accident waiting to happen.

But police work, thank God, wasn't only a matter of forensics. There were other considerations here. Three of them.

Again, Aiken went through the files and jotted down his thoughts. Outside on College Street it was raining, and when he looked out of his window all he could see were the tops of umbrellas. A streetcar rumbled by, sparks flashing from the overhead wire. Cars splashed up water from the gutters.

First of all, Aiken noted, the victims hadn't been husband and wife, as the investigators and media had first thought. The husband, Lloyd Francis, had flown back from a business trip in Vancouver—giving himself a nice alibi, by the way—as soon as he had heard the news the following day, and he was doubly distraught to find out that not only was his wife dead, but that she had died in bed with another man.

No, Lloyd had said, he had no idea who the man was, but it hadn't taken a Sherlock Holmes to discover that his name was Ray Lanagan, and that he was a sometime actor and sometime petty crook, with a record of minor fraud and con jobs. Lanagan had been clean for the past three years, relying mostly on TV commercials and bit parts in series like *Da Vinci's Inquest,* before the CBC canned it, and *The Murdoch Mysteries.* But Aiken knew that didn't necessarily mean he hadn't been up to something. He just hadn't been caught. Well, he had definitely been up to one thing—screwing Lloyd Francis's wife—and the penalty for that had been far more severe than for any other offense he had ever committed. He might have been after the broad's money too, Aiken speculated, but he sure as hell wasn't going to get that now.

The second thing that bothered Aiken was the insurance and the money angle in general. Not only were the house and Laura Francis's life insured for hefty sums, but there was the post-production company, which was just starting to turn a good profit, and Laura's inheritance, which was still a considerable sum, tied up in stocks and bonds and other investments. Whoever got his hands on all of that would be very rich indeed.

And then there was Lloyd Francis himself. The young beat cop who rang the alarm bell had thought there was something odd about him when he had accompanied Lloyd to the ruins of the house. Nothing obvious, nothing he could put his finger on, but just that indefinable policeman's itch, the feeling you get when it doesn't all add up. Aiken hadn't talked to Lloyd Francis yet, but he was beginning to think it was about time.

Because finally there was the one clear and indisputable fact that linked everything else, like the magnet that makes a pattern out of iron filings: He found out that Lloyd Francis had spent five years working as a heating and air-conditioning serviceman from just after he left school until his early twenties. And if you knew that much about gas furnaces, Aiken surmised, then you didn't have to bloody well be there when one blew up.

• • •

Lloyd felt a little shaken after the policeman's visit, but he still believed he'd held his own. One thing was clear, and that was that they had done a lot of checking, not only into his background, but also into the dead man's. What on earth had Laura seen in such a loser? The man had *petty criminal* stamped all over him.

But what had worried Lloyd most of all was the knowledge that the detective, Aiken, seemed to have about his own past, especially his heating and air-conditioning work. Not only did the police know he had done that for five years, but they seemed to know every job he had been on, every problem he had solved, the brand name of every furnace he had ever serviced. It was all rather overwhelming. Lloyd hadn't lied about it, hadn't tried to deny any of it—that would have been a sure way of sharpening their suspicions even more—but the truth painted the picture of a man easily capable of rigging the thermostat so that it blew up the house when someone turned it on.

Luckily, Lloyd knew they had absolutely no forensic evidence. If there had been any, which he doubted, it would have been obliterated by the fire. All he had to do was stick to his story, and they would never be able to prove a thing. Suspicion was all very well, but it wasn't sufficient grounds for a murder charge.

After the funeral, he had lain low in a sublet condominium at Victoria Park and Danforth, opposite Shopper's World. At night the streets were noisy and a little edgy, Lloyd felt, the kind of area where you might easily get mugged if you weren't careful. More than once he'd had the disconcerting feeling that he was being followed, but he told himself not to be paranoid. He wouldn't be here for long. After a suitable period of mourning he would go to Vancouver and decide he couldn't face returning to the city where his poor wife met such a terrible death. He still had a few colleagues who would regret his decision to leave, perhaps, but there wasn't really anybody left in Toronto to care that much about Lloyd Francis and what happened to him. At the moment, they all thought he was a bit depressed, "getting over his loss." Soon he would be free to "meet" Anne-Marie and start a new life. The money should be all his by then too, once the lawyers and accountants had finished with it. Never again would he have to listen to his wife reminding him where his wealth and success came from

The Silver Birch explosion had not only destroyed Lloyd's house and wife, it had also destroyed his car, a silver SUV, and he wasn't going to bother replacing it until he moved to Vancouver, where he'd probably buy a nice little red sports car. He still popped into the studios occasionally, mostly to see how things were going, and luckily his temporary accommodation was close to the Victoria Park subway. He soon found he didn't mind taking the TTC to work and back. In fact, he rather enjoyed it. They played classical music at the station to keep the hooligans away. If he got a seat on the tram, he would read a book, and if he didn't, he would drift off into thoughts of his sweet Anne-Marie.

And so life went on, waiting, waiting for the time when he could decently, and without arousing suspicion, make his move. The policeman didn't return, obviously realizing that he had no chance of making a case against Lloyd without a confession, which he knew he wouldn't get. It was late November now, arguably one of the grimmest months in Toronto, but at least the snow hadn't come yet, just one dreary gray day after another.

One such day Lloyd stood on the crowded eastbound platform at the St. George subway station wondering if he dare make his move as early as next week. At least, he thought, he could "go away for a while," maybe even until after Christmas. Surely that would be acceptable by now? People would understand that he couldn't bear to spend his first Christmas without Laura in Toronto.

He had just decided that he would do it when he saw the train come tearing into the station. In his excitement at the thought of seeing Anne-Marie again so soon, a sort of unconscious sense of urgency had carried him a little closer to the edge of the platform than he should have been, and the crowds jostled behind him. He felt something hard jab into the small of his back, and the next thing he knew, his legs buckled and he pitched forward. He couldn't stop himself. He toppled in front of the oncoming train before the driver could do a thing. His last thought was of Anne-Marie waving goodbye to him at Vancouver International Airport, then the subway train smashed into him and its wheels shredded him to pieces.

Someone in the crowd screamed and people started running back toward the exits. The frail-looking old man with the walking stick who had been standing directly behind Lloyd turned to stroll away through the chaos, but before he could get very far, two scruffy-looking young men emerged from the throng and took him by each arm. "No you don't," one of them said. "This way." And they led him up to the street.

• • •

Detective Bobby Aiken played with the worry beads one of his colleagues had brought him back from a trip to Istanbul. Not that he was worried about anything. It was just a habit, and he found it very calming. It had, in fact, been a very good day.

Not because of Lloyd Francis. Aiken didn't really care one way or another about Francis's death. In his eyes, though he hadn't been able to prove it, Francis had been a cold-blooded murderer, and he had received no less than he deserved. No, the thing that pleased Aiken was that the undercover detectives he had detailed to keep an eye on Francis had picked up Mickey the Croaker disguised as an old man at the St. George subway station, having seen him push Francis with the sharp end of his walking stick.

Organized Crime had been after Mickey for many years now but had never managed to get anything on him. They knew that he usually worked for one of the big crime families in Montreal, and the way things were looking, he was just about ready to cut a deal, amnesty and the witness relocation plan for everything he knew about the Montreal operation, from the hits he had made to where the bodies were buried. Organized Crime were creaming their jeans over their good luck. It could mean a promotion for Bobby Aiken.

The only thing that puzzled Aiken was why? What had Lloyd Francis done to upset the mob? There was something missing, and it irked him that he might never uncover it now that the main players were dead. Mickey the Croaker knew nothing, of course. He had simply been obeying orders, and killing Lloyd Francis meant nothing more to him than swatting a fly. Francis's murder was more than likely connected with the post-production company, Aiken decided. It was well-known that the mob had its fingers in the movie business. A bit more digging might uncover something more specific, but Aiken didn't have the time. Besides, what did it matter now? Even if he didn't understand how all the pieces fit together, things had worked out the right way. Lanagan and Francis were dead and Mickey the Croaker was about to sing. It was a shame about the wife, Laura. She was a young, good-looking woman, from what Aiken had been able to tell, and she shouldn't have died so young. But those were the breaks. If she hadn't being playing the beast with two backs with Lanagan in her own bed, for Christ's sake, then she might still be alive today.

It was definitely a good day, Aiken decided, pushing the papers aside. Even the weather had improved. He looked out of the window. Indian summer had come to Toronto in November. The sun glinted on the apartment windows at College and Yonge, and the office workers were out on the streets, men without jackets and women in sleeveless summer dresses. A streetcar rumbled by, heading for Main station. Main. Out near the Beaches. The boardwalk and the Queen Street cafes would be crowded, and the dog-walkers would be out in force. Aiken thought maybe he'd take Jasper out there for a run later. You never knew who you might meet when you were walking your dog on the beach.

PETER ROBINSON was born in England and now splits his time between Toronto and Richmond, North Yorkshire. He is the author of the Inspector Banks series of novels, the latest of which is *All the Colors of Darkness*, and of many short stories, one of which, "Missing in Action," won the MWA Edgar Award in 2000.

Lucky

BY CHARLAINE HARRIS

Amelia Broadway and I were painting each other's toenails when my insurance agent knocked at the front door. I'd picked Roses on Ice. Amelia had opted for Mad Burgundy Cherry Glace. She'd finished my feet, and I had about three toes to go on her left foot when Greg Aubert interrupted us.

Amelia had been living with me for a month, and it had been kind of nice to have someone else sharing my old house. Amelia is a witch from New Orleans, and she was hanging out with me because she had a magical misfortune she didn't want any of her witch buddies in the Big Easy to know about. Also, since Katrina, she really doesn't have anything to go home to, at least for a while. My little hometown of Bon Temps was swollen with refugees.

Greg Aubert had been to my house after I'd had a fire that caused a lot of damage. As far as I knew, I didn't have any insurance needs at the moment. I was pretty curious about his purpose, I confess.

Amelia had glanced up at Greg, found his sandy hair and rimless glasses uninteresting, and completed painting her little toe while I ushered him to the wingback chair.

"Greg, this is my friend Amelia Broadway," I said. "Amelia, this is Greg Aubert."

Amelia looked at Greg with more interest. I'd told her Greg was a colleague of hers, in some respects Greg's mom had been a witch, and he'd found using the craft very helpful in protecting his clients. Not a car got insured with Greg's agency without having a spell cast on it. I was the only one in Bon Temps who knew about Greg's little talent. Witchcraft wouldn't be popular in our devout little town. Greg always handed his clients a lucky rabbit's foot to keep in their new vehicles or homes.

After he turned down the obligatory offer of iced tea or water or Coke, Greg sat on the edge of the chair while I resumed my seat on one end of the couch. Amelia had the other end

"I felt the wards when I drove up," Greg told Amelia. "Very impressive." He was trying real hard to keep his eyes off my tank top. I would have put on a bra if I'd known we were going to have company.

Amelia tried to look indifferent, and she might have shrugged if she hadn't been holding a bottle of nail polish. Amelia, tan and athletic, with short glossy brown hair, is not only pleased with her looks but really proud of her witchcraft abilities. "Nothing special," she said, with unconvincing modesty. She smiled at Greg, though.

"What can I do for you today, Greg?" I asked. I was due to go to work in an hour, and I had to change and pull my long hair up in a ponytail.

"I need your help," he said, yanking his gaze up to my face.

No beating around the bush with Greg.

"Okay, how?" If he could be direct, so could I.

"Someone's sabotaging my agency," he said. His voice was suddenly passionate, and I realized Greg was really close to a major breakdown. He wasn't quite the broadcaster Amelia was—I could read most thoughts Amelia had as clearly as if she'd spoken them—but I could certainly read his inner workings.

"Tell us about it," I said, because Amelia could not read Greg's mind.

"Oh, thanks," he said, as if I'd agreed to do something. I opened my mouth to correct this idea, but he plowed ahead.

"Last week I came into the office to find that someone had been through the files."

"You still have Marge Barker working for you?"

He nodded. A stray beam of sunlight winked off his glasses. It was September, and still very warm in northern Louisiana. Greg got out a snowy handkerchief and patted his forehead. "I've got my wife, Christy, she comes in three days a week for half a day, and I've got Marge full-time." Christy, Greg's wife, was as sweet as Marge was sour.

"How'd you know someone had been through the files?" Amelia asked. She screwed the top on the polish bottle and put it on the coffee table.

Greg took a deep breath. "I'd been thinking for a couple of weeks that someone had been in the office at night. But nothing was missing. Nothing was changed. My wards were okay. But two days ago, I got into the office to find that one of the drawers on our main filing cabinet was open. Of course, we lock them at night," he said. "We've got one of those filing systems that locks up when you turn a key in the top drawer. Almost all of the client files were at risk. But every day, last thing in the afternoon, Marge goes around and locks that cabinet. What if someone suspects what I do?"

I could see how that would shiver Greg down to his liver. Did you ask Marge if she remembered locking the cabinet?"

"Sure I asked her. She got mad—you know Marge—and said she definitely did. My wife had worked that afternoon, but she couldn't remember if she watched Marge lock the cabinets or not. And Terry Bellefleur had dropped by at the last minute, wanting to check again on the insurance for his damn dog. He might have seen Marge lock up."

Greg sounded so irritated that I found myself defending Terry. "Greg, Terry doesn't like being the way he is, you know," I said, trying to gentle my voice "He got messed up fighting for our country, and we got to cut him some slack."

Greg looked grumpy for a minute Then he relaxed. "I know, Sookie," he said. "He's just been so hyped up about this dog."

"What's the story?" Amelia asked. If I have moments of curiosity, Amelia has an imperative urge. She wants to know everything about everybody. The telepathy should have gone to her, not me. She might actually have enjoyed it, instead of considering it a disability.

"Terry Bellefleur is Andy's cousin," I said. I knew Amelia had met Andy, a police detective, at Merlotte's. "He comes in after closing and cleans the bar. Sometimes he substitutes for Sam. Maybe not the few evenings you were working." Amelia filled in at the bar from time to time.

"Terry fought in Vietnam, got captured, and had a pretty bad time of it. He's got scars inside and out. The story about the dogs is this: Terry loves hunting dogs, and he keeps buying himself these expensive Catahoulas, and things keep happening to them. His current bitch has had puppies. He's just on pins and needles lest something happen to her and the babies."

"You're saying Terry is a little unstable?"

"He has bad times," I said. "Sometimes he's just fine."

"Oh," Amelia said, and a lightbulb might as well have popped on above her head. "He's the guy with the long graying auburn hair, going bald at the front? Scars on his cheek? Big truck?"

"That's him," I said.

Amelia turned to Greg. "You said for at least a couple of weeks you'd felt someone had been in the building after it closed. That couldn't be your wife, or this Marge?"

"My wife is with me all evening unless we have to take the kids to different events. And I don't know why Marge would feel she had to come back at night. She's there during the day, every day, and often by herself. Well, the spells that protect the building seem okay to me. But I keep recasting them."

"Tell me about your spells," Amelia said, getting down to her favorite part.

She and Greg talked spells for a few minutes, while I listened but didn't comprehend. I couldn't even understand their thoughts.

Then Amelia said, "What do you want, Greg? I mean, why did you come to us?"

He'd actually come to me, but it was kind of nice to be an "us."

Greg looked from Amelia to me, and said, "I want Sookie to find out who opened my files, and why. I worked hard to become the best-selling Pelican State agent in northern Louisiana, and I don't want my business fouled up now. My son's about to go to Rhodes in Memphis, and it ain't cheap."

"Why are you coming to me instead of the police?"

"I don't want anyone else finding out what I am," he said, embarrassed but determined. "And it might come up if the police start looking into things at my office. Plus, you know, Sookie, I got you a real good payout on your kitchen."

My kitchen had been burned down by an arsonist months before. I'd just finished getting it all rebuilt. "Greg, that's your job," I said. "I don't see where the gratitude comes in."

"Well, I have a certain amount of discretion in arson cases," he said. "I could have told the home office that I thought you did it yourself."

"You wouldn't have done that," I said calmly, though I was seeing a side of Greg I didn't like. Amelia practically had flames coming out of her nose, she was so incensed. But I could tell that Greg was already ashamed of bringing up the possibility.

"No," he said, looking down at his hands. "I guess I wouldn't. I'm sorry I said that, Sookie. I'm scared someone'll tell the whole town what I do, why people I insure are so . . . lucky. Can you see what you can find out?"

"Bring your family into the bar for supper tonight, give me a chance to look them over," I said. "That's the real reason you want me to find out, right? You suspect your family might be involved. Or your staff." He nodded, and he looked wretched. "I'll try to get in there tomorrow to talk to Marge. I'll say you wanted me to drop by."

"Yeah, I make calls from my cell phone sometimes, ask people to come in," he said. "Marge would believe it."

Amelia said, "What can I do?"

"Well, can you be with her?" Greg said. "Sookie can do things you can't, and vice versa. Maybe between the two of you . . ."

"Okay," Amelia said, giving Greg the benefit of her broad and dazzling smile. Her dad must have paid dearly for the perfect white smile of Amelia Broadway, witch and waitress.

Bob the cat padded in just at that moment, as if belatedly realizing we had a guest. Bob jumped up on the chair right beside Greg and examined him with care.

Greg looked down at Bob just as intently. "Have you been doing something you shouldn't, Amelia?"

"There's nothing strange about Bob," Amelia said, which was not true. She scooped up the black-and-white cat in her arms and nuzzled his soft fur. "He's just a big ole cat. Aren't you, Bob?" She was relieved when Greg dropped the subject. He got up to leave.

"I'll be grateful for anything you can do to help me," he said. With an abrupt switch to his professional persona, he said, "Here, have an extra lucky rabbit's foot," and reached in his pocket to hand me a lump of fake fur.

"Thanks," I said, and decided to put it in my bedroom. I could use some luck in that direction.

After Greg left, I scrambled into my work clothes (black pants and white boatneck T-shirt with MERLOTTE'S embroidered over the left breast), brushed my long blond hair and secured it in a ponytail, and left for the bar, wearing Teva sandals to show off my beautiful toenails. Amelia, who wasn't scheduled to work that night, said she might go have a good look around the insurance agency.

"Be careful," I said. "If someone really is prowling around there, you don't want to run into a bad situation."

"I'll zap 'em with my wonderful witch powers," she said, only half-joking. Amelia had a fine opinion of her own abilities, which led to mistakes like Bob. He had actually been a thin young witch, handsome in a nerdy way. While spending the night with Amelia, Bob had been the victim of one of her less successful attempts at major magic. "Besides, who'd want to break into an insurance agency?" she said quickly, having read the doubt on my face. "This whole thing is ridiculous. I do want to check out Greg's magic, though, and see if it's been tampered with."

"You can do that?"

"Hey, standard stuff."

• • •

To my relief, the bar was quiet that night. It was Wednesday, which is never a very big day at supper time, since lots of Bon Temps citizens go to church on Wednesday night. Sam Merlotte, my boss, was busy counting cases of beer in the storeroom when I got there, that was how light the crowd was. The waitresses on duty were mixing their own drinks.

I stowed my purse in the drawer in Sam's desk that he keeps empty for them, then went out front to take over my tables. The woman I was relieving, a Katrina evacuee I hardly knew, gave me a wave and departed.

After an hour, Greg Aubert came in with his family as he'd promised. You seated yourself at Merlotte's, and I surreptitiously nodded to a table in my section. Dad, Mom, and two teenagers, the nuclear family. Greg's wife, Christy, had medium-light hair like Greg, and like Greg she wore glasses. She had a comfortable middle-aged body, and she'd never seemed exceptional in any way. Little Greg (and that's what they called him) was about three inches taller than his father, about thirty pounds heavier, and about ten IQ points smarter. That is, book smart. Like most nineteen-year-olds, he was pretty dumb about the world. Lindsay, the daughter, had lightened her hair five shades and squeezed herself into an outfit at least a size too small, and could hardly wait to get away from her folks so she could meet the Forbidden Boyfriend.

While I took their drink and food orders, I discovered that (a) Lindsay had the mistaken idea that she looked like Christina Aguilera, (b) Little Greg thought he would never go into insurance because it was so boring, and (c) Christy thought Greg might be interested in another woman because he'd been so distracted lately. As you can imagine, it takes a lot of mental doing to separate what I'm getting from people's minds from what I'm hearing directly from their mouths, which accounts for the strained smile I often wear—the smile that's led some people to think I'm just crazy.

After I'd brought them their drinks and turned in their food order, I puttered around studying the Aubert family. They seemed so typical it just hurt. Little Greg thought about his girlfriend mostly, and I learned more than I wanted to know.

Greg was just worried.

Christy was thinking about the dryer in their laundry room, wondering if it was time to get a new one.

See? Most people's thoughts are like that. Christy was also weighing Marge Barker's virtues (efficiency, loyalty) against the fact that she seriously disliked the woman.

Lindsay was thinking about her secret boyfriend. Like teenage girls everywhere, she was convinced her parents were the most boring people in the universe and had pokers up their asses besides. They didn't understand *anything.* Lindsay herself didn't understand why Dustin wouldn't take her to meet his folks, why he wouldn't let her see where he lived. No one but Dustin knew how poetic her soul was, how fascinating she truly could be, how misunderstood she was.

If I had a dime for every time I'd heard that from a teenager's brain, I'd be as rich as John Edward, the psychic.

I heard the bell ding in the service window, and I trotted over to get the Auberts' order from our current cook. I loaded my arms with the plates and hustled them over to the table. I had to endure a full-body scan from Little Greg, but that was par for the course, too. Guys can't help it. Lindsay didn't register me at all. She was wondering why Dustin was so secretive about his daytime activities. Shouldn't he be in school?

Okay, now. We were getting somewhere.

But then Lindsay began thinking about her D in algebra and how she was going to get grounded when her parents found out and then she wouldn't get to see Dustin for a while unless she climbed out of her bedroom window at two in the morning. She was seriously considering going all the way.

Lindsay made me feel sad and old. And very smart.

By the time the Aubert family paid their bill and left, I was tired of all of them, and my head was exhausted (a weird feeling, and one I simply can't describe).

I plodded through work the rest of the night, glad to the very ends of my Roses on Ice toenails when I headed out the back door.

"Psst," said a voice from behind me while I was unlocking my car door.

With a stifled shriek, I swung around with my keys in my hand, ready to attack.

"It's me," Amelia said gleefully.

"Dammit, Amelia, don't sneak up on me like that!" I sagged against the car.

"Sorry," she said, but she didn't sound very sorry. "Hey," she continued, "I've been over by the insurance agency. Guess what!"

"What?" My lack of enthusiasm seemed to register with Amelia.

"You tired or something?" she asked.

"I just had an evening of listening in to the world's most typical family," I said. "Greg's worried, Christy's worried, Little Greg is horny, and Lindsay has a secret love."

"I know," Amelia said. "And guess what?"

"He might be a vamp."

"Oh." She sagged. "You already knew?"

"Not for sure, I know other fascinating stuff, though. I know he understands Lindsay as she's never been understood before in her whole underappreciated life, that he just might be The One, and that she's thinking of having sex with this goober."

"Well, I know where he lives. Let's go by there. You drive; I need to get some stuff ready." We got into Amelia's car. I took the driver's seat. Amelia began fumbling in her purse through the many little Ziplocs that filled it. They were all full of magic ready to go: herbs and other ingredients. Bat wings, for all I knew.

"He lives by himself in a big house with a FOR SALE sign in the front yard. No furniture. Yet he looks like he's eighteen." Amelia pointed at the house, which was dark and isolated.

"Hmmm." Our eyes met.

"What do you think?" Amelia asked.

"Vampire, almost surely."

"Could be. But why would a strange vampire be in Bon Temps? Why don't any of the other vamps know about him?" It was all right to be a vampire in today's America, but the vamps were still trying to keep a low profile. They regulated themselves rigorously.

"How do you know they don't? Know about him, that is."

Good question. Would the area vampires be obliged to tell me? It wasn't like I was an official vampire greeter or anything.

"Amelia, you went looking around after a vampire? Not smart."

"It wasn't like I knew he might be fangy when I started. I just followed him after I saw him cruising around the Auberts' house."

"I think he's in the middle of seducing Lindsay," I said. "I better make a call."

"But does this have anything to do with Greg's business?"

"I don't know. Where is this boy now?"

"He's at Lindsay's house. He finally just parked outside. I guess he's waiting for her to come out."

"Crap." I pulled in a little way down the street from the Auberts' ranch style. I flipped open my cell phone to call Fangtasia. Maybe it's not a good sign when the area vampire bar is on your speed dial.

"Fangtasia, the bar with a bite," said an unfamiliar voice. Just as Bon Temps and our whole area was saturated with human evacuees, the vampire community in Shreveport was, too.

"This is Sookie Stackhouse. I need to speak with Eric, please," I said.

"Oh, the telepath. Sorry, Miss Stackhouse. Eric and Pam are out tonight."

"Maybe you can tell me if any of the new vampires are staying in my town, Bon Temps?"

"Let me inquire."

The voice was back after a few minutes. "Clancy says no." Clancy was like Eric's third in command, and I was not his favorite person. You'll notice Clancy didn't even ask the phone guy to find out why I needed to know. I thanked the unknown vampire for his trouble and hung up.

I was stumped. Pam, Eric's second in command, was sort of a buddy of mine, and Eric was, occasionally, something more than that. Since they weren't there, I'd have to call our local vampire, Bill Compton.

I sighed. "I'm going to have to call Bill," I said, and Amelia knew enough of my history to understand why the idea was so traumatic. And then I braced myself and dialed.

"Yes?" said a cool voice.

Thank goodness. I'd been scared the new girlfriend, Selah, would answer.

"Bill, this is Sookie. Eric and Pam are out of touch, and I have a problem."

"What?"

Bill has always been a man of few words.

"There's a young man in town we think is a vampire. Have you met him?"

"Here in Bon Temps?" Bill was clearly surprised and displeased.

That answered my question. "Yes, and Clancy told me they hadn't farmed out any new vamps to Bon Temps. So I thought maybe you'd encountered this individual?"

"No, which means he's probably taking care not to cross my path. Where are you?"

"We're parked outside the Auberts' house. He's interested in the daughter, a teenager. We've pulled into a house for sale across the street, middle of the block on Hargrove."

"I'll be there very soon. Don't approach him."

As if I would. "He thinks I'm stupid enough—" I began, and Amelia already had her "Indignant for You" face on when the driver's door was yanked open and a white hand latched on to my shoulder. I squawked until the other hand clamped over my mouth.

"Shut up, breather," said a voice that was even colder than Bill's. "Are you the one that's been following me around all night?"

Then I realized that he didn't know Amelia was in the passenger's seat. That was good.

Since I couldn't speak, I nodded slightly.

"Why?" he growled. "What do you want with me?" He shook me like I was a dustcloth, and I thought all my bones would come disjointed.

Then Amelia leaped from the other side of the car and darted over to us, tossing the contents of a Ziploc on his head. Of course, I had no idea what she was saying, but the effect was dramatic. After a jolt of astonishment, the vampire froze. The problem was, he froze with me clasped with my back to his chest in an unbreakable hold. I was mashed against him, and his left hand was still hard over my mouth, his right hand around my waist. So far, the investigative team of Sookie Stackhouse, telepath, and Amelia Broadway, witch, was not doing a top-flight job.

"Pretty good, huh?" Amelia said.

I managed to move my head a fraction. "Yes, if I could breathe," I said. I wished I hadn't wasted breath speaking.

Then Bill was there, surveying the situation.

"You stupid woman, Sookie's trapped," Bill said. "Undo the spell."

Under the streetlight, Amelia looked sullen. Undoing was not her best thing, I realized with some anxiety. I couldn't do anything else, so I waited while she worked on the counterspell.

"If this doesn't work, it'll only take me a second to break his arm," Bill told me. I nodded . . . well, I moved my head a fraction of an inch . . . because that was all I could do. I was getting pretty breathless.

Suddenly there was a little *pop!* in the air, and the younger vampire let go of me to launch himself at Bill—who wasn't there. Bill was behind him, and he grabbed one of the boy's arms and twisted it up and back. The boy screamed, and down they went to the ground. I wondered if anyone was going to call the police. This was a lot of noise and activity for a residential neighborhood after one o'clock. But no lights came on.

"Now, talk." Bill was absolutely determined, and I guess the boy knew it.

"What's your problem?" the boy demanded. He had spiked brown hair and a lean build, and a couple of diamond studs in his nose. "This woman's been following me around. I need to know who she is."

Bill looked up at me questioningly. I jerked my head toward Amelia.

"You didn't even grab the right woman," Bill said. He sounded kind of disappointed in the youngster. "Why are you here in Bon Temps?"

"Getting away from Katrina," the boy said. "My sire was staked by a human when we ran out of bottled blood substitute after the flood. I stole a car outside of New Orleans, changed the license plates, and got out of town. I reached here at daylight I found an empty house with a FOR SALE sign and a windowless bathroom, so I moved in. I've been going out with a local girl. I take a sip every night. She's none the wiser," he sneered.

"What's your interest?" Bill asked me.

"Have you two been going into her dad's office at night?" I asked.

"Yeah, once or twice." He smirked. "Her dad's office has a couch in it." I wanted to slap the shit out of him, maybe smacking the jewelry in his nose just by accident.

"How long have you been a vampire?" Bill asked.

"Ah, maybe two months."

Okay, that explained a lot. "So that's why he didn't know to check in with Eric. That's why he doesn't realize what he's doing is foolish and liable to get him staked."

"There's only so much excuse for stupidity," Bill said.

"Have you gone through the files in there?" I asked the boy, who was looking a little dazed.

"What?"

"Did you go through the files in the insurance office?"

"Uh, no. Why would I do that? I was just loving up the girl, to get a little sip, you know? I was real careful not to take too much. I don't have any money to buy artificial stuff."

"Oh, you are *so dumb."* Amelia was fed up with this kid. "For goodness' sake, learn something about your condition. Stranded vampires can get help just like stranded people. You just ask the Red Cross for some synthetic blood, and they dole it out free."

"Or you could have found out who the sheriff of the area is," Bill said. "Eric would never turn away a vampire in need. What if someone had found you biting this girl? She's under the age of consent, I gather?" For blood "donation" to a vampire.

"Yeah," I said, when Dustin looked blank. "It's Lindsay, daughter of Greg Aubert, my insurance agent. He wanted us to find out who'd been going into his building at night. Called in a favor to get me and Amelia to investigate."

"He should do his own dirty work," Bill said quite calmly. But his hands were clenched. "Listen, boy, what's your name?"

"Dustin." He'd even given Lindsay his real name.

"Well, Dustin, tonight we go to Fangtasia, the bar in Shreveport that Eric Northman uses as his headquarters. He will talk to you there, decide what to do with you."

"I'm a free vampire. I go where I want."

"Not within Area Five, you don't. You go to Eric, the area sheriff."

Bill marched the young vampire off into the night, probably to load him into his car and get him to Shreveport. Amelia said, "I'm sorry, Sookie."

"At least you stopped him from breaking my neck," I said, trying to sound philosophical about it. "We still have our original problem. It wasn't Dustin who went through the files, though I'm guessing it was Dustin and Lindsay going into the office at night that disturbed the magic. How could they get past it?"

"After Greg told me his spell, I realized he wasn't much of a witch. Lindsay's a member of the family. With Greg's spell to ward against outsiders, that made a difference," Amelia said. "And sometimes vampires register as a void on spells created for humans. After all, they're not alive. I made my 'freeze' spell vampire specific."

"Who else can get through magic spells and work mischief?"

"Magical nulls," she said

"Huh?"

"There are people who can't *be* affected by magic," Amelia said "They're rare, but they exist. I've only met one before."

"How can you detect nulls? Do they give off a special vibration or something?"

"Only very experienced witches can detect nulls without casting a spell on them that fails," Amelia admitted "Greg probably has never encountered one."

"Let's go see Terry," I suggested "He stays up all night."

• • •

The baying of a dog announced our arrival at Terry's cabin. Terry lived in the middle of three acres of woods. Terry liked being by himself most of the time, and any social needs he might feel were satisfied by an occasional stint of working as a bartender.

"That'll be Annie," I said, as the barking rose in intensity "She's his fourth."

"Wife? Or dog?"

"Dog. Specifically, a Catahoula. The first one got hit by a truck, I think, and one got poisoned, and one got bit by a snake."

"Gosh, that is bad luck."

"Yeah, unless it's not chance at all. Maybe someone's making it happen."

"What are Catahoulas for?"

"Hunting. Herding. Don't get Terry started on the history of the breed, I'm begging you."

Terry's trailer door opened, and Annie launched herself off the steps to find out if we were friends or foes. She gave us a good bark, and when we stayed still, she eventually remembered she knew me. Annie weighed about fifty pounds, I guess, a good-sized dog. Catahoulas are not beautiful unless you love the breed. Annie was several shades of brown and red, and one shoulder was a solid color while her legs were another, though her rear half was covered with spots.

"Sookie, did you come to pick out a puppy?" Terry called. "Annie, let them by." Annie obediently backed up, keeping her eyes on us as we began approaching the trailer.

"I came to look," I said. "I brought my friend Amelia. She loves dogs."

Amelia was thinking she'd like to slap me upside the head because she was definitely a cat person.

Annie's puppies and Annie had made the small trailer quite doggy, though the odor wasn't really unpleasant. Annie herself maintained a vigilant stance while we looked at the three pups Terry still had. Terry's scarred hands were gentle as he handled the dogs. Annie had encountered several gentleman dogs on her unplanned excursion, and the puppies were diverse. They were adorable. Puppies just are. But they were sure distinctive. I picked up a bundle of short reddish fur with a white muzzle, and felt the puppy wiggle against me and snuffle my fingers. Gee, it was cute.

"Terry," I said, "have you been worried about Annie?"

"Yeah," he said. Since he was off base himself, Terry was very tolerant of other people's quirks. "I got to thinking about the things that have happened to my dogs, and I began to wonder if someone was causing them all."

"Do you insure all your dogs with Greg Aubert?"

"Naw, Diane at Liberty South insured the others. And see what happened to them? I decided to switch agents, and everyone says Greg is the luckiest son of a bitch in Renard Parish."

The puppy began chewing on my fingers. Ouch. Amelia was looking around her at the dingy trailer. It was clean enough, but the furniture arrangement was strictly utilitarian, like the furniture itself.

"So, did you go through the files at Greg Aubert's office?"

"No, why would I do that?"

Truthfully, I couldn't think of a reason. Fortunately, Terry didn't seem interested in why I wanted to know. "Sookie," he said, "if anyone in the bar thinks about my dogs, knows anything about 'em, will you tell me?"

Terry knew about me. It was one of those community secrets that everyone knows but no one ever discusses. Until they need me.

"Yes, Terry, I will." It was a promise, and I shook his hand. Reluctantly, I set the puppy back in its improvised pen, and Annie checked it over anxiously to make sure it was in good order.

We left soon after, none the wiser.

"So, who've we got left?" Amelia said. "You don't think the family did it, the vampire boyfriend is cleared, and Terry, the only other person on the scene, didn't do it. Where do we look next?"

"Don't you have some magic that would give us a clue?" I asked. I pictured us throwing magic dust on the files to reveal fingerprints.

"Uh. No."

"Then let's just reason our way through it. Like they do in crime novels. They just talk about it."

"I'm game. Saves gas."

We got back to the house and sat across from each other at the kitchen table. Amelia brewed a cup of tea for herself, while I got a caffeine-free Coke.

I said, "Greg is scared that someone is going through his files at work. We solved the part about someone being in his office. That was the daughter and her boyfriend. So we're left with the files. Now, who would be interested in Greg's clients?"

"There's always the chance that some client doesn't think Greg paid out enough on a claim, or maybe thinks Greg is cheating his clients." Amelia took a sip of her tea.

"But why go through the files? Why not just bring a complaint to the national insurance agents' board, or whatever?"

"Okay. Then there's . . . the only other answer is another insurance agent. Someone who wonders why Greg has such phenomenal luck in what he insures. Someone who doesn't believe it's chance or those cheesy synthetic rabbits' feet."

It was so simple when you thought about it, when you cleared away the mental debris. I was sure the culprit had to be someone in the same business.

I was pretty sure I knew the other three insurance agents in Bon Temps, but I checked the phone book to be sure.

"I suggest we go from agent to agent, starting with the local ones," Amelia said. "I'm relatively new in town, so I can tell them I want to take out some more insurance."

"I'll come with you, and I'll scan them."

"During the conversation, I'll bring up the Aubert Agency, so they'll be thinking about the right thing." Amelia had asked enough questions to understand how my telepathy worked.

I nodded. "First thing tomorrow morning."

We went to sleep that night with a pleasant tingle of anticipation. A plan was a beautiful thing. Stackhouse and Broadway swing into action.

• • •

The next day didn't start exactly like we'd planned. For one thing, the weather had decided to be fall. It was cool. It was pouring rain. I put my shorts and tank tops away sadly, knowing I probably wouldn't wear them again for several months.

The first agent, Diane Porchia, was guarded by a meek clerk. Alma Dean crumpled like a fender when we insisted on seeing the actual agent. Amelia, with her bright smile and gorgeous teeth, simply beamed at Ms. Dean until she called Diane out of her office. The middle-aged agent, a stocky woman in a green pantsuit, came out to shake our hands. I said, "I've been taking my friend Amelia around to all the agents in town, starting with Greg Aubert." I was listening as hard as I could to the result, and all I got was professional pride . . . and a hint of desperation. Diane Porchia was scared by the number of claims she had processed lately. It was abnormally high. All she was thinking of was selling. Amelia gave me a little hand wave. Diane Porchia was not a magical null.

"Greg Aubert thought he'd had someone break into his office at night," Amelia said.

"Us, too," Diane said, seeming genuinely astonished. "But nothing was taken." She rallied and got back to her purpose. "Our rates are very competitive with anything Greg can offer you. Take a look at the coverage we provide, and I think you'll agree."

Shortly after that, our heads filled with figures, we were on our way to Bailey Smith. Bailey was a high school classmate of my brother Jason's, and we had to spend a little longer there playing "What's he/she doing now?" But the result was the same. Bailey's only concern was getting Amelia's business, and maybe getting her to go out for a drink with him if he could think of a place to take her that his wife wouldn't hear about.

He had had a break-in at his office, too. In his case, the window had been shattered. But nothing had been taken. And I heard directly from his brain that business was down. Way down.

At John Robert Briscoe's we had a different problem. He didn't want to see us. His clerk, Sally Lundy, was like an angel with a flaming sword guarding the entrance to his private office. We got our chance when a client came in, a little withered woman who'd had a collision the month before. She said, "I don't know how this could be, but the minute I signed with John Robert, I had an accident. Then a month goes by, and I have another one."

"Come on back, Mrs. Hanson." Sally gave us a mistrustful look as she took the little woman to the inner sanctum. The minute they were gone, Amelia went through the stack of paperwork in the in-box, to my surprise and dismay.

Sally came back to her desk, and Amelia and I took our departure. I said, "We'll come back later. We've got another appointment right now."

"They were all claims," Amelia said, when we were out of the door. "Every one of them." She pushed back the hood on her slicker since the rain had finally stopped.

"There's something wrong with that. John Robert has been hit even harder than Diane or Bailey."

We stared at each other. Finally, I said what we were both thinking. "Did Greg upset some balance by claiming more than his fair share of good luck?"

"I never heard of such a thing," Amelia said. But we both believed that Greg had unwittingly tipped over a cosmic applecart.

"There weren't any nulls at any of the other agencies," Amelia said. "It's got to be either John Robert or his clerk. I didn't get to check either of them."

"He'll be going to lunch any minute." I said, glancing down at my watch. "Probably Sally will be, too. I'll go to the back where they park and stall them. Do you have to be close?"

"If I have one of my spells, it'll be better," she said. She darted over to her car and unlocked it, pulling out her purse. I hurried around to the back of the building, just a block off the main street but surrounded by crepe myrtles.

I managed to catch John Robert as he left his office to go to lunch. His car was dirty. His clothes were disheveled. He slumped. I knew him by sight, but we'd never had a conversation.

"Mr. Briscoe," I said, and his head swung up. He seemed confused. Then his face cleared, and he tried to smile.

"Sookie Stackhouse, right? Girl, it's been an age since I saw you."

"I guess you don't come to Merlotte's much."

"No, I pretty much go home to the wife and kids in the evening," he agreed. "They've got a lot of activities."

"Do you ever go over to Greg Aubert's office?" I asked, trying to sound gentle.

He stared at me for a long moment. "No, why would I do that?"

And I could tell, hear from his head directly, that he absolutely didn't know what I was talking about. But there came Sarah Lundy, steam practically coming out of her ears at the sight of me talking to her boss when she'd done her best to shield him.

"Sally," John Robert said, relieved to see his right-hand woman, "this young woman wants to know if I've been to Greg's office lately."

"I'll just bet she does," Sally said, and even John Robert blinked at the venom in her voice.

And I got it then, the name I'd been waiting for.

"It's you," I said. "You're the one, Ms. Lundy. What are you doing that for?" If I hadn't known I had backup, I would've been scared. Speaking of backup . . .

"What am I doing it for?" she screeched. "You have the gall, the nerve, the, the, *balls* to ask me that?"

John Robert couldn't have looked more horrified if she'd sprouted horns.

"Sally," he said, very anxiously. "Sally, maybe you need to sit down."

"You can't see it!" she shrieked. "You can't see it. That Greg Aubert, he's dealing with the devil! Diane and Bailey are in the same boat we are, and it's sinking! Do you know how many claims he had to handle last week? Three! Do you know how many new policies he wrote? Thirty!"

John Robert literally staggered when he heard the numbers. He recovered enough to say, "Sally, we can't make wild accusations against Greg. He's a fine man. He'd never . . ."

But Greg had, however blindly.

Sally decided it would be a good time to kick me in the shins, and I was really glad I was wearing jeans instead of shorts that day. *Okay, anytime now, Amelia,* I thought. John Robert was windmilling his arms and yelling at Sally—though not moving to restrain her, I noticed—and Sally was yelling back at the top of her lungs and venting her feelings about Greg Aubert and that bitch Marge who worked for him. She had a lot to say about Marge. No love lost there.

By that time I was holding Sally off at arm's length, and I was sure my legs would be black-and-blue the next day.

Finally, *finally,* Amelia appeared, breathless and disarranged. "Sorry," she panted, "you're not going to believe this, but my foot got stuck between the car seat and the doorsill, then I fell, and my keys went under the car anyway, *Congelo!*"

Sally's foot stopped in midswing, so she was balancing on one skinny leg. John Robert had both hands in the air in a gesture of despair. I touched his arm, and he felt as hard as the frozen vampire had the other night. At least he wasn't holding me. "Now what?" I asked.

"I thought you knew!" she said. "We've got to get them off thinking about Greg and his luck!"

"The problem is, I think Greg's used up all the luck going around," I said. "Look at the problems you had just getting out of the car here."

She looked intensely thoughtful "Yeah, we have to have a chat with Greg," she said. "But first, we got to get out of this situation." Holding out her right hand toward the two frozen people, she said, "Ah—*amuus cum Greg Hubert.*"

They didn't look any more amiable, but maybe the change was taking place in their hearts. *"Regelo,"* Amelia said, and Sally's foot came down to the ground hard. The older woman lurched a bit, and I caught her. "Watch out, Miss Sally," I said, hoping she wouldn't kick me again. "You were a little off balance there."

She looked at me in surprise "What are you doing back here?"

Good question. "Amelia and I were just cutting through the parking lot on our way to McDonald's," I said, gesturing toward the golden arches that stuck up one street over. "We didn't realize that you had so many high bushes around the back, here. We'll just return to the front parking lot and get our car and drive around."

"That would be better," John Robert said. "That way we wouldn't have to worry about something happening to your car while it was parked in our parking lot." He looked gloomy again. "Something's sure to hit it, or fall on top of it. Maybe I'll just call that nice Greg Aubert and ask him if he's got any ideas about breaking my streak of bad luck."

"You do that," I said. "Greg would be glad to talk to you. He'll give you lots of his lucky rabbits' feet, I bet."

"Yep, that Greg sure is nice," Sally Lundy agreed. She turned to back into the office, a little dazed, but none the worse for wear.

Amelia and I went over to the Pelican State office. We were both feeling pretty thoughtful about the whole thing.

Greg was in, and we plopped down on the client side of his desk.

"Greg, you've got to stop using the spells so much," I said, and I explained why.

Greg looked frightened and angry. "But I'm the best agent in Louisiana. I have an incredible record."

"I can't make you change anything, but you're sucking up all the luck in Renard Parish," I said. "You gotta let loose of some of it for the other guys. Diane and Bailey are hurting so much they're thinking about changing professions. John Robert Briscoe is almost suicidal."

To do Greg credit, once we explained the situation, he was horrified.

"I'll modify my spells," he said. "I'll accept some of the bad luck. I just can't believe I was using up everyone else's share." He still didn't look happy, but he was resigned. "And the people in the office at night?" Greg asked meekly.

"Don't worry about it," I said. "Taken care of." At least, I hoped so. Just because Bill had taken the young vampire to Shreveport to see Eric didn't mean that he wouldn't come back again. But maybe the couple would find somewhere else to conduct their mutual exploration.

"Thank you," Greg said, shaking our hands. In fact, Greg cut us a check, which was also nice, though we assured him it wasn't necessary. Amelia looked proud and happy. I felt pretty cheerful myself. We'd cleaned up a couple of the world's problems, and things were better because of us.

"We were fine investigators," I said, as we drove home.

"Of course," said Amelia "We weren't just good. We were lucky."

CHARLAINE HARRIS is the *New York Times* bestselling author of the Southern Vampire novels, which were turned into the HBO series *True Blood* in 2008, and the Harper Connelly series. She's been nominated for a bunch of awards, and she even won a few of them. She lives in southern Arkansas in a country house that has a fluctuating population of people and animals. She loves to read.

A Sleep Not Unlike Death

BY SEAN CHERCOVER

Gravedigger Peace was already sitting up when his eyes opened. It had been years since the nightmares, but his face and forearms were clammy with perspiration and his heart was racing, so he assumed there'd been one. Truth was, Gravedigger Peace didn't remember his dreams these days. Not ever. Not one.

A sleep not unlike death.

Gravedigger drank from the water glass on the bedside table. The digital clock said 3:23. He stood, peeled off his moist T-shirt, wiped his face and arms. Tossed the shirt into the laundry hamper, then shuffled to the kitchen. Instant coffee with a couple ounces of Jim Beam. Final drink of the night.

He sat on the couch in the living area and drank his bourbon-laced coffee and listened to the rain drumming on the metal roof. He stared at the dead grey television screen. No point turning it on; he knew what he'd seen and nothing would have changed in the last three hours. He turned it on anyway. The set came to life right where he left it, tuned to CNN. The news hadn't changed. The bodies, what was left of them, were back in the United States. Next of kin had been notified, and the names of the five civilian contractors slaughtered in Ramadi had been released to the public.

Civilian Contractors. A family-friendly euphemism for mercenaries. The euphemism had never bothered him when he was in the business, but it bugged the shit out of him now.

The television screen showed heavily compressed digital video that had originally aired on Al Jazeera. Five bodies, dumped together in a heap in the middle of the street. Burning. A couple dozen young Iraqi men dancing around the fire, chanting *God Is Great* and *Death To America* and other things Gravedigger could not understand. Then the television showed photos of the five Americans. Four white kids in their late 20s, and one black man in his late 40s.

Gravedigger took a deep breath and blew it out, and consciously relaxed the white-knuckle grip that threatened to shatter the coffee mug in his right hand. He didn't recognize the younger men on the television screen, but he knew Walter Jackson, and had served under him in Nigeria a decade earlier. Back in another life, when Gravedigger Peace was still Mark Tindall.

• • •

The barracks smelled like cigarettes, stewed goat, and the collective body odor of seven testosterone-rich men. No breeze came through the screened windows, and the cigarette smoke hung like a fog in the dim light.

Mark Tindall tossed three .45 caliber bullets into the center of the table. "Raise it up, ladies."

"Fuckin' Africa," said Walter Jackson, and tossed his cards in. "I fold." He wiped his ebony torso with an olive green T-shirt. "Never cools down, not even at night."

"I thought you were from the Southland, Sarge," said Raoul Graham. "Heat shouldn't bother you." Then, to Mark, "I'll call your bullshit." Raoul tossed three bullets into the pot.

Walter Jackson leaned back in his chair and grabbed a Coke from the cooler, "Milledgeville's hot but you get a break every now and then." He popped the bottle cap with the edge of his Zippo, gulped down half the bottle. Then held the cool bottle to his chest, rolling it across a faded blue tattoo. The Insignia of the 1st Special Forces was still legible—Two crossed arrows, with a fighting knife in the middle, pointing skyward, above the motto: *De Oppresso Liber.* Liberate From Oppression.

Underneath the motto, Walter Jackson had added: . . . *Or Not.*

Mark Tindall never asked what had turned Jackson's army life to dog shit, but he knew that Jackson was bitter about it and saw the military as no more noble than the world they now inhabited. Fighting for whichever side offers the most money.

Mark had never served in the military, and he hadn't become a mercenary for the money. He just wanted to kill things. To inflict pain on others. Like his dad inflicted pain.

Around the table, the other three men folded their hands in turn, and Mark shot a hard look to his only remaining opponent.

"How many?"

"Three," said Raoul, and Mark flicked three cards face-down across the table.

"And Dealer takes one," said Mark.

"You're gonna miss that straight-draw," said Raoul, grinning.

God, Raoul had a knack for pissing him off without even trying. "Flush-draw, asshole," Mark sneered. He separated six bullets from his pile, added them to the pot. "And it'll cost you six to find out I made the nut."

Walter Jackson stood and got a fresh shirt from his footlocker, put it on. "Tindall, when you're done taking Graham's money, I need you. Perimeter survey. Bastards are gettin' closer every day."

Brian Billings sat up on his cot and closed the book he was reading. "I'll go, Sarge."

"No you will not."

"Aw, how come Golden Boy always gets the glamour jobs?"

"Fuck you, Billings," said Mark, without looking up from his cards.

Jackson spoke before Billings could answer. "Tindall goes because Tindall is better than you. Quietest white boy I've ever seen, outside Special Forces."

"Thanks a heap, Sarge," said Mark Tindall. "Raoul, you gonna play, or what? I gotta go."

"Just trying to decide between a call and a raise."

Mark Tindall dropped his cards facedown. "Take it." He stood from the table and strapped on his sidearm.

Raoul giggled and raked in the pot. "I *knew* you missed your flush."

"Wrong again, genius. I was bluffing all along. Didn't have shit."

Walter Jackson slung an M-16 over his shoulder, "Let's go, Golden Boy."

• • •

In the morning, Gravedigger avoided the television altogether. Queasy from the hangover, he made a solid breakfast. Three eggs, four rashers of bacon, three slices of whole wheat. And coffee. Always coffee. He considered a slug of bourbon, just to smooth out the rough edges, but the urge itself was a red flag. Sure, he'd been drinking the night before, but now it was morning. It had been years since he drank before the day's work was done. He deferred to his better judgment, taking his coffee black. He could feel Mark Tindall creeping around in the back of his skull, and it worried him. He'd killed that guy years ago, and he was fucked if he'd ever go back.

I am Gravedigger Peace, he reminded himself as he washed the dishes. *That's who I am.*

It had been raining for two days straight, and it was still falling at a steady pace. He put on a plastic poncho and walked to the groundskeeper's shed, where he assigned the day's muddy tasks to his crew. There was his assistant, Sam, who'd worked at Mount Pleasant Cemetery for longer than anyone could remember, and Sam's son Bobby, who was approaching 30 but had the mental capacity of a 12-year-old. Larry and Jamie were a couple of black kids who'd just graduated from high school and were working to save money for college.

And then there were the losers—Tweedledum and Tweedledee, Gravedigger called them. They didn't get the reference and seemed to enjoy the nicknames. A couple of teenage metalhead stoners, they'd barely made it out of high school. But most people don't want to work in a cemetery, and Gravedigger had given them a chance. The latest in a long series of small acts, since he'd killed off Mark Tindall. Small acts to confirm his status as a member of the human race.

So far, the stoner kids had worked out okay. Just barely. They weren't going to set any records for speedy work, they sometimes called-in hungover on Mondays, and he suspected that they often smoked-up on their lunch breaks. But graves were getting dug, bodies buried, and the grass was getting mowed. So he'd decided to keep them on for the rest of the summer, but wasn't planning to invite them back next season.

Gravedigger made it through the morning meeting on autopilot, and dismissed his crew. The walkie-talkie on his belt crackled to life, summoning him to the office. He hopped on an ATV and drove through the hot summer rain to the main building near the cemetery's entrance. Without a word, the receptionist ushered him in to see the boss.

"Thanks for coming, Gravedigger. Can I get you anything? Coffee?"

"No thanks." Why thank him for coming? And why the solicitous tone? The boss sounded like he was talking to a customer.

"Reason I called you in, we have . . . well, we have a body, just arrived for burial. No funeral, just burial. Employer's picking up the tab."

"Okay."

"The deceased put it in his will, to be laid to rest here, because you're the head groundskeeper." He looked at a sheet of paper, put it aside. "His name was Walter Jackson. I guess he was a friend?"

The room spun and Gravedigger closed his eyes.

"I'm sorry, Gravedigger. Take a few minutes to collect yourself, I'll wait outside."

• • •

A silver sliver of a moon provided just enough light to move. More light would make them more vulnerable, while a moonless night would force them to use flashlights, which was even worse. This was perfect.

Mark Tindall and Walter Jackson made it out to the perimeter—five hundred yards from the barracks—at an easy pace. But the perimeter survey would be tediously slow. As Jackson so often said, "You can go fast or you can go quiet, but you can't go both."

Silence demands a kind of slow that very few men have the discipline to achieve. The vast majority of military men could never sustain it, but it is mastered by Navy SEALS and Special Forces. And few mercenaries. Mark took a justifiable pride in his ability. Still, he berated himself for every cracked twig underfoot, for the rustle of his pant legs, for the very sound of his own breathing. But there was none quieter, and even Walter Jackson could not hear him.

It took over an hour to make one hundred yards along the perimeter. Mark walked point, with his commander ten yards back, following—quite literally—in his footsteps. The night vision goggles were a necessity, but in this heat Mark had to take them off every few yards and wipe the sweat out of his eyes. Each time they made twenty yards, Mark stopped and Jackson slowly closed the distance between them. They used hand signals to communicate the All Clear. Then Mark started again, ever so slowly.

At two hundred yards, Mark saw the camp. Both the sight and sound of it had been blocked by a small hill, and by the time it appeared, they were close. Too close.

Mark held up a hand to stop Jackson from approaching, hunkered down in the tall grass, and took stock. Five small tents stood in a circle, a campfire in the center. Nine men sat around the campfire. Six wore sidearms and three cradled machetes on their laps, but Mark saw no long guns.

And then came the soft breeze. It blew gently across the campsite, and the fire crackled and threw off more light. But it blew the smoke straight toward Mark, and his eyes began to sting and water, and his nose tickled.

Mark Tindall sneezed. The night shattered.

• • •

Gravedigger stood in the rain and, using a spade, separated the grass from the earth below. The area around the head grounds-keeper's residence was taken up mostly by old mausoleums, but he wanted to bury Walter Jackson nearby, so he commandeered this spot, about ten yards from his front door. Once he'd placed the sod to one side, he used a small backhoe to dig the hole, dumping the wet soil on a tarp to the other side.

The casket arrived, and the crew lowered it into the hole. Because of the persistent rain, the ground was waterlogged and there were a couple of feet of standing water below. The sealed casket floated aimlessly in the grave.

Gravedigger sent Sam off to get the sump pump, and then retreated to his residence, where he rummaged through an old shoebox and found a photograph of Mark Tindall and Walter Jackson. It was the only thing he had kept from his former life. He'd thrown everything else away when he killed Mark Tindall and became Gravedigger Peace, but Jackson had saved his life and he could never bring himself to get rid of it. Now he would lay it to rest with his old friend.

He left the photo on the kitchen table and, in the bedroom, stripped off his sodden clothes. Walter Jackson would have no funeral, only a burial. But at least he would have one mourner. Maybe it was a useless gesture, but Gravedigger didn't care. He opened the closet, and put on his only suit.

He tied his tie in front of the bathroom mirror, and tried not to look beyond the knot. But he couldn't help himself. Avoiding his own eyes, he examined the thin white scar that ran from his left cheek down to his jaw. The scar made by a machete in Nigeria. And when he made eye contact, Mark Tindall stared back at him. *Shit! Fuck!* He swung open the door of the medicine cabinet, displacing the mirror, and fled the bathroom, thinking *I know who I am. I know who I am. I know who I am . . .*

Photograph in hand, Gravedigger headed back out into the hot summer rain. Fuck the poncho, he would stand in his suit in the rain and give Walter Jackson a proper sendoff. It was coming down harder now, blowing in his face, forcing him to look at the ground as he walked to the graveside. He looked up, and dropped the photograph.

They were coffin-surfing. Tweedledum stood on top of the casket, rocking it with his legs, creating a wave beneath. He struck a surfer's pose, and sang the theme from *Hawaii Five-O*. Tweedledee stood off to one side, laughing.

Gravedigger screamed and lunged forward, then caught himself. He trembled as adrenaline coursed through his veins.

Tweedledee stopped laughing and said, "Oh, shit."

Tweedledum jumped off the casket and out of the grave. "We were just having some fun, man."

"You're fired. Both of you."

"What difference does it make," said Tweedledee, "dude's already dead."

It took all of Gravedigger's willpower to keep his voice from breaking. "Get the fuck out of my graveyard. Now. Before I hurt you."

• • •

Nigeria is a very bad place to do prison time, especially for a white man. Walter Jackson endured his share of torture, but his cell had a cot, and a hole in the floor served as a toilet. Mark Tindall did harder time. The guards beat him daily, sometimes breaking ribs and once breaking his left arm. He was given just enough food and water to keep him alive, and days would sometimes pass between meals. His cell had nothing in it at all, not even a drain in the concrete floor, so he lived in his own filth.

Sometime around the fourth month, the guards took Mark Tindall's boots away and whipped him on the soles of his feet. His feet soon became infected, purple and swollen and oozing puss. He was given no medical attention and his fever soared. Hallucinations came regularly, and he started to lose himself. Some days he would be lucid, but other days he was stark raving mad, smearing himself with his own shit, howling at the walls and twitching like an epileptic having a seizure. Then he would pass out, and wake up relatively sane again. Until the next time.

On the six-month anniversary of their capture, the guards hauled Mark Tindall from his cell and hosed him down and put him in the cell with Walter Jackson. A man in a crisp military uniform came into the cell.

"Tomorrow morning," the man said, "one of you will be sent back to America. It is for you to decide which one." The man handed a pack of Marlboros and a book of matches to Walter Jackson, and left.

Jackson lit a cigarette and put it between Mark Tindall's lips, then lit one for himself. They smoked in silence for a few minutes.

"You don't look so good, Golden Boy," said Jackson.

Mark Tindall let out a crooked smile. "You're lookin' a little skinny yourself, Sarge."

"Hey, I'm livin' high on the hog. This is the fuckin' Ritz Carleton compared to your crib."

"Yeah. It's pretty nice. I could stay here awhile."

Walter Jackson stubbed his cigarette out on the floor and lit another. "Shit. You gonna lose those feet if we don't get you out of here."

"Might lose 'em anyway." The two men nodded at each other, and silent tears began to stream down Mark Tindall's face.

Jackson slid over and put his arms around the younger man's shoulders, holding him like a protective father. "When you get out of here tomorrow, put it behind you, Mark. Don't look back."

Mark didn't even try to argue.

• • •

Gravedigger Peace woke to the sound of his own voice. "Sorry I sneezed, Sarge." *Sorry I sneezed. Shit. Sorry I left you behind. Sorry I lived.*

The bedside clock said it was just past midnight. He had slept only three hours. After the stoners had left, he'd sumped the water out of Walter Jackson's grave and covered it with earth by hand, using the spade. He needed to work off the adrenaline. Once the grave was filled, he went home, tossed his ruined suit into the trash, and lay in the bathtub with a long drink. He tried to make himself cry a little, but he hadn't cried in years and he couldn't summon the tears. Finally he gave up, finished his drink and went to bed.

Now he was up again, and his nerves felt raw, exposed. He tried to read, couldn't. He got a beer from the fridge, but didn't open it. Sat in front of the television, but didn't turn it on. The rain had stopped at last, and the silence rang in his ears.

Then he heard it. A sound from outside. Voices.

He opened the coat closet and reached for the Mossberg shotgun that he kept there, then reached deeper into the closet and pulled out a machete instead.

The moon was almost full, and Gravedigger's eyes adjusted to the light as he walked toward Walter Jackson's grave, holding the machete in his right hand and a flashlight in his left. Tweedledee stood pissing on the grave, then put his dick back in his pants. Beside a nearby mausoleum, Tweedledum stood with a can of spray-paint in his hand. Painted on the wall was, *I rode Gravedigger's bitch!*

Gravedigger flicked the flashlight on, and both boys froze. They should have run away. But instead, they charged.

And Mark Tindall cut them to pieces.

Formerly a private investigator in Chicago and New Orleans, **SEAN CHERCOVER** now writes full-time. His debut novel, *Big City Bad Blood*, won the Shamus, Gumshoe, Crimespree, and Lovey awards for best first novel, and was shortlisted for the ITW Thriller, Arthur Ellis, Barry, and Anthony awards. His short story, "A Sleep Not Unlike Death" is an Edgar Award nominee. His latest novel is *Trigger City*. When Sean's not on the road, you can find him in Chicago or Toronto.

The First Husband

BY JOYCE CAROL OATES

1.

It began innocently: he was searching for his wife's passport.

The Chases were planning their first trip to Italy together. To celebrate their tenth anniversary. Leonard's own much-worn passport was exactly where he always kept it but Valerie's less frequently used passport didn't appear to be with it so Leonard looked through drawers designated as hers, bureau drawers, desk drawers, the single shallow drawer of the cherrywood table in a corner of their bedroom which Valerie sometimes used as a desk, and there, in a manila folder, with a facsimile of her birth certificate and other documents, he found the passport. And pushed to the back of the drawer, a packet of photographs held together with a frayed rubber band.

Polaroids. Judging by their slightly faded colors, old Polaroids.

Leonard shuffled through the photographs, like cards. He was staring at a young couple: Valerie and a man whom Leonard didn't recognize. Here was Valerie astonishingly young, and more beautiful than Leonard had ever known her. Her hair was coppery-red and fell in a cascade to her bare shoulders, she was wearing a red bikini top, white shorts. The darkly handsome young man close beside her had slung a tanned arm around her shoulders in a playful intimate gesture, a gesture of blatant sexual possession. Very likely, this man was Valerie's first husband, whom Leonard had never met. The young lovers were photographed seated at a white wrought iron table in an outdoor cafe, or on the balcony of a hotel room. In several photos, you could see in the near distance a curving stretch of wide, white sand, a glimpse of aqua water. Beyond the couple on the terrace were royal court palm trees, crimson bouvainvillea like flame. The sky was a vivid tropical blue. The five or six photographs must have been taken by a third party, a waiter or hotel employee perhaps. Leonard stared, transfixed.

The first husband. Here was the first husband. Yardman?—was that the name? Leonard felt a stab of sexual jealousy. Not wanting to think *But I am the second husband.*

On the reverse of one of the Polaroids, in Valerie's handwriting, was *Oliver & Val, Key West, December 1985.*

Oliver. This was Yardman's first name, Leonard vaguely remembered now. In 1985, Val had been twenty-two, nearly half her lifetime ago, and she hadn't yet married Oliver Yardman, but would be marrying him in another year. At this time they were very possibly new lovers, this trip to Key West had been a kind of honeymoon. Such sensual, unabashed happiness in the lovers' faces! Leonard was sure that Valerie had told him she hadn't kept any photographs of her first husband.

"The least we can do with our mistakes," Valerie had said, with a droll downturn of her mouth, "is not keep a record of them."

Leonard, who'd met Valerie when she was thirty-one, several years after her divorce from Yardman, had been allowed to think that the first husband had been older than Valerie, not very attractive and not very interesting. Valerie claimed that she'd married "too young" and their divorce just five years later had been "amicable" for they had no children and had not shared much of a past. Yardman's work had been with a family-owned business in a Denver suburb, "dull, money-grubbing work." Valerie, who'd grown up in Rye, Connecticut, had not liked Colorado and spoke of that part of the country, and of that phase of her life, with an expression of distaste.

Yet here was glaring evidence that Valerie had been very happy with Oliver Yardman in December 1985. Clearly Yardman was no more than a few years older than Valerie and, far from being unattractive, Yardman was extremely attractive: dark, avid eyes, sharply defined features, something sulky and petulant about the mouth, the mouth of a spoiled child; the kind of child a woman might wish to spoil to see that mouth curve upward in pleasure. There was a revealing Polaroid in which Yardman pulled Valerie playfully toward him, a hand gripping her shoulder and the other hand beneath the table, very likely gripping her thigh. His hair was dark, thick, damply touseled. Faint stubble showed on his jaws. He wore a white T-shirt that fitted his muscled, solid torso tightly, and what appeared to be swimming trunks; his legs were thickly muscled, covered in dark hairs. He was barefoot, his toes curling upward in delight. So this was Oliver Yardman: the first husband. Not at all the man Valerie had suggested to Leonard.

He'd thought it was strange, but attributed it to Valerie's natural reticence, that, in the early months of their relationship Valerie had rarely asked Leonard about his past. She hadn't even asked him if he had been married, Leonard had volunteered the information: No.

And no children, either. He'd been careful about that.

It had been something of a relief, to meet a woman without a trace of sexual jealousy. Now Leonard saw that Valerie hadn't wanted to be questioned about her own sexual past.

Leonard stared at the Polaroids. He supposed he should simply laugh and replace them in the drawer where he'd found them, taking care not to snap the frayed rubber band, for certainly he wasn't the kind of man to riffle through his wife's private things. *Nor* was he the kind of man who is prone to jealousy.

Of all the ignoble emotions, jealousy had to be the worst! And envy.

And yet: he brought the photos closer to the window, where a faint November sun glowered behind banks of clouds above the Hudson River, seeing how the table at which the young couple sat was crowded with glasses, a bottle of (red, dark) wine that appeared to be nearly depleted, napkins crumpled onto dirtied plates like discarded clothing. A ring on Valerie's left hand, silver studs glittering in her ear lobes that looked flushed, rosy. In several of the photos, Valerie was clutching at her energetic young lover as he was clutching at her, in playful possessiveness. You could see that Valerie was giddy from wine, and love. Here was an amorous couple who'd wakened late after a night of love, this heavy lunch with wine would be their first meal of the day; very likely, they'd return to bed, collapsing in one another's arms for an afternoon siesta. In the most blatant photo, Valerie lay sprawled against Yardman, glossy coppery hair spilling across his chest, one of her arms around his waist and the other part hidden beneath the table, her hand very likely in Yardman's lap. In Yardman's groin. Valerie, who now disliked vulgarity, who stiffened if Leonard swore and claimed to hate "overly explicit" films, had been provocatively touching Yardman in the very presence of the third party with the camera. Her little-girl mock-innocent expression was familiar to Leonard: *Not me! Not me! I'm not a naughty girl, not me!*

Leonard stared, his heart beat in resentment. Here was a Valerie he hadn't known: mouth swollen from being kissed, and from kissing; young, full breasts straining against the red fabric of the bikini top and in the crescent of shadowy flesh between her breasts something coin-sized gleaming like oily sweat; her skin suffused with a warm, sensual radiance. Leonard understood that this young woman must be contained within the other, the elder who was his wife: as a secret, rapturous memory, inaccessible to him, the merely second husband.

Leonard was forty-five. Young for his age but that age wasn't young.

When he'd been the age of Yardman in the photos, early or mid-twenties, he hadn't been young like Yardman, either. Painful to concede but it was so.

If he, Leonard Chase, had approached the young woman in the photos, if he'd managed to enter Valerie's life in 1985, Valerie would not have given him a second glance. Not as a man. Not as a sexual partner. He knew this.

After lunch, the young couple would return to their hotel room and draw the blinds. Laughing and kissing, stumbling, like drunken dancers. They were naked together, beautiful smooth bodies coiled together, greedily kissing, caressing, thrusting together with the abandon of copulating animals. He saw them sprawled on the bed that would be a large jangly brass bed, and the room dimly-lit, a fan turning indolently overhead, through slats in the blinds a glimpse of tropical sky, the graceful curve of a palm tree, a patch of bougainvillea moistly crimson as a woman's mouth . . . Leonard felt an unwelcome sexual stirring, in his groin.

"She lied. That's the insult."

Misrepresenting the first husband, the first marriage. Why?

Leonard knew why: Yardman had been Valerie's first serious love. Yardman was the standard of masculine sexuality in Valerie's life. *No love like your first.* Was this so? (In Leonard's case also, probably it was. But Leonard's first love had not been a sexual love and his memory of the girl, the older sister of a school friend had long since faded.) The cache of Polaroid's was Valerie's secret, a link to her private, erotic life.

Hurriedly he replaced the Polaroids in the drawer. The frayed rubber band had snapped, Leonard took no notice. He went away shaken, devastated. He thought *I've never existed for her. It has all been a farce.*

• • •

In Rockland County, New York. In Salthill Landing on the western bank of the Hudson River. Twenty miles north of the George Washington Bridge.

In one of the old stone houses overlooking the river: "historic"—"landmark." Expensive.

Early that evening as Valerie was preparing one of her gourmet meals in the kitchen there was Leonard leaning in the doorway, a drink in hand. Asking, "D'you ever hear of him, Val? What was his name, 'Yardman'. . ." casually as one who has only been struck by a wayward thought, and Valerie, frowning at a recipe, murmured no, but in so distracted a way Leonard wasn't sure that she'd heard, so he asked again, "D'you ever hear of Yardman? Or from him?" and now Valerie glanced over at Leonard with a faint, perplexed smile, "Yardman? No," and Leonard said, "Really? Never? In all these years?" and Valerie said, "In all these years, darling, no."

Valerie was peering at a recipe in a large, sumptuously illustrated cookbook propped up on a counter, pages clipped open. The cookbook was *Caribbean Kitchen*, an expensive book that had been a Christmas gift from friends in Salthill Landing with whom the Chases often dined, both in their homes and in selected restaurants in Manhattan. Valerie was preparing flank steak, to be marinated and stuffed with sausage, hard-boiled eggs, and vegetables, an ambitious meal that would involve an elaborate marinade, and a yet more elaborate stuffing, and at this moment involved the almost surgical "butterflying" of the blood-oozing slab of meat. This was a meal Valerie hoped to prepare for a dinner party later in the month, she was determined to perfect it. A coincidence, Leonard thought, that only a few hours after he'd discovered the secret cache of Polaroids, Valerie was preparing an exotic Caribbean meal of the kind she might have first sampled in Key West with the first husband twenty years ago, but Leonard, who was a reasonable man, a tax lawyer who specialized in litigation in federal appellate courts, knew it could only be a coincidence. Asking, in a tone of mild inquiry, "What was Yardman's first name, Val?—I don't think you ever mentioned it," and Valerie said, with an impatient little laugh, having taken up a steak knife to cut the meat horizontally, "What does it matter what the name is?" Leonard noted that, though he'd said was, Valerie had said is. The first husband was present to her, no time had passed. Leonard recalled an ominous remark of Freud's that, in the unconscious, all time is present tense and so what has come to dwell most powerfully in the unconscious is felt to be immortal, unkillable. Valerie added, as if in rebuke, "Of course I've mentioned his name, Leonard. Only just not in a long time." She was having difficulty with the flank steak, skidding about on the wooden block, so Leonard quickly set down his drink and held it secure, while Valerie, biting her lower lip, pursing her face like Caravaggio's Judith sawing off the head of the wicked king Holofernes, managed to inset the sharp blade, make the necessary incisions, complete the cut so that the meat could now be opened like the pages of a book. As Leonard watched, fascinated, yet with a sensation of revulsion, Valerie then covered the meat with a strip of plastic wrap and pounded at it with a meat mallet, short deft blows to reduce it to a uniform quarter-inch thickness. Leonard winced a little with the blows. He said, "Did he—I mean Yardman—ever re-marry?" and Valerie made an impatient gesture to signal that she didn't want to be distracted, not just now. This was important! This was to be their dinner! Carefully she slid the butterflied steak into a large, shallow dish and poured the marinade (sherry vinegar, olive oil, fresh sage, cumin, garlic, salt and fresh-ground black pepper) over it. Leonard saw that Valerie's face had thickened, since she'd been Oliver Yardman's lover; her body had thickened, gravity was tugging at her breasts, thighs. At the corners of her eyes and mouth were fine white lines and the coppery-red hair had faded, yet still Valerie was a striking woman, a rich man's daughter whose sense of her self-worth shone in her eyes, in her lustrous teeth, in her sharp dismissive laughter like the sheen of the expensive kitchen utensils hanging overhead. There was something sensual and languorous in Valerie's face when she concentrated on food, an almost childlike bliss, an air of happy expectation. Leonard thought *Food is Eros without the risk of heartbreak. Unlike a lover, food will never reject you.*

Leonard asked another time if Yardman had remarried and Valerie said, "How would I know, darling?" in a tone of faint exasperation. Leonard said, "From mutual friends, you might have heard." Valerie carried the steak in a covered dish to the refrigerator where it would marinate for two hours. They never ate before 8:30 P.M., and sometimes later; it was the custom of their lives together for they'd never had children to necessitate early meals, the routines of a perfunctory American life. Valerie said, "'Mutual friends.'" She laughed sharply. "We don't have any." Again Leonard noted the present tense: *Don't.* "And you've never kept in touch," he said, and Valerie said, "You know we didn't." She was frowning, uneasy. Or maybe she was annoyed. To flare up in anger was a sign of weakness, Valerie hid such weaknesses. A sign of vulnerability and Valerie was not vulnerable. Not any longer.

Leonard said, "Well. That seems rather sad, in a way."

At the sink, which was designed to resemble a deep, old-fashioned kitchen sink of another era, Valerie vigorously washed her hands, stained with watery blood. She washed the ten-inch gleaming knife with the surgically sharpened blade, each of the utensils she'd been using. It was something of a fetish for Valerie, to keep her beautiful kitchen as spotless as she could while working in it. As she took care to remove her beautiful jewelry to set aside, as she worked.

On her left hand, Valerie wore the diamond engagement ring and the matching wedding band Leonard had given her. On her right hand, Valerie wore a square-cut emerald in an antique setting, she'd said she'd inherited from her grandmother. Only now did Leonard wonder if the emerald ring wasn't the engagement ring her first husband had given her, which she'd shifted to her right hand after their marriage had ended.

"Sad for who, Leonard? Sad for me? For *you*?"

• • •

That night, in their bed. A vast tundra of a bed. As if she'd sensed something in his manner, a subtle shift of tone, a quaver in his voice of withheld hurt, or anger, Valerie turned to him with a smile: "I've been missing you, darling." Her meaning might have been literal, for Leonard had been traveling for his firm lately, working with Atlanta lawyers in preparation for an appeal in the federal court there, but there was another meaning, too. He thought *She wants to make amends.* Their lovemaking was calm, measured, methodical, lasting perhaps eight minutes. It was their custom to make love at night, before sleep, the high-ceilinged bedroom lighted by just a single lamp. There was a fragrance here of the lavender sachets Valerie kept in her bureau drawers. Except for the November wind overhead in the trees, it was very quiet. *Still as the grave,* Leonard thought. He sought his wife's smiling mouth with his mouth but could not find it. Shut his eyes and there suddenly was the brazen coppery-haired girl in the red bikini top waiting for him. Squirming in the darkly handsome young man's arms but glancing at him. Oh! she was a bad girl, look at the bad girl! Her mouth was hungry and sucking as a pike's mouth seeking the young man's mouth, her hand dropped beneath the table top, to burrow in his lap. In his groin. Oh the bad girl!

Leonard had the idea that Valerie's eyes were shut tight, too. Valerie was seeing the young couple, too.

• • •

"I found your passport, Valerie. I found these Polaroids, too. Recognize them?"

Spreading them on the table. Better yet, across the bed.

"Only just curious, Val. Why you lied about him."

She would stare, her smile fading. Her fleshy lips would go slack as if, taken wholly unaware, she'd been slapped.

". . . why you continue to lie. All these years."

Of course, Leonard would be laughing. To indicate that he didn't take any of this seriously, why should he? It had happened so long ago, it was *past.*

Except: maybe "lie" was too strong a word. The rich man's daughter wasn't accustomed to being spoken to in such a way, any more than Leonard was. "Lie" would have the force of a physical blow. "Lie" would cause Valerie to flinch as if she'd been struck and the rich man's daughter would file for divorce at once if she were struck.

Maybe it wasn't a good idea, then. To confront her.

A litigator is a strategist plotting moves. A skilled litigator always knows how his opponent will respond to a move. Like chefs, you must foresee the opponent's moves. Each blow can provoke a counterblow. Valerie was a woman who disliked weakness in men. A woman with a steely will, yet she presented herself as uncertain, even hesitant, socially; she knew the value of seeming vulnerable. Her sexuality had become a matter of will, she delighted in exerting her will, even as she held herself apart, detached. In all public places as in her beautifully furnished home she was perfectly groomed, not a hair of her sleek razor-cut hair out of place. Her voice was calm, modulated. It was a voice that could provoke others to be cutting but was never less than calm itself. Leonard had witnessed Valerie riling her sister, her mother. She had a way of laughing with her eyes, mocking laughter not uttered aloud. She was a shrewd judge of others. If Leonard confronted her with the Polaroids, the gesture might backfire on him. She might detect in his voice a quaver of hurt, she might detect in his eyes a pang of male anguish. He was sometimes impotent, to his chagrin. He blamed distractions: the pressure of his work which remained, even for those of his generation who had not been winnowed out by competition, competitive. The pressure of a man's expectations to "perform." The (literal) pressure of his blood, for which he took blood-pressure pills twice daily. And his back, that ached sometimes mysteriously, he'd attribute to tennis, golf. In fact out of nowhere such phantom aches emerged. And so, in the vigorous act of love, Leonard might begin to lose his concentration, his erection. Like his life's blood leaking out of his veins. And Valerie knew, of course she knew, the terrible intimacy of the act precluded any secrets, yet she never commented, never said a word only just held him, her husband of only nine years, her middle-aged flabby-waisted panting and sweating second husband, held him as if to comfort him, as a mother might hold a stricken child, with sympathy, unless it was with pity.

Darling we won't speak of it. Our secret.

Yet, if Leonard confronted her over the Polaroids, that were her cherished sexual secret, she might turn upon him, cruelly. She had that power. She might laugh at him. Valerie's high-pitched mocking laughter like icicles being shattered. She would chide him for looking through her things, what right had he to look through her things, what if she searched through his desk drawers would she discover soft-core porn magazines, ridiculous soft-core videos with titles like *Girls Night Out, Girls At Play, Sex Addict Holiday*, she would expose him to their friends at the next Salthill Landing dinner party, dryly she would dissect him like an insect wriggling on a pin, at the very least she might slap the Polaroids out of his hand. How ridiculous he was being, over a trifle. How pitiable.

Leonard shuddered. A rivulet of icy sweat ran down the side of his cheek like a tear.

So, no. He would not confront her. Not just yet. For the fact was, Leonard had the advantage: he knew of Valerie's secret attachment to the first husband, and Valerie had no idea he knew.

Smiling to think: like a boa constrictor swallowing its living prey paralyzed by terror his secret would encompass Valerie's secret and would, in time, digest it.

• • •

The anniversary trip to Italy, scheduled for March, was to be postponed.

"It isn't a practical time after all. My work . . ."

And this was true. The Atlanta case had swerved in an unforeseen and perilous direction. There were obligations in Valerie's life, too. ". . . not a practical time. But, later . . ."

He saw in her eyes regret, yet also relief.

• • •

Doesn't want to be alone with me. Comparing me with him isn't she!

• • •

". . . a reservation for four, at L'Heure Bleu. If we arrive by six, maybe a little before six, we won't have to leave until quarter to eight, Lincoln Center is just across the street. But if you and Harold prefer the Tokyo Pavilion, I know you've been wanting to check it out after the review in the *Times*, and Leonard and I have, too . . ."

In fact, Leonard disliked Japanese food. Hated sushi that was so much raw flesh, uneatable.

This passion for gourmet food, wine! Expensive restaurants!

Where love has gone, he thought bitterly.

Listening to Valerie's maddeningly calm voice as she descended the stairs speaking on a cordless phone to a friend. It was nearly two weeks after he'd discovered the Polaroids, he'd vowed not to look at them again. Yet he was approaching the cherrywood table, pulling open the drawer that stuck a little, groping another time for the packet of Polaroids that seemed to be in exactly the place he'd left it and he cursed his wife for being so careless, for not having taken time to hide her secret more securely.

(*His* small cache of soft-core porn, pulpy magazines, X-rated videos, evidence of a minor, minimal interest in porn and hardly a consuming passion, he'd taken care to secret away deep in one of the locked drawers of his filing cabinet downstairs amid documents of stultifying dullness pertaining to IRS payments, stock holdings. *His* secret he was sure Valerie would never discover!)

"'Oliver and Val, Key West, December 1985.'"

With what childish pride, Valerie had felt the need to identify the lovers!

At a window overlooking a snowy slope to the river and the glowering winter sky he examined the photographs eagerly. He had seen them several times by now and had more or less memorized them and so they were both familiar and yet retained an air of the exotic and treacherous. One of the less faded Polaroids he brought close to his face, that he might squint at the ring worn by the coppery-haired girl—was it the emerald? Valerie was wearing it on her right hand even then, which might only mean that, though Oliver Yardman had given it to her, it hadn't yet acquired the status of an engagement ring. In another photo, Leonard discovered what he'd somehow overlooked, the faintest suggestion of a bruise on Valerie's neck, or a shadow that very much resembled a bruise. And Oliver Yardman's smooth-skinned face wasn't really so smooth, in fact it looked coarse in certain of the photos. And that smug, petulant mouth, the fleshy lips, Leonard would have liked to smash with his fist. And there was Yardman wriggling his stubby yet long toes, wasn't there a correlation between the size of a man's toes and the size of . . .

Hurriedly Leonard shoved the Polaroids into the drawer and fled the room.

• • •

"The time for children is past."

Years ago. Should have known the woman hadn't loved him if she had not wanted children with him.

". . . a kind of madness has come over parents, today. Not just the expense: private schools, private tutors, college. Therapists! But you must subordinate your life to your children. My husband—" Valerie's voice dipped, this was a hypothetical, it was Leonard to whom she spoke so earnestly, "would be working in the city five days a week and wouldn't be home until evening and—can you see me as a 'soccer mom' driving children to—wherever! Living through it all again and this time knowing what's to come, my God it would be so *raw*."

Valerie laughed, there was fear in her eyes.

Leonard was astonished, this poised, beautiful woman was speaking so intimately to him! Of course he comforted her, gripping her cold hands. Kissed her hair where she'd leaned toward him, trembling.

"Valerie, of course. I feel the same way."

He did! In that instant, Leonard did.

They'd been introduced by mutual friends. Leonard was a highly paid litigator attached to the legal department of the most distinguished architectural firm in New York City, its headquarters in lower Manhattan on Rector Street. Leonard's specialty was tax law and within that specialty he prepared and argued cases in federal appeals courts. He was one of a team. There were enormous penalties for missteps, sometimes in the hundreds of millions of dollars. And there were enormous rewards when things went well.

"A litigator goes for the jugular."

Valerie wasn't one to flatter, you could see. Her admiration was sincere.

Leonard had laughed, blushing with pleasure. In his heart thinking he was one in a frantic swarm of piranha fish and not the swiftest, most deadly, or even, at thirty-four, as he'd been at the time, among the youngest.

The poised beautiful young woman was Valerie Fairfax. Her maiden name: crisp, clear, Anglo, unambiguous. (Not a hint of "Yardman.") At CitiBank headquarters in Manhattan, Valerie had the title of vice-president of Human Resources. How serious she was about her work! She wore Armani suits in subdued tones:

oatmeal, powder-gray, charcoal. She wore pencil-thin skirts and she wore trousers with sharp creases. She wore trim little jackets with slightly padded shoulders. Her hair was stylishly razor-cut to frame her face, to suggest delicacy were there was in fact solidity. Her fragrance was discreet, faintly astringent. Her handshake was firm and yet, in certain circumstances, yielding. She displayed little interest in speaking of the past though she spoke animatedly on a variety of subjects. She thought well of herself and wished to think well of Leonard and so had a way of making Leonard more interesting to himself, more mysterious.

The first full night they spent together, in the apartment on East 79th Street where Leonard was living at the time, a flush of excitement had come into Valerie's face as, after several glasses of wine, she confessed how at CitiBank she was the vice-president of her department elected to firing people because she was so good at it.

"I never let sentiment interfere with my sense of justice. It's in my genes, I think."

• • •

Now, you didn't say *fired*. You said *downsized*.

You might say *dismissed*, *terminated*. You might say, of vanished colleagues, gone.

Leonard typed into his laptop a private message to himself:

Not me. Not this season. They can't!

• • •

Another time, in fact many times, he'd typed *Yardman* into his computer. (At the office, not at home. He and Valerie shared a computer at home. Leonard knew that, in cyberspace, nothing is ever erased though it might be subsequently regretted and so at home he never typed into the computer anything he might not wish his wife to discover in some ghost-remnant way.) Hundreds of citations for *Yardman* but none for *Oliver Yardman* so far.

He meant to keep looking.

• • •

". . . first husband."

Like an abscessed tooth secretly rotting in his jaw.

In his office on the twenty-ninth floor at Rector Street. On the 7:10 A.M. Amtrak into Grand Central Station and on the 6:55 P.M. Amtrak out of Grand Central returning to Salthill Landing. In the interstices of his relations with others: colleagues, clients, fellow commuters, social acquaintances, friends. In the cracks of a densely scheduled life the obsession with Oliver Yardman grew the way the hardiest weeds will flourish in soil scarcely hospitable to plant life.

Sure he knows. Knows of me: second husband. What he must remember! Of her.

Had to wonder how often Valerie glanced through the Polaroids in the desk drawer. How frequently, even when they'd been newly lovers, she'd shut her eyes to summon back the first husband, the sulky-spoiled mouth, the brazen hands, the hard stiff penis thrumming with blood that would never flag, even as she was breathless and panting in Leonard's arms declaring she loved *him*.

Since the discovery weeks ago in November he'd looked for other photos. Not in the photo album Valerie maintained with seeming sincerity and wifely pride but in Valerie's drawers, closets. In the most remote regions of the large house where things were stored away in boxes. Shrewdly thinking because he hadn't found anything did not mean that there was nothing to be found.

"Len Chase!"

A bright female voice, a Salthill Landing neighbor leaning over his seat. (Where was he? On the Amtrak? Headed home? Judging by the murky haze above the river, early evening, had to be headed home.) Leonard's laptop was opened before him and his fingers were poised over the flat keyboard but he'd been staring out the window for some minutes without moving. ". . . thought that was you, Len, and how is Valerie? Haven't seen you since, has it been Christmas, or . . ."

Leonard smiled politely at the woman. His opened laptop, his document bag and overcoat in the seat beside him, these were clear signals he didn't want to be interrupted, which the woman surely knew, but had come to an age when she'd decided not to see such signals in cheerful denial of their meaning *Please leave me alone, you are not of interest to me, not as a woman, not as an individual, you are nothing but a minor annoyance.* Melanie Roberts was Valerie's age, and her frosted hair was razor-cut in Valerie's style. Very likely Melanie was a rich man's daughter as well as a rich man's wife but the advantage she'd held as a younger woman had mysteriously faded, even so. Melanie seemed to think that her neighbor Leonard Chase might wish to know that she'd had lunch with friends in the city and gone to see the Rauschenberg exhibit at the Metropolitan Museum and then she'd dropped by to visit her niece at Barnard. Melanie was watching Leonard with sparkly expectant eyes in which dwelled some uneasiness, a fear of seeing in Leonard's face exactly what he was thinking. He had to concede, he saw in Melanie Roberts' face that he might still be perceived as an attractive man, in his seated position he appeared moderately tall, with a head of moderately thick hair, graying, but attractively graying; his skin tone was slightly sallow, but perhaps that was just the flickering Amtrak lighting; his face was dented in odd places, and loosely jowly in others; his nostrils looked enlarged, like pits opening into his skull; his eyes behind wire-rimmed bifocal glasses were shadowed and smudged; yet he would seem to this yearning woman more attractive than paunchy near-bald Sam Roberts, as others' spouses invariably seem more attractive, since more mysterious, than our own. For intimacy is the enemy of romance. The dailyness of marriage is the enemy of immortality. Who would wish to be immortal, if it's a matter of reliving just the past week?

Melanie Roberts's smile was fading. Amid her chatter, Leonard must have interrupted. ". . . hear you, Len? It's so noisy in this . . ."

The car was swaying drunkenly. The lights flickered. With a nervous laugh Melanie gripped the back of the seat to steady herself. Another eight minutes to Salthill Landing, why was the woman hanging over his seat! He yearned to be touched, his numbed body caressed in love, so desperately he yearned for this touch that would be the awakening from a curse, but he shrank from intimacy with this woman who was his neighbor in Salthill Landing. On his opened laptop screen was a column of e-mail messages he hadn't answered, in fact hadn't read, as he hadn't for most of that day returned phone messages, for a terrible gravity pulled his mind elsewhere. *The first husband. You cannot be first.* Melanie was saying brightly that she would call Valerie and maybe this weekend they could go out together to dinner, that new seafood restaurant in Nyack everyone has been talking about, and Leonard laughed, with a nod toward the window beside his seat where some distance below the oily-dark sprawl of the Hudson River was lapsing into dusk, "Ever think, Melanie, that river is like a gigantic boa constrictor? It's like time, eventually to swallow and digest us all?"

Melanie laughed sharply as if not hearing this, or hearing enough to know that she didn't really want to hear more of it. Promising she'd tell Sam hello from him, and she'd call Valerie very soon, with a faint, forced smile lurching away somewhere behind Leonard Chase to her seat.

• • •

He would track down the first husband, he would erase the man from consciousness. He would erase the man's memory in which his own wife existed. Except he was a civilized human being, a decent human being, except he feared being apprehended and punished, that was what he would do.

• • •

Early November when he'd discovered the Key West photos. Late February when his CEO called him into his office in the "tower."

The meeting was brief. One or two others had been taken to lunch first which had not been a good idea, Leonard was grateful to be spared lunch. Through a roaring in his ears he heard. Watched the man's piranha mouth. Steely eyes through bifocal glasses like his own.

Downsized. Stock options. Severance pay. Any questions?

He had no legal grounds to object. Possibly he had moral grounds but wouldn't contest it. He knew the company's financial situation. Since 9/11, they'd been in a tailspin. These were facts you might read in the *Wall Street Journal.* Then came the terrible blow, unexpected, at least Leonard believed it to be unexpected, the riling in Atlanta: a federal court judge upheld a crushing $33 million award to a hotel-chain plaintiff plus $8 million punitive damages. The architectural firm for which he'd worked for the past seven years was hard hit. Conceding yes, he understood. Failure was a sickness that burned like fever in the eyes of the afflicted. No disguising that fever, like jaundice-yellow eyes.

Soon to be forty-six. Burnt-out. The battlefield is strewn with burnt-out litigators. His fingers shook, cold as a corpse's yet he would shake the CEO's hand in parting, he would meet the man's gaze with something like dignity.

He had the use of his office for several more weeks. And the stock options and severance pay were generous. And Valerie wouldn't need to know exactly what had happened, possibly ever.

• • •

". . . seemed distracted lately, Leonard. I hope it isn't . . ."

They were undressing for bed. That night in their large beautifully furnished bedroom. Gusts of wind rattled the windows, that were leaded windows, inset with wavy glass in mimicry of the oil glass that had once been, when the original house had been built in 1791.

". . . anything serious? Your health . . ."

From his corner of the room Leonard called over, in a voice

meant to comfort, of course he was fine, his health was fine. Of course. "Damned wind! It's been like this all day." Valerie spoke fretfully as if someone were to blame. Neither had brought up the subject of the trip to Italy in some time. Postponed to March, but no specific plans had been made. The tenth anniversary had come and gone.

In her corner of their bedroom, an alcove with a built-in dresser and closets with mirrors affixed to their doors, Valerie was undressing as, in his corner of the bedroom, a smaller alcove with but a single mirrored door, Leonard was undressing. As if casually Leonard called over to her, "Did you ever love me, Valerie? When you first married me, I mean." Through his mirror Leonard could see just a blurred glimmer of one of Valerie's mirrors. She seemed not to have heard his question. The wind buffeting the house was so very loud. "For a while? In the beginning? Was there a time?" Not knowing if his voice was pleading, or threatening. If, if this woman heard, like the frightened woman on the train she would laugh nervously and wish to escape him.

"Maybe I should murder us both, Valerie. 'Downsize.' It could end very quickly."

He didn't own a gun. Had no access to a gun. Rifle? Could you go into a sporting goods store and buy a rifle? A shotgun? Not a handgun, he knew that was more difficult in New York State. You had to apply for a license, there was a background check, paperwork. The thought made his head ache.

". . . that sound, what is it? I'm frightened."

In her corner of the room Valerie stood very still. How like an avalanche the wind was sounding! There had been warnings over the years that the hundred-foot cliff above Salthill Landing might one day collapse after a heavy rainstorm and there had been small landslides from time to time and now it began to sound as if the cliff might be disintegrating, a slide of rock, rubble, uprooted trees rushing toward the house, about to collapse the roof . . . In his corner of the room Leonard stood as if transfixed, his shirt partly unbuttoned, in his stocking feet, waiting.

They would die together, in the debris. How quickly then, the end would come!

No avalanche, only the wind. Valerie shut the door of her bathroom firmly behind her, Leonard continued undressing and climbed into bed. It was a vast tundra of a bed, with a hard mattress. By morning the terrible wind would subside. Another dawn! Mists on the river, a white wintry sun behind layers of cloud. Another day Leonard Chase would endure with dignity, he was certain.

2.

"'Dwayne Ducharme,' eh? Welcome to Denver."

There came Mitchell Oliver Yardman to shake Leonard's hand in a crushing grip. He was "Mitch" Yardman, realtor and insurance agent and he appeared to be the only person on duty at Yardman Realty & Insurance this afternoon.

". . . not that this is Denver, eh? Makeville is what this is here, you wouldn't call it a suburb of anyplace. Used to be a mining town, see. Probably you never heard of Makeville back east, and this kind of scenery, prob'ly you're thinking ain't what you'd expect of the West, eh? Well see, Dwayne Ducharme, like I warned you on the phone: this is east Colorado. 'High desert plain.' The Rockies is in the other direction."

Yardman's smile was wide and toothy yet somehow grudging, as if he resented the effort such a smile required. Here was a man who'd been selling real estate for a long time, you could see. Even as he spoke in his grating mock western drawl Yardman's shrewd eyes were rapidly appraising his perspective client "Dwayne Ducharme" who'd made an appointment to see small-ranch properties within commuting distance of Denver.

So this was Oliver Yardman! Twenty-one years after the Key West idyll, the man had thickened, grown coarser, yet there was the unmistakable sexual swagger, the sulky spoiled-boy mouth.

Yardman was shorter than Leonard had expected, burly and solid-built as a fire hydrant. He had a rucked forehead and a fleshy nose riddled with small broken veins and his breath was meaty, sour. He wore a leathery-looking cowboy hat, an expensive-looking rumpled suede jacket, lime-green shirt with a black string tie looped around his neck, rumpled khakis, badly scuffed leather boots. He seemed impatient, edgy. His hands, that were busily gesticulating, in twitchy swoops like the gestures of a deranged magician, were noticably large, with stubby fingers, and on the smallest finger of his left hand he wore a showy gold signet ring with a heraldic crest.

The first husband. Leonard's heart kicked in his chest, he was in the presence of his enemy.

In the office, that was hardly more than a store front, and smelled of stale cigarette smoke, Yardman showed Leonard photographs of "ranch-type" properties within "easy commuting distance" of downtown Denver. In his aggressive, mock-friendly yet grudging voice Yardman kept up a continual banter, peppering Leonard with facts, figures, statistics, punctuating his words with Eh? It was a verbal tic of which Yardman seemed unaware or was helpless to control and Leonard steeled himself waiting to hear it, dry-mouthed with apprehension that Yardman was suspicious of him, eyeing him so intimately, ". . . tight schedule, eh? Goin back tomorrow, you said? Said your firm's 'relocating'? Some kinda computer parts, eh? There's a lot of that in Denver, 'lectronics, 'chips,' these are boom times for some eh? Demographics're movin west, for sure. Population shift. Back east, billion-dollar companies goin down the toilet, you hear." Yardman laughed heartily, amused by the spectacle of companies going down a toilet.

Leonard said, in Dwayne Ducharme's earnest voice, "Mr. Yardman, I've been very—"

"'Mitch.' Call me 'Mitch,' eh?"

"—'Mitch.' I've been very lucky to be transferred to our Denver branch. My company has been 'downsized,' but—"

"Tell me about it, man! 'Downsize.' 'Cut-back.' Ain't that the story of these United States lately, eh?" Yardman was suddenly vehement, incensed. His pronunciation was savage: *Yoo-nited States.*

Leonard said, with an air of stubborn naiveté, "Mr. Yardman, my wife and I think of this as a once-in-a-lifetime opportunity. To 'relocate' to the west from the crowded east. We're Methodist Evangelicals and the church is flourishing in Colorado and we have a twelve-year-old boy dying to raise horses and my wife thinks—"

"That is so interesting, Dwayne Ducharme," Yardman interrupted, with a rude smirk, "—you are one of a new 'pioneer breed' relocating to our 'wide open spaces' and relaxed way of life and lower taxes. Seems to me I have just the property for you: six-acre ranch, four-bedroom house for the growin' family, barn in good repair, creek runs through the property, fences, shade trees, aspens, in kinda a valley where there's deer and antelope to hunt. Just went on the market a few days ago, Dwayne Ducharme this is serendip'ty, eh?"

Yardman locked up the office. Pulled down a sign on the front door: CLOSED. When he wasn't facing Leonard, his sulky mouth yet retained its fixed smile.

Outside, the men had a disagreement: Yardman wanted to drive his perspective client to the ranch, that was approximately sixteen miles away, and Dwayne Ducharme insisted upon driving his rental car. Yardman said, "Why'n hell we need two vehicles, eh? Save gas. Keep each other company. It's the usual procedure, see." Yardman's vehicle was a new-model Suburban with smoke-tinted windows, bumper stickers featuring the American flag, and a dented right rear door. It was both gleaming-black and splattered with mud like coarse lace. Inside, a dog was barking excitedly, throwing itself against the window nearest Leonard and slobbering the glass. "That's Kaspar. Spelled with a 'K.' Bark's worsen his bite. Kaspar ain't goin to bite you, Dwayne Ducharme,

I guarantee." Yardman slammed the flat of his hand against the window commanding the dog to "settle down." Kaspar was an Airedale, pure-bred, Yardman said. Damn good breed, but needs discipline. "You buy this pretty li'l property out at Mineral Springs for your family, you'll want a dog. 'Man's best friend' is no bullshit."

But Leonard didn't want to ride with Yardman and Kaspar; Leonard would drive his own car. Yardman stared at him, baffled. Clearly, Yardman was a man not accustomed to being contradicted or thwarted in the smallest matters. He said, barely troubling to disguise his contempt, "Well Dwayne Ducharme, you do that. You in your li'l Volva, Volvo, Vulva, you do that. Kaspar and me will drive ahead, see you don't get lost."

In a procession of two vehicles they drove through the small town of Makeville in the traffic of early Saturday afternoon, in late March. It was a windy day, tasting of snow. Overhead were massive clouds like galleons. What a relief, to be free of Yardman's overpowering personality! Leonard hadn't slept well the night before, nor the night before that, his nerves were strung tight. In his compact rental car he followed the military-looking black Suburban through blocks of undistinguished store fronts, stucco apartment buildings, taverns, X-rated videos, opening onto a state highway crowded with the usual fast-food restaurants, discount outlets, gas stations, strip malls. All that seemed to remain of Makeville's mining-town past were The Gold Strike Go-Go, Strike-it-Rich Lounge, Silver Lining Barbecue. Beyond the highway was a mesa landscape of small stunted trees, rocks. To get to Yardman Realty & Insurance at 661 Main Street, Makeville, Leonard had had a forty-minute drive from the Denver airport through a dispiriting clog of traffic and air hazier than the air of Manhattan on most days. He thought *Can he guess? Any idea who I am?*

He was excited, edgy. No one knew where Leonard Chase was.

Outside town, where the speed limit was fifty-five miles an hour, Yardman pushed the Suburban toward seventy, leaving Leonard behind. It was to punish him, Leonard knew: Yardman allowed other vehicles to come between him and Leonard, then pulled off onto the shoulder of the road, to allow Leonard to catch up. In a gesture of genial contempt, Yardman signaled to him, and pulled out onto the highway before him, fast. In the rear window of the Suburban was an American flag. On the rear bumper were stickers: BUSH CHENEY USA. KEEP HONKING, I'M RELOADING.

Yardman's family must have been rich at one time. Yardman had been sent east to college. Though he played the yokel, it was clear that the man was shrewd, calculating. Something had happened in his personal life and in his professional life, possibly a succession of things. He'd had money, but not now. Valerie would never have married Yardman otherwise. Wouldn't have kept the lewd Polaroids for more than two decades.

If he guessed. What?

The Suburban was pulling away again, passing an eighteen-rig truck. Leonard could turn off at any time, drive back to the airport and take a flight back to Chicago. He'd told Valerie that he would be in Chicago for a few days on business and this was true: Leonard had a job interview with a Chicago firm needing a tax litigator with federal court experience. He hadn't told Valerie that he'd been severed from the Rector Street firm and was sure that there could be no way she might know. He'd been commuting into the city five days a week, schedule unaltered. His CEO had seen to it, he'd been treated with courtesy: allowed the use of his office for several weeks, while he searched for a new job. Except for one or two unfortunate episodes, he got along well with his old colleagues. Once or twice he showed up unshaven, disheveled, most of the time he seemed unchanged. White cotton shirt, striped tie, dark pinstripe suit. He continued to have his shoes shined in Grand Central Station. In his office, door shut, he stared out the window. Or, clicked through the Internet. So few law firms were interested in him, at forty-six: "downsized." But he'd tracked down Yardman in this way. And the interview in Chicago was genuine. Leonard Chase's impressive resume, the "strong, supportive" recommendation his CEO had promised, were genuine.

Valerie had ceased touching his arm, his cheek. Valerie had ceased asking in a concerned voice *Is anything wrong, darling?*

This faint excitement, edginess. He'd been in high altitude terrain before. Beautiful Aspen, where they'd gone skiing just once. Also Santa Fé. Denver was a mile above sea level and Leonard's breath was coming quickly and shallowly in the wake of Yardman's vehicle. His pulse was fast, elated. He knew that after a day, the sensation of excitement would shift to a dull throbbing pain behind his eyes. But he hoped by then to be gone from Colorado by then.

Mineral Springs. This part of the area certainly didn't look prosperous. Obviously there were wealthy Denver suburbs and outlying towns but this wasn't one of them. The land continued flat and monotonous and its predominant hue was the hue of dried manure. At least, Leonard had expected mountains. In the other direction, Yardman had said with a smirk—but where? The jagged skyline of Denver, behind Leonard, to his right, was lost in a soupy brown haze.

The Suburban turned off onto a potholed road. United Church of Christ in a weathered woodframe building, a mobile home park, snail asphalt-sided houses set back in scrubby lots in sudden and unexpected proximity to Quail Ridge Acres, a "custom-built"—"luxury home"—housing development sprawling out of sight. There began to be more open land, "ranches" with grazing cattle, horses close beside the road lifting their long heads as Leonard passed by. The sudden beauty of a horse can take your breath away, Leonard had forgotten. He felt a pang of loss, he had no son. No one to move west with him, raise horses in Colorado.

Yardman was turning the Suburban onto a long bumpy lane. Here was the Flying S Ranch. A pair of badly worn steer horns hung crooked on the opened front gate, in greeting. Leonard pulled up behind Yardman and parked. A sensation of acute loneliness and yearning swept over him. *If we could live here! Begin over again!* Except he needed to be younger, and Valerie needed to be a different woman. Here was a possible home: a long flat-roofed wood-and-stucco ranch house with a slapdash charm, needing repair, repainting, new shutters, probably a new roof. You could see a woman's touches: stone urns in the shape of swans flanking the front door, the remains of a rock garden in the front yard. Beyond the house were several outbuildings, a silo. In a shed, a left-behind tractor. Mounds of rotted hay, dried manure. Fences in varying stages of dereliction. Yet, there was a striking view of a sweeping, sloping plain and a hilly terrain, a mesa?—in the distance. Pierced with sunshine the sky was beautiful, a hard glassy-blue behind clouds like gigantic sculpted figures. Leonard saw that, from the rear of the ranch house, you'd have a view of the hills, marred only by what looked like the start of a housing development far to the right. Almost, if you stared straight ahead, you might not notice the intrusion.

As Leonard approached the Suburban, he saw that Yardman was leaning against the side of the vehicle, speaking tersely into a cell phone. His face was a knot of flesh. Kaspar the purebred Airedale was loose, trotting excitedly about, sniffing at the rock garden and lifting his leg. When he sighted Leonard he rushed at him barking frantically and baring his teeth. Yardman shouted, "Back off, Kaspar! Damn dog *obey*!" When Leonard shrank back, shielding himself with his arms, Yardman scolded him, too: "Kaspar is all damn bark and no bite, din't I tell you? Eh? C'mon, boy. Fuckin sit. *Now*." With a show of reluctance Kaspar obeyed his red-faced master. Leonard hadn't known that Airedales were so large. This one had a wiry, coarse tan-and-black coat, a grizzled snout of a muzzle and moist dark vehement eyes like his master.

Yardman shut up the cell phone and tried to arrange his face into a pleasant smile. As he unlocked the front door and led Leonard into the house he said, in his salesman's genial-blustery voice, ". . . churches, eh? You seen 'em? On the way out here? This is strong Christian soil. Earliest settlers. Prots'ant stock. There's a Mormon population, too. Those folks are serious." Yardman sucked his fleshy mouth, considering the Mormons. There was something to be acknowledged about *those folks*, maybe money.

The ranch house looked as if it hadn't been occupied in some time. Leonard, looking about with a vague, polite smile, as a perspective buyer might, halfway wondered if something, a small creature perhaps, had crawled beneath the house and died. Yardman forestalled any question from his client by telling a joke: ". . . punishment for bigamy? Eh? 'Two wives.'" His laughter was loud and meant to be infectious.

Leonard smiled at the thought of Valerie stepping into such a house. Not very likely! The woman's sensitive soul would be bruised in proximity to what Yardman described as the "remodeled" kitchen with the "fantastic view of the hills" and, in the living room, an unexpected spectacle of left-behind furniture: a long, L-shaped sofa in a nubby butterscotch fabric, a large showy glass-topped coffee table with a spiderweb crack in the glass, deep-piled wall-to-wall stained beige carpeting. Two steps down into a family room with a large fireplace and another "fantastic view of the hills" and stamped-cardboard rock walls. Seeing the startled expression on Leonard's face Yardman said with a grim smile, "Hey sure, a new homeowner might wish to remodel here, some. 'Renovate.' They got their taste, you got yours. Like Einstein said, 'There's no free lunch in the universe.'"

Yardman was standing close to Leonard, as if daring him to object. Leonard said in a voice meant to be quizzical, "'No free lunch in the universe'?—I don't understand, Mr. Yardman."

"Means you get what you pay for, see. What you don't pay for, you don't get. Phil'sphy of life, eh?" Yardman must have been drinking in the Suburban, his breath smelled of whiskey and his words were slightly slurred.

As if to placate the realtor, Leonard said of course he understood, any new property he bought, he'd likely have to put some money into. "All our married lives it's been my wife's and my dream to purchase some land and this is our opportunity. My wife has just inherited a little money, not much but a little," Dwayne Ducharme's voice quavered, in fear this might sound inadvertently boastful, "and we would use this." Such naive enthusiasm drew from Yardman a wary predator smile. Leonard could almost hear the realtor thinking *Here is a fool, too good to be true.* Yardman murmured, "Wise, Dwayne Ducharme. Very wise."

Yardman led Leonard into the "master" bedroom where a grotesque pink-toned mirror covered one of the walls and in this mirror, garishly reflected, the men loomed over-large as if magnified. Yardman laughed as if taken by surprise and Leonard looked quickly away shocked that he'd shaved so carelessly that morning, graying stubble showed on the left side of his face and there was a moist red nick in the cleft of his chin. His eyes were set in hollows like ill-fitting sockets in a skull and his clothes, a tweed sport coat, a candy-striped shirt, looked rumpled and damp as if he'd been sleeping in them as perhaps he had been, intermittently, on the long flight from New York to Chicago to Denver.

Luckily, the master bedroom had a plate-glass sliding door that Yardman managed to open, and the men stepped quickly out into fresh air. Almost immediately there came rushing at Leonard the frantically barking Airedale who would certainly have bitten him except Yardman intervened. This time he not only shouted at the dog but struck him on the snout, on the head, dragged him away from Leonard by his collar, cursed and kicked him until the dog cowered whimpering at his feet, its stubby tail wagging. "Damn asshole, you blew it. Fuckin busted now. Every one of 'em in the fuckin' family, ain't it the same fuckin' story."

Flush-faced, deeply shamed by the dog's behavior, Yardman dragged the whimpering Airdale around the house to the driveway where the Suburban was parked. Leonard pressed his hands over his ears not wanting to hear Yardman's furious cursing and the dog's broken-hearted whimpering as Yardman must have forced him back inside the vehicle, to lock him in. He thought *That dog is his only friend. He might kill that dog.*

Leonard walked quickly away from the house, as if eager to look at the silo, which was partly collapsed in a sprawl of what looked like fossilized corncobs and mortar, and a barn the size of a three-car garage with a slumping roof and a strong odor of manure and rotted hay, pleasurable in his nostrils. In a manure pile a pitch fork was stuck upright as if someone had abruptly decided that he'd had enough of ranch life and had departed. Leonard felt a thrill of excitement, unless it was a thrill of dread. He had no clear idea why he was here, being shown the derelict Flying S Ranch in Mineral Springs, Colorado. Why he'd sought out "Mitch" Yardman. The first husband Oliver Yardman. If his middle-aged wife cherished erotic memories of this man as he'd been twenty years before, what was that to Leonard? He was staring at his hands, lifted before him, palms up in a gesture of honest bewilderment. He wore gloves, that seemed to steady his hands. He'd been noticing lately, these past several months, his hands sometimes shook.

Just outside the barn, Yardman had paused to make another call on his cell phone. He was leaving a message, his voice low-pitched, threatening and yet seductive. "Hey babe. 'Sme. Where the fuck are ya, babe? Call me. I'm here." He broke the connection, cursing under his breath.

At the rear of the barn, looking out at the hills, Yardman caught up with Leonard. The late-afternoon sky was still vivid with light, massive clouds in oddly vertical sculpted columnar shapes. Leonard was staring at these shapes, flexing his fingers in his leather gloves. Yardman swatted at his shoulder as if they were new friends linked in a common enterprise; his breath smelled of fresh whiskey. "Quite a place, eh? Makes a man dream, eh? 'Big sky country.' That's the west, see. I lived a while in the east, fuckin' hemmed-in. No place for a man. Always wanted a neat li'l ranch like this. Decent life for a man, raise horses, not damn rat-race 'real estate' . . . Any questions for me, Dwayne? Like, is the list price 'negotiable' Or—"

"Did you always live in Makeville, Mr. Yardman—'Mitch'?" Dwayne Ducharme had a way of speaking bluntly yet politely. "Just curious!"

Yardman said, tilting his leathery cowboy hat to look his client frankly in the face, "Hell, no. The Yardmans is all over at Littleton. Makeville is just me. And that's tem'pry."

"'Yardman Realty & Insurance' is a family business, is it?"

"Well, sure. Used to be. Now, just me mostly."

Yardman spoke with an air of vaguely shamed regret. *Burnt-out,* Leonard was thinking. Yardman's sulky mouth seemed about to admit more, then pursed shut.

"You said you lived in the east, Mitch . . ."

"Not long."

"Ever travel to, well—Florida? Key West?"

Yardman squinted at Leonard, as if trying to decide whether to be bemused or annoyed by him. "Yah, I guess. Long time ago. Why're you askin, friend?"

"It's just, you look familiar. Like someone I saw, might have seen, once, I think it was Key West . . ." Leonard was smiling, a roaring came up in his ears. As, in court, he had sometimes to pause, to get his bearings. "Do you have a family?—I mean, wife, children . . ."

"Man, I know what you mean," Yardman laughed sourly. "Some of us got just as much 'family' as we need, eh? See what I'm saying?"

"I'm afraid that I—"

"Means my 'private life' is off limits, friend."

Yardman laughed. His face crinkled. He swatted Leonard on the shoulder. "Hey, man: just joking. A wife's a wife, eh? Kid's a kid? Been there, done that. Three fuckin' times, Dwayne Ducharme. 'Three strikes you're out.'"

It was risky for Dwayne Ducharme to say, with a provocative smile, "'No love like your first.' They say."

"'No fuck like your first.' But that's debatable."

Now Yardman meant to turn the conversation back to real estate. He had another appointment back at the agency that afternoon, he'd have to speed things up here. In his hand was a swath of fact sheets, did Dwayne Ducharme have any questions about this property? Or some others, they could visit right now? "'Specially about mortgages, int'rest rates. There's where Mitch Yardman can help you."

Leonard said, pointing, "Those hills over there? Is that area being developed? I noticed some new houses, 'Quail Ridge Acres,' on our way here."

Yardman said, shading his eyes, "Seems like there's something going on there, you're right about that. But the rest of the valley through there, and your own sweet little creek running through it, see?—that's in pristine shape."

"But maybe that will be developed too? Is that possible, Mr.—Mitch?"

Yardman sucked his teeth as if this were a serious question to be pondered. He said, "Frankly, Dwayne, I doubt it. What I've heard, it's just that property there. For sure I'd know if there was more development planned. See, there's just six acres in your property here, of how any hundreds the previous owner sold off, land around here in prox'mity to Denver is rising in value, with your six acres you're plenty protected, and the tax situation ain't so stressful. These six acres is a buffer for you and your family, also an investment sure to grow in value, in time. Eh?"

Yardman swatted Leonard's shoulder companionably as he turned to re-enter the barn, to lead his client through the barn and back to the driveway. His patience with Dwayne Ducharme was wearing thin. He'd uttered his last words in a cheery rush like memorized words he had to get through on his way to somewhere better.

The pitchfork was in Leonard's hands. The leather gloves gripped tight. He'd managed to lift the heavy pronged thing out of the manure pile and without a word of warning as Yardman was about to step outside, Leonard came up swiftly behind him and shoved the prongs against his upper back, knocking him forward, off-balance, and as Yardman turned in astonishment, trying to grab hold of the prongs, Leonard shoved the pitchfork a second time, at the man's unprotected throat.

What happened next, Leonard would not clearly recall.

There was Yardman suddenly on his knees, Yardman fallen and flailing on the filthy floor of the barn, straw and dirt floating in swirls of dark blood. Yardman was fighting to live, bleeding badly, trying to scream, whimpering in terror as Leonard stood grim-faced above him positioning the pitch fork to strike again. With the force and weight of his shoulders he drove the prongs, dulled with rust, yet sharp enough still to pierce a man's skin, into Yardman's already lacerated neck, Yardman's jaws, Yardman's uplifted and still astonished face. A few feet away the leathery cowboy hat lay, thrown clear.

Leonard stood over him furious, panting. His words were choked and incoherent: "Now you know. Know what it's like. Murderer! *You.*"

• • •

Emerging then from the barn, staggering. For he was very tired now. He'd last slept— Couldn't remember. Except jolting and unsatisfying sleep on the plane. And if he called home, the phone would ring in the empty house in Salthill Landing and if he called Valerie's cell phone there would be no answer, not even a ring.

In the driveway, he stopped dead. There was the Suburban parked where Yardman had left it, the Airedale at the rear window barking hysterically. The heavy pitchfork was still in his hands, he'd known there was more to be done. His hands ached, throbbed as if the bones had cracked and very likely some of the bones in his hands had cracked, but he had no choice, there was more to be done for Yardman's dog was a witness, Yardman's dog would identify him. Cautiously he approached the Suburban. The Airedale was furious, frantic. Leonard managed to open one of the rear doors, called to the dog in Yardman's way, commanding, cajoling, but the vehicle was built so high off the ground it was difficult to lean inside, almost impossible to maneuver the clumsy pitch fork, to stab at the dog. Leonard glanced down at himself, saw in horror that his trouser legs were splattered with blood. His shoes, his socks! The maddened dog was smelling blood. *His master's blood. He knows.* Something was sounding violently inside Leonard's ribcage. Had to think clearly: had to overcome the faintness gathering in his brain. Calling "Kaspar! Come here!" but the wily dog scrambled into the front seat. Awkwardly Leonard climbed into the rear of the vehicle, tried to position the pitchfork to strike at the dog, thrusting the implement but catching only the back of the leather seat in the prongs as the furious barking seemed to grow even louder. Leaning over the front seat trying to lunge at the dog, cursing the dog as Yardman had cursed the dog half-sobbing in frustration, rage, despair as somehow, in an instant, the dog managed to sink his teeth into Leonard's wrist and Leonard cried out in surprise and pain and hurriedly climbed out of the Suburban dragging the pitchfork with him. In the driveway that seemed to be tilting beneath him he stared confounded at his torn and bleeding flesh, that throbbed with pain—a dog bite? Had someone's dog attacked him?

Glanced up to see a pickup approaching on the bumpy lane. A man wearing a cowboy hat in the driver's seat, a woman beside him. Their quizzical smiles had turned into stares, as they took in the pitchfork in Leonard's hands. A man's voice called, "Mister? You in need of help?"

JOYCE CAROL OATES'S most recent works include the novel *My Sister, My Love* and co-editing *The Ecco Anthology of Contemporary American Short Fiction*. She is a member of the American Academy of Arts and Letters and is the Roger S. Berlind Distinguished Professor in Humanities at Princeton University.

Between the Dark and the Daylight

BY TOM PICCIRILLI

His face was so anguished it was writhing. That was Frank Bradley the first time I saw him, about sixty feet off the ground.

His feet twined above me while we both dangled from the safety-line ropes. His forlorn moans echoed across the front-range hills, and he'd bitten through his bottom lip. Blood misted on the wind and flew down against my forehead.

The balloon smacked broadside into a pine tree and shook the other two guys on the ropes loose. Neither of them screamed on their way down. One landed on his back, and the impact drove him three feet underground. The other smacked a boulder that shattered his pelvis, severed his spinal column, and saved his life. He pinwheeled off the rock and came to rest on his face along the dog walk, in front of an elderly woman clutching a Pomeranian. I held on, just like Frank Bradley, who shrieked at me, "Don't let go! My son, my boy! Johnny!"

I wasn't letting go. You can make decisions in an instant that will forge the direction of the rest of your life. You can perform acts that will curse you with a hellish mark forever. You can sell your conscience by making a single mistake. You can do your best and still not make things right. Spinning in the wind, I couldn't see the kid in the basket, but I could hear him crying. He sounded terrified and very young. Maybe only six or seven. Too damn young to work the controls and hit whichever valve had to be pressed to lower the thing. I thought, *What kind of father takes a child that young up in a hot-air balloon? And how the hell did the idiot get outside of it on the ropes with the kid still in the basket?* A lot goes through your mind when you're six stories in the air and rising.

Despite his misery, I wanted to beat the hell out of Bradley—whose name I didn't know then—all across the park meadow speeding by below us. Except I was still holding the line, and we were running out of acreage fast.

The balloon caromed into another stand of pine, and thick branches brutally scraped across Bradley's back, breaking his grip. His fists opened and he flailed, slipping fifteen feet until he was side by side with me, holding the other rope. He screamed, "Don't let go!"

I'd hold on as long as I could, but eventually I would have to let go. We'd both have to, and the idea scared the hell out of me. I had the rope in a death grip and didn't want to wind up like the guy who'd be found planted half as deep as his casket would be. They were going to have to dig him up just to bury him again. "There's no way to do it!" I shouted.

"Don't let go!"

"Listen—"

"Don't let go!"

I wanted to shout, *Stop saying that!*

The balloon bounded from pine to pine, nothing slowing it. You'd think maybe the branches would've pierced the silk, but somehow—miraculously, really, if you could call it that—they didn't. We had about another couple thousand feet of parkland forest to go and then there'd be nothing but empty fields until the first break of front-range stone ridges. After that, there were the canyon cliffs and brutal mountain winds working up for another fifteen miles until we'd be high in the Rockies.

I kept thinking, I never should've moved out West.

I kept thinking my crappy apartment in the East Village really hadn't been so bad.

We couldn't bring the balloon down by ourselves. It bounced into another huge tree and the awful, overwhelming crashing sound was harrowing around us. The balloon shook insanely and the ropes twisted. I cracked sideways into the trunk and pine needles tore at my face. My feet touched branches. Then I was standing on air, and then there were branches again. I had to drop. It was something you couldn't think about, you just had to do it.

Another vicious collision nearly ripped my arms from the sockets and Bradley and I both let go at the same moment. We clung to thick tree limbs seventy-five feet off the ground. He let out a screech. I think I did, too. He glared at me with his agonized eyes and edged his way across the branch looking toward the balloon, which had almost cleared the trees and started to rise again.

The basket slipped free of the last limb with an enormous scraping noise, but the silk still hadn't been pierced. Bradley worked like a maniac to get up to the basket, hand over hand as wads of bark came off and rained down to the ground. His palms were shredded. There was no way for him to get to it.

The boy inside cried out and a sob broke in my own throat. He whimpered, *"Daddy, please, Daddy—"* He was petrified but still thought his father could save him.

But he never raised his head over the top of the basket. I wanted to see his face, if only for an instant. It was extremely important to me, and I didn't know why.

Bradley screamed, "Johnny!"

He and I watched the balloon soar away until we couldn't hear his son anymore. It lifted higher and higher, caught on the canyon winds, occasionally bouncing against the cliff walls until it was over them and almost out of sight.

We were both breathless from our exertions, but he had enough left in him to turn back and glare at me some more. He said, "You let go!"

"So did you. We had no choice."

"You could've held on!"

"We couldn't have."

Talking to the guy this high in the air, covered in pine bristles and sap, his blood drying on my face—just hanging there and waiting for the next moment to happen as his son floated away.

• • •

It took me twenty minutes to climb down out of the tree.

Bradley stayed up there wailing and cursing me as I cautiously clutched at branches and lowered myself. By the time I hit the ground there were two ambulances, a fire truck, and eight cruisers parked at the edge of the woods, cops and park rangers prowling everywhere.

The shock of what had happened hit me all at once, before I'd taken two steps toward anybody. A heaviness thickened in my chest and my hands started to tremble badly. My legs weakened and I could feel the blood draining out of my head. A wash of blackness passed across my eyes and I might've toppled over if a cop with the name badge Kowalski hadn't grabbed me.

He had gray eyes and some real muscle and power to him. He held me up with one hand and said, "Sit down."

"I'll be okay."

"Yeah, but sit down."

But I didn't want to sit anywhere among the pines. I scanned the sky and didn't see the balloon anywhere.

"The kid?" I asked.

"What kid?"

"The one in the balloon."

"Somebody was in there?"

"The hell do you think we were all trying so hard to hold on to it for? Is anyone following it?"

"It's gone over the tree line and ridge of the canyon."

"You've got to get some rangers up there."

He thumbed his radio but there was already lots of buzzing going on, people squawking and more sirens erupting in the distance. They were coming in from Fort Coffins and Greeley and other nearby towns, everybody driving to the wrong place. I saw a helicopter go overhead.

Kowalski said, "Tell me what happened."

"There's not much."

"Tell me anyway."

We recognized each other as former New Yorkers transplanted to Colorado for reasons we still weren't sure about. We both had the same general air of confusion and homesickness about us, mired in a false toughness and a general who-gives-a-damn attitude to hide our fears. It took one to recognize one. It was pretty obvious that somewhere along the way he'd made a misstep and it had fouled up his life so badly that he had to move two thousand miles away to get clear of it. Some kind of scandal—he'd taken money from the wrong guy or hadn't given a cut of it to the right one. Whatever the mistake, it was costing him now and it would for the rest of his life. I was a different story.

A ring of cops stepped in close but no one said anything.

I explained how I'd been in the park staring off at Long's Peak trying to find inspiration for the next story or song, the way I usually did when my thoughts ran dry.

I'd been sitting around the park a hell of a lot lately and not much had been shaking loose inside my head. I'd written one line—*Between the Dark and the Daylight*—knowing I was lifting it from somewhere but not caring so long as something else followed. Nothing did.

So I tried to sweat the next sentence out, staring into the white of the page. Sitting there like that for a while, waiting for something to guide my hand.

Instead, a tremendous shadow crossed over my notebook and a man howled and two guys ran past directly in front of me.

I looked up and there was the balloon, with Bradley dangling off one of the safety lines and shouting for help, the other two guys doing their best to catch up, reaching for the trailing ropes as the balloon swung low but still didn't hit the ground.

You're sitting there waiting for your next sentence and instead you get this.

I hadn't seen a hot-air balloon since I was kid on Long Island and couldn't figure out how anybody could lose one.

I got to my feet and started stumbling in that direction, the sheer forceful oddity of the situation sort of pulling me after it. The guy who'd eventually be paralyzed from the neck down looked back to me while he ran and shouted, 'There's a boy in there! We have to get it back down!"

I hesitated another second. It's normal, it would happen to anybody. We don't trust unfamiliar conditions and unknown people, it's easier to sit back down and fight the empty page. But the kid let out a murmuring whine that caught on the wind and somehow that got me moving.

I sprinted maybe fifty yards across the park before I finally caught up to the lines. By then, Bradley had actually managed to climb up a few more feet, almost to within reaching distance of the basket, and the other guys had grabbed hold of the ropes. I did a weird flying dive that should have made me land on my head, but somehow it worked. I was on a safety line draping from the basket, flitting there, sort of flying along with three other men, and we were rising.

There should've been about ten emergency shut-offs and built-in features to prevent this sort of thing from happening. Without anybody working the burner, the balloon should've been lowering, even in the wind. I looked up, but couldn't see anything but the bottom of the basket. Then the rope I was on flailed outwards a few feet and I spun around.

There were health nuts in the world that did this sort of thing for fun, I was sure. I craned my neck and saw that the burner was still lit, a lick of orange and blue flame igniting. Something had gone seriously wrong, and I'd jumped right into it. The balloon wasn't going to come down on its own.

It was already too late to jump. We were over the small lake in the center of the park. Pretty but man-made, only about four feet deep. If any of us cut loose now, even over the water, we'd hit with enough force to drive our kneecaps up through our chests. My father used to tell me about parachuting soldiers who'd leaped out over the Nam jungles and landed wrong. Twenty years later and the images were still sharp and bright in my mind. On top of everything else, I wanted to clock my father.

The kid was crying and Bradley was moaning, unable to climb any higher. He didn't sound smart or sane or even human. He should've been yelling to his kid to hit the kill switch. I opened my mouth to shout and could barely hear myself. The rushing wind drove my voice back into my throat.

If you're lucky, you get to puzzle out your what-the-hell-am-I-doing moments later on in the game. You look back and you can't believe it occurred, and you've got no idea how it was you wound up there, doing that thing.

Now I'd made it down again intact. The other two guys who'd lent a hand hadn't.

"What the hell happened?" I asked. "Who is this guy? Where'd this balloon come from?"

There was a second when Kowalski almost gave me the "I'll ask the questions, sir" speech, but he could see it wasn't going to work on me the way it did on the rich retirees waiting out the end of then-lives up in Estes Park.

A lot of yelling was coming from Bradley's tree. It took three firemen on cherry pickers working up into the pine to finally grab hold of him and pull him down. He screamed as they lowered him and went wild when he hit the ground. He started seething and throwing punches and hissing worse than an animal, calling for Johnny like the kid might be just a few feet behind him, just out of eyeshot.

He spun on his heels and began to laugh in a way I'd never heard anybody laugh before, not even the schizos and addicts in the East Village alleys. It was so chilling it brushed me back a step. Kowalski felt it, too, and he puffed his chest out and held his chin up as a way to defend himself against it.

Three officers joined the firemen and they all wrestled Bradley onto his belly and got the cuffs on him.

I said, "Hey, come on . . . !" but Kowalski just scowled at me and started listening to and talking into his radio again. It looked like Bradley had slugged and elbowed a few of the cops. Blood speckled their faces. They'd follow procedure when it came down to somebody attacking their brother officers. It didn't matter where you went, cops would always be the same about that.

They carried him to a cruiser and tossed him into the back. As it pulled across the field, Bradley turned in the backseat to stare at me. He wasn't laughing anymore, but that goddamn chill stayed with me.

"Tell me what you people know so far," I said.

Kowalski tightened his lips and then shrugged. "Information is still coming in. Looks like this one, his name's Frank Bradley. Used to run some book in Nevada before he took a fall for bank robbery."

"What?"

"Yeah, his wife split with the son. He figures it's because he's not making enough cash. So he walks in, grabs a manager by the throat, forces the guy to clear a couple of the tills. Sets off about five silent alarms. He gets something like three grand, walks outside, the dye pack explodes, and he's standing there in the parking lot turning purple when the local PD arrives. He's not what you call one of your better planners."

I shook my head. "That's more than just stupidity. This guy's crazy."

"Yeah, well, maybe. He did two years in the state pen. Gets out and goes looking for his wife. Finds out she's split the state and come to Colorado. Tracks her to Berthoud. Grabs the kid and wheels off with him. Tells the boy he's going to get him ice cream and toys and balloons. They drive by the spring carnival down there, off 17 and 287. They've got a hot-air balloon set up."

"My God. So he hijacks it?"

"Figured he'd be funny, I guess. Probably tells his boy, 'Look at the balloon I got you.' Anyway, the thing is roped to the ground it's just supposed to go up twenty feet or so, then back down. But Bradley takes the kid up and unties the safety lines, forces the carnival guy to fire it all the way up. They start hovering and catch a stiff breeze. The carnival guy jumps out the other side of the basket, falls ten feet, and sprains his ankle. Bradley tries to screw around with the controls and the next thing you know—"

"The maniac is drifting over Loveland Park, holding on to one of the ropes himself."

"Yeah."

"Any chance the kid might be okay?"

"Maybe, if we can find him in time."

It wasn't going to happen.

He knew it and I knew it. I looked at the expanse of the Rockies, thinking about how far the balloon had already traveled, up from Berthoud. If the wind hadn't been from the east, and the balloon had instead carried out toward Greeley, they could've tracked him no matter how long it took. There was nothing for thirty miles in that direction except farmland.

But heading west from the foothills, with the balloon drifting higher from the jammed burner, it would float across the range and just keep going until it hit a cliff and dumped the kid across a thousand feet of mountain.

Kowalski stared off in the direction the cruiser had gone with Bradley. I looked that way too, the chill working against me, tightening the skin on the back of my neck. That laugh. Jesus.

• • •

I made a full statement at the police department and signed the paperwork. They escorted me to my apartment and didn't look back after they'd dropped me off. While I sat on my couch drinking a tumbler of whiskey—feeling the walls closing in on me, my hands twitching as if I were still holding on to the line, thinking I'd maybe never sleep again—I slept and dreamed of the boy.

He was dying, but not quite there yet. He stood in front of me, one small hand pressed against my chest. But his head was turned completely around. He spoke, and his words faded out behind him. I heard "Daddy," and "Help," and even my own name. It was one of those dreams where you couldn't run or speak or do any damn thing at all. I knew I was asleep but couldn't break out of it. I could feel myself gripping the cushions someplace far away, and heard a voice that wasn't entirely my own, mewling there. I grabbed the kid by the shoulder and tried to spin him around, but his head kept turning away from me.

• • •

The media went nuts. It was a big story for Colorado. Bizarre and full of human interest. You looked at it one way and you saw a bunch of strangers trying to help out a kid, one of them losing his life, another paralyzed from the shoulders down. His name was Bill Mandor and he was on every channel. Half his face was bandaged and around the edges it looked like he'd been scraped to the bone when he hit the dog walk. The one good thing about his being paralyzed was that he couldn't feel his shattered legs and spine and didn't need painkillers. He looked clear-headed and spoke like the kind of heroes I remembered from when I was a kid. Men who could staunchly handle the worst events and injuries through willpower and nobility. He made me shake my head.

Reporters camped out on the lawn in front of my apartment manager's door. I took the phone off the hook and didn't answer the door for three days. Eventually the camera crews got bored and left.

I watched cable news programs every waking moment hoping there'd be information about the boy, but despite hundreds of volunteers hiking all over the front range, the canyons, and the east side of the divide, nobody had seen the balloon. It seemed impossible.

At night, helicopters buzzed through the skies, heading up to the national park and the thousands of square miles of mountain terrain and forest land.

Kowalski called me five days later, on an afternoon full of sirens, and said, "Bradley's loose."

"What's that mean?"

"What do you think it means?"

"A former bank robber out of the joint only a couple of days hijacks a balloon that causes the death of a good Samaritan, and you spring him?"

"Blame your judicial system, not me. He was obviously out of his head, so they put him under guard at the hospital, in the mental wing. They said it was depression brought on by grief. You can't help but feel sorry for the guy, his kid gone and all. He got flowers and prayer cards by the truckload. He slept for ninety-six hours straight, cuffed to the bed. What they call nonresponsive. Not a coma, just a deep sleep. They thought he might be dying. Losing his will to live."

"Cripes."

"Like he was forcing himself to kick the bucket. He started going into respiratory failure, so they got a crash cart in there, defibrillator, oxygen mask, the whole works. Five minutes after they got him breathing normally again, he woke up, kicked the hell out of a nurse, and stole a car from the parking lot."

I think I hissed. "This is terrific."

"Anyway, Bradley knocked over another bank an hour after he got free, still wearing his hospital gown. Nobody knows where he got the gun. This time he smartened up some. Got almost thirty grand, no dye pack, though he set off an alarm. But he was out of there in a hurry, and now he's on the run."

I thought about the kind of man who would stop off somewhere for a gun but not put on a pair of pants before committing grand larceny.

"He's going to come after me," I said. "He thinks I killed his kid because I let go of the rope."

Even if I hadn't been a paranoid writer with an exaggerated sense of self-importance, I would've thought that. It had been that laugh of Bradley's. It wasn't only insane. It had that see-you-later quality to it.

Kowalski grunted. "He's a nut. If he goes anywhere, it'll be back to his ex-wife's place."

"No, he only went there for his son. Any word on the kid?"

"No, no sign of the balloon. Maybe it held to the front range and came down in somebody's field. I don't know. We probably won't know for a while yet."

"Listen—"

But he was done. Kowalski was the type of cop who got bored easily and always had to be in charge of a conversation. "I picked up one of your books," he said. "I read about half of it. I didn't like it. So I gave it to my wife."

"Listen—"

"She reads everything. She didn't like it either."

"Listen to me. Bradley will show up here next."

"It's a possibility."

"More than that, he just walked in my door. He's got a gun on me. Gotta go."

I hung up and Bradley smiled at me from my apartment doorway. I figured the apartment manager had gotten tired of dealing with reporters trying to get into the building and had disconnected the buzzer wiring. I was going to die because I hadn't double-checked it. I'd gotten slack in Colorado. I wasn't paranoid enough anymore, just bored, like Kowalski, and waiting for the end.

Bradley started in with that hideous laughter until every muscle in my body had tightened to the point of trembling. At least he'd put on pants, I was glad to see. How awful it would've been to get snuffed by a guy in a hospital gown. The noise got louder and I started breathing *so* fast that I got light-headed. For a second I saw the kid with his backwards head standing behind his father, still saying "Daddy," his white hand pointing at me.

I'd had my run-ins with maniacs before. Most people in the world have, but definitely everybody in New York. They were common maniacs, but still pretty "out there." With me, it had mostly been ex-girlfriends who started off talking about taking care of me for the rest of my life and ended up setting fire to my cars. I'd had an obsessive stalker who claimed one of my horror stories had opened a portal to hell and released his father. He'd shown up at my apartment in Manhattan with a switchblade and tried to stab me with it overhand instead of slipping it between my ribs. I had a half-inch-deep scarred gouge from where the knife had deflected off my sternum. It was one of the reasons why I'd left home.

Frank Bradley held a snub-nosed .38 on me. It wasn't a Colorado gun. The guys out here carried Colt .45s and rifles, but nothing as slick as a snub .38. You didn't show off to your cowboy barroom cronies or go hunting elk with a .38. There was only one purpose to it. You put it up to somebody's forehead and you took him out of the game fast.

We stood there like that for two minutes. It was a long two minutes. It gave me time to think about my regrets. There were a lot of them. Bradley's laughter eventually died out, but he kept sneering at me. It was an expression I'd seen many times in my life, and it infuriated me as much now as it always had before.

Up close now I saw the kind of man he was—had been, would always be. Every smashed hope etched into his features. The lost chances, the missed turnoffs. The failed efforts, the stupid moves, and the mistakes that shouldn't have cost him as much as they had. All of them his own fault, by his own hand. All of them covered by a hundred excuses and scapegoats. You didn't have to look hard to see it all there.

"Bradley, think about—"

"Don't talk. I don't want to hear you talk."

So we stood there for another few minutes. It gave us both more time to think about the past, to wonder if there'd be a future.

You can get used to anything if you endure it long enough. Even with the gun trained on me, I started to relax. The longer someone doesn't pull a trigger, the more you believe it won't happen. Anything was better than listening to that laugh.

"Let's go," he said, gesturing with the barrel.

I moved down the hall and out into the parking lot with all the false dignity of an aristocrat heading for the guillotine. He pointed to a Mustang with the engine running. "You drive."

"Where?"

"Don't talk, I'll tell you."

I drove as he directed me. We roamed the area for a while in a strange pattern that I eventually recognized as the path the balloon probably took from Berthoud up 287 to the park. I saw the empty grounds where the carnival had set up. We slipped back into town and around the park and the lake before he aimed us toward the mountains.

I drove the canyon roads heading higher and higher into the Rockies, wondering if I should try something stupid like crashing into the narrow cliff walls. My mind was stuffed with dumb thoughts and I kept trying to cycle through them until something intelligent hit me. Nothing did.

"Why are you here?" he asked.

"Because you've got a gun on me."

"Here, in this town."

"I've been trying very hard to figure that out."

He swiped the pistol barrel across my head. I was lucky it was only a snub-nose. Despite his silence and his outward relative calm, he was wired and explosive. He really didn't know how to handle a gun. He barely tapped me, but I didn't take it lightly. The fact that he didn't know what he was doing meant he might crack my skull open next time, or the .38 might accidentally go off.

"Do you know what you did?" he asked.

"Got involved," I said.

"You killed my boy."

"I tried to help. I held on to a rope sixty feet in the air for as long as I could."

"Not long enough! You couldn't hold it long enough!"

"Neither could you."

He shoved the barrel into my ribs this time, growling and groaning, speaking words that weren't words except maybe in his nightmares. For four days he'd forced himself to sleep, on his way toward death, but had woken up just so he could make this play for me, the scapegoat for his own stabbing conscience.

I noticed an odd sound, a tiny ringing in the car. I glanced over and saw that he was spinning a key on a chain. He noticed me looking and held it up, but said nothing. It was a bus-station locker key. I'd seen plenty of them when I was roaming the country, trying to settle down somewhere to find my art again. Sometimes you start to drift and you just keep going, for no reason you can name. You ride and ride and hope the right thing appears around the next corner, even though you have no idea what it might be. He shoved the key back in his pocket.

We kept climbing higher until we were in the switchbacks. The temperature had dropped twenty degrees over the last several miles. Another thousand feet and we'd be able to see our breath. We'd left the towns and the cabins behind and kept threading through the mountains. The car started puttering, the thin air fouling the engine. You were supposed to do something to the timing or the spark plugs or the air filter, who the hell knew. Bradley was getting more and more excited, as if he knew we were heading to a special, secret place where he'd put his past to rest.

Snow started to appear on the ground, on the rock. The air thinned but held in the cold, the atmosphere lush and vibrant around us. I'd never been up this far. The wind tore at the car, rocking us on our shocks. The trails thinned. Finally, we ran out of road.

"Now what?" I asked.

"Get out. Climb."

We got out and he prodded me forward across the rugged, stony landscape. I'd been in Colorado five years and had never hiked through the national park, or anywhere else for that matter. Now he had me clambering up rocks like those adrenaline junkies who scaled sheer bluff faces. I was out of shape and I wouldn't last long. Not that Bradley would need me to. I knew he was leading me to an edge someplace. His edge, my edge. Maybe he'd been here himself before, ready to throw himself off the rim. Maybe he was walking as blindly as me, just waiting for the next thing to come along.

We came to a slope that dropped off into nothingness. We were so high up that there was an electrical buzzing in my fingers and toes and chest, an assaulting awareness that one foot further would be a step into oblivion.

The wind slithered around us. Bradley jabbed the gun into my back again. "Move."

"No."

"Then I'll kill you."

"You know, Bradley . . . you give a man two choices at death and he's going to choose the one that makes you work a little harder for it."

"It's just pulling a trigger."

"It's better to make you do it than do it myself." I didn't know why that was the case, but I knew it was true. I still wasn't all that worried—maybe it was altitude sickness, or maybe I'd had a death wish for a while and only now was starting to realize it.

"Move! To the edge!"

"I'm not going down there."

"Yes, you are. We both are."

"Why are you doing this?"

He rushed me and jabbed the barrel under my chin. It hurt like hell. "I want you to know what it was like for my son."

I growled, "You're the one who put *him* in it. You're the one who took *him* up."

"Shut up!"

"You're the one who let go, same as me. We had no choice."

"Shut up, damn you!"

He jabbed the barrel harder into my throat until I gagged.

"Now, jump! Do it or I'll put one in your brain."

"How is that supposed to scare me at this point?"

"You might survive if you jump."

"At twelve thousand feet? Yeah, right."

Twelve thousand feet. One hundred and twenty stories. We were higher than the Empire State Building.

Not only had he gone insane with his rage and grief, but he really hadn't thought about the end game at all. There wasn't enough thrill in it for him. He was starting to understand that my death wouldn't take away an ounce of his agony. It was descending on him very quickly now and an unbearable horror came with it. He'd be alone soon with nothing but his guilt. The fear in him was much greater than my own. I saw the realization grow in his eyes along with his terror.

My feet were slipping out from beneath me on the icy rock. I was gearing up for some kind of a stupid move. Everybody thinks it's easy, you just attack, you just spin and kick, punch and whirl and karate chop. These people, the kind who never say boo to the boss, let their relatives roll over them, and take every gram of garbage force-fed to them through their entire lives. These people, they think it's easy to make your move on death.

Then I saw it, no more than fifty feet from us, down in the rocks, nearly at the rim. I'd been expecting it the whole ride up, because when facing your fear you also face your fate, and in that moment, any damn thing can happen.

I pointed over his shoulder and said, "There's the balloon."

• • •

It had drifted twenty miles and more than six thousand feet thanks to the front-range winds. It was impossible, I thought. It had to be. There was no way the balloon could have gotten up this high. Even with the updraft carrying the kid along, it never should have made it this far. Even if the kid had accidentally gotten the burner opened up all the way, it shouldn't have been enough to get the balloon this high.

It should have bounced into one of the cliffs miles ago. The silk would have torn and the whole thing would have plummeted down in the middle of the mountains. But somehow the flight of the balloon had missed every jagged rock. Hiding behind the ridges and within the thinning tree line of the national park so nobody could see it, dancing so close to the craggy banks that he just kept rising. With hundreds of volunteers searching for him and nobody seeing.

The balloon had wedged into a tight stony niche. The basket had folded in half and the deflated silk had collapsed on top of it. When you saw a hot-air balloon you saw a beautiful mammoth thing. This you could've fit in your closet.

Bradley let out a cry that was part despair and part elation. He dropped the gun and forgot about me. I had to keep reminding myself that he was crazy.

He ran up to the niche and started yanking at the silk, trying to pull the basket free. He screamed his son's name, and the echoes swarmed across the cliffs like a thousand distressed men calling out the names of their thousand dead sons.

I picked up the pistol and tossed it over the edge.

Bradley yelled, "Help me!" I stared at him for a moment and then climbed over there.

It wasn't for him. I wanted to see the boy's face. It still felt very important that I actually see what the kid looked like.

Bradley gripped one end of the basket and I took hold of the other and we pulled until we got it open wide enough that he could climb in. He ducked low for a second and I lurched aside until I could peer into the cramped space.

The dry, cold mountain climate had preserved the boy these last several days. At this elevation, no animals or insects had been at him in the crags. Even though the basket had struck the mountain hard enough to crumple in on itself, his skin hadn't been touched. He wore a T-shirt and shorts and sneakers with holes in the big toes. The basket had folded around him like a cocoon, without actually coming in contact with his flesh. It was another miracle, depending on whether you saw it that way. He was still facing away from me.

From what I could see, except for his coloring, he looked like a perfectly healthy, sleeping child.

Bradley screamed, "Johnny!" He took the boy in his arms and fell against the side of the basket.

It started to slide. I had a chance to dive, maybe grab ahold of it, but I didn't see much point anymore. It skidded across the rock ledge and the deflated silk washed across the rocks and rippled like river water.

The basket began to tip but bumped an outcropping and righted itself. The silk flapped out as if trying to inflate, but failed.

For a moment, Bradley hung there in space with his arms around his dead little boy.

He stuck his hand out to me. I reached and he clutched my right forearm. I had maybe five seconds to haul him out of the basket before it flopped over the rim.

I stared into his eyes and thought, *He's just as insane now as he was a half-hour ago. Maybe more so. He still blames me. He'll never see it any differently, especially after the kid falls into the chasm and his body is lost forever.*

You can make decisions in an instant that will forge the direction of the rest of your life. You can perform acts that will curse you with a hellish mark forever. You can sell your conscience by making a single mistake. You can do your best and still not make things right. I kept thinking, *Here it is.* I kept thinking, *One last chance.*

I wondered if Bradley could see the same things in my face that I saw in his—the foolishness, the screwed-up attempts, the ridiculous efforts and disappointments.

I never should've let the stalker scare me out of New York. I shouldn't have lost my dream. I could've made it through the fire if only I'd held strong.

I snaked my free hand into his pocket and snagged the locker key.

It's where the money would be. Thirty grand would help me get home again. A little start-up fund to make something right happen for once. A demo reel, time to write another book. One that would sell well enough that I could feel vindicated for all the hours I wasted glaring into the abysmal white of the endless empty page.

I leaned in closer and said, "You're an idiot for putting your kid in a stolen hot-air balloon, you bastard."

I had to snap my forearm hard aside twice before I broke his grip.

The basket dipped another foot over the edge, the silk whispering like a child. Bradley could've done something—made a wild dive the way I had the afternoon I caught the rope—but I could see he just didn't have the resolve for it. He really had lost the will to live. Imagine.

He stood there with his lost son in his arms, no expression on his face, as he tipped out of sight.

The key chimed faintly in my hand, like the final small toll of every man's wasted life. I still hadn't seen the boy's face, but it would be with me forever, on every page of my life and work from here on out.

I figured I could handle it.

TOM PICCIRILLI is the author of more than twenty novels, including *The Cold Spot*, *The Midnight Road*, *Headstone City*, and *A Choir of Ill Children*. He's a four-time winner of the Stoker Award and has been nominated for the World Fantasy Award, the International Thriller Writers Award, and Le Grand Prix de L'Imaginaire. Learn more about him and his work at his website www.tompiccirilli.com.

Cheer

BY MEGAN ABBOTT

We were all in the car and by then Coach had a darty look in her eye and it was a little like when she talked Kim into doing that basket toss move for the game against Western and then all the sudden Kim was about to do it and maybe it wasn't such a good idea after all once we saw the hard floor in the Mohawks' gym but it was too late and Kim had gritted herself into it and she was going to do it and there was nothing Coach could do but watch, which she did. Kim ruled the school that night. Coach took her out to celebrate, even paid to get the tiny Stallions tattoo on Kim's lower back. Everyone was jealous.

But now in the car that look was there and I wondered who would be risking landing hard that night, or if it was Coach this time.

Next to me, with her forever-wad of foamy gum in the side of her mouth, an acid shot of grape in the air every time she cracked it, Kim was itemizing with her fingers the times she'd made her little self sick with booze, the Blackberry brandy from her parents' kitchen cabinet, the Strohs' metallic rind spun on the tongue, in Tony Marino's basement, it went on like this.

Beth was in the front seat, next to Coach, and was wearing a tank top that tied in the back, the strings dangling with little beads on each end. Smoking one of Coach's joints, she looked bored, but I knew she wasn't. We couldn't wait.

• • •

We all talked about Coach a lot, how she was kind of beautiful and had a righteous car and her husband bought her everything she wanted and worked all the time in a gleaming tower downtown and she had bright white teeth and a waist whittled down to nothing and things twisted in her eyes and you could see that too and it made her more interesting even than the tennis bracelet and perfect highlights in her butter-blonde hair.

She didn't seem old at all. She was maybe 26, but she'd already taken the squad at St. Regina to state last year and we all wanted that, even the lazy girls or the ones like Beth, and so we would do whatever she said, even after things started getting funny with her and anyway it wasn't like partying with Mr. Simmons, the science teacher, since Coach was almost one of us, only not at all.

Before she came, we'd had it pretty easy and we ran things as we felt. Beth was the Squad Captain and she did as she pleased. When Coach came on, she said there'd be no captains, she was the only captain and she was whipping us into shape. No more hours spent talking about the Master Cleanse and who had an abortion during summer break. She said we'd best get our act together and part of us liked it. If we looked sloppy we knew we'd be doing bleacher sprints, hammering up and down those steps to the pulse of her endless whistle. We could feel it in our shins the next day. We got a lot better and no injuries either because we were running a tight routine.

But Coach, she had a lot going on and you were always wondering about her. We talked about her at our lockers and jammed into our cars and on the phone at night, about what her husband might be like and what her house was like and if she cheered in college and where she went to college. It was hard to ask her because she was all business, at first. You had to try to sneak it in there when she had a moment, when she'd say something like, "I spent all weekend thinking through this routine," and we'd say, "What did you do over the weekend, Coach, did you go to the movies with your husband?"

It was just as football season was ending that it changed and everything she kept tight just flung forward and we were ready, wouldn't miss any of it. Coach and Sergeant Stud together, it was all we could talk about. We thought of them in her Audi, her legs up high and bright blondeness just coming off them both. We wondered about his muscly hardness and if she let him do anything he wanted—why wouldn't she? He was Mr. Movie Star and Beth said she'd join the Guard just so she could roll around with him. A lot of the girls liked to hang around his recruiting table in front of the cafeteria and finger the brochures. Spread Your Wings, they said. Beth never talked about him before, but now she was saying how she wanted to press up against him and feel his weapon. She said once she passed him in the hall and twitched her cheer skirt up and he told her he liked what he saw.

It had happened like this: it was time for practice and we were waiting on Coach and she was late and the other girls were doing fortunes and French braids, taunting Steph's pudgy thighs and chugging diet pop, and Kim and Beth and I went stalking halls.

After school the place always felt different, more than the cloggy bleach and disinfectant, but other things. There were kids, teachers, but strange lurking pockets of them in places other than the gym, you never knew when or where, a knot of physics grinds on the third-floor landing timing the velocity of falling superballs, the barking Forensics Clubbers snarking about capital punishment in the language lab, shaggy burnouts slouching at far ends of long hallways, the flash of nervous Mrs. Fowler, the art teacher, flitting out of the ceramics room.

We were walking toward the fourth-floor Teachers' Lounge when we heard the growly sound, like when your dad reads you a bedtime story about a tiger and does all the voices himself.

Beth had a gleam in her eye and I figured that she was probably right and she pushed the door open, which I would not have, and we saw it all, right there. She had not a stitch on and he still wore his uniform, dress green, everything but the beret and his pants dropped to the floor. Most of seeing them was not the crazy, jerking movements, the sight of her, on hands and knees on the skidding area rug. It was the dreamy look on her pinkening face, all elation and mischief and wonder, like I never saw in her, like she'd never been with us, so strict and exacting and distant, like a cool machine. Her breasts were shuddering whitely and his hand was buried in her hair, blonde and triumphant.

• • •

In her office later, she pulled the blind down on the door and shook out a handful of cigarettes and lit up one for herself. We took ours and I remember she lit mine and when she did I looked in her eyes and they were jumping. She didn't know what we would do. Beth was slouching in her seat, kicking her legs up and propping her feet against the front of the desk.

We all puffed away and she, flush-faced, a stray gold hair sticking to her forehead, explained how it was and how we had to understand that it was a love thing with her and the Sarge, only she called him Don, and that he gave her the only smiles in her life, stuck all day rousting chickens—not like us, she said, we were different, but like Carrie and Shannon and Jen and Kelly—rousting them on the shellacked floors of the Dwight D. Eisenhower Memorial Gym, their hapless ponytails flying, smarting off, being lazy, spitting gum on the floor, whining about periods and boys. She spent all day like this and then home to her kid—we knew she had one, had spotted her with her once at the parking lot at the ice-cream shop—pucker-mouthed and red-faced, a day of sugar and agitation in pre-school, and her husband at work until the nightly news some times, home filled with irritation and woe, his hair falling out at 31. Who wouldn't need the ministrations of the likes of Don, face as pretty as someone on TV, the kind of tanned, soft-lipped man you saw on commercials bringing grateful women flowers everywhere, light haloed behind his head, teeth gleaming with understanding and rescue?

Maybe this didn't seem to have a lot to do with what Don was doing to Coach on the floor of the Teachers' Lounge, but maybe it did. We decided it did. We took long understanding drags on our cigarettes and decided it did.

After that, we were all really close, even Beth. After practice, sometimes we'd go to the mall. We liked Coach's jeans and she took us to where she got them and we spent hours there, leaving with shopping bags spilling over with curl-edged tank tops, stiff, fine-stitched jeans, pokey-heeled boots, the long glitz of dangling necklaces.

A few times we went to her house after and she threw steaks on the grill and opened bottles of wine and we sat on the deck as the sky grew dark and her husband came home around eleven and we were all pretty drunk by then, even Coach maybe, because when Kim took her top off and ran around the yard, shouting into the bushes for boys, Coach just laughed and said it was time we met some real men, and that's when Brian, her husband, showed up and we all thought that was hysterical, except Brian, who looked tired and flipped open his laptop and asked us if we could be quiet, which we couldn't possibly be.

Beth, who kept saying she wasn't drunk at all but she would never admit being drunk, sidled up to him and kept asking him questions about his job, and if he liked it, and what his commute was like. He just looked at her and asked if her parents would be worried and he kept throwing these looks at Coach, who finally said she'd drive us home and on the way we decide to pick up a six-pack and go to the lake for one last hurrah but there were some guys standing around their trucks at the lake, rough-looking dudes.

They looked like they worked at the plant, wore those thick-soled boots like the auto workers did. They were cute, though, and Coach, she kept making comments to them, saying stuff like, did they like her posse, that kind of thing. One of them had a moustache like some old TV star even though he was young and he liked Coach and kept trying to get her to come into his truck but she shook her head and smiled, said she had better things to do with her time. We knew she'd never get near a guy like that no matter how cute and no matter he said he had some great smokes and he could take her in his souped-up car for a drive to the casinos downtown. Like any of us would ever want to go to casinos, or downtown.

Kim and I were having a great time, but Beth was getting bored and kept rolling her eyes and she told the guy he was wasting his time and why not try the bowling alley or the Seven-Eleven for someone in his league. Then the guy got red in the face and he threw a bottle down and Coach said let's go and we tore off and Coach was laughing and so were we and Beth maybe a little too. It was a fun time.

The next day, Beth told us we should've known how it would go, that that was Coach's type of guy, and that Sarge Don, without the uniform, was probably that type of guy too. She said she'd better enjoy it while she can because in a few years she'd probably pop out another kid and her hips'd spread like rising dough and before she knew it, she'd be coaching field hockey instead.

• • •

On Monday, Coach gave Beth a really hard time at practice, which is something the last coach, who was a hundred years old, had a teenage daughter of her own, never would've done. Beth usually did as she pleased but Coach was slanty-eyeing her and showed her she knew what she was up to and the dark settled in both their eyes and it was no joke for either of them.

"Hey, Coach," she said. "I know someone who knows you."

"Lanfield," Coach said, "aren't you supposed to be doing sprints up the bleachers." Because she was. She was late for practice and that was what you did.

"My sister's boyfriend. He says he knows you. Tom Kendall."

"Well, I don't know him," Coach said, "and you can toss that gum, Lanfield. I'm tired of seeing your tongue lapping." We all snickered a little.

"The thing is," Beth said, cracking that gum regardless, "he knows you from high school." She was grinning.

Coach had gone to our school, we all knew it, but it was ten years past.

"Yeah, well, I don't remember him," Coach said, looking at Beth like she had three seconds to make this matter.

Beth was taking her time, though. "He showed me his yearbook. You'd never been on cheer, huh?"

"Lanfield," Coach said, "stop wasting all our time."

"Okay, Coach," Beth said, with almost a smirk. It was in the locker room later that she showed us the yearbook of Coach, feathered hair and thick glasses with pink frames and a roll of pudge under her chin from one ear to the other. She didn't have any activities listed under her name and Beth said that Tom said everybody called her Tubs, if they paid any attention to her at all.

We said we didn't care much. We liked Coach and who even knew what the story was. Beth kept talking about how lame the picture was and how Coach was a big loser and wasn't that a riot and why should we listen to someone who hadn't even made cheer in high school. That's how Beth was.

It's like Beth thought the yearbook was worse somehow, worse than catching her with Sergeant Don, a hundred times worse. And she talked about it so much and it just seeped in a little and when we looked at Coach, it was like we could almost start to see the dumpy girl she'd been, even as she looked so tight, so sleek, so blonde and cool and perfect. It was like all her clothes and everything, those French-manicured nails and creamy tan and hard lines, were just a disguise, and could all fall away in an instant. Maybe we started to feel that way even if we couldn't explain it. It was just there.

The next practice, things felt different. It was like we were waiting for Coach to mention it, even though it didn't seem like she would, or for Beth to start up with it again. But no one said anything and Beth said she had to leave early to go shopping with her mom for a new bikini for their Christmas trip to Captiva and Coach acted like she didn't even hear and Beth just shrugged her shoulders and smiled sweetly and left at 4:30. And she pulled some of that kind of stuff for a while and it seemed like Coach was going to have to lay the hammer on, like she'd done with Kelly once for giving a girl on the opposing squad the finger during a game. But she never did, and it all started to fade away.

• • •

It was right before Christmas when Coach kept us all late after practice. We all smoked in her office and Kim sat on top of her desk, swinging her legs and waving her cigarette around like on some soap opera.

Coach said she had to make a call and we could tell from her voice, sticky as honey, that she was talking to Don. After she got off the phone she wondered if we'd all like to go to a party that night with some other guardsmen and we all said hell, yeah, and Beth said she'd wear her new top and steal Don away and Coach said, good luck, broom stick, and we all laughed.

• • •

In the car, the nerves were shooting. We couldn't believe it. Soldier boys, Kim kept shouting.

The hotel was on the eastern ridge of town and it wasn't very nice, but Don had gotten a two-room suite with a little kitchen and connecting doors and there were four other Guardsmen and they were just wearing jeans, which was kind of disappointing.

But they had a big bar laid out, with bottles of rum and mixers and everything. They looked really glad to see us and Coach said, boy, don't you boys owe me.

Maybe it was an hour or two later, Kim and I had been playing quarters with two of them, Sheppy and Prine, who kept pounding his fist on the table, and I knew I had to stop because the room was spinning.

I went to get some water and that was when I saw Beth and Coach talking in the kitchenette and Coach had cocaine on her fingers, I'd seen it before, once, twice, the football players had some, but we didn't do it, it was the kind of thing you get thrown out of school for. But Beth was itching for it. Lemme Coach, she was saying and Coach kept shaking her head but finally she said she could have some if she just put it on her teeth, which Beth did. Beth was so drunk I knew we couldn't take her home. We'd have to call her mom and say she was sick and was staying at my place, or Kim's.

"Well, I'll keep her away from Prine," Don said, rubbing Coach's back. "Prine'd have a bite out of her. He can't control himself. He'd gnaw at her leg like a wishbone."

• • •

Then, Coach and Don were crawling all over each other on the couch and finally they went into one of the bedrooms and I thought, there goes our ride. Beth seemed like she was about to pass out, even though she kept shouting things at the boys and asking where were their weapons and what kind of soldiers were they, really.

Prine, he was weaving as he stood, and he was eyeing Beth, whose top was nearly slipping off her tan shoulders. "Maybe you'd like some of this," he said to Beth and Beth's face grew white and it seemed like it was time to leave.

I didn't like the way things were going, but Kim was dancing with Shep and she didn't seem to care and they tried to get me to dance with them, so I did, and before I knew it Beth was gone and so was Prine.

• • •

I stood at the door of the bedroom, knocking, asking for Coach but she wouldn't come out of the bedroom and I even thought I heard her giggle, tinkling like a girl. She wouldn't come out at all. I knocked and knocked and knocked.

Over by the bathroom, I could hear Beth starting to get sick and I thought that might make him stop, but it didn't sound like he was stopping.

Shep kept saying everything was okay but suddenly he started to realize it wasn't and he said Prine was such a loser and he came over and started pounding on the door. Prine opened it and he was pulling on his pants and Beth was lying on the floor and you could see she'd been sick everywhere.

Prine's face was red and he'd turned on the water and was trying to clean his shirt, which was covered in vomit. He was shouting that she was such a dumb kid and that she was lucky he hadn't taught her a real lesson. But her jeans were curled around her ankles and her underwear too and I couldn't figure out what other lesson he might have to teach her.

Kim tried to help Beth with her clothes and Beth's eyes fluttered open and she looked like I'd never seen her, like I'd never seen anyone. Shep said Sarge was going to kick their asses and Prine said, fuck that, he brought 'em here. When Don came out of the bedroom, he was mad and he told Shep and Prine they were real fuckups and he would talk to them outside.

He'd left the door open and I looked in the bedroom and saw Coach on the bed, lying under a sheet and stretching her arms in the air like a princess.

I asked her why she hadn't opened the door when I knocked and she looked at me, shook off the hot haze glazing her eyes and looked at me.

I said Prine had done something to Beth in the bathroom. I could feel my teeth chattering like it was cold. It felt so cold in the bedroom, like the air was on high and my chest hurt with it.

"He did something to her?" Coach said. "Well, what did he do?"

And I didn't know what to say, I thought, isn't my face saying it. I thought, how do you say what he's done?

There was a glint on her mouth, her lip, like she might almost smile. That's when I knew, and it was like she was standing in the gym, whistle hanging from her neck, so serene as we pounded up and down those bleachers, pounded them until she said stop and it seemed like she never would.

"Coach," I started, but I didn't finish.

MEGAN ABBOTT is the Edgar®-winning author of the crime novels *Queenpin*, *The Song is You* and *Die a Little*, and the nonfiction study, *The Street Was Mine: White Masculinity in Hardboiled Fiction and Film Noir*. A 2008 Pushcart nominee, her stories have appeared in *Wall Street Noir*, *Detroit Noir*, *Storyglossia*, *Queens Noir* and the upcoming *Phoenix Noir*. She is also the editor of the collection, *A Hell of a Woman: An Anthology of Female Noir*. A Detroit-area native, she has taught literature at the New School University and New York University. Her new novel, *Bury Me Deep*, which is loosely based on the Winnie Ruth Judd "Trunk Murderess" scandal of the 1930s, comes out in July 2009. She lives in Queens, New York.

Babs

BY SCOTT PHILLIPS

"Visitor's Center call you about a room?" I say to the woman behind the counter. It's 11 o'clock at night, and I've been in the car since 4 in the morning. I haven't yet hit the stage where the white crosses that have kept my eyes open have turned against me, but the time will be coming soon and I'll crash and sleep the sleep of the damned, and I have business to take care of before that happens.

"Oh. You're Mr. Gandy, hello. You're lucky to get something. They got the Consumer Electronics show going on right now, good thing you thought to stop at the Visitor's Center." She's shaped like a gourd, her hair long with ends split and dyed a shade of black that doesn't occur in nature. Between the elastic of her paisley slacks and the bottom of her blouse, little black hairs dance obscenely around the milky white vortex of her navel. She takes a key hanging in front of a cubby in which three envelopes sit aslant and hands it to me.

"There's mail in that slot," I point out.

"There's a fellow always gets this room when he comes through. Salesman."

So I'm subletting someone else's rented room, basically. I don't care. I'm lucky to be getting anything, as the ladies at the

Visitor's Center pointed out to me when I pulled into town. It's a modest little motel, the Visitor's Center lady said, but super clean; you could eat off of those floors. I climb the open staircase to the second-floor balcony overlooking a swimming pool filled with cloudy water the color of urine. A couple are sitting next to the water smoking and glaring at one another without saying anything, and as one they swing their gazes upward toward me.

"What the fuck you staring at, faggot?" the woman says. She has on a shirt that says, I SUFFER FROM CRS. Her nipples are sticking straight out through the cotton, and at this moment there may not be a pair of tits on the planet I would less rather see, short of maybe Mother Teresa's; this one can't weigh much more than eighty pounds, with the emaciated face of a lifelong smoker. Even with her Jackie O shades on, her eyes look sunken.

"Seems like someone's looking to get his ass kicked," her companion says. He's so obese I can't imagine him able to get out of the lawn chair he's overflowing from, but I stare straight at him and sense that he's serious. I picture the fight and figure it could go either of two ways: He gets me down and crushes me under four hundred pounds of suet, or I dance around him and tire him out until he has a heart attack.

"Sorry!" I yell, and I head down the balcony looking for number 36. It's around the corner, facing the back ends of some houses. A dog in one of the yards starts a vicious barking jag as soon as I come into view, and keeps it up once I get into the room.

Clean enough to eat off the floors, I think after a quick walk-through, wishing I could force-feed the chipper Visitor's Center lady a nice, greasy fried egg off of the gritty shag carpet.

There's a ratty terry cloth bathrobe hanging from the clothes hook inside the bathroom door, presumably the salesman's. He must be balding, because there's hair all over the goddamned place: on the pillow, in the toilet, around the tub drain.

I'm not here for a vacation. Having spent the last few months tending bar for my stepfather's strip club in Wichita, I'm on my way back to L.A., where I am foolishly expecting to be able to pick up my old life where it left off. When I called my friend Skip to alert him of my return, he had a proposition for me: If I was coming through Vegas, he'd give me two hundred dollars to pick up a package from a stripper named Babs.

I didn't have to ask Skip to know I'd be carrying crystal methamphetamine. I'm more of a pothead myself, with a taste for the occasional hit of acid or pharmaceutical speed. Meth makes my teeth itch. But I can use the two hundred, and Skip is a good guy. (Within a couple of years, though, he'll transform into a violent monster whose ass I'll be forced to kick off my couch and out of my house in a futile effort to save my marriage. Said marriage hasn't happened yet, either, at this point.)

When I call the number Skip gave me, Babs doesn't bitch about the hour or seem surprised, just gives me directions to a bar called the Tumblin' Dice a few blocks off the Strip and says she'll meet me in half an hour. I tell her I'll be wearing a Dodgers cap.

It's past midnight and my new friends are still out by the pool. I stare as I pass by them and wink at the lady, who gives no sign of remembering me from twenty minutes ago. Her boyfriend doesn't react, having by this time fallen asleep.

• • •

The Tumblin' Dice is a monument to skank. No one here looks close to sober, particularly the lanky, disheveled bartender, whom I take at first for the victim of some exotic neurological disorder. After a long wait, he lurches over in my direction and braces himself on the bar with a big bony hand, a large bandage stretched across his right knuckles, blood starting to seep through the beige fabric.

I order a draft beer and park myself in front of a nickel video poker machine with hearts and diamonds faded to a cheerful, blurry pink. I play one nickel at a time, which proves to be a mistake.

"Fuck a duck, baby, you gotta play more'n a nickel a pop, you're fucked that way if you hit a big hand." The woman next to me is small and junkie-thin, with puffy dark circles under her eyes. I have no theoretical designs at all on the woman I'm supposed to be meeting but I can't help hoping that this isn't her.

"I'm just killing time, waiting for a friend."

"Fuck, I'll be your friend," she rasps, and then slaps my back harder than I would have thought possible, cackling. "Just kidding. I will, though. I'm Nicki." She rolls up her sleeve to reveal an amateur tattoo of a nickel the size of a silver dollar on her upper bicep. Jefferson looks pissed, like he's not happy about being tattooed onto a junkie's arm, or maybe it's the big infected whitehead erupting from his cheek. "Short for nickel's worth, get it?"

I shake my head no, even though I do.

"I done time, baby. Five big ones. Know what I did?"

"No."

"I'm not gonna tell you, either. Not till I know you better."

"Okay," I say, cursing the inborn Midwestern politeness that keeps me involved in the conversation and darting my eyes back and forth between the door and the machine. I drop another nickel and draw three nines and two queens, pat.

"Fuck, man, see that? You ain't getting shit for that, baby. You should've bet five nickels, that's the way you build up a bankroll."

"Like I say, killing time." Her short blond hair is spiky, but a stale odor emanating from her scalp makes me suspect that its body comes from a lack of washing rather than some salon product.

"What's your name?"

"Tate."

"Is your friend a lady, Tate?"

"Uh-huh."

"A lady friend, like? Like a sex partner?"

I take a good look at her, trying to figure out exactly what she's fucked up on. There's glee in her face, childish and idiotic, and I can't say whether it's malicious or not.

"Probably not."

"Cause I don't want you getting any big ideas about me, cause I'm one hundred percent dyke, baby."

"That's okay with me." I draw four clubs and a diamond, and trade the diamond for a spade.

"Aw, baby, that's a heartbreaker there. Not that it matters when you're betting nickels. You ever play one of those five-dollar machines?"

"No."

"My girlfriend, the one who died, she won a cool two grand one time. She was trying to pay me back all the money she stole."

The smart thing would be not to rise to the bait, but I'm finding her more fun than the nickel poker so I do the callous thing and bite. "How'd she die?"

Nicki leans toward me and hisses the answer in my ear, filling my nostrils in passing with a bouquet redolent of tobacco, stale beer, and gum disease. "I had her killed."

"No shit," I say, nodding, trying to strike the perfect balance between looking impressed and credulous and sympathetic.

"Bitch ran up a thirty-thousand-dollar tab on my fucking MasterCard. I said, *Bitch, you ain't getting away with that.* But I fucking loved her. It fucking broke my heart."

"Is that what you got sent up for?"

"Fuck no, that was just a little cocaine beef. This deal with Betsy was just last week. Don't you fucking tell anyone what I just told you, got it? Cause I'd hate to have to have you killed too."

"I won't tell anyone," I say, wondering how worried this should make me and cursing the white crosses popped in the course of the day's drive. Five? No, six. Seven? No, six. Three at 4 in the morning at the first motel, and three in Utah. Was it Utah?

"Cause I really would fucking hate that, cause I like you, baby. You're pretty good-looking, you know that?"

"Thank you very much," I say, the way my mother taught me to respond to a compliment.

"When I said I was a hundred percent lesbian, I meant more like eighty, if you know what I mean."

"Oh."

"You have really big lips. Just like a spade's, almost. Anybody ever told you that before?"

"Not in those exact words." I look over at the bartender, but this apparently isn't the kind of place where patrons are discouraged from bothering one another

"I can't help thinking how they'd feel on my pooss-ay. You like the taste of pooss-ay, Tate?"

In fact, pussy is one of my favorite flavors in the entire world, at this juncture, however, my gag reflex is struggling with the back of my throat, trying to force it open to disgorge the beer I've swallowed.

A strange hand on my shoulder ought to come as a relief, but it makes me spill my beer on the foul carpet. I turn to face a woman with long, dark hair drawn up behind her long, graceful neck in a ponytail.

"Tate?" she says, her voice high and surprisingly sweet. "I'm Skip's friend, Babs." She looks over at Nicki. "Sorry, Nicki, I need your new friend."

Babs is apparently higher than Nicki in the pecking order, because Nicki scurries back to the bar without a word. "I came in a cab," Babs says. "Can you drive?"

• • •

"Sorry about that," Babs says as we leave the parking lot. She struck me immediately as pretty, with the kind of sweet, big-eyed face I love, but the more I look at her the more character her face shows; the truth of it is she's a beauty. "If I'd've known I was going to be that long in coming, I would've told you someplace nicer." She spends a few seconds appraising my appearance, which makes me a little nervous, since I'm wearing the clothes I slept in last night. "You're a big guy. That's good."

I don't know how to interpret the remark, favorable though it seems, so I file it away for future obsessive, feverish rumination. "Kind of hard to picture you as a regular back there."

"I'm not, exactly. I own it."

"Really?" *Skip said you were some kind of stripper,* I almost add. Because I've been expecting somebody more like Nicki and less like Babs. She has on a loose-fitting shirt and jeans and not much makeup, and I can't help thinking that she sounds smarter than any woman I've talked to in months.

"Yeah, the last owner died and my boyfriend was a regular there, and I thought, what the fuck, I'll buy it and let him run it. Well, that didn't work out, did it? That was him behind the bar."

"The, uh, that guy tonight?"

"Yeah, the shitfaced guy. He didn't used to be like that. Guess I shouldn't have bought him a bar."

"I guess not." I'm stopped at a long light and a tiny old woman shuffles across. She doesn't look like she belongs in Vegas at all, let alone out on the street at 1:45 in the morning.

"Look at that poor old gal," Babs says. "We should offer to take her home, except we'd probably scare her into a heart attack. So what brings you to Vegas?"

"Going back to L.A. Bugged out after the Northridge quake and spent a few months tending bar in Wichita."

"Wichita? Are you kidding me?"

"No."

"I grew up in Wichita! For a few years anyway. My dad was stationed at McConnell. I had a little dog named Teenchie."

"Teenchie? You a *Song of the South* fan?"

"Yeah, I love it. I know it's supposed to be all politically incorrect and it probably is, but I saw it when I was little, so I can't be objective. The other one I really love is *Saludos Amigos.* Ever see that one?"

"Part of it. I wrote my master's thesis on Disney animation." As a matter of fact I didn't, my cousin did at USC, but I do know more than the average guy on the subject, and I'm truly bowled over to be asked such a nerdy question by this magnificent creature.

"Just loved all that shit when I was little. When I first started dancing, I used Teenchie as my stage name, can you believe that?"

So she is a dancer after all. I'm slightly more than half in love with her at this point in our ten-minute-long acquaintance, and I figure if the lush behind the bar at the Tumblm' Dice is my competition, I'm in like Flynn.

But it's late, so the aforementioned Midwestern politeness fails to stop me from asking the first question that pops into my head: "How can you afford to buy a bar on what a dancer makes?"

"Who said I was still a dancer?" She grins, a lopsided thing that shows a big expanse of teeth. She has, I finally notice, a slight overbite that makes her face perfect. She doesn't offer any more than that, so I don't pursue it further. "Turn left up here."

Something that should have been nagging me all along starts doing so. "Hey, you know that gal Nicki I was talking to?"

"God, do I."

"She told me she had her girlfriend murdered." When I say it, I can feel microscopic particles of Dexedrine racing up my spinal cord to my brain.

Babs snorts. "Jesus."

"Said this girl ran up a thirty-thousand dollar tab on Nicki's MasterCard."

"Think about it, Tate. If you were the bank, would you give that crazy bitch a MasterCard with a thirty-thousand dollar limit?"

"I guess not."

"I mean, what would she put on the application where it says *occupation*? Crack whore? Meth cook?"

This sends the Dexedrine particles back down out of my brain, and a feeling of relative calm comes over me. We're heading into a nice neighborhood now, a strangely empty subdivision. There aren't any cars on the street, not even parked, and there aren't any lights on anywhere; no late-night TV viewers or insomniac readers or dog walkers.

Finally, we get to a McMansion with all its lights blazing and two cars parked on the street in front despite a three-car garage. "Did you ever see *The Omega Man*?" I ask. "This is sort of like his place."

"Kind of spooky, isn't it? The subdivision went bankrupt before it was all the way finished and the developer's on trial. They managed to rent out a few of 'em to people who sublet the extra rooms."

"Is this where you live?" I ask, hoping she's bringing me home, even as I recognize the pathos of the fantasy.

"Hell no. I own, in a hell of a lot better nabe than this. This is where we're getting your present for Skip. Park on the street, not too close to the streetlamp." She opens up her bag and hands me a pistol. I'm a Kansas boy and I've hunted since I was little, but I've never had a real pistol in my hands, and to her consternation I hold this one like it's a live fish.

"Hold it straight up and keep your index finger on the trigger guard."

"What's this for?" I ask.

"This guy's an asshole. I just want you to stand there and look big, and if things get tense you pull the grip out of your waistband so he can see it."

Not that I like anything I've heard in the last thirty seconds, but the thing I like least is the part where I stick a firearm down my pants. I can't stand the idea of looking weak in Babs's eyes, though, and by this time she's out of the car, so I follow her to the door.

When the door opens, an expressionless woman about seventy years old lets us in without a word. She has on a tank top and a pair of shorts that reveal a big scab on her shin. It looks like she slid all the way down her driveway with only one leg of her pants on.

There are three medium-to-hot young women in the living room watching *Cops*. The action is taking place in North Las Vegas, and they're excited because the bust onscreen is happening on a street they know.

"There's Lonnie's, look," one of them says. She has long, frizzy red hair and freckles as big as moles, and like the old lady, she has a big scab on one knee. She's picking at it with one long, red fingernail as she watches.

"I've totally seen that dude," one of her friends says.

"Which? The cop or the pimp?"

"Wannabe pimp, more like. He comes in for a drink when he's got cash."

"Gross."

"Where's Kleindienst?" Babs asks, and when they ignore her she grabs the remote and shuts the TV off, which prompts a volley of protest until she asks again, louder.

The redhead stops picking at the scab and half rises. "In the dining room, bitch. Gimme my fucking remote."

Babs throws the remote behind the television to another chorus of abuse, and I follow her through the kitchen into a dark room where a man in what I take to be a blackjack dealer's vest and starched white shirt sits with an overhead light shining down on him.

He's playing solitaire and wearing a clear green visor, which gives him the pallor of a reanimated corpse and makes him look to my eye more like a dealer from a film than a real one. Remembering my role, I lean against the doorframe and fold my arms across my chest while Babs walks up to the table. I'm expecting something out of a movie, a tense, quiet negotiation followed by a quick exit, so I'm feeling suave and invulnerable, especially with the gun down my pants. It feels pretty cool, actually, like a second dick.

Babs opens with, "You lying, ripping-off piece of shit."

This gets the man to glance up from his game for the first time. "You owe me, Kleindienst."

"I don't owe you shit." He looks over at me. I rise to my full height and move my hand toward my crotch. The adrenaline is pumping. "Who's this cunt?" he asks. "One of your Johns?"

He has just insulted the woman I sort of love, and I'm still feeling the effect of too many cross-tops—I just remembered numbers seven and eight, popped at a filling station around 8 p.m. just in case—and between those and my instinctive gallantry and the drama of the thing, I commit what will in retrospect seem an error in tactics: I pull out the gun and point it at Kleindienst's face.

Babs looks at me for a millisecond, stricken. Then she pulls another pistol out of her bag and points it at the man's face as well. "Turn the light on, Tate."

"Tate?" Kleindienst says. "Your muscle's name is Tate? Oh, my goodness gracious."

I turn the light on. "Family name," I say, trying to sound like a killer.

The room is white with brass fittings and mirrors. It doesn't look as cool now as it did in the dark, and I see that Kleindienst is quite a bit younger than I'd imagined, maybe thirty or thirty-five. "Tell that bitch Darva to get in here with everything you got," Babs tells him.

He yells through the kitchen and a girl appears who looks like a teenage runaway in a TV movie, complete with cutoff hot pants and a shirt tied at the midriff. "Run fetch me the whole batch," he says. Then the three of us stand there feeling awkward, or at least the two men do. Babs looks perfectly comfortable.

A minute later, Darva reappears in the doorway holding up four good-sized packages wrapped in aluminum foil.

"Take 'em," Kleindienst says. "No hard feelings?"

"You douchebag," Babs says, and she opens one of the packages, snorts a little bit off the end of her finger. Jangly as I am, I'm relieved when she doesn't offer me a taste, and after a cursory glance at the other three packages, she seals them back up. "Don't ever fuck around like that again."

We start toward the living room and before we get there Kleindienst yells something at us. I turn to find him holding a big fucking gun pointed in our general direction. I yelp and pull the trigger, and to my horror it just makes a clicking sound. I click again and again in Kleindienst's direction as Babs fires, hitting him in the knee. He drops his gun, which sounds like a dumbell hitting the wooden floor, and falls clutching the gory knee, howling in an almost canine register. Poor Darva stands in the doorway of the dining room looking like she's waiting for someone to tell her what to do.

"You're going to need to take Billy to the hospital," she says to the paralyzed trio of Cops fans on the way out.

We run to the car and I peel away from the curb. I don't speak until we pull out of the subdivision. "How come mine didn't go off?" I ask, mortified by my own whining tone.

"Yeah, like I'm going to give you a loaded gun. I don't even know you," she says, and though my heart breaks a little, the events of the last five minutes have prepared me for the idea that there may be more to Babs than I previously fantasized. "Jesus, I didn't tell you to pull the fucking gun on him. That could have gotten us both killed."

"Is the mob going to hunt you down now?" I ask.

"What mob? Why?"

"For robbing a big-time dealer?"

"Billy Kleindienst? Give me a break. Billy's a fucking courier. Was until tonight, anyway, now he's just a crippled blackjack dealer. He's about as low as you on the totem pole. What we took belongs to me and my friend Sandra anyway."

"You think they're going to drive him to the hospital or call an ambulance?"

She shakes her head. "Don't give a shit, really. I did feel kind of sorry for that little Darva, though. I think she's his girlfriend, which is just as pathetic as can be." She looks over at me, shaking her head. "It all came out good, though, except for him getting it in the leg," she says with a rueful, easy smile. "Billy fuckin' Kleindienst."

I drive her to her house, in another subdivision. It's on a rise, and we can see the lights of the Strip in the distance. She's calmed down considerably, and the conversation is back in the realm of friendly flirtation. "You want to come in and taste some of this?" she asks.

"No thanks," I reply. I halfway think she's going to insist, that the taste of speed is just a pretext for taking me inside and fucking me, but she doesn't push it, just hands me Skip's share of the crank and opens her door.

"Nice meeting you," she says

"If you ever come out to L.A., call me and we'll go see an old movie," I tell her. I wait until she gets inside before backing out of her driveway.

Heading into town, I watch those lights blinking and illuminating the early-morning sky, no longer dreading the crashed-out sleeping jag that lies ahead, and for the first time it occurs to me that there's something I really like about Las Vegas.

SCOTT PHILLIPS is the author of three of the most highly acclaimed crime novels of recent years. His debut novel, *The Ice Harvest*, was a *New York Times* Notable Book of the Year and won a California Book Award. Its follow-up, *The Walkaway*, continued his success, with the *New York Times* calling it "wicked fun." His third novel, *Cottonwood*, was published by Ballantine.He lives and works in Webster Groves, Missouri.

Ms. Grimshanks Regrets

BY NANCY PICKARD

My dear niece Sarah,

While I do appreciate your mother's effort to encourage you to write thank-you notes, I regret to say that your latest one was a bit of a mess. I mean this literally, not cruelly, dear. I realize you are "only" ten, but that is no excuse for sloppy work. Even a child such as yourself, with a so-called "learning disability" can surely do better than that.

Let me list the ways:

Wash your hands before you begin. Fingerprints, at your age, are no longer "precious."

The book I gave you is entitled Anne of Green Gables, *not* Ann of Green Gables. *Proofreading is next to cleanliness, my dear.*

You wrote that you read the book and "loved it", but a few examples of things you liked would go a long way toward proving the truth of that claim.

Do not ask an old woman, "How are you?" The answer is rarely, "Fine." Write, instead, "I hope this finds you well."

I hope this letter finds you willing to do better next time.

Your loving Great-Aunt,

Phyllis

P.S. Please tell your mother not to waste her budget on such fine stationery next time. You are but a young girl. Dime-store writing will do just fine for you.

• • •

Phyllis Shank laid down her fountain pen, folded the notepaper in half, and inserted it in its matching envelope, which she then addressed, sealed, and stamped. She had only two more mailings to prepare on this lovely, sunny Saturday morning in June, and a stack of similar notes already completed. She would have looked forward to this weekly task were it not for the sad fact that the world needed so much improvement and she had so little time to devote to it, what with her gardening and volunteer work now that she was retired from teaching. But at least now that she was no longer molding 9th-grade minds—or what passed for minds—she had this opportunity to address others who might benefit from her counsel.

• • •

Dear Mrs. Carson,
Your novel, Love's Mystery, *came highly recommended to me by a person I had long considered to be a friend. After reading only the first chapter, I now know two things that I did not know before:*

No one who would recommend any of your books to me could possibly know me very well. Apparently, she is not the friend I thought she was, a mistake for which I do not blame her, but only myself. You may rest assured that I have also written to her to tell her so.

Publishing standards have declined shockingly, which I pointed out in my letter to your publisher. It is clear that you have some talent, which makes it even sadder that you would waste it on such a tasteless story with such offensive language in it. I'm sure you do not use those words in your own life, so I cannot imagine why you would inflict them on your would-be readers.

I regret to tell you that I will never check out any of your other books from the library, nor can I in good conscience recommend them to my acquaintances.

Yours truly,
Phyllis Shank

• • •

Proofread. Fold. Insert. Address. Seal. Stamp.

From the stack of offenses she had collected from the past week, Phyllis picked up the thickest pile. It was composed of several articles from the local newspaper, each article marked up with strong red ink—grammar, punctuation, and spelling corrected, questions of fact circled, composition corrected with examples of improved style. When necessary, beside the reporter's byline she wrote in legible block letters, "AAH?" which stood for "Affirmative Action Hire?" She did not have to explain the acronym, or even pen an accompanying note for this mailing, because the editor, Marvin Frolich, could count on receiving a full packet from her every Monday. He was, by now, after several years, cognizant of her abbreviations. The source of this latest mailing would pose no mystery to him.

Phyllis sat back, satisfied with her morning's labor.

Then she gathered the creamy white envelopes into a neat stack and marched them outside to her mailbox for her post woman, Diane Stevens, to pick up. Phyllis always tried to time her arrival at the box with Ms. Stevens's arrival, so that she could let her know of any problems with previous deliveries, or remind the girl to tuck in her blue shirt or comb her hair. Yes, it was a hot job, and yes, it was no doubt difficult to keep one's clothing tidy while carrying a heavy bag, but that was no excuse for arriving looking as if she had dressed in her truck. She was, after all, an official representative of the United States Postal Service and the residents along her route were her employers.

Lately, they seemed to miss each other, sometimes by what seemed to Phyllis to be only seconds.

This time, Phyllis lingered longer than usual by the mailbox. When Ms. Stevens still didn't come, Phyllis sighed, raised the flag to indicate there was mail to pick up, and returned to her house.

It seemed a mere moment later when she glanced outside and saw that the flag was down again.

• • •

On Monday, Sarah Bodine read the note from her Great-Aunt Phyllis and started to cry. When her mother, Amy, took the note from Sarah's shaking hands, she started to rage.

"I could kill her for doing that!" Amy told Sarah's dad that evening.

"How bad was it this time, and how did Sarah get hold of it?"

"You read it, you'll see how bad it is! Sarah read it because she got home before I did and picked up the mail before I could get to it first and throw the damned thing away."

"Why does your aunt do things like that?"

"Because she's a bitter, nasty old witch who doesn't have a kind bone in her body! She called Sarah's learning disability 'so-called'—"

"What? My God—"

"Yes, and she said our stationery was too good for Sarah." Amy's face, tearful by now, twisted with bitterness. "According to Aunt Phyllis, dime-store paper is good enough for Sarah." She blew her nose on the tissue her husband handed her. "Sarah and I picked out that stationery together, and we picked the best we could afford, because we agreed we wanted to show people how much we appreciate it when they give us presents."

"If there is such a thing as karma . . ." her husband said, letting the implication linger. His wife took up his sentence and finished it for him, ". . . then my Aunt Phyllis is going to die of a thousand paper cuts!"

He almost laughed at that, because it sounded so silly, but then he looked over at a photo of their ten-year-old daughter, thought of how hard reading was for her, how she struggled with spelling words and composing paragraphs, and a rage to equal his wife's came over him.

"She was a teacher!" Hal Bodine was indignant. "For how many years?"

"A hundred and fifty," Amy said with a half-sob, half-laugh.

"Would you mind if I had a word with dear Aunt Phyllis?" he asked, his tone dripping cold contempt for the woman.

"No!" Amy exclaimed, and then she said gratefully, "I wouldn't mind at all. Somebody needs to say something."

• • •

Sybil Carson opened the creamy envelope with some trepidation.

Fan mail was such a mixed blessing. On the one hand, it could lift her spirits on a bad writing day. It could propel her back to her writing feeling as if she had magic in her fingers. Mail like that made her feel blessed and grateful to get to do what she did for a living, however small that living was these days. But it could also plunge her into black despair on days like today. She was already teetering on the edge of giving up on her latest novel, even though she couldn't afford to give up. One more hard knock might bowl her over. It wasn't as if she could easily find another line of work. For one thing, she wasn't young, and for another she didn't have any other skills. She'd been writing novels for thirty years, always thinking the next one would make enough money to let her relax a little bit. So far, that hadn't happened. People assumed writers were all rich, but she made just enough to barely hang on until she fulfilled her next book contract. And she wasn't even doing that this time. This book had been due three months earlier, but the story just wouldn't come. She had tried every writing trick she knew to fool herself into getting going again, and still nothing happened on the page that anybody would ever want to read. If she didn't meet her deadlines, she didn't get paid. If she didn't get paid, neither did her bills . . .

Please, she thought as she slowly opened the pretty envelope, please be a nice note. I just can't take any criticism right now Nasty "fan" mail felt like a slap out of the blue, like a hand shoving out of the envelope or computer to strike her hard enough to leave marks on her psyche, if not on her face.

Sybil pulled the notepaper out and unfolded it.

Maybe I shouldn't read any fan mail right now, she thought, before looking down at the words. Maybe I shouldn't take the chance of letting it demoralize me. But then she chided herself, *Don't be a baby. Sticks and stones . . .*

Sybil read it clear through, and then laid it gently down in her lap

Words can never hurt me?

What an abominable lie that was and always had been.

Maybe, she thought, as a sob rose in her throat, *I should write a novel about killing one of my readers . . .*

• • •

"Hey, Boss, Ms. Grimshank rides again."

Marvin Frolich's secretary tossed the weekly Monday missive onto his desktop with a grin. They had dubbed their "volunteer" editor "Ms. Grimshank" as a play on her real name, which was Phyllis Shank. Once a week, like clockwork—which she would have derided as cliché—her copies of their articles arrived, all marked up in blaring red ink.

"Sometimes," Marvin admitted to his secretary "I like to imagine that all that red ink is her blood . . ."

"Boss!" His secretary laughed. "You'd never get away with it."

He sighed. "I know, but wouldn't it be nice."

What really ticked him off was that she was sometimes correct in the letter, if not the spirit, of her corrections. He had even learned a few things from her "editing." But that learning wasn't worth the price of how nasty it all seemed, and it wasn't worth the pain it caused the reporters who had seen that awful acronym,

"AAH." Affirmative Action Hire? What colossal arrogance! One of the victims had been a young black reporter with budding talent, but no confidence to match. The bigoted remark had set her back months. Only last week, it had infuriated an editor who may have fit the definition of "handicapped" in terms of his paralyzed legs, but who was anything but handicapped when it came to brains and ability. Marvin had never meant for either of them to see the mailings from Ms. Grimshank, but both of them had, by accident.

"One of these days," Marvin predicted to his secretary, "our Ms. Grimshank is going to get what's coming to her."

She grinned. He didn't.

"And what is that, Boss?"

"She's going to get edited out."

• • •

When Diane Stevens didn't find the usual stack of ivory envelopes in Ms. Shank's mailbox on Monday, she sensed that something was wrong. Maybe the old biddy was out of town, but Diane doubted it, because Phyllis Shank never seemed to venture beyond her own mailbox. She even had her groceries delivered.

Probably so she can tell the boy to tuck his shirt back in, Diane thought.

"Or maybe," she muttered to herself as she stared at the small house down the short walkway, "so she can tell him that canned goods really should be double bagged, and what was he thinking to put the frozen vegetables in with the loaf of bread?"

Diane tried to get herself in hand. The old woman could be sick in there.

She went up the walk, hurrying to make up for her previous ill will. But when she reached the front door, she took the few seconds required to make sure her uniform was on straight and to pat down her hair. Not that either action would silence dear Ms. Shank. No, no, if your uniform looked good, and you'd got your hair done, she'd still ask you if you really thought those shoes were suitable.

Diane smiled a little as she rang the bell.

It was funny, really, the way she hid from this resident so they wouldn't meet at the box. There was a conveniently placed tree, wider than Diane's own butt (which Ms. Shank had remarked could benefit from the exercise of the job!), where she could wait until she heard the front door close and the locks click. Then she counted to ten, ran to the box, opened it, pulled out the letters, stuck in the new stuff, and ran off to the neighbor's house before she could get caught. If the Postal Service had an Olympics for fastest mail carrier, Diane thought she might win it.

When Ms. Shank failed to answer the ring, Diane called her supervisor.

And when the neighbor lady came over to open the house for the police, they found the homeowner lying at the foot of the stairs, with strangulation marks around her scrawny neck. Red marks, red as the ink in her pen.

When informed of the identity of the victim, the chief of police—who had been receiving his own regular envelopes from Ms. Shank for years—exclaimed, "Good God, this will be the longest suspect list in history!" He didn't add what else he was thinking, "And the most sympathetic jury, too."

• • •

If they catch me, it will have been worth it.

Arnold Sullivan sat in his studio apartment and stared at the hands that had held the bitch's neck and squeezed. It had been the most satisfying few moments of his life. Again and again he reviewed in his memory how he had lunged, how she had gasped, and how she had looked as life struggled out of her.

"I have finally figured out who you are," she had said to him on Sunday.

He had put down the grocery sacks and asked politely, "Excuse me?"

She'd put a finger to her nose. "Who is that grocery delivery boy, I kept asking myself, because there was something about you that looked so familiar. And now I know. You're Sam Sullivan's older brother, aren't you?"

The grocery "boy," who was seventy years old, said simply, "Yes."

She had smiled her vicious smile, the one she used every week when she handed him a dime. One dime. As if he were ten. As if it were 1928, instead of 2008. It was also the smile his brother Sam had said she'd had on her face when she read his essay aloud in class, the one in which Sam confessed to his feelings for another boy. She had encouraged them to write passionately, tell something secret and deeply true, and she had promised nobody else would ever see it.

It had been 1957. Sam was a small boy, physically, and a naïve one socially. Arnold remembered his brother as being a sweet and innocent thirteen years old, too trusting for his own good.

Three hours later, Sam had hanged himself in the basement.

She had worn that smile at his funeral.

"You're the older brother of that gay boy, aren't you?" she'd asked him this past Sunday. "I wonder what your parents did wrong, that they would have one son who killed himself and another who didn't amount to a hill of . . ." She'd pointed triumphantly to the contents of one of the grocery sacks ". . . beans."

And so he'd lunged. With these hands.

The same hands that had cut his brother down before their parents could see Sammy like that. He hoped he had left fingerprints on her neck. He thought he might like to get caught, so he could tell the world what kind of person she was. Maybe they didn't know. Maybe they'd be surprised.

• • •

Marvin Frolich read over his reporter's story about the murder of the retired teacher. They still hadn't arrested anybody, because there were just so many likely suspects, including himself. The district attorney had confided to Marv, "You know, even if we find who did this and bring him to trial, the defense attorney will have a field day proving how many other people hated her. And that's all any jury will need to acquit based on reasonable doubt."

Marvin edited the article gently, with faint pencil marks, remembering how harsh red ink could appear.

His secretary came in to take it from him.

"What did you say?" she asked, when he muttered something.

"Ding, dong," he said, with profound and unashamed pleasure. "Ding. Damn. Dong."

NANCY PICKARD, creator of the Jenny Cain series and the Marie Lightfoot series, has won Agatha, Anthony, Barry, Shamus, and Macavity awards. She is a 4-time Edgar Award nominee, most recently for her novel, *The Virgin of Small Plains,* which was named a Notable Kansas Book of 2006. Several of her stories have appeared in previous editions of the year's best mystery and suspense. She currently lives in the Kansas City area.

Skinhead Central

BY T. JEFFERSON PARKER

So we moved up here to Spirit Lake in Idaho, where a lot of Jim's friends had come to live. After forty years in Laguna Beach, it was a shock to walk outside and see only a few houses here and there, some fog hovering over the pond out front, and the endless trees. The quiet too, that was another surprise. There's always the hiss of wind in the pines, but it's nothing like all the cars and sirens on PCH. I miss the Ruby's and the Nordstrom Rack up the freeway. Miss my friends and my children. We talk all the time by phone and e-mail, but it's not the same as living close by. We have a guest room.

We've had mostly a good life. Our firstborn son died thirteen years ago, and that was the worst thing that's ever happened to us. His name was James Junior, but he went by JJ. He was a cop, like his father, and was killed in the line of duty. After that, Jim drank himself almost to death, then one day just stopped. He never raised a finger or even his voice at me or the kids. Kept on with the Laguna Beach PD. I had Karen and Ricky to take care of, and I took meds for a year and had counseling. The one thing I learned from grief is that you feel better if you do things for other people instead of dwelling on yourself.

We're living Jim's dream of hardly any people but plenty of trees and fish.

There's some skinheads living one lake over, and one of them, Dale, came over the day we moved in last summer and asked if we had work. Big kid, nineteen, tattoos all over his arms and calves, red hair buzzed short, and eyes the color of old ice. Jim said there was no work, but they got to talking woodstoves and if the old Vermont Castings in the living room would need a new vent come fall. Dale took a look and said that unless you want to smoke yourself out, it would. Two days later, Dale helped Jim put one in, and Jim paid him well.

A couple of days later, I went to dig out my little jewelry bag from the moving box where I'd kind of hidden it, but it was gone. I'd labeled each box with the room it went to, but the movers just put the boxes down wherever—anyway, it was marked "bedroom," but they put it right there in the living room, where Dale could get at it when I went into town for sandwiches and Jim went outside for a smoke or to pee in the trees, which is something he did a lot of that first month or two. Jim told me I should have carried the jewelry on my person, and he was right. *On my person.* You know how cops talk. Said he'd go find Dale over in Hayden Lake the next day—skinhead central—what a way to meet the locals.

But the next morning, this skinny young boy shows up on our front porch, dark bangs almost over his eyes, no shirt, jeans hanging low on his waist and his boxers puffing out. Gigantic sneakers with the laces loose. Twelve or thirteen years old.

"This yours?" he asked.

Jim took the jewelry bag—pretty little blue thing with Chinese embroidery on it and black drawstrings—and angled it to the bright morning sun.

"Hers," he said. "Hon? What's missing?"

I loosened the strings and cupped the bag in my hand and pressed the rings and earrings and bracelets up against one another and the satin. It was mostly costume and semiprecious stones, but I saw the ruby earrings and choker Jim had gotten me one Christmas in Laguna and the string of pearls.

"The expensive things are here," I said.

"You Dale's brother?" asked Jim.

"Yep."

"What's your name?"

"Jason."

Come on in.

"No reason for that."

"How are you going to explain this to Dale?"

"Explain what?"

And he loped down off the porch steps, landed with a crunch, and picked up his bike.

"Take care of yourself."

"That's what I do."

"We've got two cords' worth of wood and a decent splitter," said Jim.

Jason sized up Jim the way young teenagers do, by looking not quite at him for not very long. Like everything about Jim could be covered in a glance.

"Okay. Saturday."

Later I asked Jim why he offered work to Jason when he'd held it back from Dale.

"I don't know. Maybe because Jason didn't ask."

• • •

The way JJ died was that he and Jim were both working for Laguna PD—unusual for a father and son to work the same department—but everyone was cool with it, and they made the papers a few times because of the human interest. "Father and Son Crime Busters Work Laguna Beat."

If you don't know Laguna, it's in Orange County, California. It's known as an artist colony and a tourist town, a place prone to disasters such as floods, earth slides, and wildfires. There had been only one LBPD officer killed in the line of duty before JJ. That was back in the early fifties. His name was Gordon French.

Anyway, Jim was watch commander the night it happened to JJ, and when the "officer down" call came to dispatch, Jim stayed at his post until he knew who it was.

When Jim got there, JJ's cruiser was still parked up on the shoulder of PCH, with the lights flashing. It was a routine traffic stop, and the shooter was out of the car and firing before JJ could draw his gun. JJ's partner had stayed with him but also called in the plates. They got JJ to South Coast Medical Center but not in time. One of the reasons they built South Coast Medical Center forty-seven years ago was because Gordon French was shot and died for lack of medical care in Laguna. Then they build one, and it's still too late. Life is full of things like that, things that are true but badly shaped. JJ was twenty-five—would be thirty-eight today if he hadn't seen that Corolla weaving down the southbound lanes. They caught the shooter and gave him death. He's in San Quentin. His appeals will take at least six more years. Jim wants to go if they execute him. Me too, and I won't blink.

• • •

The next time we saw Jason was at the hardware store two days later. I saw his bike leaned against the wall by the door, and I spotted him at the counter as I walked through the screen door that Jim held open for me. He had on a knit beanie and a long-sleeve black T-shirt with some kind of skull pattern, and his pants were still just about sliding off his waist, though you couldn't see any boxers.

"Try some ice," the clerk said cheerfully.

Jason turned with a bag of something and started past us, his lips fat and black. His cheeks were swelled up behind the sunglasses.

Jim wheeled and followed Jason out. Through the screen door, I could hear them.

"Dale do that?"

"No."

Silence then. I saw Jason looking down. And Jim with his fists on his hips and this balanced posture he gets when he's mad.

"Then what happened?"

"Nothing. Get away from me, man."

"I can have a word with your brother."

"Bad idea."

Jason swung his leg over his bike and rolled down the gravel parking lot.

The next evening, Dale came up our driveway in a black Ram Charger pickup. It was "wine thirty," as Jim calls it, about six o'clock, which is when we would open a bottle, sit, and watch the osprey try to catch one of the big trout rising in our pond out front.

The truck pulled up close to the porch, all the way to the logs Jim had staked out to mark the end of the parking pad. Dale was leaning forward in the seat like he was ready to get out, but he didn't. The window went down, and Dale stared at us, face flushed red, which with his short red hair made him look ready to burst into flames.

"Dad told me to get over here to apologize for the jewelry, so that's what I'm doing."

"You beat up your brother because he brought it back?"

"He deserved every bit he got."

"A twelve-year-old doesn't deserve a beating like that," said Jim.

"He's thirteen."

"You can't miss the point much further," said Jim.

Dale gunned the truck engine, and I watched the red dust jump away from the ground below the pipe. He was still leaning away from the seat like you would back home in July when your car's been in the sun and all you've got on is a halter or your swimsuit top. But this was Idaho in June at evening time, and it probably wasn't more than seventy degrees.

"Get out and show me your back," said Jim.

"What about it?"

"You know what it's about."

"You don't know shit," said Dale, pressing his back against the seat. "I deal with things."

Then the truck revved and lurched backward. I could see Dale leaning forward in the seat again and his eyes raised to the rearview. He kept a good watch on the driveway behind him as the truck backed out. Most young guys in trucks, they'd have swung an arm out and turned to look directly where they were driving. Maybe braced the arm on the seat. JJ always did that. I liked watching JJ learn to drive because his attention was so pure and undistractible. Dale headed down the road, and the dust rose like it was chasing him.

"Someone whipped his back," I said.

"Dad."

"You made some calls."

Jim nodded. Cops are curious people. Just because they retire doesn't mean they stop nosing into things. Jim has a network of friends that stretches all the way across the country, though most of them are in the West. Mostly retired but a few still active. And they grouse and gossip and yap and yaw like you wouldn't believe, swap information and stories and contacts and just about anything you can imagine that relates to cops. You want to know something about a guy, someone will know someone who can help. Mostly by Internet but by phone too. Jim calls it the Geezer Enforcement Network.

"Dale's father has a nice jacket because he's a nice guy," said Jim. "Aggravated assault in a local bar, pled down to disturbing the peace. Probation for assault on his wife. Ten months in county for another assault—a Vietnamese kid, student at Boise—broke his jaw with his fist. There was a child-abuse inquiry raised by the school when Dale showed up for first grade with bruises. Dale got homeschooled after that. Dad's been clean since '93. The wife sticks by her man—won't file, won't do squat. Tory and Teri Badger. Christ, what a name."

I thought about that for a second while the osprey launched himself from a tree.

"Is Tory an Aryan Brother?"

"Nobody said that."

"Clean for thirteen years," I said. "Since Jason was born. So, you could say he's trying."

Jim nodded. I did the math in my mind and knew that Jim was doing it too. Clean since 1993. That was the year JJ died. We can't even think of that year without remembering him. I'm not sure exactly what goes through Jim's mind, but I know that just the mention of the year takes him right back to that watch commander's desk on August 20, 1993. I'll bet he hears the "officer down" call with perfect clarity, every syllable and beat. Me, I think of JJ when he was seven years old, running down the sidewalk to the bus stop with his friends. Or the way he used to comb his hair straight down onto his forehead when he was a boy. To tell you the truth, sometimes I think about him for hours, all twenty-five years of him, whether somebody says 1993 or not.

That Saturday Jason came back over and split the wood. I watched him off and on from inside as he lined up the logs in the splitter and stood back as the wood cracked and fell into smaller and smaller halves. Twice he stopped and pulled a small blue notebook from the back pocket of his slipping-down jeans and scribbled something with a pen from another pocket. The three of us ate lunch on the porch even though it was getting cold. Jason didn't say much, and I could tell the lemonade stung his lips. The swelling around his eyes was down, but one was black. He was going to be a freshman come September.

"Can your dad protect you from your brother?" Jim asked out of nowhere.

"Dale's stronger now. But mostly, yeah."

Jim didn't say anything to that. After nearly forty years of being married to him, I can tell you his silences mean he doesn't believe you. And of course there were the broken lips and black eye making his case.

"If you need a place, you come stay here a night or two," he said. "Any time."

"You'd be welcome," I said.

"Okay," he said, looking down at his sandwich.

I wanted to ask him what he wrote in the notebook, but I didn't. I have a place where I put things for safekeeping too, though it's not a physical place.

Later that night, we went to a party at Ed and Ann Logan's house on the other side of Spirit Lake. It was mostly retired SoCal cops, the old faces from Orange County and some Long Beach people Jim fell in with whom I never really got to know. I've come to like cops in general. I guess that would figure. And their wives too—we pretty much get along. There's a closedness about most cops that used to put me off until JJ died and I realized that you can't explain everything to everybody. You have to have that place inside where something can be safe. Even if it's only a thought or a memory. It's the opposite of the real world, where people die as easily as leaves fall off a tree. And the old cliché about cops believing it's them and us, well, it's absolutely true that that's what they think. Most people think that way—it's just the "thems" and the "usses" are different.

A man was stacking firewood on the Logans' deck when we got there. He was short and thick, gave us a level-eyed nod, and that was all. Later Jim and I went outside for some fresh air. The breeze was strong and cool. The guy was just finishing up the wood. He walked toward us, slapping his leather work gloves together.

"I apologize for Dale," he said. "I'm his dad. He ain't the trustworthiest kid around."

"No apology needed," said Jim. "But he's no kid."

"He swore there was nothin' missing from that bag."

"It was all there," I said.

Badger jammed the gloves down into a pocket. "Jason says you're good people. But I would appreciate it if you didn't offer him no more work. And if he comes by, if you would just send him back home."

"To get beat up?" said Jim.

"That's not an everyday occurrence," said Badger. "We keep the family business in the family."

"There's the law."

"You aren't it."

Badger had the same old-ice eyes as Dale. There was sawdust on his shirt and bits of wood stuck to his bootlaces, and he smelled like a cord of fresh-cut pine. "Stay away from my sons. Maybe you should move back to California. I'm sure they got plenty a'need for bleedin' heart know-it-alls like you."

• • •

We left the party early. When we were almost home, Jim saw a truck parked off in the trees just before our driveway. He caught the shine of the grill in his headlights when we made the turn. I don't know how he saw that thing, but he still has twenty-fifteen vision for distance, so he's always seeing things that I miss. A wind had come up, so maybe it parted the trees at just the right second.

He cut the lights and stopped well away from our house. The outdoor security lights were on, and I could see the glimmer of the pond and the branches swaying. Jim reached across and drew his .380 automatic from its holster under the seat.

"We can go down the road and call the sheriff," I said.

"This is our home, Sally. I'm leaving the keys in."

"Be careful, Jim. We didn't retire up here for this."

I didn't know a person could get in and out of a truck so quietly. He walked down the driveway with the gun in his right hand and a flashlight in the other. He had that balanced walk, the one that meant he was ready for things. Jim's not a big guy, six feet, though, and still pretty solid.

Then I saw Dale backing around from the direction of the front porch, hunched over with a green gas can in one hand. Jim yelled, and Dale turned and saw him, then he dropped the can and got something out of his pocket, and a wall of flames huffed up along the house. Dale lit out around the house and disappeared.

I climbed over the console and drove the truck fast down the driveway and almost skidded on the gravel into the fire. Had to back it up, rocks flying everywhere. I got the extinguisher off its clip behind the seat and walked along the base of the house, blasting the white powder down where the gas was. A bird's nest up under an eave had caught fire, so I gave that a shot too. Could hear the chicks cheeping. I couldn't tell the sound of the extinguisher from the roaring in my ears.

After that I walked around, stamping out little hot spots on the ground and on the wall of the house. The wind was cold and damp, and it helped. My heart was pounding and my breath was caught up high in my throat and I'm not sure I could have said one word to anyone, not even Jim.

An hour later Jim came back, alone and panting. He signaled me back into our truck without a word. He put the flashlight and automatic in the console, then backed out of the driveway fast, his breath making fog on the rear window. There was sweat running down his face, and he smelled like trees and exertion.

"He'll come for his truck," Jim said.

Then he straightened onto the road and made his way to the turnoff where Dale's truck waited in the trees. We parked away from the Ram Charger, in a place where we wouldn't be too obvious.

• • •

We sat there until sunrise, then until seven. There were a couple of blankets and some water back in the king cab, and I'm glad we had all that. A little after seven, Dale came into view through the windshield, slogging through the forest with his arms around himself, shivering.

Jim waited until Dale saw us, then he flung himself from the truck, drawing down with his .380 and hollering, "*Police officer,*" and for Dale to stop. Dale did stop, then he turned and disappeared back into a thick stand of cottonwoods. Jim crashed in after him.

It took half an hour for him to come back. He had Dale out in front of him with his hands on his head, marching him like a POW. Their clothes were dirty and torn up. But Jim's gun was in his belt, so he must not have thought Dale was going to run for it again.

"You drive," Jim said to me. "Dale, you get in the backseat."

I looked at Jim with a question, but all he said was "Coeur d'Alene."

Nobody said a word to Coeur d'Alene. It wasn't far. Jim got on his cell when we reached the city and got the address for army recruitment.

We parked outside.

"Tell Sally what you decided to do about all this," said Jim.

"I can join the army or get arrested by your husband," said Dale. "I'm joining up."

"That's a good thing, Dale," I said.

"Name me one good thing about it."

"It'll get you out of trouble for a few years, for starters," I said.

We walked him into the recruitment office. There were flags and posters and a sergeant with a tight shirt and the best creased pants I've ever seen in my life. He was baffled by us at first, then Jim explained that we were friends of the family, and Dale had decided join up but his mom and dad weren't able to be here for it. Which didn't explain why Dale's and Jim's clothes were dirty and more than a little torn up. The sergeant nodded. He'd seen this scene before.

"How old are you?" he asked.

"Nineteen."

"Then we've got no problems. Notta one."

There were lots of forms and questions. Dale made it clear that he was ready right then, he was ready to be signed up and go over to Iraq, try his luck on some ragheads. He tried a joke about not having to cut his hair off, and the sergeant laughed falsely.

Then the sergeant said they'd have to do a routine background check before the physical, would take about half an hour, we could come back if we wanted or sit right where we were.

So we went outside. The wind was back down and the day was warming up. Across the street was a breakfast place. The sun reflected off the window in a big orange rectangle, and you could smell the bacon and toast.

"I'm starved," said Dale.

"Me too," said Jim. "Sal? Breakfast?"

We ate. Nothing about Dale reminded me of JJ, but everything did. I hoped he'd find something over in that blood-soaked desert that he hadn't found here.

And I hoped that he'd be back to tell us what it was.

T. JEFFERSON PARKER was born in Los Angeles and has lived in Southern California his whole life. He graduated from the University of California, Irvine. He began his writing career as a reporter and published his first novel in 1985. He is one of only three people to have won the Edgar Award for best mystery twice.

The Bookbinder's Apprentice

BY MARTIN EDWARDS

As Joly closed his book, he was conscious of someone watching him. A feeling he relished, warm as the sun burning high above Campo Santi Apostoli. Leaning back, he stretched his arms, a languorous movement that allowed his eyes to roam behind dark wrap-around Gucci glasses.

A tall, stooped man in a straw hat and white suit was limping towards the row of red benches, tapping a long wooden walking stick against the paving slabs, somehow avoiding a collision with the small, whooping children on scooters and tricycles. Joly sighed. He wasn't unaccustomed to the attentions of older men, but soon they became tedious. Yet the impeccable manners instilled at one of England's minor public schools never deserted him; and besides, he was thirsty; a drink would be nice, provided someone else was paying. The benches were crowded with mothers talking while their offspring scrambled and shouted over the covered well and a group of sweaty tourists listening to their guide's machine-gun description of the frescoes within the church. As the man drew near, Joly squeezed up on the bench to make a small place beside him.

"Why, thank you." American accent, a courtly drawl. "It is good to rest one's feet in the middle of the day."

Joly guessed the man had been studying him from the small bridge over the canal, in front of the row of shops. He smiled, didn't not speak. In a casual encounter, his rule was not to give anything away too soon.

The man considered the book on Joly's lap. "*Death in Venice.* Fascinating."

"He writes well," Joly allowed.

"I meant the volume itself, not the words within it." The man waved towards the green kiosk in front of them. Jostling in the window with the magazines and panoramic views of the Canal Grande were the gaudy covers of translated Georgette Heyer and Conan the Barbarian. "Though your taste in reading matter is plainly more sophisticated than the common herd's. But it is the book as *objet d'art* that fascinates me most these days, I must confess. May I take a closer look?"

Without awaiting a reply, he picked up the novel, weighing it in his hand with the fond assurance of a Manhattan jeweller caressing a heavy diamond. The book was bound in green cloth, with faded gilt lettering on the grubby spine. Someone had spilled ink on the front cover and an insect had nibbled at the early pages.

"Ah, the first English edition by Secker. I cannot help but be impressed by your discernment. Most young fellows wishing to read Thomas Mann would content themselves with a cheap paperback."

"It is a little out of the ordinary, that accounts for its appeal. I like unusual things, certainly." Joly let the words hang in the air for several seconds. "As for cost, I fear I don't have deep pockets. I picked the copy up from a second hand dealer's stall on the Embankment for rather less than I would have paid in a paperback shop. It's worth rather more than the few pence I spent, but it's hardly valuable, I'm afraid. The condition is poor, as you can see. All the same, I'd rather own a first edition than a modern reprint without a trace of character."

The man proferred a thin, weathered hand. "You are a fellow after my own heart, then! A love of rare books, it represents a bond between us. My name is Sanborn, by the way, Darius Sanborn."

"Joly Maddox."

"Joly? Not short for Jolyon, by any chance?"

"You guessed it. My mother loved *The Forsyte Saga*."

"Ah, so the fondness for good books is inherited. Joly, it is splendid to make your acquaintance."

Joly ventured an apologetic cough and made a show of consulting his fake Rolex as the church bell chimed the hour. "Well, I suppose I'd better be running along."

Sanborn murmured, 'Oh, but do you have to go so soon? It is a hot day, would you care to have a drink with me?"

A pantomime of hesitation. "Well, I'm tempted. I'm not due to meet up with my girlfriend till she finishes work in another hour . . ."

A tactical move, to mention Lucia. Get the message over to Sanborn, just so there was no misunderstanding. The American did not seem in the least put out, as his leathery face creased into a broad smile. Joly thought he was like one of the pigeons in the square, swooping the moment it glimpsed the tiniest crumb.

"Then you have time aplenty. Come with me, I know a little spot a few metres away where the wine is as fine as the skin of a priceless first edition."

There was no harm in it. Adjusting his pace to the old man's halting gait, he followed him over the bridge, past the shop with all the cacti outside. Their weird shapes always amused him. Sanborn noticed his sideways glance. He was sharp, Joly thought, he wasn't a fool.

"As you say, the unusual intrigues you."

Joly nodded. He wouldn't have been startled if the old man

had suggested going to a hotel instead of a bar for a drink, but thankfully the dilemma of how to respond to a proposition never arose. After half a dozen twists and turns through a maze of alleyways, they reached an ill-lit bar and stepped inside. After the noise and bustle of the *campo,* the place was as quiet as a church in the Ghetto. No one stood behind the counter and, straining his eyes to adjust from the glare outside, Joly spied only a single customer. In a corner at the back, where no beam from the sun could reach, a small wizened man in a corduroy jacket sat at a table, a half-empty wine glass in front of him. Sanborn limped up to the man and indicated his guest with a wave of the stick.

"Zuichini, meet Joly Maddox. A fellow connoisseur of the unusual. Including rare books."

The man at the table had a hooked nose and small dark cruel eyes. His face resembled a carnival mask, with a plague doctor's beak, long enough to keep disease at bay. He extended his hand. It was more like a claw, Joly thought. And it was trembling, although not from nerves—for his toothless smile conveyed a strange, almost malevolent glee. Zuichini must suffer from some form of palsy, perhaps Parkinson's disease. Joly, young and fit, knew little of sickness.

"You wonder why I make specific mention of books, Joly?" Sanborn asked with a rhetorical flourish. "It is because my good friend here is the finest bookbinder in Italy. Zuichini is not a household name, not even here in Venice, but his mastery of his craft, I assure you, is second to none. As a collector of unique treasures, few appreciate his talents more than I."

A simian waiter shuffled out from a doorway, bearing wine and three large glasses. He did not utter a word, but plainly Sanborn and Zuichini were familiar customers. Sanborn did not spare the man's retreating back a glance as he poured.

"You will taste nothing finer in Italy, I assure you. Liquid silk."

Joly took a sip and savoured the bouquet. Sanborn was right about the wine, but what did he want? Everyone wanted something.

"You are here as a tourist?" the American asked. "Who knows, you might follow my example. I first came to this city for a week. That was nineteen years ago and now I could not tear myself away if my life depended on it."

Joly explained that he'd arrived in Venice a month earlier. He had no money, but he knew how to blag. For a few days he'd dressed himself up as Charlie Chaplin and become a living statue, miming for tourists in the vicinity of San Zaccaria and earning enough from the coins they threw into his tin to keep himself fed and watered. But he'd hated standing still and after a few hours even the narcissistic pleasure of posing for photographs began to pall. One afternoon, taking a break in a cheap pizzeria, he'd fallen into conversation with Lucia when she served him with a capuccino. She was a stranger in the city as well; she'd left her native Taormina after the death of her parents and drifted around the country ever since. What they had in common was that neither of them could settle to anything. That night she'd taken him to her room in Dorsoduro and he'd stayed with her ever since.

"Excellent!" Sanborn applauded as he refilled his new young friend's glass. "What is your profession?"

Joly said he was still searching for something to which he would care to devote himself, body and soul. After uni, he'd drifted around. His degree was in English, but a career in teaching or the civil service struck him as akin to living death. He liked to think of himself as a free spirit, but he enjoyed working with his hands and for six months he'd amused himself as a puppeteer, performing for children's parties and at municipal fun days. When that became wearisome, he'd drifted across the Channel. He'd spent three months in France, twice as long in Spain, soon he planned to try his luck in Rome.

"I wondered about learning a trade as a boat-builder, I spent a day in the *squero* talking to a man who builds gondolas." He risked a cheeky glance at Zuichini's profile. "I even thought about making masks . . . ."

"An over-subscribed profession in this city," Sanborn interrupted. "I understand why you didn't pursue it."

"Well, who knows? One of these days, I may come back here to try my luck."

"You have family?"

"My parents dead, my sister emigrated to Australia where she married some layabout who looked like a surf god. So I have no ties, I can please myself."

"And your girlfriend?" Sanborn asked. "Any chance of wedding bells?"

Joly couldn't help laughing. Not the effect of the wine, heady though it was, but the very idea that he and Lucia might have a future together. She was a pretty *prima donna*, only good for one thing, and although he didn't say it, the contemplative look in Sanborn's pale grey eyes made it clear that he'd got the message.

"You and she must join us for dinner, be my guests, it would be a pleasure."

"Oh no, really, we couldn't impose . . ."

Sanborn dismissed the protestations with a flick of his hand. He was old and deliberate and yet Joly recognised this was a man accustomed to getting his own way. "Please. I insist. I know a little seafood restaurant, they serve food so wonderful you will never forget it. Am I right, Zuichini?"

The wizened man cackled and nodded. A wicked gleam lit his small eyes.

"Well, I'm not sure . . ."

But within a couple of minutes it was agreed and Joly stumbled out into the glare of the sun with the American's good wishes ringing in his ears. Zuichini's small, plague-mask head merely nodded farewell; he'd uttered no more than two dozen words in the space of half an hour. Joly blinked, unaccustomed to wine that hit so hard; but the pleasure was worth the pain.

When he met up with Lucia, she made a fuss about the dinner. It was in her nature to complain, she regarded it as a duty not to agree to anything he suggested without making him struggle.

"With two old men? Why would we wish to do this? After tomorrow we will be apart, perhaps forever. Are you tired with me already?"

Exaggeration was her stock-in-trade, but he supposed she was right and that they would not see each other again after he left the city. The plan was for him to travel to Rome and for her to join him there in a fortnight's time when she'd received her month's pay from the restaurant. He'd arranged it like that so there was an opportunity for their relationship to die a natural death. He hated break-up scenes. It would be so easy for them not to get together again in the Eternal City. If he wanted to return to Venice, he would rather do so free from encumbrances, there were plenty more fish in the sea. As for their argument, in truth she found the prospect of a slap-up meal at a rich man's expense as appealing as he did and after twenty minutes she stopped grumbling and started to deliberate about what she might wear.

They went back to her place and made love and by the time she'd dressed up for the evening, he could tell she was relishing the prospect of meeting someone new. Even if the men were old, she would love parading before them; admiration turned her on more than anything exotic he tried with her in bed. At first he'd found her delightful, he'd even managed to persuade himself that she might have hidden depths. But in truth Lucia was as shallow as the meanest canal in the city.

Against his expectations, the dinner was a success, early awkwardness and stilted conversation soon smoothed by a rich, full-blooded and frighteningly expensive red wine. Sanborn, in a fresh white suit, did most of the talking. Zuichini remained content to let his patron speak for him, occupying himself with a lascivious scrutiny of the ample stretches of flesh displayed by Lucia's little black dress. Her ankle tattoo, a small blue heart, had caught the American's eye.

"In honour of young Joly?" he asked, with an ostentatious twinkle.

Lucia tossed her head. "I had it done in Sicily, the day of my sixteenth birthday. The first time I fell in love."

"It is as elegant and charming as the lady whom it adorns." Sanborn had a habit of giving a little bow whenever he paid a compliment. "Take a look, Zuichini, do you not agree?"

The wizened man leaned over to study the tattoo. His beak twitched in approval, the gleam in his dark eyes was positively sly. Even Lucia blushed under his scrutiny.

Sanborn said smoothly, "I have long admired the tattooist's art and your heart is a fine example."

Lucia smiled prettily. "Thank you, Mr Sanborn."

"Darius, please. I like to think we are friends."

"Darius, of course."

She basked in the glow of his genial scrutiny. Joly broke off a piece of bread and chewed hard. He was revising his opinion about their host's sexual orientation. Perhaps the old goat fancied trying his luck once Joly had left town. Fair enough, he was welcome to her.

"Do you know, Zuichini, I rather think that young Lucia's heart is as elegant as Sophia's dove. What do you say?"

The bookbinder paused in the act of picking something from his teeth and treated Lucia to a satyr's grin. "Uh-huh, I guess."

He didn't speak much English and his accent was a weird pastiche American. Perhaps he'd picked it up from watching old movies. His idea of a matinee idol was probably Peter Lorre. Why did Sanborn spend so much time with him, if they were not lovers, past or present? Joly asked if Sophia was Sanborn's daughter.

"Good heavens, no. Alas, like you, I have no family. Sophia was a young lady whom Zuichini and I came to know—what?—two or three years ago. She worked behind a bar down the Via

Garibaldi. We were both very fond of her. And she had this rather lovely neck tattoo, in the shape of a flying dove with broad, outstretched wings. As with Lucia's lovely heart, I have no doubt that it was carved by a gifted artist."

"You admire well-made creations?" Lucia asked, preening.

Sanborn patted her lightly on the hand. "Indeed I do, my dear. My tastes are not confined to fine books, although my collection is the most precious thing I possess."

"Tell us more," Joly said, as the food arrived.

Over the meal, Sanborn told them a little about his life. He'd inherited money—his grandfather had been president of an oil company—and he'd devoted years to travelling the world and indulging his taste for curios. Although he had never visited Venice until he was fifty years old, as he sailed into the lagoon and drank in the sights from the Bacino di San Marco, he resolved to make the city his home. By the sound of it, he lived in some grand *palazzo* overlooking the Canal Grande, and kept his income topped up with the rent from apartments that he'd been wise enough to buy up as the years passed. For all the talk of flooding, you could make good money on property in the city. Demand would always exceed supply.

"I always had a love of books, though it was not until I met Zuichini here that I started to collect in earnest. Are you a reader, Lucia, my dear?"

She shook her head. "No, I am too young. I tell this to Joly. He is of an age where there should be no time to read. He should live a bit."

"Well, books are not simply a delight for desiccated old rascals like me or Zuichini here. You must not be hard on your young man. Seems to me he does pretty well for himself, living the *dolce vita* on a budget while indulging in old books whenever he finds a moment to spare."

Joly caught Zuichini peering down the front of Lucia's dress. Their eyes met briefly and the little man gave his toothless smile.

Perhaps even he would find time to break off from binding books if only he could spend a night with Lucia. It wouldn't happen, though, unless Sanborn was in a mood to share. Joly savoured his swordfish. He didn't care. The American was welcome to her. If he showered her with money and presents, there was little doubt that Lucia would be content to do his bidding until she got bored. She'd confided in Joly that she'd worked in a lap dancing club in Milan and finished up living with the man who owned the joint. He was something high up in the Mafia, but after a few weeks he'd tired of her complaining and she'd managed to escape him without a scratch. Joly reckoned there wasn't much she wasn't willing to do, provided the price was right.

He felt his eyelids drooping before Sanborn snapped knobbly, arthritic fingers and asked the waiter to bring coffee. Before he knew what was happening, Lucia had accepted Sanborn's offer that they dine together again as his guests the following night. He didn't object—it was a free meal, and who cared if Sanborn was a dirty old man with an ulterior motive? Already he had spent enough time in the American's company to know that he was both persuasive and determined. If he wanted to spend his money, if Lucia wanted to sell her favours, who was Joly to stand in their way?

Sanborn insisted on paying a gondolier to take them back to a landing stage not far from Lucia's apartment. On the way home, she prattled about how wonderful the American was. Joly knew it was unwise to argue, but in the end he couldn't resist pointing out that she was the one who had been unwilling to waste her evening in the company of two old men. Now she had committed them to a repeat, on his very last night in the city, when he would have preferred them to be alone.

"And you would have been able to match Darius's hospitality? I do not think so, Joly."

• • •

The next day was even hotter. Lucia went out to work early on and was intent on shopping during the afternoon. After lunching on a ham sandwich—no point in spoiling his appetite for the evening's feast—Joly embarked on a last stroll around the gardens of Castello. Finding a seat beneath a leafy tree, he finished *Death in Venice*, then ambled back through the alleyways, absorbing the smells of the fish-sellers' stalls and the chocolate shops, wondering how long it would be before he returned to La Serenissima. He understood what had kept Sanborn here. Once you became intoxicated with the beauties of Venice, the rest of the world must seem drab by comparison. But he was keen to sample Rome and after the previous night, he was more than ever convinced that this was the right time to make a break with Lucia. Sanborn was welcome to her.

When he arrived back at the flat, Lucia was short-tempered in the way that he now associated with her rare attacks of nervousness. She was bent upon impressing Sanborn, and she'd bought a slinky new red dress with a neckline so daring it bordered on indecent. It must have cost her a month's wages. A carefully targeted investment—assuming she had footed the bill, that was. Joly wondered if she'd met up with Sanborn during the day and managed to charm the cash out of him. He wouldn't put it past either of them. So what? It was none of his business, soon he would be out of here.

The American and his sidekick were waiting for them at the appointed time, sitting at a table inside a restaurant close to Rialto. Sanborn's suit tonight was a shade of pale cream. Zuichini was scruffy by comparison, his face more reminiscent of a scary carnival mask than ever.

• • •

"Lucia, you look dazzling!"

Sanborn kissed her on both cheeks and Zuichini did likewise. Joly had never seen the bookbinder show such animation.

The little dark eyes seemed to be measuring Lucia's tanned flesh, no doubt wondering what she might look like when wearing no clothes. His attention pleased her. Perhaps she was hoping the two old men would fight over her. Even the waiter who took their order allowed his gaze to linger on her half-exposed breasts for longer than was seemly. The restaurant specialised in the finest beef steak and Sanborn ordered four bottles of Bollinger.

"Tonight we celebrate!' he announced. "Over the past twenty four hours, we have become firm friends. And although Joly is to move on tomorrow, with the lovely Lucia to follow, it is my firm conviction that all four of us will be reunited before too long."

As their glasses clinked, Lucia's eyes were glowing. While they ate, the conversation turned to Joly's plans. He made it clear that they remained fluid. It was his style, he said, to trust to luck. Sanborn challenged this, arguing that even a young man needed roots.

"Learn from my mistake, Joly. Until I discovered the wonders of this marvellous city, my life lacked direction. You need something to anchor your existence. A place, firm friends, perhaps a trade."

Zuichini nodded with unaccustomed animation. "Right. That is right."

"Listen to this good man. He knows the joys of a craft, the unique pleasure that comes with creation. This is where you can steal a march on me, Joly. I am proud of my collection of books, undeniably, but I have never experienced the delight of creating a masterpiece of my own. I cannot paint, or compose, or write to any level of acceptable competence. I lack skills of a practical nature. But you, my young friend, are different. If you were to put your talents to good purpose . . ."

"I have an idea!" Lucia clapped her hands. Champagne went to her head. After a single glass, already she was raising her voice and her skin was flushed. "Once you have seen Rome, you could come back here and train as Zuichini's apprentice!"

The plague doctor's face split in a horrid smile, while Sanborn exclaimed with delight.

"Perfect! There, Joly, you have your answer. How clever you are, Lucia. That way two birds could be killed with one stone. Joly would learn from a master at the height of his powers, and Zuichini would have a good man to whom he could pass on the tricks of his trade before it is too late." Sanborn lowered his voice. "And there is something else that I have omitted to mention. Zuichini, may I? You see, Joly. This good fellow here, as you may have noticed, is afflicted by a dreadful malady. Parkinson's attacks the nervous system and he has been suffering stoically for some time. But it becomes increasingly difficult for him to work. An utter tragedy, sometimes I despair. Not only because Zuichini's disability saddens me, but also from a selfish motive. For who will succeed him in business, who will practise his very special skills, so as to keep me supplied in fine books? In you, perhaps I have found the answer to my prayers."

"I don't think so," Joly said slowly.

"Oh, but you must!" Lucia exclaimed. "Such an opportunity, to learn from a genius!"

Sanborn must have primed her with this idea and asked her to offer support. They'd met during the day, not only so that Sanborn could pay for the new dress. The American was, Joly thought, like the most demanding parent. He wanted to have the young folk beholden to him, at his beck and call and used his control of the purse strings to make sure they did not escape.

"I suppose I can mull it over, when I am in Rome."

He'd expected Sanborn to suggest that he abandon his trip, but the old man surprised him, giving a broad smile and murmuring that he could not say fairer than that. Zuichini went so far as to give him a playful punch on the shoulder.

"Good apprentice, yes?"

While Joly tucked into the succulent beef, Sanborn talked about the art of binding books. He spoke of the pouch binding of Japanese books and the unique technique of *nakatoji*, of Jean Groller's leather-bound tomes covered with intricate geometric paterns, inlaid with coloured enamels and books bound in the flayed skin of murderers and highwaymen. He told them about cheverell, a goatskin parchment transformed into a binding both supple and strong with a bold, grainy pattern, popular in Italy during the fourteenth century, he described methods of fatliquoring leather, he explained . . . .

"Joly, wake up!"

He became aware of Lucia's sharp elbow, digging into his side. Sanborn was beaming at him like a benevolent uncle, surveying a favourite nephew who has overdone the Christmas pudding. Zuichini was savouring his wine, still casting the occasional frank glance at Lucia's ample cleavage.

"Sorry, must have dropped off."

"Please do not apologise, I beg you," Sanborn said. "Put your sleepiness down to a combination of the wine and the weather. Perhaps accompanied by a tinge of *tristesse*—am I right, young man? This is your last night in La Serenissima for a little while and who could fail to experience a *frisson* of regret at departing from here?" He refilled their glasses, taking no notice when Joly shook his head. "So let us drink to our good friend Joly, and express the sincere hope that soon he will be back here for good!"

He reached out and patted Joly's arm. Blearily, Joly tried to focus on how to interpret the old man's behaviour. His hand did not linger. Had it been unfair to impute to him some sexual motive for such generosity? Perhaps in truth Sanborn's generosity did not amount to anything out of the ordinary. For a rich man, the cost of a couple of meals and a few bottles of fine wine was small change. Was it possible that Sanborn was no more than he seemed, a lonely old millionaire, keen to share the company of the young and beautiful, as well as that of his ailing friend, and that he had no ulterior motive at all?

Sanborn made some remark and Lucia laughed long and loud, a noise that reminded Joly of a workman drilling in the road. She had a good head for drink, Joly knew that from experience, but even she was beginning to lose control. He remembered her telling him about her last night with the Mafia boss. She'd plucked up the courage to put a small knife in her bag. If he'd attacked her, she'd steeled herself to fight for her life. Joly did not doubt the strength of her survival instinct. If she thought herself threatened, she would lash out without a moment's hesitation. What would happen if Zuichini made her afraid with the clumsiness of his overtures?

He yawned. His head was spinning and he couldn't keep worrying about what might happen between consenting adults. *Que sera, sera.*

• • •

Next thing he knew, someone was tapping him on the arm. Through the fog of a hangover, he heard Sanborn's gentle voice.

"Joly, my boy. Are you all right?"

Even the act of opening his eyes made him want to cry out, it hurt so much. Christ, how much had he drunk? He had no head for champagne, but he'd never felt this bad before. He blinked hard and tried to take in his surroundings. He was lying on a hard bed in a small, musty room. The sun was shining in through a small high window but he had no idea where he might be. Sanborn was standing beside the bed, arms folded, studying him. Suddenly, he felt afraid.

"Where am I?"

"Listen, my friend, you have nothing to fear. You just had rather too much to drink, that's all."

"The drinks were spiked." Nothing else could explain how he had come to black out, this had never happened to him before.

"No, no, no." Sanborn had a first class bedside manner, though Joly was sure he was lying. "You overdid it, simple as that. And you threw up all over Lucia, which frankly wasn't such a good idea."

"Lucia?" He gazed at the peeling wallpaper, the unfamiliar cupboard and door. "Where have you brought me?"

"Listen, it's all right. Lucia was upset, that's all. Zuichini took care of her, no need to worry. As she wouldn't entertain you in her bed last night, I volunteered to bring you here. Now, you need to get up and dressed. I think you said you plan to take the one o'clock coach from Piazzale Roma?"

A wave of panic engulfed him. Effectively, he was the old man's prisoner.

"You haven't told me where you've brought me."

"There's no secret, Joly, keep your hair on, my dear fellow. This is an apartment I bought six months ago. Hardly the lap of luxury, but it's only a stone's throw from the restaurant. It seemed like the best solution, we could hardly leave you to your own devices, the state you were in, and Lucia was in no mood to take you back with her."

Joly coughed. "Then—I'm free to go?"

Sanborn's parchment features conveyed benign bewilderment. "I don't understand. Why should you not be? I was only striving to do you a good turn."

I've been a fool, Joly thought, this isn't a man to fear. The question is—what happened between Lucia and Zuichini? Did he try it on, did she let him get away with it?

"Sorry, Darius. I'm not myself."

"Not to worry, these things happen. There's a bathroom next door. No gold taps, I'm afraid, but you'll find the basic necessities. I'll leave you to it, if I may. Your bag's over by the door, incidentally. I went over to Lucia's this morning to pick it up."

"Thanks," Joly whispered.

"Here's the key to the front door. Would you be kind enough to lock up for me? I have a little business to attend to, but I'll be there at the coach station to see you off, it's the least I can do."

Joly stared at the old man's genial expression. Hoarsely, he said, "Thanks."

"Think nothing of it. That's what friends are for, don't you agree?"

Two hours later, Joly arrived at the Piazzale Roma, bag in hand. Within moments he caught sight of Sanborn by an advertisement boarding and the American lifted his stick in greeting before limping to greet him. He had a black velvet bag slung over his shoulder.

"You're looking much better. Remarkable what wonders can be worked by a simple wash and brush up."

"I'm very grateful to you," Joly said humbly, handing over the key to the apartment.

"Think nothing of it." Sanborn cleared his throat. "Actually, I talked to Lucia before I made my way over here. There isn't an easy way to put this, Joly, but I don't believe she has any intention of joining you in Rome. I'm sorry."

Joly took a breath. "Maybe things had run their course."

Sanborn bowed his head. "That was rather the impression that I had gained. Well, I don't care for prolonged farewells. I hope you will reflect on our conversation last night and that soon we shall see you again in La Serenissima."

Forcing a smile, Joly said, "Who knows, I might take Zuichini up on his kind offer. There are worse ways of making a living than binding fine books, I guess."

A light flared in Sanborn's old eyes. Voice trembling, he said, 'Joly, the moment I first saw you, I knew you were made of the right stuff. In fact, I'll let you into a secret. I'd seen you a couple of times at the Campo Santi Apostoli before I made so bold as to introduce myself."

"Is that so?" Joly didn't know whether to be puzzled or flattered. "So did you see Lucia as well?"

"As a matter of fact, I did. Such a pretty creature, with that gorgeous dark hair and honey skin. Oh well, there are many more lovely girls in Venice. Despite my age, I can guess how sad you must feel. I felt the same about my friend Sophia, after I'd talked to her for the last time. But she and I were not lovers, the physical loss makes it doubly hard for you."

"These things happen."

"Yes, life goes on. And you will never forget Lucia, of that I am sure. But your life will be so much richer if you take up Zuichini's offer. Truly, his craftsmanship is unique. Think of it! You could follow in his footsteps. Make a name for yourself and earn a not inconsiderable fortune."

"Is Zuichini rich?"

"My dear fellow, do not be deceived by appearances. If—no, *when* you return, you will have a chance to visit his splendid home near the Rialto. Even though he and I are close associates, he never fails to drive a hard bargain. But I, and others like me, are willing to pay for the best. For something unique."

They shook hands and Sanborn pulled out of his shoulder bag a parcel wrapped in gift paper. He thrust it at Joly.

"I want you to have this. A token of our friendship. And a reminder of the esoteric pleasures that lie in store, should you accept Zuichini's offer to help you learn his trade."

"Thanks." Joly's cheeks were burning. He'd harboured so many false suspicions and now he couldn't help feeling a mite embarrassed. "I'm not sure that bookbinding is . . ."

"Think about it. That's all I ask." Sanborn smiled. "I have seen enough of you in a short space of time to be confident that you would relish the chance to become a craftsman in your own right. As you told me, you have a taste for the unusual. And with your love of books . . . ah well, you must be going. Goodbye, my friend. Or as I should say, *arivederci.*"

Joly found himself waving at the old man's back as he limped away. At the notice board, just before he moved out of sight, Sanborn raised his stick in salute, but he did not turn his head. The bus was waiting and Joly found himself a seat by the window. As the driver got into gear, Joly tore the wrapping paper from his present. He stared at it for a long time.

The present was a book, carefully protected by bubble wrap and old newspapers and that came as no surprise. The title was *A*

Short Treatise on the Finer Points of Bookbinding. But it was not the text that seized Joly's attention, though deep down he knew already that, one day, this would become his Bible.

The front cover was tanned and polished to a smooth golden brown. He'd never come across anything quite like it. To the touch, it had slight bumps, like a soft sandpaper. The spine and back cover felt more like suede. But what entranced him was not the texture of the binding.

At first sight, he thought the cover bore a logo. But with a second glance, he realised his mistake. In the bottom corner was a design in blue-black. A picture of a flying dove, with broad outstretched wings.

He held his breath as he recalled kissing Lucia's toes. Recalled the delicate heart shape traced in ink upon her ankle. Recalled, with a shiver of fear and excitement, Zuichini's admiration of the tattooist's work, the way those dark and deadly little eyes kept being drawn to Lucia's tender, honey-coloured skin.

He settled back on the hard seat. The countryside was passing by outside, but he paid it no heed. Sanborn understood him better than he understood himself. After searching for so long, he'd finally found what he was looking for. Soon he would return to La Serenissima. And there Zuichini would share with him the darkest secrets of the bookbinder's craft. He would teach him how to make the book that Sanborn craved, a book for all three of them to remember Lucia by.

MARTIN EDWARDS' Lake District Mysteries include *The Coffin Trail* (short-listed for the Theakston's prize for best British crime novel of 2006), *The Cipher Garden* and *The Arsenic Labyrinth* (short-listed for the Lakeland Book of the Year award in 2008.) The first of his eight Harry Devlin novels, *All the Lonely People,* was short-listed for the CWA John Creasey Memorial Dagger for the best first crime novel of the year. He has also published

Take My Breath Away, and a novel featuring Dr. Crippen, *Dancing for the Hangman*, which, like the latest Devlin novel, *Waterloo Sunset*, appeared in 2008. He completed Bill Knox's last book, *The Lazarus Widow.* His short stories include "Test Drive," shortlisted for the CWA Short Story Dagger in 2006, and "The Bookbinder's Apprentice," which won the same award in 2008. In addition, he has edited 16 anthologies and published eight nonfiction books.

I/M-Print

A Tess Cassidy Short Story

BY JEREMIAH HEALY

Tess Cassidy, carrying her crime scene unit duffle bag over a shoulder, heard the uniform at the house's front door say to Detective Lieutenant Kyle Hayes, "Bad one, Loot."

Hayes just nodded, then, almost as an afterthought, glanced back at Tess. "How's your stomach, Cassidy?"

Stung by the implied dig at her professional ability, she said, "Never had a problem so far."

Hayes moved past the patrol officer. "Always a first time."

As Tess followed the detective, she noticed the uniform was a little green at the gills, and, suppressing a shiver, she remembered what the other techs in the CSU called a "debut": covering your initial homicide and autopsy.

"Well," said Hayes to the uniform inside the den, "I don't think we have to wait for the ME on cause of death."

Tess looked at the body sprawled over an oriental throw rug, then looked away, drawing a deep breath.

The house—a McMansion—had a huge living room they'd had to cross before reaching the den, which was more a library. Floor-to-ceiling bookshelves, and not the artsy, leather-bound volumes she'd seen in other rich people's places. No, lots of novels and travel guides, jackets worn, even torn from being handled, and, Tess figured, read more than once. She wasn't that involved in books herself, thanks to dyslexia. In fact, Tess nearly flunked seventh grade before her big sister, Joan, made the principal see what their parents had ignored. But Tess always, secretly, admired anyone who loved reading.

As, apparently, the dead man on the rug had. Hayes said to the uniform, "We got a name?"

"Decedent's Zederberg, Martin, middle initial 'D' as in 'David.'"

"Who found the body?"

"His wife. Nanette. Rollings is with her in the kitchen."

Tess knew Rollings, an empathetic patrol officer and a widow herself.

"Other family?"

"Just a son, Steven, with a V. We reached him, and he's on his way."

Hayes nodded. "How about a weapon?"

"Negative so far, sir."

"Cassidy, what would you say?"

Tess didn't mind being called by her last name. Appreciated it, in fact, as a badge of "blue" respect. But she also knew that "Kyle" used it to buffer his own emotions, because he called her sister—the lieutenant's preferred investigation partner—"Joan." The older Cassidy was out on maternity leave three weeks prior to having her baby, which Hayes wished was his baby, too. Despite his romantic hopes, Joan had chosen the law over law enforcement for a husband, marrying an attorney named Arthur.

And now Joan was at the hospital, about to deliver, while Tess was wading into a grisly crime scene commanded by a scorned, pissed-off detective.

"Cassidy," said Hayes, "Am I talking to myself here?"

"Sorry, Lieutenant." Tess forced herself to look at the body. "From the way his skull's caved in, I'd guess an axe. Or, with that big RV in the driveway, a camp hatchet?"

"Might be hope for you yet, Cassidy. That's my take, too." Hayes squatted next to the slight man's torso. "No defensive wounds on the hands or forearms, so I'm guessing this one in the back of the head was Blow Number One. Then, after the vic fell and landed sideways, Numbers Two through—what, Six, maybe?—on the floor." Hayes rose. "Barefoot, too, and bloody soles but no tracks in the living room, so probably he was already here in the den when attacked, rather than being chased into it."

Tess thought out loud. "Or running for it."

"What?"

She looked around the library. "If Mr. Zederberg knew somebody was going to kill him, maybe he wanted his books to be the last things he saw."

Detective Lieutenant Kyle Hayes just stared at Tess. "Cassidy, you are one odd duck."

Consider the source, sister Joan would have told her, so Tess took that as a compliment.

• • •

Dusting for latent prints at the threshold of the kitchen, Tess Cassidy could hear Hayes interviewing Nanette Zederberg, but not actually see them. It was like listening to a play being read aloud on the radio.

HAYES Did your husband have any enemies?

ZEDERBERG No. No, Marty was in medical supplies. He was always helping people, not hurting them.

HAYES Anybody else you can think of who might want to hurt him?

ZEDERBERG Just the man I told Officer Rollings about.

HAYES The man?

ROLLINGS Mrs. Zederberg was driving down the street, saw a quote, "hulking man," unquote, walking toward her—meaning northward—about two doors up from the house here.

HAYES Mrs. Zederberg, can you describe him for us?

ZEDERBERG Not really. I mean, as she just said, he was . . . well, "hulking," the size of a professional wrestler? But also kind of mean.

HAYES Mean?

ZEDERBERG The way he walked. And moved his head. Like he was really angry about something.

HAYES Did you get a good look at his face?

ZEDERBERG No. I . . . I really only glanced at him. He stared at me, I know, but I was . . . well, frankly, scared of the way he seemed, so I just kept driving. Then I found the front door open here, and Marty—Oh, God, Marty in . . .

ROLLINGS Here you go, Ma'am. These tissues will help.

• • •

Good cop, Rollings.

Tess was almost finished dusting when she heard from behind her, "Cassidy, you know where the Loot is?"

The green-gilled uniform they'd met at the front door. "In the kitchen, with the widow."

"The son is here. Where should I put him?"

"Ask Hayes, but maybe call him out blind first. He might want to interview the guy without his mother knowing. Or in earshot."

• • •

"Stepmother, actually," said Steven Zederberg.

Now Tess was working the entrance to the library, and she could see Hayes with the younger man in the living room, sitting across from each other on matching armchairs. The son took after his father, slight frame and black, curly hair, with a Jewish skullcap bobby-pinned to the back of his head.

Looked a whole lot better than blade wounds. Thinking back to the corpse, though, Tess didn't remember any cap on or around the victim.

Hayes said, "You realize I have to ask some awkward questions?"

"Lieutenant, my father's just been brutally murdered, and you've told me I can't see Nanette until after you've interviewed me. So, please, ask away and be done with it so I can go to her."

Tess thought, kid's got some guts.

Hayes said, "We haven't found a weapon so far. Do you know if your parents keep an axe or a hatchet on the premises?"

"If you mean the house, no. But I'm sure Dad has one—had one in the camper."

"The recreational vehicle outside?"

"Yes. My father traveled a lot in his business, but mainly via airplane to convention cities and big hospitals. He always yearned to see the rest of the country, and so when he got a good offer for the medical supply company, Dad sold it."

"Can you tell me how much he got for it?"

A pause. "Is that really necessary for your investigation?"

"Yes."

Another pause. "All right. My father asked me to work with his lawyer on the deal."

"Why?"

"I'd just gotten my accounting degree, and Dad thought it would be good experience for me. And it was. Overall, we netted about three million."

"'We?'"

Tess looked up to see Zederberg clench his teeth. "My father did, that is." A shake of the head. "They were going to put the house on the market, too, though I told them he'd take a wicked hit—God, I'm sorry."

The son began rubbing his eyes with his fists, like a little kid. Tess's heart went out to him, but her job meant returning to the dusting.

Hayes said, "I know this is difficult for you."

"Yes," Tess hearing what she thought could be palms slapping thighs, "yes, you probably do, Lieutenant, because this is your job. But it's our lives."

Tess thought: The son's got guts and humanity.

Then Steven Zederberg made a noise that sounded almost like a laugh. "The bizarre thing is, Dad was always afraid he was going to die by fire."

"Fire?"

"Yes. The hospital he was born in burned to the ground like a week later. Then my father's first warehouse was struck by lightning when he was at his desk on the second floor of it. And, just before Dad decided to sell his company, he got caught in a hotel fire in Rochester, New York." The son hung his head. "Never thought he'd be killed like . . . this."

Hayes cleared his throat. "When you said your father and stepmother were going to 'take a wicked hit . . .'?"

"Uh, taxwise." Zederberg raised his face to the lieutenant. "While they'd lived here way beyond the minimum period for capital-gains forgiveness, the house has also appreciated to the point—"

Tess couldn't follow the rest of what Steven Zederberg said, but it sounded interesting, so she resolved to ask her brother-in-law, Arthur the Attorney, about the issue.

If she ever get done with this crime scene, that is, so she could go visit Joan at the hospital.

• • •

"You look way too cute to be a cop."

Puh-leeeze, thought Tess. *Where do guys find such garbage lines? Could there be a "dumb-ass.com" somewhere on the Web?*

She was at the step-up entrance to the RV, about to go in to look for the camp hatchet Steven Zederberg had mentioned. The male, forties and balding, stared back at her over the bordering fence, focusing less on her face and more on her butt.

Tess said, "And you'd be?"

"Pete."

"That's your last name?"

"No." A husky laugh. "First. Pete Odabashian."

Zero hope of remembering that one. "Can you spell it for me?"

He did.

Tess said, "And you live next door?"

"Why I'm standing where I am."

"What can you tell me about the Zederbergs?"

"Well, they were quiet, that's for sure. No wild parties, probably because she's way younger than he was."

"By how much?"

"Actually we happened to talk about that once."

Tess heard his "happened" the loudest.

Odabashian said, "We were all like ten years apart."

"The 'we' being?"

"Well, Marty was the oldest, at fifty-six. I'm next at forty-seven, then Nan at thirty-six, and Stevie at twenty-five."

Using "Nan," not her full first name. "Anything else about your neighbors?"

Odabashian shrugged. "Not very religious, though I think the kid's decided to be, since he wears a yarmulke all the time."

Tess remembered that was the religious word for the skullcap. "How'd the family get along?"

"Fine, far as I could tell. I'm guessing Marty and Nan had to help Stevie out, starting a new business with student loans, an office, his own apartment, and so on. Then Marty decided to pull the ripcord on owning and running the company, and they bought this camper here. He was always puttering around in it, even forgot to close the door sometimes."

"Lock it, you mean?"

"No, not even click the door shut. I'm surprised he didn't get a squirrel or skunk building a nest in there."

"How about Mrs. Zederberg?"

Odabashian squinted. "In what way?"

A careful reply. Tess inclined her head toward the RV.

"Roughing it?"

"Ah, right. I got the impression Marty was a little higher on the great outdoors than Nan was."

"Mrs. Zederberg told you that?"

"Not in so many words. But I remember they took the camper out for a trial run, toward really touring the country in it. When Nan came back, all I heard was her not feeling safe driving it, banging her head or elbow into things. Even though the camper's enormous to look at, when Marty invited me to take a Cook's tour, it's kind of like a submarine inside, and I kept banging into cabinet corners and doorways myself. Plus there's the poisoned ivy and bug bites Nan got on their maiden voyage."

"Was that the only point the Zederbergs disagreed on?"

"Why don't we have a drink together, and I'll tell you everything you want to hear?"

God. "Like whether Mrs. Zederberg had any . . . male friends?"

"Aside from me, you mean?"

Consistency is not always a virtue, especially when it hints at a motive for killing the woman's husband. But all Tess said was, "Yes."

"How about that drink first?"

"Actually, I'd rather start by holding hands."

Odabashian seemed stunned. "You would?"

"Yes. If you were inside this camper, I need to take elimination prints from your fingers."

"That's not exactly what I had in mind."

"Tough luck. You can hop over here now, or you can cool your heels for a night or two in jail until a judge gets around to making you cooperate."

Pete Odabashian gave Tess a sour look. "Somehow, you're not so cute anymore."

• • •

Coming through the CSU door at headquarters, Detective Lieutenant Kyle Hayes said to Tess, "The vic's wallet was gone, but the stash of cash he kept in that library—and the wife kept in the kitchen—are both still there."

Suggesting a killer/robber not familiar with the household's habits. Then Tess looked up from logging in the evidence baggies used at the crime scene. Hayes was carrying two folders of different colors, neither of them ones the department used.

Tess said, "What are those?"

"Personnel files. From the vic's former business and the wife's job at the museum. She's a docent."

"What's that?"

"Cassidy, you have to get out more. A 'docent' is like a tour guide."

Tess kept her temper. "Thanks."

Hayes laid the folders on the counter next to her. "The family'd like to have the decedent in the ground by nightfall."

"What's the rush?"

"Religious thing. The ME knows about it, and he's putting Zederberg at the top of his list. Though, if it was up to the wife, we'd be looking at burning, not planting."

"Cremation?"

"Only the son's gotten pretty devout over the years, and he said it was also a religious thing to bury, and the funeral director's agreeing—naturally, since he'll get more money on the deal."

Tess was trying to think all that through when Hayes said, "I'm gonna get some coffee. Be back in ten to see how you're doing."

No "Can I get you something, too?" Tess said, "I'll be here."

As soon as Hayes closed the door behind him, Tess moved over to the folders. She was a little surprised that the owner of a company had a personnel file on himself. Opening "Zederberg, Martin," Tess read about his selling of medical supplies, some correspondence on him in turn selling his company, and some more letters about retirement options.

Then she turned to "Zederberg, Nanette." Given date of birth, she was a good twenty years younger than her husband, as Odabashian had told Tess. And not much employment history: nurse's aide, restaurant hostess, "docent" at the museum.

Luckily, Tess was back at her logging by the seven-minute mark, because Hayes burst through the door early. And empty-handed.

"Where's your coffee?"

"Cassidy, we've got a weapon."

"The weapon?"

"Well, that's something we're just gonna have to find out, aren't we?"

Silently, Tess said good-bye to witnessing the birth of her first niece or nephew.

• • •

The uniform assigned by Dispatch to investigate a bloody hatchet had enough sense to leave it on the ground.

Hayes said to her, "Any identification on the caller?"

"I can check with Dispatch, Lieutenant, but they didn't tell me squat on that."

Tess lowered her duffle bag to a patch of grass maybe ten feet removed from the weapon. She had a gut feeling the tipper stayed anonymous, though she also knew that 911 had caller ID, so they at least could trace the number.

Probably to an equally anonymous pay phone.

"Cassidy, you want to process this thing?"

Looking forward to it all day. "Yessir."

Tess bent down, trying to picture how the hatchet got there. "We're about three miles from the Zederbergs' house, right?"

"Ballpark. And in the direction the widow saw her 'hulking man' walking."

There were two huge prints, probably thumbs, in blood on the handle, but any others seemed too smudged to matter. "I don't remember Mrs. Zederberg saying anything about him carrying a bloody hatchet."

"You didn't interview the woman. She was upset, likely to miss stuff. Especially since she just 'glanced' at the guy."

"Only other people could have seen him, even focus on a big man acting odd. Why would he bring the murder weapon this far?"

"The guy could have it in a bag. Or he could just be a crazy."

"But why not wipe the thing off? Or hide it, even bury it?"

Hayes and the uniform both laughed.

Tess said, "What?"

"Cassidy," the lieutenant still chuckling, "you are a mite slow. 'Bury the hatchet?'"

"Oh."

• • •

At her computer, Tess cursed. After taking preservative close-up photos of the hatchet's handle, she'd lifted both latents perfectly from the surface. However, neither of them was in the state or federal databases.

And there were no prints in the house that didn't belong to one of the three Zederbergs, and none in the RV beyond theirs and those of the neighbor, Pete Odabashian.

Tess ran all four people through the computer. Zip also, which meant nobody had a criminal record, served in the military, or applied for any of a dozen kinds of licenses or permits.

The good news was that Tess had done all she could on the case, so now there was nothing official keeping her from going to the hospital.

"It's a boy," the new papa said, beaming in the gleaming corridor, a piece of cardboard in his hand.

Tess smiled at her brother-in-law. "That's terrific. How's Joan doing?"

"Great, just great. Still a little groggy, but only because they had to do a Caesarian section."

Meaning general anesthetic, so that made sense.

Arthur held up the cardboard. "And isn't this just the cutest thing?"

Tess glanced at "the cutest thing," then began to stare at it, and finally read the label. "What does 'I/M-Print' mean?"

He told her.

Tess nodded once. Twice. Three times. "Arthur, what happens when a married couple goes to sell their house?"

"What happens?"

"Taxwise," said Tess Cassidy, "and keep it simple."

• • •

She had to give Detective Lieutenant Kyle Hayes credit. He was willing to do what Tess asked.

They were both in the Zederbergs' living room with Nanette, son Steven, and neighbor Pete Odabashian.

The widow checked her watch and spoke with an edge to her tone. "Okay, my husband's funeral starts half an hour from now. What's this about?"

Hayes said, "Cassidy?"

Tess had already drawn and released a deep breath. "I want to take prints of all your . . . big toes."

"Our what?" Odabashian said.

"We found impressions on the handle of a hatchet, and the blood on its blade matches the decedent's DNA."

The son said, "So?"

"The prints are either the thumbs of a 'hulking man,' like the one your stepmother reported to Officer Rollings, or the big toes of somebody else."

Mrs. Zederberg said, "I don't understand."

Tess looked at her. "I got the idea when I visited my sister in the maternity ward a few hours ago. The hospital takes an 'I/M-Print,' meaning 'Infant/Mother-Print.' Or 'prints.' The mother's thumb and the infant's foot. So there's no question about somebody going home with the wrong baby."

Steven Zederberg said, "I repeat myself, but so?"

"The prints on the murder weapon weren't in any of our databases. So if the 'hulking man' wasn't the source of those prints, maybe one of you is."

Odabashian said, "Should I be calling a lawyer?"

Hayes—God bless him—chimed in, "Just let Cassidy here take prints of your big toes, okay?"

Nanette Zederberg sighed, but began to take off her shoes.

"This is absurd," from her stepson, who nevertheless began to do the same.

Odabashian said, "Not until I talk to an attorney."

Now Hayes put some steel into his voice. "You can cooperate, too, or sit in a cell until a judge tells you to comply."

Tess thought, *Just what I already told Odabashian about his fingerprints*. "I'll only be a minute, and this way you'll avoid any legal fees."

Odabashian gave her another sour look, but he bent to untie his shoelaces.

When all three were barefoot, Tess "rolled" their big toes. However, when she compared their prints to her latents from the hatchet, there was no match.

"So," said David Zederberg, wiping the ink off his toes with a cloth from Tess's duffle, "all this was a waste of time."

"I'm afraid so," Hayes shaking his head.

Tess decided on one last try, using what her brother-in-law had told her at the hospital. "Mr. Zederberg, as an accountant, what happens when a married couple sells their house?"

"I explained all that to the lieutenant."

"Can you explain it again?"

A sigh, much like his stepmother's. "So long as they lived in a principal residence long enough, the net equity from the transaction is protected from taxes up to a certain point. And Dad said he didn't care about the surplus profit. He'd rather pay the capital gains hit on it so he could start his new life as," a tilt of the head toward the driveway, "an RV nomad."

Tess said, "And if one of the spouses dies before the sale?"

"Then the survivor gets a 'stepped-up basis,' all the way to the fair-market value of the deceased spouse's half of the property as of the date of death, thereby saving sometimes hundreds of thousands in capital . . . ." The son looked from Tess to Hayes and back again. "Wait a minute. What are you saying?"

The lieutenant nodded, and Tess continued. "Given your new accounting business and student loans, office and apartment expenses, that house money you'd inherit without all the capital gains tax could come in very handy. Not to mention the proceeds from your father's sale of his medical supply company."

"Oh," from Odabashian, "this is really good stuff."

Steven Zederberg's face twisted. "Nanette?"

His stepmother blinked, and Tess could see a tear slide down the side of the woman's nose. "And if I had been here to die with Marty, you'd have gotten this 'stepped-up basis' from both of us, wouldn't you?"

"Nanette, how can you possibly believe—"

"Only," said Tess, "We don't think it happened that way."

Odabashian crossed his arms, nearly hugging himself. "Just better and better."

Tess looked toward the widow as she ticked off the facts on her fingers. "First, you're twenty years younger than your husband, and you didn't like the prospect of spending your prime and his money as a nomad in the camper. Second, your stepson, not you, volunteered the capital gains information to Lieutenant Hayes."

"Steven's an accountant. Of course he'd bring it up."

"Third, you were pretty quick just now to dump the 'hulking man' theory in favor of your stepson as the killer."

"This is—"

"Fourth, you were alone with your husband in this house before he died, and you found the body all by yourself. Fifth, you were a nurse's aide, so you'd know about the I/M-Print procedure. Sixth, the hospital your husband was born in burned down, so there'd be no record of his I/M-Print, meaning we'd never be able to identify the print. A nice little piece of misdirection."

Tess watched Nanette Zederberg's complexion drain of color. "Seventh, you wanted the decedent cremated, despite him being terrified of fire all his life, and his son's desire to see his father buried."

Hayes said, "When we found your husband's body, the soles of his feet were bloody. Nothing more is going to happen at the funeral home before Cassidy here can take prints of his big toes."

Tess watched the son's features crumble in doubled grief as Nanette Zederberg began to curse and cry at the same time.

JEREMIAH HEALY, a graduate of Rutgers College and Harvard Law School, is the creator of the John Francis Cuddy private-investigator series and (under the pseudonym "Terry Devane") the Mairead O'Clare legal-thriller series, both set primarily in Boston. Jerry has written eighteen novels and over sixty short stories, sixteen of which works have won or been nominated for the Shamus Award. He served a four-year term as the President of the International Association of Crime Writers ("IACW"), and he was the American Guest of Honour at the 35th World Mystery Convention (or Bouchercon) in Toronto during October, 2004. Currently he serves on the National Board of Directors for the Mystery Writers of America.

The Devil's Acre

BY STEVE HOCKENSMITH

Urias Smythe
Smythe & Associates Publishing, Ltd.
175 Fifth Avenue
New York, New York

Dear Mr. Smythe:

I trust this letter finds you and your associates well. I can only assume it finds the lot of you mighty *busy,* as I have yet to hear your reaction to the book I submitted to you last month: *On the Wrong Track, or Lockhart's Last Stand, An Adventure of the Rails.*

Not that I am in the slightest impatient to have you get to it. Quite the contrary. Like a fine wine—or, to be more democratically minded, a jug of corn-mash moonshine—my book can but ripen with age. Though I could perhaps add that the public's interest in sampling said concoction might likely diminish as the events that precipitated its distilling recede ever further into the past. Even as dazzling an episode as the commandeering of a Southern Pacific express train fades with time, just as fine wine and moonshine alike eventually turn to vinegar.

But why point this out to you? As a successful publisher, you are no doubt well aware of the importance of striking while the (in this case, railroad) iron is hot. So I leave it to you to proceed at what I assume is your usual measured, deliberate, dawdling pace.

By no means rush yourselves on my account—or your own!

No, I write to you today not to urge undue (or due) haste in your reply. Rather, it's because, while my book has lain fallow, I have not.

As I mentioned in my last letter to you, based on sheer quantity of thrills, chills, and close scrapes, the heroes of your own *Deadwood Dick Magazine* and *Billy Steele: Boy Detective* seem like elderly shut-in spinsters compared to my brother and myself. While ol' Dick or little Billy manage to get themselves into some kind of dustup each and every month, hardly a day passes without a new threat to life and limb for me and Gustav. Why, I'm sometimes reluctant to so much as get out of bed to make water for fear I'll be attacked by rampaging Apaches or kidnapped by pirates on my way to the privy.

As a case in point, allow me to relate the latest near-calamity to befall us—a tale, incidentally, that I think would fit quite snugly in the pages of one of your magazines. *Jesse James Library,* say. Or, even better, *Big Red and Old Red Library.*

To refresh your memory, Big Red and Old Red would be me and my elder brother Gustav. We picked up our nicknames on the cattle trails we once worked as cowboys, though our handles have little of the drover's usual irony about them. A fat cowhand may be "Skinny," a thin one "Tubby," or a dumb one "Professor," but I am with no uncertainty about it *big.* Old Red's not old per se, having put in a mere twenty-seven years on this earth of ours, but he does tend to act aged, often coming across as crotchety as Methuselah suffering a flare-up of lumbago. As for the "Red," our hair accounts for that, it being . . . well, as you might assume, not exactly powder blue.

Having recently lost our jobs as Southern Pacific rail dicks (the railroad frowning upon the mislaying of company property, be it a coffee mug, a signal lantern, or—*ahem*—a locomotive),

Old Red and I found ourselves jobless, friendless, and near-penniless in the S.P.'s hometown: San Francisco. Naturally, we wouldn't be welcome at the Palace Hotel along with the Rockefellers and the Rothschilds and whichever other visiting fat cats might be on hand. So we ended up instead in the neighborhood known as "the Barbary Coast" . . . along with the sailors and the macks and the rest of the wharf rats.

Of course, the Coast has a certain reputation, what with its dance halls, deadfalls, footpads, floozies, and all-around atmosphere of iniquity. And it lives up to said reputation—or perhaps I should say sinks *down* to it. But once you've seen a pack of young drovers cut their wolves loose at the end of a five-month cattle drive, there's little in the way of wildness that can shock you anymore. Take Dodge City of a Saturday night, switch all the Stetsons to sailor's caps and derbies, and multiply the noise and chaos by a factor of four, and you'll get the Barbary Coast. We figured we could handle it.

We chose for our lodgings a rooming house on Pacific invitingly named The Cowboy's Rest. The *Cockroach's* Rest would have been more accurate, as we saw more *cucarachas* than cowpokes thereabouts. But shoddy and shantylike though the place might be, it offered several advantages as a base of operations, the foremost being (in my brother's mind) the cheapness of its rooms and (in mine) the cheapness of the drinks served in the saloon downstairs. The Rest is also a mere twenty-minute walk from the local office of the Pinkerton National Detective Agency, and it was there we intended to go as soon as the scrapes and bruises we'd collected during our brief run as railroad detectives had healed.

Old Red, you'll recall (assuming you've read my book by now and are merely in the process of securing the huge sums of money required to properly publicize its publication), had it in his head that he'd make a top-rail sleuth. He'd picked up this seemingly peculiar notion from the tales of the late, great Sherlock Holmes that have been appearing of late in the pages of one of your competitors. I say *seemingly* peculiar because, as it turns out, Gustav really does have a natural talent for detectiving . . . even if his attempts to prove it tend to end in disaster.

Come to think of it, they can *begin* disastrously, too—which was almost the case here.

When not sniffing around after an actual mystery, you see, Old Red likes to practice his craft on strangers, sizing them up for clues he can use to piece together the particulars of their lives. "Just got throwed out by his wife," he might say to me, nodding at a glum-looking gent with rouge on his cheek and a wrinkled shirttail hanging from his carpetbag. Or "Best lock up the silver when she's in to clean" as we pass a shifty-eyed woman in a maid's uniform—just before she veers off into a pawnshop, a muffled, metallic clinking coming from the bundle tucked under one arm.

It was with this pastime in mind that Gustav and I secured for ourselves a corner table in the barroom of the Cowboy's Rest the other day. My brother would sharpen his wits with observation and deducification, I would dull mine with steam beer, and thus we might wile away a pleasant afternoon.

And pleasant it was, too . . . right up to the moment someone got it in his head to kill us.

The someone in question was a fellow of the type the Frisco papers have taken to calling a "hoodlum"—a young, oily-haired hooligan wearing an oversized frock coat, a red velvet vest, a rakishly tilted felt hat, and a plain old-fashioned sneer. He'd been seated with a similarly slicked-up and scowly compadre a few tables over, and their hissy whispers and low, dark laughter had about them a most definitive air of skullduggery. This, of course, attracted my brother's undivided attention . . . so undivided, in fact, it eventually drew some attention itself.

"What's your problem, m________?" one of the hoodlums snarled, addressing my brother with a term your typesetters would no doubt refuse to put in print.

"I ain't got no problem," Gustav replied.

"You sure as h__ do."

The hood rose from his chair. He probably topped out at a mere five foot four . . . but when he whipped out his six-inch knife he may as well have been Goliath.

"Why you been staring at us, a____?"

"Look, friend," I cut in, "I can't speak for the a____ here, but *I'm* starin' at one heck of a big pigsticker. And frankly, I'd rather I wasn't. So why not put it away and let me buy you a beer, huh?"

"Shut up, c_______. I was talking to *him."* The young thug took a step toward our table, his glare locked on my brother. "Why the eyeballing? You some kind of g_______ copper?"

"Nope," Old Red said . . . and said no more. My brother may be a mighty slick thinker, but when it comes to talking there are times he's about as slick as flypaper. Not that it really mattered just then.

As the hood took another step toward us, his friend stood to join him. This second fellow was bigger than his buddy, and a gold band gleamed across one of his curled fists—brass knuckles. Maybe not quite so deadly as a knife, yet still a good sight more dangerous than the bare skin-and-bone knuckles we had to defend ourselves with.

Obviously, *slick* wasn't going to get us spit with these hombres. The only thing they'd understand was *rough.* So that's what I aimed to give them.

"All right, you stupid q_______-b________ z________s," I growled, coming to my feet. "You asked for it."

The hoodlums froze, looking confused. Apparently, they'd never been called q_______-b______ z_________s before.

I picked up my chair.

"Y'all might wanna clear out," I said to the only other patrons in the place—a pair of pea-coated sailors who sat leering at our little standoff as if we were the cancan dancers at one of the melodeons up the street. "There's gonna be an awful lotta wood and brain and such flyin' around here in a second."

The sailors scooted their seats back a few feet.

"Thank you." I pivoted and swung the chair up over my head, facing the hoodlums like a baseball batter awaiting the first pitch. "I do like to have me a little extra elbow room when I'm about to serve up a whuppin'."

"Put down the chair, Brother."

I peeked back at Old Red. Not only was he still in his chair, he sat so motionless he could have been mistaken for a piece of furniture himself.

"For a feller who prides himself on his powers of observation, you seem to be missin' something a tad obvious," I said. "Like, for instance, that those ain't fresh-picked posies them b_____s got in their hands."

"Oh, I ain't worried about them two," my brother said.

The smaller of the two hoodlums spat out a cackle. "You oughta be, f______."

"Nope. Y'all ain't gonna lay a hand on us." Gustav jerked his head to the left. "It's that scattergun makes me nervous."

"Scattergun?"

I craned my head around to get a better look over my shoulder.

There was our landlady, one "Cowboy Mag," standing behind the bar with a sawed-off shotgun in her hands.

"It might be pointed at you two, but still . . ." Old Red went on, talking to the hoods. "Them things got quite a spray to 'em. Never know who's gonna pick up a pellet when the buckshot flies."

"Ma'am," I said with a polite nod to Mag, and I set my chair gently on the floor and took a seat.

"Ha!" the thug with the blade barked without bothering to turn for a look himself. "Like I'm gonna fall for that!"

"Listen up, you *p*_____ *v*______s!" Mag boomed, and just in case she wasn't speaking loud enough, she let her shotgun get in a word, too—by thumbing back the hammers. "No h____ f_____s gonna l____ with my j___-y____ customers in my w_____ place. So you'd better t____ s______ your v____ r____s outta here . . . and you can go l___ your u___ g___s up your d____m _____s while you're at it!"

Now, we drovers might not be the worldliest fellows, but when it comes to cursing we're as learned as any man jack on this earth.

"Q___-b_______ z_______s" not something you'll pick up on any old street corner, you know.

For sheer width and breadth of filth, though, Cowboy Mag had me beat by a country mile. To be truthful, I didn't understand half of what the woman had just said.

Her intentions were clear enough, though: If those hoods didn't skedaddle, they'd soon find their "d____m _____s" filled with lead.

The hoods skedaddled—*pronto.*

"G_____," Mag chuckled as she put her double-barreled bouncer back beneath the bar. "That'll teach those t_____ h______s to p_____ around in my b____ m____."

(As I assume you have by now fully absorbed the flavor of conversation in the Coast, I won't bother with any more _____ s. Just insert your own d_____ or s_____ or some such between every other word and you'll be getting the talk pretty much as Gustav and I heard it.)

"Thanks kindly for the help," I said.

Mag leaned forward onto the bar. She was an oversized woman in body as well as spirit, and for a moment there it looked like her bosom was about to spill from her low-cut dress like twin pumpkins from a cornucopia.

"If I thought you two were coppers, it's *you* I would've run off," she said. "Cowboys, ain't you?"

"Ma'am," I said, "you are a regular Sherlock Holmes."

Old Red rolled his eyes . . . beneath his big white Boss of the Plains. We may have been spitting distance from the Pacific, yet he still insisted on dressing like we were moving cattle up the Chisholm Trail. And while I'd tried to citify myself with a cheap suit and a new bowler, I knew I couldn't pass for a slicker just yet—not with my Plains drawl and sun-darkened skin.

"Got a soft spot for punchers, do you?" I said to Mag.

"Ol' Mag's nothing *but* soft spots!" she roared back, giving her shoulders a shake that set her bosom to quivering like we were in the midst of a California earthquake. "But yeah . . . they don't call me "Cowboy Mag" cuz I'm crazy about *tailors.* Used to have hands coming through the Coast all the time, bringing cattle in from Monterey and Sonoma. Not so much anymore. Which is why I'm sō pleased to have a couple real buckaroos like yourselves around for a while. So . . . what brings you thisaway, anyhow?"

"Bad luck, mostly," I said, and I offered up a heavily expurgated version of our woes (the full tale being offered exclusively to Smythe & Associates . . . for the moment).

"So now you're broke, huh?" Mag said when I was done.

As "Would we be stayin' in this dump if we weren't?" struck me as more than a trifle rude, I offered up a simple "Yup" instead.

"Well, I can help you with that. Cowboys can always get work on the docks, you know. You're handy with knots and ain't afraid to work up a little sweat. Tell you what—"

Mag produced a stubby pencil from somewhere in her voluminous gray-black hair and began scribbling across the front page of that day's *Morning Call.*

"Just say Cowboy Mag sent you."

She ripped off a strip of paper and held it out to me. On it, I saw once I'd walked up to take it, were scrawled these words:

NO. 35 PACIFIC STREET—ASK FOR JOHNNY

"Feel like tryin' your luck as a deckhand?" I said to Old Red.

My brother shrugged. "I reckon I don't feel like starvin'."

I finished my beer with a gulp, Gustav took two to polish off his, and off we went.

Outside, the sky above was clear and blue . . . and the street below it crowded and befouled. Our little corner of the Coast was so jam-packed with dens of sin, folks had dubbed it the "Devil's Acre," and certainly this day it had every appearance of being one of Hell's more swarming quarters. Great herds of drunken men staggered from saloon to dance hall, dance hall to brothel, and then brothel back to saloon to begin the cycle anew. They paused only to piss, puke, or pass out, and no matter which it was they were likely relieved of their wallets in the process. For once, it was almost an advantage being flat busted, as the pick-pockets had little to pick from ours but lint.

It took us nearly a quarter-hour to slog through this quagmire of corruption to No. 35 Pacific Street, and in that time we laid eyes on more decadence and depravity than most Christians see in a lifetime. I wasn't sure exactly what to expect at journey's end—a union hall or shipping office, maybe. So when it turned out to be yet another dive drinkery, I was surprised less by this discovery than by my own naïveté. The natives wouldn't have stood for an actual place of work in the Barbary Coast. Why, it would be an affront to community standards.

"After you," I said to Old Red . . . which meant I was kept waiting on the sidewalk a spell, for my brother made no move to go inside. He just stood there staring at the entrance to that watering hole.

"It's called a 'door,'" I explained helpfully. "Folks put 'em in the sides of buildings so you don't have to climb down the chimney to get inside. Wanna give it a try?"

Gustav nodded at the saloon. It was a deadfall—an unlicensed groggery of the sort that so skimps on pretense it doesn't even bother having a name. You know it's a place for drinking simply because a steady stream of men stumble in drunk and stumble out drunker.

"Kinda seedy, ain't it?" Old Red said.

"As a watermelon. But that'd be about right for fellers workin' the piers, wouldn't it?"

"Them and certain others."

"You got a certain 'certain others' in mind?"

My brother shook his head. "Not *certain* certain, no."

"What is it, then? Your Holmesifyin' givin' you pause somehow?"

"Nope. Just my gut." Old Red turned to spit in the street, then squinted again at the door to the deadfall. "You know how there's *certain* roadhouses, *certain* ranches you hear whispers about. The ones the smart fellers ride around."

"Sure."

"Well . . ."

Gustav spat again—then reached up and tugged my bowler down hard over my ears.

"Hey!" I protested.

My brother leaned first to the right, then to the left, examining the back of my head.

"Naw, that won't do at all. Them little derbies ain't got enough brim to 'em."

"What in the world are you babblin' about?"

Old Red tilted my hat back so it rode up high on my forehead.

"Your hair," he said. "I'd try to hide mine, but that wouldn't do us no good with my moustache to give us away."

He scowled at me a moment, then nodded gruffly.

"All right. I reckon that just might work. It's a good thing we don't look much alike, aside from bein' redheads."

"Yeah, I thank the good Lord for it every day. Now you wanna tell me what you're playin' mad hatter for? Why's it so important to cover up my hair?"

"Cuz we ain't goin' into that there dive together."

"We ain't?"

"No, we ain't. I'll go in first and do me a little scout before askin' for 'Johnny,' whoever he is. Then you mosey in a little later and make like we don't know each other. If everything looks to be on the up and up, I'll take off my hat, and you can just come on over and introduce yourself But up till then, I want you hangin' back . . . just in case."

"Just in case *what?* Ain't nothin' gonna happen to us in a saloon in the middle of the day."

Gustav turned toward the deadfall again.

"We'll see what kinda day it is," he said grimly. Then he went inside.

I passed the next few minutes watching the half-clothed strumpets across the street try to entice passersby into their cathouse "cribs" for a little "fun." I'm not opposed to fun on general principle—far from it—but personally I don't consider a raging case of crabs to be a barrel of laughs. I was not tempted.

In any event, I reckoned Old Red didn't need much time for his reconnoiter: From the outside, at least, that saloon looked about as roomy as your average outhouse. You could probably scout the place out without so much as turning your head.

So soon enough, I was striding inside . . . and quickly realizing I'd been only half right. Sure, the place was small, with only five or six scattered tables, a bar barely the length of a couple coffins, and a ceiling so low it'd put splinters in my lid if I walked with too much spring in my step. But it was dark and noisy in there, too, and I needed a moment to get my bearings before I could even begin to look for my brother.

If ever there was a tavern intended exclusively for the use of bats and hoot owls, this was it, for it was hard to believe anyone else could be expected to navigate in such a gloom. I stumbled to the bar and ordered a beer from a man I could barely see, and when he plonked it down a moment later I found it more by sound than sight. My eyes adjusted to the murk as I worked on my beer, though, and after a few sips I spied Old Red. He was at the far end of the bar, on the other side of a dark-suited man so broad, squat, and round he could've passed for a pickle barrel. I assumed this was "Johnny," as he and Gustav were hunched over the bar together, sipping drinks and talking in low voices.

My brother's Boss of the Plains was still perched atop his head. I nursed my beer and did my darnedest to eavesdrop. Unfortunately, the boisterous har-har-harring of the other patrons—most of them foreign sailors, local drunks, or the hoodlums who made both their prey—drowned out whatever it was Old Red and Johnny were whispering.

After I'd been there maybe five minutes, tippling with the dainty sips of a society dame at a tea party, the bartender stopped across from me and shook a dirty finger at my glass. "You drinkin' that or waitin' for it to evaporate?" I scooped up my beer, poured it down my throat, and slapped a nickel on the bar. "Another, please."

The barkeep filled my glass from a froth-topped pitcher that was almost—*almost*—as grimy as he was himself.

"This is a bar," he snarled, putting the pitcher down hard. "You just want something to lean against, go find yourself a streetlamp." I nodded and took a healthy gulp of my fresh beer. (Well, freshly poured, anyhow. It tasted so stale I wouldn't have been surprised to learn it had come to America aboard the *Mayflower.)* As the bartender stalked away, I sneaked a peek to my right, hoping I hadn't drawn too much attention to myself by *not* behaving like a boozy ass. Johnny was turned away from me, toward Gustav, his wide back blocking my view. As for my brother, all I could see of him was his hat. He was still wearing it, that much I could tell, but the angle of it seemed odd. It was tilted forward, the brim almost in a straight line up and down, as though Old Red was hunched over the bar to read something—which I knew couldn't be the case, since he reads about as well as a catfish plays poker.

I was just about to lean back and try for a better look when the barkeep barked out, "Keys! *Keys!*"

I followed his gaze to a scratched-up old piano at the back of the room. A gangly, unshaven old-timer was drooping on a stool beside it, head on chest, eyes closed.

"Wake up, Keys!" the bartender roared. "Time to earn your keep!" "Yeah, come on!" someone shouted. "Play us a tune, Keys!" "How about 'Auld Lang Syne'?" someone else called out. Most of the customers roared with laughter. The rest—like me—watched with wary half-smiles as Keys blinked himself wearily awake and began dragging his stool around to the front of the piano. This was apparently part of some comical custom of the place, but the guffaws had a cruel edge to them, like the cheers at a bullfight.

The old man brought his long arms up over his head, held them there a moment, then crashed his hands down upon the keyboard.

He wasn't just banging away, though. He'd struck a chord—one with a low, ominous tone. He repeated it twice, loud and quick, then let it float there in the air like a black cloud.

Then came a ray of sunshine cutting through the gloom—a bright melody that echoed out of the piano ragged and off-tune yet still merrily—almost manically jaunty.

"London Bridge Is Falling Down."

There was more laughter, and a few men actually started to sing along. But the recital didn't last long. One quick run-through of the song and Keys was done. He dragged his stool back around to his resting spot, slumped against the piano, and closed his eyes.

As floor shows go, it was pretty pathetic. Certainly, the Bella Union and the other big concert saloons had nothing to fear from this place. Yet the performance brought down the house: Men were still clapping and stomping their feet even as the geezer slipped back into his slumber.

I glanced toward the end of the bar, thinking I might share a little eye-roll or shrug with my brother. But there was nothing to share . . . because there was no one to share it with.

Old Red was gone.

Johnny was leaning over to share a whispered word with the barman, and I could finally see around his stout frame just fine.

Yet all I saw was wall. I jerked my head this way and that, searching the rest of the room. In vain.

It had been all of a minute since I'd turned to watch Keys tickle the ivories (or give them a good beating, more like), and in that time Old Red had left somehow. Yet he couldn't have gone out the front door without walking right past me, and the back door was over by the piano—I'd have seen him leave thataway, too.

Now, my brother can be cantankerous, and I'll admit there have been moments I wished he'd just go away. But never had I ever dreamed he might actually up and do it—simply vanish without so much as a puff of smoke. So sudden was his disappearance, in fact, that I might have doubted my own sanity, worrying that this "Gustav" was a figment of my imagination much as my crazy Uncle Franz once befriended a potato he addressed as *"Herr Berenson."*

I quickly spotted proof that I wasn't loco, though—and that something foul was afoot.

When I glanced back where Old Red had been standing, I noticed that there were two half-full glasses on the bar next to big, burly Johnny. The barkeep picked one up, emptied it out beneath the bar, then began giving the glass a vigorous spit-shine with a filthy rag.

If my brother had heard the call of nature and slipped off to the w.c. (or, given the character of the place, the back alley), why would the bartender be cleaning out his glass? And if Gustav had simply elected to leave, why wouldn't he have collected me on the way out?

Which meant Old Red was gone, but he hadn't left. He'd been *taken.*

I looked down at the bartender's feet, leaning forward as far as I could without tipping head over heels and landing atop his brogans. Unlikely as it was, I had to make sure Gustav wasn't down there behind the bar trussed up like a beef ready for the brand.

He wasn't, of course. All I saw was a slop bucket, what looked like a tap handle (perhaps for the secret stock of *drinkable* beer squirreled away for specially favored patrons), boxes filled with assorted bottles, and—good information to have—a short-barreled shotgun just like Cowboy Mag's. It must be a regulation in *The Barkeeper's Handbook,* right between "Water down whiskey" and "No credit to cowboys": "Keep scattergun under bar."

The bartender caught me gaping his way and shot me a glower so sour he could have poured it out and sold it as lemonade.

I forced myself to smile.

"Don't worry about me, mister—I learned my lesson." I picked up my beer and splashed half of it over my tonsils. "Glug glug glug, right?"

The barman didn't bother responding, which was fine by me. What I needed right then was to be ignored. I had me some heavy-duty thinking to do . . . *fast.*

Of course, the person best suited to bust such a puzzle was Old Red himself, and I couldn't very well consult with him on his own kidnapping. And turning to the law wasn't an option. The Barbary Coast's a precarious place for policemen, and they usually don't go there at all except in squads of ten or more. I'd probably walk a dozen blocks before I saw a single cop.

Yet there was someone I could turn to, I realized, though he wasn't on hand, either: Mr. Sherlock Holmes. True, Gustav was the expert on Holmes, but he only knew of the man through me—I read him John Watson's tales of the great detective each and every night. Whatever my brother had heard about deducifying, I'd heard, too. It was just a matter of putting it to work.

I closed my eyes and dredged up Old Red's favorite Holmes quotes.

"It is a capital mistake to theorize before you have all the evidence."

Useless.

"Little things are infinitely the most important."

Useless.

"There is nothing more deceptive than an obvious fact."

Useless . . . and pretty danged silly.

"When you have excluded the impossible, whatever remains, however improbable, must be the truth."

Which might lead me to conclude that—as my brother could not have flown through the ceiling or dug down through the floorboards—Johnny and the bartender must have *eaten him* while I had my back turned.

Useless useless useless.

Unless . . .

I *had* turned my back, hadn't I? And why? To watch a sorry old sot flail away at a piano—because the barkeep told him to.

Keys's little routine might have been a distraction. But a distraction from what? He hadn't blocked anyone's view of either door. He'd just made a lot of noise.

So maybe it wasn't the sight of something he was covering up so much as the sound. The opening of a hidden door, perhaps, or the workings of some secret mechanism.

"Exclude the impossible," Holmes had said. All right. If my brother hadn't been taken out to the left or the right, that left only up or down. Maybe one wasn't so impossible after all.

I threw back my head to guzzle the last of my beer—and get a peek up at the ceiling over the spot where Gustav had been standing. There was nothing to see but rafters and cobwebs.

I put down my glass and dug a dime from my pocket.

"Shot of rye for the road," I said to the bartender. Then "Dagnabbit" as I let the coin slip betwixt my fingers. After bending down to retrieve my money, I took a good look at the floor at the far end of the bar.

When I stood up again, I was grinning—and gritting my teeth.

"Here you go, my good sir," I said with as much cheer as I could muster considering how much I wanted to pop off the barman's head like the cork from a bottle. I dropped the dime in front of him. "And you'll see no sippin' from me this time, I promise you."

Silent, scowling, the bartender thumped down a shot glass and sloshed it full of liquid the color of tobacco juice. Which was pretty much what it tasted like, too.

I tossed it down with one swiping swig and set the glass back on the bar.

"Keep the change."

I got no thanks. The barkeep just snatched up my shot glass, gave it a single swipe with his ratty little rag, and set it aside, ready for the next paying customer. He was drifting back toward his big buddy Johnny as I turned to go.

Heading for the door, I kept myself to an easy amble when what I really wanted to do was dash. It was torture not glancing back to see if Johnny and the barman were watching me—and maybe noticing the wisps of short-cropped cherry-red hair peeking out from under my bowler. But if little things *are* the most important, then even such a trifling show of nerves might be all it would take to arouse suspicion . . . and quash what slight chance I had of saving my brother.

I finally knew where he was, and I couldn't very well get there myself with a bucketload of buckshot in my back.

I managed to keep my gaze straight ahead.

The sunshine was blinding-bright when I stepped outside, but a few blinks and the ink spots disappeared. I set off down the street still keeping myself to a mosey, just in case.

Before I reached the first corner, though, I finally allowed myself that look over the shoulder. I saw drunks, chippies, and rowdies aplenty, but no sign of Johnny or the barman.

I spun around and hustled back toward the deadfall.

I didn't go inside again, though. Instead, I turned down a narrow alley that ran along the side of the saloon. A dozen quick strides brought me to an angled doorway jutting out from the building—the entrance to a storm cellar. I bent down and gave the rickety twin doors a cautious tug.

Locked. Bolted from the inside.

I paused to consider my options . . . and sighed when I realized how bad the best one stunk.

I knocked. Lightly, politely at first, then rougher when I remembered that nobody did anything politely in the Barbary Coast.

"Who is it?" a man called out from down below.

I chanced an answer, praying it didn't call for a brogue or falsetto or some other giveaway trait.

"Johnny."

"Already?" Muffled, shuffling footsteps drew closer to the door. "Bit early, ain't it?"

"So?" I grunted, hoping Johnny didn't have a lisp. The doors rattled.

I stepped back, rattled myself but knowing there was but one way to proceed.

"It's just that it ain't dark yet . . ." the man said.

The doors began to swing open.

". . . and we've only got four *EEP!*"

By the time he saw my face, my kick had almost reached his.

As Old Red is fond of pointing out, I manage to put my foot in my mouth pretty regular-like. This was the first time I'd ever put it in someone else's, though. It didn't go in far, of course. Just enough to send the man flying back into the cellar minus his front teeth.

I jumped down after him, giving him a toe to the stomach twice before he could so much as let out his first groan. He was a scrawny, grubby little fellow, and I might've felt bad about treating him so rough if not for what I spied piled up in the shadows farther back in the basement.

Men. Four of them, splayed out on a rotten old mattress directly below the lines I'd noticed in the saloon floor—the trapdoor.

From underneath, I could see the wooden slat that pulled out to drop it open and the jointed rods leading up through the ceiling, perhaps to that extra beer tap tucked away beneath the bar.

I didn't care about the *how* just then, though. It was the *who* that truly troubled me, for stretched out atop that mound of men was my brother, his body as limp and lifeless as the barman's rag.

I glowered down at the little fellow I'd just put the boot to and brought my foot up again without so much as thinking to do it. I can't even say what thoughts were in my head at that moment. It's as if there were no thoughts at all, just an explosion of red and black and a great, awful noise like the scream of a steam whistle. I'm not sure what I was about to do—stomp the poor pipsqueak to a pulp, I suppose. Certainly, that's what *he* assumed.

"No, mishter! Shtop!" he cried out, mush-mouthed with blood. "They ain't dead! I work for the Chicken!"

I froze with one foot hovering over the man's face, wondering if my first kick hadn't knocked something lose in his head.

"What are you talkin' about?"

"The Chicken—the *Shanghai* Chicken! Johnny Devine! Thish ish hish plashe! We're crimpsh, not killersh!"

I set my foot back down on the dirt floor.

"Crimps?"

The word tickled a memory of newspaper and magazine articles I'd read about the Coast. "Shanghai," too.

"You mean you aimed to sell them fellers off to crew sea ships?"

The little man nodded. "Jusht got an order from a Norwegian whaler. A dozen men jumped ship the shecond they made port, and they need replashementsh."

I stared hard at Gustav and the men beneath him, noticing only now the slight up-down of their chests and the raspy sound of ragged breathing.

"We jusht drug 'em. Laudanum in their drinksh. They wake up later with headachesh, that'sh all."

"Yeah, sure," I said, starting toward my brother. "Wake up on some leaky tub in the middle of the Pacific, you mean."

As I drew closer to the Chicken's victims, I noticed another pile in a darkened corner beyond them—a heap of a good two dozen *hats,* with my brother's white Stetson up top like the snow-cap on a mountain.

Then I saw the swollen purple bump on Gustav's forehead. Those headaches weren't brought on by laudanum alone.

I spun around just as the little crimp staggered to his feet and started toward me with his blackjack raised high.

"Thank you, friend," I said. "Now I don't have to feel bad about *this."*

"This" being a swift kick to the unmentionables followed by a roundhouse that flattened the man's nose and blew out his candle.

I left the crimp lying in Old Red's spot atop the stack of soon-to-be sailors. I wasn't happy about leaving those other fellows to the Chicken's not-so-tender mercies, but even so large a man as me can only manage so much dead weight at once, and acts of charity would only get us shanghaied all over again . . . or worse.

I toted Gustav home draped over my back, something that surely would've aroused a touch of curiosity just about anywhere else. This being the Barbary Coast, though, all I got was the occasional wisecrack along the lines of "Good thing *one* of you can handle his liquor!" By the time we were back in our room at the Cowboy's Rest, Old Red was starting to stir.

"You all right, Brother?" I asked once I had him stretched out on our bed.

Gustav's eyelids fluttered, then went wide. He pushed himself up to a sit, one hand pressed to his head.

"What the h___ we doin' *here?"* he groaned.

That's right: "What the h___ are we doin' here?" Not "Thank you, Brother." Not "How'd you find me?" Not "I owe you my eternal gratitude and will never give you guff again so long as I shall live."

"What are we doin'?" I said. "Well, you are sittin' up when you should be lyin' down. And me, I'm thinkin' I liked you better unconscious."

Old Red waved a limp hand at the war bags we kept piled up in the corner.

"Best get those packed up quick. We gotta go."

I started to ask "Why?" but didn't even make it through the "Wh—"

"Oh," I said. And I set to packing.

Not five minutes later, I was helping Gustav hobble down the stairs. Our clomping drew Cowboy Mag from her barroom.

"How about a little hair of the dog, boys?" she asked, friendly as can be—until she noticed the bags I was dragging behind us. Lickety-split, her smile spun around into a frown.

"Ain't no dog done my brother like this. It was a Chicken . . . and a snake," I said. "Speakin' of which, I been tryin' to remember— how'd you say you got your nickname again?"

Cowboy Mag planted herself before the door. With her plump arms and legs akimbo, she made quite a formidable roadblock.

"Don't think you're leavin' without settlin' up with me first."

"We wouldn't dream of it," Old Red said, his voice still hoarse and trembly. He gave me a pat on the back. "Brother, would you mind?"

"Certainly not."

And I propped him up against the wall, put down our bags, and truly settled accounts with ol' Mag.

Now, for the record, let me state that I have never struck a lady, and I never will.

Let me add, however, one obvious and important fact: Cowboy Mag was no lady.

With best wishes of (and hopes for) publishing success,
O. A. Amlingmeyer
The Cosmopolitan House (Hotel), Oakland, Calif.
August 8, 1893

STEVE HOCKENSMITH is the creator of mystery-solving cowboys Big Red and Old Red Amlingmeyer. The Amlingmeyer brothers first appeared in *Ellery Queen* in the story "Dear Mr. Holmes," and the Sherlock Holmes-worshipping drovers have returned to *Ellery Queen*'s pages three times since then. In addition, Hockensmith has completed three novels about their adventures. Thanks to the first, *Holmes on the Range*, Hockensmith was a finalist for the 2007 Edgar, Anthony and Shamus Awards in the Best First Novel category. The second (*On the Wrong Track*) was published in March 2007, and the third (*The Black Dove*) hit shelves in February 2008. Hockensmith is currently at work on a fourth Big Red/Old Red novel. Though he considers himself a Midwesterner at heart, Hockensmith currently lives in California's Bay Area. He shares his home with the perfect wife, the perfect daughter, the perfect son and a slightly imperfect cat.

The Instrument of Their Desire

BY PATRICIA ABBOTT

In 1931, my brother raised the money to hold on to our house by hiring out our older sister to a dozen men in town. Ronnie lay down with twelve men over a period of a few weeks that winter, saving us from the soup line, the poor house, the end of the line.

When the last man left her bed, Jim took the crumpled five and added it to the money in the Typhoo tea tin. Bills worn to velvet from the callused hands of the men of Coryell's Crossing. He placed the seventy-odd dollars in the same envelope our father put his goodbye letter in a few months earlier, resealing the envelope and placing it in the mailbox. He hoped Mother would think that Daddy, wherever he was, had found a way to pass along some money. Which was what happened the next day when Mother waved the bills triumphantly in our faces. She made the back payments on the house, cleared up an outstanding bill or two and filled the icebox.

Later that year, Mother got a real job in a hospital, and we took a step back from the precipice where we had teetered. I doubt it ever occurred to Mother that Daddy hadn't sent us the money. She'd often speculate aloud about the circumstances of his . . . gift, wondering what he had gone without to raise it. Later still, she wondered why he never sent another cent. Despite that disappointment, his single act of generosity made her soft on him, and whenever Jim said something harsh, she'd defend Daddy, reminding us of his sacrifice. Jim probably had to swallow down the truth, telling himself it was better she didn't know. How could he tell her that poor Ronnie had saved us?

Of course, I wasn't supposed to know either. Eleven-year old girls in 1931 weren't allowed to know about sex. But the booted feet of men tramping up wooden steps a few feet from my bed was difficult to disguise in a house the size of ours as were the noises associated with sexual intercourse. I should have been asleep when the visitors came, but I fought to remain awake, acting like some sort of sentry in my mind. And despite Jim's worried, "Hush!" it was the creak of foot on board rather than the deep voices of men that awoke me. I counted twelve visitors on the staircase that February, each one noisier than the last. In the morning, the tin with its growing booty told the truth when I reached inside Jim's nightstand to check it.

Jim and I never discussed what happened upstairs that winter, but it put both a bond and a wedge between us. Whenever I thought kindly about Jim's accomplishments over the following years, I would inadvertently harken back to 1931 and what he had done to Ronnie. But conversely, whenever I felt adrift from him, which happened often since our separations were so lengthy, I would rediscover the bond that sharing such a secret created, or I'd realize just what our fate would have been without the scheme he set in motion.

My memories were a child's though, and each passing year deepened the veneer, blurring the truth. Seventy years later, I'm hard pressed to separate what I remember from what I have invented or imagined. A particular scent, a scuffling noise, the color of the sky on a winter's day and I am back in my mother's bed listening with the sharp ears and faulty reasoning of childhood.

None of Jim's actions would have been possible if our mother hadn't taken a job sitting up nights with a dying woman across town. She was gone from dinnertime until early morning, putting our plates on the table with her coat already buttoned. She earned two dollars and fifty cents a night, considerably less than her daughter earned upstairs.

"Don't forget to put the plates away, Rose," she'd say to me each night when she left the house. "Dry them and put them in the cupboard." It saddened her to come in at breakfast and find the dishes still in the rack, the oilcloth on the table sticky with dried up food. "And don't forget to lock up," she'd remind Jim. "Desperate men pass this way after dark."

We'd both nod, taking another bite of our dinner. Before she could get out the door, Ronnie would chime in with her oddly formal, high-pitched voice saying, "And what should I do, Mother?"

"Keep an eye on the children," Mother told her every night. "You're the oldest, Veronica."

Ronnie would nod her head solemnly, looking to us for confirmation. She was seventeen that year, but couldn't read or write or tie her shoes. There were few programs for dirt-poor, retarded children anywhere in 1931, fewer still in a rural community. Children like Ronnie ended up in institutions for the feebleminded, the term used then. Ronnie had attended school for as long as the teachers tolerated her disruptions in their classrooms. Then, in about third grade, I guess, Mother and Daddy held a mock graduation one June, telling her she was now grownup and needed at home. After that, she stayed home nearly all the time; Mother fearing the stinging words and careless hands of other children would hurt her.

In some ways, Ronnie didn't seem that different. She could hold a conversation if the subject was simple and the questions direct, and she knew everything there was to know about flowers. She was neat and spoke clearly. Oddest of all was her ability to play the piano by ear, which she did every Sunday at church. My sister looked like an angel sitting on the raised platform, hands poised over the piano, and that was where the men in town grew a bit obsessed with her most amazing characteristic: her beauty. She was simply the prettiest girl any of us had ever seen. Neither Jim nor I were attractive at all. The tradeoff seemed fair considering her deficits.

As long as Daddy was around, no men came near our place. Our father wasn't particularly big, but he was unpredictable, and that gave him an edge in protecting both himself, and later, us. Men in town remembered peculiar skirmishes in his youth, times he had kept punching someone long after the fight was won, times he ambushed boys who thought he had taken their quips with good humor, and didn't want to provoke him. Myths surfaced that he wouldn't hesitate to bite off a nose or ear should the need arise. I remember him as remote, uneasy with hugs and kisses, preoccupied with how to earn a dollar from men who had none to spare. And he was a drinker, of course.

But once he left town, men began to come around. Most didn't realize Ronnie was retarded, and somehow such a thing meant less then. Low intelligence was not necessarily a fatal flaw in farm wives who spent their lives raising children, food and animals. Ronnie's handicap was apparent to anyone who spent time with her, but in church, the only place most people saw her, she was the picture of competence at the piano waiting for the minister to nod her cue to begin. None of us could take our eyes off her.

I don't think any of the men who made their way up our road that year intended any harm to Ronnie. But more than once the autumn before, Jim had come home to find a man hanging around, watching hungrily as Ronnie tended her mums or swept the porch. Once Jim came upon an out-of-work mechanic waltzing her around the yard, both of them out of breath with laughter. There were many men that year with nothing to do, men who hadn't had time on their hands since childhood and who only knew childish ways to fill it. But winter came finally, and once it grew cold, Ronnie stayed inside.

Over the last seventy years, I have spent countless evenings thinking about where Jim's idea of using Ronnie to solve our financial problems came from. I think Jim tried to find a job, called relatives in the area, tried to track Daddy down. Mother seemed incapable of doing anything, he said later. In retrospect, she must have counted on Daddy to return at some point and bail us out. That was why the money in the tin box a few weeks later didn't surprise her.

Sitting in church week after week, watching men's faces slacken or go tight when Ronnie walked up the aisle to play "The Old Rugged Cross," Jim must have believed the only solution to our problems lay in her desirability. Or perhaps it was Mr. Tyson, his high school English teacher, who spawned the idea. Certainly it was Charles Tyson I saw climbing the stairs that final night. Trying to put the pieces together in hindsight nearly drove me crazy, and Jim neatly avoided my attempts in later years to divine the whole truth.

Our town was small and even if the men who came to our house that winter meant to keep the secret, one of them did not. Sometime that spring, our family physician, Dr. Large, under the guise of a routine examination, told Mother that Ronnie was no longer "intact" suggesting rather firmly that she should be sterilized as soon as possible.

"She'll be carrying someone's child by autumn," he predicted dourly to our shocked mother.

The case of Buck v. Bell was only a few years in the past and the sterilization of retarded girls was a routine procedure. "Feeblemindedness" in the age of Social Darwinisn and eugenics was looked on harshly, with society seen as in need of protection rather than the afflicted individual. The state bore down on the poor, the sick, the injured putting them out of sight in many instances, rendering them impotent, helpless before its power. "It's your duty," Dr. Large continued, "to insure that another child with Ronnie's . . . deficiencies . . . isn't born."

The reverence of nurses for both doctors and their "scientific pronouncements" made Mother susceptible to Dr. Large's strong-arming advice. So Ronnie was spirited away one day on the pretext of a shopping trip and the procedure took place in a doctor's office in a nearby city. Mother never told Jim the specifics of the trip, but Ronnie, frightened of doctor's anyway, must have suffered. The men in our town had effectively punished their victim for their own weaknesses. All of them could shake their head at the wantonness of feeble-minded girls, looking at Ronnie with both pity and disgust.

She returned three days later, proudly holding a wicker birdcage with a salmon-colored canary in it, a lasting reminder to us, if not herself, of what she'd lost. The canary, Sweetie Pie, whistled "Life is Just a Bowl of Cherries" incessantly, a popular song that year. It was soon all any of us could do to listen to it.

When the four of us had settled back into the semblance of a normal life, and most of all when I was a little older, I began to blame Jim for much of what happened. Why had he embarked on such an extreme course of action without consulting anyone? Before I was old enough to ask, he left Coryell's Crossing suddenly, taking a job at the Navy Yard in Norfolk Virginia. A few engineering courses at the local college won him a position there, and he rarely came home afterward. The war, with its dependence on the "inventions" of men like Jim, put even more distance between us.

In 1937, an older man with grown children asked for Ronnie's hand. I was in high school by then and stood up for Ronnie at her wedding. Mother and I were both uneasy about it, fearing what a man might want from a girl (for she would always be a girl) like Ronnie, fearing her ability to be a wife. But Ed was a good man. He had some money and hired a woman to look after things in the daytime. Ronnie tended the garden, fed the chickens and played the piano he bought for her. If Ed ever wondered why no children came, he never asked. Mother remarried during the war, when she could finally divorce Daddy for desertion, and found some happiness of her own.

I became a teacher but never married. Good looks turned out to be more important than a high IQ to most men, but to be fair, marriage never interested me very much. I centered my life on my students, my books, and a long line of tabbies and was never the worse for my choices.

Jim and I rarely saw each other over the next sixty years. As I write that number, it seems impossible. But it's true. When he did come home, it was only for a day or two, and other family members always surrounded him, with Ronnie hanging on tightest of all. His only lengthy visit occurred when Ronnie died in the late 1970s. I was working my way up to asking him . . . something . . . the day of her funeral when someone—I forget who—commented on the advanced age of the attendees. "There's not a soul here under fifty," the friend of a relative observed to the small circle of mourners at the back of the room. We all looked around and saw the truth in her remark.

"The average age in this room is dead," a cousin added.

"Well, none of us had children." I said defensively. "For whatever reason." We all looked at our shoes for a minute.

"Rose never married," Jim finally said, his voice gruff. "And I married late—with the war and all." He cleared his throat. "Of course, there was no way we could allow Ronnie to . . . ." He said it regretfully, but with a finality that convinced me once and for all that it was Jim who went to Dr. Large about Ronnie. A queer, creeping cold crept up my spine at that moment, and I believed then that I could never forgive my brother. He had used our sister horribly and I felt like his accomplice in keeping the secret. It was bad enough he had used her to raise money, but unforgivable that he had exacted such a price when it was over.

• • •

Last week I decided it was time I called Jim. His wife died a year or so ago, and we were both alone. Only a few hundred miles separated us, a distance that didn't seem so large, but we hadn't met in nearly a decade, my first illness precluding my attendance of Betty's funeral. Since my doctor has assured me recently that I didn't have another decade, or even another year, I knew it was time to talk.

"It's me," I said when he picked up the phone. Ten years must have altered my voice because the pause was lengthy.

"Rose?" he asked finally. I could hear the weariness of age in his voice. "Rose," he said again.

"It's me," I repeated, my voice gruff with feeling too. We talked a bit—about family and friends, the events of the day. And then I told him about my prognosis.

He sighed. "I knew you wouldn't call just to talk."

"We never did have that find of . . . relationship." I've always hated that word.

"Sunday? After church?"

"How about the Sunday after?" I asked him. "Still driving these days?"

"If the Olds decides to start."

We agreed on the next Sunday afternoon, and I did all I could not frighten him with my appearance. I had my hair trimmed and curled, putting on my best dress with a care I hadn't exercised in months. I took an extra capsule from the prescription the doctor gave me and sat waiting quietly for my brother. Each time I heard a car turn down the street, I craned my neck, but it wasn't until the agreed upon hour that he arrived.

Holding the door open, I was heartened by his appearance. For a man in his mid-eighties, his color was good, his weight much the same. He was dressed in the pale blues and beiges my generation—or is it just the old—seem to favor. Certainly, he seemed destined to outlive me, and for that I was grateful. There would be one family member to mourn my death.

I showed Jim the garden, accepting his compliments on my lilies, the astilbe and bee balm, and after we talked about the few relatives still alive, we went back inside the house and I poured us an iced tea.

"Do you know what day it is?" I asked when we had both sat down.

He looked at me for a minute, and then nodded. "She's been dead—what—twenty-two years? And Mother's been dead thirty-five years, Daddy nearly forty. Did you ever think you'd know more people dead than alive?" he asked, rubbing his cheek thoughtfully. He put down his iced tea, gazing out the window where the twinkling yellow of the coreopsis framed his view.

"She didn't have such a bad life after all though. With Ed, I mean. Nobody expected much for . . . for girls like her in those days. She had her own home, her own piano, and nobody ever treated her shabbily."

I let it pass, watching a cardinal alight on the dogwood through the window just behind him. "Remember that damned bird she brought back from the city?"

Jim laughed, but there was no joy in it. "What song did it whistle?" he asked. "'On the Sunny Side of the Street?'"

"Life is Just a Bowl of Cherries. Sweetie Pie never learned another song. Too bad, too, the way that Ronnie loved music. She was probably hoping for duets."

"Your memory's as good as ever," he said, admiringly. "I wanted to throw a cover over its cage more than once."

Of course I remember every detail, I thought impatiently; my future was set in stone that year. I stabbed at his pain relentlessly, "Ronnie cried her heart out when that bird died."

Jim got up and opened the window wider. "Someone bought her a dog after that, right? Buster, wasn't it? A real junkyard dog, though I almost preferred his endless barking to that bird's eternal trilling." He unbuttoned the top button on his shirt. "Phew, it's gonna be a hot one! Why don't you have air, Rosie? You could put a unit in here for peanuts."

"I'd miss the smell of summer." He nodded as I hurried on. "Jim, what exactly happened that winter? The one after Daddy went away?" Awkward, but finally said. It was out in the open for us to pick at with our arthritic fingers. I eyed him furtively as he walked back to his chair.

Sinking back into his seat, he shook his head again. "I have nothing but regrets when I think back on that year."

"Can't have been easy to keep it to yourself all this time," I said feigning a sympathy I didn't quite feel.

"You won't think better of me after hearing the story. No matter what you think happened, it was worse." He looked at his wristwatch, comparing its time with the clock on my mantel.

"Two minutes slow," I told him. "And as to your story, anything is better to me than dying ignorant." I sat rigidly expectant in my straight-backed chair.

He nodded wearily. "I see you're playing hardball."

"Dying has some cachet then?"

"You think that's funny?" he asked scowling. Without waiting for my reply, he began. "Daddy left for good after I found him in Ronnie's bed. I unknowingly saw to it by walking through that door." Determined to show I could take it, I nodded, realizing then I had suspected it for some time.

"I'd wondered about it," Jim said echoing my thoughts, "He was so careless . . . so thoughtless, banging that headboard into my wall like it was a percussion instrument in the school band. Then pretending surprise that I'd heard them."

"Did Mother know what was going on?" The last quarter-century had taught us that mothers often look the other way, but I hated to think that of mine

"I doubt it. She was gone so much. I don't think she'd have tolerated . . . that, although she put up with pretty much everything else from him."

"Did you tell him to leave on the spot?"

Jim flushed. "No, I couldn't get a word out. Stood there frozen while he scrambled for his clothes. Fifteen was awfully young then, and Daddy could be so . . . crazy." I nodded, remembering how he could fly off the handle at the smallest thing. "Ronnie was naked, and Daddy didn't even try to cover her," Jim continued. "He mumbled some nonsense about Mother never being around when he 'needed' her. It was sickening." His lips puckered with distaste.

"So he left—when? The next day? Without saying anything?" I tried in vain to remember what his letter had said.

Jim nodded. "And a night or two later, I turned over to find Ronnie in my bed."

I shuddered involuntarily, and Jim turned his head. "I didn't touch her, of course. I was repulsed, but I tried not to show it. She could be very sensitive about things like that." I nodded. "All I could think was to send her back to bed, but she turned up the next night and the one after. I don't know if it was a game to her, or if she had grown used to the sex. Who knows what was in her mind?" He struggled with it. "She probably just liked the warm body in her bed. It could get pretty cold in that house."

"She didn't come to my bed," I reminded him.

"I should have told someone."

"Who could you tell?" I finally said.

"Right. Who could I tell?" He got up and began to pace. "Certainly not Mother."

"Mr. Tyson?" I guessed. He turned around startled, then nodded. "You always went to him with all your problems, didn't you?"

He laughed harshly. "Yes, I went to Mr. Tyson. All the kids with problems turned up in his classroom after school."

I nodded, wondering if every high school had a Mr. Tyson. Certainly the school where I spent forty years did—a Mrs. Philpot—but it was usually a man, and one the other teachers loathed.

"And he came up with the idea of finding men who would pay to sleep with Ronnie," I said rushing now to get the words out.

I didn't even realize I had said it aloud until I saw Jim staring at me, his face full of shock. "What men?" So Jim was still going to shade the truth, I thought angrily. There would be certain parts of the story that went unexplained. "I went to Mr. Tyson," Jim continued, ignoring my interruption, "and he agreed to come home with me to tell Ronnie that her behavior was inappropriate, or whatever the phrase was then. I had no doubt he could make her understand. He seemed omnipotent to me at fifteen."

"So you brought him home?"

He nodded. "You were in school, and Mother was out on a job. Mr. Tyson asked me to leave them alone, which made sense. I didn't want to hear what he said to Ronnie anyway, so I went out into the yard and fed the chickens or something. Then, after a bit—maybe fifteen minutes—I went back in."

"He hadn't harmed her?" I asked, dreading his reply.

"No," Jim said hesitantly and I saw from his eyes he was back in that front room. "Ronnie was already gone and Mr. Tyson was sitting on the couch."

"Probably scared her to death." I remembered Tyson as an ugly man, nearly trollish with impossibly red hair.

"He assured me he'd made some progress although 'feeble-minded girls' don't learn easily. His words. Then he asked about our financial problems."

"You told him about our debts?"

"I had a strange need to tell him everything, I'm afraid."

"Then how did it come around him seeing Ronnie alone again?"

Jim frowned. "It didn't come around to Ronnie, Rose. It was me he wanted."

"Oh, no."

He cleared his throat. "Wasn't a complete surprise. Overtures had been made in the months before. And when I told him about

Ronnie, suggesting that he come home and speak to her, it may have looked like . . . something else."

"You're being too easy on him." I said shuddering. "Children always think they bring these things on. They never do."

"I was used to his hand on my shoulder, a pat on my head. I had stopped flinching months earlier." I nodded. "When it was over that day, he placed a five-dollar bill on the table. I let it sit there until he started the car. Then I shoved it in my pocket. He came back again and again. Until I had the money for Mother. I forget how many times."

"Twelve," I told him. We were both sobbing quietly. Neither of us was good at it though, and we stopped as quickly as we started, looking at each other with tear-stained faces.

"He left little notes for me in my locker. Saying he'd be free that night. Signing them with his initials—in some ornate script. Like I might mistake them as notes from someone else." Jim shook his head. "He wasn't very good at it, the sex, I mean. It was always over quickly, with him looking embarrassed, anxious to get back to talking about a book he wanted me to read. Or a piece of music he'd heard. Sometimes he just wanted to hold me . . . for as long as I let him." He paused. "That was even creepier to me, not understanding the need for tenderness at fifteen."

"So it was you who saved us? All these years, I thought it was Ronnie."

"I put that in your head, I guess. Couldn't bear to have you know it was Tyson and me up there." Our eyes floated up simultaneously. We sat silently for a few minutes, remembering the events of that year. "Jim," I finally said, "then why did Dr. Large have Ronnie sterilized? Why did you go to him if she wasn't sleeping with men?"

"She continued coming to my bed," he admitted. "I could resist her advances, but someone else might not. She was alone in that house too much."

"So when Dr. Large saw she was no longer a virgin he suggested sterilizing her?"

Jim nodded. "He didn't once ask me who it was. I'm sure he thought it was some neighborhood boy. Or me. I still think it was the right thing for Ronnie. She could never have raised a child."

I wasn't sure about that but let it pass. "Well, you were right not to tell me, I guess. I don't think I would have understood any of it for years. I wonder what happened to him? Mr. Tyson."

"I'm sure he's dead."

"Then you never had the chance to even things up? To get your revenge?" I looked at him closely. He was examining the clock again. "He just disappeared? And then you took off too."

"I did even things up," Jim said, his voice shaky. I nodded hesitantly, afraid he'd say he'd murdered Tyson. "I kept all his—assignation notes, I guess you'd call them that—in that Typhoo tea can where I had stowed the money and when I was ready to leave a few years later, I handed them over to the police. All eleven of them." He shuddered a bit.

"Did they do anything? The police?" In those days, men were given more leeway than now.

"You know how things like this were dealt with back then. Or maybe you don't." He sighed. "They convinced me a trial wasn't in my best interest, that they would take care of it themselves—quietly. When I put up a bit of a fuss, they reminded that he'd probably done it again. With some other desperate kid." Jim took a breath. "And then I remembered seeing another younger boy following him to his car several times. I finally agreed to let them handle it. I think they probably did something pretty awful."

"They wouldn't just let him go on to another school."

"No. Anyway, I never saw Tyson again after that. The locker door in his classroom was hanging open the next day, all his things gone. Even the teapot he always kept on his desk, his books, the old blue cardigan he kept on the hook."

I shook my head. Jim, boy that he was, had driven off both men who threatened our family. We went along to dinner soon after, my brother and me, trying as hard as we could to pretend were like anyone else out to a Sunday dinner. We ordered wine, dessert and an after-dinner brandy. From the smiling and attentive service we received, I'm sure the waitress thought we were an elderly married couple out on an anniversary or a birthday, with children and grandchildren waiting our safe return before dark.

PATRICIA ABBOTT has published more than fifty short stories in various literary and crime fiction publications including *Murdaland*, *Plots with Guns*, *Pulp Pusher*, *The Thrilling Detective*, *Hardluck Stories*, *Spinetingler*, *Beat to the Pulp* and *Thuglit*. Her story "My Hero" won a 2008 Derringer Award and her story "A Saving Grace," (The Thrilling Detective) was included in *A Prisoner Of Memory*, an anthology of 2007's best crime fiction. She lives and works in Detroit, Michigan. Visit her at http://pattinase.blogspot.com.

Crossroads

BY BILL CRIDER

They hadn't killed anybody in three weeks. Roy Barker, for one, was getting bored.

"Let's go on back to Fort Worth," he said. He bounced up and down a couple of times in the back seat of the flathead Ford. "I'm tired of hicks and sticks."

Roy, Dub Dooley, and Jack Scratch had spent a lot of time in west central Texas lately, always on the move, passing through dusty little towns with names like Eden, Rising Star, Mullen, and Zephyr, spending the nights in Brownwood and Ballinger, drifting as far as Abilene and San Angelo, knocking over a hayseed bank now and then but never having any fun, at least not enough for Roy.

"They don't like us much in Fort Worth," Dub said, and he grinned.

Dub was the driver. He was thick-waisted and wide-shouldered, with muscles like steel cables. He had a high voice, almost like a woman's, not that anybody would ever mention that to him, not if they knew him. Roy had seen him break a man's back over a saloon chair once, just because he didn't like the way the man looked at him. It didn't take a lot to set Dub off.

"The cops in Fort Worth would just as soon kill us as put us in jail," Dub said. "Sooner."

A month ago, they'd robbed a bank in Fort Worth and killed a couple of guys, one of them the bank guard. Cops didn't like that kind of thing, but it didn't bother Roy any. Didn't bother Dub, either. Roy didn't think it bothered Jack, but Jack kept telling them it wasn't time to go back to Fort Worth, like he had something in mind, but if he did, he never said what it was.

"How about it, Jack," Roy said. He clasped his pudgy fingers almost as if he were praying. "What say we go back to Fort Worth, have us a little fun?"

Jack Scratch looked as if he needed a shave, but he always looked that way. He sat in the passenger seat, looked out the window at the brown, dry pastures.

"Not yet," he said without turning around.

Roy sighed.

It didn't do to get Jack upset. He didn't have a temper like Dub's, but if you got him upset, he'd take care of you, all right. Jack was the boss. They'd all agreed to that. There hadn't been any argument about it. They did what Jack said.

Roy settled back in the seat and shut up. It was hot in the car, and the wind coming in through the open windows didn't help any. Roy's shirt was sticking to him under his suit coat. He wished he had a beer, or anything cold to drink, even if it was just water, but he didn't see any stores around. He didn't see much of anything but flat brown land and cotton stalks sucked dry and turned brown by the sun.

The Ford wheeled on down the dirt road, dragging a roostertail of dust behind.

• • •

The old man sat with his chair tipped back against the wall of his little one-pump service station and store that was the only building at the crossroads. He wore a blue cotton work shirt and overalls faded almost white. The boards behind him were weathered gray where the paint had peeled off.

The sun had come up behind the building a couple of hours earlier, but the old man was still in the shade. He looked down the road and saw the kid coming.

This was the third day in a row the kid had showed up at just about the same time of morning. The old man had been more or less expecting him.

An armadillo ran out of a field of dead weeds and dried cornstalks where a scarecrow hung on a cross. Its clothes weren't much more than rags, and it had a rope for a belt. The old man didn't think it had scared any crows, but the corn crop had been so bad it didn't matter.

The armadillo stopped at the edge of the dirt road and sat still, looking like a ridged brown rock. It was almost as if it had been waiting for the kid. The previous day when the kid came along, a hawk had appeared out of nowhwere. It had swooped down from the sky and landed on the fence, and the day before that a jackrabbit had come loping up from somewhere or other. All of them had given the kid a good long look.

The old man didn't blame them. This was the kind of kid who bore watching. He'd showed up at the store with a pistol sticking in the waistband of his pants, pulling them way down on his hips. The pistol was an old M1911 that someone, maybe the kid's daddy, maybe not, had brought home from the war twenty years ago. What the old man could see of it was black and shiny, like it had been taken good care of.

"What you doin' with that gun," the old man had asked the first day. "You worried about desperay-does?"

The kid didn't crack a smile. He wasn't more than thirteen. The freckles across his face and the cowlick in his red hair made him look even younger, but he was big for his age.

"Not worried about a thing," he said. "Brought it with me in case a bear got after me."

There hadn't been a bear in that country in the old man's lifetime, and he doubted if there had ever been one. But the kid didn't appear to be funning him.

"I got me a nickel for a co' cola," the kid said. "You got one for sale?"

They had gone inside, where the old man's wife stood behind the counter near the cash register. That was her job, standing there and taking the money for cash purchases. She had a wooden chair that she sat in sometimes, but mostly she stood up so she could watch and make sure the infrequent customers didn't try to make off with a can of beans. She didn't say anything as the old man got the kid a coke from the red and white cooler. "Ice Cold" it said on the side, which was right because the bottles were kept on ice, mostly melted since the delivery the day before. The old man popped the cap off the coke in the opener on the side of the cooler and the cap pinged into the catcher.

"You gonna show Ma that nickel, or you gonna stick me up?" he said.

The kid reached in his pocket and brought out the nickel. The old man nodded at his wife, and the kid took her the coin. She looked at it and rang up the sale. The cash register dinged, and the drawer slid open. The old woman dropped the coin into a space in the wooden drawer, then shut it.

The kid walked back to the old man and took the coke. The old man went back outside and sat in his chair.

"He say anything to you?" the old man asked his wife that night. They lived in a couple of small rooms in back of the store.

"Never a word," she said. "Just drank down the coke and looked around at the stock."

There wasn't much stock to speak of. Nobody around those parts had enough money to buy much more than a candy bar every now and then, or a few groceries when they had to have something they couldn't grow for themselves. Wasn't much growing, though, what with the dry weather. Some people went hungry. More than a few.

"What you reckon he's doing here?" the old man said.

His wife shook her head. "I wouldn't know. I think he's the Martins' boy."

The old man knew about the Martins. So poor, they'd make church mice look richer than Ben Gump. They'd moved onto the old Fallon place a month or two ago. They never came to the store because they didn't have the money, and they must have known they couldn't get anything on the credit.

"Long as he's polite and don't bother us, I don't mind him coming by," the old woman said. "His money's good as anybody's, even if he does have a gun stuck down his pants."

"I guess so," the old man said, but he worried about it.

That was the way it had gone for two days now. The old man wondered where the kid got the nickels. Surely not from his folks, not if they were the Martins.

And then there was the pistol, but the old man didn't ask how the kid had come by it, and the kid didn't say. He just showed up with his pistol and his nickel, hung around like he was waiting for something while he drank his coke, and then left.

He was right on time this morning. He stopped and looked at the armadillo. The 'dillo looked back at him, then took off at a scoot. People didn't think 'dillos could run, but they could. Fast, too, and this one disappeared into the cornstalks as if he hadn't ever been there. The kid plodded on toward the store.

The old man shook his head and tilted the chair forward until its front legs hit the ground. Then he got up and went inside to get the kid his co' cola.

• • •

Dub swerved the car, trying to hit the armadillo that appeared out of the field and ran in front of the car. Dub didn't like animals that interfered with his driving. He missed the armadillo, but the swaying of the car tossed Jack and Roy around in their seats.

"Dammit," Roy said. "Be careful, Dub. You're liable to throw me out of this thing."

Dub half-turned his head so he could see Roy. "You trying to tell me how to drive?"

Roy was sorry he'd said anything. Dub was hot and touchy.

"I didn't mean to criticize," Roy said.

"You better not mean to."

Roy thought about how he'd like to punch Dub, break a few of his teeth or his nose.

"There's a store at the crossroads up ahead," Jack Scratch said, breaking up Roy's train of thought. "You can get yourself a cold drink there, Roy."

Roy knew the store would be there, just the way Jack said it would. Sometimes Jack knew things that he shouldn't have any way of knowing. Roy thought it was creepy, but he didn't say so. It didn't seem to bother anybody else.

"You want something, Dub?" Jack said.

"Wouldn't mind a co' cola."

"That'd be good," Roy said. His fingers twitched. "We gonna pay for 'em?"

"Sure we are," Jack said.

Roy frowned and started to say something, but Jack didn't let him. "I mean it. Mind your manners. We're just three law-abiding gentleman, enjoying a day in the country."

"Right," Dub said in his woman's voice.

Roy figured Dub didn't like the idea of having to pay for anything any more than Roy did, even if it was just a coke. They had guns, and they liked to use them. Out in this godforsaken country, there wasn't anybody to stop them. Except for Jack Scratch.

"There it is," Dub said.

Sure enough the store was just down the road a way. Roy saw it though a shimmering haze of heat. It looked like a half-strong wind would blow it over on its side.

"We're about out of gas," Dub said.

Jack told him to pull up by the pump, and Dub did. An old man came out of the store. He started toward the car, then stopped when Jack got out. Roy pushed the seat over and got out of the back, and Dub got out on the driver's side. They all wore black suits with the coats on so the pistols in their shoulder holsters wouldn't show.

"Fill 'er up," Dub said.

The old man blinked and swallowed a couple of times.

"Move it, old man," Dub said.

The old man swallowed again. Dub took a step forward.

The old man moved it. He walked over to the pump, removed the nozzle, and turned the crank to run the counter back to where the zeros showed.

The three men ignored him then and went into the store. It was lit by one small bulb that hung from the ceiling on a short frayed cord. The kid stood by the candy case, looking at the Baby Ruths and drinking his coke. The old man's wife was behind the cash register.

"Can I help you?" she said.

The kid looked up at her, then turned around as if he hadn't heard the men come inside. Maybe he hadn't, but his eyes widened when he saw them. Nobody said anything about the pistol stuck in his waistband.

"Can I help you?" the woman said again.

The men paid her no attention. Dub and Roy went to the cooler and opened it.

"You want a co' cola?" Dub said.

"They got a Dr. Pepper?"

"No, they don't have a Dr. Pepper. They got co' colas. You want one or not?"

"I want one."

Dub took two cokes from the box and closed the lid. He tossed one bottle to Roy and popped open his own.

Roy looked at the bottle, then at Dub. "You shouldn't have thrown it. It's gonna fizz all over me."

Dub didn't say anything. He drank half his coke in one swallow.

Roy walked over to the cooler and popped the cap off his coke. It fizzed out of the bottle and over his hand.

"Dammit," Roy said.

"You shouldn't talk like that in front of a lady," Dub said.

"Don't tell me how to talk," Roy said.

He was tired of Dub pushing him, tired of being afraid of Dub, tired of not getting to use his pistol.

"You going to do something about it?" Dub said.

"Yeah," Roy said, and he dropped the coke bottle.

• • •

The old man knew who was inside the store with his wife and the kid. The Jack Scratch gang. Couldn't be anybody else. He'd heard about them on the radio, how they were on the loose in West Texas. He didn't have a telephone, didn't know what to do.

He thought about the kid's pistol. He ran back to the store and jerked open the door.

Two of the men were facing each other with their own pistols out, their faces ruddy and twisted with anger. The screen door hit the wooden wall like a shot, and the men turned. Both of them fired at the same time. The old man flopped back outside. He looked surprised. The front of his shirt was crimson.

The woman screamed. Roy turned and shot her in the head. She fell down behind the counter. Blood spattered the tin cans on the shelf behind where she'd stood.

Roy laughed. His ears rang from the gunshots, but he was having fun and feeling good. Things had been about to get ugly, but they'd turned out all right, thanks to the old man, who'd taken Dub's attention away from Roy.

Trouble was, they'd probably gone and gotten Jack upset. He'd told them to mind their manners, and they'd killed two people. Jack wasn't going to like that.

Roy turned just in time to see Dub shoot Jack. Jack's .38 spun backward and broke a bottle of bleach. The strong odor of the bleach blended with the smell of gunsmoke.

Dub sprinted out the door. He jumped over the body on the ground and made a dash for the Ford.

Roy had two choices. He could run into the room where the old couple lived and see if there was a back way out of the place, or he could finish off Jack.

It wasn't much of a choice. Dub would be at the car by now, and Roy wanted a ride. Too bad for Jack.

Jack sat on the floor in a puddle of bleach. That wouldn't be good for his suit. His right hand was mangled, and blood dripped off his fingers into the liquid on the floor.

"Sorry, Jack," Roy said. "You know how it is."

Jack didn't answer. He looked at the kid.

The kid nodded, as if this was something he'd been waiting for. He pulled the .45 from his pants and tossed it to Jack as if it didn't weigh more than a bath sponge.

Roy watched as if it were all happening in slow motion, the slow arc and turn of the pistol, Jack's left hand reaching to snatch it out of the air.

The next thing Roy knew, Jack had shot him three times. After that Roy knew nothing.

• • •

The old man hadn't stopped the pump, but Dub didn't notice the gasoline overflowing onto the ground. He was too worried about Jack. He knew Jack would be coming after him, even if he'd been hit. Dub had shot to kill, but somehow he'd missed. He couldn't figure out why, and he didn't have time to wonder about it.

Dub turned the trunk handle and jerked the trunk open to get the Tommy Gun. It was bundled in an old quilt tied up with twine. Dub pulled at the bow knot in the string and flipped the edges of the quilt out of his way.

Instead of waiting for Jack to come for him, he whirled around and began firing. The heavy .45 caliber slugs tore into the building. They smashed straight through the weathered boards and sent splinters flying.

Inside the store cans and bottles exploded. Their contents

splattered the walls and the floor and glittered in the rays of sunlight that slanted in through the holes in the wall.

Jack and the kid lay flat, keeping their faces out of the bleach and trying not to breathe too deeply.

When there was a pause in the firing, Jack stood up. He went to the door. Dub sat in the Ford. He ground the starter as he tried to fire up the motor.

"Dub!" Jack said.

Dub looked through the passenger window. His face blanched. The starter caught, and Dub jerked the car into gear. His foot slipped off the clutch, and the motor died before the car had gone a yard. The pump nozzle came out of the tank and spewed gasoline across the ground.

Dub made a dive for the passenger seat where he'd tossed the Tommy Gun.

Jack fired three more shots, all into the Ford's back fender. The shots set off sparks that ignited the gasoline fumes. In seconds the car was burning, and flames raced over the ground where the gasoline had spilled.

Dub raised up and stuck the Tommy Gun out the window just before the car exploded. Hot metal rained down as Jack went back into the store.

The kid heard the car parts hitting the roof and saw Jack coming. The flames were right behind him, as if he were walking along a trail of fire. The old man's shirt was afire.

Jack tossed the pistol to the kid, who caught it easily and gripped it as if he'd been born with it in his hands.

"It's yours now," Jack said.

"Was mine before," the kid told him.

"Not like it is now."

The flames had reached the walls of the store, and they started to burn.

"There's an old hoopie out back," the kid said. "I don't know if it'll run."

"It'll run," Jack said. "Can you drive?"

"Never learned how."

"I'll teach you."

Jack held up his right hand. There didn't seem to be much wrong with it now. He bent over and picked up his pistol from the floor. He opened his coat and holstered the gun.

"You ready to leave?" he asked the kid.

The kid nodded, and they went through the store. The kid looked down at the old woman when they passed her. There wasn't much left of her face.

"Bother you?" Jack asked.

"Nope," the kid said.

The car was in the back of the store, just like the kid had said. It was an old Model A coupe, dark green and covered with dust. Jack got in the driver's seat, and the kid got in opposite him.

Jack fiddled with the gas valve and the timing lever. He pulled the throttle, worked the choke, and pressed the starter with his foot. The car cranked right up.

"Where we goin'?" the kid said.

"Everywhere," Jack Scratch told him, and the kid smiled.

Jack pulled the car away from the now flaming store just before the gas pump exploded. A ball of fire rose in the air, and the store burned like paper.

An armadillo sat and watched the car until it was swallowed up in a swirl of dust. Then he was gone.

BILL CRIDER is the author of more than fifty published novels and numerous short stories. He won the Anthony Award for best first mystery novel in 1987 for *Too Late to Die* and was nominated for the Shamus Award for best first private-eye novel for *Dead on the Island.* He won the Golden Duck award for "best juvenile science fiction novel" for *Mike Gonzo and the UFO Terror.* He and his wife, Judy, won the best short story Anthony in 2002 for their story "Chocolate Moose." His story "Cranked" from *Damn Near Dead* (Busted Flush Press) was nominated for the Edgar award for best short story. His latest novel is *Murder in Four Parts* (St. Martin's). Check out his homepage at www.billcrider.com, or take a look at his peculiar blog at http://billcrider. blogspot.com.

The Kim Novak Effect

BY GARY PHILLIPS

Here I was, running a sweet little hustle, not really hurting anybody, and yet I find myself strapped spread-eagle, chest down, across a piece of three-quarter-inch plywood plunked across two sawhorses. My pinpoint Oxford Raffaello shirt was in tatters. This gruff cornfed ol' boy in a cowboy hat standing behind me, ready to wail on my bare, bleeding back again with his heavy-buckled belt. The other ruffian leaned on a beam of the unfinished wall of the tract house. This one bopped his head to *The Best of Warren Zevon* playing on his iPod.

"'Roland the Headless Thompson Gunner,'" Leaning Man mouthed as Hat Boy took another chunk out of me. "Talkin' about the man . . ." He smiled, absently scratching his threadbare beard. He took another swig of his bottled water.

Hat Boy cocked back again like Roger Clemens goofy on the juice and let another one go. The leather sizzled on my flesh and the edge of the buckle dug another groove.

"Ke-Rist," I screamed into the gag tied around my mouth.

"He looks about primed," Leaning Man said, yawning. He straightened from the skeletal wall, wire conduits snaking through the holes cut into the framing lumber. He removed his earpieces and methodically wrapped them around his iPod. He then placed it carefully on a juncture of wood beams.

"Yeah?" Hat Boy said dubiously. "A few more love taps would make sure."

Eager bastard.

"He's got to be conscious when Bishop George gets here," Leaning Man pointed out. "That sonofabitch'll skin our hides if sugar lips here isn't conscious."

"I suppose," his compatriot agreed reluctantly. He wiped at his forehead with his forearm, the Vegas heat particularly stuffy inside the raw plywood shell of the house's second floor. Despite this, Leaning Man wore a bulky nylon windbreaker, shades, and a baseball cap.

We were in what the blueprints indicated was the master bedroom—the homes in development on one of the higher plateaus of Red Rock Canyon. On the other side of the ridge, down in the womb of a valley, was an eighteen-hole golf course I frequented. Beyond that was the tail end of Summerlin, this where my latest operation was bivouacked.

Leaning Man walked over and doused my back with what was left of his water. It wasn't much, but I was mutely thankful. Funny how things work out, I reflected, as we waited for the big boss to arrive. Less than two weeks ago, my golf game was improving, my off-shore bank accounts were fat, and I was in my office doing, with gusto I might add, the wonderfully preserved late-'70s sexpot Jerri Rocklyn. She of the *Ava of the Underground* WWII actioners, wherein each installment included heady doses of sadomasochism.

"Thank you, kind sir," she joked as we finished up. On the lower right cheek of that gorgeous Nautilus firmed butt of hers was the mole made famous in the photo layout the real Jerri Rocklyn had done for *Gallery*, one of the slick skin mags, back in '78. Looking dreamily from that image I gazed out of my office window, which offered a view of Rainbow Boulevard. Life sure was good.

Back in her clothes, Jerri sat on my desk crossing tanned, muscular legs. She lit a blunt and inhaled. Her real name was

Helen Hobart. She was thirty-six years old, originally from Redondo Beach, California. But for the escapade we'd just pulled, she'd been modeled to look like Rocklyn, whom she happened to favor.

"Do I really have to go back under?" she asked, blowing fumes and offering me a toke.

I took the joint, sampled it, then answered, "We can't have the mark spotting you at the craps table, now, can we?"

She sighed heavily, getting off the desk with a flourish, those marvelous gel-filled breasts of hers swaying hypnotically. "But I like this look. And so do you." She sucked in more smoke and put the joint on the edge of the desk.

I stepped forward and we kissed while she guided my fingers slowly along her leg. Momentarily lost in lust, I eventually got back on track. "Doc's ready to go, baby. And we've already agreed you can keep the tatas," I murmured as I nibbled her scented neck.

"But," she started, then didn't finish. She knew I couldn't force her to get re-cut. But she also knew it would mean the end of any future lucrative assignments if she insisted on keeping the Jerri Rocklyn look. For like me, Helen was addicted to those pretty little green ones.

"Fine," she said, giving me a last peck and sauntering out of my office after putting the dead blunt in her handbag. I checked my appearance in the mirror of my tiny private bathroom, making sure my hair was just so and my eyes weren't red from the weed. Then I opened the floor safe beneath the rug upon which sat a cylindrical glass case of sports memorabilia I'd pushed aside. I took out the acrylic-encased page from the 7/21/73 program book of the Braves versus the Phillies at Atlanta. I smiled crookedly, like Mel Gibson speaking at a synagogue, and put everything back in its place. Aluminum attaché case in hand, I left.

Not forty minutes later I was sitting across from retired dental-clinic king Eldon Dudley in the Blue Velvet Lounge on Bridger. In fact, there was a Dr. Dudley Discount Dental facility several blocks away on this street. His big smiling face, circa thirty years ago, beaming down on the abscess-plagued and broken-toothed citizenry from the 3-D logo.

"Wonderful," Dudley said, examining the inauthentic certificate of authenticity I'd laid on him. I was especially proud of the hologram work on that bad rascal. That lab in Taiwan knew its stuff. He picked up the encased program page again, savoring the item. On that date in 1973, Hank Aaron hit home run number 700 in his irrefutable quest to equal, and eventually surpass, Babe Ruth's home runs. Say what you want about Barry Bonds, Hank did it without 'roiding up, while also putting up with racist death threats from jealous crackers. Sure I was a con artist, but I could appreciate the real thing when it came along.

Scouring, as I do, antiques stores and estate sales, I'd chanced upon the actual program book from that auspicious day. The rest, faking Aaron's signature and the certificate, then working the network I'd established for high-end sports memorabilia, was simply reeling in the right fish.

"Okay," he said, sipping his cranberry juice. "You've got yourself a deal."

"This," I said, reverently touching the artifact, "is not only a wise investment on your part, but a legacy to leave your children."

He snorted. "My grandkids, maybe. 'Fraid my son and I don't see eye to eye," he lamented.

He was like that, regurgitating those clichéd homilies now and then. I said nothing, merely sat back, tenting my fingers as he wrote a check for fifteen grand. The waitress came by our table.

"Can I get you gentlemen refills?"

"I believe we'll settle up," I said, adding after the right pause, "Noreen, is it?"

Dentist Dudley looked up from his checkbook.

"Yes, it was my grandmother's name." She put on a neon smile and glided away in her skimpy outfit after laying the tab on us. Naturally I picked it up. Dudley stared after her.

"You okay?' I asked.

"Yes, uh-huh," he said, handing me the payment. "Was she our server originally?"

I hunched my shoulders. "Maybe her shift just started." I rose and said my goodbye, reassuring him once again about the timeliness and efficacy of his investment. I strolled out, sure that he was staring at the waitress named Noreen as I passed near her. She was earning her tips laughing politely at the inane *Girls Gone Wild* level of word foreplay of a couple of SC frat boys. I'm sure they were in Vegas to show us hairy-knuckled droolers how to party. I got in my platinum-colored 300, put on the factory air and a Celine Dion CD—what can I tell you, I actually like the way that broad belts out a tune. I drove over to the kitchen of a downtown casino to make a pickup. Then out to see my man.

Dr. Mathias Steiner was the cat you'd cast to play the Nazi doctor if you were of a mind to make another *Ava of the Underground* flick. He was about medium height, stocky, with good-sized shoulders even at his age. Apparently back in the day he wrestled at Dusseldorf U or whatever the institution in Germany he attended was called. He wore a pencil moustache, touched up his gray locks, and his fashionable rimless glasses stood in relief over his steel-blues. His hands were long like a pianist's, and it annoyed me to no end that his golf game was better than mine, even though he had a couple'a decades on me.

"I'll have Shauna call Helen. I'll schedule her for the day after tomorrow," he told me in the hallway of his cut shop after his new receptionist had buzzed me into the back.

"Where'd this one come from?" I said, meaning the new receptionist called Shauna. She was a statuesque hottie I took to be no more than twenty-four or -five. Once upon a time, Helen had been his receptionist.

Steiner took my elbow and guided me toward his open office. He liked nothing better than thinking about, touching, smelling, and pursuing women. He had an invalid wife. While he was a sucker for female flesh, he did right by the wife when it came to care and whatnot, so he wasn't a total ogre.

"Shauna Cheung. She's studying Economics and Nineteenth Century English Lit at UNLV." We were standing just inside his office and he gazed around the room as if worried his wife had planted a bug. "She made her college money with one of those Web sites where you watch her in the morning, rant about her boyfriend, feed the cat, and all that." The tip of his tongue wet the center of his top lip as he grinned. "Of course she did these tasks mostly in short nighties and silken underthings, earning quite a few male and female subscribers."

He tipped back momentarily on his heels as he conjured up those carnal cyber images in his head.

"You hint to her about our sideline?" I asked, conversationally. Her online thing struck me as someone who had a taste for larceny. Or maybe she was just a stone exhibitionist. Either way, she seemed to be a likely candidate.

"Not yet, but yes, she certainly seems prime material. There must be plenty of these bourgeois fools who have fantasies about the Asian goddess or Dragon Lady."

Steiner was a study in contradictions. He justified his arrangement with me as a way to strike back at the nabobs of convention and conformity. Going on about his patients, the vain, jowled men and the sun-aged, vodka-breathing blondes deluded they could defy gravity and time. Yet I also knew he was spiteful that he got the low-rent chin nip or outpatient tummy tuck, with the high-end work those vodka blondes wanted flying out to Beverly Hills to get done.

"Here you go," I said, laying the packet of blow on his desk. That was the item I got from my connection at the casino. Women weren't Doc's only weakness.

He put the dope away, relocking the drawer. Randolph Scott looked down on us from behind him. Steiner was also a movie cowboy aficionado, and had several such portraits—Glenn Ford, the Duke, Eastwood, and so on—tacked to the walls. All of them were autographed. I'd sold him his Ford. Hey, Western memorabilia brings in a decent buck.

"Noreen make contact?" We were walking back out of his office.

"Yeah," I said. "I still think it was too dead-on to use the name of his dead wife."

"We all want to believe that the second chance can be had," he said wistfully. "The heart forever overrules the intellect, does it not?"

I demurred. Since my research had shown the dentist was into mysticism, it did seem Dudley was more inclined to fall for the bit the more he glommed that this Noreen could be the spirit of his departed. This was the first time we'd done the Kim Novak this nose-on, and I hoped it didn't jinx the con.

Shaking Doc's hand in front of the receptionist, it looked like I was simply some sort of pharmaceutical salesman making his rounds. Which in a way was true. I gave her a nod and she returned that with a brief smile that could be interpreted a couple of different ways. Could be Doc had let on more than he allowed. Yes by golly, she was a candidate.

• • •

The slap across my face brought me out of my daydreaming and back into my current unpleasant situation.

"Got your attention now, asshole?" Hat Boy followed his question with a jab from his steel-toed boot into my chest. They'd untied me from the makeshift table and dumped me in a corner. A brief wind rippled the blue plastic covering the cutouts for the windows.

"The bishop will be here soon," Leaning Man said, pocketing the cell he'd been talking on. He crossed his arms and looked down at my pitiful form. "Then we'll get down to it, won't we, sugar lips?"

I feebly managed to give them the finger. Instead of knocking the crap out of me, which I expected, Hat Boy and Leaning Man laughed like they were watching a Chris Rock routine. Hell, why not? They were holding all the cards.

• • •

I know I should pace my intake. I am a doctor, for God's sake. Once I was in demand, and know more than some windshield-washing addict what this heavenly narcotic does to you physically and mentally. But the feeling it purveys, that, well, that is almost like sex itself, is it not?

I know too that as I sit here in the tomblike dark of my office, Wagner softly on my stereo, the hum of the thoroughfare beyond a desensitizing lullaby of normalcy, current matters are far from that. And yet a kind of throttle of inertia embraces me as I ingest more powder, my self-image that of the immigrant gangster Pacino played in that movie all those rappers sample. The cocaine gives me spine. The coke will give me the *eier* to reach for the pistol in my middle drawer should I need to.

This I must believe because I know my erstwhile partner in the doppelgänger enterprise is not a heroic man. I dip my head and partake of more of the powder. Mein Gott, it is an amazing substance. I wipe the residue from the rim of my nostrils and lick some left off the back of my index finger. I certainly don't mean to say that he is a coward. You can't be gutless and perpetrate the sort of bold swindles he pulls off. You have to project the veneer that reflects what the person you're taking wants to see, and he certainly has that.

But what am I to him? I, who used to be a surgeon and now create cartoon heart-shaped derrieres for the self-perpetuating, self-absorbed class. I have more coke and I wait. I could go downstairs and get in my Cadillac CTS with the temperature-controlled seats and the surround sound, the vehicle purchased from the profits I made doing my part, but where would I go? I am very comfortable in my newly obtained condo in nearby Summerlin. And really, as I have more coke and analyze it further, I am an asset, am I not?

Here I was, having driven to his office to tell him the important news I'd discovered about Shauna, anxious as I was not to speak on the phone. Cocaine makes one wary. But then spying that large one with the cowboy hat taking him away forcibly. The other one I couldn't see so well at the wheel of their car. Together those Macheaths will squeeze my name along with the other particulars of the operation out of him. What if they aren't giving him the works, and will simply offer him money? Or drugs. The judicious use of psilocybin or scopolamine, that would disorient him or create fright or paranoia and that could get him babbling as well.

Yet when he does give them my name, why would they give me the treatment? It would seem to me their boss would want to keep me in the picture, assuming he wants to keep the effort going. And why wouldn't he? Whoever was in charge of the hoodlums must be a man of means, a gangster of some sort, surely. Unless it was over a personal matter that he was taken away as he was. That might be. And if so, then all my worrying is unfounded, and I should cease my consumption. I will, just after this next line.

• • •

"You do have amusing qualities," Shauna Cheung said condescendingly. She set her margarita down on the pub table and fluffed out those raven tresses. "But why should I kick back anything to you or to Herr Doktor?" She put a finger up. "More than, say, the cost of getting the remodeling done, as you call it, and some sort of finder's fee? Though when you really think about it, why are you necessary at all?"

I pantomimed for two more drinks from the waitress in the faux-moll outfit. The third-floor game room in the Riverhead

Casino was called Nitti's. Leaning just so across the pool table, Shauna steadied herself and smacked the cue ball dead-on. She dropped her solid into the awaiting hole. I appreciated a woman who could work the stick. She walked to the short side of the table, eyeing her next shot.

"It's not just setting the job in motion that matters," I said. "But lining up the marks does take a certain specialty." That had come out more harshly than I'd intended. I couldn't let this chick get ahead of me. "But sure, you're right, you don't need me. Only, who's gonna soothe that old croaker sack's nerves when you're off playing slap and tickle with the mark? Riddle me that, Green Hornet."

"It's not hard to find a crooked cutter," she said. "Half of them are sniffing their Xylocain or whiffing their patient's panties . . . or want to."

The cue ball glanced off the solid seven and it spun on its axis but didn't have much trajectory. She left me with much of nothing on the table but I was cool. I positioned myself confidently. "You figure to branch out with my idea, that it?"

She smiled radiantly. "I'm not saying that, homeboy. I could see where you might be an asset."

"Now you're just jerking me to make me miss." I did anyway. My striped ball bounced off the padded corner.

She lined up her next shot. "No. But I was thinking this hustle could be a two-way thing."

"How you mean?"

"There're plenty of lonely widows, you know. Fact is, statistically, there's more older broads with some savings than older men." She let loose with her cue stick and, banking her shot, knocked in another solid.

"I'm not taking the denture-cream money from some gummy grannies. That is not what this is," I insisted.

"My bad." She gave me that smile of hers again, well aware that it got to me despite my anger. "The point remains, you're not tapping your market's full potential."

"Maybe that's where you come in," I suggested. "Lining up some of these beefcake boys for the work."

She seemed to consider that while she sunk her last solid. "Who knows? I might take a semester off and show you how to properly expand your operation." She pointed the cue stick at the middle pocket and put the eight ball away in a smooth stroke. "See you, champ."

I stood watching her walk away, allowing as she did a bit of a swing of those wonderful hips in those designer jeans. Yeah, Ms. Cheung was a real go-getter. And if I wasn't careful, she was going to run me like she did this pool game, and put me out of the picture.

• • •

"Really, you don't need to keep doing this."

"It's my pleasure to see that look on your face," I said.

She yawned and stretched on the bed. The diamond and white-gold pendant I'd just given her was resplendent against her magnificent bronzed skin. Noreen—and I understood she wasn't that Noreen, the woman I met in those days of want in Tulsa—pulled me closer from where I stood gazing down on her.

"How will I ever thank you?" she giggled, reaching for my boxers. Oh these modern women. I was glad I no longer wore the traditional undergarments. Much too much fuss to get out of. She laid back on the bed again, giving me an eyeful of that young and fit body of hers clad only in the frilly panties I'd bought her. What a self-deluding fool I was. How pathetic I must be to this gorgeous girl who could have her way with any of those snarling boys with their bunching pectorals prowling Vegas to satiate hedonistic desires. Yet here I was, a slave to my baseness.

"What's wrong, baby cakes?"

I sat on the edge of the bed and she snuggled close. "I'm not so gone that for one minute I would suppose you have real feelings for me," I began, touching her hair. "Sending orchids and chocolate bunnies to you at that bar and grill like some teenager."

I wiped a hand over my face. "Why did you agree to see me?"

"You have to stop doubting yourself, Eldon. I told you. Men my age have grown up playing video games, blowing up monsters and making it with digitally animated babes with balloon boobs. Salivating over how they can get a house like they've seen on *MTV Cribs* and a car featured on *Pimp My Ride*."

She kissed my far too rotund belly. "I was and still am flattered a man of your experience would find me of interest."

I grabbed her by the shoulders, tighter than either of us expected. "What if I'm crazy, Noreen? I know full well you aren't her, she died some thirty years ago. There's plenty of Noreens in this world, and no doubt a fair share in Las Vegas. And sure you favor her some, but she never had a body like yours or—"

I stopped myself, ashamed and excited all at once.

"She never did this, did she, Eldon?" She pushed me onto my back and demonstrated a technique, shall we say, I'd never experienced before in sixty-seven somewhat sheltered years. Then she had me reciprocate. Oh my. But I believe that's what the article I read in the *AARP* magazine advocated—to keep your mind active in the Golden Years, you should learn something new every day to keep sharp. Well I was a damn needle that night.

Afterward, as we got dressed for dinner, I asked her, "When you decide to leave me, do it quickly, will you? I've convinced myself I can take it easier like that, as if it were a gut punch, okay?"

"Why do you always talk like that? And why would I leave someone who is so kind to me?" She was combing her hair. As I'd noticed before, she didn't look in the mirror. I suppose I assumed all beautiful women regarded themselves, primed themselves for a night out. But then, what did I know of women such as this second-chance Noreen? She patted my cheek and gave me a look that rolled the tops of my socks.

Of course at dinner, like before, there were those who ogled, wondering just what sort of relationship we had. Her laughing at my shopworn attempts at humor and me grinning like Tom Sawyer must have when he tricked others into painting that fence for him. They were envious, I convinced myself. Here I was, not particularly handsome nor commanding, yet I was the one who'd struck it rich in Las Vegas. The Wheel of Fortune had spun in my favor.

The next day in my office, as I sat and admired my Hank Aaron prize, marveling at how that transaction had brought me such luck, my private line rang.

"Bishop George," I said upon hearing his voice. "How may I help you today?" I listened. He was concerned about my being with Noreen. Her age wasn't the issue. I knew that despite the public image he cultivated for business reasons, he still practiced plural marriage. I knew too that his third wife was seventeen. Mine and Noreen's age difference wasn't the issue. This call was of a more temporal nature.

"Oh, no, she has not made such an inquiry." I listened some more. Bishop Abel George rarely raised his voice, but he was persistent in his manner. "Yes, I understand she's just a cocktail waitress. What? Why would I do that, Bishop George? I've certainly not been very strong in our ward for some time, as you are well aware. But her being a gentile is of no consequence." He talked, then I said, "It's enough that we make each other happy."

I wasn't a child. I knew that answer wouldn't satisfy him. Indeed, I was quite aware of where his probing was going. Oh, I didn't know the exact details, but I knew that he would extract what he evaluated as his due from me. Hadn't he always?

• • •

That Mormon creep was scary. Good thing he just saw me as a stupid gold digger. He doesn't know I've done *Guys and Dolls* at the Rio, and was Big Nurse in *One Flew Over the Cuckoo's Nest* in summer stock. I know how to play my part. He couldn't rattle me, even coupled with his two bodyguards looking all fish-eyed at me.

Him asking all polite and slithery with his quiet voice and the way he leans in when he's sitting with his fancy cane and all. Eldon showed some backbone, though, talked up for me, for us, really. That must be kinda new 'cause that bastard gave him a stare, that's for sure. Getting it regularly makes a man strong.

Eldon was so ready for the picking, I knew my plan was going to work.

I straddled him one more time and made all the right sounds. Sorry Eldon, but you're just a means to an end. You and that clown who actually believed I was going to kick back a percentage to him like his other girls had 'cause this was his idea and he'd set the con up. Nothing worse than a bullshitter who started to believe his own BS.

• • •

"Are you familiar with the Mormon Cricket?"

If I could talk without spitting blood, I still wouldn't have answered. When the bishop arrived, Hat Boy figured to rack up extra points with his boss, and slugged me when I tried to rise from the corner.

"The Mormon Cricket," he continued, "is not in fact a cricket, but a katydid."

The bishop glanced down at his ostrich-skin boots, then back at my battered face. He sat near me, imperial-like in a folding chair, his large hand gripping his dark wood cane topped with a silver bird of some sort. "They are a large insect, though incapable of flight. They live in and on sagebrush and alfalfa, and I've seen them decimate fields of fragrant Black-eyed Susans and Morningstars. These abominations will even eat their own." He got a misty look in his pale eyes, then refocused on me.

"The first settlement's wheat was saved by gulls eating those damned insects," Bishop George said, glaring down at me like Odin used to mad dog Thor in those worn-out Jack Kirby comics I had. My only inheritance from a long-gone mother. Back when

I was in one of the several foster homes I'd supposedly been raised in.

"Do you not see the significance of that? Here you had birds, seagulls, that came from the ocean, from California, to save us in the desert in Utah." He pointed his gull-headed cane at me.

I couldn't muster a response. What did he expect me to do, convert?

"The spirit of Joseph Smith was with us then, as it is now."

"Your Jezebel took money from Eldon Dudley and then disappeared. This was some two hundred thousand in cash reserves he kept tucked away for necessities."

"I don't know what you're talking about." Yeah, that was pretty lame, but I wasn't inclined to give him the satisfaction that I was beaten. Not only had he caught me, but the chick I'd set up as the dentist's Noreen had skipped out on me as well. How sad was that?

Given his exertions at tanning my hide, Hat Boy was wiping his face with a handkerchief. He then gulped down some bottled water Leaning Man had passed to him. Bishop George, a tall sumbitch with a mug like a knot of wood and an Abe Lincoln jaw, smiled. That was gruesome. "You make money by setting up lonely, well-to-do men with women who purport to be their lost loves."

Mostly he was correct. I did background research on the marks like you do in any long con. But I didn't coach the women to be the dead wife or high-school sweetheart, endlessly drilling them with facts and dates. That kind of pretend the chump would see through in no time. The art of my approach was for the woman to remind the sucker of the dead wife or the girlfriend. There were other guys hyped on actresses from their teenaged days. Hell, there was even one mark, a software geekonaire, who had this crush on his junior-high teacher. So I had Steiner remodel Helen just enough to suggest her features and he was hooked. We took him for more than three hundred Gs in stock options he signed over to her to save her supposedly ailing son.

This setup included a child actor we hired to wheeze and sweat in a hospital bed. His stage mother desperate to get the kid a credit. People.

See I got the idea for the con watching this Hitchcock flick *Vertigo* on TV one night in a motel room in El Monte, laying low from a grift gone south. In the movie, Jimmy Stewart has it bad for Kim Novak, who reminds him of this other woman he couldn't save because of his fear of heights. Only of course it turns out Jimmy's being played. Kim is both women, the dead bit faked to draw him into a psychological trap of sexual obsession. And thus I created the Kim Novak Effect.

I figured the big dog here must have invested money in Dudley's clinics. I knew from my due diligence the dentist was a lapsed Mormon. "How'd you get to me if my girl lit out?"

Bishop George was smoking a cigarette in one of those old-fashioned cigarette holders. On him, it wasn't gay, just eerie. "Searching for the woman's trail, I worked backwards." He blew a stream of smoke into the still air. "The bartender at the Blue Velvet told me, for a hundred dollars, you'd gotten her hired there. Said he owed you a favor over some sort of misunderstanding. One I'm sure you engineered so as to have him in your pocket when you needed him." He tapped ash. "That put me on to you and," he spread his arms wide, "here you are."

"So what do you want?"

"I'm your new partner, partner. And you will pay back the money, with interest."

Shit. "That right?"

The bishop stood, poking my leg with the end of his cane. "Yes, that is so. You will continue to do what you do, the research and selection of the woman." He showed his blunt teeth. "I have no insight into the type of devious female you seem to be able to ferret out for this work. But I do have ideas on certain businessmen and politicians that we will go after."

"Wonderful."

"Get him cleaned up," Bishop George said to his muscle. Hat Boy made to snatch me off the floor but stumbled and then went to one knee, heaving.

"The hell," he said, and keeled over like a felled rhino.

Bishop George stared at this and Leaning Man said, "Let's go," to me. There was a gun in his hand.

"What's going on here?" the bishop sputtered, gaping at his goon. He squinted, pushing his homely face toward the hood. He started to laugh. "Very good. Very clever," he said.

We left the bishop in the unfinished room, methodically tapping his cane. Out in the dusk Leaning Man helped me into the late-model Mustang they brought me in, and we rode away from those unfinished two stories in a development where the bishop was one of several investors. At a motel on 93, near the Arizona border, Helen was waiting for us as we entered a room. She was still hosting her Jerri Rocklyn look. "Guess we've worn out our welcome in Vegas," she cracked, noting my condition.

Leaning Man had already removed the bulky coat and now his shirt, revealing the wrap and sports bra Shauna Cheung wore to hide her breasts. She scrubbed off her fake beard and the glue she'd used on her eyelids to make them temporarily rounder and less of her natural epicanthal fold.

I sat on the edge of the bed. "How'd you two work this?"

"The bishop was asking around about you once he got your name from Burt," Helen said. Burt was the bartender at the Blue Velvet. "This I learned from a girlfriend who works the VIP lounge at Caesars."

I looked at Cheung, who had stripped down to her underwear. I supposed that whatever she gave Hat Boy in the bottled water to knock him out, she'd done to the hood she'd impersonated. She'd worn some padding to give her quite obvious female physique more of a manly shape. Pointing at her I said, "You two already knew each other."

"Yep," Cheung answered. "We figured you and the doc needed watching."

That was horseshit. Neither of them gave a damn about me or that cokehead. They'd been setting me or Steiner up for something, only the bishop's intervention presented another opportunity. Plus, they let me take a beating to make me grateful when they got me out of it. They wanted me for something.

"We better get down the road." Helen was up and moving.

I could have split—or tried to, since I was sure Shauna didn't just wave around that pistol for show. I should have gone on and left these two scheming honeys to work their juju on some other sucker. But I was the dude who came up with this and damned if I was going to turn over my most lucrative swindle to them for nothing.

Turns out Helen had been scamming the Leaning Man, the real one, for a while. He was too young to know about Jerri Rocklyn, but was mesmerized by that rack she sported. That's why she'd tried to beg off getting re-cut. She'd recently learned from him that the bishop had a network of non-Mormon business and elected-official types he hobnobbed with, and not just in Nevada.

• • •

Relocated to swell Laguna Beach, California, Steiner modeled me to look just enough like the long-disappeared surfer son of a widow whose Frank Gehry-designed glass-and-stone pad overlooks the Pacific. I clip her toenails, make sure she takes the right meds at the right time, and give her back rubs with lotion that, well, let's just say often leads to other duties, if you follow my meaning. Ugh.

I couldn't run now anyway. My real name and face was on some kind of Homeland Security watch list thanks to the bishop. According to this bent-lawyer acquaintance of mine, this also put getting to my funds in the off-shore accounts iffy—at least for now, until I figured that out.

Hey, I know, the situation's somewhat reversed, but I'm also lining up some of the widow's male friends for the women to do their thing. So as I sat here on the deck of the old girl's house, as she napped from our rub-down session, I sipped a merlot and watched the sky turn orange. On the sound system Celine was singing about the Last Plane Out. And I dreamed of being on one some day, no longer trapped by the Kim Novak Effect.

GARY PHILLIPS spends an inordinate amount of time concocting plots for the tales of chicanery and malfeasance he details in various mediums. When he's not doing that, he's often smoking a cigar contemplating life and his lousy poker hands. His latest efforts include editor of the upcoming *Orange County Noir* anthology from Akashic, and *Cowboys*, a crime story graphic novel from DC/Vertigo. Please visit his website for more of his stuff at: www.gdphillips.com.

The Opposite of O

BY MARTIN LIMÓN

"Never the twain shall meet," a wise man once said.

He was referring to the Occident and the Orient, but as a criminal investigator for the 8th United States Army in Seoul, Republic of Korea, I can assure you that the two worlds often meet. Usually in harmony. Occasionally in conflict. And in the case of Private First Class Everett P. Rothenberg and Miss O Sung-hee, the two worlds collided at the intersection of warm flesh and the cold, sharpened tip of an Army-issue bayonet.

My name is George Sueño. Me and my partner, Ernie Bascom, were dispatched from 8th Army Headquarters as soon as we received word about a stabbing near Camp Colbern, a communications compound located in the countryside some eighteen miles east of the teeming metropolis of Seoul.

Paldang-ni was the name of the village. It clings to the side of the gently sloping foothills of the Kumdang Mountains just below the brick and barbed-wire enclosure that surrounds Camp Colbern. The roads were narrow and farmers pushed wooden carts piled high with winter turnips, and old women in short blouses and long skirts balanced huge bundles of laundry atop their heads. Ernie drove slowly through the busy lanes so as to avoid splashing mud on the industrious pedestrians that milled about us. Not because Ernie Bascom was a polite kind of guy but because he wasn't quite sure where in this convoluted maze of alleys we would find the road that led to the Paldang Station of the Korean National Police.

Above a whitewashed building, the flag of Daehan Minguk, the Republic of Korea, fluttered in the cold morning breeze. The yin and the yang symbols clung to one another, like red and blue teardrops embracing on a field of pure white. Ernie parked the jeep out front and together we strode into the station. Five minutes later we were interrogating a prisoner: a thin and very nervous young man by the name of Private First Class Everett P. Rothenberg.

• • •

Geographically, Korea doesn't sit on the exact opposite side of the Earth from the United States, but it's pretty close. Things are different here. People look at their lives and their relationships and their place in the cosmos through a different lens than people in the States do. For example, G.I.'s new in country see Koreans waving good-bye to one another but are puzzled when no one departs. Actually, waving the hand with the palm facing downward means "come here." So what looks like "good-bye" to an American actually means "hello."

Similarly, a Korean never says "no" to another person's face. Such a bald statement of negativity damages *kibun,* the aura of congeniality that envelopes human relationships. Instead, a polite Korean will answer "yes," meaning "yes, I'll think about it." So "yes," G.I.'s soon come to find out, usually means "no."

Children also have a different attitude toward their parents. You'll never hear a Korean child saying, "I didn't ask to be born." No matter how disaffected a Korean child is with his or her parents, they always give their parents credit for at least providing them with the opportunity to be born. An opportunity they see as being quite preferable to not being born.

We all know that in Asia elders are honored rather than ignored and that the past is revered as opposed to the future. But another difference that G.I.'s run into is two women calling one another "sisters." At first we believe that two women who work together and call one another "sister" are actually sisters. Sometimes we're puzzled that the two women don't look alike—one is tall and the other is short or one has a narrow face and the other has a round face—but having heard vaguely about the workings of genetics, we write that off as the occasional anomaly that happens within families. It is only later, after a G.I. becomes seasoned in the ways of Frozen Chosun, that he realizes that when two young women call one another "sister" they are actually referring to the fact that they are close—and often inseparable—friends. Conversely, when a G.I. stumbles across two young women who actually are biological sisters, they will most often refuse to admit to any relationship. Why? Because the family is considered sacred in Korean society, and a dumb foreigner, especially a know-nothing American G.I., has no business prying into the complex interrelationships of a Korean clan.

As if all this isn't confusing enough, there is also the language barrier. And then, of course, the biggest barrier of all: American arrogance. Our refusal to believe that foreigners have anything whatsoever to teach us.

• • •

"They were sisters," Private Rothenberg told us.

"Who?" Ernie asked.

"Miss O. And the woman she shared a hooch with, Miss Kang."

"Sisters?"

"Yeah."

Ernie crossed his arms and stared skeptically at Rothenberg. Rothenberg, for his part, allowed long forearms to hang listlessly over bony legs. The three-legged stool he sat upon was too low for him and his spine curved forward and his head bobbed. He looked like a man who'd abandoned any hope of receiving a fair shake.

"Didn't it ever trouble you," Ernie asked, "that the two women had different last names?"

Rothenberg shrugged bony shoulders. "I figured they had different fathers or something."

I asked the main question. "Why'd you kill her, Rothenberg?"

He tilted his head toward me and his moist blue eyes became larger and rounder.

"You don't believe me, do you?"

"What's to believe? You haven't told us anything one way or the other."

"I told them." He pointed to the three khaki-clad Korean National Policemen standing outside the cement-walled interrogation room. Their arms were crossed, fists clenched, narrow eyes alight with malice. Rays from a single electric bulb illuminated the interrogation room, revealing cobwebs and dried rat feces in unswept corners.

"What'd you tell the KNPs?" I asked.

"I told them I couldn't have killed Miss O."

"Why not?"

Rothenberg once again allowed his head to hang loosely on his long neck. "Because I love her," he said.

Love. The classic four-letter word. Ernie smirked. Virtually every young G.I. who arrives in Korea and finds his first *yobo* down in the ville falls in love. The U.S. Army is so used to this phenomenon that they require eight months' worth of paperwork for an American G.I. to marry a Korean woman. What with a twelve-month tour of duty, a G.I. has to fall in love early and hard to be allowed permission to marry. Why all the hassles? Simple. To protect innocent young American G.I.'s from the sinister wiles of Asian dragon ladies. At least, that's the official rationale. The real reason is flat-out racism.

"Where were you last night, Rothenberg?"

"You mean after curfew?"

"Yes. But let's start from the beginning. What time did you leave work?"

I dragged another wooden stool from against the wall of the interrogation room and sat down opposite Private First Class Everett P. Rothenberg. I pulled out my pocket notebook and my ballpoint pen and prepared to write. Rothenberg started talking.

Ernie leaned against the cement wall, arms crossed, and continued to smirk. The KNPs continued to glare. A spider found its web and slowly crawled toward a quivering moth.

• • •

Our first stop was the Dragon Lady Teahouse.

Miss O had worked here. And according to Rothenberg, she was the toast of the town. The tallest and most shapely and best looking business girl in the village of Paldang-ni. The front door was covered with a brightly painted façade; a replica of a gateway to an ancient imperial palace. The heavy wooden door was locked. Ernie and I strolled around back. Here the setting was more real. Piled cases of empty *soju* bottles, plastic-wrapped garbage rotting in rusty metal cans, a long-tailed rat scurrying down a vented drainage ditch.

The back door was open. Ernie and I walked in. The odor of ammonia and soapy water assaulted our nostrils. After a short hallway, light from a red bulb guided us into the main serving room. Wooden tables with straight-backed chairs covered most of the floor. Cushioned booths lined the walls, and behind a serving counter a youngish-looking Korean woman sat beneath a green-shaded lamp, laboring over heavy accounting ledgers. When she saw us, she pulled off her horn-rimmed glasses and stared, mouth agape.

I flashed my ID. Ernie found a switch and overhead fluorescent bulbs buzzed to life. The woman stared at my Criminal Investigation badge and finally said, *"Weikurei nonun?"*

No bow. No polite verb endings. Just asking me what I wanted. A Korean cop would've popped her in the jaw. Being a tolerant Westerner, I shrugged off the insult.

"What we're doing here," I said, "is we want to talk to Miss Kang Mi-ryul."

She touched the tip of her forefinger to her nose. Another hand gesture not used in the West. She was saying, that's me. I explained why we were here but she'd already guessed. She said, "Miss O" and pulled out a handkerchief. After a few tears, she calmed down and started to talk. In Korean. Telling me all about her glorious and gorgeous friend, the late O Sung-hee. About Miss O's amorous conquests, about the job offers from other teahouse and bar owners in town, about the men—both Korean and American—who constantly pursued her.

Miss Kang closed the accounting books and, after shrugging on a thick cotton coat, walked with us a few blocks through the village. It was almost noon now and a few chop houses were open. The aroma of fermented cabbage and garlic drifted through the air. Miss Kang led us to her hooch, the same hooch she and Miss O had shared. She allowed us to peruse Miss O's meager personal effects. Cosmetics, hair products, a short row of dresses in a plastic armoire, tattered magazines with the faces of international film stars grinning out at us. Then Kang told us that Miss O's hometown was Kwangju, far to the south, and that she'd come north to escape the poverty and straightlaced traditionalism of the family she'd been born into. When I asked her who had killed Miss O, she blanched and pretended to faint. But it was a pretty good act because she plopped loudly to the ground and a neighbor called the Korean National Police, a contingent of which had been following us anyway.

In less than a minute they arrived and glared at us as if Miss Kang's passing out had been our fault. One of the younger cops stood a little too close to Ernie and Ernie shoved him. That caused a wrestling match and a lot of cursing until the senior KNP and I broke it up.

So much for good relationships between international law enforcement agencies.

As we left, Miss Kang was still crying and two of the KNPs, God bless them, were still following us.

• • •

Camp Colbern wasn't much better.

Rothenberg worked in the 304th Signal Battalion Communications Center. Electronic messages came in over secure lines and were printed, copied, and distributed to the appropriate bureaucratic cubbyholes. Apparently, Camp Colbern had two functions. First, as a base camp for an army aviation unit, boasting a landing pad with a dozen helicopters and associated support personnel, and second, as a relay station for the grid of U.S. Army signal sites that runs up and down the spine of South Korea. When I asked the signal officers a few technical questions, they clammed up. I didn't have a "need to know," they told me.

"How do they know what we 'need to know'?" Ernie asked me. "This is a criminal investigation. We don't know what we need to know until after we already know it."

I shrugged.

Private Rothenberg had been a steady and reliable worker, I was told. A good soldier. He had no close buddies because his off-duty time was spent out in the village of Paldang-ni, apparently mooning over Miss O Sung-hee.

Ernie pulled a photograph from his pocket, one he'd palmed while we rummaged through O's personal effects at Miss Kang's hooch. It was of Miss O and Miss Kang standing arm in arm, smiling at the camera, in front of a boat rental quay on the bank of a river. The sign in Korean said NAMHAN-KANG, the Namhan River not far from here. Miss O was a knockout, with a big beautiful smile and even white teeth and a figure that would make any sailor—or any G.I.—jump ship. Miss Kang, by comparison, was a plain-looking slip of a girl. Shorter, thinner, less attractive.

And her smile didn't dazzle as Miss O's did; it looked unsure of itself, slightly afraid, wary of the world.

Atop her head, at a rakish angle, Miss O wore a black baseball cap. Using a magnifying glass, I examined the embroidery on the front. It was a unit designation: 545th Army Aviation Battalion, Company C. In smaller print on the side was a shorter row of letters. It took stronger light for me to make them out. Finally I did: Boson. I handed the photograph back to Ernie.

Ernie took another long look at the gorgeous Miss O and then slipped the photo back into his pocket. Something told me he had no intention of letting it go.

• • •

The air traffic controllers at the Camp Colbern aviation tower told us that Chief Warrant Officer Mike Boson was due in at sixteen thirty. Four thirty p.m. civilian time. Ernie and I were standing on the edge of the Camp Colbern helipad when the Huey UH-1N helicopter landed. As the blades gradually slowed their rotation, a crewman hopped out, and then the engine whined and the blades slowed further, and finally the co-pilot and then the pilot jumped out of the chopper. Chief Warrant Officer Mike Boson slipped off his helmet as he walked toward us and tucked it beneath his arm.

"The tower told me you wanted to talk to me," he said.

Ernie and I flashed our identification. I asked if there was a more comfortable place to talk.

"No," Boson said. "We talk here. What do you want?"

The chopper's engine still buzzed. The crewman and the co-pilot hustled about on various errands, all the while listening to what we were saying. Boson, apparently, wanted it that way. We asked Boson where he had been last night, the night of the murder.

"In the O Club." The officers' club here on Camp Colbern. "For dinner, a couple of beers, and then to the BOQ for a good night's rest." The bachelor officers' quarters.

"You didn't visit Miss O Sung-hee?" Ernie asked.

"No."

"Why not?"

Boson shrugged. "I don't run the ville when I have duty the next morning."

"You were scheduled to fly?"

"Yes. To Taegu to pick up the 19th Support Group commander. And then south from there."

"When did you hear Miss O was dead?"

"Just before I left out this morning. Everyone was talking about it."

"Did you realize you'd be questioned?"

"No."

"Why not?"

"Because I knew her, but a lot of other guys knew her too."

"Like who?"

He shrugged again. "I don't know their names."

We continued to question Warrant Officer Boson and he finally admitted that he'd spent more than just a few nights with Miss O Sung-hee and that he'd also escorted her and Miss Kang to the Namkang River the day the photograph Ernie showed him had been taken. They'd rented a boat and rowed to a resort island in the middle of the river and a few hours later returned to Paldang-ni, where Boson spent the night with Miss O.

"In her hooch?" I asked.

Warily, Boson nodded.

"It's tiny," Ernie said. "So where did Miss Kang sleep?"

For the third time, Boson shrugged. "I don't know."

"But she lived there, too, didn't she?"

"Yes. But every time I stayed with Miss O, she'd disappear. I figured she bunked with the landlady who owns the hooch."

"But you weren't sure?"

"Why would I care?"

We asked if he knew Rothenberg. He didn't.

"You don't know a lot of things," Ernie said.

Boson bristled. "I'm here to fly helicopters. Not to write a history of business girls in the ville."

"And not to murder anyone?"

Boson dropped his helmet and leapt for Ernie's throat. I thrust my forearms forward, blocked him and, although it was a struggle, managed to hold Boson back. The chopper crewman and the co-pilot ran over. I shoved Chief Warrant Officer Boson backward, they held him, and I dragged Ernie off of the helipad.

• • •

Night fell purple and gloomy over the village of Paldang-ni. But then a small miracle happened. Neon blinked to life: red, yellow, purple, gold. Some of it pulsating, some of it rotating, all of it beckoning to any young G.I. with a few dollars in his pocket to enter the Jade Lady Nightclub or the Frozen Chosun Bar or the Dragon Lady Teahouse. Tailor shops and brassware emporiums and drugstores and sporting goods outlets lined the narrow lanes. Rock music pulsated out of beaded curtains. A late autumn Manchurian wind blew cold and moist through the alleyways, but scantily clad Korean business girls stood in miniskirts and hot pants and low-cut cotton blouses, their creamy bronze flesh pimpled like plucked geese.

The women cooed as we passed, but Ernie and I ignored them and entered the first bar on the right: The Frozen Chosun. They served draft OB, Oriental Brewery beer, on tap. We jolted back a short mug and a shot of black market brandy, ignored the entreaties of the listless hostesses scattered around the dark enclosure, and continued on to the next dive. At each stop, I inquired about Miss O Sung-hee. Everyone knew her. They all knew that she'd been murdered brutally and they all assumed that the killer had been her jealous erstwhile boyfriend, an American G.I. by the name of Everett P. Rothenberg. But a few of the waitresses and bartenders and business girls I talked to speculated further. Miss O had Korean boyfriends. A few. Mostly men of power. Business owners in the bar district. But one of the men stood out. It was only after laying out cash on an overpriced sweetheart drink that one underweight bar hostess breathed his name. Shin, she said. Or that's what everyone called him: Mr. Shin. He was a dresser and a player and had no visible means of support other than, she'd heard, playing a mean game of pool and beating up the occasional business girl who fell under his spell.

"A *kampei,*" I said to her. A gangster.

She shook her head vehemently. "No. Not that big. He small. How you say?" The overly made-up young woman thought for a moment and then came up with the appropriate phrase. "He small potatoes."

In addition to buying her a drink, I slipped her a thousand *won* note. About two bucks. The tattered bill disappeared into the frayed waistband of her skirt.

• • •

When Ernie and I entered the King's Pavilion Pool Hall, all eyes gazed at us.

There was no way for two *Miguks* to enter the second-story establishment surreptitiously. It was a large open room filled with cigarette smoke and stuffed with green felt pool tables from one end to the other. Narrow-waisted Korean men held pool cues and leaned over tables and lounged against walls, all of them puffing away furiously on cheap Korean cigarettes and all of them glaring at us, eyes narrow, lips curled into snarls, hatred filling the air even more thickly than the cloud of pungent tobacco smoke. This pool hall wasn't for G.I.'s. It was for Koreans. The G.I.'s had their bars, plenty of them, about two blocks away from here in the foreigners' bar district. Nobody, not even the man who collected money at the entranceway, wanted us here.

Ernie snarled back. "Screw you too," he whispered.

"Steady," I replied.

In Korean, I spoke to the bald-headed man collecting the fees. "Mr. Shin?" I asked. *"Odiso?"* Where is he?

The man looked blankly at me. Then he turned to the men in the pool hall. From somewhere toward the back, a radio hissed and a Korean female singer warbled a rueful note. I said again, louder this time, "Mr. Shin."

The snarls turned to grimaces of disdain. Korean cuss words floated our way. A few men laughed. More of them turned away from us, lifting their cues, returning their attention to eight balls and rebound angles and pockets. Nobody came forward. Nobody would tell us who Mr. Shin was or, more importantly, where to find him.

Ernie and I turned and walked back down the stairway. At the next pool hall, we repeated the same procedure. With the same result.

• • •

Later that night, we stood at the spot where Miss O had been murdered.

The site was located atop a hill overlooking both Paldang-ni and Camp Colbern. On the opposite side of the hill, to the north, moonlight shone down on the sinuous flow of the Namhan River. One or two boats drifted in the distance. Fishermen on their way home to straw-thatched huts. On the peak of the hill stood a tile-roofed shrine with a stone foundation and an enormous brass bell hanging from sturdy rafters. No one was there now, but I imagined that periodically Buddhist monks walked up the well-worn path to sound the ancient-looking bell.

"When did they find her?" Ernie asked.

I pulled out a penlight to read my tattered notebook.

"Zero five hundred this morning," I said. "Just before dawn. By two Buddhist monks who came up here to say their morning prayers. She was lying right here."

I pointed at the far edge of the stone foundation, nearest the river.

"Stabbed in the back once," I continued. "And then four or five times in the chest. She bled to death."

"And the murder weapon?"

"Never found. The KNPs assume it was a bayonet for two reasons. The size and depth of the entry wounds and the fact that Rothenberg, being a G.I., would've had access to one."

"His bayonet was found in his field gear."

"He could've stolen another one. Happens all the time."

"Or," Ernie replied, "the killer could've bought one on the black market."

I nodded. Ernie was right. The KNPs were taking a big leap in locking up Rothenberg. So far, they had no hard evidence linking him to the murder. Still, public opinion had to be mollified. When a young Korean woman is murdered, someone has to be locked up, and fast. Otherwise, the public will wonder why they're spending their hard-earned tax dollars on police salaries. Someone has to pay for the crime. Like the yin and the yang symbols on the national flag, harmony in the universe must be restored. Someone is murdered, someone must pay for that murder. Everett P. Rothenberg wouldn't be the first American G.I. convicted in Korea of something that there was no definitive proof he'd actually done. But if that's the case, harmony will come to his defense. If there's little or no evidence proving that he did it, Rothenberg will receive a light sentence. Maybe four years in a Korean jail and then deportation back to the States. So far, no one—including me and Ernie—had any real idea who'd murdered Miss O Sung-hee.

Rothenberg's alibi was sketchy. After finishing the day shift at the 304th Signal Battalion Commo Center, he'd eaten chow, showered, changed clothes, and headed to the ville. At about eighteen hundred hours, he'd arrived at the Dragon Lady Teahouse. There, he'd sat in a corner sipping on ginseng tea while Miss Kang and Miss O Sung-hee worked. Miss Kang doing most of the actual serving and preparation. Miss O sitting with customers—

Korean businessmen, small groups of American officers—adding beauty and charm to their evening. Before the midnight curfew, according to Rothenberg, Miss O convinced him that she was too tired to see him that evening and he should return to Camp Colbern. He did. Since he returned to his base camp before the midnight-to-four curfew, the M.P.'s at the main gate didn't bother to log in his name. Lights were already out in the barracks. In the dark, he'd undressed, stuffed his clothes and wallet in his wall locker, and hopped into his bunk. None of the other G.I.'s in the barracks had any recollection of his arrival.

Ernie walked over to the bell and rapped it with his knuckles. A low moan reverberated from the sculpted bronze, like the whispered sigh of a giant. We started back down the trail. It was steep. Boulders and thick brambles of bushes blocked our way on either side. We stepped carefully, inching forward, watching our step in the bright moonlight.

"Why'd we bother coming up here?" Ernie asked.

As he spoke, the earth shook. Just slightly. As if something heavy had thudded to the ground. I looked back. I could see nothing except Ernie staring at me quizzically, wondering why I had stopped. Then two more thuds. One after the other. Shallower this time, as if something were skipping forward, becoming louder, rolling toward us.

It emerged from the darkness above Ernie's head, looking for all the world like a steamroller from hell.

"Watch out!" I shouted.

I leapt to the side of the trail and Ernie, not yet fully understanding, followed suit. He dove into a thicket of branches and I landed atop a small boulder and scrambled over it to the opposite side, away from the trail.

The noise grew deafening. One crash after another, and then an enormous metal cylinder flew out of the night, rolling down the trail, careening to the right and then left, barreling down the trail, and smashing everything in its path. It clipped the edge of the thicket and missed Ernie by a couple of feet. I crouched. The huge metal rolling pin crashed against the boulder and the cylinder flew over, only inches above my head. After it passed, Ernie and I sat up, staring at moonlight glistening off the cylinder. The careening monolith continued its pell-mell rush down the side of the hill, smashing an old wooden fence outside a small animal shelter and then hitting the shelter itself. Lumber flew everywhere. The cylinder kept rolling until it slowed and finally landed in a muddy rice paddy with a huge, sloppy *splat.*

"What the hell was that?" Ernie asked.

I rose slowly to my feet, checking uphill to make sure nothing more was coming at us. "The bell," I said.

"The what?"

"The bronze bell. Come on."

We ran back up the pathway. At the top of the hill, the shrine stood empty. Using my penlight, I examined the weathered ropes hanging beneath splintered rafters.

"Sliced," I said.

"With what?" Ernie asked.

"Can't be sure, but with something sharp. Maybe a bayonet."

• • •

Mr. Shin found us.

So did about five of his pals. Light from a yellow streetlamp shone on angry faces, all of them belonging to young punks with grease-backed hair and sneers on their lips.

"Why are you looking for me?" Shin asked in Korean.

We stood in an alley not far from the King's Pavilion Pool Hall Ernie and I had stopped in earlier today.

"Your girlfriend," I told him, "Miss O Sung-hee, was murdered last night. Where were you while she was being killed?"

Shin puffed one time on his cigarette—overly dramatically—and then flicked the flaming butt to the ground. Ernie braced himself, about one long stride away from me, his side to the Korean man nearest him. He was ready to fight. Five to two were the odds, but we'd faced worse.

"Not my girlfriend," Shin said at last, switching to English. "No more. Break up long time ago."

"How long?"

"Maybe one month."

A long time all right. "Miss Kang didn't mention your name to the Korean police. Why not?"

"She no can do."

"'No can do?' Why not?"

"She my . . . how you say? . . . sister."

"She's your sister?"

"Yes. Kang not her real name. Real name same as mine. Shin."

"So you met Miss O through your sister?"

"Yes."

"Why'd you break up with Miss O?"

Shin shrugged. "I tired of her."

I didn't believe that for a minute. Shin was a tough guy all right, and like tough punks all over the world there would be a certain type of woman available to him. Women who thought little of themselves. Women who, in order to build up their self-esteem, flocked toward men who were on the outs with the law. Men who they considered to be exciting. Korea, like everywhere else, had its share of this type of woman. But from everything I'd heard about Miss O Sung-hee, I didn't believe she was that type. She went for cops and attorneys and helicopter pilots. Men of power. Men of real accomplishment. Not men who were broke and hung around pool halls.

"She dumped you," I said.

"Huh?"

"Miss O. She think 'I no like Shin anymore.' She tell you *karra chogi.*" Go away.

Shin's sneer twisted in anger.

"No woman tell Shin go away."

Ernie guffawed and said to me, "Is this guy dumb or what?" He stepped past me and glared at Shin. "So you took Miss O to the top of the hill and you used a knife and you killed her."

Shin realized that he was digging a hole for himself.

"No. No way. I no take. That night, I in pool hall. All night. Owner tell you. He see me there."

Shin mentioned the pool hall owner's name because even he knew that nobody would believe the testimony of him and his buddies. I crossed my arms and kept my gaze steady on Shin's eyes. He was a frightened young man. And when he'd heard that Ernie and I were looking for him, he'd voluntarily presented himself. Both these points were in his favor. Could he have murdered Miss O Sung-hee? Sure he could have. But something told me that his alibi would hold up. Otherwise, he wouldn't be standing here anxious to clear his name. If he'd murdered her, he'd be long gone. Still, I'd check with the pool hall owner as soon as I could.

Ernie had his own way of testing Shin's sincerity. He stepped forward until his chest was pushed up almost against Shin's. Ernie glared at Shin for a while and then snarled. "Out of my way."

Shin seemed about to do something, to punch Ernie, but indecision danced in his glistening black eyes. Finally, he sighed and stepped back, making way for Ernie and me. Grumbling, his pals made way too.

• • •

We ran the ville.

Shots, beers, business girls on our laps. Ernie was enjoying the rock music and the girls and the frenzied crowds and gave himself over to a night of mindless pleasure. Me, I sipped on my drink, barely heard the music, and ignored the caresses of the gorgeous young women who surrounded me.

"What the hell's the matter with you?" Ernie asked.

I shook my head.

"Come on," he coaxed. "What could possibly be wrong?

We're away from the headshed, on temporary duty, we have a pocket full of travel pay, and we're surrounded by booze and bands and business girls. What more could you possibly want?"

"A clue," I answered.

"A clue?"

"A clue as to who murdered Miss O Sung-hee."

Ernie shrugged. "Maybe the KNPs were right all along. Maybe it was Rothenberg."

And maybe not.

When the midnight curfew came along, G.I.'s either scurried back to Camp Colbern or paired up with a Korean business girl. Ernie found one for me, and the four of us went to their rooms upstairs in some dive. In the dark, I lay next to the girl. Ignoring her. Finally, I slept.

Just before dawn, a cock crowed. I sat up. The business girl was still asleep, snoring softly. I rose from the low bed and slipped on my clothes, and without bothering to wake Ernie, I walked over to the Korean National Police station.

• • •

The sun was higher when I returned. After gathering the information I needed at the police station, I'd walked over to Camp Colbern. There, in the billeting room assigned to me and Ernie, I'd showered, shaved, and then gone to the Camp Colbern snack bar. Breakfast was ham, eggs, and an English muffin. Now, back in Paldang-ni, I pounded on the door to Ernie's room. The business girl opened it and let me in. Ernie was still asleep.

"Reveille," I said.

He opened his eyes and sat up. "What?"

"Time to make morning formation, Sleeping Beauty."

"Why? We don't know who killed Miss O, so what difference does it make?"

"We know now."

"We do?"

I filled him in on the testimony I'd received this morning from Private First Class Everett P. Rothenberg. When I finished, Ernie thought about it. "You and your Korean customs. Why would that mean anything to anybody?"

"Get up," I told him. "We have someone to talk to."

Ernie grumbled but dressed quickly.

• • •

We wound our way through the narrow alleys of Paldang-ni. Instead of American G.I.'s and Korean business girls, the streets were now filled with children in black uniforms toting heavy backpacks on their way to school and farmers shoving carts piled high with garlic or cabbage or mounds of round Korean pears. We passed the Dragon Lady Teahouse, and just to be sure, I checked the doors, both front and back. Locked tight. Then we continued through the winding maze, heading toward the hooch of Miss Kang.

What I'd questioned Rothenberg about this morning concerned his friendship with Miss Kang. How they'd both sat up nights in the hooch waiting for Miss O. But Miss O would stay out after curfew and then not come home at four in the morning and often Rothenberg had to go to work before he knew what had happened to her. But sometimes she'd be back early with some story about how she stayed at a friend's house and how they were having so much fun talking and playing flower cards that the time had slipped by and she hadn't realized that midnight had come and gone and she'd been trapped until after curfew lifted at four in the morning.

"You knew it was all lies, didn't you?" I asked.

Rothenberg allowed his head to sag. "I guess I did."

"But Miss Kang knew for sure."

"Yeah," Rothenberg said. "Miss O had a lot of boyfriends. I realize that now."

Private Everett P. Rothenberg went on to tell me that sometimes Miss O made both him and Miss Kang leave the hooch completely.

"She'd tell us that family was coming over for the weekend. And she didn't want them to know that a G.I. like me was staying in her hooch. So Miss Kang helped out, she took me to her father's home near Yoju. It was about a thirty-minute bus ride. When we arrived at her father's home they were real friendly to me. I'd take off my shoes and enter the house and bow three times to her father like Miss Kang taught me. You know, on your knees and everything."

"You took gifts?"

"Right. Miss Kang made me buy fruit. She said it's against Korean custom to go 'empty hands.'"

"And you prayed to her ancestors?"

"Some old photographs of a man and a woman."

"And you went to their graves?"

"How'd you know? To the grave mounds on the side of the hill. We took rice cakes out there and offered them to the spirits. When the spirits didn't eat them, me and Miss Kang did." He laughed. "She always told me that food offered to the spirits has no taste. Why? Because the spirits take the flavor out of it and all you're left with is the dough."

"Is that true?"

"It was for me. But I never liked rice cakes to begin with."

I stared at Rothenberg a long time. Finally, he fidgeted.

"Hey, wait a minute," he said. "If you think there was something between me and Miss Kang, you're wrong. Sung-hee is my girl. Miss O. I was faithful to her."

"You were," I said softly.

His head drooped. "Right," he said. "I was."

• • •

Miss Kang wasn't in her hooch.

"She go pray," the landlady told us.

"At the shrine at the top of the hill," I said, pointing toward the Namhan River.

Her eyes widened. "How you know?"

I shrugged. Ernie and I thanked her, walked back through the village, and started up the narrow trail that led out of Pal-dang-ni, over the hills, and eventually to the banks of the Namhan River. On the way, we passed the bronze bell. It still hadn't been moved and sat amongst a pile of rotted lumber.

At the top of the hill, we found her. She squatted on the stone platform of the shrine, just below where the bell would've been. Ernie walked up to her quickly, shoved her upright, pressed her against one of the wooden support beams, and frisked her. He tossed out a wallet, keys, some loose change, and finally an Army-issue bayonet.

Miss Kang squatted back down, covering her face with her hands. Narrow shoulders heaved. She was crying.

Ernie backed away, rolling his eyes, exasperated.

After she shed a few more tears, maybe she'd open up to us. I was about to whisper to Ernie to be patient when, behind me, a pebble clattered against stone. Ernie was too busy staring at the quivering form of Miss Kang to notice. As I turned, something dark exploded out of the night.

Ernie shouted.

For a moment, I was gone. Darkness, bright lights, and then more bright lights. I felt myself reeling backward and then I hit something hard and I willed my mind to clear. The darkness gave way to blurred vision. Ernie slapped me on the cheek.

"Sueño, can you stand?"

I stood up.

"Come on. He hit you with some sort of club and when I lunged at him I tripped on this stupid stone platform. He and Kang took off."

"Who?"

"Mr. Shin."

I followed Ernie's pointing finger. Fuzzy vision slowly focused. The early morning haze had lifted, and more sunlight filtered through bushes and low trees. In the distance, two figures sprinted down the pathway, heading back toward Paldang-ni.

"Come on!" I shouted.

"My sentiments exactly," Ernie said. "But watch out. She took the bayonet."

And then we were after them.

• • •

A crowd had gathered in the central square of Paldang-ni. It was like a small park, surrounded on either side by produce vendors, fishmongers, and butcher shops. No lawn, but a few carefully tended rose bushes were ringed by small rocks. Under the shade of an ancient oak tree, old men wearing traditional white pantaloons, blue silk vests, and knitted horsehair hats squatted on their heels and smoked tobacco from long-stemmed pipes. Groups of them gathered around wooden boards playing *changki,* Korean chess.

Halabojis they were called. Grandfathers.

One *halaboji's* horsehair hat had fallen into the dust. So had his long-stemmed pipe. Shin held him, his back pressed firmly against the trunk of the old oak. Miss Kang stood next to him, the sharp tip of her bayonet pressed against the loose flesh of the grandfather's neck.

"Get back!" she screamed at me in English. "We'll kill him."

I stood with my arms to my side. Ernie paced a few cautious steps away to my left. I knew what he was thinking. Could he pull his .45 and take a clear shot at Kang's head before she could slice the old man's throat? But at that distance, over ten yards, it would be risky.

"Put the knife down," I told Miss Kang.

"Go away!" she shouted. "My brother and I will leave Paldang-ni. We'll never come back."

A crowd of local citizens had started to gather. Their mouths were open, shocked at what they were seeing. Elders were revered in Korea, never abused like this. Mumbled curses erupted from the crowd.

"The KNPs are on the way," I said. "Put the knife down."

Of course I had no idea if the KNPs had been alerted, but they would be soon. Ernie was inching farther to the left, attempting to evade Kang's direct line of sight. I had to stall for time, before Ernie chanced a shot or Miss Kang decided that one less grandfather wouldn't be missed one way or the other.

"You had good reason for what you did," I told Miss Kang.

Her eyes widened. Perspiration flowed down her wrinkled forehead, forming a puddle beneath her eyes. "Yes," she said, surprised. "That's what I told my brother. I had good reason. Miss O made me do it."

People were shutting down produce stands now, running to the back of the crowd to stand on tiptoes to see what was going on.

Miss Kang kept talking. "She was using him."

"Who?" I asked.

"Miss O. She was using Everett."

She meant Private Rothenberg. "How so?" I asked.

"She tricked him. Took his money. Never slept with him. Only had fun, changing from one boyfriend to another. Making me leave my own room. Never paying her share of the rent. So I took Everett. I was nice to him. He met my family. He prayed at our grave mounds. He liked me."

Using her free hand, the one without the bayonet, Miss Kang wiped flowing perspiration from her eyes and stared directly at me. "He liked me. I know he did."

"But you talked to Miss O one night. Atop the hill at the shrine with the bronze bell. You argued."

"No!" Miss Kang shook her head vehemently. "We didn't argue. I told Miss O about everything she did wrong. She didn't argue. She agreed. She knew she was doing wrong. But after I told her everything and told her she should leave Everett alone, she laughed at me."

Miss Kang stood incredulous, lost in her own story. Lost in the memory of the unbridled temerity of the arrogant Miss O Sung-hee. "She said that she would take Everett's money and use him for as long as she wanted to and there was nothing I could do about it."

Shin looked about frantically, knowing that as the crowd grew his chance of escape grew less. He shouted at his sister to shut up. Her head snapped back toward him.

Ernie by now had the position he wanted, on the extreme left of Shin's peripheral vision. He reached inside his jacket and unhooked the leather shoulder holster of his .45. Miss Kang's head was bobbing around, while the old man leaned his skull backwards, trying to avoid the sharp tip of the bayonet that pointed into his neck. Tears rolled down the *halaboji's* face.

Maybe it was the sight of these tears that enraged the crowd most. Whatever it was, suddenly a barrage of garlic cloves was heaved out of the crowd. They smacked the trunk of the oak tree, barely missing Shin and the old man. Enraged, Miss Kang shouted back at them to stop. The crowd roared. This time it was a head of Napa cabbage that exploded at Kang's feet. She hopped. Ernie pulled his .45, held it with both hands in front of him. Still no shot. I took a couple of steps forward. Miss Kang swung the tip of the bayonet my way.

That was the signal for the crowd to unleash its rage. Amidst shouts of anger, more produce flew at Shin and the grandfather and Miss Kang. Garlic, persimmons, fat pears, even a few dead mackerel.

Then the enraged citizens of Paldang-ni surged forward. Ernie raised the barrel of his .45 toward the sky, holding his fire. I tried to run at Miss Kang, but a woman bumped me, and to avoid falling on top of her, I slowed. The entire mob pushed forward, some of them brandishing sticks, some hoes, some with nothing more than their bare fists.

For a second, Miss Kang held her ground. Her eyes were wide with fright, her bayonet pointed forward. But then, like a swimmer being drowned by a tidal wave, the crowd enveloped her. Shin screamed and let go of the old man and tried to run. He didn't get far.

Fifty people surrounded the old oak tree. Kicking, screeching, pummeling.

Ernie fired a shot into the air. No one seemed to notice. Rounding a corner at the edge of the square, a phalanx of KNPs ran across pounded earth. Wielding riot batons, swinging freely, they forced the crowd to disperse.

Only Miss Kang and Mr. Shin lay in the dust. Shin was hurt. His leg was broken—a compound fracture—and maybe an arm. I knelt next to Miss Kang Mi-ryul. Her nose was bashed in, the one she'd pointed to only yesterday. Also bashed in was her forehead and the side of her skull. Using my forefinger and thumb, I pinched the flesh above her carotid artery. The skin was still warm but the flow of blood, the force of life-giving fluid, had stopped.

• • •

Back at 8th Army I typed up my report. Private First Class Everett P. Rothenberg had already been released by the Korean National Police. Mr. Shin, the pool player, had been taken to a hospital and was recovering nicely, although he was facing hard time for the Korean legal equivalents of aggravated assault and aiding and abetting a murderess.

Miss O Sung-hee was scheduled to be buried by her family in a grave mound back in Kwangju. Miss Kang Mi-ryul, on the other hand, would be cremated. That's all her family could afford.

What they did with her ashes, I never knew.

MARTIN LIMÓN retired from U.S. military service after 20 years in the U.S. Army, including ten years in Korea. He and his wife live in Seattle, Washington. He is the author of *Jade Lady Burning* and *Buddha's Money*, which will be published in the Soho Crime series in 2009.

Patriotic Gestures

BY KRISTINE KATHRYN RUSCH

Pamela Kinney heard the noise in her sleep, giggles, followed by the crunching of leaves. Later, she smelled smoke, faint and acrid, and realized that her neighbors were burning garbage in their fireplace again. She got up long enough to close the window and silently curse them. She hated it when they did illegal burning.

She forgot about it until the next morning. She stepped out her back door into the crisp fall morning and found charred remains of some fabric in the middle of her driveway. There'd been no wind during the night, fortunately, or all the evidence would have been gone.

Instead, there was the pile of burned fabric and a scorch on the pavement. There were even footprints outlined in leaves.

She noted all of that with a professional's detachment—she'd eyeballed more than a thousand crime scenes—before the fabric itself caught her attention. Then the pain was sudden and swift, right above her heart, echoing through the breastbone and down her back.

Anyone else would have thought she was having a heart attack. But she wasn't, and she knew it. She'd had this feeling twice before, first when the officers came to her house and then when the chaplain handed her the folded flag that just a moment before had draped over her daughter's coffin.

Pamela had clung to that flag like she'd seen so many other military mothers do, and she suspected she had looked as lost as they had. Then, when she stood, that pain ran through her, dropping her back to the chair.

Her sons took her arms, and when she mentioned the pain, they dragged her to the emergency room. She had been late for her own daughter's wake, her chest sticky with adhesive from the cardiac machines and her hair smelling faintly of disinfectant.

And the feeling came back now, as she stared at the massacre before her. The flag, Jenny's flag, had been ripped from the front door and burned in her driveway.

Pamela made herself breathe. Then she rubbed that spot above her left breast, felt the pain spread throughout her body, burning her eyes and forming a lump in the back of her throat. But she held the tears back. She wouldn't give whoever had done this awful thing the satisfaction.

Finally she reached inside her purse for her cell, called Neil—she had trouble thinking of him as the sheriff after all the years she'd known him—and then she protected the scene until he arrived.

It only took him five minutes. Halleysburg was still a small town, no matter how many Portlanders sprawled into the community, willing to make the one and a half hour each-way daily commute to the city's edge. Pamela had told the dispatch to make sure that Neil parked across the street so that any wind from his vehicle wouldn't move the leaves.

And she had asked for a second scene-of-the-crime kit because she didn't want to go inside and get hers. She didn't want to risk losing the crime scene with a moment of inattention.

Neil pulled onto the street. His car was an unwieldy Olds with a souped-up engine and a reinforced frame. It could take a lot of punishment, and often did. As a result, the paint covering the car's sides was fresh and clean, while the hood, roof, and trunk looked like they were covered in dirt.

The sheriff was the same. Neil Karlyn was in his late fifties, balding, with a face that had seen too much sun. But his uniform was always new, always pristine, and never wrinkled. He'd been that way since college, a precise man with precise opinions about a difficult world.

He got out of the Olds and did not reach around back for a scene-of-the-crime kit. Annoyance threaded through her.

"Where's my kit?" she asked.

"Pam," he said gently, "it's a low-level property crime. It'll never go to trial and you know it."

"It's arson with malicious intent," she snapped. "That's a felony."

He sighed and studied her for a moment. He clearly recognized her tone. She'd used it often enough on him when they were students at the University of Oregon and when they were lovers on different sides of the political fence, constantly on the verge of splitting up.

When they finally did, it had taken years for them to settle into a friendship. But settle they did. They hardly even fought anymore.

He went back to the car, opened the back door and removed the kit she'd requested. She crossed her arms, waiting as he walked toward her. He stopped at the edge of the curb, holding the kit tight against his leg.

"Even if you somehow get the DA to agree that this is a cockamamie felony, you know that processing the scene yourself taints the evidence."

"Why do you care so much?" she asked, hearing an edge in her voice that usually wasn't there. The challenge, unspoken: *It's my daughter's flag. It's like murdering her all over again.*

To his credit, Neil didn't try to soothe her with a platitude.

"It's the eighth flag this morning," he said. "It's not personal, Pam."

Her chin jutted out. "It is to me."

Neil looked down, his cheek moving. He was clenching his jaw, trying not to speak.

He didn't have to.

Somewhere in her pile of college paraphernalia was a badly framed newspaper clipping that had once been the front page of the Portland *Oregonian.* She'd framed the clipping so that a photo dominated, a photo of a much-younger Pamela with long hair and a tie-dye T-shirt, front and center in a group of students, holding an American flag by a stick, watching as it burned.

God, she could still remember how that felt, to hold a flag up so that the wind caught it. How fabric had its own acrid odor, and how frightened she'd been at the desecration, even though she'd been the one to set the flag on fire.

She had been protesting the Vietnam War. It was that photo and the resulting brouhaha it caused, both on campus and in the State of Oregon itself, that had led to the final breakup with Neil.

He couldn't believe what she had done. Sometimes she couldn't either. But she felt her country was worth fighting for. So had he. He joined up not too many months later.

To his credit, Neil didn't say anything about her own flag burning as he handed her the kit. Instead he watched as she took photographs of the scene, scooped up the charred bits of fabric, and made a sketch of the footprint she found in the leaves.

She found another print in the yard, and that one she made a cast of. Then she dusted her front door for prints, trying not to cry as she did so.

"A flag is a flag is a flag," she used to say.

Until it draped over her daughter's coffin.

Until it became all she had left.

• • •

"I called the local VFW, Mom," her son Stephen said over dinner that night. Stephen was her oldest and had been her support for thirty years, since the day his father walked out, never to return. "They're bringing another flag."

She stirred the mashed potatoes into the creamed corn on

her plate. The meal had come from KFC. Her sons had brought a bucket with her favorite sides and told her not to argue with them about the fast food meal. She wasn't arguing, but she didn't have much of an appetite.

They sat in the dining room, at the table that had once held four of them. Pamela had slid the fake rose centerpiece in front of Jenny's place, so she wouldn't have to think about her daughter.

It wasn't working.

"Another flag isn't the same, dumbass," Travis said. At thirty, he was the youngest, unmarried, still finding himself, a phrase she had come to hate.

The hell of it was, Travis was right. It wasn't the same. That flag those people had burned, that flag had comforted her. She had clung to it on the worst afternoon of her life, her fingers holding it tight, even at the emergency room when the doctors wanted to pry it from her hands.

It had taken almost a week for her to let it go. Stephen had come over, Stephen and his pretty wife Elaine and their teenage daughters, Mandy and Liv. They'd brought KFC then, too, and talked about everything but the war.

Until it came time to take the flag away from Pamela.

Stephen had talked to her like she was a five-year-old who wanted to take her blankie to kindergarten. In the end, she'd handed the flag over. He'd been the one to find the old flagpole, the one she'd taken down when she bought the house, and he'd been the one to place the pole in the hanger outside the front door.

"The VFW says they replace flags all the time," Stephen said to his brother.

"Because some idiot burned one?" Travis asked.

Pamela's cheeks flushed.

"Because people lose them. Or moths eat them. Or sometimes, they get stolen," Stephen said.

"But not burned," Travis persisted.

Pamela swallowed. Travis didn't remember the newspaper photo, but Stephen probably did. It had hung over the console stereo she had gotten when her mother died, and it had been a teacher—Neil's first grade teacher? Pamela couldn't remember—who had seen it at a party and asked if she really wanted her children to see that before they could understand what it meant.

"I don't want another one," Pamela said.

"Mom," Stephen said in his most reasonable voice.

She shook her head. "It's been a year. I need to move on."

"You don't move on from that kind of loss," Travis said, and she wondered how he knew. He didn't have children.

Then she looked at him, a large broad-shouldered man with tears in his eyes, and remembered that Jenny had been the one who walked him to school, who bathed him at night, who usually tucked him in. Jenny had done all that because Stephen at thirteen was already working to help his mom make ends meet, and Pamela was working two jobs herself, as well as attending community college to get her degree in forensic science and criminology. A pseudoscience degree, one of her almost-boyfriends had said. But it wasn't. She used science every day. She needed science like she needed air.

Like she needed to find out who had destroyed her daughter's flag.

"You don't move on," Pamela said.

Her boys watched her. Sometimes she could see the babies they had been in the lines of their mouths and the shape of their eyes. She still marveled at the way they had grown into men, large men who could carry her the way she used to carry them.

"But," she added, "you don't have to dwell on it, every moment of every day."

And yet she was dwelling. She couldn't stop. She never told her sons or anyone else, not even Neil, who had become a closer friend in the year since Jenny had died. Neil, a widower now, a man who understood death the way that Pamela did. Neil, whose grandson had enlisted after 9/11 and had somehow made it back.

She was dwelling and there was only one way to stop. She had to use science to solve this. She couldn't think about it emotionally. She had to think about it clinically.

She had her evidence and she needed even more.

The next morning, the local paper ran an article on the burnings, and listed the addresses in the police log section. So Pamela visited the other crime scenes with her kit and her camera, identifying herself as an employee of the state crime lab.

Since *CSI* debuted on television, that identification opened doors for her. She didn't have to tell the other victims that she had been a victim too.

She took pictures of scorch marks on pavement and flag holders wrenched loose from their sockets. She removed flag bits from garbage cans, and studied footprints in the leaf-covered grass to see if they looked similar to the ones on her lawn.

And late that afternoon, as she stepped back to photograph yet another twisted flag holder beside a front door, she saw the glint of a camera hiding in a cobwebby corner of the door frame. The house was a starter, maybe twelve hundred square feet total. She wouldn't have expected a camera here.

"Do you have a security system?" she asked the homeowner, a woman Travis's age who looked like she hadn't slept in weeks. Her name was Becky something. Pamela hadn't really heard her last name in the introduction.

"My husband put it up," Becky said, her voice shaking a little. "I have no idea how it works."

"When will he be back?" Pamela asked.

Becky shrugged. "When they cancel stop-loss, I guess."

Pamela felt her breath slide out of her body. "He's in Iraq?"

Becky nodded. "I put the flag up for him, you know? And I haven't told him what happened to it. I've gotta find someone to fix the holder, and I have to get another flag."

Pamela looked at the house more closely. It needed paint. The bushes in front were overgrown. There were cobwebs all over the windows, and dry rot on the sills. Obviously the couple had purchased it expecting someone to work on it. Either the money wasn't there, or the husband had planned to do the work himself.

"I can fix the holder," Pamela said. "If you have a few tools."

"My husband does," Becky said.

"I have a few things to finish, and then you can show me," Pamela said.

She dusted for prints, and then, for comparison, took Becky's and some off the husband's comb, which hadn't been touched since he left. Then Pamela went into his workroom, which also hadn't been touched, and took a hammer, some screws, and a screwdriver.

It took only ten minutes to repair the flag holder. But in that time, she'd made a friend.

"How'd you learn how to do that?" Becky asked.

"Raised three kids alone," Pamela said. "You realize there's not much you can't do if you just try."

Becky nodded.

Pamela glanced at the camera. Untended since the husband left. It was probably in the same state of disrepair as the rest of the house.

"Can I see the security system?" she asked.

"It's not really a system," Becky said. "Just the cameras, and some motion sensors that're supposed to alert us when someone's on the property. But they clearly don't work anymore."

"Let me see anyway," Pamela said.

Becky took her past the workroom, into a small closet filled with electronics. The closet was warm from the heat the panels gave off. Lights still blinked.

Pamela stared at it all, then touched the rewind button on the digital recorder. On the television monitor, she watched an image of herself fixing the flag holder.

"It looks like the camera's still working," she said. "Mind if I rewind farther?"

"Go ahead."

Backwards, she watched darkness turn to day. Saw Neil inspect the hanger. Saw Becky crying, then the tears evaporate into a stare of disbelief before she backed off the porch and away from the scene.

Back to the previous night. No porch light. Just images blurred in the darkness. Faces, not quite real, mostly turned away from the camera.

"Got a recordable DVD?" Pamela asked.

"Somewhere." Becky vanished into the house. Pamela studied the system, hoping that she wouldn't erase the information as she tried to record it.

She rewound again. Studied the faces, the half-turned heads. She saw crew cuts and piercings and hoodies. Slouchy clothes worn by half the young people in Halleysburg.

Nothing to identify them. Nothing to separate them from everyone else in their age group.

Like her, her hair long, her jeans torn, as she stood front and center at the U of O, a burning flag before her.

She made herself study the machine, and figured out how to save the images to the disk's hard drive so that they wouldn't be erased. Then she inspected the buttons near the machine's DVD slot.

"Here," Becky said, thrusting a packet at her.

DVD-Rs, unopened, dust-covered. Pamela used a fingernail to break the seal, then pulled one out and inserted it in the slot. She managed to record, but had no way to test. So she made a few more copies, feeling somewhat reassured that she could come back and try to download the images from the hard drive again.

"Will this catch them?" Becky asked while she watched the process.

"I don't know," Pamela said. "I hope so."

"It's just, they got so close, you know." Becky's voice shook. "I didn't know anyone could get that close."

It took Pamela a moment to understand what she meant. Becky meant that they had gotten close to the house. Close to her. The burning hadn't just upset her, it had frightened her, and made her feel vulnerable.

Odd. All it had done to Pamela was make her angry.

"Just lock up at night," Pamela said after a minute. "Locks deter ninety percent of all thieves."

"And the remaining ten percent?"

They get in, Pamela almost said, but thought the better of it. "They don't usually come to places like Halleysburg," she said. "Why would they? We all know each other here."

Becky nodded, seemingly reassured. Or maybe she just wanted to abandon an uncomfortable topic.

Pamela certainly did. She wanted to play with the images, see what she could find.

She wanted a solid image of the culprits, one that she could bring to Neil.

Maybe then he would stop complaining that this was a petty property crime. Maybe then he might understand how important this really was.

But it was her own words that replayed in her head later that night as she sat in front of her computer.

They don't usually come to places like Halleysburg. We all know each other here.

She had lied to make Becky feel better, but the words hadn't felt like a lie. Thieves really didn't come here. There was no need. There were richer pickings in Portland or Salem or the nearby bedroom communities.

Besides, it was hard to commit a crime here without someone seeing you.

Except under cover of darkness.

Her home office was quiet. It overlooked the backyard, and she had never installed curtains on the window, preferring the view of the year-round flower garden she had planted. At the moment, her garden was full of browns and oranges, fall plants blooming despite the winter ahead. She had little lights beneath the plants, lights she usually kept off because they spiked her energy bill.

But she had them on now. She would probably have them on for some time to come.

Maybe Becky wasn't the only one who felt vulnerable.

Pamela put one of the DVDs in her computer, and opened the images. They played, much to her relief, so she copied the images to her hard drive and removed the DVD.

Her computer at home wasn't as good as her computer at work. But it would have to do.

She didn't want to do any work on this case at the state crime lab if she could help it. The lab was so understaffed and so overworked that it usually took four months to get something tested. When she last checked, more than six hundred cases were backlogged, some of them dating back more than nine months. Those cases were bigger than hers. The backlogs were semen samples from possible rapists and blood droplets from the scene of a multiple murder case.

She couldn't, in good conscience, bring something personal and private to the lab. She would work here as long as she could. Then if she couldn't finish here, she might be able to convince herself that the time she took at the lab would go toward an arson case—a serious one, not a petty property crime, as Neil had called it.

Petty property crime.

Funny that they would be on opposite sides of this issue too.

Pamela went through the images frame by frame, looking for clear faces. Her computer didn't have the face recognition software that one of the computers at the lab had, but she had installed a home version of image sharpening software. She used it to clean out the fuzz and to lighten the darkness, trying to find more than a chin or the corner of an ear.

Finally she got a small face just behind the flag, a serious white face with a frown—of disapproval? She couldn't tell—and a bit of an elongated chin. Enough to see the wisp of a beard, a boy's beard, more a wish of a beard than the real thing, and a tattooed hand coming up to catch the flag as the person almost blocking the camera yanked the pole out of the holder.

She blew up the image, softened it, fixed it, and then felt tears prick her eyes.

They don't usually come to places like Halleysburg.

No. They grew up here. And worked at the grocery store down the street to pay for their football uniforms at the underfunded high school. They collected coins in a can on Sunday afternoons for Boosters, and they smiled when they saw her and respectfully called her Mrs. Kinney and asked, with a little too much interest, how her granddaughters were doing.

"Jeremy Stallings," she whispered. "What the hell were you thinking?"

And she hoped she knew.

• • •

Neil wouldn't let her sit in while he questioned Jeremy Stallings. He was appalled she'd even asked. "That sort of thing belongs on TV and you know it."

But she also knew he probably wouldn't do much more than slap the boy on the wrist, so what would be the harm? She hadn't made that argument, though.

Instead, she waited on the bench chair outside the sheriff's office conference room, which doubled as an interview room on days like this, and watched the parade of parents and lawyers as they trooped past.

No one acknowledged her. No one so much as looked at her. Not Reg Stallings, whose brother had sold her the house, or his wife June, who had taken over the PTA just before Travis got out of high school. No one mentioned the friendly exchanges at the high school football games or the hellos at the diner behind the movie theater. It was easier to forget all that and pretend they weren't neighbors than it was to acknowledge what was going on inside that room.

Then, finally, Jeremy came out. He was wearing his baggy pants with a *Halo* t-shirt hanging nearly to his knees. He wore that same frown he'd had as he took the flag off from Becky's front door.

He glanced at Pamela, then looked away, a blush working its way up the spider tattoo on his neck into his crew cut.

His parents and the lawyers led him away, as Neil reminded all of them to be in court the following morning.

Neil waited until they went through the front doors before coming over to Pamela.

She stood, her knees creaky from sitting so long. "He confess?"

Neil nodded. "And gave me the names of his buddies."

Pamela bit her lower lip. "Funny," she said, "he didn't strike me as the type to be a war protestor."

Neil rubbed his hands on his pristine shirt. "Is that what you thought?"

"Of course," Pamela said. "Every house he hit, we're all military families."

"Who happened to be flying flags, even at night." There was a bit of judgment in Neil's voice.

She knew what he was thinking. People who knew how to handle flags took them down at dusk. But she couldn't bear to touch hers. She hadn't asked Becky why hers remained up, but she would wager the reason was similar.

And it probably was for every other family Jeremy and his friends had targeted.

"That's the important factor?" she asked. "Night?"

"And beer," Neil said. "They lost a football game, went out and drank, and that fueled their anger. So they decided to act out."

"By burning flags?" Her voice rose.

"A few weeks before, they knocked down mailboxes. I'm going to hate to charge them. There won't be much left of the football team."

"That's all right," Pamela said bitterly. "Petty property crimes shouldn't take them off the roster long."

"It's going to be more than that," Neil said. "They're showing a destructive pattern. This one isn't going to be fun."

"For any of us," Pamela said.

Her hands were shaking as she left. She had wanted the crime to mean something. The flag had meant something to her. It should have meant something to them too.

God, Mom, for an old hippie, you're such a prude. Jenny's voice, so close that Pamela actually looked around, expecting to see her daughter's face.

"I'm not a prude," she whispered, and then realized she was reliving an old argument between them.

Sure you are. Judgmental and dried up. I thought you protested so that people could do what they wanted.

Pamela sat in the car, her creaky knees no longer holding her.

No, I protested so that people wouldn't have to die in another senseless war, she had said to her daughter on that May afternoon.

What year was that?

It had to be 1990, just before Jenny graduated from high school.

I'm not going to die in a stupid war, Jenny had said with such conviction that Pamela almost believed her. *We don't do wars any more. I'm going to get an education. That way, you don't have to struggle to pay for Travis. I know how hard it's been with Steve.*

Jenny, taking care of things. Jenny, who wasn't going to let her cash-strapped mother pay for her education. Jenny, being so sure of herself, so sure that the peace she'd known most of her life would continue.

To Jenny, going into the military to get a free education hadn't been a gamble at all.

Things'll change, honey, Pamela had said. *They always do.*

And by then I'll be out. I'll be educated, and moving on with my life.

Only Jenny hadn't moved on. She'd liked the military. After the First Gulf War, she'd gone to officer training, one of the first women to do it.

I'm a feminist, Mom, just like you, she'd said when she told Pamela.

Pamela had smiled, keeping her response to herself. She hadn't been that kind of feminist. She wouldn't have stayed in the military. She wasn't sure she believed in the military—not then.

And now? She wasn't sure what she believed. All she knew was that she had become a military mother, one who cried when a flag was burned.

Not just a flag.

Jenny's flag.

And that's when Pamela knew.

She wanted the crime to mean something, so she would make sure that it did.

She brought her memories to court. Not just the scrapbooks she'd kept for Jenny, like she had for all three kids, but the pictures from her own past, including the badly framed front page of the *Oregonian.*

Five burly boys had destroyed Jenny's flag. They stood in a row, their lawyers beside them, and pled to misdemeanors. Their parents sat on the blond bench seats in the 1970s courtroom. A reporter from the local paper took notes in the back. The judge listened to the pleadings.

Otherwise, the room was empty. No one cheered when the judge gave the boys six months of counseling. No one complained at the nine months of community service, and even though a few of them winced when the judge announced the huge fines that they (and not their parents) had to pay, no one said a word.

Until Pamela asked if she could speak.

The judge—primed by Neil—let her.

Only she really didn't speak. She showed them Jenny. From the baby pictures to the dress uniform. From the brave eleven-year-old walking her brother to school to the dust-covered woman who had smiled with some Iraqi children in Baghdad.

Then Pamela showed them her *Oregonian* cover.

"I thought you were protesting," she said to the boys. "I thought you were trying to let someone know that you don't approve of what your country is doing."

Her voice was shaking.

"I thought you were being patriotic." She shook her head. "And instead you were just being stupid."

To their credit, they watched her. They listened. She couldn't tell if they understood. If they knew how her heart ached—not that sharp pain she'd felt when she found the flag, but just an ache for everything she'd lost.

Including the idealism of the girl in the picture. And the idealism of the girl she'd raised.

When she finished, she sat down. And she didn't move as the judge gaveled the session closed. She didn't look up as some of the boys tried to apologize. And she didn't watch as their parents hustled them out of court.

Finally, Neil sat beside her. He picked up the framed *Oregonian* photograph in his big, scarred hands.

"Do you regret it?" he asked.

She touched the edge of the frame.

"No," she said.

"Because it was a protest?"

She shook her head. She couldn't articulate it. The anger, the rage, the fear she had felt then. Which had been nothing like the fear she had felt every day her daughter had been overseas.

The fear she felt now when she looked at Stephen's daughters and wondered what they'd choose in this never-ending war.

"If I hadn't burned that flag," she said, "I wouldn't have had Jenny."

Because she might have married Neil. And even if they had made babies, none of those babies would have been Jenny or Stephen or Travis. There would have been other babies who would have grown into other people.

Neil wasn't insulted. They had known each other too long for insults.

Instead, he put his hand over hers. It felt warm and good and familiar. She put her head on his shoulder.

And they sat like that, until the court reconvened an hour later, for another crime, another upset family, and another broken heart.

KRISTINE KATHRYN RUSCH is an award-winning mystery, romance, science fiction, and fantasy writer. She has written many novels under various names, including Kristine Grayson for romance, and Kris Nelscott for mystery. Her novels have made the bestseller lists–even in London–and have been published in 14 countries and 13 different languages. Her awards range from the Ellery Queen Readers Choice Award to the John W. Campbell Award. Her short work has been reprinted in thirteen Year's Best collections. In 2007, she became one of a handful of writers to twice win the Best Mystery Novel award given for the best mystery published in the Northwest (for her Kris Nelscott books). She lives and works with her husband, Dean Wesley Smith, on the Oregon Coast.

The Quick Brown Fox

BY ROBERT S. LEVINSON

The quick brown fox jumps over the lazy dog.

The quick brown dog jumps over the lazy fox.

The lazy brown dog—

As far as Gus Ebersole got before deleting the most words he had put on the computer screen in the fifteen, no, now sixteen months he'd been fighting the good fight against writer's block.

Writer's block, hell.

He was suffering a doomsday bomb that had exploded in his head while he slept, taking out those parts of the brain responsible for creativity. The right side. No, the left side. One of the sides. He'd know which if it were still functioning, instead of the side he was stuck with now, the side forcing him to consider abandoning his writing career, check Craigslist for work more suited to his current mental status.

He thought about McDonald's, maybe the kitchen assembly line, squirting on the mustard and the ketchup, layering the beef patties with tomatoes and lettuce; or maybe manning the deep fry, pumping out those devilishly delicious, blood-congealing Frenchies, and—

Now is the time for all good men to come to the aid of their country.

Now is the time for all good men to come to the aid of Gus Ebersole.

Now is the time for all brown dogs—

The cell phone sang out, interrupting his train of thought.

He punched on hungrily, happy for the distraction.

Nobody he knew.

A Commander Dennis Foley of the Los Angeles County Sheriff's Correctional Services Division apologizing for his call at what might be an inconvenient time, in a nicotine-damaged voice that reeked of authority.

"I am in the middle of something," Ebersole said, "but I'm never too busy for those who protect and serve."

"A new story in your Inspector Phogg series, I hope."

"Possibly the greatest adventure of the inspector's life," Ebersole said, flattered by this proof he hadn't been entirely forgotten or forsaken since the creative well turned drier than the Mojave.

"Wonderful, he's my favorite, even more than grand old Mrs. Marlowe, although it's hard for me to imagine how you'll ever be able to top the last Phogg, *Strangers on a Plane.* Been what, two or three years since I read it in *Crime & Punishment Magazine?* Or anything, not even another Bogey Brothers, L.L.C."

Ebersole muttered something about interrupting the flow of short stories to focus on a novel and pushed the commander to explain the reason for his call.

"Over to our Men's Central Jail, got a classroom full of wannabe writers looking for a pro to steer them in the right direction—no pun intended—and my first thought naturally was you, Mr. Ebersole. An hour or two at one of the Tuesday or Thursday meetings would sure do the trick."

Ebersole hummed his way through a minute, playing at having to think hard about the invitation, masking his delight over this unexpected excuse to avoid, even if for only a couple of hours, the torture of staring at a blank, snow white computer screen, unable to untangle ideas he once translated so effortlessly into a tale well told.

"It doesn't pay much," the commander said, misinterpreting his silence. "An honorarium certainly nowhere close to what your time must be worth, sir."

"Hmmmmm . . . Send it to your memorial foundation, Commander Foley. I'm honored to *accept* and to serve," Ebersole said. *Accept and to serve.* Wordplay on law enforcement's motto. A positive omen the fires of creativity still burned inside him, yes?

Yes!

No McDonald's for Gus Ebersole, not yet, anyway.

• • •

Ebersole reached Men's Central Jail during morning visiting hours and angled his SUV into the reserved space waiting for him a half block away in the public parking lot on Bauchet Street, a mangy stretch of street within sight of the 101 and 110 freeways, full of stiff-backed law enforcement personnel and a United Nations of civilians who'd come to share time with inmates at Central or its neighbor across the way, the Twin Towers Correctional Facility, a complex built and christened before its name took on a significance far more tragic than any story any prisoner could tell.

He was no stranger to his surroundings, but it had been six or eight years since his last visit to Central, a research tour that formed the basis for his series of "High Security" stories. Twin Towers was no country club, but it was Central, the largest jail in the free world, where they housed the high-risk population.

Commander Foley was waiting at the check-in desk, looking nothing like he'd sounded on the phone, in a uniform that might have fit him twenty pounds ago, his ear-to-ear smile half lost under a thick salt-and-pepper mustache that fit above his mouth like a limp hot dog.

He shook Ebersole's hand like he was pumping for water and led him off and briefed him on the writing class members during the ten minutes it took to reach the meeting room, a space about ten by twelve feet, the walls bare except for a green chalkboard mounted behind a scarred teacher's desk fronting a semicircle of cheap student tablet chair-desks.

Applause greeted their arrival, led by an inmate in the white top and blue bottom uniform combination that identified him as a trustee. He'd been using the teacher's desk as his own. He was in his mid-to-late sixties, maybe five five or six feet in height and a hundred twenty pounds on a rail-thin frame, his angelic face home to a halo of hair, as bedsheet white as his complexion, hanging in a knotted braid past his shoulder blades.

He matched Foley's description of Chester "Smiley" Burdette. A career criminal halfway through a ten-year sentence for first-degree armed robbery, and one of dozens of prisoners transferred to Central when the county ended its contract with the state.

"Smiley's also a fan of yours and the one who's been fronting the program since he got here," Foley had said. "He's first-rate when it comes to keeping the others in line, *if* anyone gets out of line for any reason."

"Like what kind of reason?"

"You never know until it happens," Foley said.

"If you're trying to scare me, Commander, it's working."

"Just making conversation, Mr. Ebersole. We haven't lost an author yet." He showed off his smile again. "Of course, there's always a first time," he said, turning his smile into a burst of laughter and giving Ebersole's shoulder a series of reassuring pats.

Ebersole was not reassured.

He thought about canceling out then and there, fleeing Central Jail, but that would have meant returning home to a blank computer screen.

• • •

Ebersole wrote his name on the board in large block letters and launched into a lengthy introduction, sparing his audience no adjective or noun that enhanced his reputation and standing in the literary fraternity; much of what he said was true.

Then it was their turn.

Smiley Burdette went first, playing his own history like stand-up comedy, drawing his biggest laughs describing the armed robbery that got him back behind bars. "Was meant to be burglary, which is my specialty," he said. "Climbed into the Bar None through a window off the alley, not thinking to check first if the joint was still open for business. It was, so that made my burglary a robbery and how I found myself staring down the barrel of the barkeep's twin-gauge. My priors turned my sentence into five years times two, so here I am, my swan song to a home away from home."

He took a bow and spread his arms grandly to the applause he'd generated from seven of the eight other inmates.

"Plain stupid, you ask me," said the lone dissenter, earning a unanimous chorus of hisses as he dismissed Burdette with a throwaway gesture.

Burdette said, "I didn't ask, but you definitely are, Cooke. Nothing's more stupid than a dirty cop who gets caught stepping over the line. You bend over a lot in the shower or why else do they let you out of segregation and into the general pop for our class?"

Al Cooke pushed up from his seat, unfolding a six-foot frame and a weightlifter's ripple of muscles inside the orange uniform that identified a connection to law enforcement. He reared back, fists clenched, cold-cocking Burdette with his pit bull eyes, and stepped toward him.

Burdette rose to the challenge and egged Cooke forward with his hands.

Two of the inmates leaped to their feet and blocked Cooke's way, while another latched onto Burdette's arm and urged him to shut up and settle down, insisting, "Smiley, a DRB or the hole's nothing you need right now."

The air remained heavy with acrimony. Burdette and Cooke grunted between labored breaths, neither man showing any inclination to step away from a fight and be seen as a loser.

Ebersole wiped at the fright sweat blanketing his forehead and upper lip and reached over to press the call button installed on the underside of the desk. It would bring guards running, the commander had told him.

Burdette recognized the move and shook his head at Ebersole.

Pumped a laugh to the ceiling and sank into his chair.

Said, "Only playacting, Mr. Ebersole, maybe give you something to write about in one of your Bogey Brothers stories. Our way of showing our thanks for your being here today, ain't that so, Cookie?"

Cooke hesitated before answering. "Why not?" he said, and waved off the inmates who had blocked his access to Burdette. "What's to know about me, I'll make it short and sweet. I'm a bad cop who got caught, honored the Blue Wall and refused to turn state's, got sentenced to the max, and is now sitting out an appeal hearing among this bunch of losers." A cacophony of nasty sounds erupted. Cooke answered them with a wagging upright middle finger. "I've been writing a book I'm calling *Cop-Out.*"

"Cop-In more like it," somebody said, winning applause.

Cooke ignored the interruption. "So I went and scored this program hoping to maybe pick up a handy hint or three along the way from a writer like you," he said, and sat down.

Ebersole thanked him and pointed to an inmate who'd seemed more interested in playing with his fingernails than being in the class. Early-to-mid forties, Coke-bottle glasses on an otherwise ordinary face.

He didn't bother standing but remained focused on his nails. "Name's Bob Rauschenberg, no relation to the painter of the same name," he said, like he was sharing a state secret. "Been writing all my life. Checks mainly. What helped get me here. What I call *creative enterprise,* others call forgery." He blew on his nails, brushed them on his uniform, and signaled he was through.

"Who'd like to speak next?" Ebersole said, any fears for his personal safety erased by the realization these inmates were a garden of story ideas ripe for picking.

He listened to their histories with a growing intensity, anxious for the session to end so he could tell Commander Foley he wanted to return, not just once, but as often as the inmates would have him.

• • •

Five of the inmates were genuinely interested in writing. They were the ones who asked the questions. The others were using the program to kill time or as an alternative to sweating in the kitchen or laundry or off sewing prison gear. They were the ones who seemed to sleep with their eyes open, whose breath stank of pruno, the illegal alcoholic drink made in their cells from fermented food.

Ebersole was supposed to report the fakers and the flakes—that's how the system worked—but a short story Ricardo Ramirez read during his second visit was all the convincing he needed to ignore the mandate. Ricardo, who hid a high IQ under a body load of gang tats, had written in near-flawless prose about an execution-style killing on an afternoon when black clouds hung over the exercise yard—blood and guts spilled by a kid doing drug time, who ratted out a gang member for snatching his fish kit and won a snitch's reward, a shiv fashioned from a toothbrush handle drilled into his carotid artery after it ripped open his belly.

The verisimilitude of the story made Ebersole wonder if it was fact wrapped in fiction, and if Ricardo perhaps was the convict who had wielded the homemade weapon, but those were not questions he asked. That would have been inviting Ricardo to snitch on himself, a thought that amused Ebersole as much as he was excited by his plan to rewrite the story in his vaunted style and submit it to *Crime & Punishment Magazine.*

Nothing he'd mention to Ricardo, of course.

That would be like Gus Ebersole snitching on himself. Hah, hah.

Instead, Ebersole gently poked away at his story structure, his overuse of street vernacular, and his cliche-riddled plot reminiscent of one of those old Warner Bros, movies starring Cagney, Bogart, and Pat O'Brien as either the softhearted warden or the kindhearted priest.

Ricardo appeared to take the criticism well, the suggestion of a grin dancing at a corner of his mouth. "I thought I was doing what you told us the last time, to write what you know," he said.

"You know about a killing like that?"

Holy crap!

The question had just slipped out.

The room suddenly turned into a monastery for monks committed to an oath of silence as all eyes switched from Ebersole to Ricardo, who briefly played into the oath before saying, "Only what I know from the old movies, *jefe.*"

• • •

When the session ended after two hours and the inmates were lining up single file for the march back to their cells, Ricardo tossed his manuscript, handwritten in a bold, elegant cursive script, the kind they teach in elementary school, into the waste basket.

Ebersole waited for the room to empty and retrieved it.

• • •

Two days later, on Thursday, Ebersole had finished packing reference materials for his next session at Central Jail and was halfway to his SUV when the call came from Commander Foley's office, a gum-chewing deputy relieved to have caught him in time to advise that all the programs were cancelled for the duration.

"Had ourselves a murder up on the exercise roof, so we're in lockdown mode," he said. Ebersole pressed for details. "Ugly screw-up," the deputy said. "A K-10 Red, sexually violent predator fresh in from the state, who should have been in isolation because of his 'keep away' status. Word got out who he was, and that's all she wrote. Somebody waltzed over, sliced his throat, and just as quick disappeared back into the pack. Me, I'd have gone for the K-10's balls first, then his throat."

"Any suspects?"

"We're down to sixty-eight hundred inmates, sir. Central's capacity."

• • •

Ebersole returned to his class on Tuesday of the following week. By then the killing had been reduced to a cursory mention on the evening news and two tight paragraphs on a back page of the *Times'* "California" section, more attention than it was getting at Central, where violence was as common as a yawn.

He had struggled at the computer the last five days, failing time and again to better the bones of Ricardo's story. Nothing worked, except for improving the title, from "A Cutthroat Death" to "A Snitch in Time." He'd had better luck keeping the quick brown fox jumping over the lazy dog.

Last night, during another siege of sleepless tossing, he realized why.

He was wrong about the quality of Ricardo's story.

It was no damn good, not worthy of Gus Ebersole's time or effort.

He rolled out of bed, padded across to the den, fixed himself a tall vodka over ice at the bar, and raised his glass to the notion that something better would come along.

It was waiting for him when he strolled into the classroom, a story without a byline, written on fourteen sheets of blue-lined yellow pages from a legal-size pad, hand-printed in precise, microscopic capital letters.

He read the first two pages of "Unnecessary Lives" to himself and didn't dare continue. What followed an electrifying opening sentence turned him breathless, as if he were running the last mile of the L.A. marathon on guts alone.

"Whose is this?" Ebersole said, flashing the pages once he was sure of his voice. "Who wrote this?"

Heads swiveled, eyes questioned eyes, some shrugs, but no one took credit.

Ebersole, satisfied he'd done his due diligence, stashed the manuscript in his attaché case, twirled the combination lock, and launched into a discourse on the top ten clichés of crime fiction writing to be avoided.

Rauschenberg called out "Here, here!" to all but the one item on the list that decried the use of bizarre names for characters, suggesting, "They couldn't get any more bizarre than what passes for names for real nowadays. If you don't believe me, ask my daughter, Snowflake, when she comes to visit. Her mother's decision, seeing as how she was born during a snowstorm back home in West Virginia and her daddy was a flake."

"*Is* a flake," Cooke said, his only contribution of the morning.

Smiley Burdette said, "Takes one to know one, Cookie."

Cooke shut his eyes, swallowed a breath, and said, "You'd know that better'n me, old man."

"About a lot of things," Smiley said, his expression emulating his nickname.

"Here's the next cliché," Ebersole said, reasserting himself before Cooke and Burdette could take their feuding to the next level.

George Murdock, a craggy-faced airline pilot in his thirties sitting out a start date on his trial for the murder of his ex-wife and her lover, had been a silent presence during the first two meetings, taking notes but not participating in the discussions. He shook his head when Ebersole decried villains that routinely walk around in unnecessary disguises, like characters in a comic book. Murdock tore a sheaf of the yellow legal-size sheets in half.

That left Ray Lemmon the only inmate with something to read, of itself a surprise. Until now, the sad-eyed inmate with movie star looks, nearing release on a sentence for driving under the influence, had been one of the silent minority, hardly a shadow on the classroom wall.

"It came to me like in a dream after the last meeting," he said, and began reading:

There's no trick to being dead, once you get the hang of it.

Dead is a lot like living, only different.

Four pages later, as much as he'd written, everyone wanted more about a murder victim and his guardian angel, a boy with a penchant for stray dogs, who are assigned to commute from Heaven to solve crimes that appear unsolvable.

Smiley was amused. "Obviously the LAPD is their beat, wouldn't you say so, Cookie?"

Cooke half rose from his seat, then thought better of it. He called to Ebersole, "Any way you can get this fudge monkey to shut his flap trap before I do some permanent damage?"

"You hear?" Ricardo said. "Instead of the other way around, the cop needs somebody to protect and serve him."

Catcalls surrounded Cooke and Smiley, championing one or the other in equal measure and no sense of quieting down despite Ebersole's pleas for order. He pressed the call button to summon the guards and sat patiently while they cleared the room, in truth, anxious to be on his way home to an early start on reading the mystery manuscript. If it ended as well as it started, it would be pouring out of his computer and on its way to *Crime & Punishment Magazine* before nightfall.

• • •

The normal nesting time for a story submission at *C&P* was two or three months, maybe a month for the regular contributors who could be counted on for two or three stories a year, the way Ebersole once had been, before the magazine's editor, Syd Moretti, began inundating him with rejection notes that grew progressively disheartening, from your basic "Not for us this time around" to a heart-sinking, "Where is your talent vacationing, Gus? Did it get there on a one-way ticket?"

He heard from Moretti in less than a week and not in writing, on the phone, Moretti's Midwest roots betrayed by a flat, homespun Iowa twang that embraced a pronounced stammer whenever he got excited, like now.

He said, "Saw your byline and almost didn't bother with a read, Gus, but I did, thank the Lord for giant favors. You are back bigger and better than ever, my friend. 'Unnecessary Lives' is a most necessary buy for us. What else do you have that could be a fit?"

Ebersole thought about it. "I just finished one I call 'A Snitch in Time.'"

"Love it already."

"It's not as complex as 'Unnecessary Lives,' but—"

"No buts,' Gus. Upload it to me now." An hour later, Moretti was on the phone again, saying, "You're now officially batting a thousand, my friend. Both contracts will be in the mail first thing in the a.m."

Ebersole celebrated over a vodka and was halfway through a second when he fixated on Ricardo Ramirez. He thought about the sexual predator whose throat was cut and his lingering suspicion that Ricardo was responsible. His hand trembled at the thought of Ricardo's reaction when he discovered "A Snitch in Time" was, word-for-word, his story "A Cutthroat Death." He chugalugged what remained of his drink and pondered his options over swipes straight from the bottle.

• • •

The next three sessions at Central went badly, Ebersole losing his train of thought every time he caught Ricardo looking at him with more than casual interest, which was every time he caught Ricardo staring at him, like Ricardo already knew about *Crime & Punishment* and was already planning how to extract punishment on him for his crime, the theft of Ricardo's story, and—

Smiley Burdette recognized his mind was warped by his imagination and called him on it, hanging back during the pee-

and-puff break, saying, "Who are you, kid?"

"Meaning what, Smiley? I don't understand."

"Meaning yourself you ain't been for a while," he said. "Getting worser and worser, and I'm not the only one noticing. I got a shoulder for you to lean on, you feel like spilling your woes to old Uncle Smiley, and if there's anything I can do to help you . . . ?" He plugged the offer with a question mark, took a step away from the desk to give Ebersole thinking room.

Ebersole popped a breath mint and weighed the offer, what was left of his jagged, picked-upon fingernails typing out a nervous tune on the desk's surface.

Despite his age and diminutive size, Smiley was one feisty individual, not intimidated by the bigger, stronger, bullying likes of a Cooke. Confronting Ricardo on his behalf, if it became necessary, was not outside the realm of possibility.

Would it make a difference with Ricardo? It was worth a try, he supposed.

He confessed to Smiley and asked, "You think I might be overreacting?"

Smiley didn't have to think about it "No," he said "Stealing's the misdemeanor here. Taking and selling the story as your own after you filleted his ego by putting the story down, that's a felony where Ramirez comes from." He ran a finger across his throat.

"Maybe I should just quit, get the hell out of here before the issue comes out and—"

"And hide where? He has people on the outside who know how to find people. Street justice ain't pretty, but it is permanent."

"What do I do, Smiley?"

"Cancel out the sale. Get the story back. Give the magazine something else. You have a new Bogey Brothers? I told you how much I like them Bogey Brothers stories."

"That wouldn't work," Ebersole said, leaving it at that. No desire to explain his terminal writer's block. If he could write a Bogey Brothers, anything at all, he wouldn't be in this mess

Smiley pushed out a noisy sigh, shook his head, and rolled his eyes at the ceiling. “Okay, in here these things have a way of taking care of themselves sometimes, but meantime, I’m on it.”

“‘On it.’ What’s that mean, Smiley7” The inmates were filing back into the room.

Smiley said, “Ask me that when we meet again on Tuesday.” He zipped his lips and retreated to his seat.

• • •

Ebersole survived the weekend on volcanic nerves and vodka, most of the time stretched out on the sofa in the den, watching old movies on the wall-mounted TV. Monday was no better, Tuesday morning worse. He cursed a mammoth migraine impervious to poppers and prayer on the bumper-to-bumper rush hour drive to Central he measured in inches.

Anxiety was an even worse enemy by the time he reached the reception desk, where the overweight deputy who regularly escorted him to the classroom, Don, waited with his usual cheery smile and chatterbox gossip.

Don said, “I suppose you already heard how the lockdown was only lifted last night or else you’d still be home right now and I’d be talking to myself.”

“First I’m hearing.”

“Didn’t raise much of a fuss on the news this time around. Another killing in the exercise yard, another throat cut with a toothbrush shiv. Nobody saw anything, of course. Some wise asses suggested we make sure to check everyone with dirty teeth.” He laughed. Ebersole didn’t. “Commander Foley said to tell you there might be a swell Inspector Phogg story here, seeing as how you knew the victim, him being in your class and fancying himself a writer.”

“Who?” Ebersole said, feigning shock while he fought back a grin as his mind conjured an image of Ricardo Ramirez stretched out on the yard’s concrete surface, his head resting at an impossible angle on a pillow of his blood. Now he understood what Smiley had meant. He owed him a big payback.

"Nice old bird too. Burdette. Smiley Burdette."

"What? What about Smiley?"

"The vic I was telling you about," Don said. "Him. Smiley Burdette."

They had reached the classroom.

Ebersole pushed a hand against the corridor wall for support and battled to keep his legs from collapsing under him while he imagined what must have happened on the yard.

Playing intermediary, Smiley approached Ricardo and explained about the story sale to *C&P.* Instead of placating Ricardo, he only made him angrier. In the absence of Ebersole, Ricardo took out his fury on Smiley, the toothbrush his weapon of choice, like before

Ebersole was now more certain than ever it was Ricardo who murdered the sexual predator. And who next?

Him. Gus Ebersole would be his next victim, for insulting him in class about his story—then stealing it.

He wanted to run, flee, quit this place, the class, as far away as possible from Ricardo.

Ebersole remembered what Smiley told him about Ricardo having people who know how to find people. *Street justice ain't pretty, but it is permanent,* he'd said.

The deputy pushed open the classroom door for him.

Ebersole made the sign of the cross, then a second time. He took a tentative step inside. Quit. Wheeled around. Said, "I need to speak to the watch commander. Now!"

• • •

"You're saying Ricardo Ramirez did it?"

"Murdered Smiley, yes," Ebersole said.

The watch commander moved his tac boots off the desk, sat upright, and studied Ebersole over his coffee mug. "And you know this how?"

Ebersole had an answer ready "Smiley told me so," he said. "He and Ramirez had been having bad words between them—over what, he didn't say—but he said Ramirez threatened to get him, told him to watch his back."

The commander tweaked his bulbous nose and thick brush mustache and nodded like he was weighing Ebersole's response. After a few moments, he said, "You suppose, instead of his back, Smiley should have been guarding his neck?" He angled his face at Don and winked.

Ebersole bit down hard on his back teeth to suppress his anger. "Commander, you're treating this as a joke? Smiley Burdette is the second inmate killed like that, his throat slashed out on your exercise yard."

"And you're saying Ramirez was also responsible for that death?"

"Draw your own conclusion."

"Tell you what, Mr. Ebersole. I'll pass word up and see what comes down, but I think there's something you should know." He bit off a hunk of the jelly doughnut camped on a pile of blue-jacketed file folders and washed it down with a slug of coffee. Rolled his tongue around his lips "What happens when we're on inmate overload, a couple hundred receive early release, a "Get Out of Jail" card. Ramirez was one of the lucky ones sent home the day before Smiley was killed." The watch commander smiled benevolently. He finished the rest of his jelly doughnut and hand-toweled off his mouth, used a glance to send a message to Don, who caught it immediately.

"Mr. Ebersole, you got a class waiting for you," Don said.

Ebersole wanted to quit the program. There and then. Run and hide. Where? Definitely not home, where Ricardo could be waiting for him. Maybe he'd get into the car and drive—

He put the brakes to his panic.

Supposing Smiley never had a chance to talk to Ricardo?

That being the case, Ricardo wouldn't know to come after him until the story appeared in print. If Smiley did talk to Ricardo, there still was time to eliminate the problem with a call to the magazine.

Ebersole berated himself for overreacting, for overlooking the obvious.

He said, "Lead the way, Don."

• • •

The inmates quit the quiet chatter among themselves when Ebersole walked through the door. He settled at the desk, faked a smile apologizing for his tardiness, and said, "Anyone have something new to share?"

Cooke said, "Call on Smiley Burdette, why don't you? Oh, wait, the old pain in the ass has quit the class permanently." His laughter drowned out a round of hisses and boos.

Rauschenberg stood. "Maybe next time," he said and sat back down.

George Murdock looked up from the legal-size yellow pad he'd been studying and raised his hand for attention. He cleared his throat. Screwed self-doubt onto his face. Dismissed the idea of reading with a gesture.

Ray Lemmon had another four pages in the story he'd been working on about the dead detective. The inmates applauded him after he finished and Ebersole gave him an encouraging critique.

Absent volunteers from among the slackers, Ebersole read them a locked-room mystery from one of the old issues of *C&P* he carried in his attaché case and talked briefly about story structure before signaling the guard that class was ending early today.

• • •

Ebersole reached his home off Ventura Boulevard, behind CBS Studio Center in the flats of Studio City, within the hour. His worries about Ricardo Ramirez had resumed and consumed him throughout the drive, eviscerating his earlier common sense conclusions, building a fear that compelled him to circle the shade-tree-lined block twice in search of strangers hunkered down in unfamiliar cars. He exercised similar caution entering the house and exploring the rooms before he felt safe, secure, and comfortable enough to pour himself a double vodka and dial Syd Moretti at C&P.

His solution to the problem with Ricardo was simplicity itself.

He would tell Syd he had to renege on the contract for "A Snitch in Time," having only now remembered that the story was sold earlier in the year to *C&P's* major competitor, *Killer Thrills & Chills,* by his ex-agent. He'd stress the *ex.* Apologize profusely. Assure Syd there was no problem with "Unnecessary Lives." He'd have to endure some serious flak, but it beat anything Ricardo would have in store for him.

"I was just thinking to call you," Syd said, hopping on the line. "Got good news, buddy. Great news. You sitting down?" Before Ebersole could answer, Syd said, "I somehow came up a story light for the next issue. 'A Snitch in Time' was a perfect fit. We're on the presses now, and as a bonus, your name's plastered on the cover . . . Gus, you there? You hear me? You sharing the excitement, Gus?"

"Sharing, Syd," Ebersole said, trying to sound excited, trying to remember where he had stored the .38 Special he learned to use while doing research at the Police Academy for an early Inspector Phogg story. He found it in the W-X-Y-Z drawer of the metal file cabinet m the guest bedroom he'd turned into his office after buying the house six years ago. The .38 needed a lube job. Bullets too. By evening he had it in prime working condition, in easy reach on the nightstand when he stumbled into bed.

• • •

Three weeks later, the program quit Ebersole before he could quit the program.

He was relieved to get Commander Foley's call, the commander using "attrition" as the cause, with no mention of the times Ebersole had shown up nursing a hangover and launching disjointed lectures that may have made sense to him, but to no one else.

The class was down to the sleepy silent minority and, if one were to believe Foley, the current jail population lacked anyone anxious to fill the desk seats vacated by Cooke, Murdock, Rauschenberg, Lemmon and, of course, Smiley Burdette and Ricardo Ramirez

Cooke had waltzed out on bail after his appeal hearing was granted. Murdock's lawyers had successfully argued for a change of venue, and their client was now resident at the Presley Detention Center in Riverside. Rauschenberg had completed his sentence. Lemmon was among the latest beneficiaries of early release.

And Ebersole was getting no writing done.

None.

Not for lack of trying.

Every story idea petered out after a page or two, every creative thought supplanted by the quick brown fox, every noise or vodka-burnished notion reminding him the mail would bring the new issue of *C&P* any day now, and a visit from Ricardo Ramirez in its wake.

• • •

Instead, Ricardo showed up a week before the magazine arrived, in his mug shot on the six o'clock news, tied to a report about an attempted armed robbery turned deadly at a 7-Eleven in Koreatown.

The clerk had been quicker with the double-barrel shotgun under the counter than Ricardo was with his Saturday Night Special, a Raven Arms MP-25 semiautomatic handgun.

R.I.P. Ricardo.

Ebersole toasted the screen with his vodka and, loaded down with renewed energy and enthusiasm, stumbled to the computer. The quick brown fox quickly overpowered his euphoria, but he slept through the night for the first time in months.

• • •

The noises that awakened Ebersole two nights after *C&P* hit the newsstands sounded like breaking glass at the rear of the house, followed by the squeak of rusty door hinges, then footsteps cautiously advancing along the hardwood floor leading to his bedroom.

His adrenaline kicked in. His heart took off like a jazz drum solo. His breathing matched the beat. Recently there had been a series of home invasions in the neighborhood. One, a block over, had resulted in the deaths of an elderly couple. Was he about to become the latest victim? He didn't dare move as one thought after another charged through his mind, squeezing his eyes tighter when he felt the subtle heat of the flashlight beam stroking up and down his face.

The .38 Special was in the nightstand drawer.

Should he risk it?

He didn't have time to think it through before a muffled, vaguely familiar voice prompted him, "Time to rise and shine, Gus."

Gus. The intruder knew his name. This was no random home invasion. Ebersole pushed up into a sitting position. He clamped a hand over his eyes to block the flashlight's dazzle. "Please take what you want and leave," he said, answering a question he had nursed for years: How would he react if he ever found himself in this situation? The intruder made a dismissive noise. "You write better dialogue in your stories, Gus."

"You read my stories?"

"How Mrs. Marlowe was always saying, 'You naughty boy, you. I could be your dear mother.' That was a real hoot every damn time. "Your mama's dead and gone to hell, where she belongs, along with that damn maggot passing himself off as your papa."

"I can't recall writing that," Ebersole said. "Mrs. Marlowe would never speak that way."

"Not her, Mrs. Marlowe. It's in the story that just came out, 'A Snitch in Time.' Maybe you can't remember because you didn't write the story, although it has your name as the author."

"What's that supposed to mean?"

"Like you don't know without me explaining it to you?" The overhead light clicked on, momentarily blinding Ebersole. The intruder was hiding his identity inside a black woolen ski mask and a heavy olive-colored overcoat a size too small that quit at his ankles. The coat was open, exposing a poorly fitting uniform of some sort.

"That's my story, I wrote it," he said. "I named it 'A Cutthroat Death,' but nothing else was different about it except your name. Your damn name on *my* story."

"Who are you?"

"Who do you think I am? I'm my own avenging angel." He dropped the flashlight into a coat pocket, reached inside the coat, and came out with a foot-long knife.

"Maybe you remember this from the story, Gus? The black Glock Survival Knife with the six and a half inch blade sharp enough to split nose hairs in half. A utility saw on the back of the blade? My weapon of choice, but not available while I was at Central, forcing me to be inventive with toothbrushes."

"You killed Smiley Burdette?"

"Yes. And the other one, the damn predator. Perverts like him have no business walking this earth instead of feeding earth worms six feet under."

"But why Smiley?"

"He told me he was going to snitch to you about the favor Ricardo did for me by passing off the story as his own. It was nobody's business why I wanted it to be a secret, but after you tore into it like a rabid dog, I knew I had been right. Ricardo didn't mind though. He said forget it, it was only a flea bite. And I did—until I saw it in *Crime & Punishment Magazine.* Your name. You lied about my story to the class so you could steal it for yourself, making you a different kind of predator."

Holding the knife out like a bayonet, he moved in on Ebersole.

The blade cut into the pillow seconds after Ebersole reflexively rolled sideways.

He scrambled to his feet on the side of the bed opposite the intruder and pulled open the nightstand drawer. The .38 wasn't there. He cursed himself for forgetting he'd moved it back to the W-X-Y-Z file drawer the morning after celebrating the news of Ricardo's murder.

The intruder had come around the bed and was advancing on him.

Ebersole rolled across the bed, dashed out of the bedroom and down the dark hallway, the intruder in noisy pursuit. He slammed the office door shut, turned the bolt lock, and scrambled to the file cabinet, dropped to his knees, and went after the 38. The intruder was rattling the knob, pounding and kicking on the door. Ebersole padded across the room and took a shooter's stance, arms extended and two hands on the weapon. He squeezed the trigger, again, then another time, then twice more. The bullets crashed through the door, at first causing undecipherable outbursts from outside in the hallway, then nothing at all.

Ebersole, raining sweat, held his position for another minute and played catch-up with his breath. He half expected the intruder to come crashing through the door, blood spilling from his wounds, attempting another murderous charge. How many times had he written that scene in one of his short stories? How many times had he watched it played out that way in the movies and on TV? He eased his grip on the .38, but kept his finger on the trigger while unlocking and opening the door a creaking inch at a time.

The intruder was a motionless pile of bloody, bullet-riddled dead meat a few feet away, still clinging tightly to the knife. Ebersole approached the body cautiously. Satisfied, he settled on his haunches and sucked in a year's supply of oxygen before lifting the intruder's ski mask to see who owned the eyes staring blindly at him.

They belonged to George Murdock, who apparently had no problem murdering his ex and her lover, but never could bring himself to share any of the writing he brought to class. A shame, Ebersole thought now. There could have been something equal to "A Cutthroat Death" and equally worth acquiring as his own.

• • •

Two days later, Ebersole met Al Cooke for coffee. A Starbucks on Ventura, up from Laurel Canyon, a nest for writers diligently slaving over laptops on their Great American Novels and million-dollar screenplays.

"It wasn't hard tracking you down after I read in the news about that murderous creep Murdock and how you took him out," Cooke said, pumping his hand with the type of enthusiasm usually reserved for presidents and pontiffs. "An old buddy downtown was happy to do a favor for a fellow defender of the Blue Wall, if you know what I mean?"

"How is your appeal going?"

"The wheels of justice are slowly grinding to a halt. Don't be surprised when you learn the D.A.'s dropped all the charges against me and I'm back protecting and serving." He took a lick of the whipped cream on his white chocolate mocha and made a yummy face. "I'm getting out from under on the legit, where Murdock had to maneuver an escape, overpowering that guard at Presley Detention, stealing his uniform, the rest of it before he came after you like he did. Did he say why before you managed to clock him for keeps, lucky bastard that you are?"

"Murdock accused me of stealing a story from him."

"How brain dead can a person be? He never opened his mouth once in all the weeks of the program. Any truth to it, though, I could see where he might be pissed off. Happened to me, I would be tempted to do the same thing to the bastard, only I'm smarter than Murdock. Crime is easy; anyone can do it. But not everyone knows how to keep from getting caught. That's an art."

Ebersole fought to hide his discomfort. "You said you were working on a book—"

"*Cop-Out*. It's still in the works."

"But you never took it past that in class or presented a story." Cooke smiled.

"Why I phoned you. What I wanted to talk about." He worked the white chocolate mocha and spent several seconds with his eyes trained on a leggy brunette in short shorts and an overflowing halter top studying the counter menu. "I was the cop in the ointment, getting no respect, you remember? That old bigmouth Burdette with his nasty cracks, par for the course, so why run anything I wrote up the flagpole? Instead, I planted a chapter of *Cop-Out* on your desk anonymously, the one I titled 'Unnecessary Lives.' I figured you'd read and critique it, so I'd get some quality input. Instead, you stashed it in your case, never to be seen or heard about in class. So tell me, did you read it? What did you think? I'm dying to hear."

Ebersole spilled his coffee.

ROBERT S. LEVINSON, bestselling author of *In the Key of Death, Where the Lies Begin, Ask a Dead Man, Hot Paint, The James Dean Affair, The John Lennon Affair,* and *The Elvis and Marilyn Affair*, is making his fifth consecutive appearance in a "year's best" mystery anthology. He is a regular contributor to *Alfred Hitchcock Mystery Magazine* and *Ellery Queen Mystery Magazine*, whose readers have cited him in the annual EQMM Award poll three years running, while his plays "Transcript" and "Murder Times Two" were award nominees at the annual International Mystery Writers Festival at RiverPark Center in Owensboro, KY. Bob wrote, produced and emceed two Mystery Writers of America "Edgar Awards" shows, as well as two International Thriller Writers "Thriller Awards" shows. His articles have appeared in *Rolling Stone*, *Written By Magazine* of the Writers Guild of America-West, *Los Angeles Magazine*, and *Crimespree Magazine*. His work has been praised by Joseph Wambaugh, T. Jefferson Parker, Nelson DeMille, Clive Cussler, Heather Graham, John Lescroart, David Morrell, Michael Palmer, James Rollins, and others. Visit him at www.robertslevinson.com.

What Happened To Mary?

BY BILL PRONZINI

When you live in a small town and something way out of the ordinary happens, it's bound to cause a pretty big fuss. Such as a woman everybody knows and some like and some don't disappearing all of a sudden, without any warning or explanation. Tongues wag and rumors start flying. Folks can't seem to talk about anything else.

That's what happened in my town last year. Ridgedale, population 1400. Hundred-year-old buildings around a central square and bandstand, countryside all pine-covered hills, rolling meadows, and streams full of fat trout. Prettiest little place you'd ever want to see. Of course I'm biased. I was born and raised and married here, and proud to say I've never traveled more than two hundred miles in any direction in the fifty-two years since.

Mary Dawes, the woman who disappeared, wasn't a native herself. She moved to Ridgedale from someplace upstate after divorcing a deadbeat husband. Just drifted in one day, liked the look of the town, got herself a waitress job at the Blue Moon Cafe and a cabin at the old converted auto court on the edge of town, and settled in. Good-looking woman in her thirties, full of jokes and fun, and none too shy when it came to liquor, men, and good times. She had more than her share of all three in the year or so she lived here, but I'm not one to sit in judgment of anybody's morals. Fact is, I own Luke's Tavern, Ridgedale's one and only watering hole. Inherited it from my father, Luke Gebhardt, Senior, when he died twenty years ago.

Mary liked her fun, like I said, and rumor had it she didn't much care if the man she had it with was married or single. But she never openly chased married men and she wasn't all that promiscuous, even if some of the wives called her the town slut behind her back. One relationship at a time and not flagrant about it, if you know what I mean. She came into the tavern one or two nights a week and drank and laughed and played darts and pool with the other regulars, but I never once saw her leave with a man. She made her dates in private. And never gave me or anybody else any trouble.

One of the regulars gave her trouble, though, same as he gave trouble to a lot of other folks at one time or another. Tully Buford, the town bully. Big, ugly, with bad teeth and the disposition of a badger. Lived by himself in a rundown little farmhouse on the outskirts of town. Carpenter and woodworker by trade, picked up jobs often enough to get by because he was good at his work.

Thing about Tully, he was more or less tolerable when he was sober but when he drank more than a few beers he turned loud-mouthed mean. More than once I had to throw him out when he had a snootful. More than once the county sheriff's deputies had to arrest him for fighting and creating a public disturbance, too, but he never started any fights or did any damage in my place. If he had, I'd've eighty-sixed him permanently.

Worse he ever did was devil people and throw his weight around, and as annoying as that was, I couldn't justify barring him from the premises for it.

Oh hell now, Luke Gebhardt, be honest. You were afraid if you did bar him, he'd come in anyway and start some real serious trouble.

He was capable of it. Town bully wasn't all he was. Vandal, too, or so most of us believed; Ridgedale had more than its share of that kind of mischief, all of it done on the sly at night so nobody could prove Tully was responsible. Animal abuse was another thing he was guilty of. Doc Dunaway saw him run down a stray dog with his pickup and swore it was deliberate, and there'd been some pet cats, a cow, and a goat shot that was likely his doing.

So it was easier and safer to just stay clear of him whenever possible and try to ignore him when it wasn't. The only one who felt and acted different was J.B. Hatfield, but I'll get to him in a minute.

Now and then Tully tried to date Mary Dawes. Like every other woman in Ridgedale, she wouldn't have anything to do with him. Just laughed and made some comical remark meant to sting and walked away. One night, though, he prodded her too long and hard and she slapped his face and told him if he didn't leave her alone, he'd have to go hunting a certain part of his anatomy in Jack Fisher's cornfield. Everybody had a good laugh over that and Tully went stomping out. That was two days before Mary disappeared.

Disappeared into thin air, seemed like. One day she was there, big as life, and the next she was gone. The last time any of us saw her was when she left the tavern, alone, about eleven-thirty on a warm Thursday night in October.

She hadn't told anybody she was thinking of leaving Ridgedale, hadn't given notice at the Blue Moon. On Friday Harry Duncan, the Blue Moon's owner, went out to her cabin at the old auto court. Her car was there but she wasn't. She hadn't checked out and none of the other residents had seen her leave or knew where she'd gone. That's when everybody started asking the same question.

What happened to Mary?

The first time I heard foul play suggested was on the second day after she went missing. J.B. Hatfield was the one who said it.

Tully Buford was there, too, and so were old Doc Dunaway and Earl Pierce. Doc is a retired veterinarian, had to give up his profession when his arthritis got too bad; he's the quiet one of the bunch, likes to play chess with Cody Smith, the town barber, or just sit minding his own business. Earl owns Pierce's Auto Body, but he spends more time in my place than he does at his own; lazy is the word best describes him, and he'd be the first to admit it. J.B. works for Great Northwest Building Supply. Young fellow, husky, puts on a tough-guy act now and then but not in an offensive way. He's the only one who wasn't afraid to stand up to Tully Buford. Two of them were always sniping at each other. One time they went outside in the alley to settle an argument, but no blows were struck. Tully was the one who backed down, not that he'd ever admit it. J.B. got the worst of the face-off, though. It was his goat that was shot a week or so later.

The bar talk that evening was all about Mary Dawes, naturally, and J.B. said, "I wonder if somebody killed her."

"Now who'd do a crazy thing like that?" I said.

"Her ex-husband, maybe."

"Wasn't a bitter divorce. What reason would he have?"

"Hell, I don't know. But it sure is funny, her disappearing so sudden and her car still out there at the auto court."

Earl said, "Could be she went with a man one time too many."

"Picked the wrong one, you mean?" I said. "A stranger?"

"Somebody passing through and stopped in at the Blue Moon for a meal. Lot of crazies running around out there these days."

"Ain't that the truth?" J.B. said, and looked straight at Tully.

Tully didn't catch the look. He said to Doc, "Hey, Doc, you think Mary's been killed?"

"I have no opinion."

"You never have no opinion about nothing. Come on, now, you old fart. If she was killed, who you suppose done it?"

"There's no point in speculating."

"I asked you a question," Tully said, harsh. "I want an answer."

Doc sighed and looked him square in the eye. He's mild-mannered, Doc is; usually he just ignored Tully. But Tully picked on him more than most and even a quiet old gent can get fed up. "All right then," he said. "If she was murdered, the person responsible might be living right here in Ridgedale. Could even be the same coward who runs down stray dogs and shoots defenseless animals in the middle of the night."

It got quiet in there. Tully's face turned a slow, turkey-wattle red. He said, "You accusing me, Doc?"

"Did you hear me say your name?"

"You better not be accusing me. I told you before, I never run down that mutt on purpose. You go around accusing me of that and worse, you'll be damn sorry."

"What'll you do?" Doc asked. "Throw a rock through one of my windows? Pour sugar in my gas tank? Shoot some more cats in my neighborhood?"

Tully shouted, "I never done none of those things!" and grabbed Doc's shoulder and squeezed hard enough to make him yell.

"Leave him alone." That was J.B. He stood up and pulled Tully's hand off Doc's shoulder. "Doc's got bad arthritis—you know that, you damn fool."

"Who you calling a damn fool?"

"You, you damn fool."

Tully was up, too, by then and the two of them stood nose to nose, glaring. I said, "Take it outside, you want to fight," but it didn't come to blows between them this time, either. The glaring contest went on for about a minute. Then Tully said, "Ah, the hell with it, the hell with all of you," and went storming out.

Earl said as J.B. sat down again, "I was you, J.B., I'd lock up that new goat of yours and keep a sharp eye on your property from now on."

• • •

It was the next day, Saturday, the manager of the old auto court opened up Mary's cabin and found the bloodstains.

More than a few, the way we heard it, on the bed and on the bathroom floor. Long dried, so they must've been made the night she disappeared. The place was torn up some, too, from some kind of struggle. The county sheriff came out to investigate and didn't find anything to tell what had happened, but he considered the cabin a crime scene and kept right on investigating.

News of the bloodstains really stirred things up. It looked like murder, all right, and we'd never had a mystery killing in Ridgedale—no killing of any kind since one of the DiLucca sisters shot her unfaithful husband thirty-five years ago. Nobody who came into my place that night talked about anything else. Tully Buford wasn't among them, though; he never showed up.

"Blood all over the place," J.B. said. "Told you she'd been killed, didn't I?"

"Well, we still don't know it for sure," I said. "They haven't found her yet."

"Might never find her. Plenty of places to hide a body in all the wilderness around here."

"Won't make any difference if they do or don't," Earl said. "Whoever done it's long gone by now."

"Not the way I see it, he isn't."

"You think it's somebody lives here, J.B.?"

"I think it's Tully."

"Come on, now," I said. "What Doc said last night, he didn't mean it literally. Did you, Doc?"

He shrugged. "It's possible."

"I don't know. Tully's a bully and a bunch of other things, but a murderer?"

"Shot my goat, didn't he?" J.B. said. "Run over that stray dog on purpose, didn't he?"

"Big difference between animals and a woman."

"Mary might've turned him down once too often. Tully's got a hell of a temper when he's riled and drunk."

"I sure hope you're wrong."

"I hope I'm not," J.B. said.

Well, he wasn't. And we found it out a lot sooner than any of us expected.

Sunday morning, the sheriff arrested Tully Buford for the murder of Mary Dawes.

Cody Smith came into the tavern, all hot and bothered, and told us about it. He got the news from his brother-in-law, who works as a dispatcher in the county sheriff's office, and he couldn't wait to spread it around.

"Sheriff found Mary's dress and underclothes and purse in a box under Tully's front porch. Soaked in blood, the lot."

I said, "The hell he did!"

"There was a bloody knife in there, too. Tully's knife and no mistake—his initials cut right into the handle."

"Told you!" J.B. said. "Didn't I tell you he did it?"

"How'd the sheriff come to find the evidence?" I asked. "What set him after Tully?"

"Phone call this morning," Cody said. "Man said he was driving past the auto court three nights ago, late, and saw Tully putting something big and heavy wrapped in a blanket in the back of his pickup. Decided he ought to report it when he heard about the bloodstains in Mary's cabin."

"Anonymous call?"

"Well, sure. Some folks, you know, they don't want to get themselves involved directly in a thing like this."

"But the sheriff took the call seriously?"

"Sure he did. Figured at first it might be some crank, but then he got to thinking about the trouble he'd had with Tully and Tully's reputation and he decided he'd better have a talk with Tully. Got himself a search warrant before he went, and a good thing he did. Soon as he found the box and saw what was it, he handcuffed Tully and hauled him off to jail."

"Tully admit that he done it?" Earl asked.

"No. Swore up and down he never went near Mary's cabin the night she disappeared, never saw the box or the bloody clothes."

"What about his knife?"

"Claimed somebody stole it out of his truck a couple of weeks ago."

"He'll never confess," J.B. said. "He never owned up to anything he done in his entire miserable life."

Doc said mildly, "A man's innocent until proven guilty."

"You standing up for Tully now, Doc?"

"No. Just stating a fact."

"Well, I don't see much doubt. He's guilty as sin."

"They haven't found Mary yet, have they?"

"Not yet," Cody said, "but a team of deputies has already started hunting on Tully's property. If they don't find her or what's left of her there, sheriff's gonna organize a search with cadaver dogs."

Well, they didn't find Mary on Tully's property and the search teams and cadaver dogs didn't find any trace of her in the surrounding countryside. They were out combing the hills and woods five days before they gave up. Sheriff's men did find out one other piece of evidence against Tully, though. More bloodstains, small ones in the back of his pickup. All the blood was the same—type AB negative, Mary's type and not too common. They knew that on account of she'd given blood once during a drive at the county seat.

Meanwhile, Tully stayed locked in a cell hollering long and loud about how somebody was trying to frame him. According to Cody's brother-in-law, he threw out the names of just about everyone he knew, J.B. Hatfield's number one among them. But it was just a lot of noise that didn't get listened to. Nobody liked Tully worth a damn, but who'd hate him enough to frame him for murder?

None of us went up to the county jail to see him. None of us would have even if he hadn't been throwing accusations around, trying to lay the blame on somebody else.

Plain fact was, life in Ridgedale was a lot more pleasant without Tully Buford around.

There was a lot of speculation about whether or not the county district attorney would prosecute him for first-degree murder. "Bet you he won't," Earl said. "Not without a whatyoucallit, corpus delicti." Doc Dunaway pointed out that corpus delicti meant "body of the crime," not an actual dead body, and that precedents had been established for first-degree homicide convictions in no-body cases. Even so, the D.A. was a politician first and a prosecutor second, and he didn't want to lose what in our small county was a high-profile trial. Most of us figured he'd play it safe. Try Tully on a lesser crime, like manslaughter. Like as not there was enough circumstantial evidence for him to get a conviction on that charge.

Turned out that's just what he did. The trial lasted about a week, with a parade of witnesses testifying against Tully's character and nobody testifying in his favor. The public defender didn't put up much of a defense, and Tully hurt himself with enough cussing and yelling in the courtroom to get himself restrained and gagged. The jury was out less than an hour before they brought in a guilty verdict. First degree manslaughter, ten to fifteen years in state prison.

There wasn't a soul in Ridgedale didn't believe justice had been served.

• • •

Well, that was the end of it as far as I was concerned. Or it was until this morning, nearly a year after the trial ended. Now all of a sudden I've got a whole different slant on things.

It was Al Phillips gave it to me. Al is Soderholm Brewery's deliveryman on the route that includes Ridgedale; he stops in once a month to pick up empty kegs and drop off full ones. I went out to talk to him and lend a hand, as I usually do, and while we were unloading the fresh kegs he said, "I was up in the state capitol last weekend. Took my wife to the outdoor jazz festival up there."

"How was it?" I asked.

"Oh, fine. But a funny thing happened afterward."

"What sort of funny thing?"

"Well, believe it or not, I think I saw Mary Dawes."

My first reaction was to laugh. "You must be kidding."

"No, sir," he said seriously. "Not a bit."

"Must've been some woman looks like Mary."

"Could be, but then she'd just about have to be her twin," Al said. "I stopped in at the Blue Moon for lunch enough times to know Mary Dawes when I see her."

"Al, she's been dead a year. You know that."

"All I know is what I saw last Sunday."

"You talk to this woman?"

"I tried to, but she hustled off into the crowd before I could."

"Did she see you?"

"I don't know. Might have."

"If she did, why would she avoid you like that?"

Al shrugged. "Your guess is as good as mine."

"Mary," I said. "Mary Dawes."

"Yes, sir. Mary Dawes."

I didn't believe it then. I'm not positive I do even now. But after Al left I couldn't get rid of the notion that Mary might still be alive. I was still chewing on it when Doc Dunaway came in. It was early afternoon then and there weren't any other customers. I drew him a pint of lager, his only tipple, and when I set the glass down in front of him, he said, "You've got a funny look, Luke. Something the matter?"

"Well, I don't know," I said, and I told him what Al had told me.

He drank some of his beer. "It couldn't have been Mary," he

said. "A woman who looks like her, that's all."

"That's what I said. But Al sure sounded convinced. If he's right, then Tully's innocent like he claimed and somebody really did frame him—for a murder that never happened."

"Then how do you explain Mary's sudden disappearance? Where did the blood in her room come from, the blood on her clothes and Tully's knife and in the bed of Tully's pickup?"

"Well, I've been thinking about that. Suppose it was all part of a plan. Suppose whoever wanted to frame Tully paid her to disappear the way she did. Paid her enough so she wouldn't mind having herself cut and spilling some of her blood."

"Sounds pretty farfetched to me."

"Not if whoever it was hated Tully enough."

"You don't mean J.B?"

"Well, he's the first one I thought of," I said. "Only J.B. doesn't have much money and it would've taken plenty to convince Mary. And he's not too smart, J.B. isn't. I just can't see him coming up with a plan like that."

"Who else could it be?"

"Somebody with both brains and money. Somebody who was sick and tired of Tully and his bullying and carousing and killing of defenseless animals—"

I stopped. Of a sudden, the back of my scalp started to crawl.

Doc? Doc Dunaway?

No, it couldn't be. But then I thought, yes it could. He was a vet for forty years and he loved animals and he was smart as a whip and he had a nice fat nest egg put away from the sale of his veterinary practice. Old and arthritic, sure, but a man didn't have to be young and hale to steal a knife out of an unlocked truck or help mess up a cabin and sprinkle some blood around or hide a box under a porch or make an anonymous telephone call. And a vet would know exactly how and where to make a surgical cut on a person's body that would bleed a lot without doing any real damage . . .

Doc sat watching me through his spectacles. His eyes have always been soft and kind of watery; now they seemed to have a hard shine on them, like polished agates.

Pretty soon he said in his quiet way, "Won't do to go around speculating, Luke. That's how ugly rumors get started and folks get hurt."

"Sure," I said, and my voice sounded funny. "Sure, that's right."

"Chances are it wasn't Mary Al Phillips saw. And even if it was, why, she might not be in the capitol for long. Might decide to leave the state entirely this time, move back east somewhere."

"Why would she do that?"

"For the sake of argument, let's say your theory is correct. The person who conceived the plan might have kept in touch with her, mightn't he? Might offer her more money now to move away so far she'll never be seen again by anyone from this county. Then there'd be no proof she's alive. No proof at all."

I didn't say anything. My throat felt dry.

"Know what I'd do if I was you, Luke?"

". . . What's that?"

"I wouldn't mention what Al Phillips told you to anybody else. I'd just forget about it. Tully Buford belongs where he's at, behind bars. Ridgedale is better off without him." Doc finished his beer, laid some money on the bartop, and eased himself off the stool in his slow, arthritic way. Then he said, "Well, Luke? Are you going to take my advice?"

"I don't know yet," I said.

"Better think on it long and hard before you do anything," he said, and shuffled out.

Think on it long and hard? I haven't done anything but think about it. And I still can't make up my mind.

I'm a law-abiding citizen; I always try to do the right thing, always want to see justice done. It's just not right for an innocent man to be sitting in prison for a crime that never happened in the first place—even a man like Tully Buford. My duty is to go to the sheriff and tell him what I suspect.

But what can he do? Nothing, that's what. Not without proof

that Mary's alive and Tully was framed, and I don't have a shred to give him. Just a lot of unsubstantiated maybes and what ifs.

And I could be mistaken about Doc Dunaway. I don't think I am, not after the conversation we had, but I could be. There wouldn't be any justice in smearing his good name without evidence, would there? I sure wouldn't want that on my conscience.

Besides I've always liked Doc; he minds his own business, never bothers anybody, just wants to be left alone to live out the rest of his days in peace.

And there's no denying he was right about Tully. Tully might not be guilty of murder, but he's guilty of plenty of other crimes and he belongs in prison. You wouldn't get an argument about that from anybody in Ridgedale.

I don't know. I just don't know.

What would you do?

A full-time professional writer since 1969, **BILL PRONZINI** has published close to 70 novels, including three in collaboration with his wife, novelist Marcia Muller, and 32 in his popular "Nameless Detective" series. He is also the author of four nonfiction books, 20 collections of short stories, and scores of uncollected stories, articles, essays, and book reviews; and he has edited or coedited numerous anthologies. His work has been translated into eighteen languages and published in nearly thirty countries. He has received three Shamus Awards, two for Best Novel, and the Lifetime Achievement Award (presented in 1987) from the Private Eye Writers of America; and six nominations for the Mystery Writers of America Edgar Allan Poe award. His suspense novel, ***Snowbound***, was the recipient of the Grand Prix de la Litterature Policiere as the best crime novel published in France in 1988. ***A Wasteland of Strangers*** was nominated for best crime novel of 1997 by both the Mystery Writers of America and the International Crime Writers Association. Another mainstream suspense novel, ***The Crimes of Jordan Wise***, was nominated by the International Crime Writers Association for the Hammett Award for best crime novel of 2006.

Jonas and the Frail

BY CHARLES ARDAI

Jonas took the punch, as he had to—what else could he do? They were holding his arms, one man on either side of him, each of them taller than Jonas, and wider, too, though Jonas was certainly no shrimp. He'd played fullback on his high school football team, had won many a game for the Tigers by barreling through the opposition, sheer mass carrying him into and over the beefy lads from Haverfield and Oakdale. But the men holding his arms were bigger than him, and stronger, too, so he stood there and took the punch.

It was not the sort that would level a fighter in the ring, but it had force behind it and Jonas' head snapped to the side before smacking against the wall behind him with a painful *clonk*. The dapper little fireplug in front of him tugged his gloves down tighter, made practice fists a few times in the air, and then socked him a second time, this time smack on the kisser. Jonas felt his lips mash flat against his teeth, tasted blood.

"Now tell me again what my sister is to you," the man said, glowering. He wore a grey felt homburg and a black topcoat over a charcoal double-breasted suit. His cheeks were bare, his side-burns neatly trimmed. He looked like a newspaper advertisement: *Fine Menswear, Shaving Supplies. Come To Siegel's.*

"Nothing," Jonas said. The words came out mushy. "She's nothing to me, Mr. Siegel, honest."

"My sister's nothing?" he shouted. "She's nothing?" He sank a left into Jonas' gut, followed by a right, then a left again, like he was hitting the heavy bag at the gym. Spit flew from Jonas' mouth as each punch landed and he sagged forward at the waist as much as the men holding him would allow.

"I didn't mean that, Mr. Siegel," Jonas whispered, the words hardly audible. "I didn't—"

"If you touched her," Siegel said, "I will cut off your hand. If you kissed her, I will cut out your tongue. If you, god forbid, came close to her with your filthy, greasy, *goyische schvantz*, you know what I'm going to cut off?"

He waited for an answer. Finally Jonas nodded.

"So I'll ask you one last time," Siegel said, softly, politely, tugging the lapels of his suit jacket back into place. "What is my sister to you?"

"She's my job, Mr. Siegel," Jonas whispered. "She's who you told me to watch, and protect, and make sure nothing happened to. That's all. I never touched her."

"Then where," Siegel said, leaning in till his nose was less than an inch from Jonas' bruised and purpling face, "is she?"

• • •

Melissa Siegel—known to all as Missy—hung first one stocking then the other over the radiator grill, spreading the silk out with a dainty fingertip. Silk would ruin if you dried it too quickly, but a low, slow heat like this would do fine.

She pulled the negligee tighter around her, clasping it together between her breasts. Mike Donovan lay on his side in the Murphy bed, covered to the waist by the top sheet, his hat and holster on the table by his side, his shirt and pants and socks and garters strewn across the floor. Missy's dress was draped over the back of the room's one chair. Her brassiere was nowhere in sight.

Mike's eyes followed her as she strode back toward him, hips swinging lazily, the expression on her face sly and replete. She sat on the corner of the mattress and pulled her legs up under her, Indian style. "Three times, Mike," she said. "In one night. That's got to be some kind of a record, even for you."

His roguish grin widened. "Lady, you were made for breaking records."

She reached out a palm, laid it flat over the sheet where his manhood lay, quiescent at last. She patted the flesh through the fabric, felt not the slightest stir. "Ah, Mike, isn't that cute, he's sleeping."

"Knocked out is more like it," Mike said. "Like Sugar Ray Robinson took down Gene Fullmer."

"If that's how Sugar Ray took down Fullmer," Missy said, "I'm sorry I wasn't in the stadium to see it."

"You're a dirty broad, you know that?"

"Yeah?" Missy pulled her negligee apart, uncovering a pair of breasts that were heavy enough you could tell they'd start to sag by the time she turned twenty. But that was still three years away. "You didn't seem to mind earlier."

Mike reached over to the table, slipped a cigarette out of a pack. "Who would?"

Missy's face clouded over. "My brother would. If he knew—"

Mike flicked open his Zippo, touched the flame to the cigarette, flipped it closed again. "Forget about him, doll. Your brother's a little man with a little bit of business on a couple little blocks on the Lower East Side. He's nothing." Mike drew on the cigarette, handed it over to Missy, who took a drag in turn. She coughed, passed it back. "He keeps pushing the wrong people too hard and someday soon the big man's gonna give someone the nod to put some extra ventilation in him. Maybe it'll be me."

"Ah, you talk big, all you micks, but he's still alive and a dozen of you are in the river where he put you."

"That's cause he's a sneaky little yid, with a sneaky little crew, and he don't fight fair."

Missy threw her head back and laughed, a sharp sound that left her breasts quivering. "Fair. Fair's when the other guy's lying in the gutter with holes in him. Unfair's when it's your guy."

Mike reared up, the sheet falling off to one side. He rolled Missy onto her back and she wrapped her long legs around him.

"Yeah?" he said, dipping his head to kiss her hard on her throat. "I'll show you holes, baby, and I'll fill 'em for you, too."

Missy's eyes slid shut and a smile split her face. "Big talker," she said.

• • •

Jonas pressed a steak onto the mouse puffing up his right eye. The left wasn't nearly as bad. And the split lip, well—it was a split lip. Not a whole hell of a lot to do about it, he'd just have to eat carefully the next day or two.

Assuming he was still around in a day or two.

Siegel had made himself clear: He wanted his sister home and he wanted her home now. And if the reason she wasn't home now had two legs and wore trousers, he wanted those legs horizontal and in a box.

Jonas laid the steak down on a chipped plate by the sink, rinsed his hands off, and pulled on the clean shirt Hazel had left out for him.

He felt like a prize dope for letting Missy out of his sight in the first place. She'd spent the evening as she spent so many, caroming from one of Times Square's rooftop gardens to the next, swing music and champagne making a heady atmosphere in the steamy summer air. She was younger than the other women in those places and they wouldn't have let her in unescorted, but that was just as well since her brother wouldn't have let her out unescorted either. Jonas had followed her dutifully from one joint to the next, checking her wrap at the door, collecting it for her when Missy was ready to leave, and, in between, sitting beside her at a succession of little round tables and horseshoe banquettes, glaring at any man unwise enough to chance a peek down the lady's décolletage.

She'd left him for the powder room more than once as the evening wore on, the inevitable consequence of all the flutes of Dom she was downing, but she'd always returned promptly, straightening her dress beneath her as she sat and casting a resentful glance his way. Okay, she wished he wasn't there. Join the club, sister. You think it's a laugh and a half drinking club soda all night while your boss' kid sister gets tight? You think every man dreams of spending hours listening to clarinets and trombones while he ought to be at home with his wife, getting a good night's sleep?

But he knew his role and she sure as hell knew hers, and they played them out like Lunt and Fontanne.

Then came the Green Lion, where the trombones were louder and the comics nastier and the dancers less well behaved. The waiter stationed outside the swinging door to the kitchen looked to Jonas like he was packing heat. The cigarette girls fingered the packs meaningfully before handing them over and judging from the smell in the air occasionally sold one-offs that weren't filled with Virginia's finest.

And when Missy went to the powder room, she didn't come out again.

He watched—he didn't take his eye off the door, he'd swear to that later when taking his licks. But each time the door opened, it was some other woman going in or coming out. After five minutes passed, then ten, Jonas started to get anxious. Finally he burst in, ignoring the feminine squeals that erupted around him and throwing off the hand on his shoulder from the bouncer attracted by the commotion.

"Where is she?" Jonas roared at the bouncer.

"Who?"

"Missy Siegel—Harry Siegel's sister."

The man shrugged, glanced carelessly from face to face at the women in the room. "You got me, bub. She ain't in here. And you can't be in here either, understand?"

Oh, he wanted to take a swing at the smug bastard, he wanted to lay him out flat on the tile floor. But Jonas had bigger worries now than this man. Looking around, he spotted a pink-lacquered door down at the far end of the room, past the row of sinks.

Who'd ever heard of a powder room with a rear exit?

He'd raced out and down the stairs, taking them two at a time, reaching the sidewalk in nothing flat, but there was no sign of her, and none of the cabbies he buttonholed had seen anyone answering to her description. How had they managed not to notice a seventeen-year-old in a satin gown with a pair on her that made Mansfield look positively undernourished? Or were these fine gentlemen lying to him? Bracing them, one by one, with his .45 held tightly in one fist and their shirt collars in the other, Jonas concluded they were telling the truth. Which meant she was either still in the building or had stolen away through the service alley in back. Hours of hunting, first floor by floor and then street by street, produced nothing, except for the growing realization that he'd have to go back to Siegel empty-handed.

Jonas slapped the steak back on his eye for another second or two. It was cold and slimy and didn't make him feel any better. But people said it was what you were supposed to do. Steak on a black eye, slice of potato on a wart. You could make up your own rules or you could do what people told you. Jonas was the kind of guy who did what people told him.

He grabbed his keys and hat and, quietly so as not to wake his wife, pulled the door shut behind him.

• • •

Missy yawned as she drew her stockings on, clipped them to her garters, let the skirt of her dress fall to her knees. There was nothing like a lazy Sunday morning after a long night's entertainment, but while Donovan was out like a light, snoring softly into his pillow, Missy was wakeful and restless. She patted down her dress, re-pinned her hair, settled her hat on top at an angle she'd seen in a movie magazine, and stepped to the door. She had her hand on the knob when the knock came.

"Who is it?" she said.

"Missy?"

She knew the voice—oh, did she ever.

She paused only to flick one of her straps off her shoulder, letting it settle loosely on her upper arm, then opened the door.

• • •

Jonas went back to the scene of the crime, as it were: the last place he'd seen his charge before she'd pulled her disappearing act. The Green Lion closed each night at 4 a.m., but a skeleton crew remained behind to mop the place down, sweep up broken glass and cigarette butts, and evict the occasional dozing hophead from one of the toilets. Jonas pulled up in a taxi just after dawn and saw two men stumble out of the place, tuxedos unkempt and faces worse, holding onto each other for balance. He could smell their breath as they passed.

The elevator man, a one-armed veteran in a banded cap and pinned-up sleeve, resented being asked to ply his trade at such an ungodly hour. He muttered under his breath till Jonas pulled his jacket to one side to show his holster and the well-worn pistol butt it held. The muttering stopped, and a few floors later the elevator did, too.

Jonas pushed his way through the leather-upholstered swinging doors, presently unattended, where just a few hours earlier a hostess and a maitre d' had been tending to arrivals, the latter spreading a thick layer of soft soap in every direction, the former smiling dazzlingly and not noticing that the buttons on her blouse had come undone. Melissa had noticed, of course; the look the girls had given each other could have chilled a gimlet at twenty paces.

The hostess would be at home now—hers or some lucky man's. But the maitre d' would still be around, Jonas knew, supervising cleanup and bolting down a quick dinner of leftovers and bottle ends. It was one of the perks of the job, the chance at the choice leavings of chateaubriand and Veuve Clicquot.

Jonas picked his way between the tables, stepping out of the path of a kid pushing a mop, and shoved open the door to the kitchen. Sure enough, the maitre d' was bent over a serving platter filled smorgasbord-style with bits of this and that. His black bow tie was undone and dangling and a stained napkin was tucked into the collar of his shirt.

Jonas pulled his gun and thumbed back the hammer, approached calmly. The maitre d' let his knife and fork clatter to the countertop and put his hands up. "What is this?"

"What does it look like?"

"Night's receipts are gone, mister," the man said. "Long gone. Jimmy and Paul carried 'em to the bank hours ago."

"I don't want money," Jonas said.

"Then you're the first man I ever met that didn't." He untucked the napkin, balled it up, tossed it on the platter. "What is it then?" His eyes narrowed. "Got it in for Donovan? No skin off my nose. Chintzy bastard's no joy to work for, let me tell you."

"I'm looking for a girl. Seventeen years old, built like Lana Turner, you saw her here with me last night. Name's Missy Siegel. She's Harry Siegel's sister."

"That who she is?" He let out a low whistle. "Doesn't take after her old man. And you wouldn't know she was only seventeen to look at her."

"No, you wouldn't," Jonas said. "But she is. And Mr. Siegel's not happy that she didn't come home with me last night."

"Gave you what for, did he?" the maitre d' said, aiming a thumb in the direction of Jonas' swollen face.

Jonas shrugged. "It's my job. I didn't do it."

"Jeez," the maitre d' said, "the people we work for."

"Enough palaver, Skeezix. I'm not your friend. I'm a man with one question, and you've either got an answer to it or you've got a bullet coming to you. Understand?"

The maitre d' nodded nervously.

"I searched the building," Jonas said, "and I searched the neighborhood, and I didn't find her anywhere. I don't see how she could've gotten away from me so fast. What I want to know is who she left with and where she is."

"That's two questions," the maitre d' said.

"You can have two bullets," Jonas said.

"No need," the maitre d' said. "No need. She left with Donovan. Not the first time, neither. And as for where . . . did you think to check the roof?"

• • •

When Jonas stepped through the door, Missy put one long forefinger to her lips and inclined her head toward where Mike Donovan lay sleeping. This wasn't a room so much as a maintenance shed, and with the Murphy bed open there was barely room to stand, never mind for two people to talk without waking a third.

She bent forward slightly, let the top of her dress slip forward a touch, waited for his eyes to be drawn involuntarily toward her bosom, which would be all the sign she needed that she'd be getting her way.

But he wasn't having any. Jonas hooked her strap with one meaty thumb and shoved it back onto her shoulder. "Put 'em away, doll. I've already got a pair at home."

She took a step toward the door but Jonas grabbed her forearm in one fist. He wasn't letting her get away again.

"Not so rough," she hissed. "You big ape."

Donovan turned over in his sleep, the sheet slipping from his flank as he did. If Jonas had wanted any further proof of what had gone on in this room he had it now. The man was naked as the day he was born, and if there was any blush creeping up the cheek of the young woman in the room, Jonas couldn't see it.

He switched her arm from his right hand to his left and unholstered his gun.

"What're you doing?" She was still talking in a whisper, but when Jonas answered he spoke out loud.

"My job," he said, and fired one bullet into the sleeping man's haunch.

Donovan bellowed, lurched awake grimacing. He spun and reached for the table where his gun lay, but a second shot from Jonas' .45 sent the gun spinning off into a corner of the room.

"Rise and shine, pretty boy," Jonas said. "I hope she was worth it."

"Don't!" Missy screamed. She plunged her heel down hard on Jonas' foot, spoiling his aim. The third gunshot went wide, splintering a framed elevator inspection certificate hanging on the wall.

Donovan was on his knees now, clutching a pillow in front of his privates. The pillowcase was turning red at the edges.

"You're going to ruin everything!" Missy said.

"Yep, that's me, I ruin everything." Jonas pulled the trigger once more and a puff of goose feathers exploded into the air. The center of the pillowcase turned red now, or what was left of it did. Donovan's face crumpled and he fell back onto the mattress groaning. "Pillows, mattresses. Only not seventeen-year-old girls. I draw the line there."

Missy wrenched her arm from his grasp and ran to Donovan's side. "Mike, Mike," she said, leaning down to cradle his head. She stroked his hair. "You've gotta tell me, Mike. Who is it? Who's the big man that's gonna put the finger on Harry? Who?"

But Donovan's mouth was screwed shut as tightly as his eyes, his whole face a knot of agony. Tears were running down his cheeks, and his head was twitching.

"Who?" Missy said again.

Jonas pushed her roughly away from Donovan, set the barrel of his .45 against the man's forehead, and used his last two bullets to put him out of his misery.

The echoes of the gunshots seemed to hang in the air, reverberating for a minute in the closed space.

Jonas tucked the empty gun back into its holster. He turned to find Missy standing an arm's length away, Donovan's gun held in her shaking hands. It was aimed at him.

Her hair had tumbled down and her hat was askew.

"You dumb ox," she said, "do you know what you've done?"

"Yeah. I've taken away your toy."

"I'm not a *child*, damn it. I'm a grown woman."

"This is how you prove it? Sleeping with a slob like this?"

"I was getting close to him for a *reason*."

Jonas shrugged.

"I was!"

"All right," Jonas said. "So you were."

"And now he's *dead*, you stupid, stupid man."

"Yeah, he's dead. That's the way your brother wanted him."

"My brother. Without me keeping tabs on his enemies, my brother'd have been on a slab three years ago. And maybe now he will be, thanks to you."

"He told me to—"

"Yeah, he told you to. Make sure Missy's pure and clean, make sure no dirty mick's puttin' his fingers in her drawers. When at my age he was screwing half the chorus girls in Ziegfeld's, two at a time."

Jonas stepped forward, one hand extended, a reasonable look on his face. He wasn't scared, but that didn't mean he thought it was impossible she'd pull the trigger. "Give me the gun, Missy." When she didn't, he said, "We've got to get out of here, kid. Someone's bound to have noticed. No car backfires six times."

"Seven," she said, and shot him in the chest.

• • •

She wiped the gun down, tucked it into Donovan's fist, bent his stiffening fingers around it, even threaded one inside the trigger guard. It made her feel sick to see him lying there, his brains soaking into the bed. But about Jonas, who was lying on the floor in a spreading pool of blood, she felt nothing. He wasn't a man. He was a robot, like in those pulp magazines with a screaming lady on the cover, a lumbering metal man carrying her away at the bidding of its egghead mad scientist master. Jonas was all meat and muscle, no brains, like a machine you set in motion and it kept going in whatever direction you pointed it.

Well it wasn't going anywhere now.

She put her hair back up, closed the door behind her and took the stairs all the way down to street level. No point letting the elevator man see her.

Out on the street she got a look and a whistle from the driver of a lone automobile. On his way to church, no doubt. She hurried to the nearest bus stop, sat on the bench to wait for the next bus to come by. In her whisper-thin sheath with bare arms and calves and heels that lifted her a good six inches when she stood, Missy was conspicuous and she knew it. Not in a nightclub on Saturday night, perhaps—but at a bus stop Sunday morning? You didn't see girls dressed like that unless they were coming home from a night they wouldn't want anyone to know about.

She wished she had a coat, or an umbrella, or even a newspaper she could open and hold in front of her. But she had nothing, just a little handbag smaller than her palm. She sat stiff-backed and watched the horizon.

When she heard the voice behind her, she jumped in her seat. "Miss? Do you need any help?"

She turned to see a flatfoot standing with his nightstick in hand, a beat cop in more senses than one, the long night's tour of duty showing in the weight of the bags beneath his eyes.

"Actually," she said, smiling at the thought of a quick ride home in a comfy squad car, door-to-door service courtesy of the City of New York, "yes I could, thank you." And she leaned forward a touch, tilting one shoulder to let her strap fall.

• • •

The telephone was on the far side of the bed, on the floor, where it had fallen when Jonas' gunshot had knocked Donovan's gun off the table. That was only ten feet away, but ten feet might as well have been ten miles at the stop-and-start pace that was the best Jonas could manage.

His breath was coming in short strokes, and try as he might he couldn't fill his lungs. He'd vomited once already, a mix of bile and blood, and each inhalation triggered another wave of nausea. But he crawled toward the phone, a little at a time, trying not to notice the sticky trail of blood he was leaving behind him.

Halfway there, he passed the dead man's outflung hand, brushed against it. Normally the touch of a corpse would have been unpleasant to him, but now he barely noticed it. He'd be joining Donovan soon enough.

He thought about Missy as he went, and about Harry, and about the police. He'd never called the police in his life, not once, not for anything. Where Jonas grew up, you didn't talk to the police if you could help it, and the feeling was mutual. But he was tempted now. He'd seen the look in Missy's face when she'd pulled the trigger, and he knew she was bad medicine, the sort of person you can't just leave walking the streets. Harry Siegel, Mike Donovan—they were bad men, like Jonas himself was a bad man, but they were professionals, they did what their business called for, no more. Missy Siegel was a different breed. He shivered thinking about her.

So: Call the police. Tell them what happened. Let them pick her up.

Or: Call Harry. That was the other choice. He'd had a job to do and by god he'd done it. He'd found her and he'd killed the son of a bitch who'd been laying her, nailed the bastard right in his greasy, *goyische schvantz.* Harry would like that. Harry would want to know.

But when Jonas finally reached the phone—miraculously upright, miraculously still connected to the wall, miraculously still yielding an operator's voice when he tipped the handset out of its cradle and collapsed beside it, the mouthpiece by his lips—he had energy enough only for a single call and he knew it. And he didn't use it up calling Harry.

He didn't use it up calling the police either.

• • •

When the door opened and Missy walked through it, she was wearing a knit dress and a cream blouse with a jacket over it. She was almost as conservatively dressed as her brother. He rushed over to her, took her face between his gloved palms, peered anxiously into her eyes. "Missy, where were you? You know how worried I've been?" He snapped his fingers at the men posted on either side of his office door. "Get out of here. Go on."

They left, and Harry led his sister to one of the room's overstuffed armchairs. "What happened?"

She had a handkerchief clutched in one fist and artfully smeared mascara, and between realistic-sounding sobs she told him the whole sad story: How after plying her with gin in an after-hours club Mike Donovan had lured her to his room, how she'd resisted, how Jonas had shown up looking for her just in time, and how the two men had—and here she gave a little shudder—shot and killed each other. She was capable of delivering a good performance when she had to be, and she knew she had to be very good now.

"He didn't—Donovan didn't—*you* didn't—"

She forced herself to stifle the smile that wanted to rise to her lips. She shook her head timorously like a little mouse, a little virgin mouse.

Harry Siegel let out an enormous sigh of relief. "Those goddamn micks. This is the last time. They've got to be taught a lesson. They can't kill one of my men and get away with it. They can't touch you and get away with it." He pressed a buzzer on his desk. When the door swung open he said to the bruiser standing behind it, "Get everyone together. Now. We're having a war council." He turned back to Missy. "This discussion isn't over. We're going to talk some more, me and you. You could've been hurt, or killed, or . . ." He obviously didn't even want to say what the third possibility was, and she almost threw it in his face: *He could've screwed me! He could've ridden me hard in a fold-down bed on the roof of the Dover Building, and he could've done it all night long!* But she didn't say any of this, just nodded meekly and stepped outside. Let him have his war council. Let him spill some Irish blood to pay for his sister's almost-ravished innocence. It would do him some good—make the Irish take him a bit more seriously. Make them hate him that much worse, too, but . . . she could keep them from getting too close. She'd done it before. Her way.

Missy passed through her brother's outer office, then through the main entryway with their father's picture hanging in it, looking serious and grim, like the president of a bank that had just had a run on it. The one man left on duty tipped his hat to her as she stepped into the elevator. The operator was a skinny boy maybe a year younger than she was, and she saw him give her the eye. Her stare froze him where he stood and he quickly turned back to the controls, the wolf whistle dying on his lips.

When the cab settled on the first floor, the boy pulled the accordion gate open. But before Missy could step outside, another woman was pushing her way in, a matron of forty or so in an unseasonably heavy coat, her hands joined in front of her inside a matching woolen muff.

"Excuse me!" Missy said. "I'm getting out."

The woman didn't move. "Not this time," she said, and her voice shook as she spoke.

The operator said, "Hey!" and reached for the lever to take the elevator up again, but the woman had already pulled her right hand out of the muff and a pistol with it. It was a .45 just like Jonas'.

"Step away and put your hands up," the woman said. "This is between me and her."

The boy complied.

"Hold on," Missy said, "who *are* you?"

"He *called* me," the woman said, her finger tightening around the trigger. "Do you know what that was like? Listening to my husband die over the telephone?"

Missy's face paled. "I didn't do it, Donovan did—" Missy began, but Hazel's bullet was already on its way.

CHARLES ARDAI is an Edgar and Shamus Award-winning writer and the founder and editor of the celebrated Hard Case Crime line of pulp-style paperback crime novels, in which capacity he has edited the work of authors such as Stephen King, Mickey Spillane, Donald E. Westlake, Lawrence Block, Max Allan Collins, Ed McBain, and others. He was also the creator of the pioneering Internet service Juno in the 1990s and currently serves as a managing director at the D. E. Shaw group. His novels include *Little Girl Lost* and *Songs of Innocence*, both published under the pseudonym "Richard Aleas," and *Fifty-To-One*, published under his real name.

The Pig Party

BY DOUG ALLYN

I was working hotel security at the Ponchartrain in Detroit, taking a break in the third floor bar, when her face flashed on the overhead TV. Sara Silver, the network correspondent with a career as brilliant as her name. She was interviewing Kathy Bates on a news show. Noticing my stare, the guy next to me followed my gaze up to the tube.

"Beauty and the beast," he quipped, sipping his scotch.

"Yeah? Which one is which?" I asked. Which earned me a look. Kathy Bates is a great actress but she's no head-turner. "I went out with her once," I explained.

"Who? Kathy Bates?"

"No, the media babe, Sara Silver."

He started to scoff, but a glance my way changed his mind. I'm not gorilla size, but I'm big enough. And life's scuffed me up some.

"No kidding, you really dated Sara Silver?" he said, doubtfully. "Where did you take her? Las Vegas?"

"Nope, to a frat party. Roughest night of my life."

"I'll bet," he said, pointedly turning back to his scotch. I knew what he was thinking. A smalltime hotel dick dating Sara Silver? Tell me another one.

I didn't bother. He wouldn't believe me anyway. But it happened to be the truth. I really did trip the light fantastic with Sara Silver once, on the wildest night of my life. Only it wasn't a date, exactly.

Because I didn't ask her out. She asked me.

I wasn't a detective then. Just an ex dogface, a couple of years out of the Marine Corps, taking a few college courses, trying to decide what to be when I grew up.

Meanwhile, I helped pay my rent by bartending part-time at Shannon's Irish Pub, a sports saloon just off the Westover College campus in Lansing. A jumpin' joint, Shannon's, foosball tables, pool tables and pinball machines. Busy all day long, totally nuts at night.

Preppies would start popping in at noon to knock down a beer between classes, shoot pool or line the bar for the usual intellectual collegiate repartee; Freud and Kant, easy A's and easy lays.

Occasionally I'd have to eighty-six a kid who overdid but for the most part the college boys were pretty mellow.

Their women were even better. Coeds and townie girls prowled Shannon's like tigresses around a waterhole, scouting for upwardly mobile mates. But sometimes they'd settle for an affable bartender.

The first time I saw Sara Silver, I figured she was just another Westover babe on the hunt. Sat at the far end of the bar, away from the others, nursing a white wine spritzer. Attractive, but nowhere near the network knockout she is now.

Her blonde hair drawn back in a loose ponytail, held by a silver clip. Finely boned features, slim legs, her figure tomboy taut but unmistakably feminine. Her oversized glasses gave her a studious look. Figured she was waiting for an intense, long-haired type with wild eyes and wilder politics.

Wrong. She was looking for me.

"You're Tommy Malloy, right? The ex Marine?"

"Guilty," I said, sliding a napkin under her glass. "Do I know you?"

"Sara Silver," she said, keeping her voice down, making sure we weren't overheard. "I've been asking around. I understand you tend bar for a lot of fraternity parties."

"I do my share."

"Have you ever worked a Delta Omega party?"

"Once. And not recently. Why? Do you want to hire a bartender?"

"Not exactly," she said, meeting my eyes. "I need a date."

"I don't understand."

"There's a party at Delta Omega tonight. I need an escort to get in. Can you manage that?"

"Probably, but I've got a better idea. Let's make it dinner and a movie instead."

"I'm not looking for a boyfriend, Malloy, just somebody to get me into the Delta House party. Tonight. Are you interested or not?"

"Miss, I'd love to take you out. Sometime. But not to a Delta House bash, and *definitely* not tonight." It was my turn to glance around to be sure we weren't overheard. "It's a pig party," I whispered.

"I know."

"Really? Do you have any idea what that means?"

"Of course."

"I doubt that. Pig party rules say the frat boys have to bring the ugliest chicks they can find. You don't remotely qualify."

"Thanks very much. I still want to go."

"No you don't, damn it! Listen, it's a really ugly scene, and I'm not just talking about the girls. It's loud, lewd, and crude. Everybody drinks too much, the guys are jerks, the girls are desperate—"

"Sounds like you've been there."

"No way," I said. "It's not my trip. But bartenders hear things, and some of them aren't pretty. A pig party's a rough, sorry-ass spectacle. It's definitely not a party you want to crash."

"I'll pay you an even hundred bucks to get me in," she said, digging into her purse, carefully counting five tens out on the bar. "Fifty now, fifty more afterward."

I made no move to pick up the money. "Why? What's so important?"

"I write for the *Westover Wildcat*, the college paper."

"Sara Silver," I said, nodding slowly. "I thought your name sounded familiar. You did a story last semester on fake IDs. Burned some local bartenders."

"I hope you weren't one of them."

"Nope, I'm always super careful. But why bother with a story on a pig party? It may be sophomoric but it's a campus tradition. The Delts hold one every year. Most of the girls who attend know the score and it's no crime to throw a bash."

"Isn't it? There's a rumor that a girl was gang raped at a pig party. Have you heard anything about that?"

"I've picked up the same rumor. As wild as the pig parties get, I suppose it's possible. Which is one more reason why you shouldn't go."

"I'll be perfectly safe," she said mildly. "I'll be with a Marine."

Touché. Couldn't help smiling. She was not only pretty, she knew exactly which buttons to push. And I was already more interested in the girl than the money.

"Ex-Marine," I said, picking up the fifty. "Where do we meet?"

• • •

We almost didn't. Westover is a small suburban college outside Lansing. Enrollment's twenty thousand, give or take. The main campus dates from the sixties, red brick buildings designed to look older than they are, surrounded by student dorms, which are coed, plus a dozen fraternities/sororities which are not.

Silver lived at the Kappa Rho House, a converted Victorian box with a mansard roof that looked like something out of *Jane Eyre*. Kappa Rhos are ultra-bright, scholarship chicks, mostly shrill feminists. We don't see many in Shannon's and I nearly missed Sara Silver. She was sitting on a bench in the vestibule and I walked right past without giving her a second look.

"Hey, big fella," she said, standing up. "Wanna go to a party?"

I did a double take. "Holy jeez Louise," I said.

Most girls fix themselves up for a date. Sara had fixed herself down. Way down. She'd rinsed her fair hair dark, leaving it flat as a cat after a cloudburst, lank and skanky. Her makeup was backwards, too. No lipstick, no rouge. Instead, she'd darkened her brows till they looked like caterpillars perching on her zit-dotted forehead. Purple smudges beneath her eyes gave her a haggard, anorexic look.

Her smile was the finishing touch. Braces by Bela Lugosi, a tangled contraption of wires and rubber bands that gave her everted lips. Not the kissable kind. More like a carp.

"Well, how do I look?" she asked brightly, automatically checking herself in the hall mirror. "Think they'll let me in?" And in that moment, she looked so vulnerable that I swallowed, hard. Women rely on their looks far more than men. What she'd done to herself took a ton of guts.

"You look . . . stunning, miss," I said, offering her my arm. "My Jeep awaits. Shall we go?"

• • •

Delta Omega is a rich frat, mostly scholarship jocks and legacy residents. A four story faux English manor with front and rear decks, it's the largest house in Westover's Fraternity Row. And it was pumping. As I pulled into the circular drive, The house and grounds were lit up like a movie set in the autumn dusk, the thump of music pulsing in the air like a party-hearty heartbeat.

The driveway and parking lot were already jammed. No problem. I just drove my CJ-7 up over the curb and parked on the lawn next to a half dozen other jalopies.

"Come on," I said, climbing out. "The major action's around in back."

Sara'd worn a loud, flowered blouse chosen for shapelessness, cut off jeans and garish wedge heels so tall she wobbled when she walked. I was dressed campus casual, golf shirt and slacks. Wore my hair shaggy in those days, a reaction to four years of buzz cuts.

Security for the party consisted of a single campus cop stationed at the gate of the picket fence surrounding the backyard. He knew me from Shannon's, but he checked Sara's ID, rolling his eyes at me as he waved us through.

Thunderous jams were thumping from a wall of speakers stretched across one end of the tennis court. Banquet tables on the veranda were stacked with finger food but most of the activity centered around the portable bar where white-jacketed barmen were doling out beer and mixed drinks in paper cups with slick efficiency. Again, they knew me but checked Sara's ID before serving us, a wine highball for Sara, a double scotch for me.

We both stood at the rail, nursing our drinks, taking in the scene.

At first glance, the party didn't seem much wilder than the usual Delta House bash on a rough night. The tennis court was crowded with milling dancers, showing a lot more energy than grace. Most frat boys took the pig part literally, plenty of heavy duty mamas shakin' their chubby booties.

In the lighted swimming pool, a noisy water volleyball game was in full splash. Strip volleyball, muff a point, shuck your shirt, blouse, shoes, something. A few players were already down to their underwear and the game was still in the low teens.

Following Sara through the crowd, I realized she had a mini-camera concealed in her palm. She was surreptitiously taking candid photos every time she pretended to sip her wine.

A drunk goosed Sara's butt as he passed. Annoyed, I reached for him, but she grabbed my arm, pulling me back.

"Cool it, Malloy. No trouble. Yet."

"We may get it whether we want it or not," I grumbled. "Most of these clowns are already half smashed."

"Can you blame them? Check out their dates. No wonder they call it a pig party."

"No offense, lady, but you're not exactly primped for prime time yourself."

"Thanks for noticing," she said acidly. "The difference is, I worked damned hard to look this bad. These porkers are trying to look their pathetic best. Come on, dance with me."

Not a request, an order. Taking my arm, she hauled me into the swirling crush of the tennis court without waiting for a reply. I'm no Fred Astaire but the action on the floor was so frantic I found myself dancing in self defense. And managed not to embarrass myself, I thought.

Not that Sara noticed. She was dancing strictly on autopilot, her moves totally disconnected from the urban rap raging from the speakers. Seemed much more interested in scanning the crowd than grooving to the rhythm of the music. Fortunately we didn't suffer for long. The DJ punched up an old B.B. King blues grind, and things got simpler.

I usually enjoy slow dancing. I've always considered it romantic, even with a stranger. Maybe more so with a stranger.

But not with Sara. When she snuggled against my shoulder, there was nothing seductive about it. She was slyly snapping pictures as we danced, scanning the crowd between shots, steering me around the dance floor like a wheelbarrow to get the photos she wanted.

"Take it easy," I murmured, "we've got all night."

"Actually, we haven't," she said, leading me off the floor before the song ended, still scanning the crowd.

"Why not?"

"Because I've enjoyed as much of this as I can stand!" she snapped. "You were right, Malloy, this is wretched."

"Don't dally on my account. If you want to split, let's go."

"Not quite yet," she said, checking her watch. "I want to get a look inside the Delta House itself."

"Whoa up, Sara, that's a whole different deal. The yard party's open but the House is limited to members only."

"I only see one guy working the door."

"That one's enough, lady. He's Drew Braxton, the all-star linebacker for the Wildcats."

"Then start earning your money, Malloy. Knock him out or something."

"Yeah, right," I said, thinking a mile a minute. I knew Braxton from around. Big beer barrel of a guy, mean as a snake, rough as a box of rocks. A born football player with pro prospects. No chance I could mix it up with him and survive, but . . . .

"Okay," I said, taking a deep breath, "there may be a way to get past him but you're not going to like it."

"Tell me."

So I did. And I was right. She didn't like it. But we tried it anyway.

Unbuttoning her garish blouse, Sara clung to my arm as we staggered up to the door.

"Hey, Brax," I said, slurring my words. "Remember me? Malloy from Shannon's? I got me an emergency situation here."

"Porta-potties are around the side, dude," he said, unimpressed.

"I don't need a john, buddy," I said, holding out a folded twenty between my fingertips. "We need a room. Help a brother out?"

He glanced at Sara, who snuggled closer, giggling, flashing him her widest steel and rubber band smile.

"You don't need a room, sport, you need your frickin' head examined," Braxton said, palming the twenty, but checking Sara's student ID. "Ground floor guest rooms ain't locked, but you'd best knock first. Some of 'em are already busy."

"Thanks man," I said, "I appreciate it."

"Maybe now," he shrugged. "But you're gonna hate me in the morning. And yourself too."

"Jerk!" Sara muttered as we staggered through the foyer. A wide screen TV was on in the guest lounge, replaying a Michigan State game. Two couples were sprawled out on a sofa watching it, the boys more interested in the game than their plain Jane dates. They paid no attention to us at all.

Until Sara took their picture.

"Hey, what the hell was that?" one of the guys said, straightening up, bleary-eyed, but not quite as wrecked as the others. "Was that a camera?"

"Nah, cigarette lighter," I said, hustling Sara down the corridor. Yanking open the first door I came to, I pushed her inside.

"What do you think you're doing?" she said, whirling on me, furious.

"Saving our butts! If you want photos for your story, you have to be more careful! You can't just snap away at these clowns."

"They're so drunk I'm amazed they noticed."

"You'll be even more amazed if they spot that camera and decide to feed it to us," Inching open the door, I scanned the hall. Empty. "Okay, all clear. I don't think anyone followed us. Now what?"

"We give the rooms a quick check," she said, glancing at her watch. "I need—"

"That's twice you've looked at the time," I said, cutting her off. "What's going on?"

"Nothing! Except for you losing your nerve!" she said, pushing past me out the door. "Are you coming or not?"

"To do what?" I asked, following her down the hall. "We can't just crash in on people!"

"Of course we can. It's a pig party, right? We need a room so we can have our way with each other. Oops! Sorry!" she said, opening a door, then closing it again. But not before she'd snapped a quick photo.

"This is crazy," I said, following, checking our back trail. "You're going to get us stomped!"

She ignored me, continuing down the hall, opening doors.

"Oops! So sorry!" Then onto the next. Until the fourth or fifth door. When she didn't say a word. She popped the door open, then went dead white, the color draining from her face. Then she eased the door closed quietly. And leaned against the wall.

"What's wrong?"

"That girl," she said, swallowing. "She's . . ." She shook her head, clearing it. Then took a cell phone out of her purse and tapped a speed dial tab. "I've found her. We're in the Delta house, first floor."

"Sara, what the hell's going on?"

"The girl in that room is being assaulted."

"What?"

"Assaulted, Malloy! Raped! You've got to stop it!"

"Are you sure? You just glanced—"

"Do something!" she shrieked! And she wasn't the only one screaming! Sirens were howling towards Delta House like a pack of wolves as police cars roared in. Cops piling out, trying to make themselves heard over the music.

I tried the door but it was locked now! Rearing back, I kicked it open and charged in. Then dove for the floor as the frat boy inside swung a golf club at my head, barely missing me. Pure reflex! I grappled with him, grabbing him around the knees, wrestling him down. Managed to clock him with a stiff right cross as he fell. He hit the floor like a sack of cement. Out cold.

"Stop it! You're killing him!" a chunky, red-haired girl screeched. Naked to the waist, she threw herself across the unconscious kid on the floor to protect him, sobbing.

"Miss, it's all right," I said, kneeling beside her. "We're here to help you—"

"Get away from me! Leave us alone!" she screamed, snatching up the golf club, whipping it back. Raising my hands, I backed away. She wasn't kidding. Through the tears and smeared mascara, I could read pure murder in her eyes.

"Emily, come on!" Sara said, grabbing up the girl's purse, holding out her blouse. "You've got to get out of here."

But the girl was beyond reason. "You get out!" she screamed. "Help! Somebody help me!"

Somebody did. Two cops in riot gear burst through the door, nightsticks at the ready.

"Get down!" they roared together. "Down on the floor!"

"Hey, wait a minute!" I said. "We're only trying to—"

Wrong answer! One cop jammed me in the midsection, doubling me over. His partner clipped me as I fell . . . .

• • •

Somebody shook my shoulder.

"Get off me!" I growled. A stranger was leaning over me. Brushing his arm away, I sat up. Huge mistake. Huge. Felt like crap on a cracker. Glancing around, I took stock. I was sitting on a metal rack, no blankets, in some kind of a steel and concrete cage. What the hell?

"C'mon buddy, I need to have a look at ya."

I started to protest, then an acid stew of bile and beer came rocketing up. Tried to cover my mouth, Too late! Rolling off the rack onto my hands and knees, I started retching up everything but my name.

"Damn!" The guy who'd shaken me awake backed against the bars, standing on tiptoe to save his shoes. Black guy, pudgy, moon faced. In some kind of uniform.

Not a cop, though. EMT.

Finished, I wobbled slowly to my feet. Floor was uneven. The concrete sloping down to a metal drain in the center of the cell. Stood there a minute, head own, pulling myself together. At least I knew where I was now.

Drunk tank. Westover cop shop, probably. I stifled a groan as images started shouldering their way into my memory. The pig party. Delta House. The screaming girl with the golf club.

And then the cops . . . .

Whoa! Remembered getting hit, going down.

Swallowed hard, trying to remember if I'd fought back. Battery on a police officer was serious trouble.

"You done hurling?" the EMT asked.

"Sure hope so. Who the hell are you?"

"Joe Lockwood, from Sisters of Mercy Hospital. Cops called me down to look you over. Worried you might have a concussion. I need to check your pupils."

"What time is it?"

"About seven."

"In the morning?"

"Yeah. How long have you been here?"

"I'm not sure. Since . . . maybe ten o'clock last night."

"Yeah? How do you feel?"

"Worse than I look."

"That ain't humanly possible, dog. You'd be dead. Might be yet unless you let me check you over. How about it?"

"Yeah, okay, why not?" I said, sagging back down on the metal bunk.

Leaning in, Lockwood aimed a narrow flashlight beam into my eyes. It pierced my brain like an ice pick. "What happened to you, anyway?"

"Long story."

"Looks like a sad one to me. Raise up your arms." He palpated my ribs, checked both collarbones. "Okay, good news, bad news. You're bruised up some, but nothing serious, no sign of concussion. You'll probably live."

"Is that the good news or the bad?"

"Definitely the good. Bad news is, you're still in jail."

• • •

Not for long. Half an hour later I was ushered into a gray concrete interrogation room with a single metal chair bolted to the floor. A police lieutenant who looked too young to vote sat me down, read me my rights, then explained the facts of life.

The frat boy I decked could file assault charges against me but probably wouldn't. He had legal troubles of his own. The officers I had assaulted could also file charges—I tried to protest, he ignored me—but . . . if I was willing to sign a release absolving them of any liability for the . . . misunderstanding, I'd be free to go.

The 'free to go' part got my attention. "Basically, you're saying . . . it never happened? We let bygones be bygones?" I asked.

"Exactly," the boy lieutenant nodded.

"Where do I sign?"

• • •

The newspapers were already on stands when I hit the street. Campus Orgy Raided! Fraternity members charged; drunk and disorderly, furnishing alcohol to minors, and—much more seriously—statutory rape. According to the papers, one of the girls at the party was only fifteen. I was fairly sure I knew which one.

Faced with photographic evidence, the Westover administration went into top speed Cover-Your-Butt mode. Over the next few days, fourteen students were expelled or voluntarily withdrew. Drew Braxton lost his scholarship, the security guard was fired. And the boys weren't the only ones in trouble. A half-dozen girls left school as well, including the one I'd tried to rescue in that room. The papers withheld her name because of her age, but it didn't matter. I already knew her name. Emily. And Westover's a small campus.

Not all the news was grim. Sara Silver, the gutsy *Westover Wildcat* reporter who'd gone undercover to break the story became an overnight celebrity. A reporter's dream. *USA Today* carried the story of the raid with Sara's byline, *Time* and *Newsweek* both ran print interviews with her. She even scored face time on Oprah and Larry King.

With her star on the rise, Sara was already fielding offers from the networks. She'd have her pick of jobs by graduation.

But I wouldn't be around to see it. A few days after the Pig Party raid, Jack Shannon let me go. He said it was for my own good. If I stayed on, sooner or later there'd be trouble. He was right. And to be honest, I didn't much care. The fun was gone. It's tough being a bartender in a college town when the kids treat you like Benedict freakin' Arnold.

Jack gave me two weeks severance pay, plus an envelope somebody left for me at the bar.

No return address. Just fifty bucks in tens. And a note from Sara Silver asking me to meet her at the Coffee Beanery on campus the next day.

A perfect Indian summer afternoon, Westover's maples flaming red and gold. College kids strolling hand in hand. Damn. I was really going to miss this place.

I hadn't seen Sara since the bust. Scarcely recognized her. She was sitting at an open air table in front of the coffee shop, looking sharp enough to stop traffic.

The night of the pig party, she'd shocked me by turning herself into a brown wren, plain as wallpaper paste.

Now, the transformation had gone the other way. A full-blown extreme TV makeover. The cute coed had blossomed into a picture-perfect butterfly. Honey blonde hair impeccably coifed, trimmed to nape length and swept to one side. Eyebrows plucked and patterned to perfection. Ice blue contacts, Donna Karan suit. Primped, polished and ready for prime time.

"My, my, what a difference a few days can make," I said, taking the chair facing her. "You look absolutely dynamite."

"I wish I could say the same, Malloy. You look like crap."

"I had some trouble sleeping in jail."

"I got you out as soon as I could. Did my best to keep your name out of it."

"I noticed that none of the news stories mentioned me. I guess I should thank you."

"No need," she said briskly. "Mr. Shannon said you're leaving town. Because of the Pig Party? Have either of you been threatened?"

"Are you suddenly worried about my welfare, Silver? Or just looking for another byline?"

"That's unfair. If you're having problems, you certainly can't blame me for them. I never intended to cause you any trouble."

"No, I'm sure you didn't. You smelled a story and went after it without a thought to what the fallout might be for me. Much less for Emily Kaempfert."

"Who?"

"Come on, Silver, it's Malloy, remember? Your partner in crime. We both know who Emily is. Emily Kaempfert. The underage girl I hauled out of the pig party. The one you took me there to find."

"But her name was never released," she said carefully. "How do you—?"

"You called out to her at the bust, remember? And Westover's a small campus. I had no trouble finding out who she was. And where she lived."

Sara's face went suddenly still. Unreadable as a mask.

"Kappa Rho," I went on. "The sorority for promising academics. And Emily was very promising. A math whiz who graduated from high school at fifteen. Valedictorian. Precocious, but also pudgy and plain. With no social skills at all. But you know all that, don't you? Because you live at Kappa Rho, too. In fact, you're a mentor there. For freshmen like Emily. You knew her, didn't you?"

"I knew . . . who she was," Sara said carefully. "That's why I was so shocked to find her at that party."

"Bull! You knew damned well she'd be there. You helped her to get in. The security guard and Braxton both knew me but they still checked your ID. They must have checked Emily's too. The papers ran pictures of the fake ID Emily used to get into the party. Pretty lame. It wouldn't have fooled me. Don't think it would have fooled that security guard or Braxton either."

"What is it you think you know, Malloy?"

"I think Emily had a much better fake ID, maybe pro quality. But she's only a freshman and a fifteen-year-old at that. She wouldn't have a clue about how to find an ID good enough to get her past security. But you would. You did a story on it last semester."

"That's crazy."

"Is it? When you grabbed Emily's purse in the scuffle, I thought you were trying to help me get her out of there. But now I think you swapped the crude ID for the one she actually used to get into the party. The raid would be a very different story if the star reporter was guilty of setting up the crime she helped bust. My god, how could you do it?"

"Do what?"

"A chubby geek like Emily probably never had a date in her life. Certainly not at Westover. So when she told you she'd been invited to the Delta House party, she had no idea what it meant. But you did. You should have warned her, Sara. Instead, you furnished her with fake ID, then hired me to help you get pictures. Knowing that kid was headed for total humiliation, or a whole lot worse."

"Pig parties have been an open sore on this campus for years. You said it yourself. They're loud, lewd, and degrading to women. Somebody had to bring it down."

"The parties may be sophomoric but they've gone on quite awhile with no major damage done. But that's not true anymore, is it? Nearly two dozen futures smashed up and one poor shlub looking at serious jail time. Thanks to you."

"With your help."

"True, and that's what bothers me the most. That I came here looking for a fresh start and wound up wrecking a lot of innocent lives."

"Puhleeze!" she snorted. "There was nothing innocent about that party."

"Emily was innocent. God knows what'll happen to her now. The pig party was idiotic but it was just one night. The fallout from the raid will go on for years. I can understand your wanting to end it, but I can't believe you sent Emily in there, knowing what might happen to her."

"Believe what you like," she said acidly. "If you want more money, maybe we can work something out. But if you try to go public with this crock, my editors will sue you into the poorhouse."

"Don't worry, Sara, I can't talk without throwing Emily to the sharks and she's suffered enough already. I don't want to hurt anyone else. Not even you."

"As if you could," she sneered, rising. "Good luck with your career, Malloy. Maybe I'll look you up, sometime. If I need a drink."

And she walked away. The prettiest, smartest woman who's ever asked me out, or probably ever will.

And the coldest.

Oddly enough, I think I preferred the Sara from the party, braces and all, to the perfect, plastic Barbie Doll she's become.

Beauty's a tricky business. We all think we can define it, but one guy's woofer is the next guy's true, true love. In the years between, I've watched the mating game play out a thousand times and I've decided real beauty comes down to character. When people respond to each other, soul to soul, everything else suddenly becomes very small change. A plain woman in love can take your breath away. A cover girl without a heart is only a picture. And a flat one at that.

But if beauty's complicated, ugly's a lot easier. Because looks don't have a damned thing to do with it.

Pig party rules are simple. Bring the ugliest date you can find.

For most guys, that means a plain Jane or the Wicked Witch of the West, not a media babe like Sara Silver.

But for me? I've only been to one pig party. Wildest night of my life.

And I definitely took the right girl.

Award winning author **DOUG ALLYN** is a Michigan writer with an international following. The author of eight novels and nearly a hundred short stories, his first short story won the Robert L. Fish Award for Best First from Mystery Writers of America and subsequent critical response has been equally remarkable. He has won the coveted Edgar Allen Poe Award, (plus six nominations), the International Crime Readers' Award, three Derringer Awards for novellas, and the Ellery Queen Readers' Award an unprecedented eight times. Published internationally in English, German, French and Japanese, more than two dozen of his tales have been optioned for development as feature films and television.

Perfect Gentleman

BY BRETT BATTLES

You won't like me.

Whatever. I've stopped caring.

I'm not a bad guy, but you're not going to believe that. People like you never do. You hear about what I do. You see how I live. You think, sleaze or deviant or something like that. Maybe you're right. Maybe I'm all those things. I certainly don't think God's waiting for me to show up at his front gate.

Again, it doesn't matter. This isn't really about me, is it? It's about Joseph Perdue.

Now there was a guy you really hate. A real asshole. But you people only chose to see one side of him. You made him out the hero. Someday you'll probably call him a martyr for the cause. For the American way. That's what happens to the dead, isn't it? No one cares about the truth.

I remember the first time he came into the bar.

That's not really surprising. I remember every time someone new comes in. It's part of my job. First I need to make sure the guy (they're always guys) doesn't look like an obvious problem. If he's too drunk or too belligerent or has got a bad rep, I point them to another bar and say they got a special show that night and he shouldn't miss it. Works every time. If he doesn't seem like he'll be a problem then I size him up, figure out how much we can expect to get out of him, and what he might be looking for.

On the evening Perdue came in, the usual pop crap was blaring out of our far too expensive sound system. Occasionally I've been known to sneak in an old Skynyrd album or *Dark Side of the Moon* by Pink Floyd. God, I love that album. But the girls always protest, and I seldom make it through "Speak to Me" before I have to flip back to Christina Aguilera or Gwen Stefani or Gorillaz. When Perdue walked in, I'm pretty sure the song playing was "Perfect Gentleman" by Wyclef Jean.

Perhaps I should have taken that as a sign.

It was a slow night, a Tuesday. Our big nights are Thursdays, Fridays, and Mondays—the first two because around here everyone is ready to start the weekend a little early, and Mondays because that's when we hold our weekly body-painting contest. Nothing like some fluorescent paint, some beautiful young women, and a few fluorescent black-light tubes to fill up the place and bring in the cash.

Event evening or not, we still had a full complement of girls, somewhere between twenty and thirty at the beginning of the shift. That number would depend on how many girls were sick, how many had found someone for an extended absence, and how many just didn't show up.

No idea what our exact total was that night. I do know that Ellie was there. She was up on the stage with five or six others grinding away. But I've gotta say, whenever Ellie was onstage, it was as if she were dancing alone. That was her power. She was a superstar. The killer bod and the killer personality and that killer something that wouldn't allow you to take your eyes off her.

You don't get a lot of superstars. Maybe one or two per bar. Ellie was our one.

In strip bars in the States, the girls had routines, elaborate moves choreographed to the latest hip-hop favorite. But not here.

Of course, my place isn't really a strip bar. And it's nowhere near the States. It's in Angeles City in the Philippines. Perhaps you remember Clark Air Base? Used to be the biggest U.S. base outside of the States. The old main gate is only a couple miles from the door of my bar. But then there was Mt. Pinatubo erupting ash over everything, and the Filipino people threatening to erupt in anger if the U.S. didn't finally withdraw.

We withdrew.

Well, the government did. Us ex-pats, we stayed. And over the years we've been joined by more.

This is the part where you realize you hate me. Yeah, my bar is one of those kind of bars. A go-go bar. At my place, you can watch them dance, buy them a drink, talk to them, and then take a girl out for the night or for a week if you want. You just gotta pay the bar fine, and it would be nice if you tipped the girl after.

And this is the part where I tell you I take care of my girls. I try not to let them go out with jerks—it happens, but not as much as it does at other bars. I do what I can to protect them. I try to keep them out of too much trouble. I know it won't matter, but there are a hell of a lot worse *Papasans* around than me.

So go ahead and hate me, but the business will still be here. The guys will still come. And so will the girls. Because for them the money's better here, and there's always a chance they might get taken out of the life to live in Australia or the UK or America.

Perdue, if I remember correctly, glanced at the narrow stage—more like a runway down the center of the room back then before I remodeled—then took a seat in an empty booth on the far side.

He wasn't alone for long. That's not why people come to the bars in Angeles City. They come for the laughs, for the cold bottles of San Miguel beer, but most of all they come for the brown skin girls so willing and available.

A couple of my waitresses in their uniforms of tight, pink hot pants and white bikini tops approached him together. Only half interested, I watched the encounter, still unsure if the guy was one of those who was only gauging the talent and would soon be leaving, or was someone we could milk a few pesos out of, maybe even hook him up for the night.

One of the waitresses, Anna, giggled while the other one, Margaret I think, looked over in my direction and said something to our new guest. Perdue looked at me, then removed a wad of bills from his pocket and handed a couple of notes to each of the girls.

Now I was intrigued. Guys usually didn't pay for anything the moment they arrived. What happened next surprised me even more. Perdue got up from his booth and walked around the stage to where I sat at the bar.

He nodded at the stool next to the one I was sitting on. "May I?"

"Please," I said.

"Thanks. I think the view's better from over here."

Indeed it was. Superstar Ellie with the do-me-now looks was swaying back and forth less than ten feet away.

"Joseph Perdue." He held out a thin, rough hand.

"Wade Norris," I said.

His grip was stronger than I expected. Whoever Perdue was, he was more powerful than he let on.

"You American, too?" he asked.

I nodded. "Ohio. Columbus."

"Never been there. I'm from Wyoming, myself."

"Yellowstone?" I asked. It was the only place I knew in Wyoming.

He smiled at me. "Nah. Laramie. Cowboy country."

Anna walked over and handed Perdue a San Miguel, then set a cup on the bar behind him with a slip of paper inside noting the beer.

He held his bottle out toward me. "Cheers, Wade."

I obliged by clinking the bottom of my bottle against the bottom of his. We both took drinks, his deeper than mine.

"I hear you're the *Papasan.* You run things."

Run would be a good word for it, I thought. I wasn't the owner. He was thousands of miles away in the Netherlands. But I was the decision-maker, and gatekeeper.

I shrugged, then said, "You enjoying Angeles?"

"Seems pretty nice. But, you know, all these bars around here seem pretty much the same. You all got the neon, the mirrors with all the names painted on them, the big bells. The only difference I can see is the girls. Some places have a better group than others."

I couldn't argue with his assessment. There are over a hundred go-go bars in Angeles City, all offering pretty much the same thing: prerecorded music and liquor and women.

"So how does ours rank?"

"About average." He nodded toward Ellie. "Except for her. She brings your score way up."

I couldn't help but smile. The fish was circling the bait. Now all I had to do was hook him.

While Perdue took another drink, I caught the attention of Kat, the bartender. With a quick, almost undetectable motion, I indicated our new customer's interest in our superstar. Less than a minute later, Ellie had made her way off the stage and walked across the room to where we were sitting.

"Hey, Ellie," I said. "How you doing?"

"I was getting hot," she said. She pulled at her bikini top, like she needed to get air between the flimsy fabric and her C-cup breasts. She looked at Perdue and smiled. "Who's this?"

"Another Yank," I said. "Joseph Perdue."

She held out her hand and gave him a look even the most disinterested man would be hard-pressed to resist. "Nice to meet you. I'm Ellie."

"Hi, Ellie," Perdue said. Instead of shaking her hand, he kissed it, the whole time his eyes never leaving her face.

I knew the deal was done then, and twenty minutes later I was proved correct.

"He wants to pay bar fine, Papa. What do you think?" Ellie asked me. She and Perdue had moved to the booth he'd occupied when he'd first arrived. Now she had walked back over to me alone while her potential boyfriend for the night waited.

"He seems all right," I said. "What do you think?"

"I think he has money," she said.

"Then, by all means, have a great night."

It didn't surprise me when Perdue came in the next night and bar fined her again. And I wasn't particularly shocked that he'd decided to bar fine her not just for that evening, but for the rest of the week. The fish had not just swallowed the hook, but the hook and the line and the rod. Ellie was a hard one to resist.

Of course, the deal was good for everyone. I was happy to collect the cash. Ellie was happy to be out of the bar for more than just a few hours, and was definitely happy about her cut of the bar fine. And Perdue, presumably, was happy to be spending time with a beautiful girl at least twenty years younger than he was.

Honestly, after that night, I thought I wouldn't see the guy again. I figured he'd probably bar fine her for the remainder of his trip and when she came back to work, it would mean he was on the long flight home to the U.S. But two days later, he showed up in the middle of the afternoon.

It was Friday, but we wouldn't really get busy until after dark. At the time, we only had two customers, so the day shift girls—about half as many as I'd have on that night—were huddled together in cliques talking or sitting alone texting their boyfriends, both foreign and Filipino, on their mobiles.

I had only been there about thirty minutes, but as usual, my ass was glued to my favorite stool at the bar. If anyone else ever tried to sit there, Kat or one of the other bartenders made them move. "Papa Wade's chair," they'd say.

When Perdue came in, he took a few seconds for his eyes to adjust from the bright sunshine outside to the dim interior, then spotted me and walked over.

"Alone?" I asked.

"Ellie said she had to run home to take care of something. I'm meeting her at Mac's in an hour."

Mac's was the main restaurant in the district everyone ended up in. But Perdue didn't sound happy about it. In fact I'd say he was pretty annoyed. But I didn't push. My job was to make the customer feel as good as possible about his time in Angeles. Getting into the middle of a relationship between one of my girls and her *honey ko* was never a good idea. Unless, of course, it was because he was treating her badly.

Whether you believe it or not, we're a family. And a hell of a lot better one than those most of my girls had grown up in back in the provinces. We watch out for each other. We're there when times are good or times are bad. We know enough to give each other room when we need it, when to let hope simmer and not discourage it, and when to snap each other back into reality—albeit our reality—when we had to

But what we really have to do is be careful not to crush the dream. In this make-believe world of faux love and real sex, it's the dream that keeps a lot of the girls going. It's the chance that maybe, just maybe, the guy they've got temporarily wrapped around their finger might fall for them hard. Maybe they can get him to spend his entire vacation with them. Maybe they can get him to call them, and e-mail them, and send them money after he's returned home. Maybe—and this is the big one—maybe he'll even marry them and take them away from the islands.

It happens all the time. Only with thousands of girls working the business, a few a month leaving for better lives is a small percentage. Still, the dream is there. And I have always been careful not to get in the way of even that narrow chance.

"So you been having a good time?" I asked.

I figured the only answer could be yes. He would have sent Ellie back by now if he wasn't.

"Took her down to Manila yesterday. Had a little business

to deal with. Thought she might like to do some shopping." Finally Perdue cracked a smile. "I guess I was right."

I laughed. Take one of the girls shopping, and she'd stay with you for free. It was their religion, but one they seldom indulged in unless it was on someone else's dime. "So I'll take that as a yes."

The smile slipped again. "For the most part."

We drank in relative silence as the perpetual sound track of Justin Timberlake and Robbie Williams and even vintage Spice Girls played on, only at slightly reduced afternoon levels. "Can I trust you?" Perdue asked.

I looked over at him, a knowing grin on my face. "Of course," I said. It was my standard answer. Truth was, I already knew what he was going to tell me. It was going to be some variation on "Ellie's not like the other girls," or "I haven't slept more than an hour at a time since I took her home," or "Do you think you can meet someone special at a place like this?" They were all a prelude, a setup to talking himself into believing he'd fallen in love. Perhaps Ellie had actually found her ticket out of town.

But even as the thought came to me, I questioned whether it would really pan out. After you've worked here as many years as I have, you get a sense of the guys. And my sense of Perdue was that he wasn't looking for a wife.

"I'm serious," he said. "Can I trust you?"

I lifted up my beer. "You can tell me whatever you want. It'll just be between us."

For a few seconds, I thought he wasn't going to say anything. He leaned toward me. "I'm Homeland Security," he finally said, his voice barely audible above the music. In fact it was so low, I wasn't sure I'd even heard him right.

"What?" I asked.

"Homeland Security. You know what that is, right?"

I'd been living in the Philippines since the late nineties, and hadn't actually set foot Stateside since before 9/11. But with CNN International and the large American ex-pat community—

most of whom were former military—you couldn't help knowing a little bit about what was happening back home.

"That's, like, antiterrorism, right?"

"That's just part of it. But, yeah, that's our main focus."

I wasn't sure what to say. I mean, we get all types in the bar. Maybe he was trying to impress me. Homeland Security, it did sound important. Maybe I should have been impressed. But I wasn't.

"I'm here looking into a few potential rumors. We want to neutralize any problems before they develop."

"'Neutralize'?" I repeated. I think it might have been the first time I'd ever heard it used like that in conversation. "That's why you're in Angeles? Or why you're at my bar?"

"The Philippines," he said. "Mainly in the south. Two months now. I came up here for a little relaxation."

Now we were back on familiar territory. "Glad we could help you with that."

The corners of his mouth went up and down in what I could only guess was a quick smile. "When I was in Manila yesterday . . ." He let the words hang as he took a sip of his San Miguel.

"On your business," I offered.

He nodded. "On my business. I heard something disturbing. It came to us through a very dependable source. But you know how these things are."

No, actually, I didn't. And I had no idea why he was even telling me any of this. But he was the customer, so I wasn't about to stop him. Besides, it wasn't just the girls who fell into a routine. Someday I could tell this story to my other *Papasan* friends. They'd love it. *The secret agent confesses all to Papa Wade.*

"Seems there might be trouble here in Angeles," Perdue finally said.

I almost laughed out loud. Terrorism? Here in Angeles? Gangs, yes. But terrorists? Something that would concern the government of the United States of America? Not possible.

"I think maybe your source is screwing with you," I said.

"That's what I thought, too," Perdue said. "But I did a little checking this morning, and now I'm not so sure."

"We've never had any of that kind of trouble. And I'm sure we're not about to, either." I suddenly had no desire to continue talking about this. I didn't want to know. I was happy with my beer and my girls and my life. Terrorism was a problem for somewhere else.

"Yeah, well, they didn't have that kind of trouble in Bali before, but we all know what happened there."

That stopped me.

Bali was the thing someone always threw out on those rare occasions when conversation turned to terrorism. And Bali scared the shit out of me. That had been in 2002. Two bombs at nightclubs in the tourist district. A couple hundred people died. All of us in Angeles knew at the time it could have just as easily happened in front of one of our places. And then, over weeks and months, we forgot about it, pushing it out of our minds, and returning to the belief that it could never happen here.

"I'm not sure you should be telling me this," I finally said.

Perdue leaned in. "I'm telling you this for a very good reason. I need your help."

"My help?"

"I got a name and a picture from my source in Manila. He's been involved in kidnappings and executions in the south, but it appears his *comrades* have ordered him to set up shop here in your part of the country. The funny thing is, when I saw the picture, I knew I'd seen him recently. Here."

"In Angeles? It's a big city."

He shook his head. "On Fields Avenue." Fields is the main street that runs through the bar district. "I want you to look at the picture. Tell me if you recognize him."

I could feel a bead of sweat growing on my brow, not unusual for hot and humid Angeles City, but definitely unusual in my bar where I kept the AC on all the time so it was always comfortable.

Perdue reached into his pocket, and pulled out a photograph. He handed it to me.

"Well?" he asked.

I looked at the picture. It was fuzzy, out of focus. To me, and I'm not an expert at this, it looked like the picture had been taken from a distance using a zoom lens.

The subject was a man. A Filipino. I guessed anywhere from twenty-five to thirty. He was sitting on a motorcycle facing the camera. His brown skin looked extra dark, probably from spending too many daylight hours in the sun. Other than that, there was nothing to distinguish him from a couple hundred other guys who drove motorcycles in the city.

"I don't know," I said, honestly. "Could be familiar, but it's not a great photo."

"His name's Ernesto de la Cruz, does that help?"

Acting is a big part of being a *Papasan.* You've got to always be happy, always on. You've got to act like the jokes your patrons are telling you are really funny. You've got to pretend that there's never a bad day on Fields Avenue.

So when I heard the name and looked at the picture again, I didn't flinch.

"Never heard of him," I lied.

Perdue looked at me, a stupid little smile on his face, his eyes on my eyes. It was like he knew I was lying, like he was waiting for me to take it back and tell him the truth.

"Sorry," I said. "I don't know him."

He hesitated for a half second more, then broke off his stare. "You keep that picture. Maybe you can show it around. See if any of the girls know who he is. But don't tell anyone I'm looking for him."

"And if someone does know who he is?"

Perdue picked up his beer. "See if you can find out where he lives."

"I don't know if I want to get in the middle of anything here."

"You're a good American, right?"

I didn't respond right away. I didn't like the direction this was going, but when he cocked his head and narrowed his eyes, I said, "Sure."

"Then finding out where he lives isn't going to be a problem, is it?"

"I didn't say I could find out."

"I have faith in you."

After he left, I asked Kat for a match, then burned the photo. I wasn't able to relax until the last of the image blackened, then turned to ash.

I knew who Ernesto de la Cruz was. He was a local. Helped me out sometimes at the bar—washing glasses, stocking beer, that kind of thing—when one of my regular guys needed a day off. He was a good kid. Smiled a lot. Always respectful. As far as I knew, he'd never been south of Manila.

A terrorist? Not even remotely possible. Of course, the moment Perdue mentioned Ernesto's name, I knew this wasn't about terrorism.

Ernesto de la Cruz was Ellie's boyfriend. And I would bet everything I own that Perdue knew that, too.

That evening, I asked Marguerite—she was one of my girls and Ellie's best friend—to text Ellie and tell her I wanted to talk to her. I'd trained the girls to know if they received a text like that, they were to stop by the bar at their next opportunity and see me.

I didn't expect to see her until the next day, and I was right.

It was just before noon. The bar wasn't open yet, but I was already there. Ellie knocked at the front door, and I let her in.

"You want me, Papa?" she asked, once we were alone inside.

"How is everything?" I said.

She hesitated only long enough for me to notice. "Okay. Fine."

"Mr. Perdue's treating you all right?"

"Joe took me to Manila. He buy me lot of things."

"So he hasn't hurt you?"

There was that pause again. "No. Why?"

"When was the last time you saw Ernesto?"

"What?" My question obviously surprised her.

"Have you seen him this week?"

"No. Of course not."

It was a pat answer. If the girls were on an extended bar fine, the house rule was no contact with any boyfriends. The reason was to avoid exactly the problem that seemed to be developing here.

"Ellie. Tell me the last time you saw him."

"Last weekend," she said quickly. "Sunday, I think."

The girls were as good at lying as I was. But unlike their temporary boyfriends, I'd long ago developed the ability to know if one of the girls was telling me the truth or not.

"When, Ellie?"

The sparkle in her eyes disappeared as she realized she'd been caught "Yesterday," she said. "Joe went out for a while in the afternoon. I meet Ernesto at his place. But only for an hour. I don't lie."

That had probably been around the same time Perdue had stopped by the bar. "And before that, when?"

"The day before Joe take me to Manila."

"Jesus, Ellie. You know the rules."

"What? What's wrong?"

"Perdue must have seen you. He was asking about him."

"Joe wants his money back, doesn't he?" She looked horrified. "I'm sorry, Papa. I shouldn't have seen him. I'll pay you back, I promise."

I shook my head. "It's not the money."

"Then what?"

I contemplated stopping right there. I should have, but I didn't. "He wanted to know if I could find out where Ernesto lived."

"Why?"

"I don't think Perdue is a good man."

The true meaning of my words took a moment to sink in. When they finally did, she stepped away from me and turned for the door. "I have to tell Ernesto!"

I grabbed her arm, stopping her. "You can't go anywhere near Ernesto."

"But Joe will try to hurt him."

"Tell me how to find Ernesto. I'll tell him to get lost for a few days. Maybe he can go down to Manila."

"You'll do that?"

"Yes," I said. "Do you know when Joe's leaving town?"

"Monday, I think."

She told me where Ernesto lived, then, almost as if she didn't want to say it, added, "He pushed me."

"Who?"

"Joe," she said. "It was late, but I wanted to go out dancing. He said he was tired. I teased him and he pushed me into the wall."

I held my tongue as a surge of anger grew inside me.

"He said it was an accident. That he was just teasing back, but he wasn't. He pushed me. He'll hurt Ernesto."

"Go to your place," I said. "Stay there until Perdue leaves town. I'll tell him you got sick. I'll give him back his money if he asks."

"What about Ernesto?"

"I'll find him. It'll be okay."

Only it wasn't okay.

Ernesto shared a room in a dingy building about a mile from Fields Avenue. When I got there, the normal chaos of a typical Angeles street had been replaced by something much more sinister.

White vans blocked off each end of the street, but it didn't stop the curious from walking around them to see what was going on. The real action was toward the middle of the block, in front of Ernesto's building.

Whatever had happened seemed to have just ended. A dozen soldiers stood near the entrance. They were wearing full battle gear and held machine guns at the ready. At first I thought they were all Filipino, but the closer I got, I realized that though they were wearing identical dark uniforms, most of the men appeared to be either Caucasian or African-American.

My immediate thought was *Americans.*

I moved with the crowd, reaching a spot almost directly across the street from the building's entrance. I knew enough not to put myself out front, and I held back, allowing others to stand in front of me. After about ten minutes, two men appeared in the doorway. They were carrying a stretcher, complete with a sheet-draped body on top. By the way everyone was acting, I knew the dead man wasn't one of theirs. And when Joseph Perdue emerged from the building a few moments later to the back-slaps of his colleagues, it was pretty evident who was on the stretcher.

Homeland Security had gotten their man.

It was nearly 10:00 p.m. when Perdue showed up back in my bar. For the first time in a long time I wasn't sitting on my usual stool. Instead I'd taken over the back booth, and left instructions not to bother me unless it was really important.

Perdue spotted me right after he came in. He got a beer from Kat, then walked slowly back to my table, not even glancing at the girls on the stage. That was probably a good thing. While I hadn't told any of them what had happened, most had found out Ernesto was dead through other means, and had a pretty good idea Perdue had something to do with it. The looks they gave him were nothing short of venomous.

"How ya doing, Wade?" he asked

"Fine. You?"

"Doing just great."

He slid into the other side of the booth without waiting to be asked.

"Haven't been able to get anything about the guy in your picture." I figured ignorance was the best route to take.

"Don't worry about it," he said. "Problem's taken care of."

I said nothing.

"Look I'm going to be leaving town a little early. Heading out in the morning. Don't know when I'll be back."

"Have a good trip."

"Actually I came by to thank you. I had a great time. Lots of fun."

"That's what we're here for," I said, less than enthusiastically.

He took a deep swig of his beer, then set the bottle on the table. "Good-bye, Wade." He stood up. "You take it easy, all right?"

I shook his hand. Didn't want to, but there was no sense in causing a scene. He was leaving town, so I wouldn't have to worry about him anymore.

"Have a safe trip wherever you're going," I said.

"I'm heading home," he said. "Well, D.C., actually. I'm getting promoted."

"Good for you."

"Yeah, it is."

I'd been so wrapped up in wishing he'd just get out of the bar, that it wasn't until after he left that I realized he hadn't said anything about Ellie. Not one word.

Kat was the one who found her. We actually shut the bar down, and I sent the girls out in every direction. But leave it to Kat to hunt her down.

Ellie was only a few blocks from the dormlike room she shared with over a dozen other girls. She was in an alley—Angeles is rife with them—on the ground, her knees pulled up to her chest and her head lolled back with her mouth open. There was a long gash running from her left temple nearly all the way to her mouth. Blood was running from the wound, so I knew she was still alive.

The story I got later was that when she heard Ernesto was dead, she went crazy. All she could think about was killing Perdue.

She got a knife and went to Perdue's hotel. The rest is pretty easy to imagine. She was no match for him. The only reason he didn't kill her—and I'm guessing here—is because he thought damaging her would be a worse fate.

As it was, what he had done to her in less than fifteen minutes took three operations and several months to repair. Even then it wasn't perfect. The scar that ran down the side of Ellie's face would always be with her. A reminder not only of Perdue, but of Ernesto.

• • •

"Can I ask you a few questions?" the man said.

It was a Monday evening, and in less than an hour the place would be packed for the weekly body-painting contest. But at that moment we were only half full.

"Of course," I said.

"Something to drink?" Ellie asked the man. Since returning to work a couple weeks earlier, she had asked if she could work behind the bar with Kat. Who was I to say no?

"Just some water, please," the man said.

He was the nervous type, who probably felt a lot more comfortable in a suit than in the casual wear he had on at that moment.

Ellie set a cold plastic bottle of water in front of him.

"Thanks," he said.

"I'm Wade Norris," I said.

"Curtis Knowles." He held out his hand and we shook.

"What can I do for you, Curtis?" I said, already knowing what he was going to ask.

"I'm with the FBI," he said.

"A little out of your territory, aren't you?"

He smiled. "I'm just part of an investigation, that's all."

"And your investigation brought you here?"

Knowles looked around. "It is one of the more unusual settings I've been in. I'll tell you that much." He unscrewed the top of his water, but didn't take a drink. "I'm looking into the disappearance of a federal employee."

"Don't tell me," I said. "Joseph Perdue, right?"

"I realize someone's already talked to you about this."

"You're the third person in two months. One of the others told me Perdue'd been kidnapped."

"We don't know anything for sure."

"He said it was in retaliation for that kid he killed, if I remember right."

"Terrorist."

"What?"

"The terrorist he killed. Perdue had uncovered information that linked the man to potential attacks that would have happened right here on your street, Mr. Norris."

"Really?" I said. "Hadn't heard that part."

"It was in the paper."

"I stopped reading the paper years ago. Too depressing."

Knowles removed a small notebook from his breast pocket, and opened it to one of the pages. "According to my notes, you said you remember Perdue coming into the bar twice, is that correct?"

"I haven't thought about this since the last time one of you guys came by. But that sounds about right."

"People have reported seeing him with . . . a woman."

I smiled. "So he was getting in a little fun while he was here."

"The woman was not someone he was *seeing*," Knowles said. "Perdue was a good family man."

"Was?"

Knowles paused, caught by his own words. "At this point, we believe he is most likely dead."

"I'm sorry to hear that."

"We also believe he was in contact with this woman as a potential information source. One of the people we talked to thought she might work here."

"Get you another beer, Papa?" Ellie said.

"Yes. Thanks." I looked at Knowles. "She wasn't one of ours. I remember everyone who takes one of the girls out."

"Everyone?"

"It's my job."

Ellie replaced my old bottle with a new one.

"He probably just met her on the outside."

"I would have found out," I said, then took a drink of my beer. "Mr. Knowles, there are a couple thousand girls who work in the bars here. Who knows where she came from?"

Knowles nodded. "You're right."

"Why do you think she's so important?"

"We don't know for sure, but we think maybe she set him up."

"Sounds like you're reaching," I said, trying to appear sympathetic.

Another nod from Knowles. "I won't take up any more of your time." As he pushed himself off the stool, he said, "If we have any more questions, we'll get back to you."

"I'll be here," I said, then saluted him with my bottle. Knowles smiled, then walked around our new stage and out the front door.

I knew Perdue was trouble when he'd stared at me after I told him I didn't recognize the picture of Ernesto. There was no bluff in his gaze, no false toughness. What I had seen was the look of a man who didn't like to be crossed. I'd seen it before, back in my service days in the corps. Other marines who were more like machines than real men—in their minds, they felt like all they had to do was look at the enemy, and their adversary would crumple to the ground.

They were hard. They were single-minded. They were dangerous as all hell.

And I'd been one of them.

After Kat found Ellie and we'd gotten her to the hospital, I'd gone alone in search of Perdue. I found him easily enough. He was in his room at the Paradise Hotel. I knocked on his door, told him I was looking for Ellie and wondered if he knew where she was. Of course he let me in.

I eased the door closed behind me, then I buried the pointed metal rod I'd been holding against my leg under his rib cage and into one of his lungs. I watched his face for a moment as he realized too late the danger I represented. I was just a lazy old *Papasan,* after all. Drunk half the time, and mellowed by the women that surrounded me. He tried to grab for me, but he was already too weak. I should have probably said something damning, something to sum up his failures as a human being. Instead I pulled the rod out and shoved it up again. This time into his heart.

See, I was Homeland Security, too. It was just that my homeland extended only a couple miles beyond the door of my bar.

By morning, the old stage in the bar had been ripped out, and a hole dug deep into the ground beneath. Perdue went into the hole, along with some dirt and rocks and concrete. Then we got to work on the new stage. I made this one a little wider.

The girls love it.

"Thanks, Papa," Ellie said after Knowles had left.

"Nothing to thank me for. How about a dance?"

"Not today," she said. But this time, unlike all the previous times I'd asked her to try out the new stage, she actually smiled.

I was breaking her down. One day, she'd get up there and she'd dance again.

On that day, drinks will be on the house.

BRETT BATTLES lives in Los Angeles and is the author of three acclaimed novels in the Jonathan Quinn series: *The Cleaner*, which was nominated for a Barry Award for Best Thriller and a Shamus Award for Best First Novel, *The Deceived*, and *Shadow of Betrayal.* He is also one of the founding members of Killer Year, a group of novelists who all had their debut books come out in 2007, and a member of both International Thriller Writers and Mystery Writers of America.

BY NORMAN PARTRIDGE

PART ONE

Kim Barlow was two months in the ground when her brother first learned she was dead.

Glen got an e-mail from a deputy sheriff up in Arizona. Of course, the message had been gathering virtual dust for a couple of months in Glen's inbox, because Glen hardly ever checked his mail. Not because he couldn't. Sure, the rig was forty miles off the Texas coast, but there were computers around. What there wasn't was anyone Glen Barlow heard from that way. Except for Kim, and Kim had been pretty quiet since Glen tossed her boyfriend through her living room window last Christmas Eve.

Glen had only clocked a couple months with the company, but the Installation Manager liked him well enough to okay emergency leave. Some young suit from Houston was headed back to the mainland after touring the rig, and Glen caught a ride into Galveston on the company chopper. Seventeen hours later he parked his truck in front of the El Pasito sheriff's office. He'd already talked to that emailing deputy on a cell phone he'd forgotten in the Ford's glove compartment when he ditched the mainland for his time offshore. Glen used that cell phone about as much as he used his email account.

The deputy—whose name was J. J. Bryce—had spent most of the day waiting for Glen to show up. One look at the guy and Bryce shook his head. He shook his head when he saw Glen's pickup, too. Try to describe that old hunk of Ford in a report, he'd note the color as rust or primer, take your pick. And the guy who drove it was pretty much the same way. Headed towards forty with the years starting to show. Bryce was real familiar with the type. A drifter—one of those guys who was wiry as a half-starved animal. And that might mean you were talking jackrabbit, or it might mean you were talking coyote. Sometimes it was hard to tell going in.

But Bryce already had an opinion about this guy. He'd heard all about Barlow tossing Kale Howard through that living room window last Christmas Eve. In fact, he'd heard more about it than the talk that went around the cop shop. Not that any of that mattered right now. The way the deputy saw it, right now things were all business.

The two of them sat down in the deputy's cramped office and ran the drill. There wasn't much to look at. Not in the office. Not in the file Bryce had on Kim Barlow's death. But Glen looked, and he took his time about it, and that wasn't something the deputy much liked.

After a while, Glen closed the folder and slid it across the desk.

"Having a hard time buying this," he said.

"No buying it, really. It's what happened."

"You don't have a suspect?"

"You read the report, Mr. Barlow. You don't have a suspect in a case like this."

"You talk to that asshole Howard?"

"Yeah. I talked to Kale. Read his file, too."

"Then you know he used to beat up my sister."

"I know that. But I also know that Howard didn't do this. No man could have."

Glen just looked at the guy—kind of grinned, didn't say one word—and Bryce all of a sudden felt his pulse hammering, because it most definitely wasn't the kind of look you got from a jackrabbit.

Glen Barlow said: "You'd be surprised what some men can do."

• • •

There it was. Cards on the table, and all in the space of ten minutes. But the gents named Bryce and Barlow hadn't quite played out the deck, so they went a few more hands. Bryce reminding Glen about the restraining order, warning him how hard he'd go if Glen went after Kale Howard. Glen asking questions, the deputy batting them off or not answering them at all. The words exchanged weren't getting either man anywhere he wanted to go, or anywhere he wanted to take the other. The two of them were running neck and neck, and neither seemed to like that very much.

Finally, Glen said: "I want to see the pictures."

"Look, Barlow. I understand that your sister was your only living relative. You know the land out there. As far as we can figure it, she was alone, rock-climbing at Tres Manos. She must have taken a fall. After that . . . well, she was hurt pretty bad. She had a broken leg. It was a couple days before anyone found her. Something got hold of her before then . . . a pack of coyotes, or maybe a big cat. We had some experts in and they said—"

"I don't care what they said. Kale's mixed up in this some way. Wouldn't surprise me if he wanted a little protection after I tossed him through that window. Maybe he got himself a pit bull."

"We checked that out, Mr. Barlow. Kale doesn't have a dog."

"That doesn't change anything. I still want to see the pictures."

"Trust me on this. You don't."

"How many times you want to hear me say it?"

The deputy drew a deep breath and tried to hold his temper.

"You want me to, I'll say it again."

Bryce was so pissed off, he could barely unclench his jaw, but he got the job done. "Okay, Barlow. You want pictures, pictures is what you'll get."

The deputy yanked open a file cabinet harder than he should have and tossed another manila folder across the desk. Barlow looked at those photos for a long time—the way Bryce figured time, anyway.

"All right," Glen said finally. He closed the folder, slid it across the desk, and got up so quickly that he took Bryce by surprise. There was more that the deputy needed to say, but Barlow didn't give him the chance. He slammed Bryce's office door before the deputy could say another word, and a handful of seconds later he slammed the door to his busted-ass pickup hard enough to leave a shower of rust on the ground. Then he drove straight out of El Pasito, foot hard on the gas. Past the town's lone bar . . . past the funeral home . . . past the gun shop . . . .

Two miles into the desert, Glen Barlow laid rubber and pulled over.

The goddamn deputy was right about those pictures.

At the base of a dying yucca tree, Glen puked his guts dry.

• • •

J. J. Bryce filed the folders on the Kim Barlow case and shared the story of his run-in with her older brother with the sheriff. He sat around the office killing time, but he just couldn't take it sitting there with the sunset slicing through the Venetian blinds and the edge of the desk marred by cigarette burns from the lazy-ass deputy who'd had it before him.

So he clocked out and got in his own pickup, a brand new Ford which was a hell of a lot shinier than the one Glen Barlow drove. That didn't make Bryce feel any better, though. He was still boiling, and there wasn't much he could do about it at the moment—El Pasito only had one bar and Sheriff Randall didn't like anyone who wore a badge drinking there.

So Bryce drove out of town, south, towards Guadalupe. He figured he'd swing by a Mexican grocery store he knew in Dos Gatos. The place was about thirty miles out of his way, but that'd give him some time to cool off before heading home. Besides, you could get pork carnitas at the grocery, already marinated and ready to go. Bryce figured he'd grab a sixer and some tortillas while he was at it. Later on, he'd drop those carnitas in the banged-up cast-iron skillet he used on the barbeque, watch the stars wink on in the sky while he downed a couple of brews, and the night would go down easy.

Or easier, anyway.

• • •

By the time the deputy edged his speedometer past seventy and got the A/C cranking just right, Glen Barlow had chugged half a warm Dr Pepper that had been playing tag with a bunch of burger wrappers on the floor of his truck. The good Dr didn't do much for him besides wash the taste of puke out of his mouth. Still, that was a plus.

Glen drove south. Same road as Bryce, but in the opposite direction. He didn't plan to be on the road long. There was a crossroad just ahead, a narrow unpaved lane jagging west through creosote, coyote brush, and amaranth.

Down that road was where Glen Barlow was headed, because there was other stuff he needed to know. Stuff a guy like Bryce wouldn't tell him. But that was okay—Glen knew where he could find some answers. It was the same place he'd left a whole mess of questions when he cut out of town last December.

That thought chewed on him. He hung a left, pulled over at the side of the dirt road and took another swallow of warm Dr P. For the first time that day, he felt nervous. And that was strange, considering the cards he'd been dealt in the last few hours.

A yank on the handle and the truck door creaked open. Glen climbed out of the cab and stood there in the dry heat. He was dog-tired after a full day behind the wheel, but he couldn't relax. Still, he tried. He needed to catch his breath before going any further.

He closed his eyes for a minute. There were crickets out there somewhere . . . sawing a high, even whine that wouldn't go away. Glen was so used to being on the rig, listening to the sea and the gulls and the equipment. It was weird listening to something different. But he wasn't really listening, no matter how hard he tried. He was thinking. Remembering last Christmas Eve . . . remembering pulling to a stop right here, as a cold December moon shone above.

Right here in the same place that he was standing now. Glen churned the last gulp of soda in his mouth. He thought about that night and the nights that had come since then, and he thought about where those nights had taken him. Full circle. Right back to the place he'd begun.

He shook his head, glancing at his reflection in the banged-up driver's door mirror.

Guess you only have one gear, you stupid bastard.

Glen almost laughed at that. But he didn't. Instead, he spit warm Dr P on the dirt road. Then he climbed in the truck, keyed the engine, and kicked up some roadbed, leaving that wet patch on the ground for the thirsty red earth to drink up.

• • •

Lisa Allen was still beautiful, of course. That hadn't changed in the handful of months since Glen left town. But a whole lot had. Glen knew that coming through the door of the house they'd once shared.

No kiss for him tonight. Not even a hug. They sat in the kitchen, a couple of beers on the table. The back door was open behind Glen's shoulder, and he could smell the herbs in the little patch of garden scrabbling along the side of the house. Sage, rosemary, thyme . . . probably a whole lot of other stuff out there that Lisa's hippie parents had sung about back in the sixties when they built the adobe on a scrubby patch of Arizona notmuch. Of course, Glen didn't say that, even though it was the kind of thing that would have made Lisa laugh back in the days when his coat hung in a closet down the hall.

Back then, things were different.

Those crickets were still out there somewhere, sawing that high, even whine. But Glen ignored them. Instead he listened to the words coming out of his own mouth, surer and steadier than he could have imagined. And he listened to Lisa's answers, which were just as sure and just as steady.

"You saw those photos, Glen. Kale couldn't have done that."

"Maybe. Maybe not."

"The cops told you what they pieced together, didn't they? Kim was out at Tres Manos . . . you know how she loved it out there. They found her rock-climbing gear. She was on that wall south of the third fist, and she must have had an accident. God knows how long she was out there alone—"

"Or maybe she wasn't alone. And maybe it didn't happen that way. Maybe someone just wanted it to look like it did."

"Jesus, Glen. Did you listen to the cops at all?"

"Yeah. I listened to them tell me what made sense to them so they could slot a file into a cabinet pretty damn quick."

"So what do you plan to do about it?"

"A lot of that depends on you. I only know what my gut tells me . . . and that's that I need to get Kale Howard in a place where he's going to do some straight talking. I want to hear what he has to say about this, and I want to look into his eyes when he says it."

"You tried that before, Glen. If you remember, it didn't work out so hot."

"Yeah." Glen stared at Lisa. "I remember."

And Glen did remember. All of it. Images came at him like hard popping jabs. He and Kale had exchanged a couple of simple, unvarnished words. And then Kale Howard had thrown a punch that rocked Glen solid, and Glen's hands were on the rangy bastard, handling him the way you handle a chicken leg when you're real hungry and you just want to tear it apart at the joint. Which meant that Kale had exited the room through a plate-glass window before Glen even realized what he was doing.

"Look, Lisa. I only came here for one thing. You need to tell me where Kale is."

Surprised, she raised an eyebrow. "Who'd you talk to over at the cop shop, anyway?"

"Some joker with a roll of nickels up his ass. Guy named Bryce."

"And he didn't tell you?"

"Tell me what?"

"Things changed after you cut out of town last December. Kale moved in with Kim."

"You're kidding."

"Not a chance."

"And he's still there? That's what you're telling me? He's living in her house?"

"It's his house, Glen."

Lisa stared at him.

"Kale and Kim drove up to Vegas on Valentine's Day and got married. Kim left him everything."

• • •

A bitter laugh caught in Glen's throat. "Okay," he said. "Things are beginning to make sense now."

"Don't you think the cops thought that, too?"

"If they did, they sure as hell didn't show it. They found my sister torn to shreds out at Tres Manos. Her climbing gear was scattered around, and she had a broken leg, and they figured . . . *Gee, there are coyotes around here, aren't there?* So they did the math the easy way and wrote the whole thing off as an accident *times two*."

"Uh-uh. Not the way it happened. This may be a small town, but you've got to give the cops some credit. They grilled Kale. They were all over Kim's house. They didn't find a thing."

"Hard to find what's locked up in a bastard's head . . . unless you're willing to use the right tools, that is."

"You'd better think about that. You know the law around here. You try something like that . . . twice? And with a guy who's got a restraining order against you? It'd be crazy."

"Yeah. Maybe that's exactly what it would be. And maybe that's the way it should have been all along. The truth is that I stopped short when I tossed Kale through that window. You know that better than anyone, Lisa. I should have whipped that dog until I was sure he'd turn tail and run. If I'd done that, maybe Kim would still be alive. Hell, if I'd done that, maybe I wouldn't have had to leave."

"You never had to leave. That was your choice."

"No. It was your choice, Lisa . . . you made it when you called the cops and stopped me cold last December."

• • •

The words were out of Glen's mouth before he even knew they were in his brain. Lisa stared at him like he'd just crawled out from under a rock. Seeing that expression, Glen knew it might as well have been that night last December, with the kitchen door closed to the cold and the herbs cut back against the frost and an icy wind rattling the window at his back. His left eye throbbing from the sucker shot Kale Howard had landed just before getting his miserable excuse for an ass tossed through the living room window, Glen trying to explain to Lisa how he knew in his gut that kind of punishment wasn't enough for a guy like Howard, how a guy like that needed more if he was going to get the message.

He'd never forget that moment, just as he'd never forget the anger that flared inside him when Kim admitted for the first time how things really were with Howard, or what he was certain needed to be done with that anger, or what he'd done with it in the moments after his sister's confession. And he'd sat there that December night in Lisa's kitchen with all those things roiling inside him, and no way to get an explanation past his lips that could make sense to the woman he loved.

It didn't make sense to her now. "You're saying that if it weren't for me, everything would be okay today?"

Glen took a breath, but he didn't say a word.

"Jesus, Glen. You're not really sitting here saying I'm responsible for Lisa's death, are you?"

"No. But you're the one called the cops when I told you I was going back over there."

"And I told you I'd do that. You walked out of here with a *gun*, Glen."

"I was just going to scare him. That coward would have been across the state line by midnight."

"C'mon. You don't know how Kale would have reacted when he saw a gun. And when it comes to the cops, I would have called them anyway. Remember, I'm the one who reported Kale as an abuser. Hell, I would have let Kim move in here until things straightened out if she would have done it. I made the offer while Kale was locked up. She wouldn't even admit that they had a real problem."

"Sometimes people can't handle what happens to them."

"They have to."

"And what if they aren't strong enough?"

"You help them get strong." Lisa sighed. "But you can't live their lives for them. You can't walk through the fire they've got to walk through. And you can't burn down your own life because they're not strong enough to do the job. But that's what you did. To yourself, when you walked out of here with that gun. To me, too . . . and to us. And you paid the price for it. But it could have been worse."

"I don't see how."

"I do. If I hadn't stopped you that night, you'd probably be sitting in a jailhouse, serving time for murder. We both know that's true."

Glen shook his head.

"Maybe that's where I'll end up still," he said.

Now it was Lisa's turn to look at him without saying a word.

"Guess we're done here," Glen said.

"Yeah. I guess we are."

Glen stepped to the door. There was a phone on the counter. "Hate to do this," he said, and then he unplugged the phone, cradling it under his arm.

"One other thing before I go," he said.

"What's that?"

"Your cell phone, Lisa. Hand it over."

• • •

Glen hit the gas, bulleting down that red road. Suddenly, it was just like it had been six months before. Lisa and his life in the rearview, God knew what ahead.

At least the cops wouldn't be waiting for him at the end of that road tonight. That wouldn't happen, now that he'd taken Lisa's phones. From Lisa's place, it was a long walk to anywhere.

But he hadn't had a choice in the matter. No way he could afford a rerun of last December's action. That night, Sheriff Randall himself had responded to Lisa's 911 call. The old man had been quick about it, too, heading Glen off at the point where the dirt road that led to Kim's place met highway blacktop.

After Kale Howard got into the act, Glen ended up in lockup for a week on an assault charge. Of course, Howard had gotten the restraining order, dropped the charges—all like that.

Kale took some heat, too, but in the end he got off with probation and counseling . . . and soon he was back with Kim, who wasn't talking to either Lisa or Glen.

That wasn't the worst of it, though. Glen had issued his own sentence, and in retrospect he was one hard-ass judge. Because somehow, he had turned out to be the bad guy. In the eyes of the law, and his little sister, and in Lisa's eyes, too.

And maybe even in his own eyes. Because he was the one who hit the road, not Kale Howard. He was the one who didn't hang around when things went bad with Lisa, and with Kim. He was the one who didn't talk to either of them for months. He couldn't dodge that fact any more than he could make up for it now.

More than anything, that was what drove him forward. He cut the wheel harder than he should have and hit the blacktop, heading north. He tried to bury the regrets he'd felt while sitting at Lisa's table, and the familiar longings that went along with them. But he couldn't manage the trick. Though his gaze traveled the road ahead—tracking the painted line that gutted its center—his thoughts lingered behind.

He could still see Lisa there, sitting at that table. It had been six months since he'd seen her, but the way things had been six month ago was not exactly far-removed in his memory. He imagined what it would be like, burying his head in her hair again, touching her, going to bed with her, getting up in the morning together. That's the way it still was, in one small place inside him. And if he were another kind of guy, maybe he could have made it happen all over again . . . and just that way.

• • •

But that was the pure hell of it. Because Glen Barlow wasn't another kind of guy . . . and the worst thing about it was he knew that better than anyone. Even better than the other kind of guy who at that moment was stepping through Lisa Allen's front door.

That guy's name was J. J. Bryce.

The deputy put a sixer on the counter, and set the bag with the tortillas and carnitas he'd bought at that Mexican grocery store next to it. He undid his gunbelt and put it on a chair. Then he bent low, gave Lisa a kiss, and passed her a beer.

"Has Barlow been here yet?"

Lisa shook her head. But that was just a comment about Glen, not an answer to J. J.'s question.

The real answer took a minute . . . a popped bottle cap . . . a deep swallow.

"Oh, yeah," she said finally. "He's been, and he's gone."

• • •

J. J. sighed loud and long, staring down at the place the phone should have been.

"Jesus," he said. "This guy."

"I told you how he is. And you said you could handle him."

"For that little job, I would have needed some of those gloves the bomb-disposal boys use. Man, what a handful of dynamite. Your boy Barlow was ready to go to war as soon as he stepped into my office. One quick chew of my ass and he was out of there. I didn't get to say a word about Kale and Kim getting married—"

"Yeah. I noticed. I got to drop that bomb myself."

"Did you tell him about us?"

"Are you kidding?"

"Hell, someone's got to tell him."

"Oh, sure. That would have been a sweet follow-up to the news about his sister marrying the guy who used to beat the crap out of her. Hey, maybe we should invite him over to dinner and break the news. We could hold hands, and he could carve out his own heart with a steak knife."

"Don't play that, Lisa. Barlow walked out on you . . . *and* his sister. If he wants someone to blame for that, he can go find himself a mirror."

Lisa laughed sharply. "Funny thing is, I think he'd agree with you."

"Well, that doesn't mean squat to me. He walked out six months ago, and you didn't hear from him until today. I'll bet he didn't keep in touch with his sister, either. Now, I'm not exactly sure what happened to Kim out there at Tres Manos. Hell, I'm not even sure Kale Howard didn't have something to do with it. But one thing I'm sure of is that Glen Barlow did dirt to both of you when he left town, and now he's here trying to make things right when it's way too late to tote that load."

"Wow. You sound just like him. If he would have stuck around, I bet you would have rubber-stamped his plan for the rest of the night."

"What plan?"

J. J. sipped his beer and listened while Lisa laid it out for him.

When she was done, he took a deeper swallow.

Then he drained the bottle.

"That goddamn coyote," he said, and he stepped outside.

• • •

J. J. flipped open his cell phone and called dispatch. It was dark now, and a light breeze was blowing from the west. Lisa watched as J. J. moved over to the barbeque. He took off the lid and scraped down the grill while he talked. She couldn't hear his words, just clipped short sentences. But his tone told the story, and that tone was all business.

Across the table, an empty chair waited. Lisa saw Glen sitting there an hour before. She saw J. J.'s empty beer bottle on the table, right now. She heard the words of both men, sizing up things in ways that really weren't that different.

The breeze carried the smell of sage, rosemary, and thyme through the open door. Glen had always trimmed back the rosemary way too tight. He said it made the plant grow stronger. J. J. was the kind of guy who thought anything you put in your mouth should come from the grocery store. She wondered if he ever noticed the herb garden at all.

Lisa had been with J. J. two months. The relationship had started slow and easy, then come on fast. Bryce was a *what you see is what you get* kind of guy. You wanted to know how he felt about something, all you had to do was ask. He'd tell you. And things worked best if they operated that way from his side of the equation, too. He wanted to know something, he'd ask you straight out. It was never that way with Glen. Glen could be as silent as a shadow. Sure, the two men weren't exactly yin and yang or night and day, but Lisa definitely didn't have a problem figuring out which one was left brain and which was right—

Mr. Left Brain stepped through the door.

"Change of plans," J. J. said. "Dinner's on the backburner."

"What do you mean?"

"Jeff Keats is out sick tonight, and Einar Cerda's transporting a couple of prisoners over to county lockup. That Garcia kid from California's pretty much running the show, and he's out on a domestic dispute call. Since all I've got is a suspicion your boy Barlow is going to jump a restraining order, there's no way Glen gets priority. Besides, I wouldn't want to put the kid up against Barlow and Kale Howard, even if he was available. Not by his lonesome, anyway. You ask me, both those guys belong in straitjackets."

"Can't they call in someone from the day shift?"

"Sure. They could start with Randall, like they did last Christmas Eve. He'd love that."

"Who then?"

"Well, if someone's stupid enough to be proactive when nothing's happened yet, he might head out there. Someone with a solid knowledge of the parties involved. Of course, an idiot like that would have to put his off-duty self in the middle of things and worry about lawsuits later—"

"If you're saying that you're doing this off the clock, I'm going with you."

"Don't be crazy, Lisa. Let's leave that job to your buddy the road dog. I think he's made for it."

Bryce grabbed his gunbelt from the chair and buckled it on.

"Well," he said, "I guess I'll go catch some bad guys and get our phone back."

Lisa laughed, then kissed him.

"Thanks," she said.

"No need, darlin'. But let's not let this get too complicated. You just remember who's going to walk through the door when this is over."

"I'll remember," she said.

"Okay." Bryce stepped outside. "Be back soon. Don't worry."

"I won't."

"Liar."

Lisa laughed again. Another kiss that was too quick, and then J. J.'s truck was raising a cloud of dust as he headed for the highway. Lisa watched him go, and she kept on watching after the dust settled and the truck had disappeared from view.

The night air was cool.

The crickets had gone quiet.

Lisa sat on the back step and tried to think of nothing at all.

• • •

Behind the house he'd shared with Kim Barlow—the same house he'd once exited through a window thanks to her brother Glen—Kale Howard eyed Tres Manos.

The place the *Anglo* locals called The Hands was a sight to see, even from this distance. It was something different every time you looked at it. Red as a thickening puddle of blood in the hard light of afternoon. Black as the devil's silhouette in the hours past midnight . . . and right now, with silver moonlight creeping up its backside, it was as smoky and ethereal as a dream any fool could climb.

Kale smiled. Though he stood in darkness, that same moonlight crept up his spine like a dozen furious scorpions in a hurry to plant stings at the base of his brain. In his world, that wasn't an unfamiliar feeling, and it dug down to his core like a grave robber's shovel, churning up secrets buried in the deepest, darkest corners of the shriveled black hunk he called his soul.

There were visions in that place that would have made a sane man slash his wrists. Visions of women like Kim Barlow as they screamed their last screams, and visions of Kim Barlow herself, on the final night of her life, out there in the desert beneath a towering hunk of rock that might as well have been a gigantic tombstone.

They weren't exactly Kale's visions. Not completely. They were owned in part by the thing that lived inside him, the disease that sent those scorpions scurrying across his spine. But the visions were nothing to be feared, any more than he feared the silhouette of Tres Manos in the distance. And, hell, if he raised a hand right now, he could cover up that mother-of-all tombstones where Kim had died, and he could do the job with one little finger. This he did. And just that fast, every memory of Kim Barlow vanished from his mind except that very last one . . . and, for Kale, that was the one worth keeping.

The moonlight brought it home. As its clean halo broke over the rim of The Hands, the memory shimmered in the clear white light surrounding Kale's raised finger. Quite suddenly, his raised finger itched as if those ghostly scorpions had launched their own dark vision-quest, scrambling across the enormous sandstone tombstone that rose from the desert of Kale's hand, jabbing barbed tales into that tower, reducing it to fine grains, burrowing through Kale's flesh and blood and bone until they unearthed that bedrock of hidden memory.

Kim's final fright . . . and just as final understanding.

For Kale, that single moment defined his entire relationship with Kim Barlow. He understood that . . . just as he understood that it paid to take his time when those moments rose from the shadows. They were the ones that truly counted.

He'd taken his time with Kim, all right. Together, they'd gone to Tres Manos, sharing a picnic dinner as dusk turned to night. Kale had made sure Kim understood the lies he'd told, stripping them away from the truth with the same relish he stripped meat away from a bone. And when he was finished doing that little job he did another, taking what he wanted from Kim in the shadow of a great tombstone he could eclipse with a single finger.

He took it in a fury born of cursed moonlight and patience and spite. Under other circumstances Kale would have lingered with the memory, but it was time for it to go. His mind cremated every image, and his pointing finger curled into a fist along with its neighbors, and his fist tightened. Chrome skull rings gnashed on his fingers like five monsters grinding bones to make their bread. The moon crested about the towers. Kale extended his fingers. He had to. Each one was lengthening now, growing black claws that sliced the shadow he cast.

Those ghostly scorpions raised tails and drove spikes home, and the venom of the moon delivered fresh visions to Kale's mind . . . visions of Kim's brother. The bastard had been in Kale's head all day. Even when the moon was shining on another part of the world, he'd known Glen Barlow was coming. The scorpions had told him so, and he had trusted each sting of warning, and each scent raised by his daylight visions.

And he'd scented the bastard, all right . . . even in his visions. The oil burning in Barlow's old pickup had scalded his nostrils, and he'd smelled the bastard's sweat as he stood out there in the desert, and he'd retched at the stink of Barlow's puke as the hardcase gave up his misery in the dull heat of dusk. And now the visions were stronger. Barlow was coming closer. Barlow was almost here. That burning motor oil was a hot rag in the mouth of the night, and the stink of gun oil etched in the whorls of Barlow's fingerprints bore the raw perfume of vengeance.

The fact that Barlow had a gun didn't worry Kale, for the bullets in Barlow's pistol did not bear the acrid stench of a single grain of silver. That meant Kale had nothing to fear from the weapon. And if Kale did not fear Barlow's gun, he would not fear Glen Barlow. Not when his own fingers were tipped with razor claws that could slice flesh to ribbons. Not when growing teeth twisted and scraped in his mouth, carving a brutal path against thickening gums.

And that wasn't the end of it. Soon Kale's jaws were heavy with fangs. Black bristles of fur spiked from a dozen monsters tattooed on his arms. Moonlight poured over the desert, and Kale's shadow stretched across the sand as he grew larger—tendons cording over lengthening bone, muscles getting heavier.

But the moon was carving him down, too. It whittled away everything but the basics, the way those jabbing scorpions had chiseled at the sandstone tower in his vision . . . cutting away everything that had once protected Glen Barlow, skinning hesitation and fear from Kale's heart, tearing off every mask he had ever been forced to wear.

Moonlight carved the werewolf as brutally and efficiently as the Reaper's own predatory scythe. And what the moon left behind was the same . . . and nothing but.

PART TWO

As he neared Kim's house, Glen killed the headlights. He pulled the pickup to the side of the road, parking beneath an old mesquite tree a hundred yards from the entrance to her property. Night had dropped its veil, but there were still shadows here. The gnarled branches overhead netted the stark silver light of the full moon, casting twisted shadows on the hood of Glen's old truck.

Glen reached under the seat and grabbed his pistol. He stepped from the truck and cut a path through the night, following the road at a slow trot until he came to the rock-lined drive leading to Kim's house. He stood there for a moment, in full moonlight now. If anyone inside the house was looking through a window, they'd surely see him . . . but every window was dark, and so were the rusted railroad lanterns hanging from the heavy-beamed overhang that covered the front patio.

There weren't any other houses nearby. Just that silver moonlight, and desert that didn't so much as ripple until it ran into Tres Manos, many miles away. Quietly, Glen moved down the final twenty feet of the drive. He put a hand on the hood of Kale's Mustang as he passed by, but the car was as cold as the house was dark.

Sand crunched lightly beneath Glen's bootheels. Out on the road, a driver shifted gears. Glen ducked low, but the car didn't enter Kim's driveway. Headlights cast cold beams over the front of the house as the car passed by. Glen caught a quick glimpse of his reflection in the bedroom window, the light trapping his image on the pane for what seemed a long moment. Then the light moved on, smearing across the rest of the house, sweeping the shadows beneath the patio overhang as it passed, revealing the heavy slab of a front door and the old string of chili peppers hanging there . . . and, past that, a weathered sheet of plywood, still nailed over the front window.

Glen shook his head. Maybe Kale was too lazy to fix the window, or maybe the bastard didn't want anyone looking inside. It didn't matter to Glen. One way or another, he planned to take a good long look in the house. As the sound of the passing car's engine faded in the distance, he stepped onto the flagstone patio and crossed through the shadows beneath the overhang. Here the air was heavy with the fragrance of climbing roses; the plants wound around stout support posts like gnarled muscles, vines heavy with blooms cradled by the overhang above.

It was darker here, but Glen's night vision was good. He spotted a stack of cut piñon near the boarded-up window. Grabbing a length of it, he pressed his back to the brick wall near the heavy slab of a front door.

Glen tossed the piñon across the patio. The log clattered loudly against flagstone as it landed fifteen feet away. If anyone was inside the house, they wouldn't be able to ignore the noise.

Glen waited. No sound from within, and no lights came on. His breaths came faster now, and the butt of the pistol jammed into his jeans nudged at his belly.

Needles of silver light pierced the roses overhead as the moon rose higher.

The sweet fragrance of the flowers was heavy on the night air.

Glen filled his lungs with it.

He tested the doorknob.

It was locked.

Damn. Glen drew another breath . . . but this time he choked on it. Because suddenly there was another smell—a sour animal stink, as if something dead was trapped up there in the rose vines.

And then there was a sound. Glen jolted as a hunk of piñon clattered over the flagstones at his feet and bounced off the door—the same hunk of wood he'd tossed just a few moments moment before. He spun quickly, drawing his pistol as he turned toward the thing that had thrown the log . . . the thing that had been stalking him since he'd first stepped from his truck.

Because this was no man. Something down deep in Glen's gut recognized that before his mind could accept it. The shadow that faced him was enormous . . . and grinning . . . and red-eyed . . . and it moved much faster than Glen could possibly move.

It came straight at him. Before he could raise his pistol, the thing caught him with one hairy shoulder and hammered him against the door. The hanging chili peppers went to powder behind his back. The shadow snatched his wrist and yanked him forward, and Glen was suddenly spinning like a child launched from a Tilt-A-Whirl, heels scrapping over flagstone and then rising above it, the thing's clawed hands tight on his wrist . . . tighter still when the monster cracked the whip.

Glen's body was jerked so hard he was sure his left shoulder had popped from its socket. But it wasn't his left shoulder he needed to worry about. It was the right one, which slammed into the plywood covering the broken window with such force that the panel cracked and planted splinters in his flesh.

Glen dropped to the ground. The thing's hands were off him for just a couple seconds as it drew back. Then it charged again, fanged teeth gleaming in the patchwork light beneath the overhang.

It was almost on top of him when Glen realized he was still holding the pistol. Pain dug a trench from his wrist to his shoulder as he jacked his aching elbow into position and pulled the trigger. The gun bucked in his hand. The thing screamed and fell back. Blood splattered across the flagstone, and a wet hunk of meat smacked against the ground. Glen fired again—straight at the thing's chest this time—and fired once more as the monster stumbled back.

The 230-grain hollow-points did their work. Another slug drove the shadow-thing backward. It crashed against one of the patio posts—the overhang shuddering as the creature bucked in pain, its blood showering flagstones in wet droplets.

Glen fired again, and the monster howled.

Dead rose petals rained down.

And the shadow charged through them with renewed ferocity. Glen raised the pistol one more time, but it was too late. Before he could pull the trigger, the creature's bristling forehead cracked hard against Glen's chin. Simultaneously, a knotted shoulder drove into his gut, jamming him against the cracked plywood covering the broken window.

This time, the plywood didn't hold.

This time, Glen went straight through it.

And the werewolf followed.

• • •

Kale sprang through the gaping plywood maw. There was the bastard. Right there—a hunk of human piledriver stretched out on the hardwood floor.

Somehow Barlow had managed to hang on to his pistol. Kale slapped it away with a fistful of claws. Not that the gun did Barlow any good without silver bullets. Kale's wounds already scarring over. Lead slugs couldn't do more than slow him down.

He grabbed Barlow's collar, snarling at him. And the look on Glen's face? Man . . . it was priceless, as if someone had just lit up his flat-earthed little world with a full bucket of hellfire.

If a wolf could have laughed, Kale would have done it. The scorpion fury trapped inside him demanded that Barlow die hard.

It'd been too damn tough keeping the leash on during the year he'd lived with the bastard's sister. Caging his anger when Barlow gave him static about never holding a job for long . . . or the way he'd dip into Kim's wallet when he needed some cash . . . or a million other things. Sometimes he'd lose it, and Kim would pay the price. Sure. Had to be Kimmy who paid, because he'd kept Kim on a leash of her own.

And it was a short one. Kimmy'd had things he wanted. A damn fine little house in the middle of nowhere, and money in the bank, and not too many relatives around to muddy the water. So waiting had been the ticket. First for the marriage license . . . next for the will. And that meant that most of the time Kale bit back his anger, but sometimes he couldn't help himself. He'd let loose . . . especially when it was getting close to the full moon and the scorpions started crawling up his spine.

And that wasn't bad, really. Not all bad, anyway. The scorpions, the fights and the violence . . . they gave Kale an excuse to get the hell out of Dodge. Usually he'd head to Vegas. Enjoy a couple days on the Strip, then do a little cruising in the desert. Grab someone traveling alone, out where it didn't matter. He had his way about it, he favored himself some dark-haired little piece of sweetmeat. Maybe one with a little something extra to go with the gristle. He'd catch one alone at a rest stop or a backwater motel—some place like that. Have some fun with her, then chow down. Clean the bones and bury them. Strip her car and sell it to a chop shop while the best parts of the little skank were still warm in his belly, then head home with a fat bankroll in the pocket.

No sweat, Kimmy. I picked it up gambling. Now let me drive you over to Tucson and we'll have dinner. Hey, we can even stay the night at that place you like. I want to make things up to you . . . and I'm really sorry about that fight we had, okay?

Uh-huh. That was the way it worked.

Sweet when he needed to be.

Not so sweet when he didn't.

And right now, with Kim six feet under and most of her worldly possessions banked, Kale didn't have a shot glass worth of *sweet* in him. Barlow started scrambling, one hand reaching for that pistol on the floor. Kale grabbed him before he could reach the useless weapon, slamming Glen into the wall hard enough so that the boy damn near punched an outline in the sheetrock.

The werewolf didn't stop there. He piled into Glen before he could hit the ground, ramming him against the wall again . . . and again. Next he jammed a clawed hand under Barlow's chin, and this time he did the job right—hammering Glen's thick skull straight through the sheetrock.

A wrench of his wrist and he pulled Barlow out of the divot, twisting his neck into a patch of moonlight shining from the back window. Ruby beads rolled down Glen's sweaty face. *Yeah,* Kale thought, twisting harder. *Bring on the blood!*

He picked up Barlow and heaved him against the far wall. Glen crashed into a clean square of moonlight, grunted, tried to move. But Kale was on him before the hardcase could even twitch an inch. This was it—the final bit of business before the deed got done. Because right now, all Barlow really knew was that some kind of monster was putting him through the spin cycle. For Kale, killing Kim's brother would be useless unless the bastard realized the identity of the nightmare doing the deed.

Without that little moment of recognition, Kale's satisfaction-meter would register *zip.*

With it, that sucker would notch off the scale. The werewolf's claws snaked through Barlow's hair and gave his head an attentive yank. At the same time, Kale raised his other hand, and moonlight caught the chrome skull rings circling his black fingers.

Those fingers danced before Glen Barlow's eyes.

Fanged teeth sparkled with rictus smiles.

Hollow-eyed skulls filled with moonlight.

Barlow stared as if hypnotized, pupils dilating into deepening pools of realization. Kale howled in triumph, but Barlow wasn't even looking at him. He just kept staring at those rings.

And why wouldn't he stare?

It was a hell of a thing to figure out a few seconds before you died.

It was a hell of a thing to realize that the monster crouching over you was the man you'd come to kill.

• • •

So Glen did the only thing he could do.

He looked the monster dead in the eye.

The switchblade he'd hidden in his boot *snicked* open in the moonlight.

The werewolf caught the gleam a second too late. Glen jammed the knife between Kale Howard's ribs, burying the blade to the hilt before ripping it to the side. Black blood spilled over Glen's right hand. He pulled back and stabbed the creature again, lower this time. Kale roared as if his guts were about to spill out of his belly.

But they didn't. The werewolf's wounds were already healing. His left hand plunged downward, razor claws splayed in a driving arc that split the skin of Glen's right forearm. Muscle shredded as Kale dug those nails deep, burying four long fingers between Glen's bones.

Glen dropped the knife, and the well-honed blade dug into the floorboards as Kale closed his fist around Glen's ulna. Glen would have screamed if he could have sucked a breath. The werewolf's other hand snaked through Glen's hair, then deeper—claws digging tunnels between scalp and skull until they found purchase in the tendons at the back of Glen's neck.

The monster jerked Glen's head back, stretching his neck into the kill zone, trapping him between hands buried in neck and wrist. Wounds spilled blood across the corded length of Glen's neck. Kale's black lips drew back. A mouthful of spit slapped Glen in the face, and then Kale's jaws closed around his neck.

Savage teeth tore into muscle. Arterial blood geysered against the werewolf's pelt. Halogen headlights cored the jagged plywood hole across the room. It seemed the light would swallow Glen faster than Kale could. He closed his eyes against it, but he couldn't escape its stark power.

Outside, a car door slammed.

There were voices. The werewolf's ears perked, and he turned toward the light.

For Glen, the reprieve didn't seem to matter.

If the Marines had arrived, they were too goddamned late.

• • •

Of course, it wasn't the Marines.

And it wasn't J. J. Bryce, either.

There were three of them, and every one looked just a little bit like Kale Howard—even the one who didn't have a set of *cojones* hanging between her legs.

Glen had never met any of Kale's siblings.

But all it took was one glance, and he knew this bunch fit the bill.

• • •

The Howards were all over brother Kale in a matter of seconds. Dwayne—the largest of the boys—waded in first, backhanding the wolf with a handful of silver rings. Kale howled as if doused with acid, but he didn't turn tail. No. He spit blood and bared his teeth, but he never got the chance to test his game on his eldest brother. Joe—shorter, faster, and meaner—had already closed in from one side, skinning his belt from his jeans. Before Kale could make a move, Joe had looped that thirty-two-inch length of snakeskin around his brother's neck in one well-practiced motion.

The belt whispered through hammered silver as Joe yanked it tight. The buckle closed over Kale's windpipe like a pair of channel locks, the horrible metal burning its brand into his flesh.

Unable to breathe, Kale blacked out for an instant and started to drop.

In the second it took for him to make the trip to the floor, Kris—the oldest and roughest of Kale's siblings—stepped forward. Tanned, cougar-lean, and dressed in black jeans and a tank top, she looked like the kind of woman who should be demo-ing combat knives at a survivalist convention in Vegas. She jammed the barrel of a nickel-plated .45 against her baby brother's temple and tore a strip off him with a voice seasoned by whiskey and cigarettes.

"Make another move, dog, and I'll splatter your brains all over this room."

"Better save those silver bullets, Kris." Dwayne hovered over Glen. "Looks like this other boy's been bit."

Kale's sister swore under her breath as she turned to examine Glen's wounds. From jawbone to wrist, Barlow's right side was a shredded mess of meat and gristle. Any bastard suffering similar wounds under another circumstance would have slipped into shock by now, but Kris knew that wasn't going to happen to Barlow . . . not if the werewolf virus were pulsing through his blood.

She ignored his mangled arm, and the pistol that lay next to it, examining the flesh torn by the werewolf's attack. Yep. This was more than a claw job. Kale had put his fangs straight into the cowboy's arteries, but he hadn't finished him off. The wounded man's heart was still beating, and from the look of things the virus was already doing its work. Barlow's wounds were beginning to heal, a cuff of scar tissue slowly knitting over the flesh of his wrist. The only upside was that Barlow was freshly infected. His metabolism was operating at a slower rate than Kale's, so he wasn't an immediate threat.

"Better put a bullet in him, sis," Joe said. "That full moon ain't goin' anywhere for hours yet. I don't want to have to deal with two dogs if he turns."

"Brush up on your homework, idiot," Kris said. "It takes

longer than that for the virus to set. This cowboy won't do any turning until the next full moon. The most he'll do right now is some serious healing up."

She smiled down at Glen.

"If we let him live long enough, that is."

• • •

But there was no way in hell Kris Howard was going to let this desert rat live. She'd made that decision as soon as she'd learned that the cowboy had been bit.

Yep. That was the way it had to be. Kris was the one who made the decisions around here. She'd been doing that since her parents decided to crawl inside a bottle when she was just a kid. Even then, her deadweight brothers were just along for the ride.

And Kale, hell . . . time hadn't done him any favors. He was still her scrabble-brained little brother, half nuts even on nights when the moon was just a fingernail clipping up there in the sky. That's why she'd cleaned up after him so many times in the years since he'd gotten his ass chewed by a werewolf down in Mexico.

Of course, having a werewolf in a family of thieves was mostly a real plus, but Kris could see that this wasn't going to be one of those times. Damn . . . it'd been awhile since Kale tore up that little showgirl in Reno, but this clusterfuck tonight made that mess look like a picnic. Kale had opened Kim's brother like a can of Alpo. Anyone who watched forensic TV shows could collect enough evidence in this slaughterhouse to convict every Howard in the room . . . plus their dead-ass parents, who were back in Texas taking dirt naps.

So the whole deal sure enough screwed the pooch, but what could she do about it? Jagged wedges of Glen Barlow's skin stuck to the wall like some serial killer's warped painting; his blood was soaking into the cracked floorboards; the headbutt-pitted sheetrock was clotted with hanks of his hair. Kris was sure she'd have to burn down the house before they made a permanent exit tonight. And that really bit, because the plan had been to sell the damn thing for a good chunk of cash after Kale knocked off his latest bride. But there was more chance of their parents growing fresh livers and crawling out of their plywood caskets down there in Texas than there was of her selling this house. Kris figured the best she could hope for when she finished up this business tonight would be an empty box of matches. And the way she saw it, the bloody mess of a man at her feet had to have figured out the score about the whole deal—including the growling moron who at that moment was straining against a snakeskin leash.

Kris stared down at Glen Barlow, cocking her head in Kale's direction.

"Guess you know the family secret," she said.

"Yeah . . . and I think I figured out the family business, too."

Kris smiled. The bloody cowboy sucked a breath. Surprisingly, only part of it whistled through his windpipe. Had to be the virus was burning a trail through Barlow's torn-up excuse for a circulatory system faster than Kris had expected. But she wasn't particularly worried about that. After all, she was the one holding the gun with the silver bullets.

"So, you're the guy who tossed my baby brother through a window, huh?"

"Yeah."

"Looks like tonight you're reapin' what you sowed."

"Well, it was a dirty job . . ." he started, coughing up a thick rope of blood.

"Yeah . . . but somebody had to do it," she finished.

"You know how it goes."

"You bet I do. But there's a problem with that, Tex. Kale sure ain't the most obedient pup in the kennel, but he's my brother. And in our family, we take care of our own. I figure you can understand that."

Another cough, and maybe another *yeah* mixed in there, too.

"Sure. Add it up, we're not that different, you and me. I'm here to help Kale. You're here to do right by your sister. Hell, I understand that. Some guy chews your baby sis down to the bone and leaves her in the middle of nowhere for the buzzards to peck. Plus, he ends up with everything she owned in the world. You've got a right to go all *Charlie Bronson* on him, but you're a little late for that. To tell the truth, you're late for anything that doesn't include taking a silver bullet."

That did it. Barlow tried to rise. Just doing that, it looked like his head was going to topple off his torn-up neck and end up in his lap. Kris nearly laughed, and the only thing that stopped her were the scars closing over Barlow's wound.

He was healing faster now, but Kris knew there wasn't enough *fast* in the world to get the job done for him before she finished saying her piece. "You wanted to fix things, Barlow, you should have done it last Christmas. It's too late now. Your sister's in a hole. And if there's still a squeaky little cage turnin' in your guts, let me tell you something: that hamster's dead, amigo. Whatever you wanted to do, it's way past time to do it now."

"You said that."

"Yeah. I did. But you cost me a fat bankroll tonight, so forgive me if I take a minute to show you the error of your ways before I put a hunk of silver in your brain. See, I don't want you feeling the least little bit like a hero when you get your ass kicked into eternity. You're not any kind of hero, amigo. Let's get that straight."

Barlow was quiet now. Had to be it was sinking in. He didn't say a word.

Kris checked the pistol, chambered a round.

"Let me wrap it up for you, now that you're catching on. I've got a real simple way of looking at life. The way I see it, what you do is who you are . . . and what you don't do, too. And, buddy, when it comes to your sister, and when it comes to the guy who killed her, you didn't do much."

Barlow held his silence. All he gave her was a stare.

And that was enough. Hell, that stare was plenty.

Kris raised the pistol.

"I see you get the message," she said. "End of sermon. It's time for the piper to get paid."

• • •

The werewolf virus had jacked Glen's metabolism into a molten overdrive. His mind raced with quick-cut impressions, hundreds of them—Kris' .45 . . . and her smile . . . and the other two Howard boys watching him from across the room . . . and their snarling werewolf brother straining against the snakeskin leash, eager for another taste of Barlow's flesh—the slightest movement of each member of the Howard clan cataloged in a fraction of a second, and every image filed for action and reaction if Glen could only move.

He had to do that. If the virus set quickly enough . . . if the full moon shone at the correct angle . . . his lupine brain understood that he could move faster than he'd ever moved before. And it was happening already. His wounds were closing as if some heathen god had decided to dam him up. Scar tissue crackled over his carotid artery. New skin covered exposed muscle and tendon, cells multiplying with an insane rapidity.

Glen's dropped pistol lay just a foot away. Synapses fired as his brain ordered his hand to grab the pistol . . . but, damn . . . he couldn't even wriggle his fingers yet, let alone lift his arm.

"Don't even think about it," Kris said, kicking the gun across the room.

She bent low, pressing the .45 barrel against his temple.

"Here we go," she said. "Enjoy the ride."

Glen sucked a breath. Kris began to squeeze the trigger.

Across the room, another pistol cocked sharply.

A man's voice came from the other side of the ragged plywood hole.

"Drop the gun," J. J. Bryce said. "And do it now."

• • •

The hard-eyed woman did as she was told. One look at the bloody man on the floor and Bryce had a serious crime scene flashback—Kim Barlow dead in the shadow of Tres Manos—but this time he was looking at her brother, soaked in his own gore on a dusty hardwood floor.

"Get away from him," Bryce said.

The woman raised her hands and stepped backward, retreating from the dull illumination of the room's single standing floor-lamp. Bryce leaned through the splintery plywood gap, tracking her movement with his pistol.

That was when he noticed that the woman wasn't alone. Two men stood in the shadows on the other side of the room. One of them reached for a wall switch while the other slipped a loop from around the neck of a . . .

Jesus. Some kind of hairy *thing* . . . a thing with claws, and teeth, and—

It settled on its haunches.

In another instant it would spring—

Bryce's brain didn't need any more input. He fired his pistol. The slug punched the freak backward. The lights went out. The two men scrambled in the dark, but J. J. couldn't see them. He couldn't see anything—

Except a pair of red eyes, low to the floor then rising, closing on him like coals shoveled by the devil himself.

• • •

The nickel-plated .45 gleamed in a patch of moonlight. Glen was with it, his body trapped in the dead-white fire. And it seemed as if the pistol Kris Howard had used to control her werewolf brother were melting there on that same moonlight forge . . . its gleaming ivory grips scorching the silver slugs that lurked within.

The stink of silver nearly made Glen retch. His stomach roiled at the thought of touching the weapon, but he knew that the .45 was his only chance.

So did Kris Howard.

She grabbed for the pistol.

Glen did, too.

• • •

Several shots rang out inside the house, but J. J. Bryce was barely aware of them. Gripping his own pistol tightly in his fist, he scrambled to his feet as he came out of a tumble with the red-eyed creature.

It had rolled over the top of him, continuing across the flagstone patio before righting itself. Quickly, it launched a second attack, charging him like a freight train. Bryce wasn't set, but he fired his pistol three times in quick succession. Every slug found its target, dead center in the thing's chest. It didn't matter. The monster bit off an anguished scream and kept coming, and it slammed into the deputy so hard that he was airborne in an instant.

A glance to the side. White teeth gnashing inches from Bryce's face. His pistol clattered against the patio. Then he started to drop. He realized he'd be coming down hard on a flagstone slab a second before his skull slammed against it, realized too that the monster would be on top of him before another second could tick off the clock.

• • •

The cop landed hard.

Kale knew he had to finish him off quickly and get back inside the house. He'd heard the gunshots. Chances were they'd come from Kris' .45 instead of Glen Barlow's pistol. But who had the gun? That was the question—

"Hey, boy."

Kale spun toward the open doorway.

He had his answer.

He didn't like it.

• • •

The werewolf sprang. Eyes gleaming, teeth bared, claws ready to tear through Glen Barlow in a ferocious explosion of rage.

For Glen, it was just like staring into his own heart.

He didn't stare long.

He pulled the trigger.

In a bright blast of muzzle flash, everything went away.

PART THREE

J. J. Bryce lay on the flagstones, out cold, but Glen ignored the fallen cop.

The .45 still filled his hand. The silver bullets inside the weapon were encased in a steel clip buried beneath ivory grips. Glen knew that. Still, holding the pistol was like holding a live rattler, ready to sink fangs into his skin if he so much as twitched.

But he couldn't put the pistol down.

The truth was, he didn't know if he'd ever put it down.

Behind Glen, three people lay dead in the house. He'd killed Kris first, then the other two. He didn't even know their names. He'd killed all three of them in a matter of seconds, the animal fury of the werewolf virus surging through him as if it were in control of the gun. Kale was dead, too—his sternum shattered by a silver bullet that had torn through muscle and heart, finally burying itself in his spinal column. He lay on the flagstone patio, and looking at him there was no clue that he'd ever been anything different than the human monsters who lay within the walls of Kim Barlow's house.

But Kale had been something different. Glen knew that as he stared down at the corpse of the man he'd wanted to kill so badly, just as he knew that his rage was as dead as the cursed bastard who'd murdered his sister. Now it had been replaced by another fire, a hunk of brimstone buried inside him that was torched by the light of the full moon.

Glen wasn't the kind of man who prayed, but he hoped he wouldn't feel that fire when he watched the sun rise in just a few hours.

If he watched the sun rise.

If he stuck around long enough to do that.

Glen's grip tightened around the .45. He knew what the silver bullets in the gun could do to him, the same way he knew what the moon above would do to him the next time it rose in the night sky, full and bright.

Just one bullet. That's all it would take.

Just one, and he'd never end up like Kale Howard.

Glen raised the pistol. He placed the barrel beneath his chin.

And he waited. He waited for a sign . . . a sign from somewhere . . . or someone . . . perhaps a sign from Kim. Right or wrong, the things he'd done tonight he'd done for her. So he waited for an acknowledgement, a rush of images his brain could catalog the way it had cataloged every movement and expression of the people he'd just killed.

The ivory pistol grips were slick with his sweat. The gun barrel dug into the taut flesh beneath his chin. That brimstone fire inside him was cooking his heart now. Suddenly Glen heard words, down there in the sizzle.

But they weren't Kim's words.

They belonged to another, and he'd heard them earlier this night.

What you do is who you are . . .

The words were lost for a moment, sizzling in the brimstone roar. It was as if something inside Glen wanted to incinerate them, the same way he'd burned down the woman who'd spoken those words. But they came around again, surer this time . . . as if they were his own.

What you do is who you are . . .

Glen lowered the pistol.

. . . and what you don't do, too.

• • •

The sound of his cell phone brought Bryce around. It was still dark—a glance at his watch told him it was just past midnight.

Damn. His skull was pounding in time with the phone's insistent ringtone. J. J. reached for his cell, but it wasn't there. It was over on the patio, murky LCD light glowing as it chirped like a confused little bird. And there was his pistol, right next to it, and—

That thing he'd wrestled lay on the patio, too. Only it didn't look like a wolf anymore. Now the damn thing looked like Kale Howard. And now J. J. remembered. He'd cracked his head on the patio when he'd taken that fall. In the moment before he'd passed out, Glen Barlow had appeared in the doorway with a nickel-plated .45 in his hand. He'd looked like a refugee from a zombie movie, but he'd gunned down the monster beneath the patio overhang.

And now Kale Howard lay dead in its place.

Bryce stared at Howard's corpse for a long moment.

Goddamn, he thought. *Well . . . goddamn.*

Because there wasn't much else you could think. Not if you could add two and two. And even with a knock on the head, J. J. could do that. He moved on to the next order of business and tried to rise, but his legs wouldn't quite make the trip. And the rest of his body . . . Jesus. It felt like his right arm wasn't even there.

What the hell was going on? He was ass-down in the dirt, leaning against something hard. He couldn't move his right arm at all. Damn thing was asleep, bent above his head, stuck there as if tied.

Bryce leaned to the side and looked up. He was handcuffed to the driver's door of a truck. Not his own truck—Barlow's piece-of-shit rustbucket . . . which hadn't even been there when J. J. pulled in a couple hours ago.

Oh shit. With his free hand, Bryce patted his pocket. His keys were gone.

His brand-new Ford was gone, too.

That son of a bitch, Bryce thought. He settled back against Barlow's truck, and he stewed about it. Might be he'd have to sit here a while before someone came along. But that was okay. He was in no rush to discuss his stolen vehicle . . . or tonight's business.

Still, the wheels started turning in his head. Maybe that wasn't a bad thing. Sooner or later, he'd have to decide what the hell he was going to say.

To Sheriff Randall.

And to Lisa, too.

PART FOUR

In the months since he'd left El Pasito, Glen had a lot of time on his hands. That was good. There was a lot he needed to think about in the wake of the bloodbath out there in the desert. Things had changed for him . . . a lot of things. Everything.

But as the days closed into night, what he thought about most was Kim. He'd always felt responsible for her. After all, he was her big brother. That reaction was as natural as breathing. But he was starting to understand that Kim had made her own decisions in life, and he wasn't responsible for them any more than he was responsible for the trouble they'd brought her way. They were Kim's choices, not his. And she'd shut him out when making them, and she'd shut him out when they went bad . . . especially when it came to Kale.

And maybe that was part of the reason for his anger. She'd shut him out, and then she was dead before either of them could change the way things were. Maybe that was the reason he hadn't heard his sister's voice in the desert on the night he'd nearly taken his own life.

Maybe he hadn't know her well enough to ask for that kind of help.

Maybe she was still shutting him out.

They were brother and sister, sure. They'd shared memory, time, and blood. But Glen had never known the secrets Kim kept locked up in her heart. And he wondered if you ever could know that about someone else, no matter what ties you shared.

Just lately, he'd been thinking about that a lot. He hadn't reached any particular conclusions, but there was one thing he was sure of. In the time since he'd left El Pasito, he was beginning to understand his own secrets, and he was beginning to understand his own heart.

He wondered if someone else was beginning to understand those things, too.

• • •

It wasn't easy to find a payphone anymore, but Glen turned one up.

He had to buy a phone card from a little Cajun girl working the till in the convenience store before he could make his call. The phone was on a pole across from the gas pumps. There weren't a lot of people around, just a lot of kudzu. And that was okay with Glen. This wasn't a conversation he wanted to share with anyone.

He dialed Lisa's number.

A man picked up on the third ring. "Hello?"

Glen didn't say a word.

"Hello?" the man said again. "Hey . . . is anyone there?"

A click on the line, and the familiar voice was gone. Glen hung up the receiver.

Well I'll be damned, he thought, that voice still there in his head. *J. J. Bryce and Lisa Allen.*

He stood there a minute, thinking about it. A truck roared by on the two-lane highway, heading toward Baton Rouge. Glen shook his head, grinning. A lot had surprised him just lately, and he couldn't see a single reason why this should be any different.

But, right now, that was okay with him.

Really, it was.

• • •

Man, if there was one thing J. J. hated, it was hang-ups.

He turned away from the phone. At least it hadn't been another lawyer calling. Since the gunfight at the Barlow Corral, he'd had enough of lawyers. And administrative leave. And state and county investigators.

And the questions some of those guys asked. Especially that forensic specialist who'd discovered that the Howard clan had been gunned down with silver bullets. He'd asked if J. J. had any ideas about those. "Hell," J. J. had said. "Maybe Barlow thought he was the Lone Ranger. The guy was definitely crazy enough."

As it stood, investigators had connected the Howards to six murders in four states. Three of the victims had been married to Kale. Seemed he'd do the killing, and then his sister would come in a few months later and cash in the chips. She'd been smart enough to keep a low profile, mostly, and that had definitely been her M. O. in El Pasito. No one in town had even know that Kale had a sister—or a couple of brothers—out there at the house. Hell, that was probably why they kept the front window boarded up.

Anyway, J. J. was glad the deal was wrapping up. Next week he was going back to work. A couple months after that . . . well, the whole thing would probably be forgotten.

One could hope, anyway.

• • •

Lisa was sweeping the patio when J. J. stepped through the door. He was carrying a couple bottles of Pacifico, and he handed her one. She took a sip, and that was an improvement. The beer was good and cold.

"Who was on the phone?" she asked.

"Hang up. Don't you hate those?"

She nodded. They sat on the back step for awhile. J. J. drank his beer and talked about going back to the cop shop. She listened. After awhile, he said, "I think I'll drive over to Dos Gatos. Get some of those pork carnitas. We can have a barbeque tonight."

"Sounds good."

A few minutes later, he was gone.

Lisa sat there on the step, staring at Tres Manos in the distance. Afternoon clouds drifted in from the east, casting shadows over The Hands. Lisa sipped her beer and watched the clouds hang there. They hung a good long while, until the wind chased them off.

Lisa finished her beer, then got her clippers from the tool shed.

She worked in the herb garden.

She trimmed back the rosemary.

She trimmed it tight.

NORMAN PARTRIDGE'S compact, thrill-a-minute style has been praised by Stephen King and Peter Straub, and his fiction has received three Bram Stokers and two IHG awards. His first short story appeared in the second issue of *Cemetery Dance*, and his debut novel, *Slippin' into Darkness*, was the first original novel published by CD. Partridge's chapbook *Spyder* was one of Subterranean Press's inaugural titles, while his World Fantasy-nominated collection *Bad Intentions* was the first hardcover in the Subterranean book line. Since then, Partridge has published pair of critically acclaimed suspense novels featuring ex-boxer Jack Baddalach for Berkley Prime Crime (*Saguaro Riptide* and *The Ten-Ounce Siesta*), comics for Mojo and DC, and a series novel (*The Crow: Wicked Prayer*) which was adapted for the screen. His award-winning collections include *Mr. Fox and Other Feral Tales* and *The Man with the Barbed-Wire Fists*. Partridge's latest novel, *Dark Harvest*, was chosen by Publishers Weekly as one of the 100 Best Books of 2006. A third-generation Californian, he lives in the San Francisco Bay Area with his wife, Canadian writer Tia V. Travis.

Rust

BY N. J. AYRES

You have to keep the dark voice away. It does no good. Life breaks every man, didn't Hemingway say?

Trooper Erin Flannery, out of Bethlehem, Pennsylvania: Five-six. One-twelve, brown over brown. Red-brown over brown. Over hazel, make it, a kind of green. At her funeral, speakers said she was a loyal friend, good at her job, full of zip, had a beautiful smile. Everyone loved her, they said.

When she came aboard Troop M, even I thought of asking her out. But dating people from work—no good. The day our Commander, Paul Ooten, told us a female was joining us he warned not to engage in excessive swearing and crude remarks to see how she'd take it or to show she was one of the boys. He'd seen it before, and it was comical and juvenile, and nothing more than bias in the guise of jokes. He reminded us of the word "respect" used in the state police motto, and that our training includes the concept of military courtesy applied to civilians, peers, and superiors, whatever the gender. Unless some miscreant pissed us off while breaking the law, and then you can beat the shit out of him, he said. We laughed. Commander Paul Ooten. A lot like my dad. Upright, ethical, fair. Firm, yet fun when the time called for it. He also reminded me of my dad in the way he talked and in some of his mannerisms, like swiping a knuckle under his nose after he delivered a punch line. My father died when I was twelve. Heart attack in his police cruiser.

Everything changed.

My mother was okay for a while. Then she slowly took to drinking. By the time I was fourteen, she was into it full throttle. She dated, and each time it hardened me more. The idea of her wanting anyone but Dad sickened me.

It wasn't like she brought guys home, but she might as well have.

As soon as I was out of school and found someone to share rent with, I moved out, enrolled in community college, and later, with my AA degree in hand, applied to the Pennsylvania State Police Academy. What I really wanted was to go to Missoula where my uncle lived, study writing and film, and then wind up in California or New York, doing that scene. But I needed money from a job. I more than satisfied the physical training, aced the written and orals. Bingo, I are a cop.

Within seven years I earned a couple of medals for distinction in service. The last recognition was from the community, the "DUI Top Gun Award" for nailing forty-nine intelligent people who got behind the wheel while drunk.

Once, when I was ten, I alerted some neighbors across the street that their house was on fire. They called me a hero. I wasn't a hero. I was an ordinary kid who knew enough to realize a ton of smoke was not coming from a leaf pile in the backyard. My dad was the hero. He ran to the house with a ladder to get Mrs. Salvatore from the second floor.

• • •

I'm twenty-eight today. Today, like when you go to the doctor and the assistants ask and even the doctor asks how old are you today? Uh, yesterday I was twenty-eight, and today I'm twenty-eight also, thank you. And I'm single after a two-year marriage to a girl who couldn't dig someone who always thought he was right. I tried, really did, to see more gray instead of black and white. The marriage just wasn't meant to be. She went back to Alabama, teaches elementary school there. I wonder how she'd view me now. How old are you today? A hundred inside.

• • •

When Officer Flannery transferred over she was required to put in her time on reception. Nobody likes that duty, but there aren't enough civilians for it even though our governor is high on recruiting them. Right away the guys started testing her, seeing how available she might be. Married, unmarried, didn't matter. It's a thing guys do. I should say here I never saw our commander flirt or kid in any way that made it seem Erin was anything but another trooper.

Commander Paul Ooten's a real family man. That's what I heard all the time. I'd seen him with his family at a state patrol picnic once. Pretty wife. Two kids, about eight, ten.

And I saw him one night, behind a motel near Tannersville, coming down the stairs from the second floor, Trooper Flannery in front of him.

I had just gotten in my car after coming out of a restaurant. Parked perpendicular to the restaurant, nose in to the motel, I went to wipe moisture off the side mirror and then looked up. At first I thought my eyes were playing tricks on me. The light over the staircase and landing was fuzzy from moist air. The couple had long coats on. I watched them walk over patchy snow to her car. She got in, and a different light, coming from the motel sign near the street, hit her face, brighter, paler. Paul shut her door. She rolled down the window, and he leaned over and kissed her, then stood watching as she pulled away.

The next day I had a hard time looking at him.

• • •

A couple of weeks later, I was at my desk on a weekend. I had off, but my review was coming up and I had to get some overdue paperwork in. Ooten's door was open. Half of him was visible through the doorway, cut vertically, or I'd see him when he'd get up to go to his file cabinet.

Bill Buttons was in too. He's a kiss-up. Buttons thinks he's Bruce Willis. Shaves his head, swaggers around, crinks his mouth to smile. Sometimes when Ooten is around, Buttons makes like Bruce Willis making like John Wayne, saying, Wal, pardner, let's get 'er done. The effect: ridiculous.

That day, Paul Ooten came out of his office a couple of times, said something to Buttons, something to me. I tried forcing my feelings, tried to look at him the way I did before the night outside the motel with Erin. But I kept picturing him on her, her doing stuff to him.

When Buttons left for lunch, Paul—it's hard to call him Commander Ooten anymore—came into Room 5 where there are mail slots against the all, a supply cabinet, a small refrigerator, the coffee machine. I was pouring coffee for myself. Ooten put a memo in a slot and then took some time to mention the weather, the Eagles game, and how he'd been thinking of taking a course in Excel. I couldn't hide my lack of interest, but I guess because I had recently lost my mother to cancer, he said, "If you need to talk about it, Justin, my door's always open."

I said something like Thanks, I'm fine. His manner, the kindness behind it, touched me. And I resolved to put what I saw at the motel out of my mind.

• • •

What's bitter is that Erin Flannery didn't die from a car accident or a long-hidden disease. She died from brain trauma in her own home. Detectives interviewed the civilians in her life: family, friends, neighbors, they interviewed us at Troop M too, in due time. I wondered what Paul Ooten had told them. I wondered if the strained expression I saw each day is worry about his secret being outed, or if the tightness in his face was the shame he knew he brought to the badge. I'll say this: for some guys, if they learned the commander was boning Erin he'd only be more of a hero in their eyes.

No boyfriend turned up in the investigation. Bill Buttons said that's sure hard to believe, a piece like that.

A crime of opportunity, we concluded. It happens. Even to cops.

Kleinsfeldt said he overheard there was something odd about the evidence in her case, he didn't know what. We asked who he heard it from. He wouldn't say.

I reminded the guys that Flannery had been an LEO, a Liquor Enforcement Officer up in Harrisburg. It sounds like soft duty, but not necessarily. You go undercover to nab idiots who sell to minors. You look for cheats who avoid taxes by importing liquor from other states. You bust speakeasies. Yes, they still call them that, those enterprises too unenterprising to get a liquor license. The Bureau of Liquor Control Enforcement also goes after illegal video gambling machines, looking for operations suspected as hooked to corrupt organizations. Maybe she found one and was afraid she'd get cashed out because of it. Patrol sees our fair share of action, I don't mean we don't. It's more than spotting violations of the vehicle code. When your number's up you can get killed responding to a disturbance call as well as by some desperate speakeasy owner.

One time Erin found a note on the seat of her desk chair. It said he wished he were her seat cushion. She told me about it only because I was walking through the lobby and saw the look of disgust on her face as she studied the paper still in her hands. "Some jerk," she said. Said it quietly, almost with sadness. I don't know why that particular note would bother someone so much, but then I've never been a woman. I told her maybe it could be the computer guy, Steve Gress. He was in every week, supposedly upgrading our systems, which only created more problems.

I'd noticed the way he looked at her.

Carl Carolla had a thing for Erin too. I could tell because of his talk around her. He'd roll out some cockamamie story about which creep he had to deal with that day, what some wise-ass said. He said, "Joker like that, what you do, you rack up more offenses. Keep the dumb-ass violator from his appointed rounds, and hit him hard in the pocket." Carolla could be a suspect, maybe like if Erin told him to get lost after a clumsy pass.

Another cop, Rich Kleinsfeldt, resented her. Claimed women cops are a danger to everybody. Some dingbat can grab hold of their hair and then lift their sidearm, he said. Women's hair, according to dress code, has to be above the uniform collar points. Even so, it could be used for a handle, especially if it was in a braid. Another species, they are, says R.K. I'll agree that women offenders are the worst, you go to arrest them. They'll bite, yank, spit, what have you. "She's skeeter skinny anyway," Rich said. "You want that for your back?"

• • •

Something funny about the crime scene. Is that what Kleinsfeldt said? I knew one technician at the crime lab in Lancaster I could check with, but it would look odd, my poking around when the case wasn't mine. I let that idea drop.

• • •

Before what happened to Erin, I'd be on my runs, doing my job, and find myself thinking about Erin and Ooten. Ooten and Erin. The ring to it. Her power to lure him. I could understand it, yet not. I was just so disappointed in him. Hurt, you might say, though I cannot exactly say why. Ooten has awards of valor himself, the fact known by reputation and not by paper plastered on his office walls. From his example I did not display mine.

While Erin was at the front desk one morning and no public was in, I was getting pencils—pencils, by the way, not pencil.

My seventeenth summer I worked at a dollar store. The boss was training me for assistant manager, said I could take college classes at night, couldn't I, so I'd be free to do a full eight hours? In his instructions, he told me to keep an eye out for what the other employees might be up to. "If they aren't stealing a little, they're stealing a lot," he said. Those words came to mind as I grabbed my second and third pencil for home. I did it right in front of Buttons, whose arm was in the cabinet too, taking a stapler. He already had one on his desk. What did he need two for? I almost think I did it to show him I wasn't such an uptight asshole after all. But I did razz him about it. He razzed me back about my three pencils.

On my way back to my desk I heard Erin say on the phone she was letting her hair grow out. Who was she talking to? Her lover? I couldn't help but glance out the window to see if Ooten's car was in the lot. It wasn't. Every action or nonaction of Ooten's I couldn't help but attach to her.

• • •

My review was scheduled for the last day of the month. You always get a little anxious at that time. No one zips through with zero criticism. The review was the same week Erin was to complete her probationary period at the same time, a thing she had to go through even though she was a transfer-in and not a cadet. We're a paramilitary organization, the state police, why we're called Troopers. "Soldiers of the law," we are, and we suck it up when we get assignments we don't want or when we get treated like newbies. Erin said she was content here for the time being, mentioned how good everyone was to her, how terrific Commander Ooten was.

Did she linger on his name? How would the others feel if they got wind of her seeing him on the side? There are more minorities on the force than women. Women, in other words, still stand out. Her misbehavior would come to tarnish all other females entering the force and could severely damage Commander Ooten.

And so it was that I asked if she'd like to have coffee sometime, after shift. In my own way, maybe I was trying to be a decoy. Protect her and the commander both. I was a little surprised that she took me up on the invitation. Not that I look like something a dog won't eat. It's just that if she had Paul Ooten, why me? Maybe she saw me as an opportunity for a decoy too.

• • •

I suggested a seat near the window at a diner down the street, where we could watch the lazy snowflakes fall, the size of quarters that day. Erin's eyes showed her delight in it. She informed me that snowflakes fall at about the rate of a mile an hour, unless icy droplets form on them to increase their weight. How'd she know that, I asked. "Before I joined the Bureau of Liquor Enforcement, I thought of teaching biology. I'm a science junkie. Then I got out of BLE because the captain, a micromanager anyway, insisted on messing with a restaurant owner who allowed a singer to come in two nights a week."

"Say again?"

"The owner was licensed to sell liquor, could even allow people to dance in the aisles to jukebox or to live music if he wanted. His mistake? He paid a band that had a vocalist. That heinous deed made him in violation of Liquor Law Section Four-Nine-Three-Point-Ten, 'Entertainment on a licensed premise without an Amusement Permit'."

"You're kidding," I said. "Still, if it's on the books . . ."

"It's a stupid law."

"We're not paid to write the laws."

"Ah, but there was something else. The restaurant owner was an old high-school enemy of the captain. So it was personal. It's not the only reason I left, just the last one. And, unfortunately, my judgment may have faltered when I wrote a letter to the editor about police harassment of small businesses. I disguised my identity, of course. But they were suspicious because of the way

I'd been fuming about it. I got congratulations from the guys and glares from the brass."

"Ouch."

"Well, you learn to pick your battles. A lesson."

"I thought you were happy about the change."

"I am. But now I have to start over again."

She didn't get much of a chance to do that. Some evil character hit the delete key on her life.

• • •

Forget about the old days when people said tough guys don't eat quiche. Tough guys don't ever say the word depressed. I'll say it here so that maybe my actions could be understood, if ever they can.

After Erin died, on duty I'd sit off Interstate 80 and watch violators speed by. And one day, while off the rolls, I spotted a shoplifter out back of Sears in Stroudsburg look three ways and then languidly wheel a barbecue away and load it in the back of his SUV. Yesterday I saw that Gress guy, the computer jock, fudge his time card, look at me, drop it in the bin and walk away like saying, Challenge me, Muskrat, what you got in your den? And how did I know he stole time? The look. If he hadn't been smug, I wouldn't have gone to the bin and picked up the card. But he was right: I didn't challenge him. Something else was on my mind.

• • •

A few days after the coffee with Erin, I asked her out again, for a Saturday afternoon movie. We went to see *Jarhead.* Arrived in different cars. Paid our own tickets in. "You understand this is not a real date," she said. "You understand this is not real popcorn," I said. "It's packing foam." Afterward, we stood on the sidewalk outside the mall, discussing the movie. She saw stuff in it I didn't. In the chilly sunlight, talking about things outside of cop-dom, she was flat-out beautiful.

In the walk to our cars I finally couldn't keep the question away. "Want to make it official sometime? A genuine date?"

"Probably not a good idea."

"Yeah," I said. "Peace."

"Peace."

We went our separate ways.

• • •

I consider myself a balanced man, don't go off half-cocked. What my nature allows, my training reinforces. So I do not tell the rest of this lightly. It's not that hard to understand the primitives who believe in demons entering a person's skin. I say this because I don't know what came over me in the case of Trooper Erin Flannery and Paul Ooten: I became a spy. I felt righteous, principled, and therefore gave myself permissions I would never give someone else. It was the mystery of her drawing power I couldn't get out of my head, that force that makes a man like Commander Ooten forsake his marriage vows and teeter on the verge of disgracing his profession.

I took to rolling through Nazareth some weekends to see if I could spot her. I knew that's where she lived, but not precisely. Nazareth isn't that big a town: six thousand people. It's about ten miles from troop headquarters and under nine from where I live in Bethlehem—Steel City, a name that fit before the Bethlehem Steel mill and its support businesses fell victim to the Japanese business onslaught.

Driving down Center Street one day, I saw Trooper Flannery coming out of a drycleaners with her bagged uniforms. I am ashamed to say I followed her to see the apartment complex in which she lived.

And later, on occasion I would go off my route to drift down her street and see if I could catch sight of the commander's car, see it in the apartment parking lot. Sneering at my own bad behavior, I called it "volunteer surveillance." I hated what I was doing yet could not keep from the patrol. We were on extra alert because of a terroristic threat. Watch for violations on small refrigerator vehicles, the bulletin said. Stop and search if indicted. Drive by Erin Flannery's residence to see if Paul Ooten's car was there. Other guys were out at bars, cracking wise and watching games. I was stuck on one note and it was sour. Tomorrow I would shed this thing.

• • •

Don't ask me how a reporter for the *Allentown Morning Call* got it, but it happens sometimes. His piece told the basics of Pennsylvania State Police Trooper Erin Anne Flannery's demise. The state police spokesman was reserving comment on manner of death. I should think the public reader would conclude, as would any cop, that homicide was on the minds of investigators. I spent a restless night. The next day State Commissioner Corporal Robert Metcalfe announced before TV cameramen that Trooper Flannery's case was under investigation as murder, and he was sorry but he could not release any details.

• • •

"Honor, service, integrity, respect, trust, courage, and duty." Our motto. I am familiar with courage as it pertains to rescue, or in the midst of violent disputes, even in the frequent chaos of felony arrests. I've not only witnessed it but, if you'll excuse me for saying so, performed within its lighted shaft. But could it be that those were times not of action but reaction, mindless as a ball springing off the floor of a gym? Moral courage, there's the mark, and a harder one to hit.

It's clear that lying violates integrity. But does silence? We're not talking the silence of the citizens of Germany in World War II. Not that kind. In Erin's case, nothing will pull her up from the endless recycle machine, not even if I told I was there at the time of her death.

• • •

It broke. Mrs. Paul Ooten, given name Mallory, was a person of interest in Homicide Incident Number Ml-645-whatever. Mrs. Paul Ooten! Our troop was on fire with speculation, with rethinking impressions of her. And then, of course, there were the terrible distance, disappointment, and suspicion toward the commander himself. I must admit I was halfway pleased there was no gloating, as I might have expected.

The commander was put on administrative leave. It wasn't the first scandal or the first capital case to stain the state police. But it was here, now, among us at Troop M, a mortal wound, it seemed to me. My fellow troopers talked themselves raw. Then, steel bands slowly tightened on our hearts. We grew silent, more involved in what we were trained to do: to be soldiers of the law. We got back to business.

• • •

There was a message slip on my desk when I came in one morning two weeks later. It called me to a meeting at Bethlehem headquarters. I brought along my personal write-up detailing my performance accomplishments this year, as we are told to do at review time. I wondered who would be giving my review now that Ooten was out.

Whatever I can say about him, I'll say I have no doubt the commander would have given me a good one. The only thing he ever admonished me about was failure to properly orient a diagram sketch of an accident scene. For all my driving about, I'd put down north for a street that actually ran northeast, and he caught it.

As I approached the conference room, I saw an officer's winter coat draped on a chair. Two rank rings decorated the coat sleeve, signifying the coat belonged to a major. When I entered the room, there sat the major at the end of the table, Commander Ooten to his right. I looked from one to the other until Ooten spoke. "Good morning, Justin." Motioning, he introduced Major Bryan Manning.

"Have a seat, Trooper Eberhardt," the major said.

My heart was pounding. What kind of promotion could I be in for?

The major began by apologizing for not making it out to Troop M barracks before. "Been busy as a bartender on payday," he said. Intended to put me at ease. I'm afraid I didn't laugh. After more chat about nothing, he said, "Tell me, Trooper, what do you recall about your CPR training?"

Confused, I stumbled through a reply, first repeating "Two hands, two inches, three compressions in two seconds. Fifteen pushes, then two ventilation breaths."

"And what is the distance of travel for compressions, Trooper?"

"Two inches, as I said, sir."

"A third the depth of the chest," the major said.

"Yes sir."

"Makes a body tired, right, Trooper?" the major asked with a smile.

Ooten pitched in: "It can be brutal."

"Sure enough I busted a sweat first time I did it," Major Manning said. "Was a big guy, close to three hundred pounds. I was drippin' sweat on him."

You do the polite thing in a situation like this. Nod, chuckle. But what the hell was this, a grilling on rescue efforts you'd give a cadet? My wooly-pully was on under my uniform shirt. It felt like ninety degrees in there.

Commander Ooten sprung the next question. "You were pretty tight with Trooper Flannery, weren't you, Justin?"

"Friends. I didn't know her well. I mean, we didn't have that much time to get to know each other." I met his eyes, guessing if the probe was meant to inquire if I had slept with her. Slept with the woman Commander Ooten was cheating with. Her lunch hour went long, people said. Dentist, doctor appointments, flat tire, things like that, she would claim.

"She wasn't here but three months, sir." All along I'd considered how quickly she and Ooten hooked up.

How can I describe the look in his eyes? Seeing me, not seeing me. Assessing, reflecting. The oil of the present saturating the rust of the past.

He said, "Carl Carolla observed you tagging after Trooper Flannery, Justin, and not once but twice. Carl thought that was odd. What can you tell us about that?"

"I . . . I wouldn't know. He's mistaken." I said nothing more. Silence is a tool in interviews. And even in sales. My uncle told me that. When he'd go to close a deal, he put a pencil to his lips to signal he was through talking. "He who speaks first loses," is what he said. I recognized the tool's use now with the commander and the major, the three of us soundless while the room temp climbed even as I saw through the slats of the blinds behind the commander snow riding slanted chutes of wind.

At last Major Manning said, "Are you up to date on your CPR certification, Trooper?"

"I'd have to check the date, sir. I think I might be due."

"You've rendered CPR before, right, Justin?" Manning asked.

"No sir."

Why did I lie? I did start CPR on a victim once. It was part of an action that won me a Commendation Medal, but in the write-up it was not mentioned nor should it have been. Emergency techs had arrived at the scene seconds after I'd started, so I didn't consider it as actually "performed."

The major sat back, arms outstretched on the table, and looked at Paul, who asked me, "You usually wear a ring, don't you, guy?" Friendly, casual.

"A school ring, yes," I said, and shrugged. I hadn't put it on that day. I glanced at the commander's left hand as he toyed with a collector's pen our troop gave him last Christmas. His wedding ring was still on. I pictured his wife, Mallory, how she must look today, turmoil in her face, heartache visible in her robot motions, her walk, her interactions with her children. Commander Ooten sat there interviewing me about Erin Flannery while his family was torn apart because of his unstoppable urges toward a woman who wound up dead on the floor of her home.

No doubt his wife would be quickly cleared in Erin's case. Ridiculous, when you think about it, how she got tied to it at all. Who in this world would figure that she and Erin had in common a love of the oboe, I kid you not, a love of the oboe, which found the two of them in weekly classes at community college. Mrs. Ooten had lent Erin an old instrument her father gave her as an eleven-year-old, the name "Mallory Parsons" engraved on a gold plate on the case. The very fact that Mallory Ooten was innocently in the home of her husband's lover gave me a pang, my sympathy for her as tender as my own scoured nerves.

• • •

What I did not tell my superiors is that the night of Erin's injury she had consumed too much plum wine, and I had been the one to buy it. "I've been a little stressed out," she said. "Things."

"It can get that way."

"You know what? You're way easier to be around than I would've guessed."

"Thanks, I guess."

"It's just that on the job you're so serious."

"Is that bad or good?"

"It is what it is. Could go either way." Her hair looked like shined copper.

This was a couple of weeks after *Jarhead.* Ooten was out of town at a con-fab in Pittsburgh. Maybe that's why Erin weakened when I asked her out. I felt low about my reasons and was almost sorry she accepted. Here she was already involved in deceit with Ooten, and now she was deceiving him with me. Of course, it wouldn't go so far as to be labeled true betrayal, I wouldn't let it go that far. But even if it did, at least the two of us were single.

We met at a Japanese restaurant, a new place I said I wanted to try near the Bethlehem Brew Works. Erin insisted on separate cars again, saying she had things to do that would put her in the vicinity anyway. We sat at one of the table-sized, stainless steel grills where the food is prepared before our eyes Teppanyaki style. The flames flew high on the volcano of onions the chef built. We marveled at his antics with thrown eggs and knives, and, with others, applauded each performance.

In between I looked for a way to caution Erin about her activities with Commander Ooten. I wanted to ask her what in the world did she think she is doing. Ask in a nice way but one that left no doubt that her new friend, myself, was there to help set her straight.

While waiting for the check, I said, "I'm going to tell you something."

She tilted her head, a smile on her lips. "Okay."

"Don't take this wrong."

"Oh boy," she said. She peered into her wine glass, refilled once already, and lifted my sake cup to drain the last few sips. Then she went for the pitcher. "Guess I'll have to do without," she said, shaking it as if more would loosen and come free. "How bad is it, what you're going to tell me?"

"You can handle it."

"Ah, thank God."

"You're a mystery to me, is all."

"Come again?"

"I can't quite figure you out."

She winked at me and reached for her puffy pink jacket from the back of the chair, saying, "Have you figured out I'm a little wasted? If I had any more I couldn't drive. You'd have to arrest me." The way she said it, like a flirtation.

• • •

We stood in the parking lot by her car, talking, and then she said, "Ugh. You know, I'm really feeling sick. I don't think I can make it home without urping." She hunched in, and I stood by her and put my arm around her. This could be the most unusual of come-ons, perhaps the same as she used on the commander to get him to take her home.

"It must be the food. It couldn't be the wine and sake. A certain person kept me from that," she said, looking at me sideways, a pixie tease in her smile.

Icy mud sprayed us as a car sped by faster than the driver should have in the lot. The snow was about three inches deep, the woods woven with chalky fog ahead of us.

"Come on," I said. "I'll take you home. In the morning I'll pick you up at your apartment and we can go get your car."

When she quickly met my eyes, I realized she hadn't mentioned whether she lived in an apartment, a house, or a boxcar.

• • •

She lived just a few miles away, near a Moravian cemetery. "I go there sometimes and just wander down the lanes. All the headstones lie flat to show that everyone is equal in the sight of God. Rich next to poor, whites next to blacks next to Mohican Indians."

"I didn't know that," I said. "I'm from Montana. We stuff 'em and put 'em in museums." She gave a soft laugh. Her eyes were closed and her head was back on the seat as I'd instructed. It's where my own should have been. I could feel the hot drink still in my veins, the sweet burn that beckons so many, the frayed ends strangely comforting.

"All but the women," Erin said. "The women are buried in their own section. Separate. Inside the church, too."

Her lips shone pink in the boomeranged light. I wanted to kiss her there, then. Instead, I turned the key in the ignition and pulled out onto the road, driving well within the speed limit, sight often flicking to the mirrors. I disdained the fact that Trooper Flannery would let herself get blotto even off duty, but the truth was I also knew in saner times I would not get behind the wheel either. She did it again, that woman. Getting men to tread over boundaries.

• • •

She seemed to feel better, once inside. "I guess it was the wine after all," she said. "I didn't eat lunch today. Hey, want some ice water? Or coffee? I'll be glad to make some." I said yes to the coffee.

That's when she got up from the couch we were sitting on. Perhaps I was sitting a little too close for comfort. I shifted to be farther away when she returned, but then I stood up and went into the kitchen with her. She faltered as she took a step, galumphing forward off the rug and slapping soles onto the tile. Laughing, she said, "Holy shit. I really am drunk . . . or something. You know what? I'm sorry, but I think I should just go on up to bed."

Sure, sure, I told her, meaning it.

"Just help me get upstairs and I'll be fine. Thank you, Justin. Thank you, really."

Was it this way with Ooten? But then she also seemed really embarrassed. Who was she? How could one woman do this to two men?

With my help she managed to mount four of the stairs. "Just flip the lock on the way out, will you, Justin? I can make it the rest of the way."

She smiled and thanked me again. I started to go down but then reached the next step up before she did, hardly aware of my action. I brought her around and pulled her to me and sank into her lips. "No," she said . . . and let me kiss her again.

What I wanted to do . . . what I intended to do . . . was scoop her up like Rhett Butler did Scarlett O'Hara in *Gone with the Wind,* but it didn't turn out that way, oh no, it didn't. She jerked back and then . . . as I try to recall this, I am not sure just what happened. All I know is I tried to grab her to keep her from falling. Instead, as she sank she twisted, and my fist connected to the left jaw. In her dive down, her head shot against the square platform of the end stair-rod, and then she flipped and her head went *smack!* on the tile, a gray tile with tan swirls in it until joined with the brightest of red.

Even as early as then I wondered if I'd let her fall. If I'd caused her to fall. My reactions are supposed to be quick. How could I let her slip by?

She was on the floor with her eyes rolled partway up. I began CPR.

• • •

You might suppose it crossed my mind to eat the hornet. Oh, I practiced caressing my weapon the way I'd seen it done in movies. And I drew other dramatic scenarios in my mind. My illicit favorite: death by scumbag. I would insert myself into a bad street scene and, while making like a hero, arrange for my own end.

I even imagined a sequence where my body would be found among the homeless at the Bethlehem mill. Once, on a perimeter canvass after a series of home break-ins, I went in at a downed section of fencing near the rear of Blast Furnace Row. Inside the steel skeleton crows flutter. Cat eyes gleam in the alcoves. Scruffy-looking souls, both men and women, cook their meals over fifty-five-gallon drums, glance at you with little interest, as though even in uniform you're just another wanderer there. That is where I belonged. Now I lay me down to sleep . . . forever. But to involve them in my final act would be to pile wrong upon wrong.

Again I was summoned to headquarters. It was a whole month after the first interview with Major Manning and the commander. This time it was two sergeants from the homicide unit.

I won't drag it out. What they laid on me I knew was coming; knew it yet pretended it wasn't imminent, that each day I awakened would be like any other before the incident.

At the autopsy for Erin Flannery it was discovered that her sternum and two ribs were cracked from the compressions I had rendered. When I first began, I did not want to remove her bra. To do so would seem a trespass of its own variety. Because I didn't remove it, the first several thrusts downward scored the flesh over her sternum. In due time I also heard a crackling, like the sound of a cereal bag being pinched tight, but I thought it was interference from the bra. With clumsy fingers, I unhinged the plastic hook in front and just kept on pumping, calling her name before I put my mouth to hers to force in another breath.

It must have gone on for thirty minutes, or so it seemed. And then, when I had no positive response, no reaction at all, curse me, I looked around trying to think of anything I'd touched, and then I fled.

• • •

The medical examiner, upon noting those injuries to the chest, instructed her assistant to swab around the mouth and to perform another separate swab on the lips of the deceased. Even this action, through DNA testing, would not have implicated me, save for the fact I volunteered a sample in one of the extra criminal investigation classes I took after joining the force. The sample was sent to the state laboratory as though it were any other, not a student's. It would be held as an unidentified profile. These are kept in the database in the hope that someday they will "hit" in another case that had other trace evidence with which to bust a suspect. Like Mrs. Ooten's fingerprint on the oboe case, my identity would not be known from that saliva sample—except that eventually my superiors pressed for a new sample to be taken. And of course, I complied. There was the ring the commander asked about—the twist in the garrote, you might say. Nothing at the scene of Erin's death would have pointed my way. I left no fingerprints. I had not touched a glass, nor the banister. I did open the door with Erin's key, but I had on gloves, as I did when I left. Even while rendering CPR, I avoided the blood on the floor. But the ring . . .

The sergeant who studied the evidence seized on a peculiar mark on Erin's jaw, a curved flame shape with a slight space below, and beneath that a kind of pear shape, a teardrop with a touch of high waist. Two of each shape. Sergeant Geerd Scranton showed me a photo of it. "What does that look like to you, son?"

"I don't know, crooked carrots? With a blotch below?"

"I took up an interest in Indians when I was a boy."

"Did you," I said. Where was this going?

"My name," he said, "means 'spear brave' in Dutch. Piscataway Indians used spears. They'd hunt fish and bear with them."

"Are you onto something, Sergeant?" I asked, feigning only an intellectual interest in the case.

"It's part of a bear print. The nails, the pads. See? Perfect in the photo." He turned the photo my way. "You could be right."

"I'm told you wear a ring with a bear print on it, Justin. Trooper Buttons says you always have it on."

"Hah. I do. Or almost always. I guess I left it on the sink this morning." I smiled. "I spent some time in Montana with my dad and uncle. God, what beautiful country. Have you ever . . . ? The grizzly is the state mascot. Lots of people wear it on jewelry." I said.

He nodded, waited a few beats, or maybe it was minutes, or maybe it was an hour, before he said, "Why don't you just tell me about what happened, Justin? It must be very uncomfortable for you. Sergeant Kunkle, myself, Major Manning—we know there must have been some pretty powerful extenuating circumstances or you would have done the right thing. Isn't that so, son? Look, we know that sometimes we get pushed to extremes. Maybe you tried to romance her? Maybe you had a little too much to drink?"

I sat looking at him, stunned he would suggest such things, but not arguing because arguing would only deepen what he already believed.

Again he went on like that, and I shook my head as if I just couldn't believe what test they were putting me through now. I did say I was clueless as to what response they wanted.

And then he used the tool of silence. Crows could have been squalling in the steel mill shadows. The wails of warning cats went chasing their own echoes around. The hollow laughter of the homeless kept piercing my ears.

• • •

There is a certain terror in the veins of those who would do right always. I am the junior to the senior, our standards so high there is no true escape.

Perhaps my father knew that, and maybe that's part of why he left us, his daily companions a fifth of whiskey, a bottle of bennies, and tricked-up tubing duct-taped to the exhaust pipe of his cruiser, snaked into his window on the passenger side as it sat hub-deep in mud on the side of a cornfield, a stand of trees blocking the scene from the main road, no reason known, no final written note to tell us why.

As a child, nights, I'd be in bed listening to my parents argue, my mother's voice loud and clear, my father only sometimes shouting back. After his death I tried recalling what all they argued about. I couldn't then, but today I remember a woman's name. An odd name, to me even then: Clarabelle. I remember my mother calling her "whore" and my not knowing what the word meant but that it had an awful sound, the way a roar issues deep from within a throat. Perhaps I should have known, but I was a quiet child and did not hang with any special friends.

It wasn't until I was twenty and spent a final summer with my uncle outside of Butte that I learned the real story of my father's death. Until that time, and even after, I kept hearing of what a good man he was. How positive. How good, how perfect. A model of a man. My image of him was forever ruined by what my uncle revealed and, later, by other things I came to know. I longed to be better than Enoch "Eddie" Eberhardt, and determined to shape my longing into action to become, if it is possible in this world, the truly moral man.

Commander Ooten became my model. I would learn to be like him. Anything or anyone that got in the way to diminish the image I had must only be possessed of a fierce and terrible magic. In my obsession to know what the power was that did trip him up, I laid out a woman who in no way deserved an early end, whose only fault was to be a friend to a family and to a lonely madman.

To this day I do not know if I deliberately put my fist to her jaw. But does it even matter? I either committed or omitted, failed to do what I should have, and encouraged what I should not.

It may be two years now that I've lived on the banks of the Pocono River, there until weather drives me and my fellow campers to find a collapsed barn, a forgotten shed, a building in wait for a bulldozer. Days, we hook fish and toss whatever's left to forever-hungry cats skulking in the bushes. We keep watch on our meager holdings and quickly drive out any offenders. Draw straws to see who will go buy the wine. Days are good. Blackbirds chainsaw the nights. I tell those of you who would listen that even the strongest of girders rust. We are all just wanderers here.

N.J. (NOREEN) AYRES is the author of three forensics-based crime novels that pre-date the CSI t.v. phenomenon. For 20 years Ayres wrote and edited complex, multi-volume technical manuals for large engineering companies and defense contractors. She now develops proposals and reports concerning lead reclamation at private and police shooting ranges. Having won a few awards for her poetry and short stories, she enjoys serving as a judge in national writing competitions and helping other writers in polishing their manuscripts. With her long-time partner, she rescues feral cats and kittens in northeastern Pennsylvania, getting them neutered and returned to their environment or adopted out (128 so far in 3 years). Another pastime is oil and acrylic painting. In summer 2009, her story "The Exquisite Burden of Bones" will appear in *Murder Past, Murder Present,* Twilight Times Books, editors Jan Grape and Barri Born. Website: www.noreenayres.com.

Skin and Bones

BY DAVID EDGERLEY GATES

New York's a city that's forever reinventing itself. In lower Manhattan, excavations for a water main or a subway line will uncover graves from a forgotten potter's field, or a shellfish midden predating the Dutch. The public library between Fifth and Sixth is built on the site of the old Croton reservoir, itself once a formidable monument to nineteenth-century ambition and ingenuity. Times change, and the landscape of the city changes with them. Where once there was a boundary between the wild and sown, for example, in Peter Stuyvesant's day, is now Wall Street. The footprints are all about, if only you take notice.

And of course New York's a place that invites reinvention. Irish and Italians, Germans and Swedes, Ashkenazi immigrants from Eastern Europe, Armenians, Levantines, and Greeks, the tidal migration north of Negroes between the wars, apple-cheeked kids from Iowa, and streetwise toughs from Jersey, all of them hungry for adventure or advancement, Anglicizing their names, rewriting their histories, imagining their own creation myth.

Dede van Rensellaer had been born Deirdre O'Donnell. The orphaned child of a whore, she grew up in the workhouses and was turned out onto the streets when she was fourteen. She fell into the natural grasp of a pimp and was jobbed out to the trade.

If you'd asked her why she didn't seek to enter service as a domestic, she would have guffawed. Where was the practical difference? In either case, you were property. She was, as it happened, rescued by one of her clients. Not so rare an event as you might think. She married above herself and never looked back. I was startled by her invitation to lunch.

We met at the Waldorf. I knew it only from the salad. But she cared little for appearances, that was plain.

"Mickey, it's been twenty years," she said, offering me her hand.

I took it. "Ma'am." She was probably the one on thin ice, not me.

"Would you care for a cocktail?" she asked.

"Better, perhaps, that I keep my wits about me," I said, as I took my seat.

Her laughter was like a chime, nothing artificial or forced about it at all. She'd certainly kept her gamine charm.

"I'd share a bottle of wine," I said, leaning against it.

She ordered a Bordeaux. The wine steward and the maitre d' apparently knew her well

She rubbed the cork between her fingers and passed it beneath her nostrils. She approved. I let her order the meal for both of us as well. We raised our glasses.

"The future," she said.

It was the shared past we were drinking to, I imagined, but we clicked rims.

Scallops, *en croute,* a green salad, beef Wellington. More pastry, in fine, than I would have chosen, given the pounds I've put on in my age. But it was her treat, and her schedule.

We came to it over coffee.

A girl, she told me. Not much above fourteen, but already slightly soiled and shopworn from the life. Undernourished, just skin and bones. Wary, a little feral, perhaps, mistrustful of solicitude.

"Why?" I asked her. I meant, what was her interest.

"Oh, Mickey," she said. "Isn't it obvious? She reminds me of me, at that age."

"Nothing further?"

She smiled and shook her head, sadly. "I see where you're going. No. She's not my illegitimate daughter, or the like. If it were blackmail, I'd face it out, or hire a private dick to break some heads."

Something she knew full well I had a name for.

"Not that, either," she said, reading my expression.

I nodded. Rented muscle is easily found. The rich have lawyers and dogs bodies to insulate them from responsibility or consequence. "Why call in an old marker, then?" I asked her.

She looked at me with level regard, and then her focus shifted past me, into some indeterminate middle distance. "I'd say *I* owed *you,* Mickey, not the other way around." She spoke without addressing me directly, or as if she weren't talking about herself. "You never took advantage of me back then. I even wondered if you were queer. For all that you're no doubt a hard man, and a wicked one, you've got a sentimental streak."

"I've a weakness for the downtrodden," I said, meaning some irony.

"You wear it lightly," she said, letting her eyes meet mine again. They were blue and transparent, like Arctic ice.

I shifted my weight, uncomfortably.

"You have boys on the street," she said. "Girls, too, for all I know." She meant the young numbers runners I used. "What I *do* know is that you don't whore them out."

I could see where this was going. "You think my kids would already have noticed her, yes?" I asked.

"Beekman Place," she said.

I knew she lived in the East Fifties. "Not our turf," I said.

But she had a whim of iron. "*You* could cozy up to her."

"I'd be a John, no more."

"You might win her trust, Mickey."

"A thankless errand," I said.

"You'd have my thanks."

"No good deed goes unpunished, Deirdre," I said.

"And don't I know it," she said, sadly.

Which, on the face of it, was sufficient. In retrospect, I should have been less credulous.

• • •

They say there's a broken heart for every light on Broadway. I couldn't tell you, but it feels anecdotally accurate. All those children who come here, wild with ambition. How many of them fall through the cracks? How many of them suffer the slings and arrows of outrageous fortune? I was a product of the West Side streets myself, Hell's Kitchen. If the mob hadn't found me and taken me under its wing, I'd have been bait for predators.

This is not merely philosophy.

It was 1949. Along the East River, ground had been broken for the United Nations. Sutton Place and Beekman were old and established, respectable addresses, and the foreign legations were eager to snap them up. Real estate values were going right through the roof. But at curbside, prices were stagnant.

"Bareback blow job, two bucks," one of my kids told me.

"Is that how she makes the rent?" I asked.

"She can always sleep on top of a heating grate, or under a cardboard box."

"You speaking specifically, or generically?"

She shook her head. "I don't know her," she said.

"Can you *get* to know her, Judy?" I asked. She looked at me suspiciously.

How much do you give away? They were sly, they were hungry, they were survivors, they'd shovel their competition under a subway train for the odd dime. I had to be frank. "It's a favor for a friend," I said. "I want her looked after."

"Would you do it for me, Mickey?" she asked.

She was thirteen, just shy of puberty. I could have turned her out and gotten a return. "Yes," I told her. It was true.

"Okay," she said. Wise beyond her years.

I protected my kids, unlike some, but it wasn't sentiment. I was investing in the future. People might tell you that there's an infinite pool of throwaway talent, the abandoned and forlorn, and in brute fact they're thrown away daily, like candy wrappers, but if we eat our own young, hope dies.

Not that the children weren't themselves carnivorous. Judy would interpret my writ however she chose, and not necessarily to my liking. All the same, I wanted her and the other canny lads to see the job through. They were my only decent chance to get at Dede's lost girl. It was a small ambition.

I worked a different angle. Two dollars, Judy had told me. What was the girl's market? Sutton Place and Beekman.

I started with the doormen.

They were a mixed lot. Insular, territorial, proprietary. Some of them were protective, some of them were condescending, some of them were hostile. All of them were for sale. It was a matter of meeting their price.

Dede's own doorman, on Beekman, had an inflated idea of his own importance. I didn't use her name, of course, which would have gained me nothing in any case, but crossing his palm with silver gained me nothing either. He was either obtuse or willfully ignorant. His knowledge of the neighborhood was sadly deficient, and none of what he shared was useful.

I had better luck with a colored man at an apartment house on Sutton. He'd been at his trade since before the war, and I put his age at above sixty. He carried himself with brittle dignity, treading that careful line between deference and pride. The name-plate on his uniform read Judah Benjamin, which I thought curiously Hebrew, but it was only coincidence, his last name the residue of some long-dead white slaveholder, his first the legacy of a Bible-thumping mother who'd spent too much time reading the Old Testament. He had a sense of humor about it. I was careful not to press a slight and ambiguous advantage.

"A white girl, maybe fourteen?"

I nodded.

"You looking to turn her out?"

I'd laid a twenty on the counter, and he'd ignored it. This was a delicate negotiation. I didn't want him to imagine insult. I put a second cautious twenty down beside the first one. "I could," I said, "if that were my object. But why then would I be so circumspect?"

He shrugged.

"I might tell you a story neither one of us would believe," I said. "Why bother?"

"But you mean her no injury."

"I'm offering what I'd imagine was a benefit."

"A mixed blessing."

"What has she got now?"

He smiled, shifting his gaze away from mine. His eyes were very old. "She has her freedom," he said.

"No," I said. "She has choices."

He looked at me again. "I know you," he said.

"Or somebody very like me," I admitted.

He was on the edge of trust, but his experience told him better. "Russians, Arabs, Jews," he said, shaking his head. "I came to Harlem a lifetime ago."

I had a notion what he was driving at. "I grew up in New York," I told him. "I was a mick from the West Side. I worked the docks and joined a union, or I signed up with the cops."

"You signed up with the mob," he said.

I nodded. "I stepped on the third rail," I said.

"I grew up in the South," he said. "My father was a jailbird. A lifer at Angola prison. You know what that means?"

I could guess, but I really couldn't imagine.

"I came North. I left my mother; I left my brothers and sisters behind. I came for the promised land. I was too old to go in the service when the war came. But let me tell you, the '30s, the '40s, the pussy was unbelievable. It was lying around like bottle caps."

"A lifetime ago," I suggested.

"Yeah," he said. "Well."

"Let me ask you something, Judah," I said. "Back in the day, the Cotton Club, the Apollo, when you were a player. Would you have used this girl and cast her aside?"

He nodded. "A stiff Johnson's got no conscience."

"Let me ask you a different question," I said. "Russians, Arabs, Jews. What'd you mean by that? I'd think the kid's natural clientele would be your own tenants, guys coming home after a hard day at the office, don't get it from the secretary, don't get it from the wife, buy a quickie on the sidewalk."

"I don't much appreciate your vocabulary," he said.

"It gives me some sleepless nights," I told him.

The two twenties vanished. His hand passed across the counter in front of him and the bills disappeared, like a magic trick. I thought I'd lost him. I didn't know how to recover my limited advantage.

"I can tell you where to find her," Judah said.

"That's a start," I suggested.

"Diplomats," he said. There was contempt in his voice.

"You talking about the UN?"

"Yeah, the You an'," he said sarcastically.

Nobody back then used the locution UN much. Most people thought the entire enterprise a joke. It was located out in Flushing Meadows, an ash dump before the 1939 World's Fair. Now it was slated to be developed on prime east waterfront.

"Money attracts money," I said.

"You ain't just whistling 'Dixie,'" he said.

I smiled. "You don't strike me as the sort of man who'd be likely to whistle 'Dixie,'" I said.

He ducked his head, concealing a laugh in his collar.

"The girl, then," I said. "She services these newcomers."

"They take it when the tray is passed," he said.

"You know her name?" I asked.

"Maggie," he said. "May not be the one she was born with."

"That's all?"

"We pass the time of day. I give her a dollar."

"Not two?"

"I don't need no blow job from a fourteen-year-old white girl," he said. "Some kid with no ass in her pants and one step away from the needle."

Skin and bones, Deirdre had said. "You know that?" I asked him. Heroin and coke weren't as common on the street as they are now. Jazz musicians, some Bohemians who smoked dope, but it was a Negro thing, or so many of us were willing to think.

"Way things are," he said. "It's how their pimps keep them under their thumb."

"So she's a hophead?"

"Not today, maybe, but tomorrow or the next. She might not be courting salvation," he said.

I agreed. "Depends what she's running away from," I said.

"Frying pan into the fire."

I agreed with that too

"You can't fix all the sadness in this world, Irish," Judah said to me. "Some of it's beyond repair."

He seemed like somebody who'd know.

• • •

I would have tried the beat cops next, but the police found me first. I'd wandered down First Avenue as far as the corner of Forty-eighth, where the UN construction site began. It was one hell of a big hole, between First Avenue and the river, and extending six blocks south, the whole of it barricaded with cyclone fencing and plywood. But there were peepholes cut in the plywood every ten or twelve feet, both at adult eye level and for kids, to accommodate sidewalk supervisors. I was looking through one of them, not able to envision much, since the footings hadn't yet been poured, let alone the concrete forms for foundation work. In fact, the crews had either hit groundwater or the East River was leaking in because the entire excavation was a muddy, sucking wound, swallowing bulldozers and back-loaders, time and money. I wondered how far behind schedule they were by now, and who'd been fool enough to post completion bonds.

I turned when I heard the car pull up at the curb behind me. It was a big prewar Lincoln, the V-12, but I knew its owner had never been inconvenienced by gasoline rationing.

A rumpled, overweight guy in a cheap off-the-rack suit got out of the passenger side. He looked irritated.

"Sergeant," I said, pleasantly enough. I kept my hands in my pockets, representing no threat. O'Toole would have been all too happy to grind my face into the pavement.

"Pat would like a word," he said, inclining his head.

O'Toole was an errand boy and a precinct bagman, all the more dangerous for being both stupid and aggrieved. He wasn't, in fine, the sort you'd want to meet if he were off his master's leash. I had no call to aggravate him further.

I got into the passenger seat of the Packard. O'Toole left the door open and drifted a few yards off.

"Mickey," the man behind the wheel said, smiling.

"Pat."

Patrick Francis Gallagher was a lieutenant of detectives. He'd started out as a harness bull, like so many others, and by virtue of luck and opportunity, and an easy way with the necessities of criminal enterprise, he made ready advancement. He was bent. I wouldn't complain if he'd been compromised by the Hannahs, my own mob, but he was in the pocket of Frank Costello and a creature of the Italians.

"What's your interest in underage whores, Mickey?" he asked me.

"Word gets around," I said, ducking the question. I'd only been canvassing the neighborhood that very morning.

"Enough of the road apples," he said. "What's your stake in

it? Are the Hannahs looking to expand their territory to the East Side?"

It was a curve ball, but it gave me an alibi. I swung on it. "I thought this was open turf, Pat," I said. "Would you be telling me different?"

He was too slippery to give me a straight answer. We were like two card players, feeling out our respective strength early in the game, trying to read each other's betting pattern before we committed our chips. Gallagher, in this case, checked. "You still answer to Tim Hannah?" he asked.

"As always," I told him.

"Then tell Young Tim to back away," he said.

This, of course, had nothing to do with the Hannahs, but a thing takes on its own momentum, and it was about to run over me like a truck with bad brakes.

• • •

I had nothing to report to Dede as yet, but it was early days, or so I thought. I'd put some feelers out myself, my kids were keeping an eye peeled, so all in all, best foot forward. Pat Gallagher might prove to be a riddle, I knew, but for the moment I figured he was just blowing smoke up my ass.

It was coming on dusk, and the kids began to trickle in. There were half a dozen countinghouses and money drops located across Midtown, but this was a storefront on Tenth Avenue, where my runners congregated at the end of the day, swapping war stories and ragging on each other. The building was owned by the Hannahs, and I'd outfitted the upper three stories: bunk beds, a community kitchen, and some semblance of privacy. They were outlaws, thrown away, and I offered them safety. Not that it didn't come at a price. They understood what we traded for, and our currency was loyalty, both up and down.

"Haven't seen her," Judy told me.

"All day?"

She beckoned another kid over. Roger Tuohy, the Artful Roger, she called him. Ten years old, he was, and already something of a slippery character. Where she'd come up with this literary label, I wasn't to know. Maybe it was accident, or she'd spent overmuch time in the public library, a warm place for the homeless and otherwise dispossessed.

"Gone," he said.

Gone from her usual haunts, I asked him, or disappeared?

"Just gone," he told me.

They had their secrets, and I wasn't meant to intrude. They had a private language, a coded vocabulary, from which I was excluded.

"Where might she go?" I asked Judy.

She shrugged.

I bit the bullet. "Somebody very much like you, a girl who grew up in the streets, she asked me to look out for Maggie."

Judy, being who she was, went straight for the weak point in my argument. "Why?" she asked. The same question I'd asked, because it was the obvious one, of Dede.

"She said the girl reminded her of herself, at the same age and in much the same circumstance."

"I never thought of you as sentimental, Mickey."

Meaning she'd felt the back of my hand in times past. "The street's a stricter discipline than mine, Judy," I reminded her.

"You want us to find her for you."

"That's what I asked of you before."

"No, you asked me if I could gain her confidence."

I smothered a smile. Kids can be very literal, almost lawyerly. It comes, I'd imagine, from their heightened sense of unfairness. "Same difference, if she's gone missing," I said.

"Okay," she said, accepting the arbitrary gap in logic.

"Work in pairs," I told her.

"One of us gets pinched, the other one's around to tell the tale?" she asked mischievously.

"I was considering your safety."

"Tell the truth and shame a liar."

"The cops are sniffing around the edges of this, so there's more to it than meets the eye. I'm thinking the Italians."

I was telling her more than she needed to know, and she saw I was residing a trust in her.

"Watch each other's back," I said. "Don't get careless."

She gave me a contemptuous thirteen-year-old's look, and turned away.

"Jude," I said.

She swung back, impatient with my second guessing her.

"Something about this doesn't feel right," I told her. "If it smells dangerous, back away."

"Every time," she said with a wink and an evil grin, then went off to round up her posse. The girl had more chutzpah than an Italian *caporegime,* and fewer doubts.

• • •

My doubts began with Dede. I'd taken her at her word, but now I was beginning to think she might have taken me for a ride.

An unworthy thought, so I put it to the test.

We met, of course, like conspirators. I couldn't very well telephone her at home and have her husband answer. I used a method we'd arranged in advance, the after-hours delivery of her dry cleaning. A private note, ten bucks to the Chinaman.

We were at a bar on Third Avenue, in the shadow of the El. This was back when there *was* a Third Avenue elevated. It was an anonymous kind of joint, but it was busy enough to give us cover. The dinner hour was fast approaching; any saloon in New York that serves liquor has to serve food, even if it's soggy steam-table discards, and the two of us together were as anonymous as the place. I was waiting on a stool at the near end of the bar, and she'd known enough to wear plaid, not mink.

Dede and I didn't bother to act surprised to see each other. I stood up, she took a seat, I sat down again. I was nursing a weak scotch and water. She ordered a Canadian Club and soda. I paid.

"Have you seen her, spoken to her?" she asked

"No," I said, "but a couple of my runners have."

"And?"

"Nobody gets close to her, from what the kids tell me."

"Could they?"

"They're not a trusting lot, themselves," I told her "And she's not one of them."

"Could you bring her into the fold, at least get her out of the life?"

"It was somewhere in the back of my mind," I admitted

"But she'd still be an outsider, not an initiate."

"All my kids were outsiders, once," I said. "That's the appeal of being in a gang, the sense of belonging. You have to understand something, Dede. They're clannish, they're tribal, they're protective of one another. It's a pack mentality. They won't accept just any stray dog who happens onto their turf."

"In time, perhaps?"

"Time we don't have," I said. "As soon as I started asking around, it put the cat among the pigeons."

"What do you mean?" She was genuinely alarmed.

"I suggested to one of my kids that she try and get close to the girl." I held up a hand, forestalling comment. "It wouldn't be clumsy sympathy, believe me. More an actively hostile approach, if I don't miss my guess, challenging the girl for dominance, or territory. It's a protocol."

"I remember."

"My own reconnaissance was less direct."

"You talked to my doorman," she said. She didn't smile

"Among others," I said "Thing is, you're not the only one he reported it to."

"You're not a physical presence that goes unnoticed."

I shook my head. "I didn't choose to make my presence

threatening," I told her. "I might not have been the soul of discretion, but I didn't see what harm could come of it. In the event, I was wrong."

"What happened?"

"Inside of two, maybe three hours, I'd attracted police attention. A lieutenant of detectives named Pat Gallagher, as crooked as they come. Not a man you'd like to have your name on his list."

"What did he want?"

"He wanted to know my interest."

"What did you tell him?"

"As it happens, he provided his own answer."

"Which was?"

"That it had to do with the Hannahs, expanding into new territory. I left him thinking that. It was the easy way. But now I want the truth."

"I told you the truth."

"You told me a half truth," I said, "which is as dangerous as a lie. And when I went into it blind, I got ambushed."

"I never meant to put you at risk," she said.

"I'll give you the benefit of the doubt, Deirdre, but you never would have come to me in the first place if you'd thought there was no risk attached."

"My husband—" she began, turning the glass in her hands.

"Your husband knows you were a whore," I said, interrupting her. It was a purposely unpleasant choice of words.

She stopped fooling with her drink and met my gaze. There was enough sorrow there, and steel, that I dropped my eyes. "My husband," she said, evenly, "has taken advantage of this girl's services, just as he once took advantage of mine. But we made a deal, something he's been gentleman enough to let me forget."

"Until now."

"We all make compromises, Mickey," she said.

"And even a van Rensellaer needs his ashes hauled," I said. "Once in a great while."

"He never felt the lack," Dede said, sad but defiant.

She was so vulnerable and forlorn, I had to relent. "How come you didn't tell me any of this before?" I asked her.

"You would have read the worst into it," she said.

"I'm reading the worst into it now," I said.

"Even if it were a half truth, Mickey, it was still honest. She reminds me of me, and the choices I had to make."

"Fair enough," I said.

"Are you going to help her?"

"She's vanished."

"How can that be?"

"My kids tell me she hasn't been seen on the street for the last day and a half." In case she missed the point, I made it more specific. "She might have slipped through the cracks, but nobody's noticed her since you came and asked me whether I could get chummy with her."

"This isn't good, Mickey," she said.

"You're telling me?"

Dede ducked her head. "I'm telling *you,*" she said.

• • •

The runaway truck flattened me about an hour later, when it came full dark, eight o'clock that night, say.

It was my own damn fault.

I'd seen her home, from a discreet distance, of course; she never knew I was there.

Then from Beekman and Sutton, I'd walked over to the UN construction site. Why it conjured much up, I couldn't say. It was still a morass.

There were cops all over the place. I should have walked away, and I started to, but O'Toole caught me looking.

First he cuffed me. Then, with my hands behind my back, he cracked me across the face.

"Give over that," a voice said. It was Gallagher.

I was leaking blood and snot, and I could do no better than wipe my nose on the upper part of my sleeve.

"You were asking about this girl," Gallagher said.

I hawked up a gob. My face hurt. "Which girl?" I asked.

"The dead one," he said. "What reason did you have to kill her?"

I was behind in the pitch count.

"Aw, now, Mickey," Gallagher said, leaning in close, "you'd be the last one to have seen her alive, I don't miss my guess."

"When would that have been?" I asked.

"Last hour or so," he said. "Back of her body's still warm to the touch."

I couldn't very well use Dede for an alibi, although she'd have been eager to give it, in spite of the embarrassment. "How do you mean, the *back* of her body?" I asked him

"After the rape, you drowned her in three inches of water," he said. "Held her facedown until she choked."

"You're telling me she's not even stiff yet?"

He shrugged. "There's no rigor to speak of. You ready to come clean with me?"

"You're sucking air, Pat," I said. "You've got no gas in the carburetor. I had no motive to kill the girl, for one, and if she died in the last two hours, I've got witnesses who'll place me elsewhere, and I don't mean the kind of witnesses I can buy. Now get over yourself. Take off the cuffs."

"It was worth a shot," he said, and signaled to O'Toole.

O'Toole unlocked the handcuffs and left my hands free.

"Get lost," Gallagher said, turning away.

I massaged my wrists. "Tell fat boy not to do that again," I said.

Gallagher swung around. I felt O'Toole's whiskey breath on the nape of my neck.

"*Fat* boy, is it?" Gallagher inquired, dangerously.

"I'll take the gun back too," I said. O'Toole had frisked me and taken the .38 Super autoloader.

There was a moment where it could have gone either way, but pride gave way to the practical. Indecision, or loss of nerve? I couldn't say. Gallagher knew I had a Sullivan Act card, which meant I could legally carry a firearm concealed. He raised his chin. O'Toole handed me the .38, butt first. I reversed it and tucked it inside my waistband at the small of my back.

"All right, then," Gallagher said, dismissively.

"Show me the victim," I said.

He hesitated, and then shrugged. "Why not?" he agreed.

We made our way down into the enormous trench. The soil was loose and the footing treacherous. Banks of emergency lights cast deep pools of shadow. Up on more solid ground, a diesel generator hammered. Gallagher and I stumbled through the muck, earth sucking at our shoes.

The dead girl was at the bottom of the slope, her clothes disordered, her limbs splayed out akimbo, the exposed skin pale and clammy, tinged with a bluish cast. Skin and bones, Dede had said. The body looked to weigh no more than eighty pounds. I glanced upslope toward the lip of the trench. There were footprints everywhere. Whatever might have been there to see, once upon a time, had been trampled across, twice over. I knelt down beside the corpse. Her hair was dark, stringy and matted, clotted with mud. I lifted a strand away from her face. Her eyes were still open, but without depth or reflection. The dead are like that, their eyes lightless. I grunted to my feet.

"What do you know about this, Mickey?" Gallagher asked.

"No more than you," I said. "Probably less." I looked up, studying the slope again. "But she didn't die down here."

"Why would you think that?"

"Educated guess," I said. "I'd imagine you could gain access to the site through a break in the boardings." I pointed up at the plywood barrier at street level. "Ease through the fencing, you'd be in darkness, have some privacy. Enough to get your business done and not be interrupted."

"Her business was on her knees," Gallagher said.

I nodded "A man your size, or mine, how much trouble would it be to strangle her with your thumbs?" I asked him. "Or break her neck? As easily as a pigeon's."

"Or a soiled dove," he remarked.

"There's bruising on her throat, Pat," I said.

"Dirt," he said.

"No," I said. "Black-and-blue marks."

He looked at his feet. "You figure he killed her up there and then slid her over the edge."

"Take her to Bellevue," I said. "Have a coroner examine the body. I doubt that she drowned or suffocated. I'd say she died before she got to the bottom of the hole."

"Waste of time," he said. "She's just another runaway."

Discarded. It put me in mind of Judy. "I'll make it worth your while," I said.

"Will you?" He looked at me, his interest rekindled "Why would you do that?"

I looked down again at the dead girl at our feet, her white limbs spilled crossways in the dirt. "A debt," I said.

"What do you owe a dead whore?" he asked me.

"The future she never had," I told him.

• • •

So there it was, for all to see. Mickey Counihan, a fool for sentiment. I didn't much care how it looked, and it might even play to my advantage. Pat Gallagher was a man who'd be quick to probe an imagined weakness.

I held a war conference. My troops were battle hardened, after a fashion, wise in the ways of grown-up perfidy, but green where politics were concerned, which I feared they might be.

The captains I chose were Judy and her Artful Roger. "It's the same assignment," I told them, "but the stakes are higher. We're fudging with a homicide investigation, and the cops won't welcome our attention. Don't tangle with either Gallagher or O'Toole. They're dangerous men. Gallagher because he's crafty and smart, but O'Toole because he's cunning and stupid."

They were both very solemn.

"Why did she die?" Judy asked me.

"I'm thinking she was in the wrong place at the wrong time, and it could happen to any of you," I said.

"But it won't," she said.

"Not if I can help it," I told her, "but you're going in harm's way, and I admit I'm putting you there."

"Is this about her, or us?" she asked.

Fair question, I thought.

"I mean, isn't this *personal* with you, Mickey?" she asked.

"Ach, it's all personal, Judy," I said. "She stands in for the rest of you."

"But she got thrown away."

Wise beyond her years. "Somebody threw her away," I said.

"And you want us to find out who."

"Find out who she *was,* first," I said.

"Maggie, that was her name on the street."

"You can call her that, then."

"*We* called her that."

I took a breath. "Judy, a girl was killed. You can decide on the name. It doesn't matter to her."

She gazed at me evenly. "Matters to us," she said.

• • •

There were too many variables.

I'd been drawn in on the oblique. Dede. And now her husband. And why was Gallagher so ready to paper it over? He was a man with an eye for the main chance, which meant it was political, in the narrow sense, that of self-interest—but all politics is about self-interest, so perhaps it boiled down to whoever, or what, Gallagher was protecting. Turf, or an investment, which probably led back to one or another of the Mafia families, but that seemed too generalized. Bid-rigging on construction, short pours for concrete, mob influence in the building unions. The UN project, for one, was an enormous undertaking, with plenty of wiggle room to inflate costs, but that in itself was either too large, or altogether insufficient, to explain Gallagher's proprietary attitude. He had something more specific in mind. It strikes me funny, now, looking back on it, that he'd been so ready to let me off the hook. The murder charge wouldn't have stuck, but he could have taken me off the streets for seventy-two hours on suspicion, or as a material witness, and he'd held his fire, he'd held his temper, he'd kept O'Toole on a short leash. I had the uncomfortable feeling he was only giving me enough rope, and the phrase that came to mind was stalking horse.

Which brought my thoughts around to Dede again. Unworthy thoughts, yes, but she was no unsoiled dove, and our history was such that I could be manipulated.

On the other hand, if I took Dede at face value, gave her the benefit of the doubt, and further, if I considered the very real possibility that Pat Gallagher might be fishing on an empty hook, trawling dark waters without any bait, then the situation presented itself in a different light. They were none the wiser than I was.

Something missing, then. A different actor, off-stage, or a different play completely. We'd come to rehearse one drama, and been given the wrong script. Somebody else had all the good lines. We were only extras.

• • •

Judah Benjamin, the Negro doorman at the Sutton Place address, wasn't on duty when I dropped by the next morning. The guy working the shift, also colored, but a younger man, was less than forthcoming about when Judah would be there, so I left it alone. I didn't want to give him reason to remember me, or draw too much attention to my movements.

Call me overcautious, but the whole business seemed to be getting too deep, and Maggie's death was in itself an object lesson. It could have been, of course, an unhappy accident, one of the hazards of her trade. I imagined otherwise.

Russians, Arabs, and Jews. Judah had meant the remark as generic shorthand, I thought. He might as well have said Danes or Canadians, but Denmark wasn't fighting a war with Canada. In late 1948, the United Nations had recognized the partition of Palestine, the establishment of Israel, and the neighboring Arab states had attacked. They got their ass handed to them, much to everybody's surprise. Or perhaps not. My own benighted people had been underwriting the IRA since before the Troubles, and why shouldn't American Jews help smuggle guns into Haifa?

The problem with this scenario was that it was too damn general, like the UN construction project. What did it have to do with the murder of a fourteen-year-old street kid? How could she have put any of it, or anybody, at risk?

The wrong place at the wrong time, I'd said to Judy. Which meant I should be looking at it through the other end of the telescope. Who and where. Opportunity first, motive after.

Dede's husband. Not the avenue I wanted to pursue, but where was I going to go next? Even a van Rensellaer needs his ashes hauled, I'd said to her. He never felt the lack, Dede had said to me. I had to wonder. What lack *had* he felt?

I decided to ask. Not that it proved easy.

He was a man with no visible means of support. He was a creature of inherited money. Which didn't dispose him in my favor, but neither did it condemn him. The world is as it is, or how we find it, and if we're not disposed to change it, then we've got no beef. I'm no Communist. A man takes the advantage he has, and fortune favors the brave.

I wanted to catch van Rensellaer at a disadvantage.

How otherwise? You might well ask.

Most of us are creatures of habit. Even if we don't report to work on an assembly line, or go to an office, we develop a routine. Tinker to Evers to Chance. August van Rensellaer was cut from the same cloth as any commoner. He rose early and went for a walk along the river, taking a small, well-mannered dog. She was, I believe, a Bichon. He went back to the apartment house, dropped the dog off with his doorman, and headed inland, to Second Avenue, where he visited a hotel barber shop to get a facial of hot towels and his morning shave. The hotel was the Mont Royal, an old-fashioned kind of place, where half the rooms were let to long-time residents, and it had a cafeteria, where van Rensellaer took a breakfast of dry cereal and coffee, black. The problem lay not in opportunity, but in my approach.

And there was a further complication.

He was under surveillance by somebody else.

I was simply trawling his wake when I noticed. I broke off immediately.

They weren't private detectives, and they weren't NYPD. Hanging back, I made a team of three, working fore and aft, one ahead of him, one behind, one working laterally, from across the street. Their discipline seemed almost military. They treated the urban environment as hostile territory, like infantry, going house-to-house. And they were too furtive to be in van Rensellaer's employ. If he'd felt in need of personal security, they would have stayed closer, where he'd recognize their presence, but they kept their distance. Van Rensellaer was the kind of man who imagined himself safe in any circumstance, insulated from harm because of money and position. He wasn't a man to watch his back. He had no need.

I should have been watching mine.

They weren't a team of three. They were a team of five. It was the woman who took me off guard. Late middle age, Jewish, enormous handbag, typical New York. She looked to be waiting for a bus. She swung back abruptly from the curb, into my path. I shifted course automatically, to slither past her. I was looking half a block ahead, and got jammed from behind. A kid stepped on my heels, I bumped into the woman, we all stood there looking at each other stupidly, and the apologetic Jewish mom stuck a .380 up against my belt buckle. The boy had another gun screwed into the base of my spine.

"Your dance, ma'am," I said to her, hands down at my side.

• • •

"'*Bei mir bist du schön,*'" she said, grinning.

I've known some tough Jews in my time. Benny Siegel, Meyer Lansky. They never shrank from the necessary. But this was the toughest bunch of Jews you'd ever want to meet.

They took me to a brownstone in the East Fifties, between Third and Lex, a leafy, upscale neighborhood, mostly residential, with the occasional discreet consulting surgeon's office tucked into the ground floor. This was one such, with a brass plaque not so much advertising any particular medical service as announcing its exclusivity. There were no patients in the reception area. I was escorted into a small windowless examining room, where the frisk was thorough. Then they left me.

The room was perhaps twelve feet by eight, brightly lit. There were no cabinets or other built-in furnishings. There was a stainless steel table, on casters, big enough for a recumbent body, which I found a little sinister. There was a drain in the tiled floor. There was a single utilitarian folding chair, like something from a parochial school annex.

In my present circumstance, I was at the whim of somebody else's schedule. I'd learn soon enough what was required of me. I sat down to wait.

Five minutes went by. Then ten. I allowed my metabolism to slow, lizard-like, and let my imagination cool. There was no point in making ill-educated guesses.

The door clicked open. I looked up.

The man in the doorway studied me for a moment. Then he stepped inside, closing the door behind him. He was short, thick through the upper body, with the heavy forearms of a boxer or a weight lifter. Lean in the hips, though, he walked on the balls of his feet, carrying himself almost like a dancer, but he had a specific gravity that kept him earthbound.

"My name is Wolf," he said. He looked it, gray around the muzzle. I put him in his middle to late fifties. I disliked the fact that he'd told me his name, which suggested I might not live to repeat it. There was that drain in the floor.

"Mine is Mickey Counihan," I said. "I work bare knuckles for the Hannah mob, on the West Side. You look like a man who'd know that line of endeavor. My guess is Irgun, or whatever you call yourselves these days, since Partition. Israeli hard boys with a recent grudge."

"Not so recent," he said, smiling. He hiked himself up on the steel table. The casters shifted under his weight. "I have a question for you, Mr. Counihan."

"Only one?"

He shrugged. "It depends how you answer it," he said.

"Van Rensellaer," I said.

He lifted one hand, palm up. It was a gesture centuries old.

"I've got no reason to waste your time," I said.

"Let's not waste it, then," he said.

"Why are you following him?" I asked.

He looked surprised, or disappointed in me.

"It's going to waste less of our time," I told him.

"*Our* time?"

"A girl was murdered last night. Her name was Maggie. She was all of fourteen years old. Van Rensellaer had, let's say, made her professional acquaintance."

"This girl in your stable?"

"I'm not a pimp."

Wolf thought about it a beat. "What are you?" he asked.

"I'm muscle," I said. "I run a numbers bank."

He got down off the table. "Give me a minute," he said.

"I'm on your clock," I said.

He nodded, and left me in the room.

I put myself to sleep again.

The wait must have been a good twenty minutes this time.

The door opened again. It wasn't Wolf, it was the kid who'd jammed me on the street with the older woman. He motioned me out. I went.

He kept me in front of him. We took two flights of stairs. He ushered me into a study on the third floor.

The door closed behind me. I looked around. It was better appointed than the examination room, walls of books, a sturdy partner's desk, tall windows looking out front and back. It ran the depth of the house. In the back, enclosed inside the block of buildings, there was a garden, shared and secret. The tulips and crocuses had a good start against the late spring. Lilacs were blooming early, the forsythia already wilting. I took none of it for a sign.

Wolf came in. He put my guns down on the desk. "In for a penny, in for a pound, Mickey," he said. "We don't trust one another worth a damn, but we might find each other useful. Does that suit your purpose?"

"Our purposes might still be at odds," I said. "What's van Rensellaer to you?"

"He's a banker."

"I didn't know he worked."

"He's a trustee on several boards."

"Serious money begets even more serious money."

There was a pause. "What do you think about Jews, Mickey?" Wolf asked me.

"Jews put their pants on one leg at a time, same as the rest of us," I said.

He pushed my guns toward me.

I picked up the .38 Super. "Christ-killers," I told him, fitting the gun to the small of my back. "That's what the priest used to tell us, back at St. Aloysius. But he was an ignorant barstid, getting drunk on Communion wine." I scooped up the 7.65, lifted my shoe onto Wolf's desk, and tucked the gun inside my ankle holster. I put my foot back on the floor.

"Not something you care about, then, one way or the other?" Wolf asked me.

"I didn't say that."

"What are you saying?"

"I never met a Jew that didn't keep his word."

"I never met an Irishman who wasn't slippery," he said.

"Tell me about van Rensellaer," I said.

"He's a rock-bottom anti-Semite."

"Jew-haters are a dime a dozen."

"That's been my experience," he said.

"Excuse me," I said. "I meant, give me something that I can use for leverage."

"There's the dead girl you spoke of."

"You've got your reasons to compromise van Rensellaer, I've got mine," I said. "I already know what mine are."

He reached down, pulled one of the desk drawers open, and came up with a fifth of rye, shy a few inches. He fished around some more and came up with two mismatched tumblers. He offered me one, and we each apple-polished them on our sleeves. Wolf poured himself a decent three fingers and handed me the bottle. I did the same. We lifted our glasses and clicked rims. I knew he was only giving himself time to think, but I appreciated the companionable peg, and it was good, smoky Canadian.

He put his glass down. I saw he'd made up his mind. He turned and went to the windows overlooking the street. "Israel needs money and weapons," he said, his back to the room. "Small arms are problematic, still, but not the main issue. I'm talking about field artillery, crew-served machine guns, tanks. We need diesel, replacement parts, tools and dies. The industry for modern, mechanized war."

"And you're running on rubber bands and spit."

He turned around. "The choke point is financial," he told me. "If we had gold on deposit with the Federal Reserve, we could borrow against it, but for the moment, we're begging hat in hand for credit. In six months, the situation might have changed, but in six months, the state of Israel might not exist, if the Arabs drive us into the sea."

"So van Rensellaer's anti-Semitism isn't academic," I said.

Wolf went to a sideboard and unlocked it. He took out a package wrapped in oiled paper, the thickness of a telephone directory, a foot and a half long. He dropped it on the blotter of the desk with a solid, metallic thump.

I knew what it was. I could smell the Cosmoline.

"Open it," Wolf said.

I unwrapped the paper. It was an ugly thing, but it looked extremely functional. I picked it up. Maybe seven pounds.

"Based on the Sten gun," Wolf told me. "For its method of manufacture. Stamped receiver, forged barrel. Fires the 9mm Parabellum, from an open bolt. Six hundred rounds a minute, on full auto. Designed by a man named Uziel Gal. If we had the factory capacity, we could produce a hundred a day, and on the cheap."

I locked the bolt back. The recoil spring felt like a good twenty pounds, but the bolt moved like butter.

"Friends up in Hartford," he said, answering the question I hadn't asked him

Hartford, Connecticut, was home to Colt. They made the gun I carried. I squeezed the grip safety and pinched the trigger, and the bolt slapped shut on the empty chamber. Ten rounds in a second, I thought. Like a water pistol with real bullets.

"You take my point," Wolf said.

I put the gun down, reluctantly. "I do," I said.

He spread his hands, inviting comment.

"Okay, let me see if I've got this right," I said. "Van Rensellaer can choke you in infancy, because his influence extends to a consortium of New York banks. Once they turn you down, you can't get financing from Switzerland or Hong Kong, for the simple reason that bankers don't make bad loans."

"We'd be blackballed."

"How can one man make that decision?"

"Let's say he's the swing vote. Elections have turned on less." Wolf shrugged. It seemed a gesture of habit, something he did for lack of an expressive vocabulary, the way another man might smile, reflexively, and not exactly mean it.

"And if you could catch him in an embarrassment—"

"It would be preferable if we swung his vote our way, yes."

"Better than arranging a happy accident," I said.

He gazed at me with what I took for placid candor. "Things have a way of redounding," he said.

"The shortest way between two points is a straight line."

"Perhaps."

"Then why haven't you had him killed?" I asked.

He smiled wolfishly. "That was my first thought," he told me. "I was second-guessed."

"We're of like minds, then," I said to him, "but neither of us is free to act according to our instincts."

"We accept discipline," he agreed.

"Grudgingly," I said.

He knew what I was suggesting. "I might trade you mine for yours," he said.

"Except that I don't want van Rensellaer dead."

"I'm willing to split the difference," Wolf said.

I picked up my whiskey glass again. There were two fingers still left in it.

"Absent friends," he said.

We clicked rims a second time.

• • •

Of course, I had no reason to want van Rensellaer dead, so far as I knew. And it would be awkward to explain to Dede. But if Wolf had been telling me the whole truth, or as much of it as he judged wise, van Rensellaer was a wolf in sheep's clothing.

Which didn't make him a murderer.

By the time I left the Israeli safe house, it was getting on toward noon. I went to Midtown, to the Horn & Hardart. Lunchtime, and close to Grand Central, it was a rendezvous point for my numbers runners. I already had a fistful of change from the cashier, and I doled out coins as they trickled in. It didn't bother me that they went straight for the Indian pudding and the Boston cream pie; I wasn't interested in the condition of their teeth. Judy, though, had sense enough to pick pot roast with a side of succotash. She made her sidekick Roger get American chop suey. She knew the value of a hot lunch.

I never thought of the automat as a marvel, but I suppose it was, from the number of visitors from out of town who made it a destination. To me, it was part of the climate, the weather of a place I knew. Of course it's gone now, like so much of the New York that I once inhabited.

They sat down with the thick china plates in front of them and tucked into their food. I gave her the chance to take the immediate edge off her hunger, but I suppose I was waiting in vain, metaphorically speaking. Judy's hunger wasn't physical—not in the sense of being satisfied by meat and potatoes.

It didn't take her long to inhale the pot roast.

"Anything of use?" I asked her, when she came up for air.

She began mopping up the pan gravy with a piece of buttered bread. She shrugged, still chewing, and cut her eyes at Roger.

I glanced over at him too.

He had his mouth full, as well, but that didn't stop him. The difference between the two of them was that Judy played her hand close to the vest until she needed to show her cards, but

Roger wasn't as artful. He was the sort, man or boy, who turned the deck faceup on the table. His eagerness was all, and his attention to detail. It had an advantage, however. He gave everything equal emphasis. He didn't interpret, or leave one thing out at the expense of something else. He left it up to me to decide.

She'd worked only the three or four blocks south of Sutton Place, he reported. She did her business in empty doorways or vacant lots. The professionals had access to cheap hotels where the desk clerks took a piece of the action for an hour's use of their sheets, and the tough older whores had chased her off more than once. It was a buyer's market.

Something about it didn't sit right. "The older women, the prossies," I said to him, "they've likely got a cold-water flat they go home to, or a hotel room, anyway. The street kids, what do they have to call home?"

"The subway," Judy said.

"A hobo jungle, in the tunnels?"

She nodded.

"Find it," I said.

Judy and Roger exchanged a quick glance. They already knew where it was, I realized, but were reluctant to tell me.

"No harm's going to come to them, Jude," I said.

She said nothing, although her doubt was easy to read. I'd meant Maggie no harm either.

The road to hell is paved with good intentions.

• • •

I tried not to trade on my friendship with Johnny Darling. We came from different worlds. He was married now and recently a dad, no longer the devil-may-care boy of those reckless days we'd shared before the war. He carried fragments of Japanese shrapnel in one knee, too, from the Pacific, and the barely perceptible limp added to his gravity. Not that he gave himself airs. Oh, and there was *his* father, the so-called Black Cardinal, an outright market monopolist who harked back to the robber barons of the Gilded Age. I'd foolishly made an enemy of him, and it was an injury he'd be unlikely to forgive.

Johnny wasn't cut from the same cloth. He was a democrat with a small D, or what you might call a natural aristocrat, one of a dwindling number.

We met at Jack Sharkey's later that afternoon.

"How's life been treating you, Mickey?" he asked.

"Not much, lately," I said.

We shook hands and took our seats at the bar. Both of us ordered Dewar's. It was a sentimental choice. In one of our previous lifetimes, we'd smuggled bootleg scotch in from Canada.

"Not a social occasion, I take it," he said.

"We're not social equals, Johnny," I said.

He started to dispute me, out of politeness, and then chose not to. He raised his drink, his expression inward.

"August van Rensellaer," I said.

His glass stopped halfway to his mouth.

"I see I've come to the right person," I said.

"What's your interest?"

"It's personal."

"Mine is financial. Or, say better, my father's is."

"Your dad's in bed with August van Rensellaer?"

"Figuratively speaking. But understand, Mickey, compared to the van Rensellaers, my family's *nouveau riche.*" He shrugged his shoulders, ironically. "Not social equals."

I picked up my drink. "Here's to unequal partnerships," I said.

He smiled, genuinely, and we touched glasses.

"What about van Rensellaer, professionally?" I asked him.

"He makes money for his stockholders," he said.

"The public be damned," I said.

It was a famous quote of Jay Gould's. Johnny took it in good humor.

"It's an unhappy mischance, your father being involved," I remarked. "Given that there's bad blood between us already, I'd sooner not cross him a second time."

"That might be, ah, impolitic," Johnny said. "I'd hesitate to call attention to myself, were I you."

"Could be unavoidable."

"Then again, if this personal matter were to have adverse *financial* consequences for the van Rensellaers—" He left the sentence unfinished.

I thought I understood his meaning. "Your father might see advantage in it," I suggested.

"Two birds with one stone," he said.

I didn't much care whether or not I got back into the Black Cardinal's good graces, but it had a certain symmetry.

"What's all this in aid of, Mickey?" Johnny asked me.

"Jews," I said.

He raised his eyebrows.

"Jews. Yids. Sheenies. You got a problem with it?"

"Quit horsing me around," he said, evenly. "Tell me what's going on."

"Money and guns for Israel. Van Rensellaer's in a position to queer the lending policies of the major New York banks."

"He would be," Johnny said. "And he would if he could."

"Apparently, he can."

"Isn't that the damnedest thing," he muttered.

"Men with money make the rules?"

Johnny laughed. "Since when did you become a Red? No. I meant this whole crazy notion of some secret enterprise, with Jewish capital pulling strings behind the scenes, using Gentiles for front men, when Israel's going hat in hand to survive."

"What's your own attitude toward Jews, Johnny?"

He stared at me. "I had Jews in my outfit in the Pacific," he said. "We served alongside *Negroes*, for Christ's sake."

"What's your point?" I asked.

"Everybody bleeds the same color," he said, primly.

"How about your father?"

He made a dismissive gesture. "My father's a creature of his class," he said. "He's anti-Semitic by reflex. Does he do business with Jews? Of course. He'd do business with Hitler."

He probably had, but I didn't say so.

"It's about profits, Mickey," Johnny said. "It's not about personal prejudice or social distinctions."

I'd never seen Johnny squirm. I didn't like seeing it now "Then what's van Rensellaer's game?" I asked.

"Who the hell knows? Maybe he just doesn't need the money. Or he's fixated. It's irrational."

"Could be," I said "Or he's in it for bigger stakes."

"What've you got on him, Mickey?"

"Sex with an underage girl, who then turned up dead."

I watched him fold it over in his mind. "Nope," he said. "One thing follows another. Doesn't mean the first thing caused the second "

"I didn't say it did."

"You're making a connection, though."

"One thing happens, and then something else happens, or happens to be part of the mix, and *then* something else happens," I said. "Guy gets his knob polished, and a girl gets killed. That's all I have. Let's call it the *first* thing, and the *third* thing. I missed out on the second act."

I had him interested, I could see that, but maybe I'd made a mistake bringing Johnny into the equation because I didn't know if he was disinterested. It hadn't occurred to me that he might have his own horse in the race.

"We've always been frank with one another," I said. "If you've got reason to hold out on me now, all you have to tell me is that you've got a reason. I don't need to know what it is."

"You've put me in a tough spot," he said.

"When did I ever betray a confidence?" I asked him. "Yours or anybody else's?"

"We've never had a conflict of interest," he said.

"Let's say your father's made common cause with August van Rensellaer's banking combine. Let's say it's a conspiracy, in violation of the laws against restraint of trade. Let's further say it's simply a scheme to cheat investors."

"For the sake of argument," Johnny said, warily.

"I don't care," I said. "If you're robbing widows and orphans, that's between you and your conscience, or between you and God. My guess is that if it were widows and orphans, or war vets, you would have already stepped in. Which tells me it's players with a serious bankroll, real money. Money they're equipped to risk."

"Nobody can afford to lose money," he said.

"Some people lose money, and they lose their homes," I said to him. "Some people lose money, they have to sell the yacht."

"You *are* going Red," he said, smiling.

"Two questions. If van Rensellaer's end of the partnership collapses, does your father sink or swim?"

"If van Rensellaer sinks, my father treads water. He'll be in position to take a controlling interest. Second question."

"Follows on the first. Why hasn't your father just cut van Rensellaer's throat?"

"Old money, new money," Johnny said. "It's a negotiation."

I nodded. A place at the table.

"It *is* about social distinctions, Mickey," he said.

"And no Irish need apply," I said.

He drew back, offended, and then realized he wasn't the one offended.

I waved my hand at him. "Jesus, boyo, you're too sensitive to imagined slights."

"Which one of us should be embarrassed?" he asked.

I shook my head. "Leave that be," I said. "Riddle me this instead. Why is August van Rensellaer dead set on putting the kibosh on bank loans to Israel?"

"He doesn't want his daughter marrying a Jewboy."

"How many Jewboys would she have the opportunity to meet? How many darkies, if they weren't carrying her luggage? How many wetbacks, or a plain and simple Catholic? How about a damn Chinaman? You're barking up the wrong tree, Johnny You've said it yourself. It's all about profits, and devil take the hindmost."

"No," Johnny said. "It's about tribes, Mickey."

That, I well understood, to my sorrow.

• • •

The thing is, in New York it's *all* tribal. Tammany and the Mafia, native born and immigrant, the privileged and the derelict. The hierarchy of neighborhoods, Jews on the Lower East Side, Italians in the Village, Negroes up in Harlem. The unions, the cops, Freemasons and Jehovah's Witnesses. Every one of them with their hand out and a mouthful of much obliged.

So it should come as no surprise that a gang of forsaken children would jungle up in some little-used section of the IRT. Lexington Ave. has the heaviest ridership of any route in the metropolitan transit web, and when the platforms were lengthened to accommodate trains with ten cars, some smaller intermediate stations were abandoned. Eighteenth Street, between Union Square and Twenty-third, for one, was closed down in late '48, and the stop between Fifty-first and Fifty-ninth had been shuttered only a few months later, this past February. The subway was just a part of it, of course. Beneath the pavement, the city is a maze of service levels that go sixty feet down or more. Sewers and aqueducts, steam tunnels and electrical, the New York Central tracks to upstate, gaslines, cast-iron water pipes to feed the fire hydrants, an entire arterial geography, a secret circulatory system known to urban engineers and sandhogs, but much of it unmapped or forgotten, lost to living memory, the original plans disintegrating in some dust-covered file cabinet, like papyrus.

Judy appointed herself my guide to the underworld

We started, oddly enough, at the Waldorf-Astoria, where Dede and I had met only two days before, but Judy didn't take me to the lobby entrance on Park. We went around the corner onto East Fiftieth. Halfway along the block, access ramps went down to the basement. There was a guard shack at street level. Judy gave the guy a wave and walked right past him, but me, he gave the fish-eye and stepped out to block my path. He was an older man, overweight, in an ill-fitting uniform, a time clock on a shoulder strap, and a .38 revolver dragging down the right side of his garrison belt. I made him for a retired harness bull, hoping to catch his second wind. I slipped him a folded twenty and he let me pass, however ungraciously.

Below ground, in the bowels of the building, there was a cavernous service area, big enough for tractor-trailer rigs to maneuver around in, and there were half a dozen backed up to the loading docks. Some of them were refrigerated trucks, with generators over the cab, their engines idling, and in spite of the high ceiling, the air was foul with diesel fumes. Judy scrambled up onto one of the loading docks and threaded her way through the traffic, not waiting to see how closely I could keep up with her. It was as busy as the sidewalks in the garment district, everybody in motion, pushing racks of hanging meat and stacking crates of iced seafood, checking in pallets of canned goods, dollying boxes of fresh produce and hundred-pound bags of pastry flour. Linens, glassware, soap and bath salts, shoe polish, candlesticks, light bulbs, match-books embossed with the Waldorf crest, mints for the pillow slips when the maids turned down your bedclothes at night. The entire enterprise seen from behind the curtain, the effort that made the hotel services seem effortless.

Twenty or thirty paces out in front of me, Judy ducked into a stairwell. I followed her down. Concrete treads, an iron handrail made from plumbing pipe. My footsteps echoed. I found myself in a further subbasement, the laundry. Like the other big New

York hotels, the Waldorf did its own wash. If you were a guest, you could get a suit dry-cleaned on the premises, or a shirt ironed, but the real work involved the thousands of sheets and towels, napkins and aprons, kitchen whites and dishrags. It was a factory operation, steamy, hot, and close. And enormous.

Here, too, an unspoken question was answered. Judy moved through the environment unchallenged. The rent-a-cop on the ramp hadn't given her a second glance. The guys on the loading docks had let her slip past with easy familiarity. In the laundry, I saw why. It was mostly women, and of every age, but there was an Italian gal of around fifty who was obviously the supervisor. She handed Judy a package, a thick manila envelope, and gave her a quick, affectionate cuff as the girl slithered by. Policy bets. They all played the numbers on a daily basis. Judy collected, and made the payouts. She was the next best thing to invisible. Or, say better, she was like a useful pet, one of a litter of feral kittens. She'd turned out to be a good mouser, and you left well enough alone.

We went down yet another stairwell. This one led to the boiler rooms, three floors below street level, where stokers fed coal-fired furnaces. Here the stoop labor was done by Negroes, bare chested and glistening with sweat. They wore bandannas across the lower half of their faces, like bandits, to protect them from inhaling the coal dust that hung everywhere in the air they breathed, but the soot caked on their damp skin, dull as cast iron. They, too, let Judy pass without comment, although I drew their wary gaze.

These, of course, were only the anterooms to Hades.

Judy led me inside.

In this day and age, coal deliveries were made by truck. The furnaces in the bottom basement of the Waldorf provided steam heat and hot water to a city block, and went through half a ton of coal a day, spilling out of gravity-fed chutes. But before the war, when the hotel was first built, it had been more practical to devise a different system, an underground shuttle from the freight yards. Long out of use, the abandoned railway line was narrow-gauge to accommodate smaller coal cars, which were then unloaded by hand. The original entry had been double doors, with a span of track passing underneath them, but they were long since rusted shut, tine hinges corroded. Judy knew a different way, an old maintenance access panel, out of sight. She slid it aside and skinnied behind it. I could barely squeeze my shoulders through. It took some effort. And once in, there wasn't nearly enough headroom for me to stand upright. I had to move forward in a crouch, knees against my chest.

It was essentially a crawl space, and it opened up after a few yards, giving out onto the old coal-shuttle spur. We were close enough to the Lexington Avenue IRT to hear the wheels of the trains grinding against the rails, but it was tricky, the way sound traveled in the tunnels. It seemed to come from every direction, and I'd already lost mine, but Judy knew the way, and beckoned me after her.

We went deeper into the vaulted tunnels.

It felt dark and close, although the overhead was high enough to let trains pass. It smelled of earth, but metallic, as well, and overheated, which I hadn't expected. The air felt charged, with static or ozone. The noise level was intense, racketing in the underground space, a constant rumble, vibrating in your skull, the clatter of the cars, the shriek of steel on steel where the wheels met the rails, the clank of switches and the hiss of brakes. I guess you got used to it, the more time you spent down there, transit workers or squatters, but it was a tiresome erosion of your wits, unceasing, metronomic.

Judy took a turning. Following her, the noise abated slightly. We were now in a utility corridor, steam pipes leaking hot vapor and electrical conduits as big around as man's waist. There were blue bulbs, protected by wire mesh, set in niches in the wall about every fifteen feet, and the half-light was chilly, giving my bare hands a ghostly, fluorescent cast, although the passage itself was clammy and hot, the curved walls sweating condensation.

I wasn't sure of the distance, but it felt like a few hundred yards before we came out at the far end into what seemed like an older set of tunnels. The rails were tarnished, not shiny, and everything smelled of disuse. Fifty-first Street is a transfer stop, local to express for the Lexington line, and a change of platforms for the Eighth Avenue local to Queens. I was disoriented, but I thought we might actually have come as far as Fifty-third. Trains groaned on the levels above us, and chips of rust filtered down from overhead. There was only ambient light, no blue bulbs or switching signals. It wasn't entirely dark, once your eyes adjusted, but it was all twilit shadows, a permanent dusk, muted and ashen.

Judy stopped abruptly, motioning me to stillness. There was something canine in her posture, alert as a dog scenting something on the wind, or hearing a frequency inaudible to the human ear. I couldn't tell what she'd felt. I was deaf and blind, my senses smothered by the close, stifling darkness, the heat, the pressure of background noise. She glanced to her right, and I looked where she was looking. There was a slight movement, a shadow against shadows. It was a Norway rat the size of a small corgi. He watched us indifferently for a moment and then slid away. We were neither live prey nor carrion.

Judy signaled me to follow her lead again.

A few hundred yards down the tracks, she glanced back, and then shuffled a step to her right, slipping sideways between two vertical supports, and vanished. I was only ten feet behind her, but she simply evaporated, like a raindrop on hot pavement, and when I drew even with the columns, I couldn't see where she'd gone. Nor could I see any sign that indicated a passage or an exit, but then I noticed a mark, in bright orange chalk or crayon, the kind of hieroglyphic bums and gandy dancers use to let each other know if a yard bull is a bully, or if it's safe. I sucked up my gut and eased between the stanchions, the buttons of my jacket scraping the corroded metal. It was a tight fit for a grown man. And then I saw I'd have to get down on my hands and knees to go after her. A rough opening had been hacked into the bulkhead, but it was only big enough to admit a girl of Judy's build, not some two hundred pound Irish thug with bad wind and joints that were no longer elastic. I worked my way through, nonetheless, my trousers and elbows catching on the rough edges of the concrete, and I felt fabric tear. Somebody was going to owe me a new suit when all was said and done. I got to my feet again, out of breath.

It was a lateral transition into another set of vaulted subway tunnels, unused, but in this case, unfinished. It must have been dug and then abandoned. The roadbed had been graded, but no track had ever been laid. How many secret underground projects still lay beneath the streets of New York, orphaned and unremembered? I wondered.

Judy stood stock-still. All around us was evidence of a hasty departure, disordered sleeping bags and blankets, cartons and corrugated cardboard, personal items discarded, toothbrushes and teddy bears. I realized we were being watched, but this time it wasn't a rat. It was a child, a boy of eight or so, his eyes glittering. Judy coaxed him out of his hiding place, but his glance in my direction was full of apprehension, so I stayed where I was

They squatted down next to each other, heads together, for all the world like two kids playing jacks. Both of them kept looking over each other's shoulders, or glancing back over their own, keeping a weather eye out. I took up station downwind, so to speak, trying not to call attention to myself. It still took Judy a while to tease the story out of him.

She came over. "Cops," she told me.

"Cops, who?" I asked, swinging around.

"Suits, uniforms."

"So some of them were plainclothes?"

"The kid can smell copper, uniformed or not," she said.

It figured to be Gallagher. "What happened7" I asked her.

"They moved in, rounded them up, and cleared them out," she said, waving a hand at the obvious signs of abandonment.

"How did they find the place?"

She gave me an up-from-under look.

"No." I shook my head "We didn't lead them here, Judy, O'Toole couldn't get his fat ass through the cracks you took me through, and Gallagher wouldn't soil his suit. They had to come in from a different direction."

She went over to the boy again and they talked.

Judy swung back. "From the East River side," she said.

"Where are we?" I asked. "Close to Grand Central?"

She shook her head. "East of Lex, below Forty-seventh "

I was completely turned around. I thought we'd been moving north, or south, but we'd been going crosstown.

"He can show us the way," Judy said.

I took a few steps in the boy's direction, keeping my hands behind my back. He moved away from me, warily, staying out of reach.

"My name's Mickey Counihan," I told him, introducing myself as if to an adult. "Judy will tell you the last thing I'd choose would be to rat you out to the cops or the youth wardens, but we pay each other's tariff. Point us the way they went."

"What's in it for me?" he asked, tilting his chin up.

I grinned. "A hot meal, a safe bed, and a cuff on the back of your head, you scut," I told him.

He cut his eyes at Judy.

She shrugged, as if to say I hadn't yet played her false.

The kid spat in his hand and stepped forward, and we shook on it, like Irish livestock buyers at a country market town.

"What do I call you?" I asked.

"Billy," he said.

"Billy the Kid?" I suggested.

He smiled.

I pointed. "Get on with you," I said.

On we went.

I found it odd, the distance you were able to cover below ground. I'd have thought the opposite, but we weren't walking the grid of streets and avenues. It still came as a surprise to me, where Billy led us, although I should have guessed.

The old graded roadbed curved, and then straightened, and then curved again. Maybe half a mile, as the crow flies? It was hard to judge. Then the two kids stopped, alert to some new signal. I caught it, too, the touch of a cool breeze, not the fetid air of the tunnels, but it carried the smell of the river, damp and nearby, an oily scent, sweet with decay.

I'd been content to follow, thus far, because the two of them were familiar with the secret byways, as if they were playing a game of Chutes and Ladders, but now I took over the lead. The breeze freshened as we edged forward, and up ahead I made out a lighter spot in the gloom. It flickered like a candle, but as we got closer, I realized it was the flare of an oxyacetylene torch. I raised a hand, and Judy and Billy went still behind me. I worked my way into a better position, moving up behind a corroded stanchion.

It was a maintenance crew, four men. They were wrestling steel plates into place, and riveting them together to block off access to the tunnel behind me.

I stepped out from cover and motioned the kids to follow in my wake.

The first of the crew to notice me reacted with a terrified double take, and slapped the shoulder of the man in front of him. I must have looked a sight, hatless, my trousers torn, the jacket of my suit smeared with grease and rust.

I adopted a jaunty air. "Chased these scamps up and down and all around," I said. I took each of them by the ear, not playfully, and shoved them past the barricade. Judy played her part, whining aggrievedly. Billy didn't realize he was supposed to be who he was, only more so, and tried to twist away. I bit down harder with my thumb and forefinger. Judy levered out with her left leg and popped him with her heel, just below the knee.

"Who's up top?" I asked the riveting crew.

They took me for police, as I'd hoped they would.

"Lieutenant of detectives," the guy with the torch told me. "Big fella, almost your size, wearing a good suit."

"And a lard-ass sergeant with a long line of mouth," one of the other guys put in.

Gallagher and O'Toole. How not?

I started to thank them, but I realized it would be out of character. Cops don't thank anybody. What the subway crew expected of me was no more than I gave them. "Get out of my damn way, then," I said, my manners as bad as possible.

I ramrodded the kids past.

"The cheaper the clothes, the tougher they talk," I heard the guy with the torch say. It didn't bother me. I'd heard the same patter before.

"Keep moving," I muttered to Judy and Billy. I'd let go of her, and she took the opportunity to kick Billy again.

"Cut it out," he said to her.

"Cut it out, yourself," I said, letting go of his earlobe.

"That hurt," he complained.

"You don't know when you've got it good," I said. I looked at Judy. "Billy the Kid's your responsibility," I told her.

Judy rolled her eyes.

"No," I said. "Get him gone. Look ahead."

She did, and saw what I'd seen.

There was a ragged hole at the end the tunnel, where earth-moving equipment had torn into the vaulted underground cavern and exposed the abandoned subway line, like breaking open a hive of bees. It was the excavation for the UN dig.

"They scattered them like birds," I said to her.

"It wasn't our fault?" she asked.

"No," I told her. "It was an accident. Fortunes of war."

She didn't entirely trust me, that was evident.

"I'm going out into the light," I said. "But once I get in the clear, the two of you skedaddle."

She understood. "You going to be okay, Mickey?" she asked.

"Not hardly," I said.

"Meet you in the sweet by-and-by," Judy said.

"Get lost," I told her.

She did, but she did it without haste, so as not to call any undue attention to herself. And she took the kid along with her. They were slippery bastards. They'd had enough practice.

Me, a different story. I ducked past the plywood hoardings that had been erected to shroud the subway tunnels, and stepped out again into the sucking mud. I saw Judy and Billy scramble away, vagabonds on the streets, fugitives below ground, adapting for their own survival.

The lights hit me. I was an understudy filling in for the lead actor, not knowing my lines. The hot, piercing glow pinned me like a butterfly.

"Mickey." It was Gallagher, calling down.

He didn't help me, he let me struggle, but when I managed to get to the lip of the trench, he held out a hand, and dragged me up the last few feet.

O'Toole stood back, watching me with vengeful eyes.

"You keep turning up, boyo, like a bad penny," Gallagher said. "How d'ye come to be here? Better question yet, why were you in the subway tunnels in the first place?"

"Same as you, Pat," I said. "Chasing runaways."

"You don't turn your kids out, Mickey," he said. "What are you about?"

"Answering to my own conscience," I said.

Gallagher stepped in close, so we were standing shoulder to shoulder. "The girl died of a broken neck," he murmured.

I nodded. "One of her clients?"

"Most like," he said.

I looked past him. August van Rensellaer stood ten yards away, at the edge of the incline, but in the shadows, not in the light. Gallagher didn't have to follow my gaze.

"I'd be guessing, mind you," Gallagher said, still speaking under his breath. "Yank my Doodle, it's a dandy."

"My first question would be how he came to be here, Pat," I said. "How much is he paying for your protection?"

"Well, now, Mickey, those kids have proved to be a nuisance and an eyesore, and a detriment to the neighborhood."

"So a complaint from a concerned and well-connected citizen would encourage you to clean house."

"We serve at the public's pleasure," he said.

"You feed at the public trough," I told him.

"Hell," Gallagher said. He waved a hand at van Rensellaer. "You can't pin the killing on him. Could have been anybody."

"Not just anybody was scared enough to call in his markers, and get a bent cop on the case."

He smiled. "Which isn't evidence. It's simple dislike for the man, on your part."

"I doubt if he's a likeable man," I said.

Gallagher stepped back. "You're welcome to talk to him," he said. "Be circumspect, if it's in your nature." He grinned. "But the more threatened he is, the better I like it."

The more money in his pocket, he meant. I walked over to van Rensellaer, the loose earth sucking at my shoes. He glanced at me, recognized that I was of no importance, and looked away.

"The kids in the tunnels," I said. "They live there because they have nowhere else, and they work the streets out of necessity. They're victims almost by design."

He didn't give me a second glance "I don't believe I know you," he said, dismissively.

"No," I said. I started to turn away, discouraged, but I thought about the look Judy might give me later, and turned around again. "I know your wife," I said. "I knew her when she was a whore."

"She's still a whore," he said. "But her price went up."

A vein began throbbing in my temple. "Her price is her own dignity," I said to him.

He condescended to make eye contact with me. "Were you the lowest bidder?" he asked.

I blinked back my anger. My temples were about to burst.

"Or did you offer rescue?" van Rensellaer asked, smiling.

I shifted my weight and kicked the earth out from under his left foot. Off-balance, he tumbled over the edge. I threw myself after him into the trench, dirt and loose stones getting up my sleeves. "God*damn* it," Gallagher shouted, waving O'Toole and the uniforms in.

I rolled over on top of van Rensellaer, straddling his lower body, and hit him once hard, on the bridge of the nose. I felt the bones in his face break, and the knuckles in my hand.

I lifted him off the ground, shaking him by his shirtfront "You *bastard*," I said. "You're not safe from *me.*"

His eyes were wide and frightened, but uncomprehending

I shook him again. "I'll kill you, Augie," I said, my face inches from his. "That's a promise you can take to the bank."

O'Toole scrambled down the slope and hauled me back.

The uniforms picked van Rensellaer up and dusted him off. He was staring at me, blood leaking out his nose, but he didn't say anything. I took it to mean he understood I'd meant exactly what I told him.

I shrugged out of O'Toole's grip.

He stayed behind me, oddly passive, and made no move to cuff me. I looked up at Gallagher, standing at the edge of the trench. He shook his head, but it wasn't in disappointment. He was a man who knew the usefulness of hate.

• • •

So the Black Cardinal, Johnny's father, went unsatisfied. He would have benefited from van Rensellaer's embarrassment, if it had turned out to be financial, not personal. But the August van Rensellaers of this world have a habit of shrugging off scandal. It's not simply the brute power of their money; it has more to do with the imperviousness their money breeds.

"So there's no justice for her death?" Dede asked me.

"There's no retribution," I said.

I didn't tell her she might be sleeping with the man who'd murdered Maggie. Justice has a way of seeking its own level. Dede had asked me to look after the girl, and I was only able to lay Maggie's ghost to rest. An unresolved conclusion.

Judy was likewise less than happy. I was turning out to be unlucky with women.

"Social Services has the lot of them," she said.

"They'll be back on the streets in a week," I said.

She eyed me leerily.

"Easy pickings, we recruit the ones with promise."

Judy studied on it, and grinned. "Okay," she agreed.

And a package came, a couple of days later. No return address, no card. It was a bottle of Canadian rye. I knew that the bank loans to Israel had been approved.

I cracked the bottle and poured myself a couple of fingers. I inhaled the scent. Good, smoky stuff.

Absent friends, I thought. I tipped back the glass.

DAVID EDGERLEY GATES lives in Santa Fe, New Mexico. His short fiction has appeared in *Alfred Hitchcock's Mystery Magazine*, *Ellery Queen's Mystery Magazine*, *Story*, and *A Matter Of Crime*, and been anthologized in *Best American Mystery Stories* and *World's Finest Mystery And Crime*. His previous work has been nominated for both the Shamus and Edgar awards, and "Skin and Bones" is a 2009 Edgar nominee for best mystery short story. "Mickey Counihan, like the bounty hunter Placido Geist, is pretty much a character who came out of nowhere; he was unrehearsed and unanticipated. The stories are essentially about his *voice*: think an old Harp at the far end of the bar, telling tall tales. Mickey is of course an invention, a narrative device, but no less real to me for that."

La Vie En Rose

BY DOMINIQUE MAINARD
TRANSLATED BY DAVID BALL

I.

On rue de Belleville, Japanese tourists who had come to see the steps on which Edith Piaf entered the world lingered under the April drizzle, protected by odd little hats of pink, translucent plastic with the logo of a travel agency on them. All the way to boulevard de Belleville, two hundred yards further down, the bright red signs in Chinese characters gleamed through the mist. Legendre turned left into the labyrinth of little cobblestone streets leading to the park, swung the wheel hard to avoid the kids playing soccer in the puddles. Anvaud was trying to drink out of the thermos of coffee his friend made when his radio had started crackling half an hour ago. They had gone to bed very late and he had a hard time waking up, but his heart jumped when he saw police cars stopped a few dozen yards up the street with their lights flashing.

Legendre parked the cat at the end of the street and winked at Arnaud.

"I have to be careful," he said. "They've seen me hanging around the neighborhood too much, one of them threatened to give me a ticket for obstruction of justice. You coming?"

When Arnaud hesitated, Legendre held out the car keys with a theatrical gesture.

"Okay, you'd rather stay warm," he said. "That's your problem. You'll find CDs in the glove compartment. But I'm telling you, man, if you want inspiration for your book, this is the place to find it."

Arnaud shrugged with a forced smile. He was almost sorry he'd told Legendre about it a few days ago, out of boredom, out of loneliness; but the truth is, even if he hadn't seen the guy since college, there was no one else he could talk to about it. At the beginning of the winter, Arnaud had gone on unemployment insurance to start writing the novel he'd been thinking about for a long time; 181 days, he'd counted them, and he hadn't even succeeded in finishing four chapters. All winter he'd paced through his apartment watching the leaves fall from the chestnut tree under his windows and onto the sidewalk, soon to become invisible. He'd felt himself sinking into the inertia and calm of his little town in the suburbs—what a cliché, he thought, a former Literature major, the ambitions, the powerlessness.

After a meal washed down with a lot of wine—he'd accepted the cigarette Legendre had offered him, and since he didn't smoke very often he was dizzy and laughed as easily as if it had been a joint—he had dropped a few words, negligently, about this novel he'd given himself till spring to finish, adding that it was coming along, it was coming along nicely. Legendre had tried to get it out of him and finally he admitted it was a *noir* novel, but he didn't want to say very much more. Even if he'd wanted to, he couldn't. He had only said his hero would be a private detective, his victim a woman, she'd live in Paris and work in the world of the night, a stripper or a prostitute. And who'll be the murderer? Legendre had asked, and Arnaud had raised his eyebrows with an air of mystery. If I tell you, there won't be any suspense, he'd answered; but the truth was, he didn't know himself. He didn't have a feel for crime, he hated to admit, and the five months he'd spent going through short news items in the newspapers hadn't changed a thing. When he tried to understand what could drive a man to close his hands around a woman's neck, he couldn't imagine it and he told himself this was a terrible start for a novelist. Would his murderer be a pimp, a customer, a serial killer? It was absurd to already have the victim and the setting and be unable to find the murderer, as if a writer could be worse than a bad cop.

He knew Legendre worked for the newspapers and that's what had led him to get back in touch with the guy: the confused hope that since his old friend had written stories about ordinary daily dramas, he had pierced this secret and could reveal it to him.

When he spoke to Legendre about his novel, his friend had slapped him on the shoulder, pointed to the radio on a shelf, and said: "Dig that: It's a police transmitter. When something happens in the neighborhood, sometimes I manage to get there before they do and I sell my photos for five or six hundred euros. Come sleep over next weekend and if something happens, I'll take you along. With a little luck you'll get to see him, your ideal killer. Don't kid yourself, though, there's not much going down right now."

But the transmitter had started crackling early in the morning, and hearing the code the police use, Legendre jumped to his feet and shook Arnaud, who was sleeping on the floor of the two-room apartment situated over an Asian produce store with its fetid stench of durian. Come on, he'd said, this is the real thing, and twenty minutes later they were turning onto rue Jouye-Rouve.

Several of the entrances to the Pare de Belleville hadn't been closed off, so they got in without difficulty. They were not alone; onlookers were crowding the paths, teenagers especially, standing on tiptoe to peer over the metal fences and the yellow police tape stretched from one tree to another. Despite the gray sky you could see all of Paris, just slightly veiled in mist, even the Eiffel Tower to the west. The catalpa trees were in bloom, tulips were standing straight up in carefully spaded triangles of soil, and the park's little waterfall was murmuring; but in the middle of the roped-off space there was a slight swelling under a gray tarp. The fine drizzle had almost stopped; only the smell of moss and undergrowth remained hanging in the wet air. The spectators crowded behind the yellow tape in a warm, motionless mass, and Arnaud almost felt good: It was the first time he had ever been so near a crime scene and he was discovering the silence interspersed with whispers, the strange complicity of the crowd, that morbid fascination, the almost superstitious fear—but also the hope that a corner of the gray tarp would be lifted to reveal a hand or a leg.

Legendre had gone off. Arnaud heard him murmuring a few yards away, moving from one bystander to another. After two or three minutes his friend came back, grabbed him by the arm, and led him away from the crowd.

"I got some information," he said in a low voice. "It's a kid, a mixed-race girl seventeen or eighteen years old, Layla M. She grew up here but she'd been living with a guy for a year. She danced in a nightclub in Pigalle and they say she also slept with the customers. She was strangled to death. See, you've got your story now! All you have to do is find out who did it and you've got your book." He glanced at the gray tarpaulin and went on: "Got something to write with? Go question the neighbors, the people who live in the old building over there—the one with the Hotel Boutha sign, on it—they might've seen something. I'm gonna stay here and try to grill these guys—discreetly. Hurry up, you got to be the first to question them. If you go in after the cops they won't want to say a thing."

Reluctantly, Arnaud walked away from the crowd. He was cold in his light jacket and he would have liked to stay in the circle, the cocoon of onlookers. "But I can't," he protested, "I've never done that. What the hell gives me the right to question them?"

And Legendre threw open his arms, exasperated. "I thought you wanted to get involved. If you'd rather sit in front of your computer tearing your hair out, that's your problem."

Arnaud felt ashamed to have hidden his secret so poorly. "But what am I going to tell them?" he insisted, and Legendre answered with a wink before he turned away:

"Tell 'em you're a private detective. They should like that and it'll give you something to think about."

Arnaud waited until Legendre went away; then he groped around in the vest pocket of his jacket, took out the notebook and pen he always carried on him, and walked to the gates of the park. Hotel Boutha was a bit higher up, and Legendre had a point: It was the only building whose windows let you see out onto this part of the park. On the facade, a notice was nailed under the old hotel sign—*Condemned Building*—but the apartments were obviously inhabited. In the lobby, overflowing garbage cans almost prevented him from going in, and the mailboxes had been broken into so often that their doors were dangling from the hinges; the names on the boxes were all faded out, illegible. Arnaud wrote down these details in his notebook and even copied the red graffiti on a wall. He felt a vague sense of shame, taking advantage of the situation to get his hands on these fragments of reality, like a petty thief. Then he made his way between the garbage cans and walked up the stairs.

He rang the doorbells on the second and third floors hut nobody answered; a baby was crying behind one door, but no one opened it. A little girl in pajamas opened the door next to it. Her hair was made up in dozens of braids; she looked at him in silence, but before he had a chance to say a word, her mother appeared, with hair braided the same way, and as quietly as her daughter, pulled the child back and closed the door. He started up the stairs again. The stairway smelled of urine and vegetable soup but he didn't have the heart to write it down any more than he'd had the heart to note the serious silence of the child and her mother. For a moment he thought of going back down and telling Legendre the building was empty, but then he heard a door open on the fourth floor and when he got up to the landing, he saw an old man watching him intently from the threshold of his apartment.

The man must have been waiting for him—or the police, more likely—because a plate of cookies was sitting on the kitchen table next to the entrance, as well as cups with coffee stains in them.

"Good morning, sir," Arnaud said, holding out his hand, "I'm a private investigator looking into the crime that just occurred down there." And the old man shook his hand with surprising gentleness.

He was wearing a big plaid jacket even though it was quite hot in the apartment, and a woolen cap he immediately took off with an embarrassed look: "I don't even know when I'm wearing it anymore. Come in, come in."

Arnaud remained in the doorway with his notebook in his hand, tapping the cover with his pen. "I don't have much time, sir," he said. "I have to question the whole building."

But then the old man smiled knowingly, as if he was well aware that no one had opened their door for him on the lower floors, and simply repeated: "Please, come on in."

Arnaud hesitated. Later, he wouldn't be able to recall how he'd guessed the old man knew something; maybe because just as he was about to refuse again, the old man's smile had hardened and he'd looked Arnaud straight in the eye. So he nodded and said, "Just five minutes," and with two steps he was right there, in the kitchen. An old dog was sleeping under the radiator, stretched out on a plaid blanket the same colors as the old man's jacket, and he didn't even open his eyes when Arnaud pulled a chair over for himself.

As the old man puttered around in the kitchen, checking that the coffee was hot, putting the sugar bowl and a glass of milk on the table, he said: "She's a kid, right?"

"Yes," replied Arnaud, looking out the window at the trees in the park. Between their branches, blobs of color— the onlookers—were pressing against the yellow tape. "Layla M., seventeen or eighteen years old, they told me. She died from strangulation." He was trying for the neutral voice of the private detective he claimed to be. "That means she was strangled, see."

The old man had his back turned. His hands were in the sink; he was mechanically running spoons and knives under the faucet. He didn't say a word.

"Seems she grew up near here," Arnaud continued. "She hadn't been living in the neighborhood for a few months, but I thought some people would be bound to remember her. You yourself—did you know her, by any chance?"

The old man still had his hands in the sink. He seemed to be washing the silverware under the faucet for an interminable length of time, and Arnaud, thinking the sound of the water might have prevented him from hearing, repeated more loudly: "You know her, by any chance?"

The old man kept his head down, hut stretched out his hand and shut off the water. Finally, still without turning around, he said: "Yes, sir, I knew her. I knew her very well. I loved her like a daughter."

Arnaud remained silent for a moment. He cursed Legendre for having put him in this situation; he had no more idea how to console a man than he knew how to grill him or judge his guilt, and he remained silent until the old man finally turned around and leaned against the sink, drying his eyes with the hack of his hand. Then he spoke again, clumsily: "She probably didn't suffer, you know, she must have passed out when she couldn't breathe anymore. And the police are there, they're going to find the bastard who did it. Don't worry, they're animals but they always get caught in the end."

The old man raised his head and stared at Arnaud without answering. He picked up the coffeepot, brought it to the table, and filled the two cups. He sat down in front of Arnaud, right next to the dog; he scratched the animal behind the ear for a long time. Then, as if he'd just made a decision, he sat up, put his two hands down on the table, and said: "I'm going to tell you a story."

2.

You see, sir, in two or three months this building's going to be torn down. I think about it every time I see it. Every time I turn the corner, I'm glad to see its old walls still standing, and then the potted geraniums of the old lady on the third floor, they're old as the building. She takes cuttings from them and puts them in glasses of water, they're all over her kitchen. During the summer, with the flowers and the wash drying outside the neighbors' windows, you'd think it's a street in Italy. That's what I tell myself, you see, even though I've never been to Italy. Every time I see the building from the street I'm happy, and relieved. As if the demolition crew might come in with their bulldozers and jackhammers before the date they've set, and there'll be nothing left of my house but a pile of rubble. They're going to build what they call a "residence," you know, one of those high-class buildings they sell to young people for a fortune because you can see the trees in the park, as if you couldn't go live in the country when you feel like seeing trees. Twenty years ago it was a hotel—you can still see the sign painted on the front—then they knocked down some inside walls and turned the rooms into apartments to rent to people who didn't mind sharing a bathroom with four other apartments and a toilet out on the landing. Yes, people like me and Layla's mother.

But I'm always afraid they'll knock down the building without any warning, and every time I go out I take a bag with my most important things in it: my papers, the money I've saved up, my watch—I don't like to wear it on my wrist—my social security card, some letters from my mother, and . . . these photos. That's Layla. Take a look. She got these snapshots done in the Photomaton at the supermarket; she gave them to me on her fifteenth birthday. You can see how beautiful she is. Nobody ever knew who her father was; her mother got married and had three other kids but Layla was the oldest, from the years when her mom was going out and having a good time. The kid was conceived who knows where and she was born who knows where, in the street, she was in a hurry to see the world, the neighbors didn't have the time to call an ambulance.

For a long time she was ashamed of it, being born in the street. The other kids in the neighborhood knew—kids always know everything—and you can bet they made fun of her. Then one day I took her by the hand—her mother asked me to watch her a lot when she was a little girl and the kid was used to coming over my place—and I took her to rue de Belleville to show her the marble plaque on number 72, where Piaf was born, you know, five minutes away from here. And then I took her to the library to show her what a great lady Piaf was, I showed her books and I made her listen to recordings too, she looked like a little mouse with those earphones—she was . . . oh, not more than five or six. I never had a record player and neither did her mother.

That story of Piaf: who was born in the street like her . . . it was a good thing for her—and a bad thing too. Because she decided right away she'd be a singer, and she did have a nice little voice. She started singing all the time. Since they couldn't handle her anymore at her place, with the three other kids squealing, she'd come to mine. She used to give me sheets of paper with the words of the songs and I had to check if she was making any mistakes, and me, I hardly know how to read, sir. When it was nice out we'd go down to the park, right next door, I'd spread out a sheet or a blanket under a tree and I'd give her what I'd made to eat, sandwiches usuallv, cheese or chicken sandwiches, and sometimes she'd run off to get Cokes at the nearby Franprix. Those days, when I listened to her sing, with the smell of the flowers all around, stretched out on the blanket with a piece of grass between my teeth—sometimes she sang so softly I'd fall asleep—yes, sir, no doubt about it, those were the best days of my life.

They should have given her singing lessons, of course, and taught her to play an instrument too, but they didn't have any money for that either. For a while she thought she'd pay for them herself and she sang in the street, especially in summer at the sidewalk cafes around Menilmontant, and there too, I'd go with her to make sure nothing happened to her; I used to take along a folding chair and I'd roll myself cigarettes until I decided it was time to go home. Yes, you see, I never had a kid, so naturally it was like she was mine, almost, what with her mother always busy with the three little ones. But she was never able to collect enough money to pay for lessons or a musical instrument.

When she grew up things got difficult. At fourteen she started changing her name all the time, saying she was looking for a stage name. She used to go to the library a lot, first with me and then alone, that's where she learned all those, names of singers and opera heroines, Cornelia, Aïda, Dorahella. Plus, you had to watch out: You couldn't make a mistake, confuse her most recent name with the old one, or she'd get mad; it was like mentioning somebody she'd had a fight with. One day, just kidding around, I told her she was like an onion, adding skins instead of taking them off, but after that she wouldn't talk to me for a week. Maybe what the girl really missed was bearing the name of a man who was a real father to her.

She hung onto the idea of becoming a singer. Her parents wouldn't hear of it, of course, they wanted her to get a real job, with a good salary. But she stuck to her guns. Then it began to go to her head, and it's my fault too, because I always encouraged her. Those years, when she was fourteen or fifteen—they were the worst. Layla wasn't going to school anymore—we learned this by pure chance because she'd steal the notes from school and imitate her mother's signature. Her stepfather gave her a beating and she went back, but not for long, she never stopped cutting classes, she'd leave in the morning with her school bag but she'd hang out in the street all day.

Things were so bad at home that she got used to sleeping here from time to time, then more and more; her parents felt secure knowing where she was. I wanted to give her my room but she said no, she made her bed on the living room sofa, over there, she'd sleep with Milou at her feet. She said she didn't want to bother me but mainly I think she wanted to be able to go in and out without my hearing her; I've gotten hard of hearing in my old age and it wasn't so easy to watch her, she wasn't a little girl anymore. And then, I didn't have the guts to bawl her out, I was afraid she'd leave, that's the way it is when you're not really the parent, you don't dare to be too strict. And then she started disappearing for days on end. We didn't know where she went. I had a feeling she was traveling with a bad crowd—when she came back her breath smelled of cigarettes and even liquor, but you see, sir, she still loved to sing. So I used to tell myself that would save her, I always thought that in the end it would save her from the worst, that's how naïve I was!

A year ago, she started telling me about people she'd met who worked in television. She told me there were shows that helped young people like her become singers or actors and she was going to try her luck, and for the first time she asked me for a little money to buy herself a dress and shoes. For the audition, she said—she's the one who taught me the word: audition. She told me it was going to be in a suburb of Paris and she'd sleep over at a girlfriend's place, a girl who dreamed of going on stage too. She told me all that sitting right where you are, with Milou's head on her lap, pulling his ears the way she liked to do when she was a little girl. At the time we already knew the building was going to be torn down and she told me that when she was famous she'd buy a big house with a garden and there'd be a room for me and a basket for the dog. Yes, that's what she said. Then she asked if she could sleep on the couch and of course I said yes. When I went to bed, she kissed me. She told me she'd keep in touch, because she'd probably have to stay a few months there in the TV studios, after the audition. She was laughing. I hadn't heard her laugh like that for a long time. The next morning when I woke up, she was gone.

Right away I knew she'd left for a long time. She'd been to her place very early and took some money from her mother's purse. Everybody was still sleeping. They thought one of the kids had left the door open and someone had snuck in. I didn't say a thing, but I was sure it was her, even if she never stole before. I was hurt, less because of what she did than because it meant she wouldn't be coming back for a long time. And also because I told myself that if I'd only given her more she wouldn't have had to steal.

I began to spend my evenings at Samir's, the grocer on the corner of rue Piat. He had a TV set in the back room and when he had customers he let me watch whatever channel I wanted. I watched all the shows Layla told me about, those shows for young people. I never thought there were so many kids who wanted to be famous, and that made me afraid for her. It's true she had a nice voice and she was very good-looking, but there were lots of other kids with nice voices too, just as good-looking. I just hoped it wouldn't ruin her life, hoped she wouldn't be afraid to come back. I got five postcards from her over the next year, look, you can see them over there on the wall. She wrote the same thing on every one of them, or just about: *I'm fine, Grandpa. Love you.*

One evening I really thought I saw her on a show. I'm almost sure of it. By that time I'd lost hope, I kept going to Samir's mainly because 1 wasn't used to staying home alone anymore, especially without much chance of Layla dropping by. The girl I saw only stayed on stage for a few minutes, they didn't even give her time to finish her song. She said her name was Olympia but that doesn't mean a thing, you know. She had heavy makeup on, with silver on her eyelids and red lips, done up in a way she never would have dared here, a shiny dress, very short. I remember thinking, *So much money for such a short dress.* But her voice sounded like Layla's and she sang a Piaf song, which is funny because the others chose much more modern music, the kind you hear blasting on young people's car radios when they're stopped at a light with their windows rolled down, or when they don't shut their bedroom windows. I couldn't get a good look at her face, it went so fast, I yelled for Samir, hoping he could help me figure out if it really was her, but by the time he got there—he was helping another customer—it was already over.

The weeks after that I kept watching the show, but the girl—Layla—she never came back. I kept hoping for months, I told myself maybe it was just the first round and we were going to see her again at some point. But I never did.

A few months later there were the rumors. Somebody claimed they saw her in a bar, a nightclub really, then somebody else, and then somebody else again. They swore it really was Layla, said she was dancing every Saturday over there, near Pigalle, then they said the words *peep show.* I didn't know what that meant either, before. Around that time, her family moved out; they didn't even leave an address—I don't know if it was the shame of the neighborhood hearing that their daughter was dancing naked in front of men. Her mother just left a box in front of my door with the girl's things. They're still there, in my bedroom.

There isn't much left to my story. One day I went there. I don't know why, I think I was sure it wasn't Layla, just as I had been sure that I'd seen her on TV at the gates of fame with Piaf's song on her lips, but I needed to see her in person The rumor had become more and more persistent and I basically knew where to look for her. I waited a few weeks, the time to get up my courage, and then I took the bus to Pigalle one evening around midnight. I didn't have to look far. There were photos of her at the entrance to one of the clubs. I looked at them for a long time, so long the guy watching the door got impatient and said, "Hey, Gramps, you coming in or you growing roots there." In some pictures she was wearing dresses with slits at her thighs and between her breasts and in others she was almost naked. I had washed her when she was a baby and when she was a little girl; it didn't bother me to see her naked. But there wasn't one single photo where she was smiling. The lipstick was like a gash across her face, she'd lost her nice round cheeks, and her black eyes looked very big. When the guy at the entrance spoke to me I was caught unprepared, I couldn't stop looking at her face after not having seen her for months, and when he said, "Well, Gramps?" I asked, "How much is it?" and I fumbled around in my wallet to pay the admission.

Inside the peep show, as they call it, it was dark and it smelled of sweat, the music was too loud, you'd think you were in one of the worst bars in our neighborhood. I stayed standing near the door of the room they pointed me to, men kept corning in, pushing each other, I was hot, and then I realized I still had my cap on and I took it off. The first girl was a blonde in a shiny pink slip, she couldn't dance but the men were whistling and yelling, some of them tried to touch her but there was a strongman watching the edges of the stage. After that I didn't have to wait long, because the next one was Layla.

I won't tell you about how she was dancing under the eyes of those men, my poor ruined little girl. I didn't stay very long, just enough to see her pace back and forth on the stage two or three times on her high heels, with a swaying walk I'd never seen from her, and then just when I was putting my cap on to leave—maybe it was my motion that attracted her attention—she saw me. She didn't stop dancing hut she dropped her arms, she'd been holding them over her head till then, and she twisted her ankle. I saw her mouth tighten in pain but nothing more because I'd already turned around, and I left without looking back.

I didn't tell anyone about what I saw. Nobody asked me anything but I think a lot of people understood, because I never went back to watch TV at Samir's. I just went out to walk the clog and shop for food. The rest of the time I stayed here sitting in the kitchen, and I tried not to think. I didn't even wonder anymore where I'd go when the building was torn clown.

I didn't think she'd come. I didn't guess it in her look when she spotted me at the peep show, all I saw was boredom and that new toughness, and the jab of pain when she twisted her foot, but I didn't see joy or sorrow at the idea of what she'd lost, and I told myself she'd put all that behind her. Still, when there was a knock on the door one evening, very late, I knew right away it was her. I'd fallen asleep on the couch; since she left that's where I usually slept, as if giving myself the illusion she was in the room next door. I went to splash some water on my face before I opened the door.

She was pale, and I realized right away she'd knocked on the door across the hall first, the door of the apartment where her family used to live. It hadn't been rented again because of the plan to demolish the building, but two guys set up house there, with candles for light and a coal stove for heat. They drank all day and begged in front of the Monoprix supermarket on rue des Pyrenees, a little further up. She must have woken them up because the younger one, a guy with a beard, was standing in the half-open doorway looking at us. When she came in, I didn't hear him close the door and I'm sure he stayed there waiting for her to come out again.

Oh yes, I know what you're thinking. You're thinking he waited for her, followed her to the park, and then what happened, happened. But you're wrong.

She didn't cross the threshold until I told her to come in, and it was strange, that mix of humility and provocation in her face, like she was defying me to criticize her for anything. I found her taller, maybe it was her high heels, maybe her thinness, she was wearing a jacket I recognized and she floated in it like a little bird. She sat down on the couch and looked at me with a funny smile on her face. I could see immediately she'd taken something, something stronger than a couple of drinks, and that was new too: She looked at me and then seemed to look *through* me, she had to make an effort for her eyes to focus on my face again. She rubbed her nose with her forefinger and then she said: "So, they left."

Her voice was like her face, just as tough, like, grated—I know I should say *grating,* but it was something else, it was like they'd both been dragged over a hard surface and they'd lost all their softness. "Two months ago, yes," I said. "But your mother left your things, they're in my room, I can go get them if you like."

She shrugged indifferently, as if none of it had any importance. She stayed slumped on the couch with that half-smile on her lips and that floating look, twisting a strand of hair around her finger.

"Layla," I said, "come back. You can stay in the bedroom, you'll be fine there, I almost always sleep in the living room now. I can help you bring over your things, if you like. We can even go there right now."

She laughed, a joyless laugh, and I thought of the night before she left, that happy laugh I'd kept inside my ear like a good luck charm while she wasn't here. "And to do *what,* huh?" she answered.

I lowered my eyes, I never felt so old, so powerless, so silly too, but I made myself go on. "You can start singing again," I said. "Samir's looking for someone to take care of the cash register on weekends, it'd do me good to get out of here a little, and it could help pay for lessons. Maybe that's all you need to make it work."

She laughed again, rolling her head against the back of the couch, and then she said: "No, Grandfather, it's over, my voice is gone, can't you hear? It's not there anymore. It's gone, that's all there is to it."

It hurt when she called me *Grandfather* because there was no tenderness in her voice like when she called me *Grandpa,* it was more of an impatient tone of voice, kind of scornful, like the kids playing soccer in the little square in front of the park when they think I'm not getting out of the way fast enough. It hurt, and then it made me mad. It was also seeing her like that on the couch, sprawled out like a doll, occasionally scratching her knee or her nose, looking like she was bored, not giving a damn about anything. 1 went and sat down next to her. "You can't lose your voice just like that," I said, even if it's what I thought when I opened the door—that grated, worn-out voice, almost unrecognizable. "It's because you haven't worked on it for a long time. I'll make you herb tea, lemon and honey, and then those powders Samir sells for colds, you'll see, it'll come back."

But she just closed her eyes and shook her head with an angry expression, and when I held out my hand to push back a strand of hair that was trailing over her cheek, she shoved it away impatiently. "No," she said. "My voice is gone. Don't you get it? It's all over. Oh, leave me alone."

She thought she was strong but she wasn't as strong as all that; she couldn't manage to brush away my hand and I left it there, near her cheek, even when she tried to push it away more impatiently, saying, "Stop it."

I slid my hand down and placed it on her throat. "Your voice isn't gone," I said. "I'm sure I'd feel it if you sang something—there, now, I can feel it vibrating under my fingers. Your neck's all cold, that's why too, but it's going to warm up."

"Come on, leave me alone," she repeated. "Leave me alone, I can't breathe." She could have screamed if she wanted to, there were neighbors, the two guys on the other side of the landing, and yet she whispered, and it was like a secret being born between us.

"Sing," I told her. "Sing something. Sing that song by Piaf you used to like so much. 'La Vie en Rose.' Sing."

Her throat vibrated under my hand when she murmured something, still softer, but I didn't hear it. We stayed like that for a long time. She hadn't opened her eyes again. She wasn't trying to push me away anymore, she had her hands on her knees, quietly waiting for something, and that smile that didn't look like hers was gone from her face. She didn't move. I thought she was asleep.

3.

Arnaud hadn't said a word while the old man was talking. He had opened his notebook and began mechanically taking notes after glancing over at the old man to make sure he didn't mind. But his notes were such a mess that later he would be unable to read them or understand what they meant, aside from the last words he'd written in the middle of one page: *La Vie en Rose.*

Now the old man was silent. Armaud watched him. Big, fat tears were flowing from the old man's eyes, like a child's tears. He never would have thought such a deeply furrowed face could have so much emotion or so much water in it. At last the old man sighed, picked up his cup of coffee, and put it to his lips, then put it back down without drinking a drop.

"When her neck began to grow cold under my palms I understood," he said. "I took away my hands and her head slipped onto my shoulder. I didn't know what to do, so I laid her down gently on the couch and I got up. It's funny what goes through your head at moments like that, sir, because I wasn't really thinking and yet I went straight to the bedroom closet where I knew that long ago I'd put away the blanket we used to take for picnics in the park. I took it, I went back to the living room and wrapped Layla in it. All that time I was wondering what I was going to do, but I must have known already. I picked her up in my arms without any hesitation—it wasn't easy, since skinny as she was, she still weighed a lot or maybe death just does that to you—and I walked to the door. The guy across the hall must've gotten tired or else he understood and didn't want any trouble, because his door was shut.

"I walked down the three flights with Layla in my arms, I went out into the street where it was still very dark, you couldn't hear a car, not even a moped, and I walked to the park gate that doesn't close very well. Everybody in the neighborhood knows there's a gate that doesn't close and all you have to do is jiggle it the right way to open it, any ten-year-old can show you how. I pushed the gate wide with my shoulder and I took the park path to the spot where we used to have picnics back then. It must have been close to dawn, because a blackbird was singing in the trees, we must've stayed on the couch much longer than I thought, I may have fallen asleep with my hands on her throat. The smell of the flowers was very strong that night, I was surprised spring was in the air. I think I'd hardly been out of the house since the night I saw Layla in Pigalle.

"I stopped at a tree we used to sit under. I kneeled down and I put her down on the ground. I picked her up a little to tuck the blanket under her, I laid her out with her legs together and her arms straight down beside her body, I buttoned up her jacket to hide the bluish necklace around her throat, and then I got up. I looked at her for a moment. Oh, we were so happy under this tree, me and her. As I was walking back home, it started to rain and suddenly I couldn't stand to think of her staying out there in the rain. I went up to get a pink nylon windbreaker she'd left behind when she went away; her mother had put it in the box she'd left on my doormat. I took it out of its plastic bag, went back down, and put it on Layla; first I slipped it over her head, then I pulled her arms through the sleeves, and finally I drew the hood over her face. I could hear the sound of the raindrops falling on the plastic. Did she have her pink windbreaker on when they found her? She didn't get too wet."

He was looking at Arnaud imploringly, and Arnaud lowered his eyes. "I don't know," he said in a low voice, "I couldn't cross the police barrier. But she was under another plastic thing, a kind of gray tarp. No, I don't think she was wet."

The old man shook his head with a pensive expression. He picked up the cap on the table next to his cup and wiped his face with it, then kept it in his hand.

"After that, I came back up here and waited for someone to arrive," he began again in a weary tone. "I waited for someone to come so I could tell my story. I will follow you to the police station. But the dog . . . I'd just like you to leave the dog at the grocery store on rue Piat."

Arnaud capped his pen and shut his notebook. The coffee must have been boiling for hours, it was much too strong; he felt as if it had ripped the skin off his mouth and his heart was beating very fast. He was thinking of all those newspapers he'd skimmed through since the fall, all those sordid crimes, stabbings, shootings, skulls cracked against walls, that search for evil he'd thrown himself into to find an ideal killer, and he remembered the incredibly gentle handshake of the old man. He was looking at them at that very moment, those two hands clenched on his cap, which he was stroking softly, the way you pet an animal. Then Arnaud glanced up again and forced himself to smile.

"I'm not the police, sir," he said. "I'm not going to put you in jail. Your story . . ." he went on hastily. "Don't say anything. Don't tell anyone anything. Layla did not come to see you. You were sleeping, you didn't hear her knock, you didn't open your door."

But the old man was staring at him as if he didn't understand. "Don't say anything," he repeated. "Why—" He had mechanically put his cap back on, he looked ready to go, to follow the police who'd come knock on his door in a few minutes or a few hours.

"I live outside Paris," Arnaud suddenly heard himself saying. "I can take you in for a while if you like. We can go there now. No one will know you were here last night. No one will suspect you."

But under the woolen cap, his face still reddened by tears, the old man was looking at him with incomprehension, almost with mistrust.

"I don't understand what you're trying to do," he said at last. "What you're telling me there, that's not my story. I don't understand what you're trying to do." He continued to examine Arnaud's face as if he was seeing him for the first time, as if he didn't know how this stranger got into his kitchen, sitting in front of him with the coffeepot between them. He pushed back his chair and got up heavily. "Go away, sir," he said. "Go away, please."

Arnaud hesitated, then did as he was told. He stood up, slipped his notebook and pen into his pocket. The old man remained standing behind the table while Arnaud walked over to the door and went out. In the stairway he found the same stench of urine and soup; the door to the apartment across the hall was slightly open, but he was not tempted to take a look inside. He walked quickly down the three flights, just as he was leaving through the doors of the building, he saw the police coming—three men who seemed to know where they were going—and he turned his face away so their eyes would not meet.

He headed back to the park. Most of the police cars had disappeared; so had most of the onlookers. When he passed through the gates, he saw that the yellow tape was still there but they'd taken the body away. He stopped on the path. He looked for a long time at the lawn, soaked by the downpour. In the grass under a tree, there was an oval in a softer green on the spot where the body had protected it from the rain. Suddenly he felt someone tap him on the shoulder. He turned around and saw his friend.

"Hey, you sure took your time," Legendre said. "I hope you came up with something, at least. Me, I drew a blank, nobody wanted to tell me a thing and then the cops threw me out. So tell me. What happened?"

But Arnaud was looking at the soft oval of grass again. He felt tears welling up in his eyes, tears that seemed to him as big and childish as the old man's. He didn't know where he got that absolute ignorance of the human psyche. All he knew, with absolute certainty, was that he would never write his book; but that wasn't what was causing this inconsolable sorrow. Legendre had lit a cigarette and was staring at him in amazement.

"For Chrissake, what's with you, man? What did you see in that building?"

Arnaud shook his bead without answering. The last onlookers were moving away, and couples, strollers, and children were coming in through the gates of the park. In a few weeks, a few months, no one would remember Layla M. except for the old man in his cell and me, he told himself. He thought of the pink nylon windbreaker the old man had taken down to cover the corpse with, and as his tears turned into sobs, he remembered the pink plastic hats the Japanese tourists were wearing a few hours earlier in front of the plaque for Edith Piaf. They had seemed so bright and cheery in the grayness of the morning.

DOMINIQUE MAINARD is a novelist, short story writer and translator and has developed her passion for New Zealand literature through the works of Janet Frame, whose writing she has translated since 1994 (*Owls Do Cry*, Joëlle Losfeld). After publishing three short story anthologies, including *Le Second Enfant*, for which she received the *Prix Prométhée de la nouvelle* in 1994 (*La Différence*), and *Le Grenadier* (Gallimard, 1997), Mainard published her first novel in 2001, *Le Grand Fakir* (Joëlle Losfeld). She received two awards for *Leur Histoire* (Joëlle Losfeld, 2002) - the *Prix du Roman FNAC* (2002) and the *Prix Alain-Fournier* (2003), a novel that was later adapted for film by Alain Corneau - *Les Mots bleus* (2005). She was born in Paris in 1967, where she returned to live after being raised in the Lyon region and later spending five years in America.

Sack O' Woe

BY JOHN HARVEY

The street was dark and narrow, a smear of frost along the roof of the occasional parked car. Two of a possible six overhead lights had been smashed several weeks before. Recycling bins—blue, green, and gray—shared the pavement with abandoned supermarket trolleys and the detritus from a score of fast-food takeaways. Number thirty-four was toward the terrace end, the short street emptying onto a scrub of wasteland ridged with stiffened mud, puddles of brackish water covered by a thin film of ice.

January.

Tom Whitemore knocked with his gloved fist on the door of thirty-four. Paint that was flaking away, a bell that had long since ceased to work.

He was wearing blue jeans, a T-shirt and sweater, a scuffed leather jacket—the first clothes he had grabbed when the call had come through less than half an hour before.

January 27, 3:17 a.m.

Taking one step back, he raised his right leg and kicked against the door close by the lock; a second kick, wood splintered and the door sprang back.

Inside was your basic two-up, two-down house, a kitchen extension leading into the small yard at the back, bathroom above that. A strip of worn carpet in the narrow hallway, bare boards on the stairs. Bare wires that hung down, no bulb attached, from the ceiling overhead. He had been here before.

"Darren? Darren, you here?"

No answer when he called the name.

A smell that could be from a backed-up foul-water pipe or a blocked drain.

The front room was empty, odd curtains at the window, a TV set in one corner, two chairs and a sagging two-seater settee. Dust. A bundle of clothes. In the back room there were a small table and two more chairs, one with a broken back; a pile of old newspapers; the remnants of an unfinished oven-ready meal; a child's shoe.

"Darren?"

The first stair creaked a little beneath his weight.

In the front bedroom, a double mattress rested directly on the floor; several blankets, a quilt without a cover, no sheets. Half the drawers in the corner chest had been pulled open and left that way, miscellaneous items of clothing hanging down.

Before opening the door to the rear bedroom, Whitemore held his breath.

A pair of bunk beds leaned against one wall, a pumped-up Lilo mattress close by. Two tea chests, one spilling over with children's clothes, the other with toys. A plastic bowl in which cereal had hardened and congealed. A baby's bottle, rancid with yellowing milk. A used nappy, half in, half out of a pink plastic sack. A tube of sweets. A paper hat. Red and yellow building bricks. Soft toys. A plastic car. A teddy bear with a waistcoat and a bright bow tie, still new enough to have been a recent Christmas gift.

And blood.

Blood in fine tapering lines across the floor, faint splashes on the wall. Tom Whitemore pressed one hand to his forehead and closed his eyes.

• • •

He had been a member of the Public Protection Team for nearly four years: responsible, together with other police officers, probation officers, and representatives of other agencies—social services, community psychiatric care—for the supervision of violent and high-risk-of-harm sex offenders who had been released back into the community. Their task—through maintaining a close watch; pooling information; getting offenders, where applicable, into accredited programs; and assisting them in finding jobs—was to do anything and everything possible to prevent reoffending. It was often thankless and frequently frustrating—*What was that Springsteen song? Two steps up and three steps back?*—but unlike a lot of police work, it had focus, clear aims, methods, ambitions. It was possible—sometimes—to see positive results. Potentially dangerous men—they were mostly men—were neutralized, kept in check. If nothing else, there was that.

And yet his wife hated it. Hated it for the people it brought him into contact with, day after day—rapists, child abusers—the scum of the earth in her eyes, the lowest of the low. She hated it for the way it forced him to confront over and over what these people had done, what people were capable of, as if the enormities of their crimes were somehow contaminating him. Creeping into his dreams. Coming back with him into their home, like smoke caught in his hair or clinging to the fibers of his clothes. Contaminating them all.

"How much longer, Tom?" she would ask. "How much longer are you going to do this hateful bloody job?"

"Not long," he would say. "Not so much longer now."

Get out before you burn out, that was the word on the Force. Transfer to general duties, Traffic, Fraud. Yet he could never bring himself to leave, to make the move, and each morning he would set off back into that world, and each evening when he returned, no matter how late, he would go and stand in the twins' bedroom and watch them sleeping, his and Marianne's twin boys, five years old, safe and sound.

That summer they had gone to Filey as usual, two weeks of holiday, the same dubious weather, the same small hotel, the perfect curve of beach. The twins had run and splashed and fooled around on half-size body boards on the edges of the waves; they had eaten chips and ice cream, and when they were tired of playing with the big colored ball that bounced forever down toward the sea, Tom had helped them build sandcastles with an elaborate array of turrets and tunnels, while Marianne alternately read her book or dozed.

It was perfect: even the weather was forgiving, no more than a scattering of showers, a few darkening clouds, the wind from the south.

On the last evening, the twins upstairs asleep, they had sat on the small terrace overlooking the promenade and the black strip of sea. "When we get back, Tom," Marianne had said, "you've got to ask for a transfer. They'll understand. No one can do a job like that forever, not even you."

She reached for his hand, and as he turned toward her, she brought her face to his. "Tom?" Her breath on his face was warm and slightly sweet, and he felt a lurch of love run through him like a wave.

"All right," he said.

"You promise?"

"I promise."

But by the end of that summer, things had changed. There had been the bombings in London for one thing, suicide bombers on the tube; an innocent young Brazilian shot and killed after a bungled surveillance operation; suspected terrorists arrested in suburbs of Birmingham and Leeds. It was everywhere. All around. Security alerts at the local airport; rumors that spread from voice to voice, from mobile phone to mobile phone. *Don't go into the city center this Saturday. Keep well away. Stay clear.* Now it was commonplace to see: fully armed in the middle of the day, a pair of uniformed police officers strolling down past Pizza Hut and the Debenhams department store, Heckler & Koch submachine guns held low across their chests, Walther P990 pistols bolstered at their hips, shoppers no longer bothering to stop and stare.

As the Home Office and Security Services continued to warn of the possibility of a new terrorist attack, the pressures on police time increased. A report from the chief inspector of constabulary noted that, in some police areas, surveillance packages intended to supervise high-risk offenders were now rarely implemented due to a lack of resources. "Whether it is counterterrorism or a sex offender," explained his deputy, "there are only a certain number of specialist officers to go round."

"You remember what you promised," Marianne said. By now it was late September, the nights drawing in.

"I can't," Tom said, slowly shaking his head. "I can't leave now."

She looked at him, her face like flint. "I can, Tom. We can. Remember that."

It hung over them after that, the threat, fracturing what had held them together for so long.

Out of necessity, Tom worked longer hours; when he did get home, tired, head buzzing, it was to find her turned away from him in the bed and flinching at his touch. At breakfast, when he put his arms around her at the sink, she shrugged him angrily away.

"Marianne, for God's sake . . ."

"What?"

"We can't go on like this."

"No?"

"No."

"Then do something about it."

"Jesus!"

"What?"

"I've already told you. A hundred times. Not now."

She pushed past him and out into the hall, slamming the door at her back. "Fuck!" Tom shouted and slammed his fist against the wall. "Fuck, fuck, fuck!" One of the twins screamed as if he'd been struck; the other knocked his plastic bowl of cereal to the floor and started to cry.

• • •

The team meeting was almost over when Christine Finch—one of the probation officers, midfifties, experienced—raised her hand. "Darren Pitcher. I think we might have a problem."

Tom Whitemore sighed. "What now?"

"One of my clients, Emma Laurie, suspended sentence for dealing crack cocaine, lives up in Forest Fields. Not the brightest cherry in the bunch. She's taken up with Pitcher. Seems he's thinking of moving in."

"That's a problem?"

"She's got three kids, all under six. Two of them boys."

Whitemore shook his head. He knew Darren Pitcher's history well enough. An only child, brought up by a mother who had given birth to him when she was just sixteen, Pitcher had met his father only twice: on the first occasion, magnanimous from drink, the older man had squeezed his buttocks and slipped two five-pound notes into his trouser pocket; on the second, sober, he had blacked the boy's eye and told him to fuck off out of his sight.

A loner at school, marked out by learning difficulties, bullied; from the age of sixteen, Pitcher had drifted through a succession of low-paying jobs—cleaning, stacking supermarket shelves, hospital portering, washing cars—and several short-term relationships with women who enjoyed even less self-esteem than he.

When he was twenty-five, he was sentenced to five years' imprisonment for molesting half a dozen boys between the ages of four and seven. While in prison, in addition to numerous incidents of self-harming, he had made one attempt at suicide.

Released, he had spent the first six months in a hostel and had reported to both his probation officer and a community psychiatric nurse each week. After which time, supervision had necessarily slackened off.

"Ben?" Whitemore said, turning toward the psychiatric nurse at the end of the table. "He was one of yours."

Ben Leonard pushed a hand up through his cropped blond hair. "A family, ready-made, might be what he needs."

"The girl," Christine Finch said, "she's not strong. It's a wonder she's hung on to those kids as long as she has."

"There's a father somewhere?"

"Several."

"Contact?"

"Not really."

For a moment, Tom Whitemore closed his eyes. "The boys, they're how old?"

"Five and three. There's a little girl, eighteen months."

"And do we think, should Pitcher move in, they could be at risk?"

"I think we have to," Christine Finch said.

"Ben?"

Leonard took his time. "We've made real progress with Darren, I think. He's aware that his previous behavior was wrong. Regrets what he's done. The last thing he wants to do is offend again. But, yes, for the sake of the kids, I'd have to say there is a risk. A small one, but a risk."

"Okay," Whitemore said. "I'll go and see him. Report back. Christine, you'll stay in touch with the girl?"

"Of course."

"Good. Let's not lose sight of this in the midst of everything else."

• • •

They sat on the Portland Leisure Centre steps, a wan sun showing weakly through the wreaths of cloud. Whitemore had bought two cups of pale tea from the machines inside, and they sat there on the cold, worn stone, scarcely talking as yet. Darren Pitcher was smoking a cigarette, a roll-up he had made with less than steady hands. *What was it,* Whitemore thought, *his gran had always said? Don't sit on owt cold or you'll get piles, sure as eggs is eggs.*

"Got yourself a new girlfriend, I hear," Whitemore said.

Pitcher flinched, then glanced at him from under lowered lids. He had a lean face, a few reddish spots around the mouth and chin, strangely long eyelashes that curled luxuriantly over his weak gray eyes.

"Emma? That her name?"

"She's all right."

"Of course."

Two young black men in shiny sportswear bounced past them, all muscle, on their way to the gym.

"It serious?" Whitemore asked.

"Dunno."

"What I heard, it's pretty serious. The pair of you. Heard you were thinking of moving in."

Pitcher mumbled something and drew on his cigarette.

"Sorry?" Whitemore said. "I didn't quite hear . . ."

"I said it's none of your business . . ."

"Isn't it?"

"My life, yeah? Not yours."

Whitemore swallowed a mouthful more of the lukewarm tea and turned the plastic cup upside down, shaking the last drops onto the stone. "This Emma," he said, "she's got kids. Young kids."

"So?"

"Young boys."

"That don't . . . You can't . . . That was a long time ago."

"I know, Darren. I know. But it happened, nonetheless. And it makes this our concern." For a moment, his hand rested on Pitcher's arm. "You understand?"

Pitcher's hand went to his mouth, and he bit down on his knuckle hard.

• • •

Gregory Boulevard ran along one side of the Forest Recreation Ground, the nearest houses, once substantial family homes, now mostly subdivided into flats, and falling, many of them, into disrepair. Beyond these, the streets grew narrower and coiled back upon themselves, the houses smaller, with front doors that opened directly out onto the street. Corner shops with bars across the windows, shutters on the doors.

Emma Laurie sat on a lopsided settee in the front room; small-featured, a straggle of hair falling down across her face, her voice rarely rising above a whisper as she spoke. *A wraith of a thing,* Whitemore thought. *Outside, a good wind would blow her away.*

The three children huddled in the corner, watching cartoons, the sound turned low. Jason, Rory, and Jade. The youngest had a runny nose, the older of the boys coughed intermittently, open-mouthed, but they were all, as yet, bright-eyed.

"He's good with them," Emma was saying, "Darren. Plays with them all the time. Takes them, you know, down to the forest. They love him, they really do. Can't wait for him to move in wi' us. Go on about it all the time. Jason especially."

"And you?" Christine Finch said. "How do you feel? About Darren moving in?"

"Be easier, won't it? Rent and that. What I get, family credit an' the rest, s'a struggle, right? But if Darren's here, I can get a job up the supermarket, afternoons. Get out a bit, 'stead of bein' all cooped up. Darren'll look after the kids. He don't mind."

• • •

They walked down through the maze of streets to where Finch had left her car, the Park & Ride on the edge of the forest.

"What do you think?" Whitemore said.

"Ben could be right. Darren, could be the making of him."

"But if it puts those lads at risk?"

"I know, I know. But what can we do? He's been out a good while now, no sign of him reoffending."

"I still don't like it," Whitemore said.

Finch smiled wryly. "Other people's lives. We'll keep our fingers crossed. Keep as close an eye as we can."

Sometimes, Whitemore thought, *it's as if we are trying to hold the world together with good intentions and a ball of twine.*

"Give you a lift back into town?" Finch said when they reached her car. It was not yet late afternoon, and the light was already beginning to fade.

Whitemore shook his head. "It's okay. I'll catch the tram." Back at the office, he checked his e-mails, made several calls, wrote up a brief report of the visit with Emma Laurie. He wondered if he should go and see Darren Pitcher again but decided there was little to be gained. When he finally got back home, a little after six, Marianne was buckling the twins into their seats in the back of the car.

"What's going on?"

She was flushed, a scarf at her neck. "My parents. I thought we'd go over and see them. Just for a couple of days. They haven't seen the boys in ages."

"They were over just the other weekend."

"That was a month ago. More. It is ages to them."

One of the boys was marching his dinosaur along the top of the seat in front; the other was fiddling with his straps.

"You were just going to go?" Whitemore said. "You weren't even going to wait till I got back?"

"You're not usually this early."

"So wait."

"It's a two-hour drive."

"I know how far it is."

"Tom, don't. Please."

"Don't what?"

"Make this more difficult than it is."

He read it in her eyes. Walking to the back of the car, he snapped open the boot. It was crammed with luggage, coats, shoes, toys.

"You're not just going for a couple of days, are you? This is not a couple of fucking days."

"Tom, please . . ." She raised a hand toward him, but he knocked it away.

"You're leaving, that's what you're doing . . ."

"No, I'm not."

"You're not?"

"It's just for a little while . . . A break. I need a break. So I can think."

"You need to fucking think, all right."

Whitemore snatched open the rear door and leaned inside, seeking to unsnap the nearest boy's belt and failing in his haste. The boys themselves looked frightened and close to tears.

"Tom, don't do that! Leave it. Leave them alone."

She pulled at his shoulder and he thrust her away, so that she almost lost her footing and stumbled back. Roused by the shouting, one of the neighbors was standing halfway along his front garden path, openly staring.

"Tom, please," Marianne said. "Be reasonable."

He turned so fast, she thought he was going to strike her and she cowered back.

"Reasonable? Like this? You call this fucking reasonable?"

The neighbor had come as far as the pavement edge. "Excuse me, but is everything all right?"

"All right?" Whitemore shouted. "Yeah. Marvelous. Fucking wonderful. Now fuck off indoors and mind your own fucking business."

Both the twins were crying now: not crying, screaming.

The car door slammed as Marianne slid behind the wheel and started the engine.

"Marianne!" Whitemore shouted her name and brought down his fist hard on the roof of the car as it pulled away, red taillights blurring in the half-dark.

Whitemore stood there for several moments more, staring

off into the middle distance, seeing nothing. Back in the house, he went from room to room, assessing how much she had taken, how long she might be considering staying away. Her parents lived on the coast, between Chapel St. Leonards and Sutton-on-Sea, a bungalow but with room enough for Marianne and the twins. Next year they would be at school, next year would be different, but now . . .

He looked in the fridge, but there was nothing there he fancied. A couple of cold sausages wrapped in foil. Maybe he'd make himself a sandwich later on. He snapped open a can of lager, but the taste was stale in his mouth and he poured the remainder down the sink. There was a bottle of whiskey in the cupboard, only recently opened, but he knew better than to start down that route too soon.

In the living room, he switched on the TV, flicked through the channels, switched it off again; he made a cup of tea and glanced at that day's paper, one of Marianne's magazines. Every fifteen minutes, he looked at his watch. When he thought he'd given them time enough, he phoned.

Marianne's father came on the line. Soft-spoken, understanding, calm. "I'm sorry, Tom. She doesn't want to speak to you right now. Perhaps tomorrow, tomorrow evening. She'll call you . . . . The twins? They're sleeping, fast off. Put them to bed as soon as they arrived . . . . I'll be sure to give them your love . . . . Yes, of course. Of course . . . . Good night, Tom. Good night."

Around nine, Whitemore called a taxi and went across the city to the Five Ways pub in Sherwood. In the back room, Jake McMahon and a bunch of the usual reprobates were charging through Cannonball Adderley's "Jeannine." A Duke Pearson tune, but because Whitemore had first heard it on Adderley's *Them Dirty Blues*—Cannonball on alto alongside his trumpeter brother, Nat—it was forever associated with the saxophonist in his mind.

Whitemore's father had given him the recording as a sixteenth-birthday present, when Tom's mind had been more full of

T'Pau and the Pet Shop Boys, Whitney Houston and Madonna. But eventually he had given it a listen, late in his room, and something had stuck.

One of the best nights he remembered having with his father before the older man took himself off to a retirement chalet in Devon had been spent here, drinking John Smith's Bitter and listening to the band play another Adderley special, "Sack o' Woe."

Jake McMahon came over to him at the break and shook his hand. "Not seen you in a while."

Whitemore forced a smile. "You know how it is, this and that."

McMahon nodded. "Your dad, he okay?"

"Keeping pretty well."

"You'll give him my best."

"Of course."

Whitemore stayed for the second set, then called a cab from the phone alongside the bar.

• • •

Darren Pitcher moved in with Emma Laurie and her three children. October became November, became December. Most Sundays, Whitemore drove out to his in-laws' bungalow on the coast, where the twins threw themselves at him with delight and he played rough-and-tumble with them on the beach if the cold allowed and, if not, tussled with them on the living room settee. Marianne's parents stepped around him warily, keeping their thoughts to themselves. If he tried to get Marianne off on her own, she resisted, made excuses. Conversation between them was difficult.

"When will we see you again?" she asked one evening as he was leaving.

"When are you coming home?" he asked. Christmas was less than three weeks away.

"Tom, I don't know."

"But you are coming? Coming back?"

She turned her face aside. "Don't rush me, all right?"

It was just two days later when Christine Finch phoned Whitemore in his office, the first call of the day. Emma Laurie was waiting for them, agitated, at her front door. She had come back from work to find Pitcher with Jason, the eldest of her two sons, on his lap; Jason had been sitting on a towel, naked, and Pitcher had been rubbing Vaseline between his legs.

Whitemore and Finch exchanged glances.

"Did he have a reason?" Finch asked.

"He said Jason was sore, said he'd been complaining about being sore . . ."

"And you don't believe him?"

"If he was sore, it was 'cause of what Darren was doing. You know that as well as me."

"Where is Darren now?" Whitemore said.

"I don't know. I don't care. I told him to clear out and not come back."

Whitemore found Pitcher later that morning, sitting cross-legged on the damp pavement, his back against the hoardings surrounding the Old Market Square. Rain was falling in fine slanted lines, but Pitcher either hadn't noticed or didn't care.

"Darren," Whitemore said, "come on, let's get out of this rain."

Pitcher glanced up at him and shook his head.

Coat collar up, Whitemore hunkered down beside him. "You want to tell me what happened?"

"Nothing happened."

"Emma says . . ."

"I don't give a fuck what Emma says."

"I do," Whitemore said. "I have to. But I want to know what you say too."

Pitcher was silent for several minutes, passersby stepping over his legs or grudgingly going round.

"He'd been whinging away," Pitcher said. "Jason. How the pants he was wearing were too tight. Scratching. His hand down his trousers, scratching, and I kept telling him to stop. He'd hurt himself. Make it worse. Then, when he went to the toilet, right, I told him to show me, you know, show me where it was hurting, point to it, like. And there was a bit of red there, I could see, so I said would he like me to put something on it, to make it better, and he said yes, and so . . ."

He stopped abruptly, tears in his eyes and shoulders shaking.

Whitemore waited.

"I didn't do anything," Pitcher said finally. "Honest. I never touched him. Not like . . . you know, like before."

"But you could have?" Whitemore said.

Head down, Pitcher nodded.

"Darren?"

"Yes, yeah. I suppose . . . Yeah."

Still neither of them moved, and the rain continued to fall.

• • •

On Christmas morning Whitemore rose early, scraped the ice from the windows of the secondhand Saab he'd bought not so many weeks before, loaded up the backseat with presents, and set out for the coast. When he arrived the light was only just beginning to spread, in bands of pink and yellow, across the sky. Wanting his arrival to be a surprise, he parked some houses away.

The curtains were partly drawn and he could see the lights of the Christmas tree clearly, red, blue, and green, and, as he moved across the frosted grass, he could see the twins, up already, still wearing their pajamas, tearing into the contents of their stockings, shouting excitedly as they pulled at the shiny paper and cast it aside.

When he thought they might see him, he stepped quickly away and returned to the car, loading the presents into his arms. Back at the bungalow, he placed them on the front step, up against the door, and walked away.

If he had waited, knocked on the window, rung the bell, gone inside and stayed, seen their happiness at close hand, he knew it would have been almost impossible to leave.

• • •

Emma Laurie appeared at the police station in early January, the youngest child in a buggy, the others half-hidden behind her legs. After days of endless pestering, she had allowed Pitcher back into the house, just for an hour, and then he had refused to leave. When she'd finally persuaded him to go, he had threatened to kill himself if she didn't have him back; said that he would snatch the children and take them with him; kill them all.

"It was wrong o' me, weren't it? Letting him back in. I never should've done it. I know that, I know."

"It's okay," Whitemore said. "And I wouldn't pay too much attention to what Darren said. He was angry. Upset. Times like that, people say a lot of things they don't necessarily mean."

"But if you'd seen his face . . . He meant it, he really did."

Whitemore gave her his card. "Look, my mobile number's there. If he comes round again, threatening you, anything like that, you call me, right? Straightaway. Meantime, I'll go and have a word with him. Okay?"

Emma smiled uncertainly, nodded thanks, and ushered the children away.

• • •

After spending time in various hostels and a spell sleeping rough, Pitcher, with the help of the local housing association, had found a place to rent in Sneinton. A one-room flat with a sink and small cooker in one corner and a shared bathroom and toilet on the floor below. Whitemore sat on the single chair, and Pitcher sat on the sagging bed.

"I know why you're here," Pitcher said. "It's about Emma. What I said."

"You frightened her."

"I know. I lost my temper, that's all." He shook his head.

"Being there, her an' the kids, a family, you know? An' then her chuckin' me out. You wouldn't understand. Why would you?

But I felt like shit. A piece of shit. An' I meant it. What I said. Not the kids, not harmin' them. I wouldn't do that. But topping myself . . ." He looked at Whitemore despairingly. "It's what I'll do. I swear it. I will."

"Don't talk like that," Whitemore said.

"Why the hell not?"

Whitemore leaned toward him and lowered his voice. "It's hard, I know. And I do understand. Really, I do. But you have to keep going. Move on. Look—here—you've got this place, right? A flat of your own. It's a start. A new start. Look at it like that."

He went across to Pitcher and rested a hand on his shoulder, not knowing how convincing his half-truths and platitudes had been.

"Ben Leonard. You talked to him before. I'll see if I can't get him to see you again. It might help sort a few things out. Okay? But in the meantime, whatever you do, you're to keep away from Emma. Right, Darren? Emma and the children." Whitemore tightened his grip on Pitcher's shoulder before stepping clear. "Keep right away."

• • •

It was a little more than a week later when the call came through, waking Whitemore from his sleep. The voice was brisk, professional, a triage nurse at the Queen's Medical Centre, Accident and Emergency. "We've a young woman here, Emma Laurie, she's quite badly injured. Some kind of altercation with a partner? She insisted that I contact you, I hope that's all right. Apparently she's worried about the children. Three of them?"

"Are they there with her?"

"No. At home, apparently."

"On their own?"

"I don't know. I don't think so. Maybe a neighbor? I'm afraid she's not making a lot of sense."

Whitemore dropped the phone and finished pulling on his clothes.

• • •

The house was silent—the blood slightly tacky to the touch. One more room to go. The bathroom door was bolted from the inside, and Whitemore shouldered it free. Darren Pitcher was sitting on the toilet seat, head slumped forward toward his chest, one arm trailing over the bath, the other dangling toward the floor. Long, vertical cuts ran down the inside of both arms, almost from elbow to wrist, slicing through the horizontal scars from where he had harmed himself before. Blood had pooled along the bottom of the bath and around his feet. A Stanley knife rested on the bath's edge alongside an oval of pale green soap.

Whitemore crouched down. There was a pulse, still beating faintly, at the side of Pitcher's neck.

"Darren? Can you hear me?"

With an effort, Pitcher raised his head. "See, I did it. I said I would." A ghost of a smile lingered in his eyes.

"The children," Whitemore said. "Where are they?"

Pitcher's voice was a sour whisper in his face. "The shed. Out back. I didn't want them to see this."

As Pitcher's head slumped forward, Whitemore dialed the emergency number on his mobile phone.

Downstairs, he switched on the kitchen light; there was a box of matches lying next to the stove. Unbolting the back door, he stepped outside. The shed was no more than five feet high, roughly fashioned from odd planks of wood, the roof covered with a rime of frost. The handle was cold to the touch.

"Don't be frightened," he said, loud enough for them to hear inside. "I'm just going to open the door."

When it swung back, he ducked inside and struck a match. The three children were clinging to one another in the farthest corner, staring wide-eyed into the light.

• • •

Darren Pitcher had lost consciousness by the time the paramedics arrived, and despite their efforts and those of the doctors at A &

E, he was pronounced dead a little after six that morning. Sutured and bandaged, Emma Laurie was kept in overnight and then released. Her children had been scooped up by the Social Services Emergency Duty Team and would spend a short time in care.

Tom Whitemore drove to the embankment and stood on the pedestrian bridge across the river, staring down at the dark, glassed-over surface of the water, the pale shapes of sleeping swans, heads tucked beneath their wings. Overhead, the sky was clear and pitted with stars.

When he finally arrived home, it was near dawn.

The heating in the house had just come on.

Upstairs, in the twins' room, it felt cold nonetheless. Each bed was carefully made up, blankets folded neatly back. In case. He stood there for a long time, letting the light slowly unfold round him. The start of another day.

JOHN HARVEY is the author of eleven Charlie Resnick novels, the first of which, *Lonely Hearts*, was named by *The Times* (London) as one of the 100 Best Crime Novels of the Century. In 2007 he was awarded the British Crime Writers' Association Cartier Diamond Dagger for sustained excellence in crime writing. He lives in London with his partner and their young daughter.

Permissions

"The Year in Mystery: 2008," copyright © 2009 by Jon L. Breen

"Father's Day," copyright © 2008 by Michael Connelly. First published in *The Blue Religion.* Reprinted by permission of the author.

"Walking the Dog," copyright © 2008 by Peter Robinson. First published in *Toronto Noir.* Reprinted by permission of the author.

"Lucky," copyright © 2008 by Charlaine Harris, Inc. First published in *Unusual Suspects.* Reprinted by permission of the author.

"A Sleep Not Unlike Death," copyright © 2008 by Sean Chercover. First published at www.thuglit.com. Reprinted by permission of the author.

"The First Husband," copyright © 2008 by the Ontario Review, Inc. First published in *Ellery Queen's Mystery Magazine,* January 2008. Reprinted by permission of the author.

"Between the Dark and the Daylight," copyright © 2008 by Tom Piccirilli. First published in *Ellery Queen's Mystery Magazine,* September/October 2008. Reprinted by permission of the author.

"Cheer," copyright © 2008 by Megan Abbott. First published on www.storyglossia.com, May 2008. Reprinted by permission of the author.

"Babs," copyright © 2008 by Scott Phillips. First published in *Las Vegas Noir.* Reprinted by permission of the author.

"Ms. Grimshanks Regrets," copyright © 2008 by Nancy Pickard. First published in *Ellery Queen's Mystery Magazine,* May 2008. Reprinted by permission of the author.

"Skinhead Central," copyright © 2008 by T. Jefferson Parker. First published in *The Blue Religion.* Reprinted by permission of the author.

"The Bookbinder's Apprentice," copyright © 2008 by Martin Edwards. First published in *The Mammoth Book of Best British Mysteries.* Reprinted by permission of the author.

"I/M Print: A Tess Cassidy Mystery," copyright © 2008 by Jeremiah Healy. First published in *At the Scene of the Crime.* Reprinted by permission of the author.

"The Devil's Acre," copyright © 2008 by Steve Hockensmith. First published in *Ellery Queen's Mystery Magazine,* February 2008. Reprinted by permission of the author.

"The Instrument of Their Desire," copyright © 2008 by Patricia Abbott. First published on www.beattoapulp.com. Reprinted by permission of the author.

"Crossroads," copyright © 2008 by Bill Crider. First published on www.hardluckstories.com. Reprinted by permission of the author.

"The Kim Novak Effect," copyright © 2008 by Gary Phillips. First published in *Ellery Queen's Mystery Magazine,* November 2008. Reprinted by permission of the author.

"The Opposite of O," copyright © 2008 by Martin Limón. First published in *Alfred Hitchcock's Mystery Magazine,* July/August 2008. Reprinted by permission of the author.

"Patriotic Gestures," copyright © 2008 by Kristine Kathryn Rusch. First published in *At the Scene of the Crime.* Reprinted by permission of the author.

"The Quick Brown Fox," copyright © 2008 by Robert S. Levinson. First published in *Alfred Hitchcock's Mystery Magazine,* October 2008. Reprinted by permission of the author.

"What Happened to Mary?" copyright © 2008 by Bill Pronzini. First published in *Ellery Queen's Mystery Magazine,* September/October 2008. Reprinted by permission of the author.

"Jonas and the Frail," by Charles Ardai. First published on www.blazingadventuresmagazine.com. Reprinted by permission of the author.

"The Pig Party," copyright © 2008 by Doug Allyn. First published in *Ellery Queen's Mystery Magazine,* March/April 2008. Reprinted by permission of the author.

"Perfect Gentleman," by Brett Battles. First published in *Killer Year: Stories to Die For.* Reprinted by permission of the author.

"Road Dogs," copyright 2008 by Norman Partridge. First published on www.subterranean press.com. Reprinted by permission of the author.

"Rust," copyright © 2008 by N.J. Ayres. First published in *At the Scene of the Crime.* Reprinted by permission of the author.

"Skin and Bones," copyright © 2008 by David Edgerly Gates. First published in *Alfred Hitchcock's Mystery Magazine,* October 2008. Reprinted by permission of the author.

"La Vie En Rose," by Dominique Mainard. First published in *Paris Noir.* Reprinted by permission of the author.

"Sack O' Woe," copyright © 2008 by John Harvey. First published in *The Blue Religion.* Reprinted by permission of the author.

About the Editors

ED GORMAN has been called "one of suspense fiction's best story-tellers" by *Ellery Queen's Mystery Magazine,* and "one of the most original voices in today's crime fiction" by the *San Diego Union.* He's been published in many magazines, including *Redbook, Ellery Queen's Mystery Magazine, The Magazine of Fantasy & Science Fiction,* and *Poetry Today.* He has won numerous prizes for his work, including the Shamus award, the Spur award, and the International Fiction Writer's award, as well as being nominated for the Edgar, the Anthony, the Golden Dagger, and the Stoker award. His work has been featured by the Literary Guild, the Mystery Guild, the Doubleday Book Club, and the Science Fiction Book Club. He lives with his wife, author Carol Gorman, in Cedar Rapids, Iowa.

MARTIN H. GREENBERG is the CEP of Tekno Books and its predecessor companies, now the largest book developer of commercial fiction and non-fiction in the world, with over 2,000 published books that have been translated into 33 languages. He is the recipient of an unprecedented three Lifetime Achievement Awards in the Science Fiction, Mystery, and Supernatural Horror genres—the Milford Award in Science Fiction, the Bram Stoker Award in Horror, and the Ellery Queen Award in Mystery—the only person in publishing history to have received all three awards.